The
Blood Mirror

Cruxer was shouting at Kip, telling him that the bridges connecting shore and ship were about to collapse – that it was too dangerous, too late.

He was right. Those men were going to die because of their own choices. Their own cowardice had led them to their chains. It made no sense for Kip to risk himself and everything he could accomplish to try a hopeless rescue. A man who can't swim shouldn't attempt to save the drowning. But Kip surged forward anyway and ran for the widening gap between the sinking barge and the sloping planks.

Ah fuck me, he thought   do I have to be so dumb?

And then he leapt.

BOOKS BY BRENT WEEKS

Perfect Shadow (e-only novella)

The Night Angel Trilogy

The Way of Shadows
Shadow's Edge
Beyond the Shadows

Night Angel (omnibus)

The Lightbringer Series

The Black Prism
The Blinding Knife
The Broken Eye
The Blood Mirror

The
Blood
Mirror

Lightbringer: Book 4

BRENT WEEKS

www.orbitbooks.net

ORBIT

First published in Great Britain in 2016 by Orbit
This paperback edition published in 2017 by Orbit

1 3 5 7 9 10 8 6 4 2

Copyright © 2016 by Brent Weeks

Maps by Chad Roberts Designs

Excerpt from *Age of Assassins* by RJ Barker
Copyright © 2017 by RJ Barker

The moral right of the author has been asserted.

A CIP catalogue record for this book
is available from the British Library.

ISBN 978-0-356-50463-6

Typeset in Sabon by Palimpsest Book Production Limited,
Falkirk, Stirlingshire

Printed and bound by CPI Group (UK) Ltd, Croydon CR0 4YY

Papers used by Orbit are from well-managed forests
and other responsible sources.

MIX
Paper from
responsible sources
FSC® C104740

Orbit
An imprint of
Little, Brown Book Group
Carmelite House
50 Victoria Embankment
London EC4Y 0DZ

An Hachette UK Company
www.hachette.co.uk

www.orbitbooks.net

*To Kristi, whose 'No.' 'Not . . . no.' 'Yes!' taught me all
I needed to know about love and publishing.*

*And to my sisters, Christa and Elisa, my stories' first
(and wildly appreciative) audience.*

Contents

Big
Jasper

Weasel Rock

Ebon's Hill

Overhill

THE GREAT
FOUNTAIN

East Bay

The Lightbringer Series Recap

In the empire of the Seven Satrapies, a small number of people are born with the ability to learn to transform light into a physical, tangible product called luxin. Each color of luxin has unique physical and metaphysical properties and innumerable uses, from construction to warfare. Trained at the empire's capital, the Chromeria, these drafters lead lives of privilege, with satrapies and powerful houses vying for their services. In exchange, they agree that once they exhaust their ability to safely use magic – signaled when the halos of their irises are broken by the colors they draft – they will be killed by the emperor, the Prism, in a ceremony on the most holy day of the year: Sun Day. The drafters who have broken the halo (called wights) go mad with the luxin coursing through their bodies. If they run away instead of surrendering, they must be hunted to death. Only the Prism can draft with limitless power, and he or she alone can balance all the colors in the satrapies to prevent the chaotic luxin from overwhelming the lands. Every seven years, or on a multiple of seven years, the Prism also gives up his or her life, and the ruling council appoints a new Prism. If the Prism refuses death, he or she is likewise hunted down.

The current Prism is Gavin Guile.

Book One: *The Black Prism*

Prism Gavin Guile learns he has an illegitimate son living in a satrapy that's threatening civil war for the second time in fifteen years. But Gavin is actually Dazen Guile in disguise; after the battle that ended the last war and killed his brother, he stole Gavin's identity. Now he has to take responsibility for his brother's bastard. Gavin travels to Tyrea with Karris, his former fiancée and now a member of his elite defensive corps, the Blackguard. They find Kip, his son, in time to save him from a rebellious satrap who is calling himself King Garadul. The king allows them to leave, but takes Kip's knife – the only thing left him by his mother. While Gavin takes Kip back to the Chromeria to begin his magical education, Karris stays in Tyrea to rendezvous with a spy in the king's army.

Karris is captured by the king's forces, and she discovers King Garadul's right hand, a wight who calls himself the Color Prince, is the one fomenting rebellion. He is her brother, whom she'd thought long dead.

Kip tests into the Chromeria's school for drafters and meets a friend from his hometown, Liv Danavis, daughter of one of Dazen's greatest generals. Gavin is focused on killing wights and finding a political solution to the war, but he must also deal with the man he's secretly imprisoned deep beneath the Chromeria: his brother. Gavin's father, Andross, tasks him with going back to Tyrea to stop the rebellion from becoming an empire-wide war and with retrieving the very knife Gavin allowed the king to take when he rescued Kip.

When Gavin, Kip, and Liv arrive at Tyrea's capital, Garriston, they meet Liv's father, former general Corvan Danavis. They realize the city is indefensible, so Gavin begins to draft an entire wall. Gavin has almost completed the wall when a cannonball destroys the gate he'd been drafting. Gavin's forces defend the retreat of Garriston's citizens as they attempt to escape via barges. Kip learns where Karris is and decides to rescue her. Liv follows him, but they are separated when Kip is captured by the Color Prince's forces.

Kip is imprisoned with Karris, and in the chaos of battle they manage to join the army marching toward the city. Kip kills King Garadul, and Liv saves both Kip and Karris by agreeing to join the Color Prince if he'll use his sharpshooting skills to prevent their deaths in battle.

Kip races to meet another threat: he knows a young poly-chrome, Zymun, has been assigned to assassinate Gavin. He doesn't stop the attack, but Gavin survives when Kip intercedes. Kip takes the dagger Zymun used and realizes it is the same blade his mother gave him. Gavin, Kip, and Karris escape the city on barges with much of the city's civilian population. Gavin is unaware that his brother has escaped the first of multiple prison chambers back at the Chromeria.

Book Two: *The Blinding Knife*

Gavin negotiates with the Third Eye, a powerful Seer, to get permission for the refugees to build a home on her island. Karris and Gavin build a harbor for the refugee fleet, and Gavin hunts the blue *bane*, a horror forming in the Cerulean Sea. If he doesn't destroy the bane, an ancient god will be reborn.

Kip returns to the Chromeria to test into the Blackguard. He befriends a few of his fellow Blackguard candidates, including Teia, a color-blind *paryl* drafter and a slave. Her owner forces her to steal valuable goods and to spy on Kip. As hard as training is, the new interest his grandfather has taken in him is worse. Andross demands Kip play a card game, Nine Kings, for high stakes.

A librarian, Rea Siluz, introduces Kip to Janus Borig, an artist who creates 'true' Nine Kings cards, which allow drafters to experience history as it happened. But it's not long before Kip finds Janus mortally injured by two assassins. Kip manages to kill both, acquire their magical cloaks, and save Janus's deck of true Nine Kings cards. Kip uses a new deck made by Janus to beat Andross in a game, winning Teia's slave contract. Kip gives the cloaks, the cards, and his mother's knife to his father, who's just returned with Karris. Gavin has destroyed the blue bane and resettled the refugees, so he's ready to manipulate the Spectrum (the ruling council of the Chromeria) into declaring Seers Island a new satrapy and make Corvan Danavis its new satrap.

Karris is given a letter from Gavin's dead mother and learns Gavin has loved her all along. He broke their betrothal so Karris wouldn't have to marry a man she might not love. Karris approaches Gavin that night, but he's already in bed with another woman – a woman he didn't invite. Enraged at losing Karris again, Gavin throws the woman onto his balcony. She tumbles over the railing and falls to her death.

Certain he'll be arrested for the murder, Gavin decides he must free his brother to take his place as Prism. But Gavin realizes his long-imprisoned brother is crazy, so he kills him. Gavin returns from the prison to find the Spectrum has declared war and that his two Blackguards, the only witnesses to the girl's death, have sworn Gavin acted in self-defense, leaving him free to be Prism.

As the trainees continue with their elimination matches, Kip almost enters the Blackguard ranks – but loses at the last moment due to cheating by some of the other trainees. But his friend Cruxer uses a loophole to get Kip in anyway.

Gavin and Karris reconcile and marry just before they go to war against the Color Prince. With the new Blackguard inductees and the Chromeria's forces, they must destroy a green bane that is birthing a new god, Atirat. Liv is still with the Color Prince's army and uses her superviolet skills to help create Atirat.

Kip, Gavin, and Karris kill the god, but lose the city and the satrapy to the Color Prince's forces.

After the battle, Kip realizes that Andross is actually a red wight. As he confronts Andross, he draws the knife his mother gave him and stabs Andross in the shoulder. Gavin tries to stop the two, but can only redirect Kip's knife into his own body. He falls overboard, and Kip jumps after him. The ship sails on, only Andross aware of what truly happened. Gavin is picked up by Gunner, a master cannoneer on a ship they'd earlier destroyed. Kip is rescued by Zymun, who says he is actually Gavin and Karris's long-lost illegitimate son. Gavin wakes to find he is completely color-blind... and a slave rower.

Book Three: *The Broken Eye*

Adrift in a boat with Zymun, Kip is able to escape before they're press-ganged by pirates. Weeks later, he makes it back to the Chromeria, after surviving the jungle, starvation, and worse.

Because she married the Prism, as soon as she returns to the Chromeria, Karris is stripped of her rank in the Blackguard and given orders to take over the spy network of the White (the head of the Chromeria). Meanwhile, Andross Guile reveals that he has been miraculously healed from being a red wight. With the absence of Gavin Guile and the war under way, the Spectrum swiftly elects him promachos – commander in chief of the Chromeria.

Teia is quickly recruited by Murder Sharp, a skilled paryl assassin for the Order of the Broken Eye. When the Order steals her slave paperwork, and then frames her for murder, Teia finds herself helpless to resist. She struggles to balance her training as a Blackguard inductee with assignments from the Order, but finally confesses everything to Ironfist and the White. They commission her to serve as the Chromeria's spy on the Order, and Karris is assigned as her handler. As Teia continues her initiation into the Order, she discovers that she is a lightsplitter, a rare drafter who can use shimmercloaks (such as the ones Kip recovered) to make herself mostly invisible.

Upon his homecoming, Kip informs the Spectrum and Karris that Gavin is still alive, but avoids implicating Andross in Gavin's accident, which gains him a powerful if untrustworthy ally. He finds himself under Karris's tutelage for drafting and reunites with his old Blackguard squad, the Mighty: Benhadad, Big Leo, Teia, Ferkudi, Winsen, Goss, and Daelos. Andross grants the group access to restricted libraries so they can research heretical Nine Kings cards and the Lightbringer, a long-prophesied savior of the satrapies, hoping they'll gain information to win the war. In the process, Kip befriends mousy Quentin Naheed, a luxiat with extraordinary skills as a scholar.

Gavin, now unable to draft any color, spends months as a galley slave on a pirate ship, rowing next to a mad prophet irreverently nicknamed after the deity he serves, Orholam. In the chaos of a sea battle with a ship they're attempting to seize, a young Ruthgari noble, Antonius Malargos, leaps aboard their ship and offers to free the enslaved rowers if they help him break his ship free. They succeed, capturing Gunner and the Blinding Knife in the process, but Antonius takes Gavin to Ruthgar, to be imprisoned by his cousin Eirene. There her ally the Nuqaba of Paria arranges for Gavin to be publicly blinded.

The Mighty discover that everything about heretical cards, and much about the Lightbringer, has been erased from the records. Kip also realizes that the weapon that allows Prisms to be made or unmade is the very knife that stabbed Gavin. When Kip reports to Karris, they have a falling out over a poorly timed joke. Soon afterward, he is approached by Tisis Malargos, Eirene's sister, who proposes marriage to tie their families together. Kip later finds the true Nine Kings cards his father hid. Mistakenly drafting near them, he falls unconscious and enters the Great Library, where he meets the immortal Abaddon. Kip absorbs every one of the cards – except the Lightbringer card. He manages to grab Abaddon's shimmercloak, but dies from drafting so many cards. Teia, however, resuscitates him. Kip then gives Teia the cloak he stole from Abaddon. She later realizes it is the master cloak, and more powerful than any of the other shimmercloaks.

Andross manipulates Kip into confessing that he found both Andross's lost deck and Janus Borig's true cards, but Kip lies, saying they were all blank. Andross tells him to marry Tisis and go to Ruthgar to serve as his spy, while Zymun (who has just come to the Chromeria and announced that he is Karris and Gavin's long-lost son) will serve as Prism for seven years.

Karris receives word about Gavin's location just in time to assemble a small crew to save him – though not in time to save him from being blinded in one eye. When they return together to the Jaspers, where the Chromeria is located, Karris sends him for healing and finds herself at the ceremony for selecting the new White – as the previous White has just died – and that she is a nominee.

Kip and Tisis agree to marry and flee the Chromeria, and the Mighty insist on coming with them. When Zymun orders the newly formed Lightguard to kill them, they fight their way free. Though Goss is killed and Daelos wounded, the rest of the Mighty escape to meet Tisis at the docks. Ironfist's brother, Tremblefist, covers their escape, but is killed in the explosion he sets to prevent the Lightguards' pursuing them. Kip and Tisis wed just before embarking on the ship, and Teia decides to stay at the Chromeria. She will be of more value in the war effort fighting the Order than with Kip.

Though it's supposed to be a random process, Karris sees the White selection has been rigged, but manages to overcome the trickery. She kills two of the other nominees who attempt to kill her, and is declared the new White.

Before Ironfist finds his dying brother, he meets secretly with his uncle: the perfidious Grinwoody, hidden in plain sight as the slave of Andross Guile, is also the Old Man of the Desert, leader of the Broken Eye. Ironfist has been part of the Order for years. He gives Grinwoody the black seed crystal that only the White and the commander of the Blackguard have access to.

Meanwhile, Liv Danavis has been hunting the superviolet seed crystal at the command of the Color Prince. But though the Color Prince tries to make her wear a black luxin choker to keep her under his control, she foils the attempt and captures the seed crystal on her own.

Gavin is kidnapped from the physicians' care on Big Jasper, and wakes in a prison cell.

The man who is content to live alone is either a beast or a god.

In regione caecorum rex est luscus.
In the land of the blind, the one-eyed man is king.
—Erasmus of Rotterdam

Chapter 1

Like a house slave sweeping dirt into a pile, Orholam had heaped together all the earth's horrors and sin. Whistling a nursery song, he gathered barbarities and cruelties and outrages as Gavin lay on his back in the center of it all, arms spread, thrashing against his bonds. Dustpan filled to overflowing with creosote sins, Orholam turned toward Gavin for the first time.

As he turned, his face was blinding bright, unknowable, a miasma of razor-edged light, but at the corner of his mouth, his beard twitched with a torturer's glee.

'*Servient omnes,*' Orholam said. All shall serve.

He upended his dustpan over Gavin's face. Gavin screamed, but his words were taken from him like silk torn from the spool in a spider's gut, unwinding until it snapped inside him, leaving him empty and shattered inside. He tried to turn, twist, look away, but his eyes were propped open. There was no escaping the bulbous, congealed ordure schloomping toward his eye.

The whole mass fell. And as it fell, it caught fire and burnt in the air, sizzling, spattering, spitting angrily.

And afire, all the world's sin fell into Gavin's eye and set his orb aflame. The fire sank sizzling into his socket, gases escaping, *tssst*, like a sigh from a disappointed father at his failure son.

And the fire lodged in his eye, burning, and he screamed for ages past counting, until his throat was raw and tongue was dry, until deserts blew barren sands into snow, and his attempts to shriek faded, and his skin grew hard and cracked, and the burning shard impaled him, pinning him to the world, cooled by temperature's reckoning but not by pain's, and the shard crystallized, and the smoke cleared, and impaling Gavin's blind eye was a black prism.

1

Gasping, Gavin woke from his dream to find himself in darkness. But his arms jerked hard against iron manacles.

He was shackled to a table, arms extended. The nightmare wasn't over.

The nightmare had just begun.

Chapter 2

Teia lowered the silk noose toward her damnation. Rope spooled out from careful fingers toward the anxious woman quietly working at the desk below. The target was perhaps thirty, wearing a slave's dress, her copper-colored hair pulled up in a simple ponytail. As Teia watched, the woman folded a piece of the luxin-imbued flash paper that all her spies used. She paused and took a sip of an expensive whisky.

Don't look up! Please don't look up.

The woman was Prism Gavin Guile's room slave. She was the White's hidden spymistress. She was Teia's former superior and her mentor. Marissia put down her whisky, and as she sealed the note, she said, 'Orholam, forgive me.'

Teia was using the shimmercloak that Murder Sharp had given her, but because she was clinging to the ironwork on the ceiling, it hung away from her body, and it didn't hide the dangling noose at all.

But Marissia didn't look up. She put the note aside and pulled out another sheet of thin paper.

As her mentor leaned forward again, Teia dexterously flipped the noose over Marissia's head and then dropped from the ceiling, holding the rope. Draped over a beam above, the noose jerked tight around Marissia's throat and hauled her to her feet. The sharp movement flung her chair backward just as Teia, holding the other end, swung down and forward. The falling chair cracked across Teia's shins a moment before she crashed into Marissia.

Somehow Teia kept from releasing the rope, and she didn't cry out. Marissia was choking, grabbing at her neck, scrambling to get her feet under her.

2

Amazing how pain shuts down your thinking. If Teia hadn't just gotten her shins destroyed, there were a dozen things she would have done. Instead she clung stupidly to the rope, gasping, tears springing from her eyes, face-to-face with her old superior.

As Marissia regained her feet, Teia saw the problem: she wasn't as heavy as Marissia. Marissia noticed it, too. Though gagging, she grabbed the rope above her head and pulled down with all her strength.

Something shimmered in the corner of Teia's eye, and Murder Sharp became visible as he took quick steps across the carpet. He buried a fist in Marissia's stomach.

Marissia's strangled cough blew spit across Teia's face. The slave woman went slack. In quick motions, Sharp took the noose from Teia, threw a sack over Marissia's head, and bound Marissia's hands behind her back in such a way that any move she made to escape would tighten the noose around her neck.

Master Sharp was gifted with knots.

He forced Marissia to her knees and checked once more that she could breathe – all the fight had gone out of her.

'Not good,' Master Sharp said, turning back to Teia. He was a lean man with sharp features, orange-red hair, and a short beard the color of fire. His most remarkable features, though, were his teeth and his too-big, too-frequent smile, which he flashed now joylessly, from mere habit. Usually the teeth he revealed with that smile were too white and too perfect. On most hunts, he wore dentures made of predators' teeth. But today, perhaps because his mission wasn't to kill anyone, he wore dentures of beaver teeth – a full, discon-certing mouth of big, wide, flat incisors. They barely fit in his mouth.

'Not very good at all. But you kept her from destroying any of the papers,' he continued, 'so I'll accept it.'

'You were here the whole time?' Teia asked. She set the chair back upright to give herself a moment of not looking at the monster who was now her master. She massaged her aching shins. Orholam have mercy, those beaver teeth made her skin crawl.

'This is too important for me to let you bungle it. She was

some kind of secretary for the Prism. Who knows what she has access to?'

Secretary? So the Order didn't know what Marissia really was. Why, then, was it kidnapping her?

And why kidnapping? Teia had thought that the Order only killed people.

Not that it wouldn't murder Marissia later.

Handing Teia the noose, Murder Sharp strode to the window to look down at the islands. Even from where she was, Teia could see a thick curl of black smoke rising to greet the morning sun.

Earlier this morning, their trainer Tremblefist had blown the black powder stores beneath the cannon tower so Kip and the rest of the Mighty could escape by sea. He'd probably given his life doing it. The squad had gotten away while Teia had chosen to stay here. And now she was doing this.

She was a fool.

'We're lucky,' Sharp said. 'The few Blackguards who weren't already on the parade route have abandoned their posts to get down to that tower. Still, no time to waste. You watch her. Break her neck if she screams.'

He shook his head at that last part. He'd said that for Marissia's benefit. He made a fist and mimed hitting her stomach. Knock the wind out of her if she screams, he meant.

Why he hadn't just gagged her, Teia didn't know, but she didn't ask. She'd learned not to push the mercurial assassin. Sometimes he had deeper plans. Sometimes he didn't think of the obvious. But he never liked being questioned, and there was no upside to Teia appearing too smart.

Sharp scooped all the papers off the table and into a sack. He opened drawers and grabbed every paper with writing on it, and thumbed through all the blank pages to make sure nothing was hidden from him.

Then he was off, searching the rest of the room.

Marissia gave two sharp little tugs on the rope in Teia's hand.

'Shhh,' Teia said.

Marissia waited a few moments and tugged again. She wanted to say something.

What was Teia going to tell her? She hadn't known Marissia outside of their work, but she'd felt a kinship and deep respect for the woman. They had both been slaves. Both were spies, and Marissia had risen as high as any slave or spy could.

Marissia had once told Teia that the Order would make her do something terrible. 'Let it be on my head – but do it,' she'd said.

But there was no way she could have guessed that the something terrible would be her own kidnapping and likely murder.

Another tug. Master Sharp had ducked into the slave's closet off the main room, out of sight and earshot. 'He's gone. Only for a moment,' Teia whispered.

'Third drawer, left side,' Marissia whispered. 'Halfway back, straight up. Push hard. Quick!'

Master Sharp had left the drawer open, so Teia had only to take one step and stoop. The surface felt flat, but as Teia pushed hard on it, she felt something snap with a slight chalky scent of broken blue luxin, and a tiny section of the wood sank in. A folded piece of parchment dropped into her hand.

Teia stepped back into place, stashing the parchment in a pocket. 'Got it,' she whispered.

'Tug when you need me—'

Master Sharp stepped back in. 'What's she saying?'

'Um? What?' Teia said. For one terrifying moment, her mind went blank. 'Oh, she's trying to bribe me.' Teia said it like she was bored.

Staring at her hard, Master Sharp ran a freakishly long pink tongue over those horrid wide teeth. 'I took a bribe...' He smacked his lips. 'Once. Had no plan to let the man go, of course, and killed him as soon as I got the coin.' Sharp tucked a package of documents tied with red or green ribbon into his sack. Teia was color-blind, so she could tell only that it was one or the other. 'No harm, right? The Old Man... disagreed. Emphatically.'

He smiled, too broadly. Something about those teeth twisted Teia's stomach more than when he'd worn a full set of wolves' fangs.

'How much did she offer?' he asked.

5

Teia froze. There was a hook in that question. Marissia the Prism's room slave *might* have squirreled away a small fortune. Marissia the spy would have saved a lot more, and with her life on the line, would she not offer a large bribe? But maybe not too large, a spymistress would be smart enough to start small—

Too long, T, don't take too long!

Teia said, 'She hadn't mentioned any figures. And I wasn't listening, anyway. I'm not in this for coin.' Change the subject, change the subject.

'Why are you, then?' Master Sharp asked.

'Are we really going to have this conversation in front of her?' Teia asked. 'Now? You said we needed to—'

'We don't need to worry about her.' His voice lowered dangerously. 'And don't question me.'

Orholam have mercy. That cemented it. If you were in the Order of the Broken Eye, there was only one reason you didn't worry when someone learned your secrets: Marissia was going to die. Teia said, 'I'm here for revenge.'

'Revenge? On who?'

Teia cocked her head as if it were an odd question. 'On all of 'em.'

He grinned, this time for real. 'You'll get plenty of that. And you'll come to the Crimson Path eventually.' The true friendliness should have made him less scary, but any comfort she might have felt was ground to paste between those inhumanly wide teeth.

He walked over to Marissia, still on her knees. 'How much would you give us?'

Tremulously, she said, 'As much as you want, I swear. I can get access to the Prism's account if we act fast. Please, sir, please.' She broke off as if terrified. It twisted Teia's guts because she couldn't tell which was real: Marissia's earlier bravery or her current terror. Maybe both.

'I've changed my mind,' Master Sharp said. 'If she yells, kill her.' Had he forgotten he'd already threatened that?

Or did he actually mean it this time?

Marissia collapsed, sobbing quietly.

'Hmm,' Sharp said, standing so close to Teia his sweet

breath washed over her face. 'How have I never noticed...'
As if it were the most natural thing in the world, he pushed
her lower lip down with a finger. 'You have a beautiful lower
left dogtooth.' He pushed her lip right and left, examining
her teeth as if she were a mare. 'No, just the one. Good color
on the rest, but boring.' He shrugged, smelled his finger, licked
off her saliva like a chef tasting soup. 'Better. You listened to
me about the parsley, didn't you? Add mint, fresh leaves when
you can. Tuck them in the gums. Don't chew or you'll get bits
in your teeth. Unsightly.'

He turned away, and she hoped he didn't notice her tremble.

He said, 'I need to check the White's room and make a
distraction. Be ready to go quick. If I'm not back in five, untie
her, throw her off the balcony as if she suicided, and make
your way out the same way we got in.' He threw his hood
over his head and pulled the laces through the grommets
quickly, cinching the mask tight over his nose and mouth,
leaving only his eyes clear, and those shadowed under the
hood. He turned and began shimmering.

On the back of his gray cloak, the image of a tufted gray
owl appeared with its wings spread and talons extended to
strike. The image shimmered out of phase with the rest of the
cloak, and disappeared last.

The door opened, showing a hallway marked with smoke
and pools of blood and scratches and divots in the stone walls
from arrows and bullets from the Mighty's battle with the
Lightguards earlier. That felt like a lifetime ago. Then the
door shut quietly.

Teia instantly shot a wave of *paryl* gas in an arc where
Murder Sharp had been standing to make sure he was really
gone. He was.

'Quickly,' Teia said, 'what do you want me to do?'

Marissia got up on her knees. Her voice was breathy with
controlled fear. 'Did he take the papers from my desk? Package.
All tied together in red ribbon.'

'Yes.'

Teia could hear the heavy sigh of despair expelled into the
hood over Marissia's head. The spymistress said, 'Teia, you
have to get those papers. I was to keep them safe for Karris.'

'What are they?'

'They're the White's instructions for her successor. They have everything Karris needs to know how to rule. Secrets. Plans. Names. There are things in there Karris can't learn any other way.'

Oh hell no. How was Teia to steal papers from Murder Sharp? 'We weren't sent for the papers, Marissia. We were sent for you. I think Sharp's just grabbing whatever is lying about.'

Marissia sagged. 'Any other day. Any other hour, and all those papers would be locked away safe...No matter. No time.' She bent for a moment. 'He'll take it all to the Old Man's office anyway. That parchment you grabbed from my desk. It's a code. Crack it. It's the combination or key word to the Old Man of the Desert's office. Teia, that office is *here*, in the Chromeria. Maybe in this very tower. That means he – or she, we don't even know for sure that the Old Man of the Desert *is* a man – is *here*. But if you open the office without using the code, it'll wash the room in fire. Everything in it will be destroyed. You can't let that happen. Not least because the White's papers will be destroyed, too.'

'I'll find it, I swear. But what—' Teia cut off at the sound of steps outside the room. She tapped Marissia's shoulder to tell her to be silent, and drafted, disappearing with her own borrowed shimmercloak.

But whoever it was walked past, and Teia heard the banging of the door to the roof. She and the squad had had quite the fight up there, only hours ago, but only a single Blackguard was standing watch now. Master Sharp said the commanders of the Blackguard would isolate the area until they could examine it to try to figure out what had happened.

'What about you?' Teia asked. 'How do we save you?'

A pause. Teia wished she could see Marissia's face, but the bag stayed perfectly still, giving no hint of her fear or her bravery or her hatred or her desperation.

'We don't,' Marissia said quietly.

'You've seen Sharp's face. They're going to kill you.'

Marissia's head bowed. 'Just...pray for me,' she said, and there was her fear again.

'At least let me give you a knife.'

'And what happens to you when this assassin finds your knife on me?' Marissia asked.

Before Teia could protest further, the door opened and closed. Master Sharp was speaking before he was even fully visible. 'Give me that cloak.'

'My shimmercloak?' Teia asked.

'It's not yours. It's the Order's, and don't forget it.'

'I'm the one who stole it! I risked everything to—'

'Now!'

Teia unclasped the choker and handed Master Sharp the burnt-hemmed shimmercloak. He lowered his own hood, threw Teia's cloak on over his cloak, attaching the choker awkwardly. He pulled his hood back up, but couldn't lace it properly. He swore.

'What are you doing?' Teia asked.

He swore again, and said to Marissia, 'You do other than what I say, and you die now, and not easy. Understand?'

Her head bobbed, the sack trembling as she wept. He slashed the rope between her neck and her wrists, and slung her over his shoulder. 'Teia, help me with the cloak.'

Teia spread out the second, bunched cloak over Marissia's body. Given that Marissia was slung over Sharp's shoulder, it covered her fully, if awkwardly.

'I have to sneak out without a cloak?' Teia asked.

'You go out the way we came in. Outside. Collect the climbing crescents as you go down. Be quick. You won't have long before people start looking up here.' He poked Marissia. 'You, when I tell you, you scream that there's a fire in the White's quarters. Because there is.'

Oh, *that* was why he hadn't gagged Marissia. The Blackguards would recognize her voice when she called out.

Still holding Marissia over his shoulder, Master Sharp stooped to pick up the bag full of papers he'd stolen.

'You want me to take the bag?' Teia asked.

He almost handed it to her, then paused. Anxiety hammered great blows against her mask of nonchalance. He said, 'Better not. Get climbing.'

'I could bring it to—'

'Now,' he said, and there was quiet menace in his voice. Without waiting, he turned his back, and far more slowly than usual, the cloaks began shimmering, the fox emblem on Teia's burnt cloak showing dark gray against the gray and then fading.

The door opened, and Teia smelled smoke.

'Fire! Fire in the White's quarters!' Marissia shouted. 'Fire!' And then the door closed behind them.

The obvious course was to hurry up and climb down the wall. Once the smoke started billowing out of the White's windows, eyes would turn toward the Prism's Tower. Teia couldn't be clinging to the walls in full view when that happened.

But Teia had a card to play that Master Sharp didn't know about.

She had her own cloak, the master cloak that Kip had given her. She pulled it out of her pack, the material thin and weightless as liquid light. She put it on. Drew the choker around her neck. Pulled up the hood, snapped it closed over her face. She could follow Sharp unseen.

But after extinguishing the fire, the Blackguards would search the tower exhaustively. If Teia followed Sharp, the Blackguards would find the climbing crescents stuck to the outside of the tower. The Order had spies in the Blackguard, so they would learn of it, and they would know Teia had disobeyed.

It wouldn't be proof that Teia was a spy, but the Order didn't need proof. They would kill her.

But if she didn't follow Sharp, they would kill Marissia.

Marissia had ordered Teia to let her die. The old Teia, the slave Teia, would have accepted that order and shrugged off responsibility for what happened next. Teia wasn't that Teia anymore.

This was war, and Teia was behind enemy lines, alone. She had to make her own decisions and live with the consequences. Like a warrior. Like an adult. Like a free woman.

In the unholy calculus of war, Teia was somehow suddenly worth more than a woman older, wiser, smarter, and better connected than she was. Teia was starting to suspect that the Order was a greater threat to the Chromeria than even the

10

Color Prince. Saving Marissia – even if Teia could figure out how – would jeopardize the Chromeria's best chance ever to destroy the Order. And only Teia knew now about the Old Man's office. Only she had the code.

It's war, T. Friends die.

Jaw clenched, heart leaden, Teia went out onto the balcony, closed the door behind her, and stepped onto the climbing crescents. She descended, taking away the evidence of Marissia's murder with each step.

It's war, T. The innocent die. And the best their friends can do is get vengeance.

Later.

Chapter 3

'Oh, my lord, what have they done to you?'

Gavin knew that voice. He opened his eye, tried to turn, but he was bound to a table, arms extended, nothing beneath them, as if on a raft over an ocean that was no longer there. His tongue was thick and parched, and a bandage covered his left eye.

Marissia came hovering into view above him, and the pity on her face told him how awful he must look.

'Wa...water,' Gavin rasped.

But the first thing she did was unbind his arms and legs. Marissia had been his room slave for more than a decade. She knew how he hated to be bound, how even the encumbrance of blankets twisted around his legs in bed made him panic and flail. Marissia, here? But where was here?

He remembered now. He must be at Amalu and Adini's, the chirurgeons on Big Jasper. He must have been panicking, delirious. It had all been nightmares. Marissia was here. There was no prison. Everything was going to be fine.

Karris had pulled him out of the hippodrome where they'd put out his eye, and he must have come down with a fever. He'd only dreamed he was in that blue hell he'd made for his brother. He'd only dreamed that his father knew everything. Fever dreams. Impossible dreams.

Oh, thank Orholam.

Marissia put a wet cloth in his mouth, and he sucked weakly. She wet it again and repeated the process, until he motioned that he'd had enough. She wiped the crusted spit from the corners of his mouth.

Only then did he try to speak. 'Marissia, where's Karris?'

'Your lady wife is safe, my lord. She's been made the White.' It was oddly formal for Marissia, but Gavin hadn't yet sorted out the blurred boundaries between his room slave and his new wife. Doubtless Marissia was upset that he had married, and who knew how Karris had been treating her? With Gavin's absence, he was lucky Marissia was even still employed in his household. A more jealous wife would have sold off the room slave who'd been so close to her husband.

But Gavin didn't have time to worry about a slave's feelings with all the problems facing him.

'The White?' he asked. 'You didn't just say...'

'Orea Pullawr has passed into the light, my lord. My lady Karris Guile has ascended to serve as the new White.'

'I thought that old crone was going to live forever,' Gavin said. But he felt an intense surge of pride at his wife's accomplishment. The White!

In retrospect, though, maybe Orea had been preparing Karris for that all along.

Orholam's balls, the other families were going to lose their minds. Andross Guile as promachos, Karris Guile as the White, and Gavin Guile as the Prism?

Well, that brought up a host of other problems. But Gavin was back, and with Karris beside him, there were few things he—'Marissia, is there something odd about the sound in here?'

'My lord.' There was a dread monotone to her voice.

With difficulty Gavin sat up. His bed was the kind of palanquin on which nobles were carried when injured, with drapes on all sides for privacy, but small and light so that slaves could navigate corners and narrow streets.

A wall was not far behind Marissia. It *curved*.

'Oh, Marissia, no.'

That gray wall curved like a teardrop or a squashed ball. Gavin tore back the palanquin's other curtains. Everywhere the one curving wall, sparkling quietly with inner light. Gavin couldn't see the blue of it, but he could see all he needed to from that winking crystalline luxin. He was in the blue hell. His gaoler had somehow brought Marissia here to care for Gavin's wounds. To keep him alive. For punishment.

'How are you here?' he asked.

'I was kidnapped. By Order assassins who were contracted by your father.'

'What?!'

'My lord, I have secrets I would tell you. I don't know how long I have.'

'You expect them to kill you.' He could see it in the tight calm of her face, like an improperly tanned hide stretched too far over a drum.

'I was allowed to see my kidnappers' faces. And High Lord Guile's. Your father brought me here himself. Alone.'

Gavin's arm shook from the mere effort of holding himself seated. He fell back on the palanquin. 'Of course he did,' he said. 'He couldn't let anyone know about this place. But someone had to care for me, and he guessed that you would know about these cells after so many years with me, so he accomplished numerous tasks at once. That's my father. May Orholam damn him.'

It was also very much Andross Guile to discard the slave after she'd served her purpose.

He wouldn't even guess that Gavin would be put out by it. Andross wouldn't think of it as murdering Gavin's lover; he would think of it as destroying a piece of Gavin's property. Gavin could always buy another room slave, one prettier and younger, even. This one had to be more than thirty years old, after all.

'Marissia, I'm—'

He could see on her face that she knew it, too. 'I don't know how much time we have, my lord. Please don't. My courage is leaking away by the moment. Please treat me like a scout or a captain in your armies, so I can think of myself

13

as a warrior, because I can't bear...' Her throat clenched as she lost her words to fear, the thief.

Gavin hesitated and then gathered himself. 'Water. The cup this time.' He didn't try to sit up. With a trembling hand, she gave him water. He took it, clumsily, his left hand missing the third and fourth fingers.

'Report,' he said when he was done, and though he lay on his back, his voice was all command.

'What I have to say is quite sensitive, my lord. What do we do about eavesdroppers?'

He thought about it. 'If my father brought you here himself, it means he isn't trusting even his closest spies to know about this place. So he would have to be eavesdropping himself. He knows I may sleep for another few days, so I doubt he'd gamble his time that way. Just sitting here, waiting for me to wake, doing nothing else while he doubtless needs to do much? No. Speaking is a risk, but it's a risk I'll take.'

She took a deep breath, bracing herself. She looked away from his eye. 'I am – that is, I *was* Orea Pullawr's spymistress.'

Gavin felt as if he'd been punched in the gut.

Marissia hurried on. 'At first I just met with a few of her contacts, but I did well. She kept expanding my role until, in the last few years, when she was losing mobility, I took over everything.'

Gavin couldn't look at her. He stared straight up. Furious, he tore off the palanquin's roof.

Marissia fell silent.

The action left him exhausted, aware again of how sick he'd been. He could only stare up – up the anus of the blue hell, as it shat bread on the poor souls within. He would be eating Andross Guile's shit-mercy for as long as he chose to live. 'And how exactly did that fit with our arrangement, Marissia?'

'I did my best to make it fit, my lord.'

He half laughed. 'You did your best?'

'I never betrayed you.'

'What did the White have over you? I was here! You're mine!' he spat. 'What could she threaten you with that I could not protect you from? I'm nothing now, but I was...I was indomitable. Do you not remember what I did for you? Do you not remember the Seaborns?'

'I remember, my l—'

'People think I killed that young asshole in a rage because he'd damaged my property. I did it so no one would ever harass you again. I killed a man and ended up having to purge his entire family – for you. For a slave. And for that – for that! – I get no loyalty? From you who shared my chambers and my bed. From you, whom I trusted more than I trusted even my own mother.'

'My lord...' She was weakening, losing whatever courage she'd gathered to tell him all this.

'What did you tell the White?' he asked, voice dangerous.

'I told her nothing that we hadn't agreed on. I swear. I *swear.*'

Marissia had been the White's gift to Gavin. A young, pretty, smart virgin to be his room slave, untainted by the politics of Big Jasper or loyalties to any other family. She was a rich gift indeed, and an unusual one. She had a passing resemblance – more pronounced in those early years – to Karris. The White had obviously thought Gavin had a type.

As a young, single Prism, he could have easily had many room slaves. Wealthy subjects were always giving gifts, looking for favor, and looking to place spies near him.

A procession of room slaves wouldn't have been a problem except for one reason: the food chute down to his brother's prison connected to his own room. Regardless of whether a room slave's duties were purely sexual or she acted as more of a chief slave, as Marissia had, a room slave was *in* one's room constantly. So rather than trust that a hundred searching eyes would all miss one hidden secret, Gavin had decided to turn one spy to his own side. He'd assumed that the young Marissia had been ordered by the White to spy on him.

But who was the White to command more loyalty than Gavin in his proud prime?

The White had asked him to kindly give the girl a few weeks to adjust to her new life. It would be bewildering for a young slave from the reaches of the Blood Forest to adjust to life here, she said. Give her time.

Gavin had gone further than that. He had plotted how to take full possession of his newest acquisition as a general might plot a military campaign. He had seduced her as if she were a princess. It was not a hard labor, and not entirely a deceitful one, either. He'd been immediately attracted to Marissia's obvious intelligence, her beauty, and – no less important to the young, arrogant man he'd been – her desire to please.

In that first year when Karris had left and he'd been so heartbroken and believed he would never see her again, Gavin had even thought that he was in love with Marissia.

As if one could love a slave the way one loves a woman.

It was the stuff of scandal. It was the subject of satirical stories and songs. An entire sequence of comedies was devoted to the dullard Old Giles, the henpecked lord who left his wife for his slave, left all his lands and titles to marry her, and had adventures as he cluelessly attempted the basic labors of farmers, or millers, or salt rakers, or brick makers, or bakers, always failing and always then having to try another occupation in the next story. Usually in another city. Usually because his lady wife had shown up at his place of business.

Other tales of masters and slaves in love were darker and not sung much in front of lords or ladies. Those were tales of the too-pretty room slave whose jealous mistress sold her off to the silver mines or the brothels, or murdered her outright. Like every good gift, beauty was a blessing for the rich, but sometimes a curse for the poor.

The frisson of danger for a lord, who might be mocked by his friends for being an Old Giles, didn't compare to what a room slave had to feel, afraid on the one hand to please her master too little, and afraid on the other hand to be seen pleasing him too much.

Gavin had decided many times that instead of feeling love-love, he loved Marissia as a master loves a favored hound. You could love a hound. A hound could love you. But loving a hound as one loves a woman? Unnatural. Disordered.

Whatever his few qualms, he had won over Marissia's heart along with his ownership of her body, and eventually, after he was sure she cared for him more than anything in the world, he'd confronted her with evidence of her spying for the White, pretending he felt betrayed by what he knew had been the point all along.

It had, of course, been unfair. How could Marissia have said no to the White herself – her owner – when she hadn't yet even met Gavin? But his scheme had worked. After shaming and terrifying her, Gavin had made his accommodation with her: Marissia would continue to spy for the White, but she would ask Gavin what she could share with Orea Pullawr first. There would be certain secrets the White could never know.

And then, by degrees, Gavin had let her learn secrets and false secrets, always watching the White to see what she knew, always testing Marissia's faithfulness. And faithful she had been, until Gavin had even trusted her with the bread. He hadn't told her it was for his brother below, but she'd understood it was some awful secret, and Orea had never learned of it.

And now the White, Orea Pullawr, was dead, and she hadn't used whatever secrets Marissia had told her to destroy him. So what kind of partial betrayal was this?

'Marissia,' Gavin said. 'Why would you do this? What loyalty did you owe her?'

Marissia straightened her back, and looked him in the eye. 'My name is Marissia Pullawr. The White was my grandmother. You were my assignment. I was never a slave.'

Chapter 4

Karris Guile, the White, the Chosen of Orholam, the Lady of Seven Towers, the Mistress of the Breaking Light, the Left Hand of the Omnipotent, stared out over the Jaspers from her apartments atop the Prism's Tower. Her word was law on every bit of land her eyes could see. Every drafter in the Seven Satrapies owed her obedience. To most people, she was a figure of near-mythic stature.

She had never felt more powerless.

She wasn't about to let that continue.

Around her the six other towers of the Chromeria rose as if in an embrace, but they were set lower than the Prism's Tower, like children hugging her legs, offering encumbrance instead of comfort. Responsibilities to fulfill, duties to attend to, and too many of both. Karris, who had always had an affinity for the blue virtues of order and hierarchy – an affinity oft buried by her wanton drafting of green and red – was making a list not just of the facts facing her, but also of the actions she would need to take regarding each, shelving her emotions for the time being.

She had only minutes before Andross Guile arrived, and she needed all her faculties for the confrontation. She had to make her own plans before he arrived, because if she weren't firmly set on her course before he began speaking, he would steer her toward his destinations so skillfully that she would come out thinking it had been her idea.

Gavin was gone. Her husband, her broken Prism – to save whom she had risked war with Paria and Ruthgar both – had vanished. As soon as she'd gotten out of the ceremony anointing her the new White, she'd sent an entire squad of Blackguards to the chirurgeons' clinic where he'd been left. It had been wrecked. Everyone gone. Blood splattered about. The door splintered off its hinges.

I have a contact who owns a tavern on that street.

☐ *Ask contact if any unusual men were in the neighborhood today.*

But what counted as unusual on a Sun Day? The city was packed with visitors for the holy day festivities; everyone from pilgrims to pirates piled into the city to celebrate.

In the distance, the cannon tower that had guarded East Bay still smoked. Seventy dead there. Sixty-four of them confirmed as Andross Guile's Lightguard thugs. Six unknown.

No, five unknown; one of the dead is reported to be Commander Ironfist himself or maybe his brother Tremblefist.

☐ *Go view the body myself to confirm which of my friends it is.*

No, that wasn't right at all.

☐ *Go view the body myself to confirm its identity.*

She breathed out slowly. Tears weren't an option now. Not when her people needed her. Her Blackguards needed to know that she was strong. Andross Guile needed to know she wasn't weak.

Next, two great crenellations had dropped from the top of the Prism's Tower, becoming counterweights for two different great escape cables that had sprung up from hidden places – escape routes that Karris had never heard so much as a whisper of. Apparently no one else had known of them, either, because no one had maintained them. One had malfunctioned.

The other had worked, though, and Kip and his squad – the Mighty, they were being called – had escaped.

☐ *Question Carver Black. (Did he know of this escape route?)*
☐ *Coordinate with Carver Black to assign engineers and slave teams to put the crenellations back in place and fix the broken mechanisms.*
☐ *Assign drafter-builders and divers to repair and bury the cables again.*

Why the Mighty had *needed* to escape was still a question that needed answering. And if Karris was furious that someone had exposed an ages-old secret of the escape route, she was more furious that they'd had good reason to do so. While Karris and the Colors and High Satraps had been sequestered to choose a new White, someone had been killing Blackguards in the very same tower.

Kip was gone. In addition to being her stepson, he had been her discipulus for nine months, and she cared for him a great deal, even if she had been wretched at showing it. According to the Blackguard, the Lightguards had attempted to murder Kip without provocation, gunning down Goss, one of Kip's Mighty. The Blackguard had apparently been ordered to stand down, and, damn them for their obedience, they had.

- ☐ *Find out who ordered them to stand down.*
- ☐ *Interview each of the watch captains.*
- ☐ *Interrogate the member of Kip's squad who was left behind, Daelos. Did he get his injury during the escape?*

Tisis Malargos, the younger sister of Eirene Malargos – the real power in Ruthgar – was gone. She was far down the list of Karris's immediate problems, but there was still a war going on, and such details couldn't be dismissed. Tisis had been the Chromeria's hostage, guaranteeing Ruthgari loyalty. Why had she fled now? A hostage's leaving without permission was a breach of treaty and thereby technically an act of war.

- ☐ *Find Tisis's friends and slaves. Interrogate.*

Commander Ironfist was missing. Promachos Andross Guile had relieved him of his position, but Karris would fight tooth and nail to reinstate him. Of course, first she had to find him, and he'd last been seen heading to the docks – which was exactly what she would have done if she'd found herself suddenly without a position and knowing Andross Guile was against her.

Dear Orholam, what if it *is* Ironfist dead down at the cannon tower?

- ☐ *Destroy the Lightguard. Failing that, place spies high within the organization.*

Regardless of whether it was Tremblefist or Ironfist dead, how had he died? What had happened?

☐ *Interrogate some Lightguards directly.*
☐ *Consult with Carver Black.*
☐ *Find locals who saw what happened.*

How would she find Ironfist? How could she bring him back?

☐ *Tell all the Blackguards to look for Ironfist. Offer a reward. Do everything. Offer him whatever he wants if he'll come back.*

Ironfist was the one person Karris could trust without reservation, because—

Marissia was gone. Hard as it was to admit, for Karris's new duties this was the worst blow of all. Marissia had been the head of all the White's spies for years until Karris had recently begun to take those over.

Karris thought they'd become something like friends, so Marissia's betrayal bit deep. And who knew what she'd taken with her?...Or whom.

Dear Orholam. What if Marissia had taken Gavin? But what could Karris do? It seemed hopeless. There were no hints at all about Marissia's whereabouts – or Gavin's. But the woman couldn't have absconded with him without help. She had no retainers or family, so that meant she had money.

☐ *Check in with all spies. Determine if each one is loyal to me or to Marissia still.*

☐ *Shift all monies to new accounts.*
☐ *Determine how much Marissia has stolen, if possible. How? By leaning on Turgal*

21

Onesto? The young banking scion will have the opportunity to prove his worth now.

The only good news was that regardless of how high she'd climbed, Marissia was still a slave. Her clipped ear meant she would have trouble keeping power if she didn't have money. Money. Money's the answer for that snake.

But all this was recovery. All this was merely treading water after a shipwreck. That wasn't enough. Karris needed to swim for shore.

She was the White now. That meant all the drafters in the Seven Satrapies were her responsibility. It meant the Chromeria and Big Jasper and Little Jasper were her responsibility. Taking care of those meant that the physical, brute-force weapons she'd loved for so long were inadequate to the task before her.

She had to win the war.

☐ *Win the war.*

She made it an item on her list, as if something so immense might be better comprehended if she wrestled it into words.

Winning battles wouldn't suffice. By sheer numbers killed, the Seven Satrapies had won battles. But their numbers bled away every night while the Color Prince added to his.

Karris's war wasn't going to be fought on battlefields. It was up to her to give the people of the Seven Satrapies reasons to fight, to bleed, to die, and to kill. Others would be the sword in this fight. She would be the lash and the pen.

She must unite the Seven Satrapies for this war. Any who opposed that goal, who opposed her, must be brought into line or crushed.

There was a knock on the door, and the now omnipresent Blackguards announced Andross Guile. He was only the first test.

Lovely to be starting out easy.

Andross Guile looked as if he had purloined all the youth Karris had lost in the last few months. It wasn't only that his little round paunch was shrinking, or that his skin, formerly pallid from being so long covered from the sun's gaze, was taking on color again. His back was straight, his head high, showing the broad Guile shoulders and strong Guile jaw. He was energized by crisis.

A good man for these times, then.

And that's the first and last time I'll ever think of Andross Guile as a good man.

'It's nice to see you smile in such fraught times, High Lady,' he said.

Karris wasn't a player of that game that Andross liked so much, Nine Kings, but at this moment, she knew she had only one card: her own attitude.

He knew more than she did, so it made sense to defer to him. If he were Ironfist, she would ask, "What must we do to win this war?" But with Andross Guile, there was no way she could position herself as the subordinate.

'Those men I killed,' she said. 'How are you going to deal with the fallout from their families?'

His face jumped off a bridge, tried to flip, and landed on its belly. 'Me?'

She looked at him levelly. He'd tried to stack the election of the White against her. During the testing, two of the candidates – secretly *his* candidates – had tried to push her off the great disks to fall to her death. It hadn't turned out well for them. 'If nothing else,' she said, 'we share a last name. That's a problem...for you.'

Then he laughed. 'Oh, that *is* an interesting play. Ha!' He looked at her for a few moments, and she had a brief fantasy that he was bald because his brain generated so much heat it had burnt off all his hair. 'I was rather hoping that you might choose to be known by your maiden name, to use the term "maiden"...loosely.'

Karris saw Blackguard Gavin Greyling's eyes go wide. He couldn't believe Andross was speaking to her that way.

And in that moment, Karris thanked Orea Pullawr for forbidding her to use red or green luxin. After years of her constantly using angry red and impulsive green, Karris's tongue had been a flame. But the months of abstaining had given her

23

new patience. Karris let the insult pass beneath her feet with blue disdain.

'Hmm,' Andross said, as if it were merely interesting that she did not take offense. As if he'd played a good card, and the play hadn't worked the way he'd thought, and thus, because he'd been countered, that was the end of it.

She wanted to be angry about it, but that was a waste, too, wasn't it? Instead she should take note: Andross will make personal insults impersonally, not because he's trying to insult you, but because he's trying to find your weaknesses.

'I'll never prove it,' she said, 'but I *know*. You tried to have me killed. Or you encouraged those who tried. Same thing, as far as I'm concerned. I merely stopped you, so in my view, you shit the bed. You clean it up.'

A frisson went through the Blackguards assigned to Karris and to Andross. They all knew how fast Karris was. They knew how good she was at unarmed combat. She was well within lethal range of Andross Guile. And the Blackguards were charged with protecting both the White *and* the promachos. What were they to do if one attacked the other? Pulling apart fighters was vastly more dangerous and complicated than simply putting down a threat.

But Andross Guile merely tugged on his nose, scratching it. He looked at the Blackguards and their weapons and their menacing stances. 'Stand down, children. You're here to make us look good, not to actually do anything.'

'While you're being an asshole for no good reason to people who can't fight back,' Karris said, 'I want to point out something.'

'Oh, please do.'

'Orea beat you. You stacked the cards against us. I know you did. You owned all six of the other candidates, didn't you?'

'All six? That would be excessive, wouldn't it?'

'You think you're the best at all your games. But Orea beat you. She *beat* you.'

Andross smiled and shrugged. 'Luck,' he said, as if Karris's selection as the White and the death of two of his cat's-paws were trifles in the course of a friendly wager between friends.

'Not luck. Orholam turns his face against the proud, Andross Guile.'

'You think the divinity himself selected you?' Andross said, amused.

'It is the point of the entire ritual, isn't it?' Karris asked.

Andross laughed, as if he couldn't believe how naïve she was. 'You drew one stone in seven. And perhaps there was no luck involved at all, depending on how far Orea stooped to get you where you are. You won. Take your victory, but to mistake that for a divine mandate on your—'

'That's exactly what it is,' she interrupted.

He paused, and saw she was serious. 'Oh, you are surprising, aren't you? I can't tell if you're bluffing or if you actually believe that. No, don't tell me. I like the uncertainty. You're not a player, but you are a fascinating card, aren't you? After all these years, I finally start to see what my son saw in you.'

'Sons,' Karris corrected. Both of them had fallen for her, after all. To the whole world's sorrow.

'I hadn't forgotten,' Andross said, his voice suddenly stone.

Oh, so this wasn't all games and feeling out weaknesses and triggers. There was a personal edge in there. Andross blamed *her* for all this? For the war, for the loss of his sons? The sheer blind audacious folly.

But Karris wasn't here to destroy Andross Guile. She was here to make a partner of him. And the truth was, their problems were mutual. Much as they both hated it, they were yoked together not only against external threats, but against internal ones as well. Three Guiles in power went against tradition, if not law. No one was going to be comfortable with one Guile as promachos, another as Prism-elect, and a third as the White.

Karris waved the Blackguards back. 'So, how about it?'

'It? You mean me smoothing over your murder of Jason Jorvis and Akensis Azmith? Surely you're joking.'

'Not murder. Summary judgment of traitors. Which is the direction I'd go in my defense if I were brought to trial.'

'Not self-defense?' Andross asked. 'A petite woman like you, against two big men?'

Any trial would be agonizing, of course. People who've

25

never been in a fight to the death always seem to think that split-second decisions can be derived rationally, and that a good person will naturally always make the best choice and then carry out what she intends flawlessly.

Self-defense would be the stronger case, as Andross knew. Karris had been targeted for assassination by those two men, each of whom was bigger and stronger than she was.

She'd been scared, she could say. If her reaction had seemed disproportionate, people had to remember that she was a small woman, and they were large, threatening men. She'd merely done as her training taught her: she'd put an end to the threat.

It was all true, but it wasn't all the truth.

Karris hadn't been afraid. Combat was scary: you could do everything right and still get killed by a stray bullet or an ally's error or dumb luck. Fighting two untrained idiots hand to hand? Not that scary.

She might have been able to save them, but she'd had time for only two thoughts as they held on, balanced at the edge of the testing platform: First, that they were the sons of noble families that were needed in the war, and thus they would get away with their treason and blasphemy and murder. Second, that she wasn't going to let that happen.

Self-defense was a perfectly good legal defense, but telling people their new White had been afraid wasn't the way she wanted to start her term.

Or she could point out that by the rules of the selection as it had been presented, other than that none of them were to draft, there *were* no rules, no laws. Whoever came back would be the White, and the White would be immune to prosecution. Another perfectly good and true defense.

But her path, alleging treason? That would tear those families apart. If, during the ensuing investigations, someone folded and admitted they'd tried to manipulate the selection of the White, Karris had no doubt the fingers would end up pointing at Andross Guile. He would have to be executed as a traitor and heretic on Orholam's Glare, along with who knew how many others.

Andross said, 'If you take that path, you'll fatally weaken our war effort.'

'Even if I succeed,' Karris admitted. Rallying allies wouldn't be easy after decimating several powerful families and showing that there was corruption at the very heart of the Chromeria. 'I've not been elected to be the Gray. I am the White. What is white without purity? Bad enough that our promachos is faithless.'

Andross Guile gave her a long, appraising glance. 'Are you suddenly so ins— so zealous?'

'Hmm,' Karris said.

After a long moment, Andross said, 'I'll take care of the Jorvises and Azmiths. A trial won't be necessary.' He nodded and moved as if to leave, then stopped. He smirked. 'May I be excused, High Lady Guile?'

She grinned a little back – no harm letting him think his charisma worked even on her – and motioned that he was dismissed.

Only after the door closed behind him did she breathe again.

↗ *Survive first meeting with Andross Guile.*

Chapter 5

It was Sun Day night when Teia discovered the note on her bed. It was simply folded and dabbed with red wax, no seal impressed on it. Teia flared her eyes to paryl, saw nothing suspicious, and picked up the note: 'Report to Cowardice 27. Now.'

No signature.

Cowardice was the nickname of the sixth floor on the dark side of the red tower, not just the apparition strangling Teia.

Here was the problem with serving two masters who demanded total discretion: Teia had no idea whether Karris or Murder Sharp had left this message.

She hoped it was Karris. She had so much to report it was ridiculous.

She also hadn't slept for two days, and she wasn't at her best. Sleep deprivation led inexorably to bad decisions. If this note was from the Order, she couldn't afford any bad decisions.

The more immediate problem was what Teia should do with the master cloak. But what could she do with it now? Leave it in the trunk at the foot of her bunk? A treasure worth empires, hanging quietly on a hook from her bedpost? She could disguise it, sure, but as what? What if the laundresses came through and grabbed it? What if laundering destroyed the magic in it?

Trainer Fisk had once badly translated an Old Parian proverb for his classes: 'A sword unneeded can be laid, but a sword needed can't be made.'

Once they deciphered what it actually meant, all the young Blackguards took the message to heart: they carried two pistols or more; they carried backup blades and hidden blades; during the entire fight to get out of the Chromeria, Teia'd kept thinking of her rope spear. She'd left it in the practice room. It was still down there. She'd made do with paryl and swords and her dagger and a blunderbuss.

Orholam have mercy on her soul, that blunderbuss. How many of those Lightguards whom she'd raked with the blunderbuss at the lift had died? She'd *killed* men. Perhaps more worryingly, she didn't feel bad about it.

But fuck them. They'd been trying to kill her friends.

She looked at the cloak, still undecided. She really didn't know much of how it worked. The Blackguard had taught her that you don't take a weapon you're unfamiliar with into battle.

She glanced around. No one. She closed her eyes and pictured a flamboyant Abornean musketeer's cloak. Looked down.

Leagues of brocade and a starry sky's worth of gold medallions on blue velour, pointed shoulder pads in burnished silver and a starched collar.

She touched it, expecting her fingers to pass through the illusion.

It was all solid. Real.

It couldn't be. It must be an insanely powerful hex, tricking not just her eyes, but her mind. Teia closed her eyes tight, waited a few breaths, and touched the cloak again, locking in her mind her certainty that the illusion would be gone.

It was solid. Real.

The master cloak didn't fuck around.

It was too dangerous to take it until she figured out how to control it. She concentrated again, and the cloak went the flat, solid gray of a Blackguard nunk's cloak, color muted with use, and too short for any of the other nunks to borrow. She hung it on the hook at the end of her bunk with a quick prayer, grabbed her actual nunk's cloak, and left.

The trip to the red tower was a quick walk across the elevated bridges that hung in the air between the Prism's Tower and the six other towers without external supports, glimmering like a spiderweb bedecked with dew. Teia jogged up the slaves' stair to Cowardice and Courage, went to the dark side of the tower, and found room twenty-seven. She knocked.

No one answered. Room twenty-seven was on the outer curve of the dark side of the tower; Teia looked down the bending hallways each way, wondering if she'd caught a glimpse of a slave leaving down the shadowy hall. Best not to be seen at all. Unless that was her contact?

He wouldn't appreciate being accosted in the open if he was, so she tried the latch instead. Unlocked. Took one breath, drew in paryl, and went in.

She was struck in the face by a beam of light, blinding her after the relative darkness of Cowardice. The light was streaming from the lightwell, the communal reserve of pure sunlight shot down the middle of each tower from the many mirrors atop them.

'Lock the door,' a voice said. It sounded slightly off, and Teia knew immediately that it was being altered. Karris had a collar that did that. But Karris wouldn't be concealing her identity from Teia now.

That meant Teia was meeting one of the Order's goons.

Oddly, the realization calmed her. At least she knew what she was up against.

She locked the door. 'You mind?' she asked, squinting. The

room was dark other than that single beam of light, and the door behind her was draped in black cloth so as to absorb the light so it wouldn't bounce around the room and illuminate it.

'Light blinds,' a figure seated in the depths of the room said.

Teia held up a hand against the beam. 'Which is why I tend not to stare straight into it,' she said. 'Who are you? I've got a lot to do. I'm not in the mood to play children's games.'

With a clatter, the shutter shut and the room was plunged into blackness.

She drafted a paryl torch immediately, flaring her eyes.

'None of that!'

She froze. 'None of what?' It could have been a guess.

There was a reptilian silence. Teia felt the stirrings of Fear, deep in his lair, twisting in her stomach like an old dragon in unquiet slumber.

'Diakoptês was a lens maker, you know,' the voice said.

When the Order spoke, it was as if it had another language. Diakoptês. Teia still had to mentally translate it to Lucidonius. To the Chromeria, he'd been the one who enlightened them when they were imprisoned in the darkness of paganism. To the Order, he was the great betrayer, the one who'd broken them.

'So I've heard,' Teia said.

Kip's father Gavin had given him some lenses supposedly crafted by Lucidonius himself, the most valuable among them sub-red and superviolet lenses that allowed any drafter to see in their respective spectra. Whether they were actually Lucidonius's work or some other genius's, those lenses had never been duplicated. But that dragon thrashed now, fully awake.

'You've got paryl lenses?' Teia asked. She couldn't believe it.

'Not stupid. Good. I require a certain bare minimum intelligence even of my Shadows, though your own master dances close to that flame.'

Of the few who knew of him, no one spoke of Murder Sharp so dismissively. None would dare, except...

Teia dropped to her knees. 'Master. My lord.'

It came easily to her, obeisance, prostration. So many years a slave.

But it was right to be afraid. This was the Old Man of the Desert himself.

He didn't move. Didn't speak for a long time.

Teia flared her eyes to sub-red sensitivity, but he was nothing more than a warm smudge in the darkness. Likely swaddled in many layers, his face so dark that he must be wearing thicker layers over it in case she used paryl and he missed it. 'My lord?' Teia asked finally.

'None may wear cloaks in my presence. Put yours on the hook by the door.'

She removed her cloak and stood slowly, certain that he had a cocked musket pointed at her. She groped around until she found the hook, and hung her cloak on it.

Right choice. I made the right choice for once, leaving my cloak back in the room.

'Pull the hook down,' he said quietly.

She pulled the hook and a mechanism snapped around the cloak with a click, securing it in place. So the Old Man of the Desert was paranoid about his Shadows and their cloaks, even when he knew (or thought he did) exactly which cloaks they had.

It was, Teia guessed, perhaps the only way to become an *old* man when one ran a network of assassins.

A light bloomed in the room, cool blue. It wasn't for her benefit. She wondered if it meant he was a blue drafter, or he merely wanted to be able to see the expressions on her face as he spoke to her.

The altered voice emerged again from his swaddling robes. 'You were seen getting individual training with Karris White Oak some time ago.'

Teia's throat tightened. 'Yes, my lord. The, uh, the Archers try to take care of each other.'

'She took a special interest in you.'

Teia couldn't tell if it was a question, couldn't tell if there were suspicions hidden in that statement. 'She seemed to like me. We trained together a couple of times.'

'Everything you've done tells me I should trust you, Adrasteia. And yet.'

She said nothing.

'A crisis is simply opportunity wearing danger's cloak. On the other hand, you know what they say about old warriors and bold warriors.'

'Uh.' She didn't.

'Ah, that's right. A slave. Not stupid, but not educated, either. No matter. I'll test your loyalty as we go. The perennial problem of a secret order, is it not? The danger of infiltration? You have risen so fast. And your gifts make you so useful, it's hard not to put you to work. It could be a purposeful temptation. Hmm.'

Heart pounding, Teia waited again. She turned her palms out, helpless, but didn't say anything. There were lines here, and crossing any of them might get her killed. On the other hand, she couldn't seem too self-controlled, too patient, too formidable.

Finally she threw her hands up in the air. She was playing the angry girl who would lash out at anyone. Might as well play her to the hilt. 'I can't do—'

But he interjected immediately, as if to spare both of them the consequences of what she might say, 'I have an assignment for you. The new White is isolated, surrounded by enemies, with all her most trusted friends fled or dead. Get close to her.'

'Close? I'm in the Blackguard. As soon as I take final vows, I'll be near her all the time.'

'I want you to be more than that. She'll need a confidante. Become that.'

It was the best news Teia could have heard, but she sagged. 'I'm...I'm a nunk. She's the White!'

'She was herself taken under Orea Pullawr's wing in just this way. Fit the mold. Make her feel she's doing good by taking you in. That's an order.'

'Yes, my lord,' she said, as if she felt it far beyond her capabilities.

'Adrasteia. You admire her, don't you? Like her, even.'

Teia swallowed. To lie or not to lie? 'I do, my lord.'

'Never forget.'

'Forget?' Teia asked. Playing a little stupid had never hurt.

'You may be called on to kill her and die doing it.'

Teia prostrated herself. 'Yes, my lord.'

'Do you have doubts?'

She nodded, still gazing at the floor.

'Good. Honest. I would have thought it strange if you didn't. Adrasteia, your work is so secret that it will be hard for you to learn the wisdom of the Crimson Path. But I can tell you this. You will matter. To the Chromeria, you're an exalted slave. For us, you are a woman who will change the world and leave it better for your sacrifices.'

'Yes, my lord.'

'You worry about Kip?' he asked.

'He said once that the Order tried to kill him. A Mistress... Hillel?'

'Indeed. She was one of our best. For who expects a fat middle-aged woman to be an assassin? Not a Shadow, though.'

'I...He was in my squad, and he was my owner, my lord. I hated being a slave – I hated being his slave – but he was kind to me. Didn't rape me.' Teia had to acknowledge her closeness to Kip. Bring part of a secret to light unbidden, and you might be mistaken for honest.

'Listen to yourself,' the Old Man said. 'He didn't rape you. Thus he's kind? Don't you see how diseased that is? Their entire system of governance, religion, society...it leads to you, saying a man is kind because he didn't rape you.'

Teia hesitated. 'I...That does seem wrong. But...you won't ask me to kill him, will you, sir? Can I ask that of you?'

'Oh no, child. That will never happen. Kip is not our enemy. Early on, we thought him insignificant, and his elimination a perfect way to get closer to Andross Guile, who wanted an inconvenient bastard removed. It was a mistake. We have learned since then. I swear this to you, Adrasteia. You will never have to act against Kip.'

The Old Man of the Desert was very good. He was very, very good. So maybe it was the voice modulator. Maybe it was that Teia had spent some time around the very best. But whatever it was, Teia could tell he was lying. Some tiny flutter in his voice, some pause a fraction shortened as if he'd practiced beforehand, the stilted lack of contractions.

For some reason, until now this had been simply an assignment. Now a sudden spark of outrage caught in her soul. You tell me I'm not a slave, but you treat me like a moron?

How stupid do you think I am?

The Old Man must be accustomed to dealing with idiots. He thought he would draw Teia slowly into his circle until she would do anything for him?

Oh, look, a little girl, a former slave, small and stupid. When it comes to deceiving her, I don't even need to try.

It was as if, as she burst from her chrysalis – nothing but that old lie 'I am a slave' – the Old Man was stomping on her before her wings could spread.

'You're young, and you know little of our faith yet. It is natural to have questions,' the Old Man said, supremely confident.

Oh. Fuck. You.

This *little girl* is going to tear you apart, Old Man. You have just become my mission in life. What had Kip said? Diakoptês didn't mean 'breaker' exactly, it was more like "the 'one who rends asunder,' the one who destroys utterly. On Diakoptês's behalf and on her own, Teia was going to wreck this bastard.

'I guess I just have one,' she said. 'Will it be worth it?'

'Oh. Oh, indeed. We will pull down all the artifice of this world and break it. We will show how hollow the Chromeria is. We will kill their very god and see them scuttle for the darkness like cockroaches exposed to the light of our fury. We will destroy the very edifice on which their power rests, and in the end, they will know we did it for good.'

Teia pursed her lips and bobbed her head eagerly. Took a deep breath, as if this were all she had ever hoped for.

These weren't madmen. They were something more dangerous. These were zealots. More dangerous than merely bad men because they would never rest, but also more foolish. Zealots always wanted to explain, to gain converts.

'And now,' the Old Man said. 'A reward for your good service. And a test, I suppose, to see if you are what you appear to be. You're a bitter child, aren't you?'

Teia looked up angrily, smoothed it over quickly. Hesitated. 'I don't like to be wronged,' she said. He'd talked to Master Sharp. Sharp must have told him how she wanted vengeance on everyone. It was her part now. She couldn't blink. Not ever, not if she was going to get in.

'Schedules will be juggled to put you in proximity with the new White. You will begin getting close to her immediately. In the meantime...in the next three days, tag one person with paryl. Whoever's wronged you, I suppose. Or whoever you wish. Only no Blackguards. No nobles. That person will be dead within the day. My gift to you.'

Chapter 6

⤢ Summon Zymun.

Karris was in no place to do this now, but there was no way she could avoid it, either. She'd rejected Zymun at birth; if she repeated the insult now, on this horrible night of all nights, there was no way he'd ever forgive her.

Forgiving herself was already out of the question.

'High Mistress?' Gill Greyling said. He must have pulled a double to be still on duty.

☐ *Accelerate promotion of new Blackguards, even at the cost of quality.*

Trainer Fisk – Commander Fisk now – would howl, but she would help him pick out those with a natural gift. The nunks would have to learn as they fought. It would mean more dead, but having veteran Blackguards who were constantly exhausted would mean more dead, too, and if they lost too many veterans, the whole force would be degraded for decades.

Let the young die, so the old can sleep.

Dammit.

She motioned for Gill to open the door. It had been too long a day. But if it had been a long day for her, it had to have been nightmarish for Zymun. He'd been called on, so soon after arriving at Big Jasper, to perform the Freeing. Seventy-five old drafters had submitted to his knife today. Karris couldn't imagine what he must be feeling.

Gill didn't obey immediately, instead giving her a few extra moments to pull herself together, and nearly commenting on her state. Despite his newness, Gill was going to be an excellent Blackguard. The best of them didn't look out only for their charges' physical well-being. Finally, satisfied, he opened the door.

Zymun Guile was seventeen years old, though he looked older dressed in his Prism-elect's finery. Stylishly combed black hair, broad shoulders, blue eyes already tinged with a rainbow of luxin, a broad nose, and the devastating good looks that seemed the Guile inheritance.

'High Lady,' he said, his bow flowing smoothly into his kneeling and touching her foot in obeisance. He looked up at her and swallowed. 'Mother.'

She stared at him, somehow unable to move, to respond. He looked so like his father's family, a dark mirror to their good looks. Could he not look like her, a little?

If he resembled her more, would that make this meeting easier or harder?

'Zymun,' she managed. She took his hand and helped him stand.

He mistook her pulling, and hugged her immediately.

She froze up, but he didn't notice.

'Mother. Mother, I was so afraid you'd not want to see me.' His voice quavered on the edge of tears.

She couldn't move. Couldn't speak.

He stepped back, getting control of himself. He dabbed at the corners of his eyes to dry tears she hadn't even seen.

'I'm, I'm sorry,' he said. 'I was out of line. That was inappropriate. Forgive me, High Lady.'

Forgive *him*? The words Karris had barely summoned were snatched from her throat.

'No...' She'd meant to say, 'No, son,' but she couldn't force the words past her lips. 'No, the offense is mine. I know your day has been much, much harder than my own.'

He looked at her blankly for a half a moment. 'Yes – yes, I...I don't really know how I'm supposed to feel about today.'

'You don't have to feel how you're supposed to, Zymun,' she said. 'How *do* you feel?'

He searched her face, then looked away. 'How did Father do it?'

'With immense loathing and terrible guilt,' Karris said. 'But, speaking confidentially of course, Gavin's faith in Orholam and the Chromeria itself was never strong. He had trouble believing Orholam would ask for the killing of innocents, whatever they'd sworn or whether they'd agreed to it. It tore his soul, every time. I didn't know if maybe it was easier for you, because you're younger or maybe have more faith than he did.'

'I only wish I did, Mother. I, I wanted to be strong for you. It was the hardest thing I've ever done in my life.' He heaved a great sigh. 'I've been trying not to think about it. But it's good to honor Orholam in this, right?' He looked up at her as if to check her reaction. 'I'm just really amazed at the faithfulness of those who I freed to the light today. They're like heroes to me. The self-sacrificing purpose with which they came to this day was so inspiring. And if I hadn't been coached so well, I couldn't have done my little part.'

Karris didn't know what it was, but something felt off in his response. He'd killed seventy-five people today.

What was the appropriate response to that?

The mind is fickle. She'd seen men who'd learned their entire families had been murdered by wights actually laugh because they simply couldn't believe it. Soldiers made rude jokes about the bodies of their dead mates. Medics laughed about spurting blood and diarrhea. When life is outrageous, the only appropriate response is an inappropriate one.

But an appropriate response, muted?

'Mother,' he said suddenly, swallowing. He whispered harshly, 'I *killed* them.' He convulsed on a sob barely contained. 'All those people.'

She felt herself suddenly warm. He'd been trying to play strong for her. Of course that was it. Thrown into a world he didn't understand, with rules he didn't comprehend, and subjected to incredible demands, he'd had to pretend.

He went on in a rush, 'I tried to tell myself that it was for the best. That they were going to meet Orholam, that I should envy them, but, but it was my hand on the knife. I never – I never asked for this. I never knew how hard this would be.'

She pulled him close and hugged him to her. He dissolved into her arms.

He wept quietly for a minute, and then pulled back, putting a brave face on. 'I...Can we not speak of that again?'

Holding on to his arms, she said, 'Only this, Zymun. You honored Orholam and those brave drafters by what you did. And me. You did right.'

He bowed his head, pursed his lips under the weight of his emotion, and nodded. 'Thank you,' he said quietly. 'I'm sorry we had to meet like this, High Lady. And I didn't mean to talk all about myself. You've just ascended to the chair. Congratulations are in order.'

'Thank you,' she said. She finally let go of him. It was as if she were slightly out of her body as she looked at him. What was she looking for? Herself? He was a seventeen-year-old man, not an infant where you pick this trait from his mother and that from his father.

Oh, look! He has a nose – like his mother does. Oh, look! He has two eyes – like his father does. What a coincidence.

But the very thought of a father made her think of Gavin.

Gavin, dear Orholam. There had been no word, all day, no word of where he was. It was as if he'd been spirited away, as if she'd never dragged his half-blind ass back from the hippodrome in Rath. No word about Marissia, either. The bitch. Karris would be meeting with the banker Turgal Onesto soon to see if he might help in tracking Marissia, but she hadn't been able to fit that in today with all the other emergencies.

She put on a smile to push both thoughts away. Zymun hadn't noticed.

'I'm really proud of you, Mother,' he said. 'The White! Don't they usually pick old crones for that? And you're hardly that. I mean, you're older for a drafter, maybe, but not *old* old. And so beautiful.'

He was not quite gifted with the Guiles' golden tongue, was he? Even Kip did better than that. But then, if he hadn't gotten the Guile charm, from which parent had he inherited that deficiency?

And he was a young man, trying to impress, and he'd been through so much. She had to make allowances.

Underneath all his bravado and awkwardness, he was probably furious with her for her abandonment and her distance, but wanting her approval, too. She was asking too much of him, even having him meet her today.

It took all the bravery in her heart to go straight at the issue, as Gavin would have. 'Let's get this out of the way, shall we?' she said.

'Mother?'

'I didn't want to leave you, Zymun, but I couldn't bear to keep you, either. I had no prospects and no friends. Or so I thought. And I was ashamed. Not ashamed of you – but ashamed nonetheless, for all the wrong reasons. But I want you to know it wasn't your fault. I didn't leave for anything you did.'

His lip quivered, and he looked away, blinking.

Orholam have mercy. Her heart broke again.

'No, I...I know that,' he said. 'I mean, how could it be my fault? I was just a baby, right? I hadn't done anything yet – good or bad, right? I mean, I don't know, maybe your pregnancy was really awful? And you blamed me for it or something? I thought about it a lot. I just wanted to know if it had been something I'd done. Or if, or if I seemed like some sort of monster to you for some reason.'

Whatever leash she'd held on her emotions slipped through her fingers. She turned her back.

How could he have thought that?

How could he not?

But he kept talking, quickly, always quickly. 'I mean, they told me I was a cute baby, but I didn't know what you thought of me. They didn't like that I was handsome, actually. At least that's one of the things they beat me for. They said I was a burden. They said I thought I was better than them. It was a lie. I just wanted to fit in. I just wanted to be accepted by someone, anyone. It all got worse when it turned out I could draft. I could show you the scars if you want? Did you get any of the letters I sent you? They said they'd send them on. They promised. They lied about so many things, but I was certain they were telling the truth about sending my letters.'

Every dream she'd had for her son. Every hope she'd nourished that he would be protected, loved, that he would grow up knowing both a mother and a father – it all burnt and broke at once. Every nightmare from her long nights stepped fully armed from the waves in an instant, invading the beachhead her fears had captured in her mind and setting up camp along the whole coast.

She'd wanted to let herself off the hook, all these years: he was with a good family, she told herself. The Ashes were her cousins, and had been close with her branch of the family for generations. She'd thought he would be far from wars and danger, that he would be loved and nurtured.

But that was all a fantasy, wasn't it? That her abandonment had somehow been beneficial to him, and not just a selfish sloughing off of a problem onto someone else. Now that hook eviscerated her, she fell to her knees, barely able to breathe through her sobs.

'Mother, mother, please…' he said, and it was as if he were speaking to her from far away. She'd thought she knew Devon and Karen Ash. They'd seemed to be such good people, but then, the real monsters had an uncanny ability to hide right in plain sight, didn't they?

'Mother, please don't turn away again,' Zymun said.

She beckoned him to come to her. He was there instantly, sitting on the floor with her, burying his head in her chest. He was taller than she was, even sitting, so it was an awkward movement, but she thought she understood. He had never been comforted by a mother, of course he would want to act like a little boy.

She brushed his hair with her fingers, and a tiny ray of sweetness penetrated all the bitterness.

He nuzzled his head in against her breast. 'Mother, please, I'm so afraid of you rejecting me.'

'No, never,' she said. 'Never again.'

'Will you promise me you'll keep me close? That you'll never send me away?'

'I swear it,' she said.

'You swear to Orholam? You swear on your hope of the light?'

It was a burden, and it invited future pain. It invited the possibility of the kind of hurt that she'd pushed away when Kip had made his innocent joke, calling her 'Mother'. She'd failed Kip then; she'd not fail Zymun now.

'I swear to Orholam, by all that is holy, by all my power and light.' And finally, as that oath passed her lips, as she finally felt that she had done one good thing for him in her life, even if it was only utter some words, something loosened in her chest, and her throat allowed her to say the word that had been denied her too long. 'I swear it...son.'

Chapter 7

'Kip, it's been four days. Four days since our wedding, and we still...'

'I know,' Kip said. He was sitting on their little bed in the captain's quarters. Another dread night was falling, and the back slapping and jokes about being a sneaky little bugger from the captain and the mate and the squad had been endured already. The public torture ended, the private one begun.

'We don't *have* to try again right away,' Tisis said.

'And you wore that because you wanted to wait until tomorrow?' Kip asked.

In her initial excitement and ardor at Getting Married and

41

Not to Some Old Guy, Tisis had packed all manner of lace and silk lingerie. She was wearing a celadon nightgown now that showcased her cleavage and curves. Kip's new wife was one of the most beautiful women he had ever seen – even during the day, when she wore baggy men's trousers and a tunic too large for her and no cosmetics. Seeing her like this only made everything more painful. 'You know the law...' she said.

'I didn't until you told me!'

She pursed her lips. She didn't like it when Kip raised his voice at her. 'Fine, then. We wait three more days, and it's over. We'll just...have to figure it out from there. I don't think Andross Guile will do anything rash—'

'No, not rash. His vengeance is anything but rash.'

She lowered her head, and Kip saw her swallow quickly. She looked at her silk nightgown. 'I'm sorry. I wouldn't have worn this, but I didn't want to tell my sister's slave to bring me something plainer. She'd ask more questions than they already have.' She mimicked the room slave Verity's nasally voice: ' "Is mistress's lord husband gentle enough?" "Does mistress have any...delicate questions?" It's not supposed to be like this, Kip. What's wrong with me?'

'Tisis, quieter? Please?' Kip said awkwardly. 'Remember...' Sound went through the walls of the captain's quarters as if they weren't even there. Maybe that was where their troubles had started. Maybe if she could just relax...

And maybe this was the stupidest thing in the world to worry about right now. The world was falling apart, and Kip – who had fought an immortal and stolen the master cloak from him, who was a full-spectrum polychrome, who was maybe, just maybe, the Lightbringer – Kip who had killed a king and a god and escaped the Chromeria itself with all the Lightguard after him, who had brought along with himself the best and brightest the Blackguard had to offer – Kip, the son of Gavin Guile, couldn't make love. With his own wife. Who seemed entirely willing – at least on one level.

It was as if her body itself was rejecting Kip.

It had all been merely mortifying until Tisis had told him that their wedding contract was automatically revoked if they didn't consummate the marriage within seven days.

42

'I'm a failure as a woman.' As she stood outside the covers in her barely-there nightgown, Tisis's skin was covered in gooseflesh.

She bares her heart to you, and you stare at her nipples. Nice.

'Maybe it's not you. Maybe I'm doing something wrong,' Kip said lamely. Neither of them believed that, now.

They were really great nipples.

She lifted her eyebrows and pulled back the covers he had bunched over his lap. His tunic covered his arousal about as effectively as Tisis's nightgown covered the fact that she had breasts. He bloused the fabric gingerly and cleared his throat.

'I'm sorry,' she said. 'I didn't mean to embarrass you. I was just... *Your* body is doing what it's supposed to, Kip. I'm the problem. I mean, there are jokes about how all a woman has to do is lie there. "Easy as falling off a log." Ha!'

Kip could tell she was heartbeats away from breaking down. Tears were not going to help their problem. 'Tisis, maybe we should slow down, take it—'

'Slow down? Kip! We've only got *three days* left!'

The law had been passed to protect children from being married off too young by their parents or to prevent marriages of convenience – part of some long-ago fight about taxation or boundaries or testimony compelled by a satrap, Tisis had said.

'Tisis, it's freezing out there. Come here. We'll figure this out together.'

She puffed out her cheeks and crawled into the narrow bed with him. He threw the covers over her. He'd been thinking she would lie down with her back to him so they could talk and cuddle, but she lay down face-to-face with him instead.

Before he could say anything, she kissed his neck, and all hope of rational conversation dimmed quickly. Kip still hadn't blown out the lamp. But her kisses were perfunctory. She broke away almost as soon as Kip went hazy. She reached for a vial on a shelf. Her expression was determined, not impassioned. She poured olive oil into her hand and tugged his clothes out of the way.

Her touch was a shock of pleasure, despite everything, as

43

she spread the oil on him. If she'd continued for very long, Kip would have lost control. But rather than saying, 'I want to make love with you,' the expression on her face said, 'I will not fail my family.' She rubbed the rest of the oil on herself, and straddled Kip, hiking up her nightgown just enough to get the work done.

There were no more preambles. No soft words or touches. She held Kip in place and lowered herself onto him.

As before, he was stopped almost immediately. She grimaced and pushed harder, harder until she was hurting both of them. She eased off, adjusting him, making sure he was in the right place, and then she banged down again, wincing each time.

Andross Guile had once used a euphemism, calling a woman's quim the Jade Gate. Kip had thought it embarrassing. Of course, talking with your grandfather about lovemaking was bound to be embarrassing, but why did all the euphemisms have to sound either dirty or childish?

Now he felt as if he were bringing a battering ram to the Jade Gate. The gate was winning.

Tisis began crying, tears streaking silently down her cheeks, making her cosmetics run, and still not giving up. She was hurting Kip, and she was definitely hurting herself.

'Tisis. Stop. Tisis!' Kip whispered.

She didn't listen to him.

He grabbed her hips and held her still. 'You're hurting me.'

'I can do this,' she hissed.

Much as he'd tried to avoid the common areas in the public baths, Kip had been around enough to know that his horn wasn't freakishly huge. It wasn't that; he doubted he could fit his littlest finger inside Tisis. She said it wasn't her hymen, either. That had broken when she was young. This was pure muscle, and it was clenched so tight that if he'd been inside her when it clamped down, he'd have been left with a jerky stick.

'Tisis, stop.'

She released her hand's death grip and sat on him, defeated. 'What do we do, Kip?' Her sitting felt far nicer than anything else she'd done, but perhaps that was just an absence of pain.

'You're beautiful,' Kip said. 'And I'm lucky to have you.'

Her expression softened from its desperate anger. She lay down on him and rested her head on his chest. She tried to speak, but then dissolved in tears.

Kip figured it was better than her sleeping with her back to him silently as she had for the first three nights. Maybe it was his own fault. With the shock of the battle and their flight and Goss's death at the Chromeria and Tremblefist's likely death at the cannon tower and Kip's declaration that he wouldn't be going with Tisis to Rath, they hadn't even tried to make love the first night.

The second night, she'd found out that he really did plan to take the Mighty to war, instead of going to Rath with her. She'd been furious with him, and he'd been mortified at the idea of having to strip naked and expose his body and his scars in front of a woman whose beauty would make a goddess cringe. She'd blown out the lamp, handed him the olive oil, and gotten in bed, legs spread, silent, her whole demeanor saying, 'Just get it over with, you animal.'

Despite a lack of personal experience, Kip hadn't been completely clueless – he'd thought. Tisis had gotten spitting mad with his fumbling, finally taking charge herself. And... nothing. He'd found nowhere to go when he was on top, not because he was an idiot; he'd found nowhere to go because there *was* nowhere to go. They'd pretended to sleep, back to back.

The crew's jokes the next morning had been unbearable. And that was when Kip had missed his opportunity. He should have confessed to... whom? One of the Mighty? None of them had even hinted that something like this was possible. The randy captain? Ugh. Someone, anyway, that things weren't going well. Or going at all.

But how stupid could you look? What kind of mockery did that invite? I took a beautiful woman to bed, and I didn't know what to do?

The third night had been better and worse. Tisis hadn't told any of her slaves, either, apparently as ashamed as Kip was. She'd failed her family too many times, she'd said. She wasn't going to fail again. But she'd decided she wasn't going to take it out on Kip, and then she'd begged his pardon.

45

They'd made some perfunctory moves at kissing and caressing – and tried and failed again. She'd been furious, but not at Kip.

I should have made love with Teia when I had the chance.

The one thing Kip had thought he'd definitely be getting when he'd agreed to marry Tisis, he was being denied.

Maybe he should let the marriage be annulled.

But Andross had assigned Kip to this task. He would assume that the failure was a deliberate betrayal. The Chromeria needed Ruthgar bound to it by the Guile/Malargos marriage. This was bigger than Kip, bigger than his frustration. Tisis and her family needed it, too, though the Guiles had gotten the better of the bargain. She had been a hostage of the Chromeria, a guarantor of the end of the Blood Wars between Ruthgar and Blood Forest. She could leave Big Jasper legally after she was married, but leaving before that without permission was a breach of the articles of peace – something damn near akin to an act of war.

In normal times the Ruthgari hostage leaving without permission would be a diplomatic gaffe understood between friends. During a war in which the loyalty of Ruthgar was in question, it would be far worse. If Eirene Malargos actually was on the brink of siding with the Color Prince, regaining her beloved sister would give her freedom to join him if she wished it. If the Chromeria handled the gaffe poorly, though, threatening her, it might actually push her into the Color Prince's camp. Annulling their marriage could mean breaking an alliance.

Tisis's sobs had quieted, and she shifted as if to get more comfortable to sleep on Kip. Which was actually really nice. Way better than frigid silence. But the motion made her leg brush Kip's horn. Great. Here for a moment he'd nearly forgotten about it. She froze.

She sat up. Her makeup had run, and her eyes were puffy, and there was clear snot under her nose. 'I should at least take care of you,' she said, her voice sniffly, right on the verge of crying again.

It was not a thought that hadn't occurred to Kip in the last four nights.

Kip the Lip was back, already speaking: 'In the history of

the world, there have been five great unromantic invitations to romance, but this...this outshone them all.'

She pounded a fist on his chest. 'Kip! Not funny!'

'You're smiling.'

'I am not.' But of course she was. Her face was a war of humor and frustration and despair and tears. 'It's either smile or cry, and I hate crying.'

'I have an idea,' Kip said.

'What?'

'Not a good idea, mind you.'

'What is it?'

'All I can promise is that it's a *little* better than crying.'

Chapter 8

If this had been any other time in his life, Gavin could have taken the shock, absorbed it silently, and gone on to the next appointment of an overfull day. In every down moment, he would have chewed through the surprise. He would have lain it down for six or ten hours, not thinking about it at all. And then, passionless, he would pick up that shock late in the day and rationally decide what to do about it.

But in this gray hell, there was nowhere to go. Nothing to do. Nothing else to think of. Little to see except the expectant face of Marissia, like a loyal hound expecting a beating.

Except not loyal.

Nor a hound.

'Not a slave?' Gavin asked. 'You clipped your own ears? Who would do such a thing?'

'I was eighteen years old when I came to serve you,' Marissia said. 'But I had been deeply in love with you for three years already. Though you'd never seen my face. From as early as I could remember, I'd heard tales from my friends, from my mother, and my grandmother. Everyone knew about the perfect Guile brothers.'

Gavin wondered sometimes if he'd been so stupid when he

was young that he hadn't seen how different his life was from everyone else's. He and his brother had taken the affection and attention as their natural due, and his mother had muted people's more exuberant gestures skillfully. In many ways, he'd had no idea that not everyone grew up as cherished as he did.

She went on. 'I didn't pay much attention to the False Prism's War. It was so far away from Blood Forest. I knew there was some horrible girl who was to blame for everything, and that the fighting was awful. I thought you must be very brave. And then the war was over, settled in some distant land, and almost immediately, the Blood War started up again.'

'Tell me. Tell me everything. Give me it all.' Maybe he could regain his equilibrium if he didn't have to speak for a while.

She still couldn't meet his eye. 'My experience of the war was almost anticlimactic. My family was wiped out by pieces, and each time, I was supposed to be at the places the raiders hit, and I simply...*wasn't*. For me, it was like my family disappeared slowly, every time I turned my back. I never saw their bodies. I never felt the heat of the burning fields, or touched the broken gates. I never smelled the forbidden magic still steaming in the air. A cousin would bring in a confirmation: he'd seen the bodies himself, there would be no ransom, there was no mistaking my sister's death, then my father's, then later my mother's. There was no false hope, but also never a chance to grieve. The land that had been taken from us was being held by enemies. There would be no visits to graves, no remembrance wreaths, no dirges or holy fires against Long Night.

'I was brought quietly to the Jaspers – and found out that after I'd left, my cousins had been killed, too. I decided I had been spared for a purpose. My grandmother Orea was more distraught than I'd ever seen her. And then you came back from Rath. You'd just ended the Blood War, which had been simmering for centuries. You simply *ended* it, with a fatal wave of your hand.

'I think my grandmother had been about to move against you, before that. But that changed her.

'She found a peace again. It was my idea, you know. Me becoming your room slave. One day, my grandmother spoke privately to your mother; Felia said you were dissatisfied with your current room slave, and she herself was unhappy because the woman was spying on you. So Orea asked your mother if she might procure a girl for her. She said she'd give you an excellent room slave as a gift to make up for past friction. I was eavesdropping, and as your mother gave her the description of what she wanted for you, I realized it fit me perfectly.'

'But to become a slave...' It was the greatest fear for every family in power. Losing a war didn't mean becoming a tradesman: nobles were either at the top, or reduced to death or the most onerous servitude possible.

'I'd lost everything, Gavin. My family. Our fortune, which wasn't large to begin with. The Pullawrs' power had dwindled since Ulbear Rathcore died. My grandmother refused to use the power of her office to help us unfairly. Her integrity was the slow ruin of us. Your father had some grudge against Ulbear, and I think he orchestrated much of our downfall. The Seaborns had bled to seize our lands, so there was no way they were going to simply give them back to anyone, certainly not to an eighteen-year-old girl with no army or fortune.'

'The Seaborns?!'

'Yes. And yes, Brádach Seaborn did recognize me. He shouldn't have. We'd never met. But he'd known my sister, and the resemblance was strong. Strong enough, apparently. I don't know if he killed her himself, or if he merely allowed her murder. But I goaded him into hitting me. I knew your vengeance would be swift and terrible. I thought you loved me. It was the first and last time I manipulated you. I'm sorry. It was the only way I could see to get vengeance for my family. I had no idea how far things would go.'

Gavin had killed Brádach Seaborn for beating Marissia and put his head on a pike. The Seaborns had eventually sided with pirates to get vengeance on the Guiles for that. Almost all of them had ended up hanged, and their lands seized.

All from one slave's lie.

Having known Marissia always as his own property, Gavin had trusted her to act in good faith, which to him had meant in his interests. After she'd passed his trials of her faithfulness against the White, Marissia had become, in Gavin's view, an extension of his own will.

Instead her own secrets had led to lies, and lies to death.

It wasn't as if she were the only one. He'd made his own choices, and the Seaborns had, too. What did it matter now?

'But Marissia, a slave?' He couldn't get past that.

'My grandmother couldn't intervene for me in the satrapies' politics. Or wouldn't. The White is supposed to be above politics, and things were so tenuous here. My prospects were limited. I'd been trained to run a large household, to manage slaves and servants, to see the proper protocols were observed, to check the books but not to keep them myself, to see that animals were properly tended but not to do the tending, to check that the cooks were performing well but not to cook myself: I knew a little of everything, but was master of nothing. I was useful as a chatelaine, but useless for all else.

'Of course, I was a fool for thinking that. One who can learn so much by eighteen can easily learn more. But I knew I would never have my dream. I would never be that high lady with six or eight children embracing her, which had been all I ever wanted. So I volunteered.

'I knew I had been saved for some great purpose, and what could be higher than serving the greatest Prism of all time, Gavin Guile? They told me that if you accepted me, I would be with you for years. Maybe many years, if I did well. It was almost a marriage, to a desperate foolish heart like mine.'

Indeed, anyone who married a Prism would know her marriage would likely last only seven years. Gavin had been with Marissia for more than ten.

'My grandmother was desperate, and I solved so many problems for her. But she never forgave herself for letting the blacksmith clip my ears. Because the moment he cut, our course was set.'

Here Gavin thought he'd tried the most insane gambit possible to save himself in the fallout of the civil war. He felt numb. Marissia. A Pullawr.

'It wasn't a bad life,' she said.

'What?'

'I served the Seven Satrapies. I got to see my grandmother,

whom I had always loved dearly, almost daily. I wouldn't have seen her ever if I'd had my old dream. She would have been here, and I would have been off somewhere, paired with some fool or other who wasn't half my equal. That's what grandmother said, when she was trying to look on the light side. And I got to be with you. And you loved me after your way, didn't you? Not quite in the way I thought you did early on, but you cared for me.'

There was something plaintive in how she said it, as if she couldn't bear to make it a question, but wanted to know the answer more than anything.

Not stupid, Marissia. Of course she'd seen through that lie, eventually. She, who was closer to him than anyone, had eventually realized what being a slave meant.

He wanted to break down in horror for what he'd done, for who he'd become, but if he did, the orange in him knew she would come comfort him. He, who had hurt her, would take from her even comfort.

Gavin had once thought his father a fool because the old man had been so close to Gavin and had never seen him for what he was. He himself had been closer still to Marissia and had never seen her at all. It was a bitter mirror to hold.

'Marissia, I did—'

But his pause, the very pause he'd taken because he had been trying to be fair to her, was too long. She took it as a negative. She swallowed, and interrupted, 'My lord, it was an honor to serve you. But not one I would repeat, given the choice.'

He squeezed his eyes tight shut – and pain lanced through his left eye. 'Marissia, please…'

'Don't lie to me now, my lord.'

'I loved you as a master loves his best slave. I was well pleased, but I took it as my due. I never saw you, Marissia.' And that says nothing about you, and everything about me.

She took it like a slap in the face, but after a moment, she breathed. 'Truth, from Gavin Guile. I should thank you for that.'

He was not exactly Gavin Guile, either. But that was a confession too far afield.

'Marissia... Marissia. You did more for me than anyone. I owe you more than I can ever repay. But I have nothing to give you for all you've sacrificed for me.'

'Then *see me* now.'

He looked at her, unsure what she meant.

'Talk to me. Talk to me like I'm a free woman. Like I'm your friend. Like I'm *here*.'

And so they talked. They talked of people they had known. They talked of Marissia's childhood, and her family, and of her grandmother. Marissia shared stories Gavin had never heard of the old woman, and not just of her. Marissia told him of intrigues in the Chromeria he had never even guessed at. She told him about times he'd almost caught her spying for her grandmother.

Something tight in Gavin's chest loosened.

Despite their situation, they laughed.

For once, Gavin imitated his mother rather than his father, and asked questions rather than giving commands. As Marissia spoke, and Gavin listened, she became more animated than he had seen her in years. She glowed beautifully, unmissable. Yet Gavin had missed her.

He saw her now.

And though time had no meaning down here, and the gray light never varied, they spoke what must have been long into the night. Finally she stood and stripped off her slave's dress, leaving only her shift. She crawled up onto his narrow convalescent's palanquin. He had a bad feeling, but she merely draped her dress over the two of them as a makeshift blanket. There was no way he could deny her the comfort of his arms, and he needed the warmth. She snuggled against him, and soon fell asleep.

His left arm was around her, with its two lopped-off fingers. His left eye was toward her, blind and seeping. He was a cripple, in the prison he himself had constructed, and he was holding the wrong woman.

'I'm sorry,' he whispered to this woman who had lived and would die for him. 'I'm so, so sorry.' But for this cold night, he cuddled close to her and thought of his wife.

Karris, will I ever see you again?

Chapter 9

This wasn't shit creek. This wasn't no paddle. This was shit ocean. This was I can't even see land.

In the three days since Sun Day, Teia hadn't had a single moment when she could go see Karris. Every waking hour had been filled. Double shifts with the Blackguard, guarding Carver Black and other members of the Spectrum as they'd investigated what exactly had happened in the city, sometimes being debriefed herself about what she knew, and then clearing rubble and scraping floors with the other nunks on the top floor of the Prism's Tower. The nunks weren't even excused from lectures, so Teia had only had a few hours' sleep each night – and no time at all to sneak away and meet Karris, even if the woman had left a response to Teia's signal that they needed to meet.

Teia had wanted to report to Karris *before* she'd talked to the Old Man. Now it was absolutely necessary – and utterly impossible. Teia was being followed. If she met with Karris and was seen, it would mean the death of both of them.

But Teia had a superpower that no one had counted on: she was completely paranoid. She had thought she was being followed a hundred times since she'd started working for the Order, so she'd figured out a thing or two.

One, she was a paranoid mess.

Two, she was pretty good at it.

She knew all the places where she could lose a tail. Whether in the Chromeria itself or on Big Jasper, she knew some good tricks, and she was always adding to her list.

So. No time to sit here gulping like a beached fish. Find the tail, lose the tail, and then report. She could worry about everything else after that.

She started walking, quickly, heading back to the barracks and the master cloak. The first thing to do was to figure out how many people were following her, and who they were.

If you were being followed by a team of professionals, it was well nigh impossible to tell. The front-follows, the hand-offs, the disguise switches – if a squad had three or four people of medium height and build in any area with decent traffic, there was no way you could figure it out.

But Teia didn't think she was being followed by a team. Whoever was following her had to be able to see paryl.

Of course, if the Old Man really had paryl-viewing spectacles, he could simply lend them to anyone.

But would he let such a priceless treasure out of his own hands? No. If the Old Man was half as paranoid as Teia was, he wouldn't dare let his only defense against the shimmercloaks out of his sight.

There weren't many paryl drafters in the entire world, so the odds that Teia was being followed by a team of them was low – though of course, the Old Man would be the one person in the world who would have access to an entire team of paryl drafters—

Agh! That way madness lies.

Teia had to make her guesses and jump. So: she was most likely being followed by a single paryl drafter. That might be wrong, but there was no sitting still in this war of shadows until she could find out for sure. She had a day to pick someone who would die, and everyone she could actually think of who might deserve it had been forbidden her. If she didn't mark someone, she would undermine her own pretense of being a peevish, vindictive woman eager to inflict her rage upon the world. Losing her disguise among the Order wouldn't be dangerous, it would be fatal.

Put simply, if she didn't pick someone else to die, she would.

It wasn't a call she wanted to make herself. Teia was no assassin.

I'm not a killer. I'm a soldier. A secret soldier, but a soldier under authority, a rightful and good authority, Karris. Karris would know what to do.

It's different from being a slave, when you choose it.

But time was running out. Her deadline for tagging someone was tomorrow morning, and Teia couldn't talk to Karris while she was being followed.

At the barracks, she shed her regular cloak, picking at an imaginary stain before tossing it in the laundry basket for the slaves to clean. She looked around, and her paranoia was piqued again. Was someone in this room secretly a paryl drafter, ready to follow her, or ready to report to those who already were? Which of the men and women here were traitors?

With her squad, the Mighty, she'd never needed to worry about that. Now she was so alone.

'Teia,' Watch Captain Fisk said gruffly as she headed out, the master cloak folded over her arm.

He was standing at the door to Commander Ironfist's office. 'Teia, get in here.'

Something about seeing him there stirred fury in Teia's soul. He didn't belong in that office. Didn't deserve to even set foot there. She walked up to him, but didn't go inside.

She stood at attention. She wouldn't have minded Trainer Fisk – it was hard not to think of him that way, even though he'd been promoted months ago to watch captain. She'd liked him, even, for his gruff competence, until they'd figured out he danced to Andross Guile's secret tune. He'd allowed the cheats that had nearly barred Kip from the Blackguard.

And now he was her commander.

'Yes, sir?' Teia asked stiffly. She didn't want to be in an enclosed space with him if she could help it.

'What's this?' Fisk demanded.

He had dark circles under his eyes, and his usual rigorous military bearing was slouched with fatigue. He was not tall, but he was a hard knot of muscle on muscle with a shaved head and short beard.

'Just tired, I guess, sir.'

'By order of the promachos, I'm acting commander of the Blackguard, Teia.'

She hesitated. 'Congratulations on your...swift rise, sir.'

'I don't like it, either,' he snarled. 'I'm the one who demanded it be only "acting commander." He was my commander, too, nunk. And my friend.'

'Yes, sir.' Neutral, noncommittal. The flat acquiescence of a slave had its uses still.

'Who would you have put in before me?' he demanded.

Maybe he'd been right. This wasn't the kind of conversation they should be having out in the open barracks. 'Sir, I'm just a soldier, raised from a slave. I don't question my betters.'

'Watch Captain Blademan was found dead this morning in East Bay. Sharks took too much out of him before his body could be recovered for us to even know how he died.'

Teia swallowed hard. Would the Order have done this? But why? Andross? So he could place Fisk as commander? The Color Prince, deliberately eliminating Blackguard leadership?

'I'd have picked him to be commander before me, even with his troubles,' Fisk said.

That was true. Teia was so accustomed to seeing plots everywhere that she was discounting the simple explanations out of hand. Blademan could have been killed in a tavern brawl. He'd been a man who ricocheted between long stretches of sobriety and short bouts of violent drunkenness – and when he got drunk, he'd earned his Blackguard name Blademan a dozen times over.

Teia ducked her head. 'I'm sorry, sir, I know he was a friend.'

'And I'd have picked Karris before him, before all this. But none of us can fill Ironfist's shoes, and he shouldn't have been relieved of command.'

'I, I wasn't saying—' Why was Fisk telling Teia this? They'd never been close. 'Sir, can we talk about this later? I'm on my way—'

'You think I'm a traitor. We need to talk,' Fisk said. He moved out of the way of the office door. '*Now.*'

It was a gut punch. Teia's expression and silence must have spoken for her. Might as well admit it and see where this went.

She stepped inside, and he closed the door after her.

She swallowed hard. When you're short and light and not that strong, being penned in was the last thing you wanted if it came to a fight. 'Not a traitor, sir. But compromised.'

'Why?'

In for a den, in for a danar. 'You called Breaker "Kip the Lip." Only his grandfather called him that. And only privately. And then you rigged the rules.'

Fisk took a deep breath. He rubbed the bridge of his nose as if he had a headache. 'Not much rigging required.'

Teia couldn't speak. Out of all the things she might have expected, a straight admission of guilt wasn't on the list.

Fisk looked down. 'I had...a relationship with another Blackguard. He found out.'

'He? Andross Guile?'

'Who else?'

'So Andross blackmailed you. For how long?'

'Just that one thing against Kip. Although he told me my failure at it meant I still owed him. But he didn't threaten any further repercussions. He seemed to understand that Orholam himself must have wanted Breaker to get into the Blackguard. The promachos may be a horrible person, but he's not irrational.'

'So is he still blackmailing you now? Is he blackmailing your lover?'

'No, and he can't. I confessed everything to the White after...'

'After?'

'After Lytos died.'

Teia twitched. Lytos? Fisk's relationship had been with a eunuch? How did that even work...?

Of course she knew of slaveholders forcing their eunuchs to serve them sexually, but otherwise a eunuch was assumed to be asexual. That was the point, wasn't it? That a free eunuch might want a sexual relationship hadn't even occurred to her – and it had to be a sexual relationship because Blackguards weren't forbidden other relations, so they couldn't be blackmailed with anything else. What sort of satisfaction would a eunuch get out of...

Then again, she didn't have to understand the mechanics of the thing. She could see the emotion of it. 'I'm...so sorry for your loss.'

The tightness around his eyes eased a little: he'd been worried she would mock him or think him a pervert for falling in love with a eunuch. 'Anyway, none of that matters,' he said. 'I stopped serving Andross after Lytos died and—'

'Lytos didn't just die, though,' Teia objected. Winsen, peerless archer that he was, had feathered Lytos's heart as Lytos had helped Buskin try to assassinate Kip. 'Andross Guile tried to make you stop Breaker from joining the Blackguard. You failed. Did Andross send Lytos afterwards to kill Kip, to stop him once and for all?'

Fisk shook his head. 'I don't – I don't think so. When I confronted the promachos, he said he not only hadn't black-mailed Lytos, he'd never even talked to him. Andross Guile said that for him to ruin a eunuch's relationship would be like an emperor stealing a gold ring from a beggar. Such a theft changed nothing for the emperor, but by whatever improbable means that beggar had gotten that gold ring, he'd never get another one in his life. Andross said it would show a meanness of spirit to ruin such happiness, no matter how puzzling he found it. The promachos is not a good man, Teia, but I believed him. I still do. He is ruthless, but he's not cruel for its own sake. At the same time, I can certainly believe that someone else found out our secret and used it to blackmail Lytos into doing…what he almost did. Neither of us could have lived with having been expelled from the Blackguard.'

'Why are you telling me this?' Teia asked.

'Because you know what it is to love someone forbidden you.'

Teia went cold. Fisk? *Fisk* had been able to see how Teia felt – before she knew it herself? She moved to object, but he spoke over her.

'I'm telling you because you're utterly loyal to Breaker, and you stayed behind anyway. I think you stayed behind on his orders. I think you stayed behind because you're spying for him.'

'I'm not—'

'You stayed behind because you know Breaker is the Lightbringer.'

'Excuse me?' Teia said.

It took the wind out of Teia's sails. Cruxer believed Breaker was the Lightbringer with the fervor of a prophet. She thought so, too, but she wasn't worried about being part of history or something grand like that. She followed Kip because he was both great and good. That was enough for her.

And it had to be enough now, because more wasn't an option now that Teats Tisis was scabbarding his sword. Plenty of men lusted after Tisis; she was tall, curvy, graceful, and rich, with exotic silky blond hair and exquisite taste. Teia wouldn't have forgiven Kip for falling into bed with that creature, but she would have understood it.

But Kip had *married* her. A total fucking stranger. Ten minutes after he'd kissed Teia, too, stirring follies she'd never known.

Asshole.

Fisk said, 'I want you to let him know that I'm on his side. If he needs the commander of the Blackguard, I'm here for him.'

Teia couldn't even decode the words for a moment.

Kip's friends had believed he was the Lightbringer. Sure, but they were dumb kids. Kids believed stupid stuff all the time, right?

This was different. Dour Trainer Fisk believing it?

'Why would you—' she started.

'We've all heard the stories. It's just that some people don't want to believe them. "He shall rise from green" doesn't have to mean coming from the Blood Forest or Ruthgar. It could mean he starts out drafting green. One of the first glimmers of Breaker's magical genius showed when he went green golem in the Battle of Garriston – he'd never even heard of going green golem. He *intuited* it on the spot. His will was so strong, he drafted a green that stopped musket balls, Teia. "He shall kill gods and kings"? He's already done both. "He'll be an outsider"? How much more outsider can you be than a mixed-blood bastard from Tyrea? Each of those things offend the luxiats, and all of them together make their blood boil – as it makes them furious that a Lightbringer would be necessary to put their worship right – but hasn't Orholam's work always offended those in power? I won't put myself on the wrong side of Orholam. "In the darkest hour, when the abominations come to the shores of Big Jasper, when Hope himself has died, then shall he bring the holy light and banish darkness." "Hope himself," Teia. That's Gavin Guile. He's dead. Our darkest hour is coming. We have to pick a side.'

Teia'd heard it translated as 'hope itself,' but that was maybe beside the point. For some reason, Teia hadn't thought through what it would mean for the world if Kip really was the Lightbringer.

If he was the Lightbringer, he would shake the pillars of the earth. At the Lightbringer's coming, the pious, the desperate, the poor, the naïve, the fools, the idealistic, the young – all those would flock not to the Lightbringer, but to their hope of what the Lightbringer would do for them. To those who had nothing, he could be everything.

What had happened to those first tribal warriors who spilled out of Paria with Lucidonius? They'd become Names. They'd ruled satrapies. Men and women who'd been thralls and stone-cutters and foresters and mercenaries and brewers had become luminaries and generals and High Luxiats.

At the same time, to everyone who had power now, he would be terrifying. He would bring rebellion even in the best of times. But now? At the very time the Chromeria needed a united front against the Color Prince, Kip might splinter it from within – without even intending it.

For purely utilitarian reasons, the Chromeria itself might want to kill Kip, who'd never shown disloyalty for a moment.

But those who kill their friends for the trouble they *might* cause don't deserve friends.

'Deserve'? Am I still thinking about power as if morality belongs in the same conversation with it?

Teia said, 'He didn't leave me here to spy. I decided my work with the Blackguard was what I was called to. But we are still friends. I don't deny that. That friendship doesn't abrogate my loyalty to my oaths, sir.'

'Not yet.'

Teia licked her lips and admitted, 'It won't. Ever. Orholam forbid that such choices ever face us.'

'But if it did...?'

'This is like you're asking a mother if they had to sacrifice one of their children, which one they'd choose. It's a cruel question and it won't happen.' She prayed.

'And if it does?' he asked.

'I'll do the right thing, sir.'

'Ha! Best answer I could imagine. Anyway, I wanted to let you know where I stand before I raise you to full Blackguard.'

'Sir?!'

'You stand vigil tonight in the Prism's chapel. At dawn you take the oath with a few of your brothers and sisters. Your first shift as full Guard will be on the White's detail tomorrow at noon. We're putting some traitors up on Orholam's Glare. I recommend you get some sleep now. It's gonna be a long couple days.'

Teia was thunderstruck. Full Blackguard? So soon? Was Commander Fisk so pressed for new bodies to fill the details, or was he trying to use his time as commander to pack as many good people into the Blackguard as possible? She mumbled a thanks and opened the door to leave.

'He hesitated, you know. Lytos,' Commander Fisk said quietly, looking away from Teia. 'At the end. Breaker didn't tell your squad about it, but he did tell the White. Lytos changed his mind, turned away from his treason. He was moving to attack Buskin to stop him when Winsen killed him. It wasn't Winsen's fault, so Kip didn't tell him. Lytos shouldn't have been there in the first place, so Breaker kept the burden of that knowledge on his own shoulders. But he wanted the White to know. When you're a leader, you protect the living first, but you honor the dead as you can. It's the kind of grace I'd expect from the Lightbringer. And...and Orholam saw to it that word of Lytos's ultimate faithfulness got to me, the one person to whom it would matter most, so I wouldn't have to remember him as a traitor. That's Orholam's mercy, isn't it?'

Chapter 10

Time is the only prison from which prison frees us. Gavin woke with a new sense of vigor. Of course, the light was still the same, so he had no idea how long he'd slept. He accepted his ignorance as a gift. He'd slept until he was no longer tired.

And he felt better. Stronger than last night, the pain faded from his eye to a dull throb. He felt almost his old self. Or, he thought as he stretched and became aware of it, maybe that was just his erection.

Somehow, despite the narrowness of the palanquin, neither of them had fallen off it in the night, and Marissia's form was plastered to his. The curve of her butt was holding down what was straining to be up.

His twitch seemed to waken her. He couldn't shift away. He'd been imprisoned nude, and with Marissia only in her light shift, she could hardly help but notice his state if he moved. Marissia knew his body like no one else in the world.

But then she made his stillness moot by shifting her own position. She hesitated, and gave a luxurious moue. She'd always loved morning sex. 'Is that for me?' she asked.

It wasn't, but it seemed rude to say so. He cleared his throat as she rolled over with impressive dexterity, anchoring a leg on his hip and looking into his face. She pulled her body close.

'You're feeling better, aren't you?' she asked.

'Much.'

A cloud passed over her face. 'Then your father will take me away soon.'

And like every freedom, the freedom from time offered by this prison was revealed to be a lie. Gavin said, 'I can pretend to be sicker than I am.'

'But we can't know when he's watching, so that's hopeless, isn't it?'

Gavin hesitated, then said, 'Yes.'

She looked into his eyes with a serenity that defied sense. 'He'll kill me.'

Gavin nodded, throat thick. She was a loose end.

'Will you do me a favor?' she asked.

'Anything.'

'Make love to me.' Her fingernails brushed lightly down his back in the way he liked. But having really seen her for the first time just last night, how could he now ignore her deep currents and see only the surface?

Easily. Oh so easily.

Her eyes were hot, intense, full of longing and grief and fear. 'One last time, please. Show me I meant something to you.'

Orholam have mercy. Gavin remembered the last time he'd made love with Marissia, just before he'd left the Chromeria, how he'd felt as if he were somehow cheating on Karris, though that was before they'd married. He'd rejected the guilt then: every lord kept a room slave. Most kept more than one. Gavin was downright abstemious by comparison with others, and certainly compared to others in his class.

That day Marissia had made love to him like fire, all longing and hidden rage and despair.

No wonder.

And she felt all that again now, and worse. She said, 'Show me I meant something to you,' but she meant, 'Let's blot out feeling and fear. Let's do what we've always done.' She would make love as if it would make him love her.

Marissia pulled her shift away from between them, and her body was hot against him. And not for the first time in his life, Gavin split. His body said what his will did not. Marissia's ears had been clipped. She had been sold, even if she'd chosen it. She had been a slave, hadn't she? She'd been treated as a slave, so that made her one, didn't it? And slaves weren't quite covered by wedding oaths, were they?

He owed her this. She'd made love to him many times when she probably hadn't really wanted to. Didn't he owe her this once?

And he did want to.

But Karris. Karris, his wife.

She would never find out. If she found out, she would understand. If she understood, she would forgive him, as she had forgiven him so many other things.

But what another will forgive is shitty ethical measurement, isn't it? Karris would understand that she'd married a faithless piece of shit. Karris would understand that you don't blame shit for being shit. It's your own fault for thinking you could polish shit and find gold.

I'm tired of being shit. Of being a liar. Of being an oath-breaker.

This wasn't about Karris. It was about Gavin and what kind of man he was.

Gavin the Liar. Gavin Get Along, who wanted everyone to

love him…and quietly cheated in the background. Gavin the Gray.

Gavin's hunger was a trumpet, blaring in his own ear. His body wanted satisfaction. It knew the pleasures of Marissia's body. He deserved this, didn't he? He should take what small comfort he could. Some sweetness. After all he'd been through.

If Marissia had made the slightest move to please him, had rocked her hips against him, had brought his hands to her breasts, had kissed his cold lips, he would have acted, he would have damned himself again, eagerly. He was that weak.

But she didn't. She knew him that well. More than that, her self-control told him that she loved him that much.

'Marissia,' he said, pained.

'Karris,' she said. It was defeat. It was heartbreak. She scooted back, unhooked her leg from over his. Her face fell.

She deserved so much more.

'My oaths, Marissia. They've been worth nothing for my whole life. This is my last chance.'

She got off the palanquin and swallowed. 'Am I always to be cast off and second best, my lord? Here at my end, is there nothing left for me?'

And then she wept. There were no corners in the spherical cell, but she huddled as far away from him as possible, knees to her chest, hiding her face. She'd wasted her whole life on him.

Where was his golden tongue now? Gavin sat up with effort, and pain lanced through his burnt eye again, leaving him breathless for a long moment.

There had to be something to say that was honest and true and comforting, but Gavin wasn't a master of words like that.

'So you live.'

Gavin nearly got whiplash looking for the source of that oddly disappointed voice. A panel had opened in the wall, and something stung Gavin's chest.

His one good eye took in his father in a split second. He wanted to lunge and kill that old bastard—

But he looked down. A dart was stuck in his chest, and it felt warm. So warm.

'Marissia,' Gavin said. But he wasn't sure what he wanted to tell her, now. His thoughts were thick, gooey. This was it. The end.

'Put these on, *caleen*,' Andross Guile said. He stood powerful, as if he'd dropped twenty years, and packed on a few sevs of muscle. He tossed a pair of manacles over to her, utterly certain she would obey. He didn't even see her.

Andross stared at Gavin, an intensity in his deep eyes, but he said no more.

'You can't. I need her,' Gavin said.

'Need her?' There was an edge of dark amusement in his voice.

'Please. Please don't kill her. I'll go mad without her.'

'*Go* mad? You're worried about *going* mad?' Andross said. He laughed, a free and open sound in the cell, and turned away, dismissive.

Gavin swung his legs over the side of the palanquin. He stood, wobbled, braced himself on the palanquin. The warmth had spread everywhere.

He blinked, suddenly on the floor, drool dribbling down his cheek. The dart in his chest was gone. The palanquin was gone. Carried out by Marissia and Andross? He tried to speak, but couldn't make words.

But Marissia and Andross hadn't left, not yet.

The last thing Gavin saw was Marissia's tear-streaked face as she was pulled out of the prison, hopeless, broken, looking back at him for what he couldn't give.

And then she was swallowed by the darkness.

Chapter 11

'Are we being bad?' Tisis asked.

'We're being naughty. There's a difference,' Kip said. The morning sun angled in through poorly sealed cracks in the walls of the captain's cabin, emphasizing how little privacy they had. 'Are you ready?'

'I better be,' she said. 'She'll be along any minute now. Take off your tunic.'

They'd been up half the night talking. But plotting was one thing, carrying it out was another.

'Oh, I just had another idea,' Tisis said, keeping her voice low. She sat up in the narrow bed and swung her slender legs over the side. She'd put her lingerie on again after their little disaster last night, adding a light robe to her camisole and underwear. 'Tunic, Kip,' she said, throwing off her robe and tossing it into a corner.

He'd seen her in beautiful underthings several times now, and she'd been nude during his very first interaction with her at his Threshing, but Kip wasn't even close to being accustomed to seeing Tisis's body. Before he'd known her, he'd actually kind of hated her for being so flawless. He'd thought at the time that she'd tried to kill him, and she *had* made him fail the Threshing. But still. Hating someone for being beautiful was kind of perverse, wasn't it?

And he was really the last person who should hate *anyone* for what she'd inherited. Kip had somehow gone from the whore's boy to the polychrome husband of the richest heiress in the Seven Satrapies – all because of his father. Of course, that he had been a hypocrite to hate her didn't make it easier.

It wouldn't be so bad if she were just beautiful. Even just among the squad, the young men had different preferences. Cruxer was a sucker for a pretty face and dark kinky hair like Lucia had had. Ferkudi waxed poetic about a bottom that could shake your house like an earthquake. Big Leo had wanted a petite girl, and when Teia had made fun of the obvious size differential that would create, Leo had said, "Yeah, petite, like you, Teia, but you know, with breasts."

Later, in training, she'd accidentally kicked Leo in the stones. Twice.

The problem with Tisis was that she was exactly the type of beautiful Kip liked most. Skin light and exotic to a boy from the hinterlands of Tyrea, the vanishingly rare true blond hair, a huge smile, radiant hazel eyes, a heart-shaped face, and that body. Those breasts.

Kip tried not to think about those.

Which wasn't easy, with them straining the silk of her camisole with its tiny straps and its deep cut into her cleavage.

Kip loved Teia, but Tisis. Holy shit. Woman, you are the reason some ugly smart guy invented language – simply so he could have some chance against better-looking men to woo you.

In typical Kiply fashion, though, he'd realized he loved Teia and then married Tisis not half an hour later.

'With my body, I thee worship,' part of their archaic wedding oath went. Well, that part was going to be easy.

She stepped close enough that she pressed that worshipped body against him. 'This'll put the cream in the kopi,' she said.

Kip was familiar with the bitter drink, and at first he thought it was sexual innuendo. He was about to say something about her skin being lighter than his, so what they were actually trying to do was put kopi in cream.

Unless by cream, she meant his—

Then he realized she meant, 'This will be the finishing touch.' Not an innuendo.

Right. Excuse *me* for going there.

'Tear my camisole,' she said.

'Nrg?'

She grabbed his hands. 'Like we were so passionate you ripped it open last night.' Her eyes sparkled as she put his hands on her chest, clearly loving the game.

The second night they'd actually tried to make love, Kip had nervously deferred to Tisis to lead things. She'd said she was only technically a virgin, so Kip figured even that made her way more experienced than he was. She'd gone quickly from tearing off clothes to attempting penetration, and after that hadn't happened and she'd been left fuming and trying to blame him, it had seemed like too much to ask to say, 'Hey, do you mind if I just play with your body a bit? I like it.'

On the fourth night of their marriage, with the addition of olive oil and a singular focus on breaching the Jade Gate lest their marriage be annulled and they start a war that no one could win and that would kill tens of thousands of innocents and be remembered ignominiously for all time, Kip hadn't gotten a chance for his playfully wandering hands to wander much at all, playfully or any other way.

'Kip?'

'Mmm?'

'The camisole?'

'Mm-hmm?' he said, lost in the gloriousness under his hands. 'Oh!'

He cleared his throat and tugged gently on the deep neckline of her camisole, trying to ignore that a camisole of this material, with this much lace, and dyed this color, might cost more than all the villagers in Rekton would have seen in a year. Inside, Kip was still the poor boy, and he wondered if he always would be.

'Oh, for Orholam's ...' She grabbed his hands in hers and helped him tear the neckline down to her navel, but then she held his hands there. They both hesitated. She did some kind of undulating feline movement into him that did all sorts of wonderful things. 'I never did take care of you, did I?' she asked.

'It wouldn't take long, I promise,' Kip said.

She looked at the door and grimaced. 'Verity'll be here any—'

Kip slid his hand from silk to silken skin, and she stopped speaking.

She looked up at him with suddenly fiery eyes, as if she were furious. She threw a leg up on his hip and grabbed his face in both hands. 'Why, Kip? Why? Why do I want to be naughty with you when I can't, but when it's perfectly acceptable and I have all night, then I can't? Dammit!' She ground her hips against him angrily, kissed him, and bit his bottom lip. Then she pushed away from him.

Never breaking eye contact, she shimmied out of her underthings and peeled off her camisole, throwing each to a separate corner of the room. She tousled her long blonde hair. She scooted into the narrow bed and pulled the covers only over her legs, as if she were totally comfortable being nude in front of her husband. Which, of course, was what Verity needed to believe.

'Ah! Idea!' Tisis said. 'Love bites. We'll have to do that

68

tomorrow. Tunic, Kip. Off. Then get over here and give me some whisker burn on my neck. Quickly.'

Kip's mother had once said that if he pulled a funny face for too long it would get stuck. Could the same happen if your horn was up for too long? What if it got stuck? Orholam, let it not be so. The Blackguard blacks that the Mighty had been allowed to take were a nice camouflaging black, but they were also *tight*.

There was a knock at the door, and Kip realized suddenly that somehow the plan had always been that he answer the door naked. And then he had to pretend to be comfortable with that. Like he was the kind of man who would answer the door naked because wow, after a night like last night, who could think about clothes?

That hadn't been his addition to the plan, he was sure of it. Even if Kip were slow-cooked in a stew of sexual satiety until he fell to pieces, he didn't think he'd ever *not* want to cover himself.

'My lady, my lord? Breakfast,' Verity said from outside.

'My lord husband, would you get the door, please, and then come right back to bed. It's so cold without you,' Tisis said loudly. She grinned at him.

Kip shucked off his tunic, acutely aware of Tisis's eyes on him. Part of him knew that his modesty was ridiculous at this point. Though he'd kept his tunic on during their abortive attempts at intercourse, she knew how he looked by now. Still, it was one thing to know he was fat, another to see it.

He held his tunic in front of him in one hand casually, covering as much of belly and groin as possible, and popped the door open. Even with that, beyond Verity, he saw a sailor try to get a glimpse beyond Kip at the nymph they all knew lay within.

Kip just gave the man a self-satisfied smile, and closed the door after Verity came in, balancing a silver tray in one hand and a steaming bucket of water in her other.

Verity was a gnarled oak stump of a woman, wider than she was short, with silver hair that had once been blonde, holding far stronger ideas of how lords and ladies should behave than any lord or lady Kip had ever met.

'Oh, is it time for breakfast already?' Tisis said. She yawned and stretched luxuriously, uncovered.

Kip forgot about the plan. He dropped his tunic from nerveless fingers.

He snatched it off the floor, almost colliding with the slave through his sudden lurch in the tiny cabin.

'Perhaps milady would prefer to bathe and dress first?' Verity asked.

Kip tried to slip around behind her just as she bent over suddenly to put down the bucket. His groin brushed against a bottom so large and wide that Ferkudi would faint.

Mercifully, his fist and the wadded tunic ran interference in the split second before Kip could twist, taking the contact on his hip rather than his horn. He made it past her, but his motion jostled her as she set down the bucket, slopping water on the floor.

Verity stood slowly, leaving the bucket on the floor. With the air of one extremely put out, she sighed, looking at the mess. Then she glared judgment at Kip, naked as he was. Kip swallowed.

'Does my lord need something?' Verity asked.

Kip had picked up on the very subtle cues that Verity didn't approve of Tisis's marrying without her sister Eirene's consent. She had extended that disapproval to Kip himself.

'Sorry,' Kip said.

She sniffed and turned to Tisis, muttering none too quietly, 'A proper lord would know not to apologize to slaves.' She raised and brightened her voice: 'Milady?'

'Only a sponge bath?' Tisis asked, disappointed.

'I fought the captain long and hard, milady. He avers fresh water is too precious on a voyage to be used for bathing.'

Verity took a folding screen and set it up to block Tisis from view, though the logic of that escaped Kip. Verity spoke aloud, too, as if the screen were a real barrier. 'I see that your lord husband has mussed your braids. I suppose we shall have to set aside a few *hours* to fix them this morning. I think you should also speak to him about procuring a room slave.'

'What?' Kip interrupted. 'Why would I need a room slave? We have you.'

'I'm not that kind of room slave, my lord. You'll need to get your own for that.'

Tisis started laughing immediately, but Kip didn't understand.

'My lord doesn't need that kind of room slave, Verity,' Tisis said. 'I'm keeping him quite contented.'

'Many a lord tells his wife that while seeking additional pleasures on the side. But a lord who strays must have the decency to do so safely, so as not to bring disease and dishonor to his house.'

'Verity!' Tisis said. 'I'll not have you speak so.'

Kip caught up only slowly. First, he wanted to laugh incredulously. Verity was worried he wanted to take *her* to bed? And then all the rest crystallized as dirty whispers, not quite directed at him, but definitely directed at him.

He had long felt like a bumpkin lost in the tightly circumscribed manners of the nobility, and the customs of slaveholding were the most opaque to him, and made him more reticent than anything else.

It was baffling to him that when he made mistakes, if anything erred on the side of being too nice – giving a gratuity or looking a slave in the eye or apologizing – slaves resented those slips most. It was as if they were saying, 'Don't break the rules. They're all we have.'

They knew how to deal with abuse, or with being ignored or taken for granted, but making them remember all the privileges of freedom was too hard.

'Hmph,' Verity said. 'You're a woman married now, Mistress, and it's time you face facts. Your duty in the bed chamber is to provide my lord with children. It is his to satisfy your carnal desires fully. But you have no reciprocal duties on that count. If he desires activities you don't enjoy or even ones you do more frequently than you wish to indulge him, he has a room slave for that. Of course, as the lady running the household, it is your duty to procure a room slave pleasing to your lord husband.'

'Orholam have mercy,' Tisis said.

'It is his mercy,' Verity said. 'What else are slaves for, but to ease the burdens on my lady?'

The old Kip would have shrunk back, would have accepted the slave's sly insinuations.

Kip swept the folding screen crashing aside. Verity was dunking a cube of soap into her bucket. Kip hauled her up and pinned her against the wall, his fire-scarred left hand around her throat.

'You listen to me,' Kip growled. 'I keep my oaths – all of them, including my wedding oaths – and if you impugn my honor again, I swear to Orholam, I'll throw you overboard for the sharks.'

'My lord, I wasn't—'

'We both know you were.'

She'd gone limp. Just another slave being abused by another master.

'Look at me. Look at me!' he shouted.

She looked at him with the cold impassivity of a woman who didn't value her life much. Or perhaps the cold terror of a woman who thought she was going to die.

'You can hate me, but you will not pour poison in my wife's ears about me. Not while I'm here. Not while I'm gone. Do I make myself understood?'

'Perfectly, my lord.'

He released her. 'If you can't stand to serve us loyally, we'll sell you immediately. I'll even let you choose which offer for you we accept. I won't send you somewhere terrible as a punishment, but I also won't have you here.'

'Yes, my lord,' she said quietly.

'Now take the laundry and get out. I'll have your answer by tonight.'

She moved around the cabin more nimbly than Kip would have imagined possible, gathering Tisis's cast-off clothing and noticing but making no comment on the tears. She mopped up the spilled water, and Kip realized then that he was still naked. Tisis was staring at him, but there was no teasing now. She was holding a cloth up in front of herself, and she looked a little scared.

Oh hells. Did I just jump the wrong way?

'My lord?' Verity asked. 'Do you wish me to launder your tunic as well?'

He was holding it in his hand still. 'Uh...yes? Yes,' he said. It did actually need laundering. He'd been training on deck daily with the squad, and though he washed himself daily, he hadn't gotten around to cleaning his clothing. At the Chromeria, you put your dirty clothes in a basket and they magically appeared the next day, clean and folded on your bed.

But he didn't hand over the tunic.

Verity handed him a towel. 'For your sponge bath, milord,' she said. It was big enough that he could hold it in front of himself while he handed her the tunic.

She walked to the door with her pile of laundry. 'Oh, milord? Just in case my lady is too delicate to speak of such things, and since you'll be washing yourself. Do make sure to clean well under your foreskin. A lady's perfumed garden ought to be fragrant, but a gentleman's oak should smell only of soap.'

Kip was so aghast that he couldn't say anything. Tisis snorted. Kip just shook his head, acknowledging that she'd scored a point.

Her mouth pressed to a line briefly to avoid smiling, Verity walked out the door. 'I'll return in due time to dress milady and take the dishes. My lord. My lady.'

It was only as she closed the door behind herself that Kip realized the parting tease had been a test, too: Was Kip the kind of master who would hurt her at any provocation, or had her adultery insinuation crossed one of a relatively small number of important lines? It was the kind of thing a slave would want to know.

He sat down on the bed, not knowing whether he'd passed or failed, or what either meant about him.

Tisis had pulled the screen back into place, and she was continuing her sponge bath. 'You scared me, but it was a good distraction.'

'Huh?' Kip asked, coming out of his reverie.

'Distracting her like that so I could wash myself. She told me yesterday I didn't smell like sex.'

'As if I'm that smart.' Kip only realized he'd said it aloud afterward, but Tisis said nothing from behind her screen. Kip pulled on his underclothes and his clean blacks.

When Tisis emerged dressed in her moss-green tunic and

73

breeches with a leather belt that emphasized her slender waist, she had an odd look in her eye. 'So you knocked down the screen because you were actually angry?'

'Yes?' Kip said. Was this a trick question? 'Am I a bully?'

'You're a lord,' Tisis said as if it were a strange question. 'The gentry know your titles, but they also know what you were before you came to the Chromeria. We'll devour you if you let us, Kip. Even our slaves. That's what we do when we're threatened.'

'Is it always to be battles and contests, even with my own side?' Kip asked.

'Only if you lose the important ones,' she said. She saw he didn't understand. 'Kip, in Lucidonius's time, Karris Shadowblinder was a theatre girl. It was considered the next thing to a prostitute by polite society. No one talks about her as a theatre girl now. She became a Name. There is no middle path for people like you and her. You're suddenly elevated greatly, and everyone wants to know if you deserve it. Me? I can be some lady born to a great family with one or two excellences, but little else worthy of comment. That path is closed to you. You come in suddenly at the top, and everyone else feels like they've been knocked down a notch. You have to prove yourself.'

'Even to slaves?'

'Slaves take not only orders but also cues from their masters. Verity was Eirene's governess. Eirene sending *her* to serve me? You think that wasn't a little dig? My sister was implying that I was acting like a child. But it's also because she trusts Verity.'

'If I'd known that, maybe I wouldn't have threatened her with death,' Kip said, grimacing.

'About that. Were you angry because it was true, or because you wanted her to think it was?'

Something about her intensity drove all thoughts out of Kip's mind. 'Because what was true?' Kip asked.

'That you keep your oaths.'

So of course Kip thought immediately of the oaths he hadn't kept: one to his mother, to avenge her rape by his father – a story that had all been nonsense from an addict. And then he'd sworn to Gavin that he would destroy Klytos Blue. He'd been doing his best to investigate the Color through the forbidden libraries, but he'd never found anything damning there, and had broken that oath, too. He said, 'Maybe I was so furious because I've failed oaths before.'

And he told her about them, without too many specifics. She was still a Malargos, after all.

'But you consider your wedding oaths binding, and plan to do all in your strength to keep them?' she asked.

'Yes! Absolutely,' he said.

'But you love *her.*'

Her. Teia. It was a gut punch. So Tisis wasn't oblivious. Kip hadn't said a word about Teia. Tisis had picked that up from what? A few glances?

Do I lie?

After a pause this long, a lie would be pointless, wouldn't it?

'Yes. I think so. I don't know. I've been infatuated with like four girls in the last two years. Always the impossible ones. Maybe that's why you're terrifying. You aren't just not impossible; you're not just possible; you're actual, and the rejection will hurt that much more when it comes, won't it?'

He'd meant to use the technique his grandfather had taught him: use his blunderbuss of a mouth to his own advantage and see how the other person reacted to whatever outrageous truth he'd fired at them.

Except that Tisis didn't respond at all. She merely looked at him.

Well, now Kip felt naked in a new way that was nearly as uncomfortable as the first.

Then she said, 'When you wouldn't take off your tunic, were you hiding your scars, or your...stomach?'

'You can say fat,' he said.

'I will not.' She said no more, and he couldn't help but be impressed by her quiet dignity.

'Did they teach that in lady school?'

He didn't mean to say it out loud. But she didn't respond. Again.

'Sorry,' he said.

'How did you get those?' she asked, as if he were being a willful child. Which was sort of fair.

'Too much pie.'

'The scars,' she said, missing his attempt at humor, though he couldn't tell whether it was on purpose or not.

'I lost a bet,' he said. He was taking the totally wrong tack here, sailing straight into the storm instead of quartering the waves.

'With some kind of animal?' she said angrily. 'Kip, there was a part of our vows that said, "Let there be no darkness between us." Why are you lying to me about stupid stuff?'

It was supposed to be the setup for a joke:

A bet?

I bet dinner that I could get out of a locked closet. The rats bet I couldn't. I was dinner.

No one had ever really laughed at that joke, but he thought that was maybe in the delivery.

Right as he was about to explain and apologize, she said, 'About those vows. If *she* showed up, and she became possible, and I would never know...'

'I'm not adding "cheater" to the list,' Kip said.

'The list?'

Damn. Caught out. And no joke was possible now, not after the ass he'd already been. 'The list of things I, uh, dislike about myself.' Loathe.

'That decides it,' she said.

'Decides what?' Kip asked.

'Reeny is going to be so furious,' Tisis said. She squared her shoulders and straightened her back. Reeny? Oh, her sister Eirene. 'But if you can't run away with your husband, who can you run away with?'

'What?' WHAT?!

'I'm not going home, Kip. I'm going with you. Wherever you go, I'm going.'

'I really don't—'

'Save your breath. There's nothing you can say that will change my mind. Try to stop me and our deal's off.'

'Empty threat?' After all that talk of failing family...

'How about this one, then?' She stepped close and grabbed his crotch through his clothes. 'This stays with me. If you choose to leave my presence, you'll go without it.'

76

'Oh, come on, it just finally went to sleep.'

'You find threats of me tearing it off arousing?'

'Not when you put it like that.'

'So it's settled. I'm going,' she said triumphantly.

He pushed her back. 'Tisis. This isn't a game. We're going to war. You're no fighter.'

'And you're no noble,' she said. 'But we'll teach each other.'

'Tisis, it's different. Nobles won't kill you—'

'If you believe that, you're a fool.'

Well, shit. Kip's very pause was an admission of defeat.

Tisis said, 'You don't know it yet, but you need me as much as I need you.'

She smiled coyly, but at least she didn't rub in the victory.

'The squad's not going to like it,' Kip said.

She pointed at him. 'Haha! I beat a Guile!'

He hoped his face was a study in Nonplussed Kip. But she only smiled beatifically for a moment, thawing him more than he would admit.

Then her mouth pursed in quick disapproval. 'Also, did you really put clean clothes on your dirty body?'

'Yes?'

She clucked in mock horror. 'My lord husband, surely you must know, a lady's perfumed garden ought to be fragrant, but a lord's—'

'Ah! Fine! I'll wash!'

Chapter 12

Teia climbed down the tower using the servants' stairs. Just a little 'Screw you' to her tail. The stairs themselves were clogged enough with servants and slaves and discipulae that there wasn't much purpose to it other than inconveniencing him and giving herself time to think.

She went to the main floor and across to the other stairs, and went down farther still. Commander Fisk had given her an idea.

In a few minutes, she was at the dungeon. Few people were kept here except a couple of drafters immediately before Sun Day. Those who'd broken the halo would be put in rooms of colors safe to them, or blackened rooms for polychromes. With Sun Day just passed, there should be no one here – except whoever was going to be executed tomorrow.

Two of Carver Black's tower soldiers were stationed in front of a heavy oaken door. As Teia approached, they stood respectfully. The tower soldiers had always had reasonably good relationships with the Blackguards, but with the influx of Andross Guile's Lightguards, whom they hated, they now treated the Blackguards like dear friends.

'You're holding the accused for execution tomorrow?' Teia asked.

'Yes, sir,' the elder tower soldier said. He was long past his prime, stiff knees and lots of experience.

He wasn't being rude at the sight of a petite young girl who – to another tower soldier – might look like the epitome of how far the Blackguard's standards had fallen. Quite the opposite, in fact.

Through a quirk of protocol, tower soldiers always addressed Blackguards as 'sir,' regardless of gender. Apparently it had originated with some gaffe or deliberate insult involving a particularly manly Archer. The Blackguards had turned it back on the tower soldiers, demanding that every one of them be called sir – when Teia had complained to Quentin that language was weird, he had speculated that it was perhaps analogous to how all magisters were called magisters regardless of gender, rather than magistri and magistrae, while the declensions of the nouns for their pupils were retained as 'discipula,' 'discipulus,' 'discipulae,' and 'discipuli,' while a mixed group of girls and boys went by the feminine plural 'discipulae.'

As Quentin had explained to Teia, 'Language isn't weird. People are weird. Language makes sense until people get their phoneme pukers on it.' Teia had no idea what that meant, but she got the gist.

The younger man looked at his officer, obviously unaware of the protocol. 'Uh...'

'Later,' the older man said. 'How can we help you?'

'I need to interview them,' Teia said.

They looked ready to say no.

'I'm on the execution detail tomorrow, and they're not telling us anything,' Teia said. 'I've got to...ascertain in what respects they may present dangers...to the assemblage.'

With soldiers, if you spoke bureaucratese, they'd assume you'd been assigned to do it. All the bullshit orders come dressed in jargon. If you just said what you wanted, they knew it was your own idea.

She switched back to her own tone. 'You know what happens if something goes wrong during the execution – it's on us. With all that's gone on recently, the Blackguard ain't takin' another hit.'

The older soldier looked as if she were asking the impossible and he hated to say no.

'Look,' Teia said. 'I'm not even a full Blackguard. I'm doing my vigil tonight. I've just been on duty, and after holding vigil all night, my first official detail is watching what everyone tells me is a horrific way to die. Orholam's Glare is the death they scare drafters with from the moment we first learn we can draft. The Blackguard's stretched thin to breaking, and it's all made worse by those Lightguard assholes running my friends off as if they're traitors. I know this isn't the normal way of doing things – but what's been normal about anything recently? You can take all my weapons, do whatever you need. I just need to talk to them so someone can check it off a list. And I'm not going to have my first official act be lying to my commander by telling him I did it if I didn't. But I don't want to start my service by failing a simple assignment, either. Can you cut me some slack?'

Momentarily, Teia was kind of impressed with her own lying.

'Not many Blackguards would let us take their weapons. Your lot tend to hold that privilege pretty fierce,' the older man said. It was a singular right: Blackguards were allowed weapons in the presence of satraps and diplomats and Colors and the Prism himself. It set them apart from everyone else, not least the tower guards like these men.

Teia quirked a grin. 'Eh, if you ask me tomorrow when I'm a real Blackguard, I might not give them up so easy!'

They laughed together, and Teia put her weapons on the table.

The old man moved to unlock the door. 'I'd not get in arm's reach of that false prophet. I know you have training and all, but madness gives 'em strength. The young luxiat mostly sits there and cries. But madness... You never know. Last one's the drafter, watch them vipers. No offense. Oh. Shoes.'

'Shoes?' she asked.

'You have to take off your boots. Put on these.'

Teia hadn't noticed, but there were slippers of various sizes on a mat. She stepped into the appropriately sized pair.

The door opened onto the strangest prison Teia had ever imagined. All the surfaces were lined with mirror. Orange lux torches provided a single dim spectrum of soft light.

The older soldier accompanied her down the shimmery hall. Even the floor was mirrored, the slippers polishing the pounded silver with every step. They approached the first door and the soldier handed Teia a mirror mounted on a handle. He demonstrated how she should use the mirror to peek around the corner to see any threat. Then, after she'd put the spectacles on, he handed her a tiny knife with an oversize handle. The blade wasn't even as long as her little finger was wide.

'Hellstone,' he said to her puzzled look. 'If they somehow draft. Drains out their luxin without killing 'em. Works on you, too, though, so don't let 'em take it from you. Oh, and if they capture you, our orders are to go in with muskets firing. We don't try to recover hostages. They know it. It's not a bluff. We've done it before.'

'Great. Thanks.'

He left and she heard the door being barred behind her.

She opened the window inset in the door of the first cell. She extended the mirror, and was surprised that she knew the man therein. She closed the window. It was the Color Prince's prophet, the spy handler she and the Mighty had surveilled months ago. He'd tried to kill Big Leo. It wouldn't bother her to see him executed or to leave a paryl tag on him for assassination. Good option, maybe.

She walked down the mirrored hall farther, little slippers scuffing a floor that really should have been cleaner. Men. It was as if they were physically blind to messes unless you pointed them out specifically: Is this floor clean? Yessir. Do you see this dirt? Yessir. Did you see it before when you just told me it was clean? No, sir.

Teia opened the next cell's window, peered in with the little angled mirror, and paused. The young man inside had his head down, ignoring the sound of the opening window. He was a disheveled mess, but there was something familiar about him, too.

Orholam have mercy.

'Quentin?' Teia asked.

He froze up, and it was an admission of guilt. A moment later, his head snapped up. 'No,' he said. 'No, no.'

'Quentin, what are you doing here?' Teia asked. She unlocked his door and stepped inside. Teia was petite, though stronger than many would guess, now. But if there was one man from whom she had nothing to fear, it was Quentin. He was skinny to the point that it was painful to look at him. He so often forgot to eat while studying, he probably weighed less than she did. He was a brilliant mind, though, a polymath who mastered subjects within months that took others a full career. He read scrolls and books within hours, and remembered nearly everything he read.

His was the kind of scholarly mind that came along once in a generation, if it was a great generation.

'Quentin, what's going on?' she asked. His cell was a cube with mirror walls and floor and a luminous orange ceiling that gave a sickly hue to the boy's skin.

He looked at her with such shame that she thought he was going to throw up. 'They found me,' he said. 'They never gave up.'

'Who? What?' she asked.

'I didn't even know her name when I did it,' he said.

'What?'

'It was supposed to be Kip,' he said. 'I didn't know him or any of you then. It was before I'd met you.'

'Quentin, what the hell are you talking about?'

'But I knew. When he gave me the orders to do it, I knew it was wrong.'

'What did you do, Quentin?'

He looked up at her as if he couldn't believe she didn't already know. 'I tried to kill Kip. Lucia stepped in the line of fire. I didn't mean to hit her...But I did try to murder him, so it doesn't really count as an accident, does it?'

'No,' Teia said, aghast. Quentin had become their friend. Twitchy, nervous, and scared a lot, but they'd written that off to his having the lopsided brain of a genius.

'It was why I swore an oath to Kip that I'd never lie to him. I was hoping he'd ask, one day. But he never did, and then he left, and I thought – I thought maybe Orholam had forgiven me. But then the Blackguards came. They'd never given up on finding who'd killed her. I was hoping they wouldn't take me alive.'

'You? *You* shot Lucia?' Teia had barely seen the hooded figure raise the musket. In her dreams, it had always been some monster. Someone eminently capable. Some assassin whose bullet had been intercepted through Orholam's will alone. Not a scared kid. Never Quentin.

'It was pathetic how easily they turned me. A little bit of threatening, a little bit of bribery. That's all it took. I knew it was wrong, Teia. They're going to execute me, and I deserve it.'

'Who sent you?' The orange light in here was making Teia feel as slippery as the Old Man of the Desert himself.

'High Luxiat Tawleb. I told the White as much. But he's sworn it's a lie, of course. And what is my word against his? I've no evidence.'

It was true; Teia could tell. There was no guile in Quentin's voice or gaze.

Teia hadn't been friends with Lucia. She could tell early on that Lucia wasn't going to make the cut to become a Blackguard. Why make friends with someone who wasn't going to be around long?

It was practical, but also somehow heartless.

'Quentin, I came down here hoping to find a solution for a dilemma. Seems I have.'

82

She tagged Quentin with a paryl marker for the assassin.

'What dilemma?' Quentin asked. 'What do you mean?'

But this murderer wasn't entitled to an explanation.

Teia left.

Chapter 13

Kip stood in the captain's cabin, trying to put on his Breaker face before he headed out to face the squad.

They were going to be rightly livid with him. After all their training, the Mighty had reached a rough equivalency with each other, a working strength. Adding Tisis to the Mighty's war party would be like adding a fifth leg to a dog. They couldn't help but trip over her, have to compensate, slow down, and get tentative as they had to protect her.

But here he was.

He opened the door to a bright shining noon, good wind and few clouds. He acted nonchalant, as a young groom would be after a wild night of connubial exertion. Just a twinge of smugness as he walked astern toward where the Mighty were working to create a skimmer.

The captain, a black-haired, fair-skinned Blood Forester with long mustache and beard like a lamprey attached to his face, grinned at him as he walked past.

'Finally found the pearl button, huh?' he asked, slapping Kip on the back and laughing.

The what? But Kip just blushed ruefully, accepting the teasing as if he didn't think the man was an asshole.

'Day five!' the captain said. 'Ha! We had bets going. You won me two danars. Seems like a smart lad, I said, and that's one eager lass he's got there if I don't miss my guess. Won't take him a whole week, I said. I was drunk. You done me right, though – and you clearly did her right last night. How many times was—'

'Hey, hey,' Kip said, putting a hand out to stop the man. 'That's my wife, huh?'

It had been four times. Four times, lying side by side, throwing their bodies around to make the bunk squeak and Tisis crying out while Kip grunted and groaned and then they tried to muffle the sounds of their laughter.

'Four times?' Kip had asked Tisis. 'Isn't that a lot?'

'Not really. I mean sometimes when I...'

In sub-red, Kip could see the heat of her blush spread through her face despite the darkness. 'When you...?' he'd asked.

'Uh, when I've heard people talk about lovemaking,' she'd said.

Even though he'd had the impression that wasn't what she was talking about, he said, 'I always thought those were exaggerations, bragging, because then I'd hear the older Blackguards joke about not being that young anymore.'

'But we *are* young,' Tisis had said.

Young enough that neither of us knows how many climaxes in a night is believable, Kip had thought. So they'd faked four for her and three for him, and laughed and plotted until the early hours. He'd had as much fun in bed as you could have without having as much fun as you want to have.

Apparently they'd hit the correct number to be believable for their age, though, because the captain raised his hands in quick surrender. 'Didn't mean no disrespect.' He grinned. 'Quite the opposite. Good day, my young lord.'

Pearl button?

The Mighty were deep in discussion at the stern, where they were building the skimmer. All wore their blacks, with the insignia of the Mighty at the collar: a powerful figure with arms outspread, radiating power, but his head downcast as if in prayer or concentration or grief. No matter how many times Kip saw it, something about that figure stirred something deeper than memory in Kip. How had Andross Guile picked this emblem? Surely that scorpion had a soul insensitive to art.

'Breaker!' Cruxer called out. The Mighty's leader was tall and slender, confident and handsome. A blue by nature as well as by the thin luxin streaks in his brown eyes, he was serious but not humorless. He always did the right thing, and he always did it quickly. It made him a great leader. Believing the best of others, he somehow brought it out. 'Breaker, would you get over here and tell Ben-hadad that he's not as smart as he thinks he is?'

Kip had expected some gibes about 'sleeping in,' but, of course, that he'd dodged gibes for the moment didn't mean they wouldn't come later. But when the squad teased him, it didn't bother him. They'd given up everything to be here with him and with each other.

'What are you destroying now?' Kip asked, joining the circle between muscle mountain Big Leo and Ben-hadad, who'd had to hop around on a crutch with one knee bound in a splint since his injury during their escape from the Lightguards at the Chromeria.

Ben-hadad said, 'I'm destroying suddenly obsolete methods of shipbuilding. And maybe sailing, too. I'm destroying old strategies of naval combat.' Struggling to handle his crutch, he took off his yellow-and-blue hinged spectacles and alternated between gesturing with them and rubbing the lines they left above his ears from how tight he wore them.

'Breaker, he destroyed the skimmer,' Big Leo said. 'Literally.'

'Wait? What?' Kip asked. 'I thought it was—' He peered over the side into the water, where he'd expected to see the skimmer they'd been building for five days. There was nothing there.

'Look! Look!' Ben-hadad said, half-apologetic, half give-me-a-chance-to-explain. 'It took me a few days to intuit the principles of hydrodynamics.'

'Hyd-what?' Ferkudi asked. Not quite an idiot, nor quite a savant, Ferkudi was the guy you could count on to snort fire pepper paste on a dare. He was the guy who'd be openly picking his nose for the next six weeks, happy to have the excuse. He was also the guy who'd throw his dopey bulk in the line of fire for you without a second thought. With an affable roundness only accentuated by his shaven head, he was their best grappler, a blue and green drafter, and solid in every sense of the word.

'The way water moves, Ferk,' Kip said.

'Duh, it moves *downhill*. You smart guys sometimes...' Ferkudi shook his head.

Ben-hadad ignored him. 'It's not an original design, it's just I didn't understand how—'

'It's not a design at all!' Big Leo said. 'You destroyed our skimmer!'

'I meant the next one. And that skimmer was garbage!' Ben-hadad said.

'You designed it! You said it was the best skimmer ever built. And *I* helped build it. Probably drafted two years off my life,' Big Leo said, pointing to the red rising like flood-waters a quarter of the way up his dark irises. 'I worked my ass off on that thing!'

'Still got a way to go before you're assless,' Winsen said quietly, giving a significant glance at Big Leo's haunches. Whereas Big Leo was by far the biggest of the elite athletes, Winsen was by far the smallest. Slight and unremarkable except for the bars of yellow luxin staining his cold blue eyes, he was the only member of the Mighty one might not be afraid of if one met him in a dark alley.

And that would be precisely the wrong reaction. Not only was Winsen the slipperiest killer of them all, Winsen simply didn't care. With his longbow, he took shots that none of them could make, and he took shots that none of them would make, because they'd be worried about the consequences of hitting civilians or friends. Winsen seemed incapable of worrying about consequences.

'True! And I was right,' Ben-hadad said, soothing Big Leo. 'But skimmers are a new invention. Gavin Guile just discovered them. That's what makes them – look, trust me! Look. I'll do all the drafting myself.'

'No, I forbid it,' Cruxer said, speaking up. He usually let them sort things out themselves, so when he intervened they instantly shut up. 'We trust you, Ben-hadad. But you're not drafting it alone. You can't burn yourself out. We share the burden of making the new one. But next time, you ask me before you destroy what belongs to the squad, understood?'

'It was my design—'

'And the squad's work,' Cruxer interrupted. 'We all throw all of what we have into the pot. For some of us, that may be just muscle—'

'That would be me,' Ferkudi volunteered. Unnecessarily.

'—on a particular project, but we all give our all. Right?'

A brief moment passed, and Kip wanted to rush in and try to make things better. Cruxer and Ben-hadad butted heads constantly. Cruxer saw everything in black and white, and Ben-hadad saw relentless shades of gray possibility.

For Ben-hadad, his life and honor were the Mighty's, but his creations were his own. He valued himself for his brilliant inventions, and that – that one thing – he didn't want to share, and he didn't see keeping that little bit as being too much to ask of a squad he gave everything else.

For Cruxer, you were either in or out.

But Kip didn't try to fix it. Later, maybe, each would be more receptive to reason, more flexible. Not in front of everyone, though.

Ben-hadad was trying to keep his temper, saying tightly, 'I'll make the best skimmer I can so the squad can be safe—'

'Cap'n! Captain! Sir!' the lookout cried out from above.

At the alarm in his voice, the squad reacted immediately. Low stances, spectacles flipped on, team fanning out, looking for threats, hands to weapons. That most of the calamities that might come upon them at sea would be impossible to oppose didn't matter; this was instinct.

The galley had no proper crow's nest, so the lookout merely stood atop the main yard, balancing himself with one hand on the rigging. Above the full-bellied sails, the man was pointing north.

'Fore!' Kip said.

They turned and looked but saw nothing.

'Go,' Cruxer ordered.

So they ran toward the prow, sliding or jumping down the steep stair-ladder from the rear castle, dodging cursing sailors, and dashing up onto the low forecastle as the captain bellowed at his sailors. The captain might be an ass, but he seemed a capable one. When they reached the prow, the Mighty spread out, each of them having drawn in his color, except Kip, who was slower. Kip was still swapping spectacles in and out of his hip case, stealing glances at the dirty white sails to soak up each color in turn.

'What is *that*?' Cruxer asked.

'Ben?' Ferkudi said.

'Uh-huh?' Ben-hadad said.

'We're looking north, right?'

'North-northwest, technically, but—'

'Why is the sun rising in the north?'

Within moments, all of them saw it. At first, it looked like the sun on the horizon, but blinding yellow like the risen sun, not red as the sun on the horizon ought to. And as it rose, the orb deformed, elongated, like the longest finger of a great hand, then simply the first burgeoning cloud of a vast cloud bank rolling into view.

'Storm!' the lookout bellowed.

The sailors sprang into action. A storm they knew how to handle. Only the Mighty were frozen. They knew this was no normal storm.

This was a luxin storm, ravager of cities, slayer of armies, Orholam's wrath, the gods' lash. And it was coming straight for them.

As the luminous cloud bank filled the horizon, the sea reflected the sky with an unnatural clarity. Tiny bright needles flashed between sea and sky, as if knitting them together with light.

This was the consequence of the Seven Satrapies' not having a Prism to balance the colors. Drafters inevitably caused imbalances, and these storms broke out spontaneously. No one understood yet why they happened where they did, what exactly sparked them, or why they ended.

'Breaker, Winsen,' Cruxer said. 'How tight is that yellow?'

Winsen licked his lips. 'Hard to tell from this distance, but uh...I think it's better than I can do.'

Kip flipped on his yellow spectacles. 'It's all over the yellow spectrum. But some of it, yes, some of it's solid.'

'Is it raining? Anyone?' Cruxer asked, though he had the best eyes of the Mighty.

They'd heard stories of a crystal storm in a little village in Atash. Blue luxin crystals the size of fists and sharp as razors had fallen from the sky and shredded everything within a day's walk, but no farther. No one had known whether the tale was true. Solid yellow would be worse.

An odd wind started blowing at their backs, blowing them toward the storm front. It was like no wind Kip had ever felt. It was utterly constant. No gusts, no variation in its strength at all, just a simple constant hard push.

The distant seas in front of the storm fell flat in an expanding circle. No chop, no whitecaps, no variation at all. The sea became a perfect mirror for the bright clouds above. The great luminous clouds running straight against the wind seemed to crash into it as if it were a wall, and then the clouds flipped over that wall in a mass like pancake batter spreading on a griddle in concentric rings.

But everywhere the clouds folded over, the bright needles flashed again. As they got closer, they were mere needles no more, but tree trunks, massive pillars from the sea to the heavens.

At each point, the flat sea pulsed, throbbed yellow, gathering like a vortex, then cratering downward before exploding into the sky. Yellow luxin shimmered into light, but each pillar was also wreathed in chasing fires, spiraling into the sky.

Each pillar pulsed light for several heartbeats, then blew apart, falling into water and light onto seas now crisscrossed with tremendous waves expanding in rings from the luxin-lightning strikes.

'Orholam have mercy,' someone said.

'This is impossible,' Ben-hadad said.

'It's happening,' Ferkudi pointed out helpfully.

'No, this is impossible,' Ben-hadad said.

'You smart guys,' Ferkudi said.

The wind died, and the sea abruptly went still and flat as the front edge of the light-storm passed over them.

'What do we do?!' the captain bellowed at them.

Kip tore his eyes away from the storm. Everything that could be secured on the ship had been. The sailors had reefed the sails, trying to give the ship enough propulsion to quarter the waves, but not so much resistance to the wind that the masts broke.

Then Kip saw that everyone was looking at him. As if he had the answers.

'Turtle,' Cruxer said.

At first, Kip thought Cruxer was talking to him, the turtle-bear, the ridiculous beast that he'd come up with as his own avatar and that had ended up somehow tattooed on his forearm, invisible except when he drafted. But the rest of the squad understood. They drew together around Kip, and the green and blue drafters among them began putting luxin shields up around them to protect all of them from the scything rain.

Going below would have been safer, but Cruxer thought Kip was going to figure this out.

We're facing a force of nature, and they expect me to *fix it*. Orholam's balls.

'Why's it impossible, Ben?' Kip asked.

'Because it's yellow.' He stopped, as if that were enough to explain the dread on his face.

'And?!' Cruxer demanded.

'The storms come from imbalances. Yellow is the center of the spectrum. It's the fulcrum. It shouldn't be possible for the center to be out of balance. So if it is, we are truly—'

But the rest of whatever he said was lost as the sailors screamed out. The captain shouted, 'Secure yourselves to—'

A few hundred paces directly ahead, the sea was cratering. Lightning bolts raced low on the water toward the crater, and were sucked in.

With a concussion that shook the galley and knocked down most everyone standing on deck, the sea exploded upward. Fire spiraled around the pillar of light, discharging into bright clouds above.

Discharging.

Kip clambered to his feet. Water and yellow luxin dropped on the ship in bucketsful, sweeping several sailors and half the Mighty off their feet. But it was liquid yellow, thank Orholam. It flashed into light as it hit the deck, blinding but not killing anyone. Whether they would be lucky enough to be hit only by liquid yellow or whether there were solid razors of yellow yet to come, Kip had no idea.

Discharging. Because it was out of balance.

Kip left the turtle, rushing to the prow just in time to feel it rise as the galley climbed a mountainous wave.

'Breaker, get back—' Cruxer shouted.

But the wave was too massive, too fast for the galley to climb. The prow dug into it instead, slowing the ship as suddenly as if it had hit a wall. Winsen was thrown off his feet. Kip snatched his wrist as he tumbled and was drafting before he knew it. He manacled one of his own wrists to a line connecting the prow and mainmast and the other to Winsen's wrist.

Then water hit them like the slap of a sea demon's tail.

Kip and Winsen were blasted back, and then up the line, into the air, halfway up to the mainmast. Blinded, and with lungs half-full of water, they were dropped, zipping down the line back to the deck as the wave crest passed and the prow suddenly dove, racing down the back side of the wave.

The rest of the Mighty were still crouched, clinging to the deck in a low, luxin-imbued circle like a tick burrowed into the ship's skin.

As soon as Kip's feet hit the deck, he was running. He threw Winsen toward the squad, not even aware of releasing the solid yellow luxin he'd drafted – solid yellow? That fast?

He leapt over the forecastle rail out onto the beakhead as the ship bottomed out between the waves, and lashed himself down with yellow luxin as the ship began its climb again.

A deep breath, and the beakhead plunged into the next wave, the waters pouring over him, scouring at him as if he were an offensive stain.

But then air. This second wave was smaller than the first had been.

Kip popped to his feet, reaching for the lens holster on his left hip. If yellow was out of balance, that meant…If the center of the spectrum was out of balance, it could be out of balance only with the ends of the spectrum. Kip's lens holster had seven pairs of spectacles, ending at sub-red and superviolet, which balanced each other.

But there was one color beyond sub-red: Teia's color, paryl. In legend, there was another in the opposite direction, beyond superviolet: *chi*. Kip had no idea how he'd draft chi. Hell, all he knew about drafting paryl was that Teia's eyes went so wide open the black of her pupils took over the entire eye. Lashing one hand onto the line that held the foreyard to the figurehead, Kip moved forward as far as he could.

There was no third wave. A bit of luck, finally.

'Breaker! Whatever you're going to do, do it fast!' Cruxer yelled.

The sea had gone still, again. An unnatural flatness that defied reason after the titanic waves that had just passed.

Lightning passed low over the waves to sizzle against the galley's hull. For the first time Kip could recall, he saw fear in Cruxer's eyes as they both realized that the next pillar of fire and light was going to spring up directly beneath the galley.

There was no way the ship or anyone in it would survive.

Kip turned to the waves. He stared straight down and widened his eyes, wider, despite the pain, despite the brightness. Into sub-red, and then beyond. It was like opening his mouth too wide, discomfort turned to pain, and the light stabbed daggers into his face.

And wider.

And wider still.

He almost gagged – and then paryl snapped into focus as if it had been waiting for him.

Paryl was racing below the waves, like clouds blowing through a storm-swept sky, and Kip's awareness was pulled along with the gale to its center, where it swirled beneath the galley. A hard knot of paryl and something else – chi? – was forming, buzzing like the lightning-catcher atop each of the Chromeria's seven towers. Kip could feel the charge building, building.

Oh hells.

The paryl and that other color were just touching, and slowly twisting together, like partners coming together to dance. Kip could feel the pressures massing behind each.

And they twisted together hard, spinning together, lightning crackling—

Kip flung them apart with all his will.

The seas exploded, and his paryl-wide eyes were blinded. Everything was lost in the twin roaring to his left and right, and great jets of water streaming skyward pressed in on him. He could feel the jets twining together in the sky above the ship like wire and discharging the imbalanced yellow.

The paryl and chi wanted to snap together, wanted to crush Kip in their embrace. Kip stood, hands extended, arms extended, shoulders knotted with effort, his screams lost in the cacophony. He wept in agony, tear water blending with seawater and brightwater, salt to salt, deep to deep, magic to magic.

Nothing but magic.

Kip barely dared blink, though the world was a wash of undifferentiated light stabbing him. He couldn't lose the colors. His head lolled, chin down, arms out, shaking, exhausted, defiant. It didn't matter where he looked with his blind eyes: the magic was everywhere. Magic was all.

And it was crushing him. It was like holding apart two rams who wanted to butt heads to show their dominance, each side lurching and twisting, ever lunging in.

Kip's arms were stone. He dropped to his knees, still holding the paryl and chi streams apart.

His arms sagged, halfway to his sides, his will almost extinguished.

He wanted to drop dead, drop into the sea, and be no more.

But before his arms fell, he felt a presence behind him, embracing him, propping his arms up. 'I've got you, Kip. Come on, Kip, we're almost through!'

Kip? Everyone on the squad called him Breaker. Who...

'Help me!' Tisis shouted.

And Kip felt another pair of hands on him. 'Breaker, you can do this!' Cruxer said, pulling him to his feet.

Kip was weeping. Oh, Orholam, it hurt. Stabs of pain shot through his eyes, down his spine. His arms were gelatinous. His will was dust.

'Another ten count, Breaker,' Cruxer said. 'Give me just another ten.'

Mumbling through his tears, Kip counted with Cruxer.

'Captain, tell me when we're through!' Cruxer shouted over his shoulder. 'Eight, nine, and – keep going, Breaker, I know you, you've got five more—'

But Kip is gone.

*   *   *

'You've got five more, I know you, Andross Guile. Plans within plans,' the young woman says. Katalina's the kind of awkward girl whose beauty has unfurled with a crack like a sail suddenly filling with wind: luminous dark skin, rare blue eyes, and a shy smile. It's Andross's luck that he's the first suitor to come pluck this flower – it's a good bit of luck, too, because he would have had to woo her regardless of her beauty or lack thereof: she has what he needs.

He waggles his eyebrows at her, and she laughs and puts another pile of scrolls on the desk. But she holds two back. 'But I can't possibly show you these two. If anyone learned, I'd lose my position here and shame my family and the entire Tiru tribe. I'm the youngest under-librarian in Paria.'

' "If anyone learned," huh?' Andross smiles recklessly. 'Oh, what could I *possibly* do to convince you of my discretion?'

She feigns a frown, and that feigned frown hits Kip like a slap in the face. He didn't recognize the smile. He didn't recognize those clear eyes. He didn't recognize the beauty. But he knows that frown.

Kip gasped.

He was weeping, blind, and hands were lifting him, carrying him. 'You did it! Kip, you did it! Orholam's mercy, you saved us,' she said.

It's not *her* speaking. No, it's Tisis. Tisis was the one who'd come to him, caught him. Saved him.

He was weeping, and he was ashamed of his weeping.

'What's wrong with his eyes? One is – and the other—'

'Cover his eyes! He's staring at the sun, you fools!' the captain shouted.

And people were shouting orders and suggestions back and forth. Kip heard a door bang open, and he was bustled inside. His knees hit what had to be his own bed, and he sat, gentle hands guiding him.

'We should strip him out of—' a concerned woman said.

'Just let him breathe, Verity,' Tisis said.

Kip looked up, and despite that his eyes were closed and now bound with cloths, he could see three figures in the room. Three?

Verity and Tisis moved about, trying to take care of him, their bodies luminous in a color beyond purple, their clothes and hair translucent wisps, any bits of metal – buckles and jewelry and hairpins – glowing bright white. He was seeing in chi.

The third figure was glassine, but in full, natural color. She smiled, her lips full, her hair a great curly halo around her head. Rea Siluz, the warrior, the librarian, the immortal somehow more real than real.

She smiled at him, glowing, literally *glowing* with pride for him. Kip had no idea how an emotion could have color, but for some reason it seemed natural.

'The enemy steered that storm toward you, so this much healing is allowed me. You won't be blinded, not today,' she said, and she extended her hand as if making the sign of the three on him, her thumb to one eye, middle finger to the other, and her forefinger touching his forehead where the eye of the mind was. Warmth shot through him, and he fell into blessed sleep.

Chapter 14

Teia had always expected her Blackguard vigil would be one of the most religious experiences of her life. After a night of prayer atop the Prism's Tower, the chosen initiate would take his or her final Blackguard oaths as the sun rose. Teia had always believed in Orholam, but she was usually too busy to pray or attend more than the mandatory chapels. Orholam was the emperor of the universe, but she paid him scant tribute.

She'd looked forward to her vigil, though, thinking it would finally give her time to pray and focus. Perhaps – it being a vigil that would shape the course of her entire life – Orholam would take special notice of her. Speak to her, even.

Instead she'd barely been able to prop her eyelids open through the night. She'd mumbled some prayers, sung a few traditional songs, and wondered if she'd made a huge mistake by staying on the Jaspers instead of going with Kip.

And from the twinges in her belly, her moon blood was going to start soon. Six months since her last cycle, and it came now? Shit.

Did I really mark Quentin for death?

He's going to die anyway. It's war. It's necessary.

Like Marissia.

How many of my friends do I have to kill before I'm on the wrong side?

I'm a soldier, a Blackguard under orders.

But Quentin? Bumbling, adorable Quentin?

Dammit.

All his nerves, all his twitching, his weird oath to Kip that he would never lie to him. His strange intensity, that he would help the Mighty no matter what.

Quentin had been trying to repent for literally as long as they'd known him. But it wasn't real repentance. Not when you wouldn't face justice.

But judging what was real repentance wasn't up to her, was it? That was Orholam's job, and the White's.

I'm a soldier, not an executioner. I can't kill him. I can't be his judge. That's not what I am. I've stepped outside my authority.

I can kill when ordered to do so, but I don't choose it myself. That's not who I am.

And just like that, she knew she needed to go fix this. Even if it meant failing her mission.

She stood and opened the door. A Blackguard named Presser was guarding her vigil, but he said nothing. A Blackguard's vigil was her own. If she left, she left.

Taking a deep breath, Teia walked out past the Blackguards at Karris's door, and to the Blackguard station guarding the steps and the lift. It was the middle of the night, but Commander Fisk was apparently checking in with his people, chatting quietly in the orangey light of their torches – the usual luxin lighting here hadn't yet been repaired.

'You're leaving?' Fisk demanded. 'You abandon your vigil, you're out. You know that.' He was taking it unusually personally, she could tell.

Ah, he'd probably taken some criticism for raising her to

full Blackguard so early. Her failing reflected poorly on him, and just as he began his tenure as commander, too.

Teia would have usually bulled right at conflict, but the orange gave her an idea. 'Not abandoning my vigil, sir. Fulfilling it. Orholam told me there's something I need to do. I've committed a transgression against my brother. I need to make it right before final vows.'

Tleros, a Blackguard Archer as skinny as the spear she carried, said, 'You're supposed to take care of that kind of thing before your vigil.'

'I didn't know I was going to be keeping my vigil until today. Which is better, delayed obedience or disobedience? Should I honor our traditions and stay all night with a guilty conscience, or should I honor Orholam and obey him now?' It was the best way she could think of not to blame Fisk for not giving her enough time.

But he got the message. Commander Fisk grimaced. 'You're right. Allowances must be made. Back before dawn, nunk, otherwise you've broken your vigil.'

'Are you serious?' Tleros asked. She hesitated. 'Err, Commander.'

'Yes,' Commander Fisk said, 'and why don't you meditate a bit on what your tone should be when you speak to your commander?'

'Yes, sir,' Tleros said. She hesitated again. 'Perhaps a shift in the scullery would help focus my mind?'

Commander Fisk merely glowered at her.

'Two?' Tleros asked.

'Whatever you think is necessary,' Fisk said.

Tleros's shoulders sagged. 'Yessir.'

Teia took the lift down, stopped a story above the main floor, took the stairs down, and down, and found the same men on duty at the mirror prison still. Thank Orholam for that.

A few pleasantries later, while checking in paryl for an assassin, and she was outside Quentin's cell.

She opened the peephole.

She hadn't expected him to be sleeping, but his body was too warm to be dead. The last remnants of her paryl marker still clung to his head. She thought about not waking him. She didn't want to talk to him. She hadn't killed him, wasn't that enough?

'Quentin,' she said before she could think too much about it.

He woke easily, but not guiltily as he used to. 'Is it time?' he asked before he even turned to the door.

'No, it's still late. You've got six or seven hours yet.'

'Teia.'

'Quentin, I hate what you did, but I don't hate you. I've taken the wrong way out myself before.'

He looked at her for a while, silent and sober. 'There's nothing I can do to make up for what I've done,' he said. 'I've cooperated with the White, I've told all I know, and it's still not even close to balancing what I did, and what I tried to do. I've got nothing more to say.'

'Fuck, Quentin.'

'I assume you have questions for me or you wouldn't have come back. I'm willing to answer.'

'Who was involved?'

'As I said, High Luxiat Tawleb gave me my orders. I believe one of the other High Luxiats may have been involved, but they told me nothing to give me evidence of that. It's purely speculation. But I know the High Luxiats fear the Guiles have grown too powerful.'

Their fear would be greater now, Teia realized. But that at least one of them had been willing to kill to keep the balance of power? Luxiats? Killing? Much less High Luxiats. What was the world coming to?

'Do you need anything?' she asked.

His calm composure cracked for an instant. 'My shriving wasn't the best. They couldn't allow any luxiats to visit me, lest they be spies or assassins. The Prism-elect Zymun came instead. He was, um, not terribly interested in...much.'

'Zymun's an asshole.'

Quentin suppressed a quick grin, then grew somber. 'I suppose I deserve no better. Indeed, worse.'

'Surely there's something I can do for you.'

He swallowed. 'There is...one thing.' He cleared his throat.

'My, uh, my mother. I was forbidden writing instruments. For good reason, I suppose. I wonder if you could send her a message. You can put it in your own words. Given that I'm a traitor, the authorities fear I'd be sending code. Tell her the truth, Teia. She lost everything in the False Prism's War, and she wanted me to stay with her more than anything. We were very close. But I felt Orholam's call. My mother sacrificed me for—' He cut off, blowing air, puffing his cheeks out to keep from crying. 'For Orholam. And I...did this. Became a murderer. Because High Luxiat Tawleb promised that I could be a High Luxiat myself. I told myself that I obeyed him because I wanted her to be proud of me, but it wasn't for her. It was for me. For my pride.'

'Fuck, Quentin,' Teia said again.

'Goodbye, Teia. Thank you for being a friend to me, though I didn't deserve it. If you'll excuse me, I think I'll spend the rest of the night in prayer.'

'Me, too,' she said. 'It's my vigil night. I'm to become a Blackguard at dawn.'

'Congratulations!' he said, and he seemed to have real joy for her. But then his face darkened once more. 'Will you...if you have time...will you pray that I'm brave? I'm not naturally courageous, and I don't want to shame myself.' There was a hitch in his voice, and his cheeks were wet. 'Further.'

'I swear it. I'll...' She cleared her throat. It was hard to speak. 'I'll be on the White's detail tomorrow. If you need strength, you just look at me, Quentin. I'll stand for you.'

Chapter 15

The Emperor of the Seven Satrapies sat upon his luxin throne impassive. Legs folded, hands draped over his knees. He shat and didn't even move. He stopped eating, and soon he didn't even need to shit.

He sat at the center of all things, moving only to stretch and lick at the trickle of water that tracked down the wall, around the curve of his cell, and down into the waste chute over which he sat.

His bread fell out of the chute above and tumbled to him. He picked it up with his left hand, and promptly dropped it because of his missing fingers. Carefully he picked up the bread again and put it in the semicircle in front of himself. It was a torture to have the bread always before him, but there was a purpose to this, to being seen to starve.

I am Guile.

Everywhere he looked, he saw only himself reflected in the walls of the cell. Had it not always been thus? Had he ever seen anyone else, ever?

She was dead. He'd killed her. For her good service, he'd rewarded Marissia with death.

He had loved her, he saw now. He'd loved her with a love as small as his own soul. He'd loved her as a man loves the hand he masturbates with. And thought as much about her.

He was not a good man, Gavin Guile.

Dazen Guile. Whichever.

A brief smile creased the arrogance that was his face. He'd fooled the old man with his disguise. He'd fooled Andross Guile once. He would do it again.

No prison can hold me, Father.

Another day. Another piece of bread. And he was weakening. His breath was foul, his skin greasy, muscles weak, eyes intermittently blurry.

All normal stages of fasting, though he wasn't sure how much his body could stand. He hadn't started healthy.

The pain of hunger was deserved. The torture of having the means to ease it within reach had been more than earned.

But more than simply deserved, the pain was necessary. One doesn't fool Andross Guile on the cheap.

And when the time came, he dreamed of Marissia, dreamed of throwing her off a balcony when Karris found her in his bed.

He dreamed and he woke, and he found he couldn't much tell the difference. Fewer leg cramps in the dreams, perhaps. *Karris*. This was for Karris.

The dreams were redolent of déjà vu. He'd dreamed of this cell when his brother had suffered down here. For sixteen years, he'd dreamed of this soothing blue hell, the facets of the blue luxin crystalline walls shimmering like sun on the sea.

Idly, Gavin wondered how his father had repaired the damage of the real Gavin's escaping. Andross couldn't draft blue, so he must have had help. But any help would have had to be taken care of afterward. If Andross had been careful enough to bring Marissia down here alone, it meant he was keeping all knowledge of these cells to himself.

It would have been a lot of murder if he'd had to fix each of the cells that the real Gavin had escaped from.

But of course Andross Guile wasn't as wasteful as his second son when it came to drafting. There was no way he would bother to maintain numerous functioning cells. He would have only two. One to hold Gavin, the other as a backup. If Gavin broke out of one, Andross would let him stay in the second until he repaired the first and fixed its weakness, and then he would move Gavin back into the first cell again. Efficient and cold.

As Gavin should have been.

He could still hear the muskets echoing in the cramped space as he'd blown his brother's head apart.

What had Andross thought when he found the corpse?

Karris! Are you looking for me? Surely, surely she must be. She'd rescued him from the Nuqaba herself. She wouldn't abandon him now. But how could she find him?

Funny. Funny how he'd obsessed over keeping this prison secret for so long, and now his only hope was that someone would find it soon.

Gavin hadn't buried his brother. Hadn't done anything for him. Just left him there to rot. Literally to rot.

Who did that?

He remembered Gavin laughing when they were children. Some prank he'd played on one of the White Oak boys. They'd put honey down the sleeping boy's underclothes. The boy, Tavos, somehow hadn't noticed until the next day, hours after waking, when he was already out in Sapphire Bay on a fishing trip with his father. The waves had been high that day and Tavos couldn't swim, so it had brought an abrupt end to the trip and the permanent ire of Tavos White Oak and his father.

How his big brother Gavin had laughed.

That Gavin would never laugh again.

But it was just another murder in the list, wasn't it? Dazen had to have killed, personally, perhaps more people than anyone in history.

He was not a man, he was an epidemic. He moved across the land snuffing out drafters young and old, broken halos traded for blood. He had spilled a river of blood – and in that river of blood, all he saw was his own reflection.

He was not a good man, Dazen Guile. He didn't deserve to escape. But he was going to. Not for himself. She deserved to have a husband, and she'd been cursed to love Dazen.

The least he could do was be there.

The bread beckoned him to give up this farce of a suicide attempt, but he didn't touch it.

One doesn't fool Andross Guile on the cheap. He scrubbed his face with his crippled hand.

In the gleaming gray wall, he saw a dead man. One eyed, smiling back at him, the dead man winked.

Chapter 16

Kip was blind for three days. He had never been more afraid in his life. What was a drafter without his eyes? How could he let everyone down by leaving the fight before they'd even really begun?

He didn't put it in words. Who would understand?

Despite the darkness, or perhaps because of it, the Nine Kings cards he'd absorbed kept triggering in his head. He lived as men who'd lost limbs. As a heretic woman who'd had her eyes put out. As a broken warrior lashing out at those who loved him.

It wasn't exactly a comfort.

Comfort. That was the name of a pistol, wasn't it? Abaddon, the King of…Locusts?

But that thought, that memory – was it even his own memory? – slipped away from him like all the others.

Tisis shared the bed with him, snuggled up against him, but she didn't seem to know how to bridge the gap. He held her close, but without his eyes to judge her expressions, he didn't trust himself not to make a fool of himself or hurt her by doing the wrong thing. They slept only.

On the third day, he sat up in bed and took off his bandages. He could see perfectly. His eyes felt well.

But those who broke the halo usually felt well. Part of the madness was believing that you weren't mad.

Verity nearly dropped her tray when she came in and found him up.

'My lord,' she said.

'My apologies, caleen.'

'Please, my lord, call me Verity.'

'With pleasure. Verity, will you look at my eyes and tell me what you see?' Best to know how bad it was immediately.

'Is that safe?'

Kip nodded, and she pulled back some heavy drapes they'd put up on the walls. Where had those been when they were trying to make love in here? Verity stared at his eyes for a long moment as he blinked. From the quality of the light, it had to be late morning.

'There's something – forgive me, my lord – there's something captivating about your eyes, as if a color beyond color shines there, but your halo's intact, if that's what you were worried about.'

Kip took heart from that, and ate his breakfast as she went about her duties, finally leaving to tell the others he was up and well.

Then it occurred to him that if he broke the halo in paryl or chi, there were only a few people in all the world who would be able to tell, and none of them were on this boat.

He could be a madman already and not know it.

Cruxer came in alone. 'Breaker,' he said, nodding his head. 'We thought it best not to overwhelm you by coming in all together.'

'Thanks. Can you, uh, tell me what happened out there?' Kip asked.

'How much do you remember?'

'Right up to where the water tornado thing was going to explode under the galley.'

'That *was* the exciting part,' Cruxer said. He cleared his throat. 'Well, it did explode – half on each side of the galley, and it kept trying to twist back together. Two enormous spinning waterspouts. And…somehow…you held them apart until the galley sailed through. The light storm passed as fast as it came. All's been well since then. You saved the ship and everyone on it.' He cleared his throat again. 'A, um, a couple of the sailors tried to worship you.'

'Ha!' Kip said. 'Funny.'

Cruxer didn't share his amusement. 'I was serious. They were, too.' He chewed on his lip. 'Breaker, I saw you sink the *Gargantua*. This was…Breaker, I froze up. I've never frozen up in the face of danger before. Tisis was the one who saved you. Shamed all of us.'

'Because she's a girl?'

'Maybe a little. But mostly because we're Blackguards. We're supposed to be there for you first. We failed you.'

'You got there in time,' Kip protested. He remembered that much now. The hands on him, the yelling.

'We got there second.'

'You got there soon enough.'

'It could have – you almost fell in the—'

'What did Commander Ironfist say about past mistakes?' Kip asked.

Cruxer grimaced. 'Look at your mistakes long enough to learn from them, then put them behind you.'

Kip lifted his eyebrows.

'Oh, shut up,' Cruxer grumbled. He picked at a fingernail for a bit. 'Tisis is saying some things that have the squad uncomfortable, Breaker.'

'What's that?'

'I guess you told her we're leaving? She's been insisting that she's going with us. She says you told her she could.'

'I did.'

'But you told me we were leaving her.'

'And then I changed my mind. I had to.'

Cruxer's displeasure had an almost physical weight to it.

'Breaker, we've got to figure something out right now. I know I said that you'd be in charge when it made sense for you to be in charge, and I'd be in charge the rest of the time, but that isn't working. I can't handle the uncertainty.'

'Uncertainty is part of—'

'Uncertainty is part of your world. Not mine. When I give orders, I have to know they're going to be followed. Or when someone tells me something, I have to know it's the truth.'

That stung.

'It's not a lie when someone tells you what they think is the truth and is wrong. Plans change. Anyway, heck, call her an honorary member of the Mighty now. She did save me,' Kip said. 'There, see? The Mighty didn't fail now. She was just the fastest of us to react.'

Cruxer grimaced. It was, Kip thought, a fairly nice dodge to save face. But Cruxer wasn't interested in dodges. Regardless, he let it go. 'It's not about that. It's not only about that, anyway. Breaker, I propose we use a different template for our squad.'

'And what's that?'

'I say we mirror how the Prism and the commander of the Blackguard interact. It's close to what we have now. As above, so below, right? You decide where we go – though I give input and register any disagreements – and I keep you alive when we go there. You're the boss, but we don't keep each other from doing our work.'

As above, so below. But for Kip to step into that place, that low mirror of the Prism, was highly suggestive of something else. 'I've never claimed to be the Lightbringer, Crux.'

'*That* uncertainty I can live with.'

'I want you to know, I think Tisis can help us, Cruxer. I wouldn't ask to bring her along if she couldn't.'

'I'm not convinced. And if we get her killed, her sister goes from a very tenuous ally to a mortal enemy. But you don't need to convince me. You don't need to ask to bring her along at all. Simply give the order...my lord.'

Chapter 17

Biggest day of my life, and all I can think about is how I have to pee.

When the complement of full Blackguards had joined Teia and the other nunks in their vigils before dawn, the one-handed new Blackguard trainer Samite had thoughtfully brought Teia and a few other Archers-to-be cups of kopi, still steaming from the kitchens. Teia had only sipped the stimulant before, and hadn't liked the taste, so she'd never had a full cup.

This morning, she'd drained it with gusto.

Now she had to pee, and she felt jittery. With the burden of Quentin's life and death off her shoulders, she'd then had something quite like the vigil she'd always hoped to have: she'd wept and then sworn at Orholam for all her problems, then beseeched him for forgiveness, then begged him for guidance, then been at peace, and then wept again. She'd had a sense, for some fragile tender minutes, that she wasn't alone, that she wasn't forsaken, that she had purpose, that he knew her. He saw her. He cared. He saved. It had been a night overfull.

Like my bladder.

Orholam, let me not wet my new blacks.

Fifty Blackguards had gathered to stand in rows with her and five other nunks on the roof of the Prism's Tower, saluting the sun as it rose. Commander Fisk turned as soon as the sun had barely cleared the horizon. It was going to be a busy day for all of them, so the ceremony would be abbreviated at best. Not that Teia was complaining.

'Adrasteia Gallaea's daughter,' Commander Fisk said, after greeting each of the others. Teia hadn't heard her mother's name since the day she'd been signed over to Blackguard training. She didn't want to think of herself as that creature's daughter, though slaves were traditionally known by their matronymic. 'The Blackguard is an ancient order, heavy with honor. We were born out of fealty and failure, out of the honor of Lucidonius's thirty mighty men and the shame of the satrapies failing to protect his widow and our second Prism, Karris Shadowblinder. Upon her death, those who remained of the thirty organized this guard to protect the Prism, and, in the last extremity, to protect the Seven Satrapies from a Prism.'

A quiet descended, the full Blackguards contemplative, the newest ones confused. Protect the satrapies *from* the Prism?

Then a crack like a musket shot rang out. Fifty pairs of hands went to weapons. Fifty pairs of eyes were covered with colored spectacles.

But it was only the propped-up replacement door falling to the ground as someone came up to the roof.

Karris Guile, Karris White Oak, now Karris White, stood in the opening for a moment to let her former brethren relax, then stepped outside. She wore the white dress of her station, but one newly made, cut to her slim, muscular figure. The points of her high collar were sharpened, reminiscent of swords, and all her accents were bright silver, not gold. The dress itself was lean cut, and if Teia didn't miss her guess, infused with luxin, as were the Blackguards' blacks. As much as a dress could be, it was one in which the former Blackguard could move. It was steel femininity, and Teia immediately recalled that just days ago, when they'd tried to throw her off the testing platform, this woman had kicked two big men to their deaths without hesitation, remorse, or much effort.

The Blackguard Karris White Oak had been small, fast, and fierce.

The only thing small about Karris White was her frame.

As the Blackguards saluted her and her attending Blackguards fanned out onto the roof, she said, 'If I may, Commander?'

'It's an honor, High Lady,' Fisk said. 'Please do.'

Karris addressed them somberly. 'Prisms don't break the halo like the rest of us, but they do go mad after their allotted time. Some of them. Others can't handle what the Freeing demands of them. Others, when the end of their term comes, and they know they're going to die, try to escape.'

Teia had never heard of that. She saw some of the others were rattled by it, too. Who could imagine being called upon to kill a Gavin Guile?

Then she realized she hadn't heard of it because the Blackguard was that competent. Prisms who shamed themselves by breaking their oaths and trying to flee were *always* quietly killed. Word never got out. Who could escape the Blackguard?

Teia asked, 'But how do they know that they're going to die? If Gavin Guile made it to his third term, how would another Prism not know if they might not have a second or a third term themselves? Or is that it? They don't know, so they flee?'

'They know. Somehow they know.' But Karris looked troubled, as if there were parts of this she didn't understand, either.

Orholam have mercy, had that been in the papers Teia had helped steal?

'Do we know, too?' another asked. 'Is there some warning?'

Commander Fisk said, 'The Colors and the Magisterium will tell you when it's likely. But it's always *possible*. None of the Blackguard now serving have ever had to hunt a Prism, and we pray we never do, but ours is the long watch. Do you have any other questions before we continue?'

Teia shook her head.

Karris said, 'Your duty is hard, but this I promise you: you shan't be asked to betray your honor.'

It was an answer to the question Teia couldn't ask with all the others there: will my attempted infiltration of the Order of the Broken Eye compromise my oaths?

But it wasn't an exact answer, was it?

I won't have to betray my *honor*, but I may have to break – or appear to break – my *oaths*. Would Karris thread so narrow a needle's eye with her words?

Karris White Oak wouldn't have. Would Karris White?

Why had Karris come up here? To bond the Blackguards further to her, to wish a former pupil well, or to make sure that Teia did take the oaths?

All of the above, no doubt. We are warriors, and this is our lot.

'Commander,' Karris said, 'may I continue with you?'

'We would be honored, High Lady. Though one may be called to other duties, one never ceases being a Blackguard,' he said, and then he turned to Teia and the others. 'The Blackguard forms an unbroken chain extending back to the time of Lucidonius himself. At induction, we recite the stories of our forebears to remind us who we have been, who we are, and to what we should aspire. At the end, we each name a Blackguard who inspires us, a patron whose qualities will help us become the best Blackguard we can be. High Lady White, will you start for us?'

'I remember Karris Shadowblinder, Lucidonius's wife and widow, and a Prism. Though our order wasn't established until after her death, it was built on the foundation she laid. Dancer, poet, theatre mummer, and, when times demanded it, finally a warrior-drafter of unmatched ferocity, she swore an oath to marry no man who couldn't beat her in will, wit, and weapons. Lucidonius failed twelve times, on twelve successive months, until she admitted he at least equaled her in will. He cheated at the contest of wits, drugging her beforehand, which she agreed showed a wit of its own. And last, with weapons, she lost – though some argue that was intentional.

'Karris Shadowblinder would later save Lucidonius's life three times, and fail on the fourth. Karris is precious to me because the heart of the Blackguard is love. Love for the Seven Satrapies, love for this brotherhood, and in the best of times love for the leader we protect. Karris Shadowblinder reminds me that in this mortal realm, even if we love perfectly, we may fail still.'

The White stepped back.

A tall, shaven-headed Blackguard named Asif stepped forward. 'I remember Finer. He was a Blackguard during the time of Prisms Leonidas Atropos and Fiona Rathcore. He struck down the Bandit King in the Battle of Ghost Flats. Handsome, funny, and loved by everyone, it was widely expected that he would one day be the commander of the Blackguard. Instead he went wight and fled. He killed four of his brothers before he could be put down. Finer reminds me of the importance of duty, and that all fame and renown count for nothing if we don't uphold our oaths.'

His cousin, Alif, stepped forward next. 'I remember Commander Ayrad, who sat quiet, judging until the time came to act. In his testing fights, he placed each time last. Forty-ninth at the end of the first week, then thirty-fifth at the end of the second, then twenty-eighth, then fourteenth, and on the last week, he fought from place fourteen to thirteen, thirteen to twelve, twelve to eleven, then to ten, to nine, to eight, to seven, to six, five, four, three, two, one. Never in our history has man or woman fought so many times or won so authoritatively. Because of his intelligence, Ayrad didn't fight harder, he isolated the weakness of each opponent, and took him or her out efficiently. Later in life, that intelligence would raise him to commander of this hallowed body, and it would save the lives of four Prisms.

'And yet,' Alif said, 'yet Commander Ayrad himself would fall to poison. The culprit was never found. Even Ayrad with all his intellect had blind spots, as do we all. I learn from him that we can never, never be off our guard.' He took a step back.

Tlatig, an Archer, stepped forward. She was not a handsome person. Her mouth turned down, eyes squinted, skin blemished, body with fewer curves than the seven towers, only when she picked up a bow did a grace came upon her. She was then a wonder as is a swallow in flight. Surreal, prescient, a walking miracle with a bow. On the training field, Tlatig wore a tiny chemise, tied tight, to show off the knotted muscles of her shoulders and the V of her back.

'I remember Commander Dauntless. She gave up her noble connections and her family's aspirations in order to serve the Seven Satrapies. She had two dreams, to be a Blackguard and to be a mother, and she sacrificed the latter to be the former. When she retired after a long and storied career – whose details I would tell you had not Commander Fisk asked us to be brief today – she tried to have a family, and, that late in life, she could not. She reminds me of the heavy price of duty, and that our forebears paid it, and lived in honor. Commander Dauntless lived in duty, and died with honor, though it cost her grievously. I remember her, and strive to meet her standard.'

Teia looked at Tlatig with new eyes. *Tlatig* wanted a family? That was her greatest longing, and the price she was willing to pay for this family? Tlatig had never seemed like the mothering type. On the other hand, from Tlatig's slightly embarrassed look, Teia could tell that she felt exposed from having shared so much – but that she shared anyway, when sharing made her feel so awkward, told Teia that she was being given something precious.

Another Archer, Piper, stepped forward. She wore her hair pulled into a knot at the back of her head, and had the straining halos and lined face of a woman on her last year before Freeing. 'I remember Massensen, and Ikkin, and Gwafa, and Mennad. Massensen defeated three great-horned iron bulls on the Melos Plain in the Jadmar Rebellion. Ikkin Dancing Spear killed the Jadmar's war chief, the giant Amazul. Gwafa demolished the Nekril, the will-casting coven that laid siege to Aghbalu. Mennad gave his life saving the Prism in Pericol when he was there to sign the Ilytian Papers. All these heroes were one man. Massensen took a new name every time he performed another act that would make any other man a legend. Where others would take a name that celebrated their heroic act to remind people of it forever, Massensen did the opposite. He took a new, plainer name each time, and refused to become even a watch captain. He believed that all glory should be reflected to Orholam, and that his own fame should be shared with his companions and his Prism. He was simply a Blackguard, and any Blackguard was his equal.

'Massensen reminds me that we wear black that we may serve in obscurity. We wear black that the light may shine the brighter. Massensen reminds me of duty with excellence.'

For some reason, it was only as Piper spoke that Teia finally stopped thinking about her bladder and was pulled into the words. These were some of the greatest heroes in history. These were people who had altered the course of satrapies, crushed kingdoms, saved Prisms and Colors, and fought monsters out of legends. This was the company she was being invited into. As an equal.

This was what she'd wanted since she could remember. All

the misgivings and questions about herself faded. They would call her a slave, but she is not a slave who chooses to serve.

As she thought, heart swelling, a tear cold in the wind on her cheeks, the normally quiet Nerra had stepped forward. She smiled shyly. 'I remember Thiyya Tafsut. She served all her days quietly, and was to retire at Sun Day on her fortieth year. She sought and received permission to become pregnant, as there was little light left for her. Pregnant, on the day before Sun Day, she hurled herself at a wight attempting the murder her Prism. She was killed, and she did not kill the wight in turn, but she slowed it enough that others did. Others in those circumstances would have hesitated, saved themselves, saved their baby. She did not. She reminds me that even those who are not great themselves can, through great sacrifice, change history.'

And that was the cost to join this company. What made them fearsome was the totality of their dedication, their readiness to pay all one could pay.

But in return, they bought a life that mattered.

Even a slave girl from the far reaches of the empire could matter.

Yes, her soul breathed, *yes*.

It was not that these heroes hadn't failed; it was that they had: all of them, sooner or later, in public or private. They were heroes despite their failures, for they had striven with their whole hearts toward the light. The Blackguard was strong because it didn't feel threatened by those failures. This was a company that would live in the light.

And by some grace, Teia didn't think how she would be a spy. She soaked up the light of the dawn, and the light of clear purpose and bedrock devotion. She only wished Kip and the rest of the squad could share this with her.

Gavin Greyling had stepped forward to be the seventh and final speaker.

'I remember Gavin Guile.'

'Gavin Guile was never a Blackguard,' Fisk snapped. 'Great though he was. Is, High Lady. My apologies. Pick another, Greyling.'

'I beg to differ, Commander,' Gavin Greyling said.

'Respectfully. Just before the Battle of Ru, when he sank the great ship *Gargantua*, Gavin Guile was given a Blackguard name by Commander Ironfist himself. Among us, Gavin is known as Promachos.'

'Neither you nor even Commander Ironfist had the authority to name a promachos,' Fisk said. 'And though our esteemed emperor held that position, he surrendered it back to the Spectrum many years ago. You're embarrassing—'

'Your pardon, sir, but it was not meant as a title, but instead as a Blackguard name that, in accordance with our best traditions, reflects the essence of the man. Earned hard and given true, it is not our way to strip a Blackguard – even an honorary one – of his name if he hasn't forfeited the right to it by acting dishonorably. Are you suggesting Gavin Guile acted dishonorably?' Gavin Greyling was pushing it, but he did so with such glee it was hard to be mad at him.

'Watch your tongue, son.' Even for Commander Fisk, apparently.

'Yessir.'

Commander Fisk hesitated, looked around, and pursed his lips. 'No one speaks of this. This circle is closed,' he barked. 'Go.'

With no small amount of swagger, Gavin Greyling said, 'I remember Gavin fucking Guile, who won the False Prism's War, who outwitted the Thorn Conspirators and ended the Red Cliff Uprising. Gavin Guile, who brought low pirate kings and bandit lords, who ended the Blood Wars with his wits and one deadly wave of his hand, who brought justice to the Seven Satrapies. Gavin Guile, who hunted wights and criminals, who built Brightwater Wall in less than a week, who aborted the births of gods, destroyed at least two *bane*, and killed a god full fledged at Ruic Head. Gavin Guile, who faced a sea demon and lived, saving all the people of Garriston and the Blackguard, too. Gavin Guile, who sank Pash Vecchio's great ship *Gargantua* with a rat. Gavin Guile, who armed us for war and gave the Blackguard the seas entire with our sea chariots and hull wreckers. Gavin Guile, heart of our heart, our Promachos, the one who goes before us in war, who came and conquered and will come again.'

The Blackguards couldn't help it; they cheered.

They'd already been out looking for him on the skimmers, Teia'd heard. Sometimes on duty, sometimes off. And they would never give up. 'For such a man, I would die twice,' Gavin Greyling said.

'Hear, hear!' a number of voices called out.

But Teia was looking at Karris. Her head was bowed, and Teia saw her swallow once, hard. But when Karris opened her eyes, her face was clear, with no hint of crying there. She nodded regally to the Blackguards.

'Thank you,' Karris said.

Commander Fisk said, brusquely, 'We've all got duties awaiting us this day, nunks. We are a storied company, but we are also slaves, nunks, though some of us are slaves with ears unshorn. We serve a term, almost like indentured servants, but our term may be extended at will by our commander, and our eventual retirement may be requested, but granting that is the commander's decision alone. Even if you save the money to buy out your papers, your commander need not accept them. We are honored slaves, but slaves. For warrior-drafters as we all are, there is no higher calling, no greater service, no possibility to rise higher than this shining company. But our lives are short and hard and lived at the direction of others.

'Teia, having taken vigil to reflect on your life and this calling, have you selected a patron to whose example you would aspire?'

'Yes,' Teia said. 'I choose Commander Ironfist, who alone silenced the artillery at the Battle of Garriston, saving countless lives, who led this company with honor and bravery, and in the end was expelled for no good reason whatsoever. Ironfist reminds me that we join the Blackguard to serve, not for our own gain. He reminds me to be as vigilant of those who wield orders as those who wield swords.'

There was some quiet muttering in response to that. Teia thought it was in agreement – no one liked how Ironfist had been discarded and had then disappeared, though that was surely the only safe thing for him to do – but frankly, Teia didn't care what they thought of her choice.

After a moment, Commander Fisk nodded, letting it go. 'Well, then, if you would bind yourself and your honor to this lauded company, repeat after me.' And Teia followed him, echoing phrase for phrase: 'I, Adrasteia Gallaea's daughter.'

'I, Adrasteia Gallaea's daughter.'

'Do swear that I will be faithful and bear true allegiance to High Lady Karris White and her successors, according to the law.'

'Do swear that I will be faithful and bear true allegiance to High Lady Karris White—' Terror, shambles! Teia forgot the words!

But Fisk prompted her gently, 'And her successors, according to the law.'

'And her successors, according to the law.' Whew.

'I will protect the Prism with my life, and in the last extremity...'

'I will protect the Prism with my life, and in the last extremity...'

'I will protect the Seven Satrapies from him or his successors.'

'I will protect the Seven Satrapies from him or his successors.'

'So help me,' he hesitated to give proper reverence, 'God.'

'So help me God.'

Then, as if Teia's life hadn't just changed forever, Commander Fisk continued on down the line.

Chapter 18

Buttoned tight, tall, rapier lean, and hawk eyed, Cruxer stood before the squad to give orders. He said, 'I'm going to explain this to you in terms you can understand: shut up.'

The Mighty were gathered on the deck, greeting Ben-hadad with his flip-down spectacles and goofy Ferkudi, who'd just successfully tested Ben's newest skimmer. They hadn't all taken the news that Tisis would be joining them well. So now they paused, thinking Cruxer wanted them to shut up so that he could explain it. But he said no more.

'Oh. Come. On,' Winsen said.

'No,' Cruxer said. 'You have your orders. You don't like them. Fine. Don't like 'em. And shut it. Since when did soldiers like the orders they got?'

'We're not exactly just soldiers,' Big Leo pointed out. When he folded his arms like that, his biceps bulged out like sides of beef.

Cruxer said, 'We are in this way: we get a task, we have to carry it out. Having to like it is nowhere in the description.'

'I'm not asking for blind obedience,' Kip said.

'He shouldn't have to,' Cruxer said. 'We've pledged our lives and honor to him. Stop acting like children and start acting like warriors. There've been lots of women in the Blackguard.'

'Every last woman in the Blackguard is a special case, and you know it,' Big Leo said, his voice low and large.

'Every last *person* in the Blackguard is a special case,' Cruxer said.

'None of that matters,' Winsen said. 'We make our own rules. We aren't Blackguards.'

It hurt all of them to be reminded. Only Ferkudi seemed unmoved. He said, 'Well, I don't want to make rules that get us killed.'

'I think us getting killed was pretty much assured as soon as we decided to go with Breaker,' Ben-hadad said. 'No offense, Breaker.'

'None taken,' Kip said. Because it's wonderful that my closest friends assume I'm going to get them killed.

Somehow, none of them noticed Tisis approach. With her blonde hair tucked up under a floppy petasos, scruffy trousers and tunic, and a belt full of weapons slung low and loose on her hips, she nearly fit in with the ship's crew. 'You should take me,' she said. 'There's only six of you. I'll be lucky number seven.'

'I'm not superstitious,' Big Leo grumbled.

'I am!' Ferkudi said. 'Ever since this one time, I talked to this old witch lady, and she said, "Son—"'

'Ferkudi!' Cruxer said.

'No, she said "son," she didn't know my name. It was already creepy enough that—'

'Ferk!' Cruxer said.

'Oh! Oh. Right.'

Tisis said, 'There are things I can do that none of you big, terrifyingly strong men can do.'

'Like what?' Big Leo asked.

Ferkudi looked pleased to be called a big, terrifyingly strong man. He flexed his pectorals in a little dance. 'She gets my vote.'

'Shut up, Ferk. Like what?' Big Leo asked.

'I can talk to strangers without scaring the hell out of them.'

'Funny,' Big Leo said. 'But we're trying to have a serious—'

'I was serious,' Tisis said. 'I know you all look at Ferkudi and think of him as a big goof. Stop that, Ferkudi. Look at him. Right now.' They turned and looked at the big goof. 'Ferkudi,' she said, exasperated, 'finger out of your nose.'

He withdrew his finger and glowered.

'There! Like that.'

'O's saggies,' Winsen said. 'I get it.'

'Get what?' Cruxer asked, clearly irritated that he wasn't understanding.

'Look at all of you,' Tisis said. 'You've known each other for years now. Some of you since you were barely walking. Look what happened to you while you weren't paying attention. You're not six boys traipsing through a foreign satrapy, looking for adventure. What do you look like?'

Kip knew what she was talking about, but he was captured by another thought. These young warriors had been cutting her off, telling her how she couldn't come with them, disrespecting her because of her beauty. Now they were listening to her quietly. She'd turned them already, and they hadn't noticed it yet.

Except maybe Winsen. He seemed unaffected by her charm, grimly amused by the whole thing.

'You look fuckin' scary,' Kip murmured.

It was true, and Kip saw it crash down on Cruxer most of all for some reason. Perhaps because he was the commander.

Somehow he'd seen himself as a junior officer – a leader whose command would surely be taken from him, who would be shuffled back under the leadership of someone older. A leader of boys. He had always known he would have to start at the bottom when he went out into the real world.

But now here he was. He'd been proud that the Mighty were the best squad among the Blackguard trainees, but he hadn't realized that now they were among the best in the world.

They would be feared, because they were fearsome. Big, grinning, chummy Ferkudi might have a permanent layer of softness around his big, round frame, but he could tear off a man's arm with the power in those big, round shoulders. Add man-mountain Big Leo, quietly menacing Winsen, graceful Cruxer with his calcified shins, sinewy and double-spectacled Ben-hadad, and Kip, and not many people would block their way in a dark alley.

'I meant you, too, Kip,' Tisis said.

He snorted, and they looked at him as if he were crazy. 'What?' he asked.

'They're calling you the Splitter of Storms,' Tisis said.

'Storm Breaker, now, actually,' Ben-hadad said. 'My suggestion.'

'Oh, hey, that's clever!' Ferkudi said.

Ben-hadad said, 'Sometimes praise from you doesn't have the intended effect.'

But Kip wasn't listening. It was always a game, right? These names were a propping up of a façade: if you're not a real hero like an Ironfist but you have to accomplish what he would, you have to borrow as many of the trappings as possible. Ergo 'Breaker.' 'Storm Breaker' fit the mold, but that had been...a fluke. Irreproducible. Luck. If he even tried to draft paryl or chi again right now, he'd only hurt himself.

But Tisis was still staring at him, as if he were a half-wit for doubting himself.

Tisis was looking at him like that? Tisis? Who'd seen his embarrassing nudity? Who'd seen the shameful scars of a man who hadn't been able to fend off small rodents?

'A couple of the sailors tried to worship you,' Cruxer had said.

It was as if all the faces around him were trying to tell him he was a different man than he knew he was.

Some men like the feel of wool over their eyes, I suppose.

That was a fine dismissal for the sailors, but his wife? His friends, who knew him far better than she did?

They had a blind spot for him, born of their love and forgiveness. Their kindly view of him was more a reflection of their characters than his.

'Right,' he said easily. 'It's beside the point. All of us, going into Blood Forest, all armed, all with the stained eyes of drafters, all with the dark skin of foreigners? We'll look like invaders or brigands.'

Cruxer sighed, and Kip could feel frustration emanating from him. Cruxer was the best of them, and the blindest. Kip loved him for it.

'She'll slow us down,' Big Leo protested, but he'd already lost.

'Any more than I will?' Ben-hadad asked, gesturing to his knee. 'Or do you want to leave me behind, too?'

'That's not what I meant,' Big Leo said.

But Kip was diverted by another problem now. Verity was walking across the deck, laden with baggage, taking up a place at the periphery of the conversation, head downcast, just a slave, invisible, thanks.

'Uh-uh,' Kip said. He grabbed his own bag from her and checked it briefly: soap, spare clothes, sundries, a pot, a plate, deck box, and coin sticks – with the correct number of coins on them. 'You're not coming.'

'I'll be most useful, my lord. Cooking, cleaning, mending, things you've gotten used to having a slave around for. I can ease your life on the trail in a hundred ways.'

'I have no doubt of it,' Kip said. He looked dubiously at the other bags she was carrying. How many of those were for her, and how many for Tisis?

'Uh, Breaker, someone to cook for us?' Ferkudi said. 'Have you ever *tried* to eat Cruxer's squirrel stew?'

'I never was good at laundry,' Winsen said.

'Is this about my former...insouciance, my lord?' Verity asked. 'Because I can promise—'

Kip held up a hand. 'It's not about that. Tisis is coming with us. Her sister is going to be furious, and I need someone whom Eirene Malargos trusts without reservation to tell her that this really *was* Tisis's choice, and at her insistence. I need someone to tell her the truth, the whole truth.'

'Lady Malargos will be furious with me, my lord.'

'And for that, I'm sorry. I assume you've tried to steer Tisis otherwise?'

She scowled. It was a yes.

'So have I.'

She took a deep breath, then bowed her head, accepting.

When Kip turned back, Winsen and Ferkudi were looking at him. Ferkudi looked glum, like a child denied a cake. Winsen, though, looked peeved. Kip realized that when he'd held up his hand for Verity to stop speaking, they'd taken it as an order for them, too.

'Have to admit, I liked it better when you were just one of us,' Winsen said. 'If I may be excused, *my lord*?' He sketched a mock bow.

'No, actually,' Kip said. 'Before we go, we have to sort one more thing out. Not just for us, but for Eirene Malargos.'

'What's that?' Winsen asked, lemon faced. He and the others glanced over at Verity, who was suddenly trying to look very nonthreatening.

'Just what the hell we plan to accomplish,' Kip said.

'I say we go fuck up the Color Prince,' Big Leo said.

'I don't think we're in the audience participation portion of the show,' Ben-hadad said.

'What?' Big Leo asked.

'Shut it, both of you,' Cruxer said.

Kip took a deep breath. 'The strength of the Seven Satrapies has always been its trade. As much as our religion and politics bind us, we've partly been strong because of the trade winds and the trade circuit and the intermingling of blood and culture and goods that's allowed us. Ilyta produces the best firearms even though they're as far as possible from the best sources of gunpowder, in Ru. Parian iron is shipped everywhere.

Ruthgari crops feed all the satrapies. That's meant even a farmer in Abornea can afford to buy fresh Tyrean oranges on occasion. But there are downsides to this, too. No one in other satrapies tries to mine silver on the scale they do at Laurion in Atash. Everyone knows the best and most salt comes from the Ruthgar coast. The shipyards of the Great River Delta are fed almost exclusively with Blood Forest's lumber. Point is – and I know I'm losing you, but give me a few more moments – point is, the Chromeria has been pretending this war isn't serious from the beginning. At every step, it's been worse than they realize, and *much* worse than they let on. The specialization that has been so helpful is going to be devastating as we lose the only places that make certain necessities for us making war. It wasn't that much of an economic blow when the other satrapies lost Tyrean oranges and Tyrean hardwoods. But now we've lost the guano mines of Ru for gunpowder and all the silver of Laurion – silver the Color Prince's Blood Robes can use to hire mercenaries and pirates.

'At the Battle of Ruic Head, we lost our navy. It's being rebuilt, but that takes time and treasure, neither of which we have in excess. But if the pagans take Blood Forest, they take away cheap, plentiful lumber that's close to our shipyards.

'That sets off a death spiral for us: If we can't get lumber, we can't build ships. If we can't build ships, we can't defend the shipyards. If they take the shipyards, they take the Cerulean Sea. If they take the Cerulean Sea, they won't need to win a single battle against us. Big Jasper and Little Jasper are *islands*, and they're nowhere near self-sustaining. A simple naval blockade would mean everyone there starves.'

'Our skimmers can sink any ship they throw against us,' Cruxer protested.

'True, absolutely,' Kip said. 'But skimmers can't haul in food, or gunpowder, or salt, or lumber, or iron, or all the tens of thousands of things Big Jasper needs every single day. And the fact is, the secret of the skimmers won't be a secret forever. How long will that be our advantage? A year? It'll take the Blood Robes a year or more to build the navy they need. What will the Chromeria do if they show up with a vast navy *and* skimmers?'

'They'll die,' Winsen said.

'Make this simple for us, Breaker,' Ben-hadad said. 'What do we need to do?'

'I'm certain – and Lady Eirene Malargos needs to know this,' he said, looking over at Verity, 'that if we lose Blood Forest, we lose the war. There was one battle already at Ox Ford, and our side lost. Grievously. Ruthgar lost thirty-five thousand men there. That, followed by Raven Rock and the worthless victory at Two Mills Junction? Ruthgar's sick of taking the brunt of every battle. Sick of sending men to die. I think everyone on our side has written off the Foresters. They're too far away, and too expensive and too hard to defend. A better line, they think, is the Great River. I think the satrapahs and the Colors will never say this out loud, but they'll send token forces to make a guerrilla war in the Forest to buy themselves time to build their own defenses, but no one's going to send tens of thousands of soldiers to die again. In short, the Seven Satrapies have already fallen. They simply don't have the will to do what needs to be done to win.'

A silence fell over them.

'Worst fight speech, ever,' Winsen said.

'But...' Kip said, grinning suddenly. 'We have a few advantages. Inside Tyrea and Atash, there were people who wanted the Color Prince to win. He threw off odious bonds and tore up bad treaties. He freed slaves. He promised wealth and a return to ancestral gods. A certain slice of the people loved him. That's not true in Blood Forest. The people here care deeply about nature, and they see wights as profoundly unnatural, defying the order of the seasons themselves by which life yields to death. Moreover, the Color Prince lost his temper here. He wiped out whole towns, and let his men ravage and rape others. This is the satrapy just across from the border town where two hundred young women jumped to their deaths off the walls of Raven Rock *with their children in their arms*. The people here are scattered, but they're tough and they know the land intimately. They're hunters and trappers and guides and lumbermen and river captains. In some areas, they've never much recognized the Chromeria, but they will recognize someone who comes in and fights a hated invader with them. We gather everyone who's willing and has something to offer, and we show the Color Prince why it's called the Blood Forest. Tisis grew up there. She knows the people and their customs. With her help, we're going to go to the Deep Forest, we're gonna raise a small army, and we're going to save the satrapy.'

'In other words,' Big Leo said, 'we're going to fuck up the Color Prince. Like I said.'

Kip punched the big man in his good shoulder. It was like hitting a side of beef. 'Exactly. I just had to use more words to explain it for the slow ones.'

'Don't you guys look at me!' Ferkudi said.

And so, nearly in sight of the capital of Ruthgar, they boarded the odd new skimmer that Ben-hadad had dubbed the *Mighty Thruster*.

Kip had shaken his head. Tisis had muttered, 'Boys.' Ferkudi had guffawed. Winsen had grinned. Cruxer had blushed and said, 'You can't call it that.'

'We're the Mighty,' Ben-hadad said. 'The propulsion units are thrusters, that's all.' The damn liar.

'I guess you'll be the first man to ride the *Mighty Thruster*?' Tisis asked.

His brow wrinkled. 'That makes it sound...'

'Make sure you take a good wide stance, legs far apart, or he'll throw you.'

'He? I didn't...'

'Do you need more instruction? Because I'm getting quite adept at riding a mighty thruster myself,' she said.

Ben-hadad blanched.

'You'll want to make sure you have a good grip, and loosen up your hips a—'

'All right! All right!'

Hours later, they sped into the mouth of the Great River – on the good skimmer *Blue Falcon*.

Chapter 19

'It's your fault. This war. This madness. All this death and insanity.'

Gavin lifted his head at the sound of the voice, but there was no speaker with him in his cell, no slot open to the outside from which a taunter could hurl word-bolas at him. He closed his eyes again. The silence was a pillow over his face.

Which was odd, considering the hard surfaces reflected back every sound he made. But motionless, barely breathing, seated with his legs crossed, his fingers splayed in the sign of the three in an attitude of prayer, he was habituated to his own little noises. It was only natural that, too long deprived of sensations, he would start hallucinating.

How did you make it so long, brother?

His brother had gone mad down here, but slowly. So slowly. Sixteen years in this monochromatic hell, and for how long had he been sane? Ten years?

Gavin didn't think he could make it two months.

Odd.

He'd barely moved since Marissia had been taken away. He had control of nothing but his own body.

Seven days. Seven days he'd eaten nothing. In the natural progression of fasting, he hadn't even been hungry since the wretched third day.

On the seventh day, water had cascaded down the umbilicus above him. First, the rush of soapy water. When Gavin had created this prison, he'd thought it was a measure of his kindness to give such a luxury. Plus, he didn't know how long a man could live in filth without getting some sort of infection, sickening, and dying. The Prisms' War had seen plenty of filth, but it had been a war measured in months. Even then, nearly as many men had died of disease as from battle.

But when he'd designed the prison, he'd forgotten about

heating the water. A rush of cold, soapy water to a naked man with no means to heat himself was no kindness.

Even my attempt at kindness was cruelty.

But Gavin endured the torrent. He rubbed some water over his wounds, but made no move to clean his beard or skin. He merely sat near the cloaca on the floor and watched as his bread was soaked sodden and sucked away.

The lime, to defend against scurvy, came next. (There were no oranges now, with the loss of Tyrea.) Gavin couldn't tell, of course, if his father had dyed it blue as he himself always had dyed the oranges he'd sent his brother.

But Gavin didn't scramble to grab the lime.

The clean water flowed next, rinsing away the soapy water and the lime.

Gavin sat, impassive, his face in his hands.

In the new cleanness of the cell, he could somehow smell afresh his own stench – deliberate, this time – and the slight chalk aroma of blue luxin. He glanced up at his reflection, pinched to inhumanly narrow proportions by the curving of the reflective wall, shimmering slightly with the crystalline facets of so much blue luxin. It looked disgusted with him.

The gaunt figure said, 'Starving yourself? You think that's an acceptable way for a Guile to go? Grow a spine.'

'I control what I can,' Gavin said.

'I didn't peg you for a coward.'

'What do you mean?' Gavin challenged his reflection. I'm unhinged, he thought.

'Make up your mind. You still have teeth, don't you? You want to live, bite the bread. You want to die, bite your wrist. Bleed out.'

Maybe it wasn't his imagination.

Gavin could imagine taunting himself, but this wasn't how he would have done it.

With his hands in front of his face, Gavin couldn't see if the reflection's mouth moved in time with his own or not. Was his sanity so tenuous?

'What am I doing?' Gavin asked aloud. Talking to oneself was one thing, talking as if one were really two different people was something else.

Then he felt a chill down his spine. He could have sworn this time the reflection didn't move quite correctly.

He tilted his head. Squinted. Sniffed. The reflection wasn't quite moving in time with him.

'You don't remember?' the reflection asked. This time, Gavin was sure its mouth moved, whereas his hadn't. But the voice was all in his head. 'Where's your perfect memory, Gavin Guile?' it asked.

'Dazen.'

'Doesn't matter now, does it? After what you did. Filicide.'

No. It didn't matter. 'What are you?' Gavin asked. 'I don't feel mad. Nor fevered. I've not been fasting so long that I should see apparitions.'

'You really *don't* remember. I'm appalled. Gavin Guile, the man so near to being a god, has forgotten his own creation? But some part of you does remember, doesn't it? Else why are you talking in your sleep?'

'What are you talking about? What are you?' And then it hit him. 'Orholam have mercy, you're the dead man.' The name itself was a distant echo. Something his brother had ranted about once, years before, perhaps?

'You still don't understand how cruel you really are, do you?'

'I wasn't cruel,' Gavin said. 'I did what I had to. I couldn't kill him, and I couldn't let him go. This was the only way. It was only supposed to be until I established my rule. Things escaped me. There was never a time I could release him safely. I thought there would be, someday. I never did anything to be cruel, though. It was never that.'

The apparition grinned, unconvinced. Like Gavin was pathetic.

'The black didn't take that much from you,' the dead man said. 'I know you wanted it to. You fed the black every obscenity you'd committed, every crime and horror. Black luxin is forgetting and madness and oblivion so it mostly worked. But one thing it is not. It isn't clean. It never works exactly as you hope, does it? You forget the wrong things, and it sticks like tar on the fingers of your mind.'

For years, Gavin hadn't even remembered that drafting

black was possible. He must have fed even his knowledge of how to draft black into the black. For years, he hadn't been able to remember what he'd done. Certainly not how. Hellishly, now – too late – it was coming back to him in bits and pieces, black stones turned over in the light, cutting memories best left on the banks of the river Regret. 'What are you?' he asked.

'You created these prisons, the first one in a single month, the rest over the course of the first year. It was a mammoth undertaking. A brilliant demonstration of your gifts, and of your monomania and your fear. But you knew. You knew he'd be down here for a long time, and you knew he would have nothing to do but figure out how to undo what you had done. And destruction is ever so much easier than creation, isn't it?

'But then you realized that wasn't true only of things, but also of men. Destruction is easier than creation. So you made me. A reflection of yourself. A distraction. A dissuasion. You knew that eventually Gavin would figure out an escape, unless you could keep him from turning his mind to the puzzle fully. So you made me, to destroy him first, so he could never destroy your prison.'

'No,' Gavin said. It was too plausible, too smart.

'You had been exploring the forbidden arts of will-casting, and so you will-cast a portion of yourself into this prison. I am indeed a reflection of you, Dazen. I am all the hatred you had for your older, stronger, more assured big brother, with his natural air of superiority, with his total ownership of father's affection and father's pride, with his easy mastery of all that came to hand. With his casual contempt for you. You only needed me to be a distraction, but you decided to go far beyond that. You made me to be an instrument of torture. Your brother lived alone, with only your hatred to keep him company for sixteen years.'

'I would never...'

'You are a crueler man than you know. Of course, then you used the black to obliterate the memory of what you had done, even from yourself. As if sin forgotten is sin forgiven.'

Gavin swallowed.

'But all magic fades, scoured slowly by the sands of passing years, and you're starting to remember, aren't you?'

It couldn't be true. But it fit. He had recently dreamed about his first Freeing as the Prism, and that dream had ended with his using black luxin. On purpose, to blot out memory.

It had worked. He had lost his memory of that night – and how many others? – for more than seventeen years.

With how much evil he could remember that he'd done, how much worse must the memories be that the old him had decided needed to be fed to the black?

'You can get out of here, you know,' the dead man said through heavy-lidded eyes.

'How?' Gavin asked.

'You know how.'

Draft black. One last time.

'Any idea that starts with the words "one last time" is a bad idea,' Gavin muttered.

'What?' the dead man asked.

'Something father used to say.'

'You're older now. More in control of yourself and your magic. You could do it safely.'

'I have no magic.'

'You can have the black again.'

'No. It is madness and poison and murder and death. It's what got me here.'

'Yes, here, *alive*,' the dead man said. 'How much do you remember about Sundered Rock?'

'Everything,' Gavin said.

'Liar.'

'I remember enough.'

'Really? I doubt that. How much truth are you ready for, "Gavin" Guile?'

'I have no illusions left.'

The dead man barked a laugh. 'Odd indeed that I am the fragment of you, when you are the one who is so thin and hollow. Gavin, Gavin. Do you remember meeting the Mirror Janus Borig when you were a child?'

'Yes.'

'Do you remember what she said?'

Vaguely. 'Yes. What does it matter? Mirrors don't see everything.'

'You don't remember.'

'No,' Gavin admitted. 'And I don't want to talk about it.'

'Oh, that is fortunate. Because I was not created to torment your brother, no. Sadly, you created me to torment a prisoner. Which now is *you*!' Gleeful, irritating little ass. Had Gavin ever been like that? Oh yes, he had. He'd honed his skills against his big brother when they were children. 'And,' the dead man said, 'I've got nothing but time, and you have nowhere to go.'

'Make your point and be done with it,' Gavin said. But his stomach turned. How long could he last with a twin self mocking himself in his hell? This apparition would know all of his weaknesses, all his secret self-loathings. The dead man would be a better tormentor for Dazen himself than he could possibly have been for the real Gavin.

'Janus Borig told you, Dazen. She told you that you could draft black.'

'Yes, so what?' Gavin had recovered the memories of that much.

'She told you that you could *only* draft black. You were a black monochrome, Dazen. You told your brother. You, who had been powerless, the one son in a powerful family who couldn't draft. You could feel father's embarrassment, his keenness that no one else know, his hope that he could fix you eventually. So when you heard that you had black, you bragged about it, and Gavin feared you. Rightly. When you began to evince your powers, your brother knew how you were doing it, because you told him. And gradually, Gavin came to understand that he had to stop you.'

'No, this isn't true.'

'Do you remember why you went to the White Oak estate, to face Karris's brothers?'

'I went there to see her. We were going to elope.'

'No, you knew she was already gone. You cared for her, somewhat, at least enough you didn't want her to die. But you never planned to marry her. You yourself leaked that you were coming to take her away.'

'No.'

But the dead man went on, heedless. 'So if you knew she was gone, why did you go to the White Oak estate? Why would you knowingly face seven brothers, seven drafters?'

'I wouldn't. That's not how it happened.' But it was so long ago now. So foggy.

'You went for the same reason that you've hunted down wights yourself. Why would a Prism himself hunt wights? When Orea Pullawr tried to stop you, it should have been a small fight – Gavin, you'll get yourself killed, she said. But you fought for the right to hunt wights as if your very life depended on it. Why would a Prism do such a thing?'

'I could hunt them safely. There was no reason for other men to die. So many had died already. It wasn't dangerous for me.'

'No, those are the lies you've told others to make yourself look good. The truth, Gavin, was that it was dangerous for you *not* to.'

'What does this have to do with the White Oaks?' Gavin demanded.

'Because between them, her brothers included drafters of every color. Because black is emptiness, but emptiness can be filled. Darkness may be filled with light. Black can hold every color. You went to the White Oak estate to murder those young men, to steal their powers. Because that's what black drafters do.'

'No.' But it came out a whisper.

'And that's why you had to hunt wights. You've been running out of power from the very first day, and it had to be replenished with the blood of drafters. In her weakness and her love, your mother denied it. Your father and brother knew the truth. They held off as long as they could, but when you murdered all those people at the White Oak estate, they knew you were a monster. They knew you had to be stopped. You, Dazen, are the Black Prism.'

Dazen had crafted his Gavin persona like a goblet of blown glass. Molten glass given shape with hot air, hardening to a fine, beautiful, brittle finish. Seeing the gold leaf twining down the delicate stem and the rich imperial purples of the wine, and hearing the melodious chime of fine crystal, the world had been blinded to the palsied hands cupping the bowl.

Now, wine sipped down to the lees, the glass slipped from drunken fingers, spun from control, and shattered – an explosion of lies, glimmering now in the light, sharp, dangerous. He stooped to pick them up, ashamed.

He picked up the shards with tremulous fingers, and they cut him. Gifted ingrate. Liar. Impostor. Murderer. Thief. Filicide. Betrayer. Villain. Blood and wine were watered with tears on the broken flagstones of his mind. False teacher, false prophet, false king. Bloody-minded, benighted, black hearted, black drafter, black Prism. Black Prism.

Chapter 20

'So, uh, Your Ladyship, what's this town called?' Winsen asked.

The Mighty were skimming up the Great River as they had been for more than a week. Winsen had been peppering Tisis with seemingly innocuous questions since they'd shot past the harbormasters at Rath.

'I don't know what this one's called, but we should be getting to a town called Verit soon. It's right at the base of Thundering Falls,' she said. 'It's where the Great River and the Akomi Nero come together – or, well, for us – split as we go upriver beyond the falls. The Akomi Nero originates in the Ruthgari Highlands.'

'Huge landmark, huh?' Winsen said.

'Huge,' she said. She was trying to play it off like Winsen's questions didn't bother her, but it was obvious to Kip that they did.

'Good to know our guide knows the big landmarks at least, I guess,' he said, not quite under his breath.

She flushed, her pale skin doing her no favors as she seethed. But she never said a rude word. Kip had asked her, awkwardly, if he was supposed to do something to defend his wife from his own friends, and she'd said no, that she had to win certain battles on her own.

But he wasn't entirely sure she meant it, and Winsen usually managed to walk right on the line where he wasn't rude, but he was calling her value into question.

'I mean, you have been down this river a few times, right?' Winsen asked.

'Winsen,' Cruxer interrupted. 'Are you being an asshole?'

The smaller young man said, 'No, sir. It is my specific intent not to be an asshole.'

'Is it also your specific intent to come as close to the line as possible?' Cruxer asked.

Winsen hesitated. One didn't lie to Cruxer. Winsen had been insubordinate once early on. Cruxer threw him off the skimmer. He'd swum ashore – through waters where alligators were known to live – and had to walk through the afternoon and night to catch up with the skimmer.

When he'd arrived, only an hour before they had to depart, Cruxer had chastised him for being late for his shift on watch. He'd stayed up, and taken his turn on the reeds, too.

'Yes, sir, it was,' Winsen said. 'Did I miscalculate, sir?'

'Oh, I don't know if you were right up to the line or over it, Win. Orholam judges the heart, and so do I. Keep your mouth shut until we make camp, why don't you?'

Winsen saluted – silently – and that was that. For now.

It didn't help that Tisis hadn't really been able to answer any of his questions. She'd told him she didn't know the lower river. He'd said, 'But surely you know it better than the rest of us, who've never been here, right?'

Seeing that they wouldn't make it to the top of Thundering Falls that night, they made camp early to avoid staying in Verit or any of the outlying towns.

The *Blue Falcon* was a wonder yet again. This would have been most of a day's journey if they'd traveled conventionally.

They'd not only passed the authorities easily, but also avoided river pirates, easily glided over snags that would have otherwise required a pilot with current charts, and been able to hunt from the deck as well.

They'd slowed their pace after getting stuck in sandbars half a dozen times, though. With drafting and a lot of muscle, they were always able to escape, but they lost hours every time. Ben-hadad had already been working on a design for the next *Blue Falcon*, and he added a shallower draft, camouflage, and a depth gauge to his designs.

That night, as he had several times before, Kip went with Tisis to a nearby village to get the news. Even this far from the fighting, Ruthgari and Forester villagers knew a lot about the world. The Great River was by far the largest arterial for goods and news between Green Haven, the Floating City of Dúnbheo, and Rath – and thence to the rest of the satrapies. Tisis usually learned whatever they knew.

Though she used aliases, the villagers always accepted her as a Forester. In the simplicity of his Tyrean village, Kip had always thought blonde hair and light skin must be pure Ruthgari traits, but the Great River made those who lived on its banks nearly as diverse as any people on the Cerulean Sea's coastlines.

Tonight they stopped at a beaten-down farm with children's playthings in the yard but no garden. As ever, they brought game with them, a sure way to find welcome at the subsistence farms they visited, and they called a hello a good distance away to announce themselves unthreateningly.

There was no lady of the house here, only a veteran of the Blood Wars and his twelve-year-old son who seemed less than well mentally, staring into the cookfire and laughing at odd moments, squawking or shrieking suddenly and then giggling, and talking nonsense, sometimes loudly.

Tisis showed no fear of the boy, though, and ended up holding one of his hands in hers, and not minding when he sniffed her hair.

When the veteran saw they wouldn't have any cruel words regardless of how his boy acted, he warmed to them. He gave them a concise analysis of the military disposition of the upper river cities, and the venues of attack the White King would likely take, given what they knew of his forces.

It was the first time Kip had heard the term.

Apparently 'the White King' was what the Color Prince was calling himself now.

By the end of the evening, Kip had asked the man to join them, but Deoradhán Wood shook his head. 'You seen my boy. His mother weren't well, neither. Different than him, but not well. In the head. Or perhaps the heart. She walked into the river two years back. You understand? Walked into the river. Didn't even leave me a body to bury, a grave to visit. Damn near killed me, too, when she done that. I live for my boy now.'

The man was suffering, but Kip couldn't help but feel that it was needless. 'You've got a clear mind and a strong back still. I'd have a place for you. A place of honor and a purpose. Is there none who can take care of the boy for a time? Six months? A year, maybe? We have gold to help, if feeding him and all is a burden.'

'Nah, he's worth his grub. Good helper,' Deoradhán Wood said. 'But I can't go. My lot ain't easy, but it's good. I'll carry this load until the Highest frees me of it one way or th'other.'

'If someone doesn't stop the White King,' Kip said, 'no one will be able to sit on their farm and live quietly, doing right.'

'I'm no coward, son. No tired old man. But big causes and crowds of strangers? What kinda man sacrifices his own son for that? Besides,' he continued, 'I gave my word that I would never leave him, no matter what. A foolish oath, perhaps, but better men have abided by worse. Orholam light your paths and guide your arrows, young warriors.'

When they got back to camp, everything was set up and a fire cheerily burning. They ate and shared what they'd learned. It wasn't much, but it was enough to help them make the next decision.

At Thundering Falls, they had to decide whether to pay to use the great locks to raise the boat to the level of the river above the falls, to pay for porters, to attempt to port the *Blue Falcon* themselves, to sell it, or to sink it and build a new one.

They had enough money to pay for portage or the locks, but Cruxer thought they might need the coin later, and porters would be able to inspect the boat closely – the first step to the Chromeria's losing its secret advantage. The *Blue Falcon* was too heavy for them to carry easily, especially because the porters were known to sabotage those who eschewed their services, loosening steps and rearranging signs to point hikers up dead-end paths constructed to take them to places where it was impossible to turn around.

It was the kind of near banditry that the Chromeria had never stamped out, and probably never would. It still pissed Kip off.

But what the old veteran turned farmer had told them let them know they'd be moving up the river a lot. It was worth it to build yet another skimmer. It broke their hearts a little to unseal the luxins and let the boat dissolve into dust, but such a military secret wasn't something to simply hand over to anyone who had the coin for it.

They made the climb easily and quickly. The porters even seemed friendly. Perhaps Big Leo's permanent glower encouraged their deference.

When they reached the top of the falls, they hiked on another couple of leagues until they found a nice secluded spot. Ben-hadad was excited to build a new ship, even if working with so much luxin meant hastening them all to the end of their halos.

'Might as well,' Big Leo said, his eyes tiger-striped red and sub-red, 'it's not like any of us are going to live long enough to worry about breaking our halos.'

It took them all day.

That night, around the campfire, Winsen started up again. 'So, Mighty Guide Lady, what's next?'

'Things get different now,' she said. 'On the coasts of Blood Forest and on the lower river are many kinds of folk, and I love them dearly. But they are more citizens of the Seven Satrapies than they are Foresters. Here, up where it isn't easy for foreigners to come, the land is wild. There are pockets of civilization here, even the two great cities, but they're lamps in the forest's night. You may see people with forked ears or a blue cast to their skin. Say nothing. They are the last of the pygmy blood, less than half-bloods. Quarters. Eighths. Don't inquire.'

'Why not?' Ben-hadad asked.

'It's never a happy story,' Tisis said.

'How so?' Winsen pressed. 'We're less likely to blunder if we know what the blunder would be.'

'You're asking me like you think I don't know,' she said calmly.

'You're damn right,' he said.

'Winsen,' Cruxer said, 'are you—'

'No, sir. Not at all this time. I'm just trying to get an honest take on what our strengths are here. Does our guide really know anything more than what you'd read out of a book in the Chromeria's libraries, because see here, I realized something the other day.'

He waited.

'Oh, please, do go on,' Ben-hadad said sarcastically. 'We're on tenterhooks.'

'You said you grew up among these people. But…you're Ruthgari, not a Forester. And you've been a hostage of the Chromeria as long as I've known you or known of you. I mean, I don't mind that you're just here to entertain Lord Guile at night, but if that's all you are, I'd rather we all not pretend you're anything other than the royal sword swallower.'

Kip was halfway across the circle before anyone could blink, but he was intercepted before he could lay out Winsen by none other than Tisis herself, who threw herself bodily against him.

'No!' she said. 'No. Let me handle this.'

Kip looked around at his friends, and saw she was right. Dubious glances met his.

'Hey,' Ben-hadad said, shrugging. 'Leadership should come with some perquisites, but Winsen's not all wrong. We deserve to know what she brings to the table – and if it's only our leader's happiness, great! But maybe if that's it, then she shouldn't be leading us…? Why are you looking at me like I'm the asshole?'

'Fuck you,' Kip said. 'You think I'd lie to you all?'

'Kip, Breaker,' Tisis said. 'Please let me explain. Let this be between me and them.'

Kip backed off. What was he supposed to do? Let his friends tell his wife she was only good for what she could do on her back? He'd not spoken of her too kindly before he married her, granted. Orholam's balls, this would make it a hundred times worse if they found out that the one thing they thought she was good for was actually not working out at all, *at all*.

'After Gavin Guile ended the Blood Wars,' Tisis said, 'by his decree all the leading families of both sides had to surrender certain lands, and were given equal lands on the other side of the river. I was raised on the new Malargos lands deep inside Blood Forest. It was my assignment from the very beginning to become one of the Foresters, so that my family might hold that land, and inspire loyalty. At ten I was selected to be a hostage of the Chromeria—'

'Ten years old!' Winsen said.

'But four months of the year I've been allowed to rotate back into my own lands while my cousin Antonius took my place as hostage. I've spent the bulk of those months in the Forest, and some part in Rath, and yes, Win, I've spent a lot of my time at the Chromeria learning about the home I've adopted.

'So yes, I'm useless in a fight. I've never pretended otherwise. I can load and fire a musket, but that's about the extent of my martial skills. But I know lots of arcane history that even most Foresters might not. Like – as you asked when you were trying to prove me a pretender – why you shouldn't ask pygmies their lineage. The answer is that it implies that you think they have human blood.'

'And that's bad why?' Kip asked.

'Because pygmy women can take a man's seed, but they couldn't bear his children. You understand?'

The young men looked at each other.

'No?' Kip said.

'It actually sounds kind of perfect if you like 'em small,' Ferkudi said.

They all looked at him.

'I mean, if you liked really, really small women – oh, hey, not like children! I didn't mean it like that! And not me! I'm not – I meant no pregnancies, right?'

'No, no,' Tisis said. 'What I meant was, they *can* get preg-

137

nant by men, but they die in childbirth. Every time. Of course, pygmy men could breed human women no problem. But in the next generation, any half-blooded daughters had the same problem. Even two half-bloods marrying often ended in the woman's death, if not on the first child, then often on the second. Even a half-blood marrying a pygmy ran a risk. The pairings were soon banned by both sides, called cursed. So the half- or quarter-bloods you see now are either the children of taboo love or the product of something my dear, lovely, may-he-burn-in-the-fires-of-all-nine-hells ancestor Broin the Cruel called "retributive rape."

'Now, male and female alike, mixed bloods are welcomed to communities – some even think they're good luck, as they've obviously dodged death – but they're utterly shunned in marriage and romance, for who would willingly pass a death curse onto their children? Even naturally tall pygmy men and women find it difficult to find partners, as everyone suspects they might have falsified their genealogies.'

'I lost you back at "retributive rape." What the hell?' Kip asked.

'Broin the Cruel lost a horse race and claimed the pygmy's jockey – a child – didn't weigh enough, and was thereby cheating. He started a war over it. He said the only way to purge the pygmies of their deceitful nature was rape. Only from virtuous blood – his and his men's, of course – could come virtuous seed, to bear virtuous fruit in befouled soil – the pygmy women. Thus he tried to make a sacrament of rape. It wasn't for his men's pleasure, you see, by his perverse doctrine, rape was for the pygmies' salvation. So they gelded the men and raped the women and condemned half the next generation – the daughters – to death as well. To say that the effects of that murderous asshole have been far reaching would be an understatement. It was partly to escape his legacy that my own ancestors left the Forest and went to Ruthgar. And now you understand why we decided to work doubly hard to fit in as Foresters again.'

Big Leo breathed a curse. 'My parents traveled the Forest for ten years, and they never spoke of such a thing.'

'It's not really something we speak of,' Tisis said. 'Many

of the pygmies withdrew to the Deep Forest after that. Some hundred years ago now. It's said free tribes of them still exist, and where we're going, we may find them. They wear a permanent smile, part of the bone structure of their faces. But they'll tear your throat out if you insult them, and it's said their will magic can turn the forest itself against their enemies. So if we meet any, Winsen, you watch your sloppy undisciplined leaky anus of a mouth for once, or your short bitter life may come to a violent end and none of *us* are going to start a war over it. You understand?'

He looked at her for a few moments, then broke off his gaze. 'Yes, Lady Guile.'

Miracle of miracles, for the first time Kip could remember, the young man actually sounded a tiny bit chastened.

Chapter 21

It was a tradition that the newest Blackguard would get some onerous duty to celebrate his or her swearing in. Teia was so exhausted that she was seriously considering asserting Archer privilege here. She *was* cramping, but the other women hated it when a girl used her moon blood to shirk unpopular duties.

''S time,' Commander Fisk barked. The other Blackguards on the roof were standing at ease, laughing and telling jokes, but Teia snapped to attention, only a little late.

Opting out of anything would be a terrible way to start. The new person was always considered useless until he or she proved otherwise. Regardless of how she'd done in training, this was a fresh start. Which was great if training hadn't gone well and you needed to show you belonged. But it was terrible if what you wanted was to take all the goodwill you'd earned in training and for once, just this one time, for Orholam's sake, by all that was holy, you really needed to go to bed, cry for approximately ten seconds, and then fall asleep.

'Got a special assignment for you, Teia,' Commander Fisk

said. 'You and I rose together, didn't we? I was your trainer when you were a scrub. I've seen you. And I know a shirker when I see one.'

Ah hells. It was so unfair. She never did less than anyone!

T. Now's the time to opt out, quick. If you wait until he says what the duty is, you'll really look bad.

But she said nothing.

'And you're no shirker,' he said. He glanced over at squat, one-handed Samite, the new trainer. Teia wondered what the significance was in that look. 'In fact, I've never seen anyone jump into their duties quite so fast, no matter what they are.'

What?! A compliment?

'You got your squad off this island alive because you were that loyal to them, and then you left them, because you're that loyal to us.'

Teia swallowed and nodded. She understood that he was shaping the story. There would be gossip among the Blackguards and questions about her loyalty, both in fighting for her squad and then in abandoning her squad. The Mighty weren't technically deserters – they'd left with the permission of the promachos and before they swore the final oaths – but they'd left right when the Blackguard really needed more people. And they'd been the Aleph squad, the best of the Blackguard recruits. Their loss weakened the Blackguard, and that had led to sore feelings that could spill over onto Teia.

The commander was putting the best face possible on Teia's split loyalty.

'I figured you'd be here this morning,' Commander Fisk said. 'We always lose some Guards right at the end, but I know you. I knew you'd stay. It's a big moment, for any of us, so I went and talked to some scholars last night. I asked what Adrasteia means. Do you know what they told me?'

'No, sir.' Teia thought her parents had liked it because they thought it sounded pretty.

'Funny thing. Sometimes you wonder if a name shapes a thing. But if you didn't know it...Adrasteia means "not inclined to run away." And apparently, you're not. Anyway, you look like hell. And you've got execution detail at noon.' He grimaced. 'Until then, you've got inspection duty.'

'Sir?'

'There's a bunk, fifth one down on the Archer side. Make sure it's up to code. Do it quickly, shouldn't take you more than four or five hours.'

A bunk? Inspecting a bunk for five hours—

Oh, that was *her* bunk!

She snapped a salute and walked toward the stairs to go inside.

'She runs toward duty, and when it comes time to leave, she walks,' Commander Fisk said. 'Get a move on, Walker! Before I change my mind!'

She started to protest, but it didn't matter. If she'd gone fast, he would have made a crack about how she was not inclined to run away unless her bunk was at the other end. This was what it was to be the newest Blackguard.

It felt...awesome.

Inspecting her bunk for five hours felt awesome.

Waking up didn't. She swore she'd been asleep only minutes when she was awakened by the Greyling twins.

'Teia, it's time. We let you sleep as long as we could. We have to go. Now.'

She sat up.

But Gavin's eyes widened.

Gill glanced at his younger brother and cleared his throat.

Teia hadn't realized that she'd stripped off her tunic before lying down, and her camisole had gotten all twisted in however she'd thrashed in her sleep, so she exposed half a breast as she sat up. Half of little being practically nothing.

'Gav!' Gill scolded as Teia hiked things back in place. He smacked his brother's shin with the haft of his spear.

'Ow! What was that—'

'You know what it was for, you ape. Glance, don't gape.'

Gavin winced. 'I know, I know. Look, don't linger. Sorry. Sorry.'

'Not to me,' Gill said.

'What?' Gavin asked.

'Don't say it to me.'

'Well, I was tryin' not to stare again—' Gavin started. 'I have a hard time controlling my eyes when, you know?'

141

'Trouble controlling your eyes? And you're a drafter?' Teia said. 'And you're the veterans I'm supposed to be looking up to?' She stood up and reached for the hem of her camisole. 'It's not battlefield rules, is it?'

'Huh?' Gavin asked. 'Oh.'

They turned away, and she stripped and dressed in fresh clothes quickly.

'I didn't mean to...I, uh, I polished your boots and belt so you could sleep a little longer,' Gavin said.

Oh no. First, Teia didn't want anyone going through her things. Second, he was a little too eager to please.

Teia said, 'Well, since you're so helpful and so interested in my personal business, take these,' she put a wad of garments in his hands, 'and put them in the bin for dirty menstrual rags.'

Gavin dropped the clothes from limp hands as if he'd been pithed.

Gill guffawed.

'I'm joking,' Teia said. 'But I am on my moon, so I'll need a minute.'

He looked queasy and still distrustful of the laundry at his feet.

'And Gavin, you're sweet and all things wonderful, but... no, not ever. I almost did that once, and I've no interest in doing it again. The rules are there for a reason, and I'm going to obey them. Nothing personal.'

He didn't look as if he understood, but she went past him and washed up in the Archers' toilets as quickly as possible. Curse cramps, anyway. Maybe his big brother would explain it to him while she was gone.

When she came back, he'd put the rest of her clothes in the basket for the slaves. She was glad that she'd remembered to change the master cloak's disguise so it looked like a Blackguard cloak now. After you were elevated, your nunk clothes were taken by the slaves, laundered, patched, and given to the next cohort. Teia didn't even want to think about what she'd have had to go through if she'd let the master cloak get mixed with every other nunk cloak at the Chromeria.

But she hadn't loused up, this time.

She threw on the cloak. She felt resplendent, proud.

'You look good,' Gill said. 'You look like a Blackguard.'

They let her check her own weapons – a Blackguard always checked his own weapons.

'I didn't mean anything like that,' Gavin said, awkwardly. 'I was just trying to give you some more time to sleep.'

His face cleared. Rejection was hard for any man. Rejection and a loss of face together were too much for most.

'Oh, my mistake, then. I'm just so excited about finally being a Blackguard, I've got a hair trigger about anything that would make me mess up, I guess. Forgive me, brother?' she asked.

Why was it on a woman to tiptoe around the feelings of men...?

'Of course, sister,' he said, and all was well.

At least men usually made up for projecting their stupidity by being easily maneuvered.

They had to jog to make it to their posts on time, forming up outside the White's apartments, and Watch Captain Tempus grimaced at them for cutting it close on this day of days. He was a wild-haired man, his roots gray. He had deep-black skin and intense blue eyes compounded with blue halos.

'On time is five minutes early,' he said.

'My fault, sir,' Gill said.

Gavin and Teia both looked at him. Gill really was a big brother. He would gibe Gavin constantly, but when it came time to take care of things, Gill was there every time.

Watch Captain Tempus handed Teia a velvet baggie no larger than a coin purse. 'Dark eye caps,' he said. 'So you don't go blind using paryl out in the full sun.'

The hallway was crowded, not only with Blackguards, but also with slaves scrubbing at the stains on the floors and ceilings from the smoke, fire, bullets, and blood. Stonemasons and carpenters were making their own measurements and estimates with their own journeymen and apprentices and slaves, and the Chromeria's slaves were trying to work among all that. Cleaning and repairing the highest floor of the Prism's Tower wasn't something that would be allowed to proceed at

143

a slower but more efficient pace. Half a dozen Blackguards stood watching the workers at all times.

The violation of this area, the White's very sanctum, the Blackguard's home, had been taken as a personal affront. Teia was sure that she would be answering more questions about that in the near future, too.

Watch Captain Tempus led them past the Guards at the door. A knot of diplomats, room slaves, an anxious luxiat, and one-handed Trainer Samite stood around the White's desk. As Teia's squad came in, Karris declared, 'Everything else will have to wait.' Her voice rose over the people crowded around her, though with her diminutive height, she did not.

'Tell Carver Black I'll meet him in two hours, and to have as many of those reports as possible. Tell the Ruthgari ambassador I won't see her until dinner. Assure her that I'm not putting her off on purpose. Have her seated with me to placate her. Clear everything out of the first two hours after noon, we'll have some urgent demands for a meeting from the High Luxiats after the executions. Are we ready?'

The luxiat attending her blanched. 'Surely you're not presiding over the execution in *that*?'

Teia still couldn't see Karris, so she didn't see what he was talking about for a moment, but the room went absolutely still at his reproof of the White.

As the diplomats nervously shrank back to let Teia's squad come forward, Teia saw what Karris was wearing, and she almost laughed aloud. Whoever was shocked by Karris's choice of clothing had no idea who they were dealing with. She wore an outfit much like what she'd worn to Teia's swearing in. White Blackguard blacks, tight fit around her athlete's body, infused with luxin, and decorated with silver thread. She had even – whimsically? – denoted her rank on her left shoulder. A Parian zero, the stylized circle looking something like an eye.

Given that her clothes were white, the outfit did reveal her curves far more than identically cut blacks would have, but to Teia's and the Blackguard's eyes, it mostly revealed that Karris hadn't let herself grow fat when she'd left her official Blackguard duties. Neither modest nor immodest, it was amodest, clothing indifferent to any man's or woman's sexual interpretation of it. Here was the body as power, as an implement of war sharp honed with use. Her clothing said, 'Remember who I am and where I came from and how I intend to rule.'

It would take a soft, lustful man like a luxiat to see this body in harness for war first as a receptacle for his illicit desire.

'I just did something shocking,' Karris told him, 'and worthy of complaint. But that thing was not what I'm choosing to wear. If you're such a fool that you use your eyes when you ought to be using your ears, you're too much a fool to advise me. You may dare correct the White, but do it for the right thing. Tell your superiors that I wish never to see your face again, and if I do, there will be consequences. For them. And for you. There are many souls beyond the Everdark Gates who crave a luxiat's wisdom.'

'High Lady, I didn't—' Sweat stood out instantly on his face.

Karris said, 'In another time, I should delight in giving you a second chance. Lust, after all, is a sin of the body. But you have gone beyond lust all the way to the depths of pride in giving reproof to another for your own sin. Thus does the weakness of your body cloud the eye of your mind. Orholam shall forgive you if you repent truly, but I have no time for you while there are still holy men and women in the Magisterium with unclouded sight who might give me true counsel. Begone.'

He looked at her for only a moment, seeing iron there. Then he looked to the Blackguards, who hadn't even stepped forward, but their eyes were walls against him. He looked to the other courtiers, and saw no aid from any of them. Some, doubtless, he had worked with for years.

He turned on his heel, back straight, and strode from the room, huffing.

Karris obviously dismissed him from her mind before he got to the door. She gestured for the courtiers to leave.

She walked toward the slaves' nook and sat in a chair there, allowing her slaves to work on her hair while she spoke. 'My

145

brothers and sisters – my *former* brothers and sisters,' she said to the Blackguards. 'I hope you will not find me impertinent in borrowing a semblance of your garb. I should have asked first. I recently fought in a dress, and it nearly cost me my life. We are at war, and I will not be helpless. I trust you to defend me, but in turn, you can trust me to be as little of a burden as possible.' A grin stole over her face. 'Plus, it's impossible to find anything else nearly as comfortable as the blacks.'

They shared her grin.

'I think offense is the last thing we feel, High Lady...' Tempus paused. It was within protocol to address the White as 'High Lady,' but he'd obviously meant to append her name, and his wits failed him. 'High Lady Karris' because of their Blackguard friendship, or was that too informal? 'High Lady Guile' because of her long-hoped-for marriage? But that had been so brief and so painful, and did that seem to ignore all she had accomplished under her own name? 'High Lady White Oak'? But did that seem to ignore her marriage?

She saw his dilemma. 'I prefer "High Lady White," thank you. I am those other names as well, but for the time Orholam has given me in this office, I am the White before all else. Caleen?'

Her slaves had finished putting the pins in her hair, and now they set a large wig and headdress on Karris's head. Luminous sea demon ivory had been carved into a seven-pointed crown. Suspended above the central point was a single winking diamond, smaller than one would expect. Platinum-white hair cascaded down around Karris's shoulders, but each tip had been dyed one of the seven colors where it swept back up to entwine with the ivory crown.

Her only nod to her origins as a green and red drafter was a single earring in each ear, a ruby and an emerald. She waved away any powders. 'I'm pale enough,' she said. 'And I care not if they see me sweat.' Even while the slaves worked, another held up a series of parchments for her to peruse. The White would nod every so often, and the slave would turn the pages. The woman was illiterate, and once Karris had to motion for her to turn the page right side up.

The White was practicing her speech, Teia realized.

'I take it back,' Karris said. 'Give me some powder.'

Captain Tempus cleared his throat. 'On most days, the White being late would be expected, High Lady White. But noon waits for no one.'

'Thank you, Captain,' Karris said, peeved. Then she sighed. 'I'm sorry. In the unexpected absence of my chief room slave, it *is* kind of you to remind me. I am well aware of the pressures of time today. Please don't act differently. I'm not accustomed to...all of this. Any of it. Orea made it look so easy.'

'She'd been doing it ten years by the time you knew her,' Samite said. 'Your first time in the sparring circle, you don't try to win; you try to survive.'

'Doesn't seem like an ideal time to be learning as I go, does it?' Karris asked.

Tell me about it, Teia thought.

Karris stood, her makeup finished. 'Shall we?' she asked.

Samite said, 'You aren't...I mean I understand dismissing some slobbering luxiats, but you aren't actually going out there like...Or do I need to find a new job?'

Karris grinned. 'Ha! I was just playing with you. I wondered how far you'd let me go. All things may be permissible, but not all are fruitful.'

She beckoned, and two slave women came from the closet, carrying a dress between them. It opened like a clamshell, sideways. Karris stepped into the sleeves as if into a jacket, and the rest was buckled tight around her.

'How did the tailor take my instructions?' Karris asked the younger of the slaves.

'I believe "apoplexy" is the word. But obedience, too.'

Karris grinned at the Blackguards. 'Pull this down. All this silk is under tension, and this razor embedded in this channel should cut it instantly. So if I need to fight – or, more likely, if I'm injured and you need to carry me away from danger or see how bad a wound is, you can cut the dress off in a matter of moments.' She turned to the slave. 'Shorter sleeves next time.'

'He said if you asked for shorter sleeves to tell you to look for another tailor, because he'll be jumping off each of the seven towers until one of them finally agrees to release him from this hell you've confined him in.'

Karris laughed. 'Is it a universal rule that the more talented the artist, the more of a pain in the ass?'

'We're all pains in the ass if we can get away with it,' Samite said. 'Great artists are just allowed to get away with it more.'

Waving away the slaves now just fluffing her skirts, Karris asked, 'How do I look? Never mind. Don't answer that. It's too late to change. Noon waits for no one.'

She stopped at the door, though.

'Some of you know already, but some of you are too young to know me. I don't look forward to this. I've killed wights and men, and I don't even like killing wights. There is a time to agonize, and there is a time to act. Today we do what must be done, and we don't shrink from the truth or from our duty. Trainer Samite, you remember Ithiel Greyling?'

'Of course. Those Blue-Eyed Demon mercs put a dung-smeared arrow through his hand,' Samite said. 'May Orholam send them to a lower hell.'

'Ithiel knew those arrows. You try to treat them, and you get gangrene. You die, always. The chirurgeon said he could just take the hand at the wrist, but you'd still risk death. If he'd done that, maybe Ithiel could have been a trainer, like you. But Ithiel had two boys. He didn't want to give up fighting, didn't want to give up the Blackguard he loved. His wife had already done that in order to marry him. But he loved his family, too, and wanted to be there for them. So we took off his arm at the elbow. Instantly.'

'Bravest thing I ever saw,' Samite said.

'To realize in an instant that you aren't going to have the life you'd hoped for, but not waste a moment complaining, instead acting instantly to save what good you can? That's more guts than I'd have had,' Karris said. Orholam have mercy, Karris hadn't been thinking of Gavin until the very moment she said the words. She pushed it away, tried to get back on track. 'He lived until just a couple years ago, didn't he?'

'Indeed. And raised two damn fine sons,' said Watch Captain Tempus.

No one was looking at Gavin and Gill Greyling, but Teia

saw tears streaking down both their faces to see their father honored so.

'What we do today, with this execution, is that cut,' Karris said quietly. 'We may cut too deep. We may kill men who could have been saved. The one is all rot, but the other two, in gentler times...Perhaps they could be treated with gentler medicine. Today we cut deep so we may save the whole body. But I want you to know, I hate it, too.'

Quentin, Teia thought. We're going to kill you. Dear Orholam, Quentin.

Chapter 22

I'm no better than my brother. But I live.

Gavin waited, starving, fasting, wondering if his father saw him or if he had been forgotten. His entire gambit rested on his father's seeing him choose death, and the water flushing the cell every week erased all evidence of that.

Nor would Gavin necessarily even know if his father came down to observe him and left.

But you can never blink when you stare down a Guile.

There was only the bland trickle of water, so slight that it usually clung to the ceiling and coursed down the wall with only the occasional drip. It had, over the years, worn a slight gutter in the blue luxin. He plugged that gutter with the two remaining fingers of his left hand, watched the water back up and spill out of the gutter and finally course around his fingers and into oblivion.

Death always finds a way.
Stop what gaps you may;
Scream defiance that you live,
Life leaks through the mortal sieve.

When he'd constructed these cells, he'd thought that there were two main problems with any prison: what comes in, and what goes out. He'd spent restless nights figuring out exactly how to deliver the food, and how exactly to take away the waste and the water.

He'd gotten it exactly backward. The problem with a prison isn't what comes and goes; it's what stays.

When he shat – rarely now, it had been so long since he'd eaten, but it had been a problem from the beginning – he had to wipe with his left hand like the barbarians of old in the Broken Lands. There was no way to wash his hand adequately after. Thus, when he ate, he had to tear apart his bread with right hand and his teeth, feral.

Once in the first days, he forgot, and ate three bites with both hands.

The Mighty Gavin Guile, the High Lord Prism, the Emperor of the Seven Satrapies, the Promachos of Orholam, the Defender of the Faith – shit eater.

He'd pondered then, for days straight, whether that was to be the end of him. Would he get some infection and shit out his life, while his father watched – or, worse perhaps, didn't? He had no idea how often his father checked on him, but it couldn't be often. Regardless of how the old arachnid did it, getting down here wouldn't be easy. Harder still to keep his passage secret and to come and have no one notice the absence.

Gavin had never gotten sick, though, which proved something profound about him or Orholam or the state of natural philosophy. What that profound something was, he wasn't sure, which definitely proved something about himself.

At the very least, the shit eating and his sick fear afterward had made the fasting more palatable.

After the first days, the hunger had passed. He almost missed it, insane as that was, for it had been a constant distraction. A blessed distraction from what that demon in the glass, his own tormenting reflection, had said. 'You, Dazen, are the Black Prism.'

He had convinced himself, somehow, that he hated Sun Day. That he hated ritually murdering all those drafters. He'd convinced himself that he was being noble when he hunted down wights personally. He was saving people's lives! He'd convinced himself that he had gone to the White Oak estate that fateful day for love.

As if a Guile knew anything of love.

He knew what love was, surely. He knew what it would look like, smell like, act like. Though never wise, he was smart enough to know the real thing. He just could never feel it. He was Guile, and that meant corruption.

Orholam forgive him. Every small thing he'd done right had been feeble atonement for the murder of thousands. He could barely remember his knife strokes on all those Sun Days now, the insincere words offered to comfort those condemned to die. He'd corrupted the holiest day of the year into just another long day of labor.

I have to work so hard, he'd thought, as he slew the best and brightest and most dedicated men and women of the satrapies.

And added to his power with every death.

He had convinced himself, recently, for a time, perhaps... that his brother had been the villain after all. His brother must have been a murderer, a cheat, a rapist, a monster. And his father! Worse, worse still.

But Gavin – nay, Dazen. Dazen False-Face. Dazen the Impostor – Dazen himself was the monster here.

He himself had been the tyrant, the lone beast who would be a god. He just hadn't been very successful. He had let his father remain in power. He had let the White oppose him. He had been less competent than he could believe.

And that stung worse than the idea that he was evil.

He was evil and he wasn't even good at it.

But.

But. He survived. He was here. Maimed and bent. Eye burnt out. Fingers cut off. They'd broken everything but his will.

As long as he had that, he could overcome. And he would.

He was the bad guy? So be it.

He was a monster? He would be the best. He would emerge. He would comfort Karris, and he would avenge himself on his enemies.

She would be better off without him. He saw that now. But she didn't see it. And she had how many years left, anyway?

151

Five, maybe? He'd kept up a pretense of goodness for seventeen years. He could do five more for her sake.

I will be sweetness and light to her eyes, and bitter gall and hellfire to my enemies.

Goddammit, Father! Come down here already!

'Want to talk?' the dead man asked.

Gavin said nothing. You don't respond to a torturer who has only words as his rack.

Finally, after what seemed like forever, his father came.

Gavin was awakened by the slight tremor that he knew signaled the cell's being lifted. He'd thought when he built the cell that it would be imperceptible. After his time here, though, the small change felt like an earthquake. He woke instantly and sat over his hole, placid, meditative.

When the slot in the wall opened from the apparently seamless blue, it wasn't where Gavin had guessed it would be. Top-quality workmanship there, hiding its location. His own workmanship.

But almost as soon as the slot opened, something slid into the gap. When Dazen had come to visit the real Gavin down here, he'd left only open air between them. Andross Guile was not so confident, or so cocky, perhaps.

Andross Guile set a window between them, sparkling, crystalline, translucent but not fully transparent – thus, likely blue luxin. He was illuminated with an icy light.

Gavin stood on wobbly legs and faced his father. The elder Guile was visible only through Gavin's own reflection. And Andross was a perverse mirror of him. He looked hale. He looked better than he had in twenty years.

In contrast, Gavin himself looked like hell. It was as if his father had stolen away all his youth. His skin was bronzed where Gavin's was pallid. The fat of all his sedentary years had now melted into his sharp Guile jaw and broad Guile shoulders. Gloves gone, spectacles gone, he didn't look anything like the invalid he had so recently been – or perhaps had merely pretended to be.

A dozen quiet expressions ran over Andross Guile's face at the speed of his thoughts. Finally, all he said was, 'Son.'

It was a kidney punch.

It shouldn't have done any such thing, but it sent Gavin spinning. For no reason at all, he thought of his own son. Though not by birth, by adoption Kip was his, and Gavin loved him fiercely. He'd warmed to the boy only slowly, true. Only seen and loved the Guile in him by degrees. Gavin hadn't been much of a father to him, but he'd done some things right. He'd gotten him into the Blackguard. He'd given Kip time amid those good people to help him grow straight and tall rather than crooked, as the other nobles' pampered sons and daughters would have turned him.

And he'd saved Kip's life, the once.

It wasn't much, but it had been solely for Kip's benefit, not his own. He had tried. In what little time he'd had with the boy, before this war had torn him away, he had tried. Once.

What had Andross Guile done for his sons, with all the time in the world? With all the wealth he'd accrued, and all the power he'd accumulated, with all the leisure he could want and limitless years, when had Andross Guile ever taken his eyes off himself and simply been a father?

'When I was a boy, why did I never go to you when I needed a father so desperately?' Gavin asked. 'You were there. But where were you? What kind of man abandons his son to this? Never mind. Putting your kin in this hell is the least of your sins.' He waved at his father-reflection dismissively. 'You call me son? No. This man-shaped grotesque is nothing to me. You are no father of mine.'

Gavin started crying, and he couldn't help but shut his eyes. Tears getting into his eye hurt so much it blinded him. He saw only a single expression on his father's face before he heard the scrape and snap of the slot slamming shut.

He staggered over to the wall, and leaned against it, whispering, 'Damn you. Damn you for all you were and all you could have been. Damn you for all you should have been and were born to be, but never were.' And because the wall was fully reflective now, he whispered to that blue mirror where his sire might not be, and where his own reflection was, 'Damn you to the hell you've built for yourself, Guile.'

Chapter 23

'Something ain't right,' Big Leo said. 'What is it that isn't right about this? Anyone?'

'No oars,' Cruxer said. 'How the hell did all of us forget oars?'

The *Blue Falcon II* had no oars; it was almost dark, and this was a problem for a luxin-propelled ship in a river with a current pulling them toward what might be enemies.

Standing at the prow of the skimmer, Big Leo said, 'Not that this. *That* this. That. Something ain't right about that.' He pointed toward the strangers waiting for them with his chin.

'It's my fault,' Ben-hadad said, still looking at the *Blue Falcon*. 'My design. My work.' He brightened. 'But...hey, I think I already know how to fix it. Orholam's shining smile, boys, it'll be beautiful.'

'Can you fix it *now*?' Cruxer asked, looking nervously toward the armed men waiting for them on shore.

'No, no, no, but on *Blue Falcon III*,' Ben-hadad said. 'If we give the oars a convex shape and modify the hull a bit, we can have them fold seamlessly and interlock into the gunwales here. See? They'll nest into each other. And if we make them of brightwater, they'd double as armor! Breaker, you think you can do that much solid yellow?'

'Ben,' Big Leo said, his voice rumbling deep in warning.

Ben-hadad clicked his lenses up. 'Hmm?'

'Shut up. Someone tell me what's wrong with this. With them. My gut's going crazy.'

'Could be fear,' Ferkudi offered.

Big Leo leveled a gaze on him like a hammer falling on an errant thumb.

'Not fear,' Ferkudi amended. 'Definitely not fear.'

No one else answered Big Leo. The skimmer drifted slowly

downstream in the late-evening water. No sunlight meant no luxin, no luxin meant no motion. No oars meant no options. So they stared at the figures on the riverbank, and the figures stared back at them.

They could crack their lux torches for a source, but those were precious and they had precious few of them. No one wanted to waste their lux torches because they were scared of a few villagers.

'The current is pushing us right to them,' Tisis said. 'And the wind isn't helping.'

An improbably large bare-chested man and a child stood at the shore, but another dozen men and women sat around a cheery fire higher up the bank, cooking dinner and talking quietly.

'We're too interesting for only two of them to be at the shore,' Kip said.

'If you do say so yourself,' Winsen said.

Kip let it go, though he was this close to punching Winsen in the nose. 'We're too dangerous looking,' Kip said. 'That's what's wrong, Leo.'

'They're trying not to spook us,' Tisis said, getting it.

'Who tries not to scare six armed men in uniform?' Kip asked.

'People who are scary themselves, that's who,' Ferkudi said.

'Quiet, all of you,' Cruxer said. He was holding the waxed leather bag that carried the Mighty's remaining mag torches. 'Winsen, I count fourteen on the beach. Are there any others in the trees?'

'They're Deep Foresters,' Tisis said. 'If there's more hiding in the trees, you'll never see them.'

'None in the trees,' Winsen said, ignoring Tisis.

Cruxer handed out the precious mag torches. 'No one crack one unless I give the order. Or unless I die, I suppose. That is one big, hairy, freckly guy.'

There was something feral about the man standing at the water's edge. He wore a brown linen shirt, but it hung fully open, unlaced to show off a pelt of red chest hair and muscles, the tails of the shirt tucked into his belt, sleeves rolled up short to show bands of polished copper around his enormous biceps. Everywhere he was covered with thick, curly red hair over freckles: chest and arms and stomach. A beard like a burning bush hung halfway down his chest, contrasting with the bald dome of his head. And though Big Leo had a full head's height on him, this warrior was chiseled from stone. Despite the fading light and the distance and hair, Kip could see veins on every muscle. And scars, as if from wild animals?

Tisis gasped, and at first Kip was needled that she was appreciating the incredible virility of that wild man, but when he turned to her, she said, 'Look at *her*!'

The child wasn't a child, but a pygmy.

Her appearance rattled something loose. A memory or—

I'm lying facedown, motionless, in the jungle underbrush in the lee of a downed tree. Loathsome things move under my belly and scuttle over my bare hands. Most of them harmless, I hope. A bird spider perches on a bough within arm's reach above. Spiders terrify me beyond all measure, but I don't move. Don't dare to. Rustling through the underbrush and trees not twenty paces away is the war party.

The war-blue pygmies carry lances and flails, but the greater danger is the great tygre wolves they ride. Standing tall enough that they look eye to eye with a tall man, they're almost too big for the pygmies to ride. They have long jaws more akin to an alligator's than a dog's, and their riders don't control them so much as direct their viciousness. Tygre wolves aren't trained mounts like a horse, they're more like an arrowhead you strap into. Barely controlled, and that only by will magic; if a rider falls off, he can expect to be eaten first. Sight hunters, so their sense of smell isn't as acute as a dog's, but it is far better than a man's.

The chi I drafted should have killed the scent of my body – give it that, the vile stuff – but there's nothing to do about my breath. I don't have it in me to draft chi again, not now. I can practically feel the tumors growing every time I do.

One of the tygre wolves comes toward me now, big wide paws silent on the greenery beneath. It growls.

My bowels turn to water, and I couldn't move if I wanted to. The tygre wolf lunges – and snaps its fangs shut on the huge bird spider above me, drool from its slavering jaws splattering across my forehead.

Its rider curses and pulls at one of its ears, and it obeys her, chomping happily. Before they turn, I see the rider well, her gaze keen, teeth bared.

She is—

Not the same woman. Very alike. Maybe an ancestor. But that woman was not this one. Or perhaps Kip's very unfamiliarity with the pygmies made them all look alike to him: sharp elfin features, imperial-purple hair, and the permanently upturned mouth and cheek depressions like smiles and dimples that had so often confounded men, who repeatedly mistook their expressions and motives, coming to call them smiling devils.

For a moment, Kip was suspended between the card's knowledge and his own.

And then, in the blinking of an eye, he was out of that time-that-is-not-time.

And then the skimmer skritched onto the pebbles of the riverbank.

'Greetings,' Kip said. 'We've come to fight.'

That came out wrong.

'Not to fight you, obviously,' he added. 'I mean, we hope not? You wouldn't happen to be fighting for the White King, are you? That would be awkward.'

'Good old Kip Silvertongue,' Winsen whispered.

'We know why you've come,' the pygmy woman said, her voice high pitched. 'We've been sent to welcome you. Kip Guile? And you, Tisis Guile, born Malargos? And the Mighty, we presume?'

'That's…right,' Kip said. She knew about Tisis and his marriage? How could she know that?

'I am Sibéal Siofra. This is Conn Ruadhán Arthur. We are of Shady Grove.'

'Shady Grove?' Tisis said. 'You are far from home indeed.'

A cloud passed over Sibéal's face. 'There is no home now. Not for us. The White King has driven out everyone before him. First we in Shady Grove welcomed refugees, then to our shame and against our traditions we turned aside refugees, then we became refugees in turn. We have lost homes and tribe and spouses and children and land and faith. We have only a thirst for vengeance. Lead us, *Luíseach*, and we will go anywhere, so long as you lead us against that abomination.'

'Lee shock?' Kip asked, butchering the accent, though terminology probably shouldn't have been foremost on his mind.

'Bringer of Light,' Tisis said.

'Oh, great. That again.' He turned to Sibéal and Conn Arthur. 'Gather your people.'

'They're not ours to command,' Conn Arthur said. 'We here are all clanless, masterless, free.'

Kip had never heard anyone say 'free' with such a mix of loathing and despair. Though he'd already had long talks with Tisis about the Foresters, apparently he was going to need to have more of them.

He waved to people at their fires, almost all of them now looking curiously toward him and the Mighty. 'I have things to say. If you want to hear me out, come here,' Kip shouted.

More than the twelve people at the fire came. The woods emptied, and over a hundred men and women and teens came from the trees.

Tisis raised an eyebrow at Winsen. 'No people in the woods, huh?'

He cursed under his breath.

And as they gathered around Kip, these people, shoeless, hopeless, bereft, eyes glazed with shock and loss, jaws set with pitiless rage, Kip realized he was slipping into the Guile role: he would use his words to sway the wills of men. It was the Guile talent more powerful than their magic. Magic requires will, but words shape will, turn it, direct it, reflect it from one target to another.

He'd seen it done. He'd marveled at it. Envied it. Been in awe of his father's profound, bedrock conviction that people would do what he wanted them to do.

But these lives weren't his to spend however he willed. He was nothing to these people, a stranger, an interloper.

How dare he come to them with promises? Much less promises he could never keep.

When they were gathered, he said, 'I am Kip Guile. If you've heard of my family, perhaps you know it is their way to sway others to their will. Sometimes for good. Sometimes not.' He shook his head. 'I'm not here to be your lord. I'm not here to turn you to my will, to manipulate you or make you my vassals or anyone else's. I'm here to fight. I'm a full-spectrum polychrome, and I've been taught to fight by the best in the world. With others – not alone – I killed King Rask Garadul of Tyrea, and with the Blackguards and Gavin and Karris Guile, I killed Atirat at the Battle of Ru just as he was attempting to assume godhood. I know how to fight, and the Mighty with me are better than I am. But we don't know this country the way you do.

'I'm going to hit the Color Prince, this pretender White King. I'm going to hit him hard, and where he doesn't expect it. I'm going to keep hitting him until one or the other of us dies. I can do a lot of damage with the Mighty alone. But alone, I don't think we can stop him. We can do more and better and live longer if you join us, if we teach each other. If you come with me, we're going to move fast and work hard for long hours and sleep little. We're going to fight and kill and die. That's it. That's all we offer. My goal is to expel the White King from Blood Forest altogether. If we can kill every last damned wight while we do it, so much the better. I don't guarantee victory, but I do think victory's possible if we fight together. So no big speech. Join us or don't. Let me know what you've decided in the morning.'

They looked at him as if they couldn't quite believe that was all he was going to say, but as he got to work setting up tents with the Mighty, the crowd slowly dispersed.

'Well, that went...' Winsen said. 'But I guess they aren't trying to kill us, so that's something.'

'Shut up, Winsen,' Tisis said. 'Kip, that was perfect.'

'I wasn't trying to be perfect. I was trying to be honest.'

'That's exactly what they need.'

'You said you were sent?' Cruxer asked Sibéal and Conn Arthur, who had remained with them. 'By whom?'

Sibéal smiled, and Kip was certain it was a smile. 'By a prophet you know as the Third Eye, and her husband, Corvan Danavis. Allies.'

'Damn,' Big Leo said behind Kip. 'You telling me we got a Seer on our side? We might have a chance in this war after all.'

Sibéal said, 'They send their greetings from a thousand leagues away, and wanted me to tell you this is all the help they can send.'

'Well, shit,' Big Leo said.

Chapter 24

Gavin waited for a long time there, leaning on the wall until the tears had passed and he was sure his father wasn't coming back. He measured three hands over and two hands up. He licked his finger and marked a spot.

It had all been for this: the days of misery and starvation, the carefully calibrated fight with his father.

This was where the luxin was sealed. He'd needed the open slot in order to locate the seal. And he'd needed to make his father angry enough that he wouldn't soon return; otherwise Gavin might start his attempt and have his father interrupt it before he could bring it to fruition.

But now came another bad part. He ate as much bread as still remained in the cell. Eating would be misery for a while after this.

Facing his father had been the worst, but Dazen had made this prison well, and blue luxin is harder than fingernail. Harder than a fist.

'What are you doing?' the dead man asked. He hadn't spoken in some time.

Gavin said nothing, taking deep breaths, bracing himself. He measured carefully. With a pinky, he stretched his lip back, and before he could think more, he slammed his face against the wall.

He shook his head. His lip was bloody and swollen.

The dead man was baffled. 'I told you if you want to kill yourself...'

Gavin slammed his face against the wall again.

It took five more attempts to loosen his dogtooth. He wobbled it back and forth, back and forth, his eyes streaming tears, and finally ripped it out with a cry.

It slipped from spit-and-blood-slick fingers. It bounced on the blue luxin, and with his depth perception ruined by having only a single eye, Gavin swiped frantically—

And caught it from the air before it could plunge down the waste hole.

He stood strong, bloodied, body broken, but determined, defiant.

Blue luxin is stronger than fingernails or fists, but enamel is stronger still, and spirit supreme. Gavin took the dogtooth between bloody fingers, and, like the lone, mad beast he was, he started chewing at the wall.

Chapter 25

Kip and Tisis were given their own tent. The idea of having some real privacy was exciting right until Cruxer said, 'I'll be right outside, taking first watch.'

He met Kip's exasperated gaze with one of his own. 'I'm like the commander, you're like the Prism, right?' Cruxer asked.

'But it's a *tent*,' Kip said.

'Thus, not even as safe as a ship's cabin,' Cruxer said.

'But it's a...tent,' Kip said.

'We know what you'll be doing in there. So what? You pretend like we can't hear, and we'll pretend like we can't hear. No comments tomorrow, no jokes. You deal with the brutal hardship of having to make love with your beautiful wife where someone else might hear the blankets rustling, and we'll deal with having to stay up all night, standing watch in the wind and the rain.'

'You make me sound like an asshole when you put it that way.'

The rest of the squad cleared their throats and avoided his gaze.

'Hey, it's not like I chose—' Kip stopped. 'Wait, I actually did, huh? Fine. I'm sorry.'

He slipped into the tent. It was small, barely big enough for them to sit up; they did plan to carry everything on their backs, after all.

Tisis already had the fresh-scrubbed look of a person who'd just bathed. She passed him a clean cloth and pointed to the small tub of water. 'Sleep clean, and we won't have to launder our blankets as often,' she said.

'If only we'd brought a slave along to worry about such things for us,' Kip grumbled.

She grinned. 'I don't hold it against you, Kip.'

'I do.'

'You're funny,' she said. 'You do the right thing, often the brilliant thing, and then you pretend you didn't want to do it. What is that?'

'I dunno. I've got a whole lotta stupid inside, fighting to get out. And, uh, thanks.'

'For what?'

'For the "brilliant" thing.'

'For calling you brilliant? It's not a compliment. It's just the truth. I don't think you got that armpit well enough.'

He scowled. Trying to sponge bathe yourself while sitting and not slop soapy water on your stuff was a pain.

'Hey, I have to sleep with you!' she said. She was teasing, but some part of it pierced Kip.

He looked away and put the cloth in the soapy water again, tried to lose himself in the mechanics of bathing.

'Wait, wait, wait. What was that?' she asked. 'Ah hells, Kip, what did I say?'

'I'm sorry,' he said. 'I know you didn't ask for any of this.'

'Stop that! Stop that. Do you even know how loused up

162

you are? Everything you believe about yourself is wrong. Orholam's toe cheese, Kip, it's so frustrating!'

'Toe cheese? Good one,' he said, grinning at her.

'Deflect and redirect. Always.' She sighed and gave up. 'They love you, you know.'

'Who?'

'The Mighty.'

'They're amazing,' Kip said.

'They respect you.'

'Well...they follow me, but that's, you know, accidents of birth and all. I'm a Guile. I'm a polychrome. It doesn't happen that often.'

'You think they love you because you're a Guile?! You... you stupid...' She lay down and rolled over so her back was toward him. 'So you know, I was planning that tonight be really good. If you weren't so infuriating...'

'Huh?' Kip said. 'I'm sorry?'

'You don't understand anything about women, I know. But here's a tip: when your wife is amorous, don't make her angry just before bed.'

'Amorous?' Kip asked. He knew what it meant, but how'd he miss—

'Good night, Kip.'

'I'm sorry? I mean, I'm sorry. Really sorry.'

'Good *night*, Kip.'

'Some people like angry sex.'

'Not me. Good. Night.'

Damn.

Kip thought of lying down, but he wasn't tired. He'd just fret. He thought about how he'd viewed that card briefly and unintentionally this afternoon. He had another deck of Janus Borig original cards in his pack, untouched since he'd put them there.

There had been two decks – one Andross had owned that Gavin had stolen from him at some point, and then the ones Kip had saved from the fire at Janus Borig's when she'd been murdered. That had been the deck responsible for this afternoon's vision. It had been the deck that had nearly killed him.

He really hadn't wanted to touch any cards ever again after

that. But the vision changed things. He was here, totally out of his depth among a new people. He should at least look at the cards to see if there were any that might help him. He didn't need to view any of them, but he'd be a fool if he didn't use such a potent tool.

Scrounging in his pack, he found the deck box readily. Pulled out the cards.

They weren't the same cards. Disbelieving, he fanned the deck on the blankets on his lap. It was a standard deck, no unusual cards, certainly no originals. As if someone had swapped it so the deck box would have the correct weight. Verity?

But there was a slip of paper among the cards.

'Please let me know how long it took you to discover the swap. I thought within the first three days. Grinwoody bet me five danars it would be closer to two weeks.' There was no doubt whom it was from, and it wasn't Verity.

Andross had known Kip was leaving with Tisis.

Andross had known which boat Tisis was taking.

Andross had put a man on the boat.

It had taken Kip more than two weeks.

Totally defeated by this dung-smear of a day, Kip flopped back onto his blankets, defeated. He landed across Tisis's long hair, tugging it painfully.

'Ow!' she said. 'What'd you do that for?'

There wasn't a big enough sigh in the world.

Chapter 26

~Gunner~

'It's not for sale,' I says.

'Who said anything about a sale?' the wrapped man asks.

'It's a holly trust.'

That one was apurpose, and he don't correct me, so he knows about Cap'n Gunner. Ergot, he's crafty. I'll have to hold my coins a-foursquare in my fists around this 'un.

But I know how to deal with conners. He's all swattled like a babe, like he's got the skin-sloughing disease maybe, but I think he's well after all. He's accosted me here, outside Lee Lee's watering hole, my favorite tavern on the swollen teat that is Big Jasper. He was waiting for me, and I'm feeling a bit too boozy for this.

'I don't believe in holy or unholy,' says he. 'I believe in having the best.'

'What's that to me?' I asks.

'I want to show you a ship. Best girl on the Cerulean Sea or any other.'

'Every captain or owner selling a ship says the same,' I says.

'Everyone says it. Some of them believe it. But one of them's right.'

'The odds that one is you are blinky indeed,' I say, but I can't help being intrigued.

'Take a look for yourself,' he says. 'I'll let you come aboard armed as you will, and you can examine it as you will.'

'What's the hook?' I asks.

'No hook. A game. I'll tell you more after you decide if she's worth your time. Though there's not been a sailor worth his salt yet who's scorned the *Golden Mean*.'

There's his bait. I've heard of this boat. The breathless wonder and slobbering are enough to turn a man's stomach. And his eyes.

'I'll take a looksie.' I wouldn't mind being the man to disprove the silliness and lies about what a wonder she is.

It's not long to her place at the dock. She's a new Ilytian galleass, but I see the stories were true. She's bone white, but with a golden sheen to her skin, like a pale Blood Forester lady riding your hips sweaty at sunset.

'Abornean teak?' I ask.

'Lightweight and stronger than any other wood known to man.'

'Too porous for decking. Your ship is shite. She'll warp and sink 'fore Long Night.'

But I don't leave, and he don't defend her.

'She's really imbibed with brightwater?' I asks.

'Just enough to fill the pores in the wood, and just on the

hull. No need to add weight where it's unnecessary. The yellow luxin imbuing the wood is segmented, though, so the wood can still flex. I'll warn you, it does mean you have to hire a brightwater drafter every ten years. A good one. They told me twenty years, but shipwrights...'

'Would swear their own mother was a virgin, before selling her to be a poxy cap'n's buttboy,' I agree.

He says, 'I'm untrusting myself, so I hired my own yellow drafter to look her over. She estimated ten years. Bonus is that with the yellow luxin coating, barnacles won't grow on the hull, which makes it faster still.'

'Eh. Means you can't keelhaul a man.' Of course, you still could, but with no barnacles, he might actually live through it. Which has its own advantages.

He says nothing again.

No barnacles means you don't have to clean the barnacles off, and that's one of the more time intensive and costly bits of maintenance for any ship.

'How many guns?'

He laughs, and it makes his bandages slide some. I can see he's almost as night-skinned as me. Older man, though, from how he moves at times. Skinny. 'You're familiar with the work of Phineas Vecchini?'

Here's where his lies are gonna get his lines wrapped round his legs. I know Phin well. 'Some,' I says. 'This from his workshop, or stamped by his hand?'

'Master Vecchini has quit working,' the man says. 'He let his daughters take over his shop.'

Everyone knows that. Guess that's not the lie to trip him, then. 'They're good, but others are their equals,' I grumble. 'Maybe one day the youngest will be her father's rival. Maybe. Guns from his daughters ain't quite the braggery you'd like to claim, though.'

He adjusts his wrappings patiently. 'I'm not bragging of guns from his daughters. I convinced Phin to go back to work, one last time. The girls didn't want him to, said he'd ruin his health, and he may well have done so. He spent a year on this.'

'Pah. How'd you do that? I heard he swore to that harpy he wedded he'd never—'

'His wife passed on two years back. His daughters were as adamant he not take the work, but then I offered him something he couldn't resist.'

'And what's that?' I ask. 'That old goat rogerer weren't swayed by neither women, wealth, nor wine. What could you offer him?'

Like the insidious stench of wine shits after shore leave, a smug aura surrounds the bandaged man. 'I told him the cannons were for you.'

Phin had spent a year, with all his forgers and smiths and cast-iron men and engravers and potboys and apprentices, his workshop belching smoke day and night? For me?

It knocks my knees a bit weak, to be forthright.

It's one thing to shout at the world that you're the best. I been doin' that since it warn't true. It's a whole 'nother fish for the best in the world to acknowledge you as the best, too.

It's like finding another barrel a' brandy in the hold two days after you run dry and got the shakes.

'How many?'

'Forty guns. Various sizes. Some with parts my cannon caster and gunner together couldn't even make sense of. Phin laughed and said you'd know what they were for, or figure it out, or – if, after all I'd promised, if the guns weren't actually for you, that we could go...sodomize ourselves.'

I'm not sure what that means, but he's a shipowner. They like fancy talk to keep 'em company while they sit on their piles of money. It sounds like old Phin gave him hell, though, and that makes me happier than the first lovelorn sailor on shore leave through the door at an understaffed brothel.

'I don't believe you,' I says. 'Who's manning her?'

'No one,' he says. 'I fired them all. I was given to understand that smugglers and pirates like to hire their own crews. And given that I may be handing this ship over to you, I wasn't planning on paying for a crew in the meantime.'

Handing it over? So he doesn't mean to pay me to captain her on some errand. 'I told you before, *it* ain't for sale. Nor trade neither. Cap'n Gunner is intergated. Integrated? Has integrated? That ain't right.' Damns, though. A sword for a boat? I got little use for one, and many for the other, no matter what that nattering Orholam said.

'Has integrity. Yes, you're known for that.'

There's a twinkle in his eye that I don't like. Like I amuse him, poncy little buttboy. I oughta jam my thumbs through them eyes. 'The answer's no, then, and you know it, and I know it...' But I don't move.

He doesn't, either.

'A look isn't going to harm anything. At least would let you know if I was telling you the truth about those cannons.'

A long moment, then I say, 'I owe it to that old goat, I s'pose. Just a looksie.'

'Of course.'

Captain Gunner is renowned for his shooting, of course, but he ain't no fool about a ship, neither. This ship is all first-rate. The last crew got a bit sloppy about some things if you look in the corners for grime, and Gunner's never allowed that hard crease to be folded on the edge of the furled sail: looks nice ashore, but gives the cloth a weak place that will eventually rip.

Most of her, though, is simply astonishing. Master Creepy gives me a lantern and stays topside. No interest in seeing it again, he says, and he don't want me nervous with him behind me.

Gunner inspects her for half an hour. She's a dream.

And then Gunner goes to the gun deck. The cannons are inmistakably Phin's work. But instead of on wheels, these cannons are on tracks. There are knobs and dials and articulated sights.

I intuitively understand some of it. It's made so one gunner – the best Gunner – can walk up and down a full row for a broadside, and make sure that every cannon is aimed exactly as he wishes, and fire each exactly when he wishes, separately or all at wunst.

In the old days, I could train my crew for it, but I could only aim one cannon perfectly myself. Here, if I understand aright, one man could direct his crews like another set of limbs, them doin' the dumber work of swabbing and reloading, and Gunner doin' the artist's bit of aimin' and boomin'.

On the forecastle, in pride of place, is a cannon engraved with a name like a punch to my belly. I sink down beside her, filled with awe and wonder and hate. Her engraving reads 'Ceres' or 'The Compelling Argument.'

She is the utter pinnacle of the cannon makers' craft, a culverin extraordinary near four paces long, with a bore wider than my own spread hand and shot as big as my balls. With this masterpiece, I could make my own legends. I spend ten minutes with her before I go up, and spit on her before I go, then rub that spit in down the long barrel as if it were my own shaft.

Guile's sword for this ship? The ship's worth a hunderd swords, no matter how bejeweled and begemmed. A hunderd at least.

I must have this ship. And I can't.

When I stole the sword, that prophet told me the sea would run with my blood if I lost the blade. I'm not a superstitious man, but I'm no fool, neither. How hard is it to keep a sword, I thought.

'Gunner's honor,' I tell the man wrapped as a leper to hide his identity, 'is not for sale.'

'Not a sale, no! I would never besmirch Gunner's name by suggesting so. But...' I can see the man's mask tug at the corners of his face as he grins beneath it. 'Even God plays dice.'

Chapter 27

Before dawn, Kip woke to an empty tent and the fear that when he emerged, he would find no one there. They'd finally wised up. He'd tried to be bold. He'd tried to take the lead, but he hadn't done it the way his father would have. And then he'd also infuriated his wife. Good old Kip Leaden Tongue.

Chest tight, he pulled on his clothes. Took a few deep breaths. It was quiet out there. None of the usual sounds of people moving about camp. Not even the early-morning sounds of someone going to relieve themselves. He tried to pat and finger comb his hair into some sort of relative order, and then went to face reality.

There were a lot of people standing there. Silent. Armed. Not just a lot of people. More than a hundred.

Everyone.

And the Mighty were, most unhelpfully, standing way back.

Everyone was staring at him.

'So what's it going to be?' Kip asked. When you've put all your coin on the table, you can't blink. 'This mean you're coming with me, or do I need to prove myself to you? You want me to wrestle a bear or something?'

Oh hells. Kip didn't know why he'd picked a bear. It must have been rattling around in his head because Tisis had told him last night that in their old tongue, Arthur meant 'bear.' Ruadhán meant 'little red.' Ergo, the giant chieftain was Little Red Bear.

I just volunteered to wrestle ol' Master Hugely McHugerson. I am dumber than words.

Conn Arthur looked troubled, as if he wasn't sure if Kip was challenging him. Oh, please, no. But the man looked toward Sibéal Siofra, who shook her head slightly.

Mercifully, the conn said nothing.

The pygmy woman stepped forward. 'The Third Eye told us impossible things, but she never told us as much as we would like.'

'Prophets,' Kip said. 'They're like that.'

'She told us to come this far to meet you, but that if we wanted any hope of defeating the White King, we would have to do battle with one of his captains at Deora Neamh...in two days.'

'And...' Kip said.

'It's a waterfall,' Tisis said, coming out of nowhere. 'It's a hundred leagues from here.'

'Ah,' Kip said. Given a marching speed through the forest of maybe ten leagues a day, or poling or rowing upriver at maybe fifteen leagues a day, that would seem impossible indeed. 'How many drafters do you have?'

Conn Ruadhán Arthur cocked his head to the side, puzzled.

'Your pardon, Lord Guile,' Sibéal Siofra said. 'We thought you knew. We're *all* drafters.'

Kip looked around. Without exception, these people were pale skinned. Only a few had any luxin staining visible on their arms at all, even the older ones. That was odd. A few were so freckled it might cover up orange or red staining, but most were not.

There were many blue-eyed people among them and a number of pygmies, and the light eyes should have made drafters doubly obvious. But he'd not noticed iris shading in any of them.

'Oooh,' Tisis said as if something was dawning on her. She looked toward Kip as if she wanted to say more, but instead she said, 'You're not just from the *town* of Shady Grove.'

'No,' Conn Arthur said. 'We're Ghosts. Look on us and tremble,' he said sarcastically. 'Is that going to be a problem?'

'Can many of you draft solid luxins?' Tisis asked.

'Yes,' Sibéal said, seeming relieved. 'We just...don't get much practice.'

Drafters who intentionally didn't draft? What was the point? 'One moment,' Kip said, and he pulled Tisis aside. Quietly he asked, 'Ghosts?'

'It's a school for drafters that's not under the authority of the Chromeria. A long time ago, when the Chromeria was consolidating control of all drafters, they declared everyone at such schools to be heretics. Those who stayed were often declared dead by their families, either to disown them or to escape Chromeria punishment for that family member's apostasy. Thus, Shady-Grove–trained drafters became referred to as Shades, or Ghosts. Since they also tend to keep a low profile lest the Chromeria renew its hunt for them, the name stuck.'

'The Chromeria hunted them?' Kip asked.

'The Magisterium, actually. Luxors.'

Kip turned back to Sibéal and Conn Arthur. 'You like blunt speaking, right?'

'It's usually faster,' Conn Arthur said. 'Isn't it?'

All right, Kip Blunderbuss. Come out and play. 'They branded you heretics. Are you?'

The conn took a displeased moment to digest that, but then said, 'We love Orholam and follow him.'

'Not to elide a painful history and many hard feelings,' Sibéal Siofra interjected. 'We do have some doctrinal differences, and don't submit to the Magisterial assertion of primacy.'

Orholam's crooked little toe, that permanent smile of hers was hard to get past. Kip thought her true expression was an uncertain, placating smile. He sighed.

'Good old Chromeria. Never failing to make its friends fearful and its enemies bold,' Kip said. 'Well, then. This is war, not an admissions test on doctrine for the Magisterium. Let's get to work.'

He broke them up into teams to start building skimmers for everyone. He organized the correct numbers of drafters of each color needed and put Ben-hadad in charge of overseeing the creation of the skimmers themselves, letting the young genius figure out the most efficient number and composition of skimmers given the number of people they had to move and the skill or lack thereof of the drafters available.

Kip went to work learning the disposition of his new forces. Most of the Ghosts here were those who had no homes anymore. Either they'd made Shady Grove their home, or their families' homes were in areas that the White King had already captured.

With Cruxer and Conn Arthur, Kip went over a map that Tisis was able to draw of Deora Neamh and its environs. She'd never visited, but she'd studied Blood Forest geography extensively, and she could draw. They showed the map to all the Ghosts who'd ever visited the town, and amended it as necessary.

Kip stared at the map. The problem with it was that the land was hilly – it was home to a tall waterfall – but the map itself did a poor job of showing the elevation changes. 'What do they want from this town?' Kip asked.

'Slaves. Loot. The regular, I suppose,' Conn Arthur said.

'No,' Cruxer said. 'There's a water mill here, below the base of the falls. Where do farmers keep their grain before and after it's been milled?'

They found someone who'd visited the town. He sketched a warehouse a ways down the rocky river, at the first place where the river was navigable for larger boats and barges. There was a good road between the mill and the docks. He hadn't even thought to add it in when shown the map before, because it was outside the scope of the paper.

Kip didn't know how long he stared at the map. They had no idea how many men and wights would be attacking the city. If it really was a foraging party, it would contain a small force of fighters meant to cow the populace, but be made up mainly of laborers and camp followers pressed into service to haul the grain back to the main camp.

'Breaker,' Cruxer said. It was almost noon, and Kip was still turning things over in his mind, visualizing the terrain. 'Ben-hadad says they're finished. He's launching the skimmers now.'

Kip didn't move. 'The thing about prototypes?'

'Milord?'

'They fail.'

'Well, these aren't the first skimmers that Ben's built.'

'They're the first ones he's watched inept drafters build for him, with so many going at once that he can't watch every step.'

Just then a spate of curses rang out from the water's edge. They turned and saw an entire section of hull had disintegrated and a skimmer was sinking rapidly.

Kip grinned at Cruxer.

'Well, you don't have to be smug about it,' he said. 'If we don't get there in time, we might lose our new allies, you know.'

'Eh, the prophecy says we *can* get there on time; therefore we *will*, right?'

Cruxer grimaced. 'I don't think it works like that. And maybe the Third Eye was lying to us just to get us to try. She could even be working for the Color Prince for all we know, and we're going to our destruction.'

'Corvan Danavis wouldn't let that happen,' Kip said.

'Well, maybe these Ghosts are lying about what Corvan and the Seer said.'

'How would they know such a lie would work on us?' Kip asked.

Cruxer just frowned.

'Why so dour, Crux? It's not like you.'

The young commander rubbed his face. 'Didn't sleep well last night.'

Well, Tisis and I didn't do anything to keep you awake, that's for sure. 'That's not so rare. Doesn't usually leave you grumpy.'

Cruxer pursed his lips. But then he spoke. 'I had this terrible nightmare about Commander Ironfist. It felt like a premonition. We were both wounded from fighting wights or something. But then we turned on each other. We killed each other, Breaker.' He shook his head. 'It felt so real.'

'If it's any consolation,' Kip said, 'I don't believe you could kill Ironfist.'

'I know, I can't imagine anything that would turn us against each other.'

'No, I mean the man could kick your ass while sipping kopi and reading the day's briefings and never spill a drop.'

An unwilling grin broke over Cruxer's face. 'You're a real flesh protuberance, you know that, right?'

'I got your back,' Kip said, patting his friend's shoulder. 'But if you fight Ironfist, I'll have it from way, *way* back.'

'Thanks a lot.' Cruxer's face fell again, though. 'I wish he were here. I wish he were leading us, not me. I mean, no offense to you, Breaker. But you know what I mean, right? I'm not making sense, I'm too tired. Sorry.'

'I know what you mean. I wish he were here...' Kip forgot what he had been about to say next as something occurred to him. 'Huh.'

He pulled on some spectacles and started drafting, swapping spectacles as necessary. In a few minutes he had a pretty good luxin model of the map they'd created.

Cruxer had immediately summoned the people who'd helped with the map earlier, and Kip held the luxin open so they could make the model accurate together.

The leadership had gathered by the time Kip expanded the model to include the surrounding countryside for several leagues.

'Avoid battle, seek victory,' Kip said. He remembered that from one of Master Danavis's books. 'They're here for grain. Conn Arthur, you mount an attack on the warehouse. You come straight from the forest here.'

'I can do it, but why do we want to go after grain? You plan to keep it? If we undermine support from the people...'

'To win, the Blood Robes need that grain, so if we threaten it, they have to defend it. Try not to actually set the warehouses on fire, though. You decide how many people you need to make the attack credible, but it must fail. Fall back and regroup – probably here – within sight of them, giving them time to call for reinforcements.'

'And...what?' Conn Arthur said. 'There's no way to get around them in this valley without being seen.'

'We don't attack them at all. This isn't a battle; it's an attack.'

'I don't...' Cruxer said.

Kip asked, 'What's the trouble with moving huge amounts of grain?'

'It's heavy, bulky,' Cruxer said.

'Right. Their goal is to transport the grain, so they may hope to take the village's barges to send the grain down the river and then back up the river to their own tributary. But I can't imagine that the villagers would be that dumb – if you're sitting on a fortune in grain, the last thing you do when you see an army coming is to leave your barges in places to make your stuff easier to steal. Naturally, if you do see barges, sink them. Thus...'

Kip looked around. Everyone was giving him their total attention, not even trying to interject. Even Cruxer looked impressed. As Tisis had said, they were turning to him. He was becoming a leader in their eyes, if not his own. What did that say?

He went on. 'Thus, the Blood Robes either have their own wagons up here above the falls, or they have more barges even farther back. With the skimmers, the Mighty can get in place without being noticed.'

Conn Arthur said, 'Why are we looking at the same thing and I see a problem, but you don't? Like you said, their barges or wagons are up a completely different tributary above the falls. If we split our forces to attack in two places at once, how do we possibly coordinate an attack? We don't have any idea how many soldiers, drafters, and wights they might have. We could get massacred.'

'The tributaries end up pinching close at Deora Neamh. When the battle starts at the warehouse, we'll be able to hear the musket fire.'

'Over the noise of the waterfall?' Cruxer asked.

'Good thought,' Kip said.

'It's not that big,' someone who'd visited the town said. 'You'd hear a musket over it.' Others agreed.

'What if something goes wrong?' Conn Arthur asked.

'Oh, something will go wrong,' Kip said. 'Even if it doesn't, we use luxin flares to communicate.'

'That gives away our position if we use them,' Cruxer said. 'And if these, uh, Ghosts use them, the enemy will see that they're using flares and suspect a trap.'

'No. They won't see them at all, because we'll use super-violet flares,' Kip said. 'Conn Arthur, tell me you've got at least one superviolet drafter.'

'Three or four.'

Kip went on. 'And before you point out that this means we have to have two people watching the sky constantly in the superviolet spectrum, we specify times instead. We each get a sand clock or a water clock – whatever Ben-hadad can make – and we check the sky at set times. Even if this captain has superviolet drafters, they won't know to be looking at all or when to look if they do, so they'll miss whatever we signal. Remember, victory for us isn't wiping them out. It isn't even fighting them at all. It's stopping them from getting food. Saving the village, saving the grain, and killing lots of Blood Robes – all nice, but very much secondary. If we sink the barges or burn the wagons and scatter their horses and they still get the grain and decide to carry it back to the main army, we'll have plenty more chances to wipe them out in the forest.'

They all thought about it for a moment. It was the best Kip could do without scouts or any real idea of the enemy forces.

'Well, it sounds great,' Conn Arthur said. 'Of course, plans usually do.'

Chapter 28

'How did the High Luxiats take it?' Andross asked, pitching his voice low and quiet. Teia was walking beside Karris White as they crossed the delicate green bridge between Little Jasper and Big Jasper toward the execution platform, so she couldn't help but overhear.

'As well as we expected they would,' the White said.

'But they'll not rebel?' he insisted.

'We'll find out presently, won't we?' Karris said.

Teia was glad she'd already applied the dark eye caps. Karris was working with Andross Guile?

Of course she has to work with him, T. She's the White, and he's the promachos. But this sounded like more, like they were on the same side. Andross Guile was an open sewer. He was the human embodiment of evil. Teia didn't want Karris any closer to him than was absolutely necessary.

But the promachos was already taking his leave. 'I despise not knowing beforehand exactly how others are going to react.'

'And imagine,' Karris said drily, 'some of us always live that way.'

'The horror,' Andross said, but Teia thought he seemed secretly pleased that his daughter-in-law was making fun of him.

Ugh. Teia didn't like it when the old man acted human.

As the Blackguards emerged from the tunnel that was the Lily's Stem, Teia saw the crowd for the first time. The muffled roar of their murmuring washed over her as if she had suddenly slipped into a full bathtub of their speculation. Though she was second in the line of Blackguards, it felt as if every eye were upon her.

The entire Embassies District was packed from building to building with bodies. The large execution platform had been built against the wall, beneath the great mirrors that were known as Orholam's Glare. Nearest to the platform in the plaza were Chromeria officials, nobles, soldiers, Lightguards, and Blackguards, but as Teia mounted the steps, she saw an ocean of humanity.

Teia had thought that there would be a big crowd. She hadn't guessed the half of it. Nearly every man, woman, and child living on Big Jasper had turned out for this event. Slave, free, Parian, or Tyrean, it didn't matter. A bobbing mass of humanity filled the plaza and the great avenue and every street that converged here throughout the Embassies District. Balconies of mansions and embassies and roofs of shops were filled to bursting with onlookers.

Everyone wanted to see what would happen. Everyone wanted to hear what the Chromeria had to say. With the death of the old White, the ascension and near murder of the new White, the unveiling of the secret escape lines from the Chromeria, and the explosion of the cannon tower, it seemed the Big Jasper and Little Jasper Islanders' veil of safety had been torn away. Everyone had heard the reading of the lists of the dead. They'd heard about the battles. But all this, plus the arrest of traitors, here?

Suddenly the reality of war had come home.

The Chromeria hadn't played off the explosion of the cannon tower as a mistake. It hadn't lied, exactly. It had merely said, 'It wasn't an accident.' Everyone assumed that the Color Prince had attacked.

Believing themselves to have been attacked, the people wanted assurances. Many wanted blood. That the people to be executed today had nothing to do with the attack seemed not to matter. This was the people's chance to hear the new White and judge her, to be soothed or to be inflamed – or to be disheartened.

No wonder Karris was nervous.

The Blackguards spread out across the platform. Teia and Stump, being the shortest, would flank Karris so as not to make her appear smaller than necessary. The commander would stand among the Colors and High Luxiats behind Karris.

The crowd fell silent as Carver Black stepped forward to introduce Karris as the new White. Teia didn't pay attention; it was all titles and trivia. She was doing what she was here for: scanning the crowd for dangers, alternately in paryl and in the visible spectrum. She had already looked through the clothes of everyone on the platform. With paryl she could see through cloth but not skin, and the very bodies of the men and women already in place could conceal weapons.

It was a discomfiting thing, being able to see through people's clothes. Most people, she decided, looked better with their clothes on. She now knew things about the High Luxiats that probably no one else knew.

From the fresh cuts and welts on his back atop old scars, High Luxiat Amazzal obviously practiced self-flagellation. It was a practice frowned on, though not explicitly forbidden unless it impeded the penitent's performance of his or her duties. High Luxiat Mohana had the stretch marks of at least one pregnancy, which might or might not be scandalous. Certain orders of luxiats were allowed to marry, but generally not those who wished to progress high into the Magisterium. Perhaps Mohana had lost her child and joined the luxiats late? Or switched orders at some point?

Secrets, secrets everywhere, and Teia didn't want to know most of them, and couldn't use others that lay open to her eyes.

It seemed unfair. Godlike. How did she have this power? This power to see, and to kill? How did she have the right?

And a year ago, I was whining that my color was useless.

Suddenly everyone was bowing, and Teia flinched. She hadn't even noticed that Carver Black was finishing his introduction. Throughout the plaza, everyone bowed or curtsied as deeply as possible.

Standing in front of those tens of thousands, Karris waited until everyone had risen. Then waited some more. Then more, until it was painful. Had she frozen up? Did someone need to do something?

Just when Teia was sure one of the Colors was going to move to rescue her, Karris began speaking in a strong, clear voice that carried well. 'War is here. Would it were not so.

Too many of us have thought of this war as something far away. The proclamations have meant nothing to us, for our own people are near. Our loved ones have been safe. So we have turned deaf ears to the widows keening at the lists. We have turned hard hearts to the weeping mothers of boys and girls who will never come back. What is some distant war to us?

'But war is here. Would it were not so. You have noticed the shortages in the markets. How long has it been since you've had a Tyrean orange? But an orange is a luxury, surely we can let that go. Then, cotton is expensive, too, from the loss of Atash, is it not? And wool, as the Ilytian traders have reconsidered the journey. But so what? What is this war to us? Perhaps more patches on our clothes, and our children having to make do with tunics and dresses they've outgrown. Builders, have you not seen the price of lumber double? Why? Because our brothers in the Blood Forest have laid down their saws to pick up swords, or turned their axes from hewing wood to hacking wights. So what? What is this distant war to us? The rest of us will put off those repairs our homes need until next year. You builders will have to charge the rich double, and pray they will pay so you can feed your families. You shipowners and fishermen, you'll be paying double for wood for the repairs without which your ships will sink, so you'll have to charge double for your goods, for your fish. But what is this distant war to us? We will pay in coin, lest we have to pay in blood. For those with money, that sounds like an acceptable trade.

'But we'll notice that a certain kind of cargo comes to our island more frequently, not less. Slavers. Starving mothers will think, better my starving daughter live as a slave than die howling here. Better that I eat from the coin of her misery than die and leave all my children orphans to fend for themselves. Tell that mother she's paying in coin, and not in blood. But what is this distant war to us?'

She paused, head bowed. And no one said anything. It was not like any rallying speech Teia had ever heard.

Karris said, 'My friends, beloved under the light, war is here, and would it were not so, but we are not innocent in its genesis. After the False Prism's War, our sisters and brothers in Tyrea begged us for the eye of mercy, and we delivered only justice instead. We took the holy command to "Love mercy and do justice, and walk humbly before the Lord of Light," and we ignored the parts we didn't like. We took our own vengeance. When we take a command and obey only the parts that profit us, that's not obedience.

'We have thought that because Orholam has blessed us, that his love and blessings belong to us, regardless of what we do. We have treated our lord as a slave to our desires. Where is the walking humbly in that? We, your leaders, are guilty.'

There was some uneasy shifting among the Colors and the High Luxiats. Karris, newly risen to her exalted position, hadn't been among the 'we' she was so pointedly impugning now. They, on the other hand, all had been. And from the rapt attention on their faces, they didn't know what she was planning to say next, either.

Except for Andross Guile, who was a cipher, as always.

'Therefore,' Karris said, 'those of us here before you, the Colors and the High Luxiats, will be mourning and fasting for the next three days. I invite those of you who are able to do so to join us, to pray for us, and ask Orholam's blessing and wisdom in our endeavors. For though we have erred, there is yet work to be done. We may repent, but the consequences of our sin remain. Would it were not so, but war is here.

'We cannot fight and take it for granted that Orholam is on our side. We must fight to make sure that we are on Orholam's side. And that means cleaning our own house first.

'Don't misunderstand. There's no time to lose in proclaiming new festivals and holy days of repentance. If we hesitate, we shall lose all of Blood Forest and Ruthgar, too. As we cleanse ourselves, we shall also prepare our armies. Those who pray will pray, and those who fight will fight, but those who lead will do both.

'So let us turn to the work before us today. The first is a symptom of our emptiness. An emptiness that has reached even into the Magisterium itself. Where there is a vacuum of true worship, it will be filled by our own venality, our lusts, our cupidity, and our pride. It is a stain upon the Chromeria and the Magisterium itself.' She slowed down. 'It must be... purged. And one way or another, it will be *purged*.'

That word, used twice, used so deliberately, sent a shiver through the ranks of luxiats. When they were commissioned, the luxors always began their purges among the luxiats first. Any luxiat with heterodox beliefs or personal failings would have much to fear if the Office of Discipline was commissioned and empowered again.

'And indeed,' Karris said, 'to my great horror, our first guilty party today hails from the Magisterium itself.' The crowd booed and hissed, and Karris seemed taken aback for a moment. Teia felt the same. It wasn't easy to distinguish boos and hisses directed at you from those directed at your subject.

But then she forged ahead. 'Quentin Naheed distinguished himself early. Among the many brilliant scholars in the Chromeria, from his earliest days here, he stood out consistently as one of the brightest. Barely one year since taking his vows and donning the black robe, he is already acknowledged as an exemplary scholar, a gifted historian, hagiographer, and translator. His excellences are many, and his mind is peerless. However, Brother Quentin Naheed is also a murderer.'

She beckoned, and Quentin was brought forward by the tower soldiers. He had been stripped to his underclothes, and he resembled a small bird drenched and shaken from its time in a cat's mouth, feathers limp, dignity taken.

Teia's heart dropped. She realized too late that though she had sworn to meet Quentin's eyes, to be his strength, with her wearing the hard, angular, opaque eye caps, her gaze would be no comfort at all. And the glue holding the caps on didn't reattach well, so she couldn't take them off and put them back on.

But an oath is an oath. She tore them away.

One of the High Luxiats, Brother Tawleb, was shifting peevishly. He murmured something to High Luxiat Selene next to him, but she said nothing.

'Brother Quentin Naheed,' Karris said. 'Are you guilty of murder?'

'Yes, High Lady,' he said, wretched. 'Murder and attempted murder, and violating my oaths before the faith and Orholam himself in so doing.'

'Has this confession been compelled from you? Have you been beaten, or threats made against your family?'

'No,' he said, puzzled.

'Louder, please,' she said.

High Luxiat Tawleb shifted again, clearly agitated, but not wanting to cause a scene.

'No, I wasn't beaten. In fact, when the soldiers showed up, I was terrified, but I was also relieved.'

Karris turned to the crowd. 'In my time, I've hunted unrepentant wights and fought rebels. You hardly seem the normal criminal. Are you giving your confession in a bid for clemency?'

Again, the shock on Quentin's face couldn't have been feigned. 'Clemency? I shot a girl in the throat while I was trying to murder your stepson, High Lady. If I seem resolute in the face of my death, it's only so I don't weep and shame myself further.'

'High Lady,' High Luxiat Tawleb interjected, 'many pardons, please. But did we not agree that it's a terrible idea to let this traitor, this, this loathsome pagan heretic, spread his lies to the people here who might be vulnerable or misled? A platform is exactly what these traitors hope to get. Look, even now, this – this posturing, as if the man who shot a young girl so she could die on the street like a dog is somehow heroic. As if there were anything noble about him. Let us put an end to this.'

'I understand why you want him silenced,' Karris said, loudly.

He blanched, but shot back quickly, 'Yes, because he was once dear to me, and I'm furious that my own discipulus would turn out to be a traitor. It is a stain to my honor, and my judgment, and, yes, an embarrassment that—'

'No, Brother Tawleb,' Karris said. She shook her head sadly. But his words rode right over hers. '—that anyone so near to me should harbor such bile in his heart, and I not notice it. But if you're going to try to say that—'

'Enough!' She held up a hand, and he finally stopped.

What was happening? Teia looked at her commanders for a hint about what to do, but they simply seemed ready for anything. Watch Captain Blunt looked at her and threw his eyebrows up.

Oh shit. With paryl, despite the pain of widening her eyes so far in this bright noon light, Teia double-checked Tawleb for a weapon.

Oh *many* shits. She'd missed it earlier. He had a dagger, held tight under his armpit with cloth, so no straps had stood out to her. Why would a High Luxiat arm himself? Should she do something now? Do you tackle a High Luxiat for being armed? He'd made no move with it.

She made the hand sign for 'knife' and tapped her armpit. The watch captain and the commander and Stump caught it.

Teia missed some bit of Karris's saying this wasn't a court, but that the High Magisterium had met and discussed some kind of evidence. Karris produced some papers, asking Tawleb to explain them.

He stepped close to examine the papers. This would be the moment he would attack, if he was going to. Teia saw the commander tensing, about to give the order to take him down regardless rather than risk it, but then Karris gave a very subtle wave-off.

Of course she knew the Blackguard hand signs, and she'd caught them going around even as she spoke. She knew.

The commander gestured a stop.

'These are worthless!' High Luxiat Tawleb said, and Teia knew then that he wasn't going to attack. 'Forgeries. You're trying to become a tyrant, Karris *Guile*. You're putting the Spectrum above the Magisterium. You're a heretic, an apostate, a pagan whore.'

Gasps went though the crowd. Murmurs, a frisson of danger. *What did he say? Did he really just—*

Karris held her hand up as – of all people – Carver Black moved forward to strike High Luxiat Tawleb to silence him. She said, 'No, please, High Lord Black, I'll strike him myself if need be. And I will, if, on this day of truth, he tells one more lie—'

'A lie?! Which?! That you're a heretic or that you're a whore—'

Teia had seen Karris train. She had fought with her and against her. The speed with which Karris moved shouldn't have been surprising.

It was.

Despite her huge amazing dress, she kicked – *kicked* – Tawleb. Not in the knee, or the gut. She kicked this man who towered over her in the side of the head. He went down instantly, and by the time everyone's gaze had bounced from the blur that was Karris to the big man bouncing off the wood at her feet, Karris was composed again, standing calmly, straightening her dress, as if nothing had happened.

Balls! Guarding this woman is either going to be really, really easy, or really, really hard.

'Brother Tawleb,' Karris said, 'stand forth and accept Orholam's judgment. The High Magisterium has voted, and the Spectrum has adjudicated the penalty. You are guilty of treason. Your penalty is death.'

He stood, shakily, and Teia and the others were twice as alert now. But again Karris waved them off.

'If you repent, and tell us of others involved in this and any other murders, you may have a private execution by the method of your choice tomorrow. If not, the time is—'

He spat on her. Or tried.

Fast as a serpent strike, Karris blocked his spit with a gloved palm.

'I have no master! I did it for all of us! All of you! You ignoramuses! I did it to save you from the Guiles' tyranny and apostasy!' He turned to Quentin. 'You incompetent! You failed me! I was going to give you everything!'

Karris gave a signal that the Blackguard was on duty to defend her once more, and a bare moment later, Tawleb scrambled to draw his dagger. It was tucked too deep for him to draw it quickly enough, especially given that they knew it was there.

The others had him down practically before Teia moved. She'd been trying to enervate his joints with paryl as Murder Sharp had done so often to her, but she was too slow, and she ended up doing nothing – standing still while her brothers worked. Dammit!

They hauled him away and bound his hands and feet, and blindfolded him.

The great metal legs of a frame had been folded out of the wall itself. A great mirror as tall as a man, like those at the tops of the seven towers, dangled from chains between them, resting for the moment on the platform. But this mirror also had shackles, themselves mirrored, and a head brace.

Fighting weakly, High Luxiat Tawleb was dragged toward the mirror. His palms were pierced briefly with hellstone to make sure he hadn't packed any luxin – though the man wasn't a drafter, it was customary.

Teia had been briefed on what would happen, and what to do. And she still didn't want to think of it.

High Luxiats Selene and Amazzal went to Tawleb, who was held on his knees. Selene spoke quiet words, expelling him from the Magisterium and excommunicating him from the faith. She was followed by an equally sorrowful Amazzal, who offered to shrive him and hear his repentance, if he desired.

Tawleb spat at him.

The tower soldiers bound him to the mirror, his head held immobile, still blindfolded and gagged. Teia helped pull the chains to lift mirror and man into place.

'Orholam is merciful,' High Luxiat Selene announced to the crowd. 'And his justice tarries, but it will not be held back forever. May we all walk rightly, that we may stand before the Lord of Light unashamed and unafraid. Let us seek never to deserve the hard light of Orholam's glare.'

Across the surface of the oceanic crowd, lights winked like the sun on the waves of Sapphire Bay as everyone from the lowest slave cook to the High Luxiats drew forth mirrors. Hand mirrors, cosmetics mirrors, signal mirrors; from expensive glass mirrors with tin-mercury backings crusted with rubies down to pieces of polished copper or bronze. Some Atashian nobles who'd lost lands and children in the war had bought hundreds of mirrors to hand out to those who couldn't afford them: a voluntary war tax they paid to support the execution of traitors and heretics and murderers and spies.

Above and around the platform, mirrors unfolded like the petals of deadly flowers opening, answering the call of the sun above. In front of a number of the mirrors, white sheets unfurled, covering them, and in front of the condemned, a black sheet unrolled, blocking him from view.

Teia saw other Blackguards donning darkened spectacles. Things were going to get bright around here.

It wasn't only the noonday sun, or the light reflected from ten thousand mirrors. In moments, the mirrors of each of the thousand star towers around Big Jasper would be focused here. The great banks of mirrors atop each of the seven towers would likewise be uncovered.

The only small mercy here was Orholam's. It was a clear day. The noon sun blazed with white-hot fury. Tawleb would die far more quickly than on a cloudy day.

Not that burning to death was an option Teia would choose.

She turned, checking her area with paryl light one last time before she would have to narrow her eyes or be blinded. She caught sight of Quentin, still on his knees between tower guards.

He looked more terrified than she had ever seen anyone look in her life. It pierced her like a splinter in her soul.

Quentin had murdered one of the Blackguard's own, but Teia had nothing of vengeance in her now.

Sadah Superviolet had come forward, and she gave the final invocation: 'Orholam, you are not deceived. Darkness is no cover from your eyes. No stain is hidden from you. We follow your gaze, O Father of Lights. Let what has been hidden by man's darkness be revealed by your light. We, your people, cast our eyes and our light upon this stain.'

Above Sadah, Tawleb was shrouded from the audience and their pinpricks of light by the heavy black cloth. As she finished speaking, she produced her own mirror, and with one hand she turned it toward the man suspended in the air above her.

Everyone else did the same, turning their mirrors either directly toward the figure hidden behind black cloth or – if they didn't have a direct line of sight – toward one of the mirrors set up to collect their light.

Not everyone in the crowd had perfect aim, of course, so it was suddenly blindingly bright on the platform. But Teia saw Sadah Superviolet's other hand extend downward.

Not being a superviolet, Teia didn't know exactly how it worked, but there was a superviolet control node here that connected all the Thousand Stars and the Chromeria's tower mirrors.

Suddenly all the hundreds of huge, perfectly polished mirrors around the island and the Chromeria flared as one, shooting beams of light in every direction before swiveling into place with a sound like heaven's gates slamming shut. At the last moment, a blade sheared the blindfold over Tawleb's eyes, though the black drop cloth was left in place.

Teia had thought the light was blinding before. It had been a candle next to the sun.

When she was a child, her parents had once taken her to the Eshed Notzetz, the tallest waterfall in the Seven Satrapies. Standing on the execution platform so near the focal point of every mirror here was like standing beside a very cataract of light. She'd never heard of light having a sound, but the intensity of it seemed to make her heart stop, ears stop, skin register nothing.

A small whoosh as of something catching fire, and then a scream, and all Teia's senses came rushing back. It was unbearably hot, the instant sweat evaporating off her skin and leaving it hotter than before. Heat so hot she actually didn't want to tear off her blacks, because she thought her skin would melt in the onslaught.

There was nothing but heat and screaming, and the screaming was worse as Tawleb roasted to death.

Teia peeked through one scrunched eye and saw the man in outline against white, dancing like an egg on a hot buttered skillet, skin popping open, juices hissing across the mirror he was bound to, turning to steam.

And then it was done.

It couldn't have been ten seconds.

It had been the longest ten seconds of Teia's life.

Sadah Superviolet stopped first, the great mirrors swinging out and away, and the intensity of the light falling off dramatically. Then the people, squinting, dazzled, turned their own mirrors away.

Above them, chained to his mirror, Tawleb had been turned into a blackened husk, half the size he had been before, burnt nearly beyond recognition even as a man.

For one moment, there was total silence.

Then, then the people – Orholam forgive them – the people suddenly cheered. Teia would have thought their horror would be greater. Not standing in the light's path themselves, they would have been able to see the whole thing, if not hear it. They had watched a man cook in moments, skin splitting like that of a sausage accidentally dropped onto the coals.

And they cheered.

Karris White strode to the front of the stage. The new White held up her hands, quieting the crowd. The noon hour was slipping, and there was yet work to be done.

'Quentin Naheed,' Karris White called, 'stand forth and face Orholam's judgment.'

If she lived to be a hundred years old, Teia would never forget the nauseous terror in Quentin's eyes. He looked at her, and she did nothing.

Chapter 29

Kip had been a very young man once.

That young fool had died in the fires of his wife's wrath when he tried to deny her something. Specifically, he'd tried to forbid her from coming along to fight.

'You don't fight,' he'd said, quite sensibly, he thought.

'I don't want to fight.'

That flashbomb of scintillating non sequitur had left him momentarily dazed. She'd thrown her things aboard the skimmer, along with another woman Kip didn't recognize.

'But...we're going *in order* to fight. We are going *so that* we can fight. We're going with the sole intention of *fighting*. Ergo, if one doesn't want to fight, where we – the Mighty – are going, is not where *you*, who are not the Mighty, should go.'

That seemed to set a kettle of rage boiling. So he kept talking.

He'd been a young man.

'You see,' he said. 'If I were not going specifically to fight, I would probably choose someplace safer to be than, you know, the middle of a battle. And since your place—'

'My place? My place?!' And a more rapid boil than Kip had expected. Here he'd kept his eye on the pot the whole time and everything. 'First things first, Lord Guile! I am too a part of the Mighty. I'm one of you now, and don't you dare take that away from me.'

'The Mighty obey my orders. I'm their—'

'You do not give orders to your wife!'

'If they're in the Mighty I do!'

He knew he shouldn't have said that.

He'd said it. He'd been young.

Thing had gone downhill from there.

Tisis had come along. With a healer. As a noblewoman, Tisis had already had a basic education in battlefield medicine – or, as it was otherwise known, how to stop your child's bleeding if no slaves are around to help.

She'd agreed to stay with Evie Cairn, the healer.

Kip counted it a win.

He was no longer a young man.

The skimmer cut up the broad river in the moist evening air. As they'd slowly gained elevation over the past days, the jungles had yielded to evergreen forests.

'Kip, you know, I can learn,' she said.

'Learn to what?' he asked.

'To fight.'

'Of course you can. And we'll brush up on your shooting and some basic attacks with green. But you'll never be a match for any of these guys. Even if you could, we don't have ten years for you to train to get there. It doesn't make sense to even try—'

Ben-hadad cleared his throat and said under his breath, 'I think you're missing the point, brother.'

Kip charged ahead. Fucking fuck. This was so simple. It wasn't a matter of feelings. It was a matter of facts. 'Look! I've been training with the best for more than a year now. Every day we worked for hours to learn how to fight this way. Every day. We've been in numerous battles, and I'm still the weakest of us. I'm *still* a liability to the Mighty, Tisis, so—'

'That's really not correct,' Ferkudi said.

'Ferk,' Cruxer said. He was working one of the reeds.

'Sure, in a fistfight any of us could take him,' Ferkudi went on, 'but battle's not a fistfight. Breaker, you don't need to be modest. I don't think any of us would want to face you one-on-one on the field of battle.'

'Orholam's chapped nutsack, Ferkudi,' Big Leo said from the other reed. 'You're not wrong, but your timing is.'

'My timing is what?' Ferkudi asked.

'Wrong.'

'Oh, I thought you were leaving me hanging there, like, "You're not wrong, but your timing is..."'

'Ferk,' Cruxer said in a tone of command that was a twin of Commander Ironfist's.

'Ah. Right, sir.'

'You see?' Tisis said. 'I need to do my part.'

'I thought we'd already agreed what your part is!' Kip said, starting to get hot again.

Ben-hadad cleared his throat again, looking blithely at the sky and trees. 'Missing the point,' he whispered again.

'Fine!' Kip said, too loudly, turning to the young man. 'What's the point, Ben?'

Ben-hadad abandoned his quiet tone, matching Kip's frustration with his own. 'She wants your respect, dumbass. You treat her like dead weight and it robs her of purpose. I understand how she feels.'

He gestured to his knee. Ben-hadad did little stretches every day to reclaim what movement he could, but the kneecap had been shattered, and every move caused him terrible pain. He used one crutch most of the time, and two when he had to move at any decent speed. 'But hell, add the cripple and the neophyte together, and you might get one warrior between us.' Bitterness roiled beneath the surface of his words like cream first poured into kopi, awaiting a single slight stir to stain every part.

'We need two drafters on the reeds to keep the skimmer mobile if we have to retreat,' Cruxer interjected. 'It's a necessary function. Plus Ben-hadad's a helluva shot if it comes to it. Tisis, you stay with Ben.'

Tisis swallowed and nodded. 'Okay.'

'That's 'Yes, sir,'' Cruxer said, with a little smirk. 'You're one of the Mighty now.'

Tisis lit up. 'Yes, *sir*!' she said. 'And sorry for being a jackass, everyone.'

'Common malady 'round here,' Big Leo muttered.

Ferkudi stared over at him.

'Universal malady?' Big Leo asked.

'Huh?' Ferkudi asked. 'I was just – you've got a booger.'

Big Leo trailed off into cursing Ferkudi under his breath and trying to dig at his nostril discreetly while the others grinned.

'Universal,' Kip said. 'Definitely universal.' He turned to Cruxer with gratitude welling up in him. Sometimes you just needed a guy to step in and assert some authority. Cruxer was so good at that. Many in power liked to assert their dominance. Cruxer liked to let people figure things out for themselves, intervening only if there was a problem he could fix that they couldn't fix on their own. It was one of many traits that made him a good man to follow. 'Thank you...Commander Cruxer.'

'Commander?' Cruxer asked.

'If we're going to do this, let's do it right, right?' Kip asked.

Cruxer stood up straight, as if donning a new cloak and feeling the weight of it settle on his shoulder. 'Commander Cruxer,' he said. A big smile spread over his face.

'Commander Cruxer,' Winsen said, nodding to him, not even a hint of sarcasm in his tone.

'*Commander* Cruxer,' Big Leo said in his basso profundo as if announcing him in a stadium.

And on they went, each adding their own little twist.

'Commander Cruxer?' Ferkudi asked.

'Commander Cruxer,' Ben-hadad said.

Tisis fluttered her eyelashes and clasped her hands like a swooning girl. 'Oh, Commander Cruxer.'

He blushed and they laughed together.

Kip suddenly felt far, far away. After all they'd been through, and what he knew he was taking them into, it was a honeyed moment that they could be silly kids together. Like a spark flying upward, their youth was bright and fading fast.

'It's time,' Ben-hadad said, abruptly professional. He'd made water clocks for them, complaining about it. He'd not had time to make their globes the correct size to correspond to hours or minutes. Instead he'd merely made the two clocks exactly the same size, so although it took about seventy minutes for them to empty rather than an hour, they were still synchronized with each other, which was all that mattered.

Kip drew his superviolet spectacles from his hip case, absorbed light, and shot a flare into the sky. It had taken them a while to figure out how to keep the flare from disintegrating immediately, superviolet was so fragile.

There was no answering flare they could see, but in the river valley, with trees draped over every shore, they hadn't expected to.

'Quiet from this point on,' Cruxer ordered.

They went silent, leaving only the whupping noise and burble of the reeds as luxin pushed water and trapped air into the water behind the boat. Kip saw Ben-hadad looking annoyed at the noise – already designing a quieter propulsion unit for *Blue Falcon III*, no doubt.

A few minutes later, they pulled the skimmer into the lee of a downed tree that would conceal it while letting the reeds remain in the water. They loaded the muskets and checked their other weapons.

The Blood Foresters had shown them how to camouflage themselves for the woods, breaking up their silhouettes by binding twigs to their clothing, dulling the bright gleam of metal or luxin, and adding streaks to their black clothes so they looked like shadows dappled with sun rather than man-shaped darknesses.

Stealth was vital for the plan. If they were spotted before the attack at the warehouse pulled away the defenders, the whole ruse would be for naught. On the other hand, they still didn't even know if they were looking for barges or wagons or even both. They didn't know how many defenders there would be. They were going in blind.

The element of surprise is no advantage if you're surprised, too.

But the longer they took to attack, the more Ghosts were going to die below.

So, quietly, as they double- and triple-checked everything, Kip reviewed their rendezvous points if they got separated, the likely fallback areas if they had to retreat, and so forth. There were only the seven of them, and Kip wished again that he had Goss, Daelos, and Teia along.

Best not to think about any of them, though. Especially Teia.

Damn, but Teia's cloak would have made scouting easy.

Then they heard it, a single, distant musket shot.

'Could still be a hunter,' Cruxer said.

'Who hunts with a *musket*?' Winsen asked, as if every archer in the world could reliably down a stag at two hundred paces with a single arrow the way he could.

There was a rattle of another dozen shots.

'Aha,' Big Leo said, breaking into a huge grin for the first time in several weeks. 'That sounds like our song.'

They put on their spectacles and filled themselves with their colors, luxin curling like smoke under their skins.

Kip got ready to lead them out, only to see a reproachful look in Ferkudi's eyes. 'What?' he asked.

'You know, I'm not as smart as you, Breaker, but sometimes you're just plain dumb.'

'What?' he asked again.

'The hell is wrong with you?' Big Leo said. 'We're going into battle. Vastly outnumbered. May all die...and you're not gonna give your wife a kiss goodbye?'

'Oh!' Kip said. 'Oh.'

They bickered, but in an overarching sense, Kip and Tisis were actually becoming friends. And for all that they'd tried to consummate their marriage any number of frustrating times, they hadn't really...kissed much.

The Mighty think I'm being dumb because I'm leaving without patching up a fight, but I think I'm actually a lot dumber than that. He'd kissed her neck – she'd liked that a lot. He'd kissed her breasts – they'd both liked that a lot. But the last girl – the only girl – he'd kissed on the lips had been Teia.

Had he really never kissed Tisis on the lips?

It was as if without really realizing it he'd been holding on to that for Teia, holding back one intimacy because he'd given away so many others. To kiss Tisis – his wife, for Orholam's sake! – seemed to finally let the latch fall closed...

The woman's voice says, "You Guile men, so intelligent with your brains, and so cluelessly, hopelessly stupid with your hearts."

My cheek is stinging from Zee's slap. Give the woman this, even at fifty, she's got arms and shoulders to make many young warriors jealous. I'm just glad she hit me with an open hand.

She says, 'Our houses and our nations need heirs to knit together the Oakenshields and the Guiles, else this war will never die. We've talked this all through. We've agreed on this course. We had our chance, Darien, all those years ago, and we missed it through our own pride. It's a closed door. Don't make us both pathetic by banging on it. You've married my daughter to give us an heir. None of us liked that choice, but we all made it. Now you act like a spoiled child, not willing to pay the price of your choice, and making everyone else miserable with you. Darien, if you give my daughter a child but not your love, you're treating her like a whore, a broodmare, nothing more than a receptacle for your seed. She's my daughter, and I won't have you treat her like that. You *will* treat her like a lady, like your wife, like a woman making the best of a bad situation, like a woman offering you not just her body but also her heart. If you spurn that, you never deserved my love in the first place.'

'But I love *you* hopelessly, helplessly.'

'The seeds of love may sprout where they will, but we

choose whether to water them and give them light or to pluck them like weeds from the soil. We always have a choice.'

'This choice seems impossible.'

'Seems,' she says, her back straight and eyes pitiless.

And in the mirror of her eyes, I see how callow, how selfish, how self-absorbed I've been. This marriage puts me in the arms of a young woman, willing to give me children and love; it puts Selene with an older man who loves her not, and breaks her relationship with her mother at the same time; it puts Zee alone, with her daughter married to the man she herself loves. As a lover, how can she wish her daughter happiness with the man she herself once loved? As a mother, how can she not?

'Is he having one of his fits?' Ferkudi asked.

'No,' Kip said, coming back to the moment. 'Just feeling ashamed for my stupidity.' Darien Guile had been more than fifty years old, and he'd loved Zee Oakenshield for more than three decades. When they'd finally made peace, she'd been too old to give him an heir, and he had no sons. He'd had to marry her daughter Selene. *Darien* had had an excuse for being an idiot.

Kip had been in love with Teia for a few months. Before that, he'd been infatuated with Liv Danavis. Before that, it had been Isa. Always, he'd panted after the safely impossible.

He walked to Tisis and looked down into her questioning hazel eyes, her face more open than he deserved, more beautiful than he could imagine. 'Forgive me?' he said.

'Just this once,' she said, smiling.

He cupped her face in his hands and kissed her gently on the lips. She reacted like red luxin just waiting for a spark. Her body molded into his as if it had been made for it. Her lips were—

Big Leo cleared his throat noisily.

—her lips were, oh, Orholam, her lips were the best—

'Hey! Newlyweds!'

'You were the one who reminded him of impending death,' Winsen said.

' "Gather ye rosebuds while ye may," and all that,' Ferkudi said. 'I mean, we do need to let the trap develop a bit. Maybe they have time for a quick throw behind those bushes over—'

'Breaker,' Cruxer said.

' "Gather ye rosebuds," Ferkudi?' Ben-hadad said, incredulous. 'You read poetry?'

'I'm a gentle soul!' Ferkudi protested.

' "And lo! they saw that the ape could speak, and they were much amazed," ' Big Leo said under his breath.

' "And sore afraid!" ' Tisis said, finally pushing Kip back. It took him a moment to realize she was finishing the quote. He hadn't read either poem. Aside from Master Danavis's scrolls of military history and tactics and drafting – boy, did some things about the general seem obvious in retrospect – there had been few books or scrolls in Rekton, and fewer people willing to let a fat kid with pie-sticky fingers handle their treasures. His mother had kept books for years, despite her addiction. Finally, most of those had been sold to fund her haze smoking and self-loathing.

'You don't look like a man who's just been thoroughly kissed,' Tisis said.

'Mmm. Just putting on a good show for the boys,' he said.

'Come back,' she said. 'And I'll put on a good show just for you.'

'Oh my.'

There was something cosmically wrong with being horny when you left your wife to go to battle. There were traditions to follow, dammit: there was supposed to be a night of passion first, then the husband left deeply satisfied, carrying a nice memory of what awaited when he returned. It was a nice incentive to live.

Of course, unrelieved horniness with the promise of relief if he lived was a nice incentive, too.

Yes, sir! Thank you, sir! I would prefer the other incentive, sir!

Chapter 30

☞ *Stand straight and tall.*

Done and done.

☐ ~~*Maintain the dignity of the White.*~~

That was probably a lost cause, considering she'd just kicked a man in the head in front of tens of thousands of people.

☐ *Speak loudly and clearly. (Don't talk fast because you're nervous.*

Karris took a deep breath. Say this for executing a man: it does rather overshadow one's fear of public speaking.

She looked out over the many thousands of faces staring at her and the charred corpse of High Luxiat Tawleb and the huddled young luxiat Quentin at her feet. She had moved out from under the shadow of Tawleb's corpse. She had fought enough to know that even a roasted body can drip fluids. Not something she wanted to wear.

But coincidentally, her move had arrayed her so that she stood in the center as judge, and the dead man hung to her left, and now to her right huddled the repentant young luxiat Quentin. It wasn't an arrangement she had planned – Gavin certainly would have thought of it, standing here like the sign of the three, but then, he'd had a lot more practice with theatrics, and he was able to pull off symbolism effortlessly. Karris would simply have to muddle through, and accept luck when it came knocking.

'Luxiat Quentin Naheed,' she said loudly. 'You have earned expulsion from the Magisterium for the violation of your vows. You deserve to be stripped of your title.'

He said nothing. He was already on his knees, and he simply slumped forward. Silent.

'Quentin Naheed, you have earned being disowned by your family for the shame you have brought upon them. You deserve to be stripped of your name. Quentin, you have earned exile from your satrapy for dishonoring the gift of your education. You deserve to be stripped of a home. And most of all... convict, you have earned death for the murder of Lucia Agnelli. You deserve to be stripped of your life.'

Two Blackguards came forward and lifted Quentin to his feet. He wasn't weeping, nor did he have the ten-league stare of the doomed. He was staring toward Teia, who had pulled off her eye caps, and was meeting his eyes, with a resolute, calm strength Karris hadn't known the young woman had. Almost too quietly for Karris to hear, Quentin was repeatedly whispering a breath prayer: 'Orholam, give me strength for the path you've laid before me.'

They took his arms, and, as he stepped into place, offering no resistance, he stepped on the foot of one of the Blackguards. 'Pardon me, sir, I did not mean to do that,' he said.

'Hold,' Karris commanded. She turned her gaze to the crowd, that restive, hungry hound, eyeing her hands for its next treat. She glanced at Quentin, but his eyes were down. To the crowd, she announced, 'We are called to do justice, but to love mercy. How do we do those things on any day? How do we do those things in war? We have not Orholam's perfect sight. The traitor we spare today may return to the fight and kill our allies tomorrow. But...

'But even a traitor may repent truly. And today I have seen a vast gulf between the attitudes of these two men doomed to die. Thus, today I will extend the hardest mercy I know. Quentin, you will not die for your crimes.'

The young man stared at her as if she were speaking a foreign tongue.

'We are at war,' Karris said, 'and I will not cast aside a weapon that can be used. Quentin, your sin was pride, a pride carefully banked in hot coals under false humility. The body can die but once, pride can die every day. You, Quentin, shall live a slave. You shall be my slave until you learn what true humility is. I expect it may take all the years of your life.

'And why my slave? Because you are to be a lash for me. We are called to do justice and to love mercy – so I will extend the mercy of your life to you. But we are also called to walk humbly in the light. And this is the lesson that too many of us have forgotten. A lesson that the Chromeria has ignored. You, Quentin, will not be ignored. Despite what you deserve, you will *not* be expelled from the Magisterium. You shall be a luxiat still. You will be a badge of their shame, for failing Orholam, for allowing darkness to enter the temple of light. You will be dressed in gold, to remind them how easy it is to love gold and to be led astray by a love for earthly pleasures. You will be assigned to study beside and tutor luxiats, to turn your brilliant mind to helping them in their work, and to helping us win this war. You will be Orholam's justice to them, you shall be a lash against their pride, and the High Luxiats and I shall continue to talk about whether this is punishment enough to cleanse the stain they have allowed into the House of Light.'

Before Karris had climbed up onto the platform, Andross Guile had reminded her that this was no amphitheater. Whatever tricks they did to project her voice, those at the back wouldn't hear a word she said. Naturally, her words were being transcribed and would be published all around the Seven Satrapies, but what could be seen should be considered separately from what could be heard. If she wasn't careful, Karris would be seen doing nothing to a traitor. That would look like weakness. So Quentin's enslavement had to be seen.

So Karris now walked over to the seated High Luxiat Amazzal. She pulled out a large ceremonial dagger and handed it to him.

'If you'll do the honors of clipping his ear, High Luxiat?' she asked.

'I prefer we handle such discipline privately,' he said.

'Oh, I know what you prefer,' Karris said. 'Orea Pullawr trusted you to handle your own affairs faithfully, and you rewarded her trust by raising at least one traitor to the High Magisterium itself. You have loved the darkness of your privacy. Now we banish darkness from the House of Light.'

He held her eye, jaw clenching.

'Don't be a fool,' Andross said to High Luxiat Amazzal from his seat, pitching his voice low so no one beyond the platform would hear him. 'Every moment you hesitate you show the people that you are reluctant to give either justice or mercy or both. Accept the loss, or change the game and fight.'

High Luxiat Amazzal flushed, but he took the knife. He took the steps toward the kneeling Quentin, and held a hand up in the sign of the three, moving it through the four quadrants in the circle of blessing, but he wasn't praying. He said, 'You will pay for this.'

He wasn't speaking to Quentin.

'Happily,' Karris said. And she meant it. There was something refreshing about the kind of man who would tell you he was angry at you. Frontal attacks were so much easier to defend against.

But something changed in his posture, and Karris's old Blackguard senses began tingling.

'By the power vested in me as High Luxiat—' Amazzal declared to the crowd.

'One moment, High Luxiat,' a voice interjected. Andross Guile's. Faster than she would have expected he could move, Andross was already standing beside the furious old man. 'Let us show that we are united in this, the promachos together with the White and the luxiats against the pagans and traitors. I will hold the boy.'

Andross put his hands on Quentin's shoulders, but then whispered to Amazzal, 'You have to move faster than that if you wish to change the game. Too late now.'

Too late for what? For a moment, Karris didn't understand. Then she did. The old man had intended to say Quentin had gone too far. He'd intended to kill him, to assert Magisterial privilege over its own, despite whatever the White wanted.

He'd intended not to have the constant embarrassment of Karris's slave's being around, humiliating his luxiats.

And Andross Guile had figured it out before perhaps even the old man had. Certainly Karris would have been too late.

The vein in Amazzal's forehead throbbed. 'And if I—'

'I swear to God I'll put you up on the Glare next,' Andross said.

Amazzal looked like a bully punched between the eyes, disbelieving. But then he saw the look in Andross's eyes – and believed.

The rage went out of the old High Luxiat in a whoosh. He spoke loudly again. 'By the power vest— vested in me...By the power vested in me, here is the Chromeria's justice and mercy, Luxiat Quentin Naheed. You are hereby enslaved.'

He sliced Quentin's ear, blood spitting out onto the High Luxiat's hands and his lambent white robes.

Amazzal was not a bad man, nor a bad luxiat. But he was a bad leader, and that made him a bad High Luxiat. He looked perfectly the part with flowing white beard, dignified disposition, speaker's voice, and gracious manners. He cared for others deeply, and offered mercy wherever he went.

But mercy ceases to be a virtue when it enables further injustice.

The tower guards dragged Quentin away, and Karris ghosted through the next speech, barely aware, condemning the traitor prophet to death on the Glare for fomenting rebellion, placing spies, and blasphemy.

Pheronike was the man who'd been confirmed to be a spy handler by the Mighty in one of their training missions. Karris had gotten a spy close to him through that operation, and just before she passed away, Orea Pullawr had had her people scoop up the lot of them. Of them, only this man was a drafter. He was a sub-red, but he'd not been Chromeria-educated, so he was probably little danger, but despite that, he was kept in the special garb for condemned drafters, which was woven with hellstones to disrupt any luxin he tried to gather; he was also blindfolded to forbid him light, and subjected to a litany's worth of other traditions that Karris didn't even know about, much less comprehend the reasons for.

But despite the strangeness of the black garb and blindfold, it was only as they lifted Pheronike onto the mirror that Karris snapped back into focus on the moment. She'd never seen a drafter executed on the Glare.

It was supposed to be the worst way for a drafter to die. Or the two worst ways, really, depending on whether you decided to draft or not. She'd heard it described as choosing whether to die of constipation or diarrhea.

On the other hand, how could it be worse than burning to death?

They moved into place, and Karris donned dark spectacles as he was lifted high. Again the people's mirrors came out, and Sadah Superviolet came forward. Again, it was only as Sadah swung the mirrors into focus that a blade sliced the blindfold from the condemned's face.

Though Karris was prepared for it this time, it was still like standing in a thunderstorm of light. It was like going from the snowy slopes of Atan's Teeth to the hottest desert of the Cracked Lands in an instant. The heat alone was a hammer. The light itself had a physical presence – a thickness, a reality so heavy that it made all the material universe seem like a ghostly realm in comparison. A concussive force pressed out Karris's breath. She wanted to drop to her knees. She wanted to hide.

In that moment, Karris believed those who swore that Orholam himself was within that beam of light, and she prayed only that he turn not his eye upon her.

The black drop cloth hiding the accused had already caught fire. The cloth was both symbolic and practical: intended to represent sin and attempting to hide from Orholam's eye, and intended as a mercy, to keep the people's mirrors from burning the condemned and torturing him before all the mirrors could come into place.

Orholam's Glare was excruciating, but it was brief.

All the light in the world illumined the traitor, and he screamed. He soul-screamed a name.

But it was impossible to catch the disembodied syllables over the flame and the pain.

The air above Pheronike undulated as he let out a huge

wave of sub-red – a beam into the sky. Unable to form luxin anywhere else because of the hellstone clothing pressing in on his skin, he tried to shed the excess heat from his face.

It was too much to handle, too much to draft artfully; it was a gush. It was also why the condemned's face on Orholam's Glare was angled skyward, so he couldn't attack the crowd around him.

The geyser of heat crackled and cracked like a flag in the wind, even flickering into flames. And it kept going.

As did Pheronike's howl, a lone, long ululation of agony as skin burnt and cartilage burnt and bone burst forth, blackening.

Then they stopped altogether, drafting and screaming both, cut off with a name: 'Nabiros,' the prophet said, a soft life-sloughing sigh. A summons.

For one heartbeat, nothing happened. It was long enough that Karris realized Pheronike's body wasn't burning.

Then his skin burst apart in a spray of gore, his head tearing apart as his neck vomited out three dogs' heads, black and red, growling and snapping. His shoulders bulged, and muscles knotted in his skinny legs, splitting the skin like a bursting boil. But his limbs stayed bound, and in the next heartbeat, he sagged, deflated, defeated, and died.

The dog's heads sizzled in Orholam's obliterating light, and his whole body burnt like any man's – at least that of any man with three blackened dogs' skulls attached to three necks.

For Karris, the moment stretched like a raindrop about to fall off a leaf, bulging, heavy with intent.

No one even breathed. The civilians had ducked back, cowering, and for this precious instant they still disbelieved. The Blackguards had weapons drawn – as did Karris herself, all unknowing, her other hand out to them, signaling no.

A collective gasp passed over the crowd in the next moment. It was disbelief. Literal incredulity: *Did I actually see that? Did* you *see that?*

But it was undeniable. The skeletal remains had three heads.

And then the collective question: What the hell was that? What the hell *is* that?

Karris gave a signal, and finally the mirrors turned away.

When the light faded, there reigned a baffled quiet. The audience held mirrors in nerveless fingers, forgetting to turn them away. Still no one spoke.

And then children started weeping – and not only children, but men and women, too.

Karris had always been fast. Not being big or strong, she'd taken to heart early the lesson her trainer had given: it's often not who hits hardest who wins, but who hits first. So she ignored the terror raging in her own stomach, the knee-weakening, bile-churning confusion.

'Orholam be praised!' she shouted, throwing her hands over her head. Don't look shaken, look triumphant.

'*Orholam invictus,*' Andross Guile said quietly behind her. Of course he was the next fastest to move. Even he hadn't expected *this*.

'*Orholam invictus!*' Karris shouted. Orholam the invincible, the unconquered.

'Orholam invictus!' the crowd roared.

What they'd seen wasn't a monster, Karris proclaimed.

What they'd seen was a monster vanquished by Orholam's light.

The crowd roared as Karris had never heard before, and the crisis was averted.

And though nothing she had done had been intended to aggrandize herself, she saw the truth of what Orea Pullawr had once told her: a small woman standing next to a great light casts a long shadow.

From that day forth, the people no longer referred to Karris as Karris White Oak or Karris Guile, and only rarely as Karris White. She wasn't the new White, or the Blackguard's White, or Gavin Guile's widow, or the girl who had caused the False Prism's War.

The people loved her.

They called her the Iron White.

Chapter 31

On the sixth day, at the fourth hour after dawn, exactly 558,032 seconds since she had first touched the superviolet seed crystal, Liv rose from the stones of the great promontory overlooking the Everdark Gates. She had once been Aliviana Danavis, daughter of General Corvan Danavis, child of Rekton in Tyrea, discipula of the Chromeria, later rebel and Blood Robe – naïf entangled in the schemes of powerful men. Who she was now, she wasn't sure.

But she'd decided she was about to become something different. Something other.

Phyros lay dead and rotting still where she'd killed him. He'd given her the option of slavery or death. Do what I want or I'll make you regret it, he'd said, as had so many men in her life.

She'd been attracted to him, before he'd betrayed her. Now she felt nothing. The insistent wind here on the mountain blew away all his stench, and she had neither time nor strength to bury him or even drag him away. Not while she had to think.

The superviolet that people thought so cold and brutally rational was to her a warm blanket. Not least literally. She was here to think and not to move until she decided which way of moving would be most efficient and which objectives would in turn attain at least a plurality of her desires, but she was still embodied. A woman could freeze to death up here in the cold wind, even on a summer night. A series of overlapping thin shells to trap a layer of air warmed by her own heat was enough for that.

Irritatingly, the body had other demands, and amid her deeper concerns, she kept forgetting about eating. She'd lost a fair amount of weight, and she'd now reached the end of the provisions she and Phyros had brought.

But she hadn't been wasting her time. The Color Prince had

wanted her to be a god *and* his slave. The slave part was simple to figure out.

The necklace Phyros had tried to force her to wear was a fragment of living black luxin, somehow controllable at a distance or imbued with will. At his command or at her removal of the necklace, the stone would cut through her neck. Presumably it would also work on gods – unless it was a very, very reckless bluff. She'd used a stick to put it in a bag, as if it were a serpent. She didn't want it anywhere close to her until she understood it.

The god portion was harder to comprehend. She was, quite clearly, no god.

Holding the seed crystal helped her think more clearly, to notice when she was going in circles mentally, and it let her see the superviolet light around her at all times without having to constrict her eyes. But that was all.

That wasn't enough.

Finally, she'd come to understand that the god portion was impossible for her to comprehend in her present state. The seed crystal was incarnitive; to harness its full powers, she needed to integrate it with her body.

To do that, she had to break the halo.

Her gut twisted again at the very thought. Growing up, she'd always thought breaking the halo was pretty much the same as dying. The two were always inextricable. Breaking the halo on purpose was tantamount to suicide.

Despite all she'd learned of the Chromeria's lies, those were still her foundational truths, ruts in the streets of her mind. To be fair, even in the Color Prince's camp, it was known to be very, very dangerous. Even the Color Prince had had to put down some drafters who attempted too much too soon.

Not that she herself was so far from breaking the halo anyway. A few more battles, or a couple of years without them. She'd used superviolet wantonly in her time with Zymun. It had stilled her terror, given her poise, and she had relied on it utterly.

Had relied on it from her own weakness, truth be told.

Her own weakness was the enemy now, and the only way to overcome that was to become a goddess.

The Danavis motto was Fealty to One. Her father had lived by that, at least for a while, and it had done him no good. Her uncles and grandparents before him had served some fool lord and lost everything. Fealty to One? More like Fealty to None. There is only one to whom I will have fealty: myself.

So she would become a goddess – for herself, not for them. The Chromeria said that the sin associated with superviolet was pride. This wasn't pride. This was power, and Liv chose power now with all her heart, mind, soul, and strength.

With the superviolet seed crystal in one hand, she streamed great gulps of alien, logical light and let it suffuse her body. She became a waterfall, a cataract of the invisible and barely visible purplish light.

She felt her body reach its boundary. No one had talked to her about this. Wasn't that strange? When the price for stepping too far was death, that no one in the Chromeria explained exactly how you could tell when you'd reached the edge of the precipice?

No, those fearmongers were ignorant. More worried about paying homage to their sky puppeteer than about paltry matters of life and death for hundreds of drafters every year.

To hell with them.

She would have said it was like giving birth – reaching a crisis and then pushing through – except she had never given birth and never would. There was a sense of building energy, building resistance, of moving with agonizing slowness suddenly, like what athletes called hitting the wall—

And then.

Parts of her mind seemed to blow apart. She felt or heard something in her, and it felt as if her eyes were bleeding.

It was like when she'd first tried ratweed and smoked far, far too much to impress some so-called friends. First was the sense of having done something really, truly wrong to her body. Then came a rush of euphoria so strong it threatened to carry her away. This felt like the way a deep draft of brandy on an empty stomach set fire to your body, except this started from her head and rushed through her limbs, her eyes hot and cold, the drafting scars on her hands freezing, every pathway through her blood alive and tingling like a first kiss.

She gulped deep breaths and tamped the corners of her hot eyes.

For a long time, she didn't dare move. Didn't dare look to see if her hands had come away from her eyes bloodied or worse. She knew that when she started, everything would be different.

Non serviam, she thought. I shall not serve.

Nor would she have to. She felt connected now, not a part of a greater whole, but the mistress of it. A spider feeling vibrations in her web. And one such vibration was before her. A magical creature of some sort? Bound to her?

She couldn't yet decipher all that her new feelings were telling her. It was like stretching a new pair of arms, opening a new pair of eyes, suddenly standing three times as tall and having to learn to run again. She opened her eyes slowly, feeling the qualities of the light streaming over her.

She looked first at her hand. It was unbloodied. Whatever had changed her hadn't injured her. Then she saw him.

Hands clasped behind his back, a tiny man who came no higher than her chin stood before her. He had golden-etched skin that sparkled in the cold sun.

'Who are you?' she asked.

'Your humble slave, Mistress. How do you wish me to address you in your magnificence?'

But she ignored the question. 'I have duties for you,' Liv said.

'Of course, Mistress.'

Chapter 32

Not many archers were brazen enough to try a head shot on a sentry. Too many bones, too many angles that could deflect even a perfectly aimed arrow. A man could turn his head fractionally even in the time it took an arrow to fly. Most archers thought such a shot was foolish. Especially on a sentry wearing a helmet. Especially in the gathering dark of an evening.

But Winsen was different. Danger was an abstraction too alien for him to grasp. Sometimes it seemed he couldn't even conceive of the possibility of his failing, much less the consequences of such a failure.

He had disappeared into the brush minutes ago, saying he'd take care of the sentry. Kip could see where Winsen had to be, but with their camouflage in the dim woods, he couldn't make him out at all.

The sentry was walking the deck of a light-hulled scout boat, which had been drawn up on the bank about fifty paces downstream from where two huge barges floated in the river, tied to the bank with many ropes, with ingenious walkways spiderwebbed out to them for loading grain.

Given how low the barges were sitting in the water, this was not the foraging party's first stop; they were laden with some cargo already. If they were sunk, it would be a more significant blow against the Color Prince than Kip had originally thought.

Kip was hiding behind a mossy stone with Big Leo and Ferkudi. The air felt humid and full. Cruxer had left to climb the ridge that separated this fork of the river from the waterfall and the village of Deora Neamh.

Cruxer crept back now, putting his back to the broad trunk of a pine tree.

'Things aren't quite going according to plan,' Cruxer told Kip. 'Conn Arthur seized the warehouse rather than attacking and falling back. Must have been a weaker defense there than we expected. He set fire to two barges identical to these at their docks. Saw three other barges burnt out, different design, though, so the town already had burnt their own. White King's people brought barges with them.'

Worse luck for them, now that the Conn Arthur had burnt them, but it also meant this foraging party was larger than Kip had hoped. 'Reinforcements?' Kip asked.

'I saw maybe two hundred soldiers from up here headed down the trail. They should be close enough to the waterfall by now that it will mask whatever noise we make. But if they look back, they'll be able to see any smoke until they get to the base of the falls. Their main camp is farther down in the valley, not up here. They have probably another two hundred soldiers and only Orholam knows how many wights and drafters down there. I don't know if Conn Arthur has any idea how many people he'll soon be facing.'

'He's got his orders. We have to trust him to figure it out.' Besides, Kip was the only superviolet drafter they had up here, and there was no time for him to climb the ridge and signal.

Cruxer made the sign of the seven and muttered a quick prayer. Kip mimicked him. They'd need all the help they could get.

Then Kip turned and peeked over the rock just in time to see a sentry's helmet fly into the air – off the head of a sentry Kip hadn't even seen. Before that helmet even landed, the other sentry dropped instantly, an arrow angled through the back of his neck up through his forehead.

Winsen popped up from the ground – he'd been lying on his back to get the right angle for the two shots, and he'd crawled into the very shadow of the scout boat to do it.

Kip and the Mighty leapt over their mossy boulder and bolted toward the boats. Before they even reached the scout boat, Winsen had scrambled aboard with the dexterity of an acrobat. A third sentry, who had been seated below, rose to see why his comrades had disappeared, only to find Winsen's knife rammed into his kidney and a hand over his mouth.

Letting go of his knife for one moment while he still held the dying man tight against himself with his left hand, Winsen waved them on – no other opposition here – so they ran directly to where the barges were moored.

A campfire was being lit not far from the planks leading to the barge, and half a dozen men were standing around or helping clean up camp, or cleaning muskets or repairing armor or preparing food.

They didn't see the Mighty zigzagging toward them, breaking the sight line with what trees they could, but mostly closing the distance as quickly as possible. Cruxer easily outpaced the rest of them until he stopped suddenly, tossing a small ball the size of his fist in a high arc. It landed just beyond the fire with a sound like shattering glass as the blue luxin Kip had drafted broke open. The men at the fire turned instinctively to see what it was – and the flashbomb's yellow luxin exploded into brilliant, blinding light.

Kip was looking at the Mighty when the flashbomb geysered its light, and the light etched every one of them in his memory. Long-legged, supple Cruxer was hurdling a fallen tree with the grace and ease of a stag while carrying a long slender spear. Big Leo ran with all the stealth of an avalanche, and just as much frightening speed. The man managed to sprint while carrying a tower shield, and his short black beard was split by his ferocious, eager smile. Big, dopey Ferkudi sprinted with each hand streaming luxin like smoke, green in his left, blue in his right. It was usually a sign of poor drafting – all that luxin lost – but it was scary as hell. Ferkudi's face showed an expression closest to regret. Ferk wasn't a born killer.

Or maybe it just pained him to be thinking so hard.

At twenty paces out, Kip threw his hands forward and hurled all his weight into shooting two brightwater missiles. He'd taken what he could draft competently and brought it together. Namely, he could now make solid yellow into unbreakable blades, and he could shoot the Great Big Green Bouncy Balls of Doom, which were good for knocking people over, but not much else. On the other hand, throwing an orb of yellow blades or a ball of yellow spikes was pretty much impossible without cutting yourself to pieces. So he encased yellow blades in a green ball and shot that from his right hand, and yellow spikes inside a green ball and shot that from his left.

They worked differently. The orb of spikes caught a man in the armpit as he staggered, covering his blinded eyes. The green luxin bent and then broke apart, and the spikes stuck into him, caving in his ribs and sticking. The orb of blades hit another man in the face, the green luxin flexing in, a blade slashing a cheek, and then it bounced off him, caroming into the neck of another man, and then off into the woods.

The transference of momentum had brought Kip to a halt, so as he prepared his next attack, the Mighty thundered past him.

Cruxer went for two men on the periphery who hadn't been

blinded. One was a blue wight, just beginning his transformation, who still had the face of a man but wore no tunic, his chest a rippling crystalline wonder better than skin, impervious to the elements.

But not impervious to steel.

Cruxer buried the spear through the wight's chest and spun, instantly, snapping off his dual-bladed spear at its blue luxin haft on purpose, like a bee leaving its stinger in its victim. The other leaf-blade of Cruxer's spear slashed through a green wight's arm and into his chest and out again, so light and thin and fast it barely slowed. The spear spun up into a javeliner's hold, flinging blood in a circle, and then Cruxer hurled it into the back of a man rushing for the camp's cone-stack of muskets.

An arrow pierced the same man before he even hit the ground, and Kip saw that Winsen had taken up an overwatch position behind them with his bow. Fifty or sixty paces was an easy shot for the little archer, and he was picking off anyone who seemed like they might be getting away or about to raise an alarm.

Before Kip, newly rearmed, could make it to the campfire to join Ferkudi and Big Leo, the battle here was suddenly over. There was a splash from one of the barges and a yelp from the other.

A man had fallen into the water at the nearest barge, and on the other, a soldier was staring at Winsen's arrow buried in his thigh. Another arrow streaked through the air above him as he stooped to look at the curious marvel. But Winsen's next arrow dove through his stomach.

Bless Winsen, his distance had helped him not get the tunnel vision Kip had.

But Ferkudi had never paused. Running across the web of planking and lines, Ferkudi got to the arrow-pierced man just after he fell out of sight behind a low gunwale.

A splash of blood answered Ferkudi's descending mace.

Then he turned and looked back at them, unseeing for a moment.

Ferkudi must have been gritting his teeth when he brained the soldier, because blood had shot across his face, and across his white teeth. There was nothing young or dopey in Ferkudi's expression now. Two images were superimposed on his face. In rapid succession, it flickered between a scary, blooded warrior, the veteran he would be; and a big child, covered in wet mortality and scared of what he had done. That young Ferkudi looked like a child caught stealing candy, his face saying this is wrong, and I've done it, and I've been caught doing it, and nothing can fix this.

But it wasn't filched candy, it was the crushed skull of a man, and being caught red-handed here was literal. Ferkudi closed his mouth as he looked at them, and his pink tongue darted out to clear his mouth, and then he blanched as he realized he was clearing his mouth of another man's blood.

'*Tsst!*' Kip hissed, waving.

It saved Ferkudi. He shook himself and got control. He looked around, signaled – no one else was standing on the decks of either barge.

'Perimeter,' Kip told Winsen, as all of them refilled themselves with luxins. 'But finish any wounded first. I can't believe we got this lucky. There may be more.' He nodded to Big Leo, who was the other sub-red/red drafter. 'You take the far barge with Ferk. I'll get the near one.' To Cruxer, he said, 'You collect Winsen's arrows and our weapons as well as you can, I want this to be a clean raid, no hints. As soon as the White King knows who he's fighting, we lose an advantage. Then you come help me.'

'That puts you alone on that barge,' Cruxer said. He had already collected the point that had snapped off his spear. Drafting blue luxin even as he spoke, he locked it back into place with a twist. 'We agreed that you would have an—'

'Then collect our weapons quick,' Kip said. 'No time.'

Kip ran out down the walkways. He heard the distant rattle of muskets as another engagement started down in the valley. Good. He made it to the barge with no trouble. Everything seemed to be going perfectly. Maybe they had plenty of time. Maybe he should wait for Cruxer.

The Mighty was too small. They simply didn't have enough bodies to do a raid like this. They were getting lucky here. More people meant more noise, more trouble with communication, more problems, but it also meant someone to watch your back.

Hell with it. You worked with what you had. Kip threw open the door to head below. A muffled explosion from the other barge was the only warning he had that the ships were defended.

He threw himself to the side as a scared young woman in front of him fumbled a linstock and fired a small cannon toward the door Kip had just opened.

Kip was deafened and saw black spots swimming in front of his eyes. The door was shredded, but somehow he rolled to his feet.

In a bit of idiosyncratic military doctrine, the Blackguards were taught to attack an ambush. They were taught that the only way to regain initiative, having lost it to the enemy, was to attack. Immediately. Ferociously. This meant you didn't give yourself time to regroup or time to think—but you didn't give it to the enemy, either. They didn't get a chance to enact phase two of their plan, because they were suddenly busy getting killed.

And Kip's training took. He charged the young woman just as she had turned her back and was trying to light another fuse. He chopped across her arms as she reached out, but given his dazed state, cut deeply across only one forearm.

It was enough to make her drop the linstock. She turned, baffled that he was still alive, bleeding, and tried to draw the pistol tucked into her sash. He rammed his yellow luxin sword through her belly, but immediately dropped it to grab her pistol as it cleared her sash.

He trapped it in his left hand and wrenched it aside. She wasn't strong enough to stop him. And with her left arm wounded, she didn't have a chance to stop his right uppercut to her jaw.

She fell to the ground, insensate, doing little more than groaning as she fell on the hilt of Kip's yellow luxin sword, driving it deeper into her gut.

Kip rolled her over and pulled his sword free. No small amount of blood followed it. The woman couldn't have been more than twenty years old, if that. Atashian dark hair and eyes, poor clothes. Just a girl taking orders.

He should have felt something. She was unconscious, bleeding, certain to die slowly if not quickly. But he only heard Trainer Fisk's voice: 'Never trust the dead. Men will faint from fear at the first charge and lie at your feet, but find their courage again when you show them your back. The mortally wounded will rise to play hero one last time. You can't always pause to make sure a dying man's incapacitated, but when you can, you damn well better!'

After Kip's sword came free of her body, he slapped it back into the side of her neck with all the emotion he'd summon to sink a hatchet into a stump after he was finished cutting firewood.

Satisfied from the sword's recoil in his hand that he had cut deep enough, he didn't even look down; he was already peering deeper into the gloom of the barge's hold.

He followed the fuse the young soldier had been trying to light. It went to a charge against the hull, and then another, and another.

What the—?

A boom shook the ship. Not an explosion here, but on the other barge. Dammit! It must have been rigged identically to this one.

But it wasn't a trap. If it had been, there would have been more than one guard.

Kip moved farther into the hold. There was nothing here except all the slaves at their oars on overcrowded benches and plenty of slaves in reserve.

Slaves, while the White King railed against the Chromeria for practicing slavery. Asshole.

There was no grain.

But if there was nothing here, why set charges so you could scuttle the boat?

For that matter, why were these barges up here at all? Kip had barely noticed in Cruxer's report, but this foraging party had already sent two barges directly to Deora Neamh...but had left these here.

Charges and separation had to mean a cargo. But what cargo?

Kip had been flickering his vision between sub-red and normal vision to pierce the darkness for any violent moves toward him, but now he held up a green orb, drafted to shimmer back to light.

Despite the darkness, all the slaves wore blindfolds.

Kip ran back to the dead girl in her spreading pool of blood, and found a key around her neck. He ran to a tall man on the first bench, his pale Blood Forester arms permanently stained blue and green and yellow with luxin. Kip pulled off his blindfold.

'Who are you?' Kip demanded. He pointedly *didn't* unlock the man's manacles.

'I'm Derwyn. I'm Aleph of the Cwn y Wawr,' the man said quietly. 'Repaid for our faithlessness here.'

'What faithlessness? Quick!' The Cwn y Wawr, the Dogs of Dawn, were Blood Forest's hidden society of warrior-drafters.

The man's stony sorrow said that he knew he was speaking his own death and he didn't care. 'We saw no path to victory, so to save our villages and families we tried to make a separate peace with the White King. He ambushed us instead. Captured us. We're being taken to him. We either give him our fealty or he takes our eyes.'

'Same on the next barge?' Kip asked.

'Yes. There's – there *were* two hundred and thirty of us.'

'You fucking traitors!' Kip exclaimed. He paused for only one moment more. He couldn't tarry here; his friends might be dying outside at the other barge even now. He said, 'Meet me at Fechín Island if you want to find your honor again. Otherwise, fuck off and at least don't fight for him.' He slammed the key against the man's chest. 'Scuttle the barge when you leave.'

No wonder the Blood Robes had set charges. A resource like two hundred and thirty neutral warrior-drafters wasn't to be scoffed at – and it certainly wasn't something you wanted to fall into the hands of your enemies.

Kip ran onto the deck in time to see the other barge list to one side, great gaping holes in the hull from the charges. Ferkudi and Big Leo were on the shore, bloodied. Kip couldn't tell how badly they were injured. But there were no slaves with them. That barge was going down with more than a hundred semi-innocent men chained belowdecks.

Cruxer was shouting at Kip, telling him that the bridges connecting shore and ship were about to collapse – that it was too dangerous, too late. He was right. Those men were going to die because of their own choices. Their own cowardice had led them to their chains. It made no sense for Kip to risk himself and everything he could accomplish to try a hopeless rescue. A man who can't swim shouldn't attempt to save the drowning.

But Kip surged forward anyway and ran for the widening gap between the sinking barge and the sloping planks.

Ah fuck me, he thought as the gap yawned wide. Why do I have to be so dumb?

And then he leapt.

Chapter 33

The seal sat in his reflection at the height of his forehead. Before he got too exhausted to be amused, it amused him to be scratching out the dead man's third eye, or his own.

It took two sweaty desperate days of cramping hands and blood to hit the seal.

He barely felt the nub when he finally reached it; his dogtooth skipped across the uneven knot of luxin like a stone across water for only a few strokes, and before he could stop, the seal broke suddenly.

A section of the prison wall as wide as his own spread arms simply disintegrated into chalky blue dust.

Freedom whispered then, but she said, 'I'm too far away. You'll never see me.'

'It's impossible,' the dead man said. 'You built these prisons too well. You'll never get out.'

The sand was draining through the glass now that Gavin had broken the cell. If he'd been more aware of the seal, he would have slept, waited, gathered his strength before he broke through. As it was, there was no time. A small alarum was rigged to ring in the chambers above if the cell's seal broke.

Gavin hadn't remade the alarum for this cell since his brother escaped, but he couldn't be sure that Andross hadn't found it, hadn't repaired it, hadn't heard it. There was no way to tell what time of day it was, so there was no way to guess when he could trigger the alarm without Andross's being in his room to hear it. If a slave heard it while Andross was out, she likely wouldn't know what it was. Gavin couldn't imagine his father's trusting anyone as much as he had trusted Marissia. Maybe his father trusted Grinwoody that much.

No. Not even him.

But it didn't matter. Gavin was committed.

The cell filled the entire space Gavin had carved out of the Chromeria's rocky heart here. He had burnt through lux torch after lux torch for the light necessary. Here there was only a small area to stand in, and then a single tunnel so low it was necessary to crawl through. A fortune's worth of hellstone was mortared into the floor and the walls.

His father, of course, had simply been able to take the vertical shaft down to the blue cell. Unfortunately, the cell itself lifted into a new place, and the only way to trigger the controls to lift it was from above. There was no way for Gavin to reach the ceiling of his blue cell – much less break through it – to try to escape that way.

He had to go through his own tunnels and cells.

It seemed Andross hadn't altered the tunnel from Gavin's original design. It curved one way into darkness, and then would swoop back so that no blue light could leak through. If Gavin could still draft, the hellstone would have been a huge problem: it would drain any blue luxin from him before he got to the next cell.

A moot point now, but the razor-sharp hellstone would still shred skin and bone if he fell against it.

But he remembered the path: crawl like a bear here on hands and feet, rest a knee here, hand there, crawl again over to here. A singular way that had to be recalled from memory once he made it past the first bend and he was fully in darkness. He rested on a knee after the second bend and reached up. It took him several minutes to find the depression overhead, and there, recessed, was another piece of hellstone, loose in its mortar's grip. Gavin pulled it free and tucked it in his mouth. It was no larger than a dogtooth, small enough to be missed. Small enough to be swallowed if necessary, and maybe still not kill him coming out the other side. Gavin continued on.

The trapdoor was still where he remembered it.

His heart sank. Apparently Andross had found this tunnel, because the trapdoor had been repaired. The latch was designed to break under the pressure of a person's weight. He'd wanted to be sure that his brother fell in, instead of triggering it and staying in the tunnel – which was a dead end anyway. But since the real Gavin fell in, it had been reset.

Gavin felt nauseated. He'd expected it, of course. His father wasn't stupid, and he would have searched thoroughly, but Gavin had hoped against reason that his father wouldn't find the other cells. If Andross had found the other cells, then he'd found his eldest son's rotting body.

Dear Orholam, forgive me.

Gavin put his full weight on the trapdoor and tumbled down into the green cell.

He stood to find that it, too, had been repaired. His brother had blown a hole in one wall, but there was no sign of that now, just perfect, slightly undulating, woody green luxin. Gray to Gavin's eye.

He stood, slightly wobbly despite that he'd expected the fall. He was not well.

'Long time no see, Guile,' the dead man said. He looked somehow different in the green wall. A worse reflection, of course, but some trick of Gavin's memory made even his voice different, as if, in a green wall, the dead man must have green characteristics. His voice husky, something wild in his leer.

'Oh, I've missed you, too, darling,' Gavin said. He walked to the wall, and pulled out the hellstone shard he'd taken from the tunnel.

'But time is different for us here.'

'Uh-huh,' Gavin said.

'Why don't we talk about this?' the green dead man said. Was there an edge of fear in that voice?

'I think we've talked quite enough,' Gavin said, and he set the hellstone against the dead man's third eye and began scratching the wall.

'You need your strength. Why don't you draft some green?' the dead man said.

'Funny,' Gavin said. He was certain now about the dead man's moving independently: the green reflection didn't even bother to try to match his movements precisely. He spoke, and his mouth moved when Gavin knew his own wasn't moving.

Part of the traps he'd laid for his brother had been dependent on his drafting. He'd thought the lure of drafting green would be too powerful for his brother to resist, and thus he would act wildly. Trapped like an animal, he would bite the bars of his cage, but never be able to gather the wits to do it mechanically. He had, unfortunately, underestimated how long the original Gavin would spend in blue, and how the blue would change him, make him more rational and cool despite his baseline hot temper and rebelliousness.

This green cell had held his brother only for a few days.

'So you've been lonely, huh?' Gavin asked, still scratching, scratching, scratching.

'You'll never get out,' the dead man said.

'You really think I'd spend a year building a prison and never once stop to think how I'd get out if I were ever trapped in it myself?'

Of course that was only half-true. He'd planned how to escape – that was why he'd placed the hellstone chip for himself. But he'd not planned how to get out without drafting.

The hellstone would get him out of green. Yellow...yellow was another question.

'How much did Mot tell you?' the dead man asked.

'Mot?' Gavin's only interaction with the god had been when he'd sunk the blue bane and run his skimmer over all the god's foul wights, turning the water red. 'Not much. I never bothered to chat with him.'

The dead man looked at him for a long while quizzically, then burst out laughing.

'We don't remember much at all, do we?' the dead man said. 'How many times did you – I mean *I* – use black luxin anyway? Do I remember? Because once shouldn't have done this much to…me.'

Of course, Gavin was in green. Of course the dead man would try madness here. Try to make Gavin think he was already mad, that he remembered things that weren't true and didn't remember things that were. Of course green would try to make Gavin wild and fearful and uncontrollable.

When Dazen had made this prison, he must have figured that his brother would be particularly susceptible to the wildness of green. That questioning his very sanity would be a good way to keep him from formulating logical plans, would infuriate him.

But one thing this creation of his did do was remind him how much the black had taken.

And then the will-casting. It was always dangerous, he knew that. Utterly forbidden for a lot of good reasons that Gavin had naturally decided didn't apply to him.

He'd been talking to the dead man here as if he were the same dead man in the blue cell. As if he were still Gavin, mocking himself.

The dead man was still a reflection of himself, of course, but Gavin suddenly understood something about his own design. He hadn't cast his will into the prison as a whole – there was magic-killing hellstone everywhere down here. If he'd made the prison a seamless whole, a failure of part of it would be a failure of all of it.

So instead he'd imbued a bit of his will into each cell. This dead man was utterly separate from the first.

That was why he'd made this dead man ask what the last one had asked Gavin. He would have wanted to know how to torment his brother more successfully. There were two facts he could glean from this: this dead man didn't remember anything he'd told the last one, and, more importantly, this one might know things the last one hadn't.

Dazen had made the blue cell in a month. He'd poured

everything into that, and he'd known that his brother was there and not making any progress in getting out for a long while. But Dazen had taken much longer creating the other cells, which meant he'd also crafted them later, when he knew more and different things.

So what did this bit of his will-cast self, this shadowy mirror of himself, know that Gavin himself had forgotten?

It was almost worth exploring.

Talk to a version of his old self that his old self had crafted purely to drive a prisoner insane?

Was he smarter back then, when he'd been cool and collected and healthy and patient, or was he smarter now, with all his experience and the wisdom of years?

He thought about it as he scratched at the wall. Here there would be no luxin seal that he could so easily find. He'd intended his brother to waste a lot of time – years, even – looking for that seal. He hadn't crafted this cell that way. All the seals here were on the outside.

His brother had been ingenious and far more disciplined than Dazen had expected. Carrying with him the blue bread from the first cell – and thus defeating the hellstone draining out his blue luxin? That was brilliant, Gavin. And drafting a tiny bit of the spectral bleed blue put off under green light so he could draft in here?

Amazing, brother.

Gavin had thought his elder brother would have been terribly frustrated in here.

But that real Gavin had escaped because he could draft and he'd had a source and he'd had indomitable will.

Dazen had only the last.

After many hours, his hand started cramping too much for him to keep going.

The next day he continued. The green dead man heckled him, but he ignored him. They would learn nothing from each other, because Gavin wasn't willing to give him more ammunition against him. Perhaps that was his wisdom, knowing that he couldn't take much more, knowing that he was fragile.

On the third day – or after the second sleep, whichever – he'd broken through the green cell wall.

Then he followed the natural grain of the woody luxin a distance somewhat less than the span of his broad shoulders, and began again.

Four days later, he cut through again.

Five days later, he cut through one more time.

And the last side of his escape box, with the wall weakened, he cut through in three days.

Before he'd left the blue cell, he'd gorged himself on all the bread he'd accumulated, but he hadn't managed to bring much along with him to this cell. In the last twelve days of the fifteen he'd been here, he'd eaten nothing.

That was good in only one way: it meant Andross Guile hadn't noticed Gavin had escaped his first cell. Water flowed through each of the cells, so he hadn't died of thirst. It was, of course, terrible because it meant he hadn't eaten in twelve days.

His brother had done better.

Gavin spent hours etching lines between his holes to weaken the wall. After many kicks that threatened to break him before he broke the wall, the panel finally gave way.

It wasn't large, but by wriggling his broad shoulders through the hypotenuse of that partial rectangle, he made it through and dropped into a dim gray-lit circular chamber.

The wall his brother had broken through had been repaired.

What had his father been thinking? Why go to so much effort and not set up alarums to notify him if Gavin escaped? Andross couldn't even draft green himself, which meant immense trouble in bringing a trusted green here. But then, Andross had certainly cultivated total blind loyalty among enough monochromes to do his dirty work when necessary.

Unless Andross knew, and was cruelly just watching every step?

No, that was paranoia. Andross had seen the broken pieces of this prison and had it repaired. He would do that first because he was cautious, just in case.

Later, when he had time, Andross would try to figure out every piece of Gavin's creation. But he would be busy in the interim, and he was an old, feeble man, after all, wasn't he?

How had he seemed so powerful and young when he'd come down to see Gavin?

It was surely only a façade of youth.

No matter. Gavin had to get as far as quickly as he could. The green prison had cost him too much time already.

He searched the underside of the outer wall of the green orb that had just been his prison. Near the base, a section yielded.

A hidden lever popped out of the granite wall.

It took him several minutes of gathering his starvation-sapped strength to pull it.

The secret door opened to Gavin's old access tunnels.

He poked his head into the pitch-black tunnel. Andross hadn't discovered all of Gavin's secrets in the construction of these tunnels, but that didn't mean he hadn't planted traps of his own.

Bet the torch is trapped.

Gavin froze, but he hadn't heard it aloud. It wasn't the dead man, it was only his own thoughts.

Not so strange, under the pressures of solitude and starvation, that he would externalize some dark mirror of himself. Still, it was too akin to madness for comfort.

Talking to yourself is one thing, not realizing both voices are yours is quite another.

There we go. That's my voice in my head. That's me. That's my own sardonic sanity speaking.

Goddammit, Karris, I miss you. I need you.

Gavin blew out a breath. Then, still outside the entrance to the tunnel, Gavin reached an arm in and found the yellow lux torch in its sconce. He hadn't trapped that one. But Andross might have trapped it. He figured that his older brother would be too paranoid to grab the first torch, and would grab the second or the third. It was still there, of course.

Gavin yanked the torch from the wall and snatched it back around the corner.

Nothing happened.

He expelled a slow breath, and examined the lux torch carefully. He peeled off the clay facing and was rewarded with soft yellow light. His own work. He could shake the torch to increase the reactivity of the yellow and get brighter light, but he didn't bother. That would make the torch burn out faster.

He stepped into the tunnel.

Nothing.

He took his time working his way up through the spiraling tunnel, climbing, slowly climbing, but watching every step. After all his privation, he tired quickly anyway.

Andross Guile would have a trap here somewhere, wouldn't he? But traps took time to craft, Gavin knew that well. How long had he been down here? How much time had Andross been able to take away from his other work?

Gavin made it to the second lux torch. He'd trapped the handle of that one with hellstone, though he hadn't thought his brother would grab it. An easy trap, and one Gavin had easily avoided.

But Gavin's slender hope that Andross Guile hadn't found these tunnels was dashed when he found the third lux torch. That was the one his elder brother had taken and used. It had been replaced, put back perfectly in place, a mockery.

Burn in nine hells, Father.

It shouldn't have shocked him that Andross Guile was a subtler torturer than he himself had ever been. But Gavin couldn't even imagine the rage his father must have felt when he found the rotting corpse of his favorite son in the yellow cell. And not an ancient corpse, either.

What a shock it must have been for Andross Guile, and he had never been a man to let an offense go unanswered.

If Andross hadn't found it, there was a stash of food hidden in the chamber ahead. Cured meat, bread in airtight containers, and wine stored in new skins that should have aged well.

His mouth watered at the mere thought. Food. It was maddening to even consider it, but Gavin couldn't hurry.

Surely I've learned patience in suffering by now.

He approached his old work chamber slowly. It was ten paces wide and blessedly square after the hellish globes Gavin had been trapped in. A small cot came into view, then a table.

Trap, I'm telling you, his sardonic self said. Trap.

He ignored the heckling, but he was careful where he aimed the light of his lux torch lest he spring his own trap as the real Gavin had.

He moved slowly forward. He'd concealed a tiny portcullis

in the ceiling above the entrance to keep his brother from fleeing back down the tunnel. It was raised again, of course, reset.

He was so close. From this chamber, he could avoid the other cells, and escape. Food and wine were here. In another hidden cache just down the next hall, weapons and clothing and bandages and ropes and grapnels and every other kind of gear he might need waited.

His father would have trapped either this room, or the very last one.

The very last room would be it: that was how his father worked. But he wouldn't expect Gavin to have weapons and rope. Gavin's options would expand exponentially once he had those, and his strength back.

Hold on.

Gavin glanced back to the cot. Where was the table and the chair? They'd been right there, last time.

What was that sound?

Gavin quieted his own breathing, even as his heart pounded. Was there someone in the chamber? If so, he couldn't fail to know that Gavin was here, with Gavin waving the lux torch in the darkness.

Gavin was at every disadvantage. No night vision, no strength, no weapon, no drafting. He was paralyzed, helpless.

But just as he shook that off with his next breath, a light bloomed in the room, full-spectrum, glorious light, almost blinding Gavin's eye.

Gavin stabbed the lux torch into a gap to keep the portcullis from slamming shut behind him, and leapt into the chamber, rolling.

It was a pitiful effort. His emaciated muscles betrayed him and he fell rather than rolling to his feet.

In the far corner, sitting in the chair, was Andross Guile. He yawned, utterly relaxed, as if he'd been sleeping.

'Son,' he said. 'I've been waiting for you.'

Chapter 34

'Hey, beautiful,' Gav Greyling said as he came onto the training pitch below the Chromeria. 'Wanna go a few rounds? You're already sweaty.' He waggled his eyebrows over deeply blue-stained eyes to show he wasn't serious.

This again?

'Yeah, sure,' Teia said, as if she'd missed the double entendre.

'Hand-to-hand?' he asked.

Right. Not only could she never beat Gavin Greyling in hand-to-hand combat, but she wasn't going to wrestle him while he was being a jackass.

'Rope spear,' she said.

He groaned. She practiced with a lead weight wrapped in leather rather than a spear point, of course, but he still had quite a few bruises from their last bout.

'Awright,' he said. 'But I'm using a sword-breaker this time.'

Weeks had passed with no contact from the Order. Teia's dread was only growing. Nor had Karris responded to the signals Teia had activated requesting a meeting. She must be being watched very, very closely. That didn't help Teia's anxiety.

She'd filled the time with work and training, both open and covert. It filled the hours, but not the loneliness. Being abruptly finished with lectures – even if they'd been mostly inapplicable – and merely working? It was discomfiting. She felt displaced even when she trained with the Blackguard.

She'd thought that her goal had always been to be in the Blackguard, but now she saw that everything she'd wanted here paled in comparison to what she'd had in the Mighty.

The rope spear was turning out brilliantly for her. It looked like and could be a distance weapon, which was excellent for a small woman. In reality, anyone who snagged the rope with a hand soon found it was also a grappler's weapon.

Snag the rope, and you found Teia flipping another loop

around your hand or head. Stagger back away from the entrapping loops, and you tightened the knot.

Then Teia was on top of you, tripping you, throwing another loop around arm or leg, and then recovering the spear blade and ending you.

They got started amid all the other Blackguards and trainees who were also practicing. This time Gav Greyling snagged the rope with his jagged sword-breaker – and threw it away from himself, a technique no one would usually try.

He rushed Teia, but her panicky jerk on the encumbered rope somehow worked, whipping the sword-breaker and spear point into Gav's legs as he charged.

He tried to jump over the blades as he stumbled, but Teia slid sideways and flipped a loop of the rope up, catching his foot. She pulled hard as he was still in midair, and he crashed flat on his face.

She rolled onto him and jabbed the spear point lightly into his back.

He groaned, but didn't curse. 'Round to you,' he said, as other Blackguards training laughed.

As he lay on the ground with Teia's elbow holding him down she said, 'You know we can't have a relationship, right?' Dammit, she'd said it too loud. Some of the others had overheard.

'Nrg. Who said anything about a *relationship*?' he said, keenly aware of the others.

They both knew how well that would go over with the commander. Fisk wasn't as inspiring a leader as Commander Ironfist had been, but he'd been a trainer. He didn't let that kind of stuff slide.

'I'm not your type,' Teia said.

'Oh? And what's my type?' he asked as he stood, retrieving the sword-breaker.

She went to stand right in front of him. She put her hands on his shoulders, then slid her hands down his arms in front of everyone. 'Hmm,' she said in an appreciative tone. 'Your arm is so strong. But just the left. So I'm guessing this is your type.' She held up his left hand and shook it back and forth, then dropped it. 'Ew.'

Everyone laughed at him, and he shook his head.

Dammit, Teia. Why'd you have to go there? She hadn't meant to take his vulnerability and beat him with it, but she had.

'Ya know, Gav,' Essel interrupted. 'I don't know why you waste your attentions on her.' She tugged down the hem of her tunic to show off more of her substantial cleavage. Essel was famously insatiable, but she was also almost twenty years older than the young Blackguard, and infinitely better looking. 'If you know where to look, you'll find those who are always up for a good ride.'

His jaw dropped. 'Really?' He couldn't help but look her up and down. She was a veritable Atirat to him.

She licked her lips, and he was entranced. Just because it was forbidden to have sex with another Blackguard didn't mean it didn't happen. And if anyone would be available for something quick and dirty and temporary, it would be Essel. In a husky voice, she whispered, 'Why don't you, uh…head to the stables?'

Gavin Greyling must have blocked his hearing with his hopes, because despite everyone's laughing at him, he said, 'You'll meet me by the stables? When?'

Gill Greyling put his face in his hands. 'For a ride, you dumbass. If you're looking for a ride…'

'Huh?' Gav said.

'I can't believe we're related,' Gill said as the rest of them laughed.

Afterward, though, Essel came to Teia, falling in beside her as she cooled down with some fighting forms. 'He flirts with you because of how you turn him down. You know that, right?'

'Why would he—'

'Because you're safe, Teia. He would never dream of actually breaking his Blackguard vows, and he knows you wouldn't, either. So your rejections don't hurt, or not as much. It's fun to flirt with someone you find attractive anyway. You're practice for him to hone his confidence and his approaches – which, let's be blunt, need practice. If you like the flirtation, fine. If you don't like it, just once, seriously, at some time when he's

230

not flirting with you, tell him that you don't appreciate it. He'll stop. But don't – *don't you* fucking *dare* take him to bed. There are ways to break even that rule, if—'

'The rule against sleeping with other Blackguards?'

'Yes. But not with him, not for you. He'd fall in love with you head over heels, and *that* is what the rules are there to prevent. Last thing we need here is tempestuous young love, and taking sides, and grand gestures, and burning resentments, and all that horse shit. That is what gets people killed.'

'Why is this my problem?' Teia asked. 'I didn't do *anything*.' She just wanted to be invisible when this sort of thing came up.

'What do you want me to say, Teia? "You're the woman. Can you imagine what kind of world it would be if we let men take the lead"?'

Teia saw she was kidding but not kidding. 'Fine. I'll take care of it.'

'No, listen, because you shouldn't go do this with a chip on your shoulder. You know the Philosopher? His concept of the *zoon politikon*?'

Teia shook her head. 'I attended my mistress's physical training, not her tutoring. My owners didn't want a slave girl to think I might be an equal to their daughter.'

Essel waved that away; it was a discussion for another time. 'We're social animals, Teia. All of us. Without a community, we can't reach our proper end, our *telos*. We can't become who we're supposed to be when we're alone. Those without a community become monsters. We can get stuck looking for a freedom that doesn't exist, because when you're part of something, the weakness of others puts a burden on you. Maybe even an unfair burden. But you'll put unfair burdens on your community, too. And let me be blunt. You do. You're inexperienced, you're uneducated, you're color-blind, you're short, and you're weak. So in this thing, you're going to help Gav Greyling. Not because you're the woman, but because you're human. You're a Blackguard. And our community, this precious little thing we have, helps each other grow and become the best us we can be. And maybe he'll never help you back, but one of the rest of us will. Or maybe we won't, and you'll go through life with your ledger slightly unbalanced. If you've got complaints about things being unfair, take them to my friends who died at Garriston in one fucking unlucky cannon shot.

'It's not fair. But so what? There was a scholar – more of a dramatist, really – who said, "Hell is other people." He was right, and he was a fool. Heaven is other people, too.' She smiled apologetically. 'Sorry. I kind of gave it to you right between the eyes there, didn't I?'

Teia said nothing, though she wasn't offended. It felt good to be treated as an equal by a full Blackguard. Apparently she didn't need to say anything, though, because Essel went on.

'It's uh, it's something I've been thinking about a lot, duty. Obligation and service and what we Blackguards owe and what we don't. I mean, I loved Gavin Guile being my Prism. He was like my big brother and father and luxiat and the lover I could never have all wrapped up in one. Believe me, I spent more than a few nights with a lover with my eyes tight shut, imagining it was him on top of me, or under me. Mm. That sounds wrong because I started with the brother-and-father thing, doesn't it?'

'I, uh, knew what you meant,' Teia said.

'I mean, he was our Prism from the time I was girl. I grew up on Gavin Guile. Most heroes get smaller the closer you get to them. But he's gone. Even if we find him – and surely he would have surfaced by now, if he lived – I saw him, Teia. He was broken. Fingers cut off, eye gouged out, starved. He can't be Prism now. I don't know if I'd want him to be, knowing what he once was. And…you know, he's married, too. That fantasy should have died long ago, but it's dead now. And I don't think I want to be a Blackguard for this new Prism. You've heard the rumors.'

'Um, no?' Ah shit. Apparently being in her own world so much had some real drawbacks in the gossip circle.

'That's right, you've mostly pulled duty with the White. Well, by order of the commander, none of the Archers are allowed to attend Zymun alone.' She tented her eyebrows at Teia, lips pursed as if it was a significant look.

Except Teia had no idea what it signified. 'Huh? Why?'

Essel sighed. 'He gets grabby. Won't take no for an answer. Samite nearly punched him in the face.'

'He laid hands on Samite?' The stocky, one-handed trainer didn't exactly seem like his type.

'Oh hell no. Gloriana. From the cohort behind yours.'

'Oh, sure, I was there at her swearing in.' It was odd to Teia to already not be the newest, but they were inducting new Blackguards as fast as they could.

'If it weren't wartime, we'd already have had a number of the Archers buy out their commissions because of him. That's actually what I'm thinking of doing. Not because of him, though. Or more that he's not Gavin. I'm thirty-five years old, Teia. I love the Blackguard. But maybe it's time for me. I mean, after the war anyway, right? I want to get married. Not kids, you know, but a husband? The same man every night used to sound too boring to me. Maybe it still does. But the same man every day? That sounds...I dunno. Warm. Safe. Nice.'

She scowled ruefully.

'But listen to me go on. I guess that's another thing about community. When someone who filled a certain place leaves it, someone else has to stand in. Karris used to listen to my whinging. Now she's the White. It doesn't seem right to bother her with all this, you know? Anyway, sorry to unload. You're a good Blackguard, Teia. A good Archer. I'm proud to call you sister. Thanks. I feel a lot better.'

Teia had said approximately two words. 'Right,' she said. Three. 'Anytime.' Four.

'And take care of the Gav thing.'

Teia winced. 'Right away.'

Chapter 35

The goddam cards. Kip had absorbed scores of the damned things – and not a one was triggered by a wall of fire or a sinking ship?

The Cwn y Wawr on the second, sinking barge weren't taking their impending deaths passively. It was the only reason they hadn't already died of smoke inhalation. They were chained, so they couldn't reach their own blindfolds, but they'd torn off each other's.

The initial explosion had blown holes in the barge's hull, but through those holes, enough light had poured to give a few of them a source for magic. Even as Kip had leapt through the air, they'd blown the upper deck off the barge, leaving most of the hold open to the evening sky.

But there was no key. It wasn't on the big man who'd triggered the explosions, so it had probably been carried by one of the sentries now dead at the bottom of the river. Nor could most of the drafters actually help. There was a source for sub-red and red from the fire, some oranges, and a bit of weak green from the trees illuminated by the fire, but the sky was too dark for the blues to draft more than a trickle.

The oranges were warding off the fire with walls of their luxin, and the sub-reds were redirecting the heat as well as they could, but it was a losing effort. The barge was on fire in every place not in their direct lines of sight – and it was sinking.

The main lock holding the chains to the deck was already submerged. It was one thing to try to pick a lock with luxin when you could see it, but holding your breath, trying to feel the lock through foul water and keep drafting long enough to work the tumblers of a well-made, huge lock?

Kip had already failed thrice.

He surfaced with a gasp.

Two rows of men chained closest to the lock had already been pulled beneath the water and fought no longer. A third row were still holding their breath, eyes squeezed tight shut or rolling with terror. The men of the fourth row were submerged to their throats. They tilted their chins up, sucking air, no longer screaming.

One drafter, three rows back, had drafted a large cone around his own neck. He was shouting at the others telling them to do the same, but between the cone muffling his voice and everyone else screaming, no one noticed. Except Kip.

The cone would buy the man time when he was pulled under the waves. Until the water reached above the top of his cone, he could still breathe. Almost every one of the men chained here could have done the same, but they hadn't thought of it.

Kip could do it for them.

But that was a distraction, wasn't it? He could save ten or twenty men so they could have another minute or three of life – but only if he abandoned the main problem: the damned sinking barge.

If ten more men had to die while he solved the problem, that was the price he had to pay.

Well, that *they* had to pay.

Come on! Not *one* of the damned cards was going to help him?

'Breaker!' Cruxer shouted from above, standing on a nonburning remnant of the upper deck. 'Not much time!'

So he'd caught up. Kip looked at him and saw Cruxer had a coil of rope in his hand. The other end stretched out beyond him toward the shore.

Immediately, dozens of voices cried out for him to save them. As if he weren't trying. As if he could.

Kip looked through the water. It was up to his neck, too. The next row went under.

He couldn't save them.

He nodded his failure to Cruxer. He had to leave. They couldn't be saved.

Cruxer threw the rope toward Kip, but immediately dozens of hands reached up to catch it.

A man grabbed it and tore the ends away from his neighbors. 'Save me! For the love of Orholam, please!'

Kip waded up the main aisle between the rowers' benches, feeling a panic build in him. He was going to be trapped here. He not only wasn't going to save them, he was going to die himself.

Bubbles came up in the water as a submerged man despaired of holding his breath any longer.

'Breaker!' Cruxer shouted. 'I believe!'

Cruxer cracked open a mag torch, and it flared shocking green.

Kip couldn't leave them. He had to do this. He was the only one who could.

He made it to the man holding the rope. 'Give me the rope. I can save you.'

But the man was fear-frozen, desperate, beyond reason.

Kip clobbered him and took the rope. He pushed back into the deeper water, took several deep breaths, and pushed under water.

He found the lock again. But the lock didn't matter. The chain was too strong to break. But the chain was just a bond, and a bond wasn't evil. A chain could be a lifeline. What mattered was what you were bound to.

By touch in the cool, murky water, Kip found the enormous metal loop that bolted the chain to the deck. He wound green luxin thick around the chain, pushing his will into that space until the green luxin filled it.

He called to mind then that boy he had been so long ago, trapped in that closet with the rats, biting, scratching. It came back all too readily. But he pushed past the remembered terror – that wasn't what he needed now – and there it was: the unspeakable thirst for freedom, the longing to break something, to get out.

Every muscle in his body flexed and he roared, bubbles erupting from his mouth, and he felt something crack.

Kip surfaced, gasped, and went down again, even as another row disappeared under the waves.

The big loop was torn loose of the decking, but only one huge nail had pulled fully free. The bolt hadn't broken; one of the clinch nails that had been pounded through the deck and then bent aside had been pulled through.

Kip pushed the chain beneath the freed side, and then moved up the submerged rows by feel.

There were identical, much smaller loops holding the chains bolted to the floor at every row.

But Kip had the process now. Attacking the clinch nails rather than the bolts, almost as quickly as he could push through the water, he tore out one after another with an explosion of luxin and wood and breath.

He surfaced again, and waded forward. The men were

shouting. They didn't understand because they couldn't feel the slack in the chains until their own loops were broken.

Finally Kip pulled the last one free, directly beneath Cruxer. He looped the rope Cruxer had given him through the chain. 'Pull!' he shouted.

And suddenly help arrived as the Cwn y Wawr from the first boat freed themselves one at a time. First a single man helped Cruxer lift men out of the hold, pulling the chain in like a fishing line, the enslaved flopping about like fish.

Then another man jumped into the hold with Kip, giving the imprisoned men a foot up to climb out. And then another came to help keep the chain from getting tangled. And others arrived, pulling the dead from the water.

The whole line was still bound together, so if any part was dragged underwater, at least half the men would be pulled down with it.

There was a sharp crack, and water gushed into the boat, but the men didn't feel it, even as the deck bucked beneath their feet.

The healthy heaved on the chain, and the chained made it to shore.

A few exhausted minutes later, Kip and everyone else had been dragged onto the bank. Nine men couldn't be revived and several others had died in the initial blasts or in their own escape attempts – at least two lay facedown on the river-bank having cut off their own arms to escape their shackles, only to bleed to death in cold freedom.

The pale Cwn y Wawr commander, the short, gap-toothed, black-haired man named Derwyn Aleph, had tried to use his barge's key on the still-chained men's locks. It hadn't worked.

He looked at the corpses bound to his men, and he looked to the forest, from which reinforcements might come at any time. He turned to Kip, who was seated on the riverbank, barely able to move.

'By your traditions, you can't defile the dead, nor can you leave them behind,' Tisis said. Kip had no idea when she'd arrived. 'But your men can't possibly carry them through the forest with the speed you need to move if you're to escape.'

The man gave a stiff nod.

'Tell your men to look away,' she said. 'Ferkudi, Big Leo, if I'm to lead these people, I can't be ritually unclean in their eyes. Cut these men free of the chains, and put their bodies on our skimmer.'

She walked around so the commander could look at her rather than seeing what Ferkudi and Big Leo did. And to their credit, the Mighty did it quickly and without question or complaint, quickly lopping off hands and feet and freeing the dead from the chains that still bound them to the living. To Kip, it was a sudden synecdoche of all that warriors do: the stomach-turning, soul-scarring butchery that society asks for the safety and squeamishness of its soft souled.

Tisis said, 'We'll lay them out on Fechín Island at the Black River confluence. Burial is yours, though.'

Derwyn looked overwhelmed with gratitude. He pointed at Kip with his chin. 'Who is he?'

'Does it matter?' Tisis asked.

'Only to spread the tales,' Derwyn said. 'A hero's due.'

'Then he is Kip Guile, leader of these Mighty, who call him Breaker. Perhaps he is the Luíseach, perhaps he is the Diakoptês, though he claims neither. He is my husband. Even were he not, he is the man I would follow to the ends of the earth.'

Derwyn looked into the wood, deep in thought or merely peering for approaching enemies, and then turned to Kip, who sat on a stump, wrung out and wet, feeling anything but heroic.

Kip's thoughts were running in the opposite direction: Wow, that was really dumb. I never should have done that. Why can't I think before I do anything? Cruxer's gonna kill me.

As his men sat or stood or stretched or bound up each other's wounds, they all watched, and the Forester said, 'These names tell me that you are a great man. I have seen great men. The chains you lifted from my wrists tell me that you are a strong man. I have known strong men. But you didn't dive into that water to save us so that we might be your weapons. You knew we'd sought a coward's peace. Most men would leave us to the hell we deserve for our faithlessness. The lives you have saved this day will testify unto eternity that you are a good man. A man who risks his life to save strangers testifies not to their worth but to his own. I have never seen or known a man to be great and strong and good as well. I will see you in three days with any who will join me. I care not what others call you; if you will have me, I will call you lord.'

Unable to quite process so much kindness at once, looking for some way to shrug it off and make a joke, Kip glanced over to find Cruxer glowering somewhere.

But Cruxer wasn't glowering. He beamed. The rest of the Mighty ranged from Winsen's expression of 'Of course we're awesome' to Big Leo's stolid approval to Ferkudi's huge smile. Ben-hadad had already processed whatever he was feeling and was back to fixing something.

Last Kip looked at Tisis, but even she didn't give him some humorous out. Her eyes shone with tears of pride. It was as if all of them were reflecting back a different man than Kip had ever thought he was. What if the story I've been telling myself about who I am has been wrong?

And a chunk of his self-loathing broke and faded away. Kip straightened his back. 'I look forward to seeing you and whoever joins you at Fechín Island,' he told Derwyn Aleph. No joke. No self-deprecatory smile.

Then, having taken all the gear and weapons and provisions they could carry from the first barge, they scuttled it. And far more readily than two hundred men carrying a hundred paces of heavy chain should have been able to, the Cwn y Wawr disappeared into the forest.

Chapter 36

'You cannot go this long without seeing me. Not ever again. Understand? I forbid it. Forbid!'

Karris had given in to the temptation to abuse her powers and decided that she was entitled to the services of the Blackguard's physicker/masseuse, Rhoda. She'd decided it was acceptable as long as she didn't take either of them away from their duties. Unfortunately, that meant they were meeting two hours before dawn.

The Chromeria was home to all sorts of strong personalities from all over the world, and with that came idiosyncratic styles of dress and cosmetics use, but even here, Rhoda stood out. Of Tyrean and Parian lineage, she had dusky skin and wavy hair that she wore in a topknot, the explosion of hair above it woven with colored beads. When outside, she wore a broad-brimmed petasos with a hole cut in it for her topknot. Of slim build, except for a round soft belly that made her look perpetually pregnant, she wore more, and more garish, face paint than anyone Karris had ever seen, but no perfume – 'That's for whores,' she said – but once she put her hands on your muscles, nothing else mattered.

Rhoda knew Karris's body like no one else in the world. She started with a quick examination of Karris's body – checking the mobility of that left ankle she'd sprained so long ago, testing how far and how evenly her limbs moved. She clucked and pulled and tweaked. She found aches Karris hadn't even been aware of, and old injuries Karris barely remembered.

Then she went to work. She was a sub-red, and her hands radiated heat deep into Karris's left shoulder, still swollen from when she'd jumped off the top of the hippodrome into the Great River. At an old hamstring injury, she pulled the heat away, as well as the heat from Karris's own body, her hands becoming as ice.

'And what is this?' Rhoda asked, her elbow working on a spot low in Karris's back. Karris grunted. She wasn't required to answer. 'Too much sitting. Feel this?'

Karris mumbled into her cushions, 'I have to hold court, you know that.'

'Iron White can talk while standing, yes? Talk standing. Also this?' Rhoda grabbed a double handful of Karris's hair. She always ended with the scalp massage. It was Karris's favorite part, the sweetest medicine of their time together. But now she tapped at Karris's hairline with one finger. 'Gray. And not just one or two. At your age. You always dyed your hair for whimsy. Now, not fun. More sleep. Is order.'

'Too much to do,' Karris said. 'Too many decisions to make.'

In fact, she should be going over her lists right now. There were so many items now that she had to write down the nonsecret ones.

'This is what happens when you stay away,' Rhoda said. 'You forget how this works. I tell you what you doing wrong. I tell you what price you paying for what you doing wrong. I tell you how fix. *Then* you ignore me.'

'I'm sorry, Rhoda,' Karris said. She sighed.

'Iron White, ha! Feel like Iron-Necked White to me.'

She was glad to hear Rhoda tease her about it, but it had had an odd effect on Karris, being called the Iron White, as if she were a Name. She had recoiled from it at first: I'm not that.

But the more she thought about it, the more she realized rejecting it was foolish as a practical matter. If she were ever to check off 'Win the war,' she had to lead. She had not the animal presence or the huge charisma of her husband. She was small. It meant something, that, even if it shouldn't. But someone small could be known for being hard and quick – not just physically, but mentally, too.

The people she led needed her to be strong. They needed her to be special if they were to follow her against gods and monsters.

So she'd made a new goal:

☐ *Become the woman they hope I am. Become the Iron White.*

Rhoda was still chattering, and Karris loved her for it nearly as much as for her amazing hands. 'There is no part where you argue. Understand? I have fired more important patients, thank you.'

'Of course, Rhoda, I – wait, more important than the White?'

Rhoda grumbled. She put her hands around Karris's neck as if to wring it. 'Do not flag-wave bull in open field!' But she was amused. 'My Iron White, here is what you should do: more sleep, less exercise so you can have regular moons by the time husband is back, more standing, some riding if you can fit it in, less wine to relax and more use of your room slave.'

I already use – oh. Karris had promoted one of Marissia's underslaves, an intelligent young woman named Aspasia, to be her room slave in Marissia's absence, but the woman served as chief slave and messenger, and she slept at the foot of Karris's bed, not in it.

Karris knew that in the absence of their husbands, it was not uncommon for women to use their female room slaves as their husbands did, for relief. Many nobles didn't consider it being unfaithful for a woman to use a female slave that way, though they believed using a male slave or even a eunuch was. But Karris had never even considered it. As a Blackguard, she hadn't had a room slave. That just had never been part of her life, except for her hating Marissia, who'd served so ably as Gavin's room slave. Apparently excelling in *all* of a room slave's duties and more.

Damn you, Marissia. The searches had turned up nothing. No one had seen her leave. The Blackguards swore she'd yelled fire, but hadn't run past them or dangled a rope down the outside of the tower. She was just…gone. Nor had Karris found any money trail. Turgal Onesto had confirmed that Marissia had access to at least one account he knew of – but it hadn't been touched. Nor had anyone seen her at the markets, at the docks…anywhere. It was as if the woman had evaporated.

Regretfully, Karris gave up on it. There were too many other things to do to waste more time on that one.

☐ ~~Find Marissia.~~

So when do I scratch off Gavin? Every criterion that justified crossing off Marissia applied to him. He'd disappeared exactly the same way and on the same day. The searches for him said exactly the same thing – nothing. Nothing. Nothing.

☐ *Find Gavin.*

She would never take that off the list. She would die first.

Karris paid Rhoda – insisting on it, since the woman had woken with her and this was in addition to her normal duties – and then threw on a robe. She hadn't even noticed her own nudity as she'd walked across her room to grab the coins. She was alone here with only her physicker and the two Blackguards at the door.

After Rhoda left, Karris said, 'Baya, what's the problem?'

'High Lady?' he asked, pained.

'We've been in the field. We trained together. You've seen me naked dozens of times. You're as nervous as a boy beckoned to a woman's bed for the first time.'

He swallowed. 'Honestly, High Lady?'

'Yes!'

'I, um, I guess you always notice. I mean, a man does, right? But I mean there's noticing and *noticing*. And I guess it's one thing to sort of...appreciate you when we were Blackguards together. I mean, I didn't stare! Tried not to? But now that you're holy, I...it makes me feel—'

She held up a hand. She needed to remember that when the White asked for total honesty, she sometimes actually got it. Some people took her orders as a religious obligation. 'Just...*pretend* not to notice. That's part of the work. Do better. Now get out. I'm angry with you. I'll be going over papers for the next couple hours until my day begins. Adrasteia can handle watching an empty room and me until then.'

Baya Niel, who'd faced the green god with her, unflinching as death came for him, practically bolted from the room.

Karris went to her desk and sat. She gave the Blackguard hand signal: 'Clear?'

Teia nodded. 'Lot of work, just to get your own Blackguard to report to you.'

'It seemed you had more to say after you gave your official report. I had some more questions.' Days ago, Teia had finally given her report about how the Mighty had been attacked and then how they'd escaped in the presence of Commander Fisk, but Karris was certain there had been more to the story that she'd held back. It just hadn't been the most important thing to find out about in the midst of all the crises she'd had to deal with every day for the last couple of weeks.

But Teia goggled. 'Are you joking?'

'Whatever do you mean?' Karris asked.

'I set the emergency meeting signal twice! Even though Marissia told me I'm never supposed to set it more than once, in case I'm being watched. And you never came!'

Karris's heart dropped into her stomach. 'Marissia never handed over the list of emergency signals before she fled. That bitch!' What else had Karris missed?

Teia paled. 'Orholam have mercy. What if those were in that package? I could be dead already if the Order was watching. And what do you mean she's a bitch?'

'What?' Karris asked.

Karris and Teia had seen each other almost every day in the last weeks, but to keep their relationship as handler and spy secret neither of them had acted out of the ordinary. It must have been killing Teia.

'Just, just report,' Karris said. 'Quickly.'

Luckily, Teia had obviously prepared herself for this in case she needed to report the essentials in only a few minutes. She told about the Lightguards' murdering Goss, and the flight down the stairs, the flight back up the lifts, and out onto the roof. She backtracked briefly with '—And you know that Andross Guile had the White assassinated, right? He hired my master Murder Sharp to do it. I overheard him offer the contract myself.'

Karris hadn't known. It was a punch in the guts. They'd had a quiet funeral for Orea Pullawr, according to her wishes – everything in her life had been public for decades, and she'd long demanded her parting be private. How Karris had wept, and thanked the old woman for the privacy so she could do so freely.

That soulless piece of shit, Andross. Orea had been dying anyway. Why hadn't Andross Guile simply let her go?

Because that wouldn't be a win over his old nemesis?

No, because he'd stacked the deck for who would become the *next* White, and he'd wanted to get his grandson approved as Prism-elect, and he feared that Orea Pullawr was going to stop him. By killing her before Sun Day, he'd gotten both – except that Orea had seen it coming.

She'd taken care of Karris. Prepared her.

'You said something about a package of letters?' she asked suddenly. 'Wait...not bound with red ribbon?'

'On Marissia's desk, yes,' Teia said.

Oh no.

Teia spun out the rest of the tale to Karris's growing horror: The discovery of the escape lines, which Orea had given Kip a hint about. The flight to the docks. Kip's hasty – Andross Guile–arranged – marriage to Tisis Malargos. Karris had known Tisis was gone, but none of her spies had been able to tell her why or where yet. The girl was supposed to be a hostage for Ruthgar's good behavior. Scratch that item off the list, and not the way Karris had hoped.

Teia then told about her own decision to stay, then backtracked to tell how Tremblefist had been the one to blow up the cannon tower to save the Mighty's ship from being sunk.

Karris had already learned about that one from other sources, but the loss was still fresh. Tremblefist had died for his young charges. Sacrificed himself for Kip.

Then Teia told her about kidnapping Marissia with Murder Sharp, and how the woman had tried to get the bundle of papers to Karris – and failed.

So Marissia wasn't a traitor. She was a martyr.

The woman Karris had been denouncing as a bitch, and whore, and disloyal had been doing everything in her power to be Karris's friend and faithful servant.

Damn me.

But why would Andross want Marissia? This Murder Sharp hadn't known that Marissia was a spymaster. But that meant only that the Order didn't know she was a spy. Andross had instructed Sharp to take her papers.

Maybe he knew or suspected what she was. Maybe he'd just gotten lucky.

Karris had felt as if she were drowning ever since she'd taken the white robe and watched a roomful of nobles prostrate themselves before her. To hear that someone had tried to throw her a lifeline – only to have it snatched away – was almost too much to bear.

I need to kill Andross.

Except he was untouchable. Too valuable. Too powerful. Irreplaceable.

'High Lady, I'm sorry to rush, but I want to make sure I tell you everything.'

Karris motioned she should go on, and then Teia told her about the Order's offering to kill whomever she'd wanted killed and how she'd tagged and then untagged Quentin.

And there we *got lucky,* Karris thought.

'Have they followed up with you about that?' Karris asked. 'Will they kill you for it?'

'I've got a plan,' Teia said. 'But if I just disappear...I'll do my best not to talk.'

It seemed surreal to be talking so blithely about such things. People didn't just disappear from the safety of the Chromeria. That was Ilyta, the satrapy of traitors and pirates and cutthroats and bad men. A young girl like Teia shouldn't have to be a warrior. She should be overanalyzing what she'd said to some boy who might reject her because of it, not analyzing what she'd said to some cultist who might murder her because of it.

This is the world we've both been thrust into now. Sink or swim, girl. And Orholam have mercy on my soul for throwing you in the water.

They talked a bit more, bringing each other up to speed and updating their dead drop and emergency drop procedures. Then, finally, Karris said, 'We're almost out of time. Any quick questions before I give you your new orders?'

'Yes. How'd you know that Quentin was telling the truth about High Luxiat Tawleb?'

Karris sniffed, amused. 'Orea Pullawr left me many tools. Not only eyes and ears; I have fingers and blades as well. My spies learned of Quentin's guilt. When he confessed, I had no one in High Luxiat Tawleb's house, but I did have people in place to see if he would do what a guilty man would do when he hears a fellow conspirator has been seized. But Tawleb didn't liquidate any of his goods or home, which either meant he was innocent or just intelligent. He did hire out an entire well-known smuggler's ship, without telling the captain what he would carry.

'Within the hour, we had that smuggler sail "on other quick business." If Tawleb's timing had been merely a coincidence, say, he was hiring a smuggler for some other illicit cargo that we didn't know about because we'd never really examined him that closely, then he would have waited for his favorite smuggler to return. He didn't. He went to another instead. This one we let stay. And then early the morning of the executions, one of my light fingers returned to me with Tawleb's diary.

'Most clever men just can't help but brag about their cleverness, even if only to themselves. His wording was always vague enough that alone, it could have meant anything. Combined with all the rest of the evidence, though, it was damning.' She paused, a chastened grin stealing over her lips. 'But perhaps I shouldn't blame anyone for boasting of their cleverness, now should I? I've just done it myself.'

'I won't tell. Promise,' Teia said, and she grinned for the first time.

'It's nice to see you smile, Teia,' Karris said. There was a quick rap on the door, and five beats later, having given Teia just enough time to take up a post against one wall, a stoic Baya Niel poked his head in. 'Breakfast and correspondence, High Lady.'

'Two minutes while I finish these papers,' Karris said.

He closed the door. Karris looked at Teia, somber once more.

'You've no hint what happened to Marissia or even Gavin?' she asked Teia. As if the girl would have held that back.

'No word at all, High Lady. Nor way to ask without arousing suspicion. Else I would have done it, I promise. I care for both of them, too, you know.'

Karris did. She was silent for a long while, querying Orholam and her own heart if she was ready for this next step. Orholam, please, this is the last moment to let me know if I'm stepping out of your will with this.

But he said nothing, and she saw nothing except that it must be done.

247

'Teia, I hoped that we could defang the Order. But serpents make poor pets. They offered a murder to you, as a gift? And allowing one of their own to kidnap the Prism's own room slave? These are not actions of a group that can be brought back into Orholam's goodness. Teia, what you've told me changes what we need to do. Much as I wish we could concentrate our forces in one direction at a time, this war must be fought on two fronts simultaneously. Are you familiar with the *bull luxiatica Ad abolendam*?'

'Uh, something to do with the luxors?'

'It's a letter sealed with lead giving certain powers to an office or a person. It's too dangerous for you to carry anything like that, so if you are challenged, yours will be hidden in my desk – in the secret compartment you found. Please don't give me occasion to have to produce it.' Dear Orholam, forgive me. Even as I denounce serpents, I'm creating one.

'What are you talking about?' Teia said. 'Why would I need such a thing?'

Will they put me on Orholam's Glare for this? Will I deserve it? Her face as still and hard as the Iron White she aspired to be, Karris said, 'In secret, I'm conferring upon you the title of *Malleus Haereticorum*. "Hammer of Heretics." You are now named and empowered as a luxor, Teia. The first named in my lifetime, and let us hope the last. Your mission is no longer merely to infiltrate the Order of the Broken Eye. You are to destroy them. Do whatever you have to do – up to and including murdering innocents. The blessing and forgiveness of the Chromeria and the Magisterium entire rest upon you for every lie and sin you deem necessary to accomplish this task. This is war. Kill the Order, Teia. Kill them all.'

Chapter 37

'Pity that by saving the village, we've destroyed it forever,' Big Leo said. 'The Blood Robes' retribution for this is going to be ugly.'

The Mighty were seated around a small fire in a hollow on an island, listening to Sibéal Siofra report what had happened below the falls as they had fought above them. The Mighty and the Ghosts would rendezvous in the morning – the battles had concluded after sunset, so there was no way the skimmers could cover all the leagues of river between them.

Sibéal had come alone overland, sneaking through the woods with the natural ease of her people. Conn Arthur had known the Mighty would want to hear how things had gone as soon as possible.

And Big Leo, bless the glowering lunk, had had the presence of mind to decide that the most vital provision that must be stolen before they scuttled the barge was wine. They passed several bulging skins around the fire, feeling young and invincible.

Except for Ferkudi. He'd been selected to be the lookout, which meant sober. He was vocal about his martyrdom.

The distraction raid below the falls, Sibéal reported, had been a huge success. She confirmed that the villagers had sunk their own barges before the Blood Robes arrived, hoping to protect their stockpiled grains. The Blood Robes, however, had brought their barges. When the Ghosts of Shady Grove attacked, they'd overwhelmed the Blood Robes' barges so quickly they hadn't needed to sink them. Instead, sparing only a few people, they'd stolen them and their nearly full load of flour.

The rest of the Ghosts had pressed on to the warehouses, seizing them as well, because the resistance was so light that the conn thought the Blood Robes would smell a trap if he pulled back.

He'd wisely shored up his defenses at the warehouses, avoiding a disaster when they discovered that there were over a thousand Blood Robes camped less than a league away – and coming fast.

'A thousand!' Cruxer exclaimed.

Instead of engaging in a hopeless battle, the Ghosts set fire to the warehouses and retreated before the reinforcements arrived.

Final tally: fifteen to twenty enemy killed. One dead and

two wounded among the Ghosts. And all of the Blood Robes' provisions either stolen or destroyed.

But Big Leo was right: The White King's men wouldn't believe that the opposing force had simply materialized without local support. There would be retribution. Conn Arthur had told the people to flee, but Sibéal said that some wouldn't listen. Some never listen.

'We can't let our fear of what they'll do to retaliate dictate what we do,' Kip said. 'If we let that work, they'll do it again and again until we can do nothing at all.'

'On the other hand,' Ben-hadad said, 'not to be coldhearted, but the more brutal the Blood Robes' retaliation, the more people will come to our banners.'

'Which brings both help and trouble,' Cruxer said, 'in logistics and loyalty. With the skimmers and a small platoon of drafters? We'll be unstoppable raiders. I've got nothing against munds, but they'll slow us down.'

Sibéal piped up, 'Like people who haven't trained to fight their whole lives slow you down?'

Cruxer looked at her flatly. 'Yes. But your Ghosts have strengths that more than balance out your weaknesses. I don't think that will be the case with...non-drafters.'

'We'll deal with that when it comes,' Kip said. 'For now, know that I see the problems coming. I don't know what we should do about them yet, but I've got them in mind.' These were things he would need to discuss with Tisis first.

The Mighty needed to sink into this country. They needed to learn the people and the land. They needed friends if they were going to stop the White King.

'First thing we need to do,' Kip said, 'is divide the loot.'

'Loot? The flour?' Big Leo asked.

'When you're hungry in the forest and someone gives you gold to snack on, I want you to think about that tone,' Tisis said.

'The loot is ours,' Kip said. 'We bled and died to take the White King's flour—'

'The White King's flour?' Sibéal asked.

'He stole it and the villagers had no way to get it back, did they? That said, after Conn Arthur makes clear that all of the flour and the barge itself is ours by the laws of war, he's going to take only two sevs for each of us – little enough that each of us can add it to our pack without us having to add wagons, and enough that each of us can split our share with those who join us soon. *Then* the conn finds whoever is in charge from the village, makes clear what is ours, and then gives all the rest and the barge itself to the village. We want to bind the survivors to us, make them grateful. Make them spread good stories about us. And for Orholam's sake, make sure they hide the barges until the Blood Robes are long gone.'

Sibéal Siofra nodded her head. 'Saving their lives means a lot. Saving their livelihoods may mean more in the coming days.'

Orholam's balls, Kip thought, they were going to need things like food and weapons and shoes and tents and cooks and everything else. Eight people could live off the forest without its slowing them too much. Especially with the skimmers. They wouldn't be able to do that with the conn's hundred and twenty added to that. And if even half the Cwn y Wawr joined? That put them at nearly two hundred and fifty souls. And two hundred and fifty mouths. Five hundred feet.

At that number, skimmers became a huge headache. With every new one they built, the quality got worse, the speed of the whole group got slower, and the likelihood of either losing one into enemy hands or having a spy steal their secrets magnified. That could have consequences for the whole war, not just the Mighty's raids here.

Then again, what use was an advantage you were too afraid to use?

'Things are going to change,' Kip said. 'It's already started. We're going to grow, and we're going to learn, and we're going to fight. We'll always have this.' He gestured to the circle of the Mighty. 'It's always going to be special, but it's going to change, too. For good' – he nodded at Tisis and Sibéal – 'but for ill, too. So tonight let's tell stories about Trainer Fisk, and Ironfist, and Goss and Daelos and Teia, and the battle we just fought, and how Ferkudi totally cheated in our placement fights—'

'Yeah,' Ferkudi said. 'Wait – what?'

'And tomorrow, we go back to war.'

So they swapped stories and embellished a few, and were called out half the time. And mostly Sibéal and Tisis were silent. They understood. It was a wake for the boys' childhood, which had been dying for a long time.

Tisis told about Kip's initiation and how she'd sabotaged him. Sibéal in particular looked stunned, though Ferkudi did, too. How he'd missed that story, Kip had no idea.

'That's how you met? And yet here you sit, together? Married?' Sibéal asked. 'I can't believe he would forgive you such a thing.'

'Kip has a remarkable ability to see the difference between an adversary and an enemy,' Tisis said. She patted his arm, and her eyes were warm.

'Oh, gag me,' Ben-hadad said.

'With wine!' Cruxer called, tossing a sack at him.

Deadpan, Kip said, 'After I saw her naked, I'd forgive her for anything.'

She smacked his arm, her face bright in the firelight.

'He does have a penchant for grabbing on to something and not letting go, doesn't he?' Cruxer said.

'Tell me about it!' Kip said, showing off his burn-scarred left hand.

They laughed, and Cruxer said, 'I was thinking about Aram, in our placement fights, and how you grabbed him until he nearly broke your neck!'

So they segued into those stories: who had been better than expected, how Teia had placed everyone before the fight, how Kip had bulled his way all the way to fifteenth place, and how Cruxer had crushed Aram's knee to disqualify him and get Kip into the final fourteen.

And suddenly the fire was rainbows of color because of the tears swelling in Kip's eyes. But he didn't avert his face. He didn't stand and go hide in the dark as he would have not so long ago.

'Wine making you maudlin?' Big Leo asked, trying to let him play it off.

'No,' Kip said, and the circle went silent, all of them looking at him. 'I had no friends growing up. I was the addict's boy.

252

The fat boy. Made fun of, beat up, the butt of jokes. The best of the townsfolk merely pitied me. I was taken on, but not taken in. I steeled myself to that. Accepted that I would always be alone. It wasn't anyone's fault, not even my mother's, who hated herself for her failures more than I ever could. I was lucky, really. In a city, I'd have been pressed into a gang or taken by slavers.

'It shouldn't have been any better with you all. I was fat and awkward and only had a place because my father had demanded it for me. But you accepted me. For the first time in my life, you made me part of something.'

'Not just part of it,' Cruxer said. 'You're the Mighty's heart.'

Kip grinned. For some reason, being called the Mighty's heart was far more meaningful than if Cruxer had called him the head. 'I would have called you the heart, Cruxer. Maybe you're the spine or the guts of us, then.'

'Well, if neither of you is the head, I guess I must be,' Ben-hadad said.

'I'm obviously the left hand,' Winsen said. 'I'll come outta nowhere and slam ya.'

'That makes me the right,' Big Leo said. 'You might be on the lookout for me, but that doesn't mean you're gonna stop me.'

'Well, what's that make me?' Ferkudi said. 'A foot?'

The Mighty looked around the circle at each other, and then they all answered in unison: 'The ass.'

'The ass?!' Ferkudi said.

'So what's Tisis?' Cruxer asked.

Oh shit. Kip remembered the nickname, apparently at the same moment a blushing Cruxer did. Teats Tisis. Cruxer opened his mouth to apologize.

'Well, obviously—' Winsen said.

'—she's the charisma,' Kip interjected.

'And...Winsen gets to live,' Tisis said flatly.

They grinned. Crisis averted.

Maybe the wine had gone to Kip's head, but he wanted to say this: 'I came from all that. But now—' He choked up, but no one said a word. Tisis squeezed his thigh, being a support. Kip said, 'Now I have this? I'm risking my life to do something that matters with people I love? This is the best night of my life.' He spoke through the tears, and looked at them each in turn. A few eyes glimmered with tears in return. 'Thank you. I love you all.'

Then he shot a wink at Sibéal. 'Except for you. I mean, I'm sure you're nice, but I barely know you.'

They all laughed, and Kip looked down at his hands. 'What the hell, why are my hands empty? Can't any of you bastards share with a thirsty man?'

'Hear hear,' Ferkudi said, reaching out an empty hand enthusiastically, trying to grab a wineskin from Big Leo, who was pointedly guzzling it so as not to share. Ben-hadad grabbed it away from Big Leo and handed the skin across, ignoring Ferkudi, but Tisis intercepted the skin.

'Uh-uh,' she said. 'You come with me. I've got something better for you than wine.'

There were cheers and hoots as she took him by the hand and led him into the woods.

He wasn't drunk – he'd been enjoying the stories and the camaraderie too much to want to dull it – but the wine and fellowship and the good-natured teasing made all the world warm for the fifty paces it took for Tisis to lead him to where she'd set up their tent.

'You set up our tent away from the others on purpose?' Kip said.

'Uh-hmm. That was…one helluva kiss this morning,' she said.

And that snake in his guts was back.

Orholam knew he wanted her, but every time they tried, she ended up furious or crying or both and then apologizing and then offering to pleasure him. At the top of Kip's list of things that filled him with erotic desire was not a weeping, furious, guilty mess of a woman.

Although if things went on this way much longer, it was going to have to do.

Pained, he said, 'You want to try again?'

'I want you…'

It took Kip a few moments to realize that maybe that was a complete sentence. 'Oh, well, yes, I want you, too—'

'...to shut up.'

'Oh, I thought that was a full—'

'And kiss me.'

'Ah. That. That I can do!' Kip said.

'Kip.'

'Yes?'

She stripped off her tunic and chemise together. 'The lips?'

As she slid into his arms, her skin warm and the night cold, it took him a moment to process the words. 'Yes?' Kip the Lips? No, it was Kip the Lip. What did she—

'Are not for talking.'

He had no idea what she meant, but found he didn't mind much as their lips came together.

The moments blurred in the welcome haze of intertwined fingers and intertwined limbs and the cold night driving them into their tent, where they made their own warmth.

And damn, it was a small tent. He was giddy, laughing aloud as she struggled to strip off her trousers and belt and underclothes and nearly knocking over the tent poles – she hadn't ever set up a tent before. Not that Kip was so dumb that he was going to criticize how she'd set up the tent.

And then with a flapping of her feet like a fish on the shore, she finally kicked her trousers off her feet. Her long blond hair had fallen over her face, but Kip's giggle died in his throat as she rolled up on her side toward him and brushed her hair back.

She sidled into his arms, and he bifurcated: part of him kissing, caressing, enjoying – and another part pulling way, way back into fear and cognition.

Orholam, are you out there? I know some men beg for a favor when they're in terror of dying. This is way more serious than that. Look. Here's the deal: I'll serve you forever if you'd just Please Don't Let Me Trigger a Card Now.

Blacking out or blanking out would be the quintessential Kip maneuver. With his luck, there was no way he could just enjoy himself like a normal man. No, Kip always had to do things backward. He was the one who'd gone to battle *not* having had sex with his bride. He was the fat kid who'd somehow made it into the Blackguard. He was the privileged bastard. He was...

Not paying attention.

Until she pulled his trousers down and pulled her lips away from his, kissing down his chest, lower.

One half of him took over all of him, utterly.

The wrong half.

He froze up. All mental. All awkward. All fear. It was all going to go sideways. Again. Another failure. He knew it.

She paused and looked up at him. But her gaze was patient, not frustrated. 'Let me do this.'

'I want to, but...'

'Let me do this,' she said firmly. 'Not just for you. For us. We need this.'

'It doesn't seem fair.'

'Oh, my husband, you beautiful soul. It's *not* fair, but that doesn't mean it's not good. A marriage breathes, and every exhalation is giving, and every inhalation is taking. It can't live without both, Kip. So...just...breathe.'

So he did.

Breathing, he decided pretty much immediately, felt *amazing*.

Chapter 38

'I thought you'd humiliate me,' Gavin said. He didn't move. He still thought it. He scanned the room. His father was leaning back in his chair, and the table was covered with food. Meat, dried fruits, sweetmeats, cheeses, bread, nuts, two flagons, two fine golden goblets. Gavin could hardly bear to look at it, and could hardly bear not to.

'Humiliate you? By springing a trap on you? Like all your others? What would that prove? That I could outthink a prisoner with no weapons, no tools, and only the light I've allowed him? That's not exactly a challenge, is it?' He hesitated. 'Or are you really still trying to prove how smart you are? Is that what all this is?'

There was no answer.

'Come. Sit,' Andross said. 'This wine shan't stay chilled forever.' Indeed, there was condensation on one of the glasses.

He'd not been here long, he was saying. Just long enough to have plenty of time to wait for Gavin. He'd predicted him that perfectly.

Andross tilted the goblet and inhaled the scent with relish.

'Marvelous. Oh, wait. Was this the one I poisoned, or the other?' He picked up the other glass and drank. 'Ah, that's right, I poisoned neither. What trivial games you play, boy. How unworthy you are of my name.'

Gavin didn't move. It didn't make sense. His father had taken such precautions last time. Why simply let Gavin step within striking range?

'You fucker,' Gavin said.

That was the humiliation. Gavin was so weak, the old man didn't fear physical violence from him. And Gavin couldn't draft. He had no power Andross need fear, neither martial nor magical nor mental.

Andross grinned, as if pleased that Gavin had figured it out. 'You know, I made a mistake with you.'

'More than one,' Gavin said.

Andross continued as if he'd not heard him. 'I thought you'd *found* this prison. I had no idea you were so insane that you'd *made* it. I didn't realize the truth until you broke out of the blue cell. Then it became obvious. And of course you'd not have made a prison without designing ways for you yourself to escape.'

'I am my mother's son,' Gavin said. Orholam have mercy, that food. His whole body ached for it. Not the hunger of the belly, but the deeper hunger felt in the throat like thirst.

Andross's face darkened, but he controlled himself. He said, 'I propose a trade.'

'A trade?'

'There is a dignity in making bargains, and you need all the dignity you can get. You know I'll abide by my word.'

Gavin said nothing. He was too hungry, too weak. His mind couldn't race as fast as Andross Guile's in this moment.

'You give me the tooth and that bit of hellstone, and you can eat your fill.'

Gavin's heart had been an eagle, mounting on strong wings, as he'd seen the chamber before him. His father's appearance had torn out his flight feathers. And now Andross plucked out his last hopes. Andross knew about the hellstone. He knew about it all. Wearing nothing but rags, Gavin had hidden both secrets in his cheeks, like a *khat*-chewer. Gavin's hopes plunged to earth, flapping wildly, helplessly, uselessly.

'Then what?' Gavin asked.

'Then you go back to a cell, of course.'

Gavin didn't so much as glance back at the lux torch he'd stuck in the works to keep the portcullis from falling. He was weak, but it could be used as a club.

His father did look at it, pointedly. 'Too far away, don't you think?'

It was.

'Even were it closer, do you think it would be enough, against me, in your present state?'

And Gavin's hopes plunged into the earth, ribs breaking, body smashed. There was nothing left for him.

Andross said, 'Come now, sit sit sit. We have so much to talk about.'

Gavin hesitated for one moment more.

'So disappointing,' Andross said. He sighed. 'It used to be your particular strength that you could see how a situation had changed and adapt to it instantly...Dazen.'

It was a horse stomping on a body already dead. Gavin had known his father had to know by now, but to hear it, to have that sick, shameful truth spoken, was more than he could bear.

'Three...two...one...and the offer's expired,' Andross said. And now he was stripping the dead for loot, breaking open Gavin's jaw to get at a gold tooth.

'But wait, I haven't—'

'I gave you a fair chance. This wasn't a trap. This food was here for you, and you had it. *Almost.*'

And now Andross was desecrating the dead, mutilating the corpse.

The word had a resonance, here, in this chamber: 'almost.'

But Gavin was already speaking, reacting, walking toward

Andross. For may not the desecrated dead rise as vengeful ghosts? 'I want you to know, Father. I didn't know if I could really go through with it and kill Gavin. But then I realized I wasn't murdering him, I was freeing him from the nightmare you'd pulled him into when he was just a child. You took him away from us and destroyed the boy he was. I was freeing him from your corruption. It was a mercy killing.'

Rage washing over his face, Andross snapped his fingers and light flared from a wall behind Gavin and to his left.

Fiery letters appeared, spelling out 'Almost' in Gavin's own hand. The very sign he'd used to taunt his brother into his trap.

But how had Andross triggered it?

Gavin didn't wait. He lunged toward the old man.

An egg of red luxin larger than his head hit him in the face and blew him off his feet.

Gavin fell flat on his back and pawed at the sticky pyrejelly covering his face, spitting, trying to breathe. He barely opened his eyes in time to see Andross standing over him, one hand aflame.

With the combustible goop on his face, if Andross brought that fire close, Gavin would burn to death.

But his father checked himself, extinguished the flame, and merely hit him with a right cross.

Gavin's head bounced off the floor and his limbs went limp. He fought to recover.

He heard a clang as Andross used luxin to hurl aside Gavin's lux torch from where it was blocking the portcullis. But there was no clatter of the portcullis dropping to the floor.

Andross cursed and shot a flaming missile at the rope holding up the portcullis.

It fell, but the floor didn't open beneath Gavin. Andross must not have reset the trap correctly.

Gavin pulled himself up to his knees, but his father saw him move and kicked. Gavin tried to block the kick, but he was too weak. Andross's foot smashed into his stomach, and another fist caught Gavin across the jaw.

He fell to the ground, and Andross stepped on his neck.

'Some trap,' the old man said. Still holding Gavin down,

Andross reached in front of him, where Gavin had spat out the hellstone fragment and the broken tooth he'd kept secreted in his mouth.

Gavin tried to scramble away, but Andross pinned him harder, exerting so much pressure Gavin thought his vertebrae would crack. Gavin caught the barest glimpse of Andross's pinprick-tight pupils.

He was drafting. He threw out a hand, and sent something beyond normal vision into Gavin's old trap. Gavin said, 'But you can't draft superviolet.'

'Can't I? It seems you know as little about me as I once knew about you.' With a light kick to Gavin's temple to stun him once more, Andross said, 'I think it's time you learn something else you didn't know. Take a look at what's waiting for you below.'

His brother's rotting corpse was below. Orholam, no. Gavin had thought his father would surely give his brother the burial he himself hadn't.

'No, please...'

The floor gave way, and Gavin tumbled into the yellow hell.

Chapter 39

The subtlety of the problem was its beauty. Kip sat in the soft light of the incipient dawn, teasing slender threads of yellow light for his project. It would be some time before the Ghosts had enough light to reach them, and watching the river change as night pulled back its covers and shivered into dawn was precious to him as last night had been precious.

He looked at the yellow cords in his hands. Something about having the peaceful light before him and having something to occupy his hands left no space for other thoughts, and sometimes thinking was the enemy.

After Tisis had pleased him last night, he'd begun to learn the mysteries of her body in turn. Joyful discoveries for an attentive novitiate. But after several rounds of delight, Tisis had sworn her body was relaxed enough to attempt intromission again.

Her Jade Gate was still firmly closed. Something in her wouldn't allow him inside, and a tiny part of him couldn't help but wonder if her body was betraying her words as lies that she really did want this marriage.

Maybe that was unfair of him.

It had certainly been unwise to say it out loud.

A magical, nearly perfect night had ended in tears and a turned back.

Eventually he'd pulled her to him, and she let him hold her against his big form, but neither had said another word.

The problem in his hands this morning was ever so much simpler. When he'd been lost and delirious the last time he'd been in Blood Forest, he'd drafted a small length of chain from solid yellow. He'd begun by drafting each tiny link one at a time. It would have taken him several years to make a mail coat that way.

If he lived long enough to finish it, it would make something lighter and much, much stronger than iron or steel. He still wasn't sure if it would stop a musket ball, though.

That uncertainty, and that he would have to spend weeks to draft a large-enough section of mail even to run an inconclusive test against a musket ball, had made him lose interest.

Tisis had been up for a while. He could hear her moving around the tent, getting dressed and ready for the day. She paused now, just inside. Gathering her courage? Kip wondered if they were going to start the day with a fight.

He glanced back down at his project as she stepped out. She stretched with a pleased sound and made a quick sign of the seven to the sun as it first peeked over the horizon, illuminating the river and her blonde hair in its ponytail. She met Kip's eye and smiled.

She came over and sat next to him, her hip touching his.

So...not a fight. Thank Orholam.

'What're you working on?' Tisis asked, a smile in her voice.

'Just something to keep my hands busy.'

'Something to keep your hands busy?'

'Little project. Was thinking of making a mail coat with it

at first. But it'd take me six months at least. I'm not sure it makes sense to plan that long term.'

She put her hand on his thigh and blew out a breath. 'Kip, I wanted to say sorry for last night. I was a brat.'

I wish more people would be a brat that way! was probably not the right thing to say. But she wasn't talking about the first part of the night and he knew it. 'I'm sorry, too,' Kip said.

'No, you've got nothing to be sorry for. Thanks for pulling me back to you. I needed that,' she said.

The rest of the camp was stirring now, and not a few people were already hard at work at morning chores, but, taking their cue from Winsen, who stood guarding Kip and Tisis from a good distance, the others didn't approach.

'I know we didn't exactly choose this,' Kip said. 'I mean, we did, but it was a pretty constrained choice. But we're in this together. I had a great time last night – the best time. You were, just, wow.'

'But,' she said glumly.

'Yeah. I want us to stop trying the other thing.'

'The normal thing, you mean?' she asked bitterly.

He wondered how much they were being careful not to say it straight out because they were outside where someone might just overhear, and how much they were just embarrassed. Who fails at having sex?

'Everything is great for us except that. Why can't we just have fun and put that aside?' Kip said. 'It's just not—'

'You know damn well why,' she said quietly. 'The contract isn't valid. I mean, at this point I've already lied to my sister, which has only worked because I haven't had to see her face-to-face. She'll know, Kip.'

'We're not going to see her,' he said. 'Not until all this is over.'

'Kip, political marriages get split up all the time. And that's when they're valid in the first place. I'm not really safely in your family until I have a baby and your grandfather decides it looks like a Guile. You think that old man wouldn't be happy to cast me off like a cheap whore again?'

Again.

She cursed under her breath. Neither of them wanted to remember Kip walking in on her stroking Andross Guile under his covers. It had been a scene Andross had set up on purpose to humiliate both of them – and precipitate this marriage, though Tisis still didn't know that part.

Orholam. No wonder she was tense, if she had to get past her memories of *that* every time she was with Kip.

'Forget that,' Kip said. 'Forget him. For now. Our vengeance on him is being happy with each other. We'll figure something out about all that other stuff later. For now, we keep doing everything that brings us joy – and that's a lot! – and we stop doing the one thing that brings us misery.'

'You want to give up,' she said.

'Is it giving up when you stop doing something that hurts us?'

She scowled at first, but then squeezed his leg. 'You said "us."'

'How many ways do I need to tell you we're in this together?' Kip asked.

She put her head on his shoulder. 'I want you to know it's not just for the contract and my sister, or for fear that you'll drop me later. I want to make love with you. You know that, right?'

'I know,' Kip said. But he hadn't, not really. Didn't, still. She was being honest, and he trusted her, but he still didn't believe her, somehow. They weren't just a boy and a girl, trying to figure something out. They never would be.

But then, if they were just a boy and a girl, Kip never could have caught so much as the eye of a girl this beautiful, so he probably should never complain ever, ever again, so long as he lived.

But she'd said that word, that word that demands response. Though she'd said only 'make love,' and that could be part of a phrase, meaningless. It hadn't been entirely meaningless. Had it? Was that a question? A test. It was still there, prickly as a caltrop for him to step on: 'love.'

He'd said, Let's have fun.

She'd said, Let's make love.

Shit.

'You're beautiful,' he said softly. 'And gracious. I really appreciate you, and I'm really coming to ... care for you. Deeply.' Orholam, that sounded so lame. He shouldn't have said anything at all. 'I'm sorry, that's ... all wrong.'

'Teia?' she asked, and hurt echoed harsh and deep into a cave of longing. 'You still think of her.' It wasn't quite a question.

'Sometimes,' he said. 'But I don't dwell on it.'

She sat up and held his face in her hands. 'You're a man who feels deeply. It's one of your best qualities. I can't hold that against you.'

'But you do. A little,' he said.

'A little,' she admitted. 'I'm getting over that slowly, too.' She took a deep breath, and Kip saw something flit through her eyes.

'I wasn't thinking about her last night while we were together,' he said. 'Not at all. Not at all.'

She expelled her breath and relief washed over her. 'I didn't want to ask. Thank you.'

And she let him off the hook, just like that. She really was kinder than he deserved.

'So if you're not making a mail coat, what's this going to be?' she asked, pointing to the length of lambent yellow luxin chain.

'Well, the chain is easy enough if I'm not hooking every link to three or four others, so I thought I'd do something harder, more subtle.'

'More subtle?' she asked.

'I'm still going to have the chain as the core, but I'm trying to make, like ... an articulated rope around it. See, rope spears are awesome because you can throw knots over your opponents' hands and do grappling and all sorts of things, but the rope itself can obviously be cut by any blade if you're not careful. A chain spear can't be cut, but it's much harder to throw loops and knots and whatnot. So I'm trying to get the best of both worlds.'

'But you never trained with a rope spear, have you?'

'No, no, it's just something to keep my hands busy.'

'Right,' she said suddenly. 'That's great. Oh, look, it's the

Ghosts. I'd better go prepare.' But she'd stiffened, and she suddenly stood and walked away. And Kip had the distinct feeling he'd loused up again.

'What'd I do?' Kip asked Winsen.

Winsen was squinting against the dawn like someone with a serious hangover. 'I am asking myself the same question. But my answer is drink way, way too much wine.'

Chapter 40

As she'd arranged, Karris was still at her dawn prayers when Promachos Andross Guile arrived. She lay prostrate before the open window facing the sun, and felt the faint stirring of the wind as the inner door opened behind her.

'Orholam,' she pleaded aloud, 'I could try to hide my ignorance, but I won't. I'm not going to act in darkness. Let it all stand before the light. Orholam, this is your empire; these are your people. You will have to fight for us, or we shall perish. Will you let your name be defamed upon the earth?'

She stayed there prone for some time, praying. She'd arranged this, but that didn't mean it wasn't real, too. She needed to look like a zealot in order to accomplish what needed doing. It was the zealots in the Magisterium who could give her the most trouble if they allied against her. But by disarming them, she could also make unnecessary the calls for luxors. She had two luxors. She had no desire for there to be any more, by her hand or any other.

But as she said the words for Andross Guile's benefit – let him think her a little crazy, it might make him careful around her – she realized she meant them, too. She wasn't fighting for herself. She didn't want power for its own sake; she wanted only to save the Chromeria and the people of the Seven Satrapies. After that was accomplished she would happily step down.

So it was only right that Orholam should take up his own fight. This war was his problem.

Finally, when she felt emptied, when she felt heard, she stood.

She hadn't realized that Andross Guile had gotten down on his face next to her.

'A prayer as fierce as you are,' Andross said, dusting his hands off.

'My apologies for keeping you waiting,' she said.

'One must know the order of one's loyalties,' Andross said, as if understanding her perfectly.

'But Orholam knows the heart. Our prayers are surely for our own reflection more than for his instruction, no?'

'A point for the luxiats to debate, no doubt. Tea?' He gestured to her slave to close the doors to the balcony.

It was a breach of etiquette for him to command her slaves, but a small one. He obviously thought she deserved it for keeping him waiting.

'We have much to discuss, but before we get started—' Karris said. She chewed on her lower lip, thinking. 'A number of months ago, I was ambushed on Big Jasper. I was beaten, efficiently and dispassionately. It was clearly intended to teach me a lesson. Maybe a man would have taken such a beating as intended. Once he realized he wasn't being beaten to death, he might simply endure it. Perhaps. But a woman made to feel utterly helpless at the hands of half a dozen men?' She paused. 'There are different fears. Lingering fears. Fears that can be crippling, if one doesn't know her history.'

'Perhaps that was the message instead? A beating is bad, but there are worse things possible?' Andross said innocently, as if just speculating, trying to find the answer with her.

'If so,' she said, 'that message was beyond ill considered, and had the opposite effect to what was intended. No one likes to feel helpless; I have a particular loathing for it. I made a foolish oath about what I would do when I found out who had done that to me. It involved flaying and honey and insects and castration. Not a fitting oath for the White to take.'

'But then, you weren't the White at the time,' he said, still so damnably innocent.

'No indeed. Do you think a White is bound by oaths she made before she was the White?'

'Hmm. Yes? – unless they interfere with her duties as the White. That oath and office supersedes all lower bonds,' Andross said.

'I agree. It becomes tricky, though. You see, with all the intelligence apparatus available to me as the White, I've uncovered who ordered my beating.'

'Indeed?' he asked. 'A curious allocation of your resources, don't you think? Still. I wish I had thought to have my own people look into that for you. What punishment may I help you inflict upon this malefactor?'

She took a breath and looked away. 'None. I forgive you.'

'*Me*?! Beg your pardon?' He didn't even sound that outraged. He wasn't even trying.

'I'll seek no vengeance against you. I consider the matter closed.'

Baffle Andross Guile.

'In return for what? Me admitting something I obviously didn't do?' Andross asked, but his expression had already betrayed him.

'It would be nice—'

'My dear, some people only know the language of blunt objects. I speak to such people in the language they understand. You, however, are not one of those.'

She held up a hand. 'I forgive you. Let it not stand between us. Clean slate.'

'Generous of you,' he said sarcastically. 'Should I forgive you in turn for seducing my sons and destroying the Seven Satrapies?'

It was so unfair it almost took her breath. Andross Guile had been the one who ordered his younger son Dazen to seduce Karris, so that he wouldn't have to marry off his elder son to her to seal their families' alliance. It had worked, too. She and Dazen had fallen in love, but then the real Gavin couldn't bear to see his younger brother so happy. What had happened next was Andross Guile's fault more than anyone's. And he blamed her? A fifteen-year-old girl at the time?

She wanted to scratch his damn eyes out. But she'd learned something in the Archers about fighting those who were bigger and stronger. Things about accounting for the trajectory of the superior force. You never try to stop it. You redirect it instead.

'Yes. Please do forgive me,' she said without a hint of sarcasm.

He stopped, suddenly emotionless. He wasn't often taken by surprise. 'Oh, I don't think I respected Orea enough,' he said finally.

She wasn't sure which he meant: that Orea had been brilliant in appointing Karris who was so surprisingly capable, or that it had been nice to deal with Orea and he hadn't noticed how nice until he had to deal with her inferior.

'A mistake I'm sure you'll not make with her successor,' Karris said.

He chuckled. 'Oh, I already have. But not again, perhaps. I make many mistakes, but few of them twice.'

'Well, now that we've gotten all that out of the way, the purpose of our meeting,' Karris said.

'Yes. Pray tell.'

Karris said, 'I looked at the faces of all the High Luxiats and the Colors on the execution platform when that…thing happened. I saw bewilderment or fear on every face. Most hiding it, naturally. But one face looked almost…'

She paused.

Andross said, 'Please don't hold back on my account.'

'Smug. Like he'd been proven right about something. Strange, don't you think?'

'That *would* be an odd expression for such a time,' Andross agreed. 'And quite astute of you to look for it.' He sipped his tea.

'I think you might find that my eye is on you more than you'd guess,' Karris said. Shit. That came out as a threat. 'To see how I should act. To take your lead.'

'To take my lead?' he asked, amused.

She wanted to kill him. She wanted justice for Orea's murder. She wanted to demand to know what he'd done with Marissia and the package of letters.

But that was all a fantasy.

Andross Guile was too dangerous to kill; he was also too valuable alive. When he wanted things done, he got them done. And diplomats who might start fights with anyone else would do anything in their power not to tangle with Andross Guile.

Which mattered. This war wasn't just going to fizzle out. Karris saw that now. The White King was making smart moves in his conquered lands, preparing to hold and keep them, to generate wealth that he could draw from to take all the satrapies.

Vengeance is yours, Orholam.

It'll have to be.

'Promachos,' Karris said. 'When you lock shields with the man next to you in a battle line, you don't first ask his opinion on the Manichean dichotomy. I don't intend to challenge your position or your power, so long as I feel we're fighting on the same side. The Color Prince has gone from a regional problem to an existential crisis. I can't fight you and him at the same time. But if I need to fight you before the satrapies can fight him, I'll throw everything against you – and I will fight you until one of us is annihilated. I can't do half measures, and I won't accept them from you. So, war. Together. Are you in, or out?' And this was where it was important he see her as a zealot.

'In.' He said it with no hesitation.

'Then start talking. What happened at the execution? What was that thing? Why haven't I heard about any of this before?'

Karris hadn't slept well since the execution. She didn't know if she'd ever sleep well again. Seeing that monster tear out of that spy's skin had been the single most frightening experience of her life. In all her battles, even hunting down wights – those she'd fought had been men at core. This was something else.

For the first time Karris had ever seen, Andross Guile looked somewhat daunted, as if he didn't know what to say, or perhaps where to start. 'Have you heard of the Thousand Worlds?'

I'm not interested in fairy stories, Karris wanted to say. But Andross Guile rarely went on tangents without good reason. 'The premise that there are many worlds like ours?'

'Not exactly like ours,' Andross said. 'The idea being that

Orholam, being a creator, wouldn't necessarily stop after making one world. Maybe he'd make twenty, or a thousand or a million. Who knows? I was ambivalent about the hypothesis. The unmasking of Nabiros has changed my thinking.'

'That thing. Delara Orange swore it wasn't a will-casting or a hex.'

'I believe her. Nabiros was real.' He rested his piercing eyes on her. 'The Chromeria and the Magisterium don't actually teach some of the things that they believe, for fear that weaker souls will be led astray. Regardless, I've been piecing together truths and making leaps of intuition for many years, but this is the truth as well as I know. Will you cry heresy if I say things you don't like?'

It wasn't a real question. What it was, Karris saw, was a plea to have his efforts recognized. Doubtless Felia had always given him assurances of his genius. But the old man's wife was gone now, and he wanted someone to appreciate his intellectual heavy lifting.

So instead of mocking him as her heart desired, Karris chose compassion: he's lost his wife, for Orholam's sake, be kind.

By the grace of Orholam alone, she painted rapt attention on her features. 'Caveats accepted. What have you learned?'

He stared hard at her, looking for mockery, and here she saw him as human again. With weaknesses. Seeking approval and praise. Not venally, but simply as part of the normal human exchange – a person does something excellent and useful, and they wish it to be recognized.

But then he accepted her interest and took it as his due, the momentary chink in his arrogance covered again.

'It was told to me as a creation story, transcribed from an old Tiru wise man in the Parian highlands, but I've no gift for stories. Mine is a mind that tears things asunder and examines the pieces. What matters for us is that before time, Orholam created six hundred immortals – or possibly six hundred legions, but let's not complicate things. Two hundred of those rejected him and sought his throne. They lost, are losing, will lose. In the meantime, they seek to ruin every joy Orholam might have of his creations, and taste every dark pleasure they may. If they may not rule all the celestial realms, they desire to rule a world. They will possess the bodies of the willing to taste what it is like to wear flesh. They will sire children. They will murder, steal, crush, and rape. They will defile any goodness they find. They will wage war and bring ruin wherever they can in their fury at losing the home that was free to them and is now forbidden forever. For rage burns hottest against a punishment deserved.'

This was nothing new, except for the specificity of the numbers. What was new was Andross's treating it as real. Karris had to guess there was some spin into heresy coming soon.

'The salient fact, though, is that these immortals are neither omniscient nor omnipresent. Here.' He reached into his pockets and pulled out a number of short scrolls, one after the other. Karris could commiserate. They were both always getting reports, and always on scrolls of uniform size, which made them stack better, but also led to the waste of having entire sheets of lambskin with only the words "Arrived safely" or something similarly concise on them. Many of the reports were deemed too sensitive for the parchments to be scraped and reused, too.

He unrolled half a dozen scrolls and laid them atop each other on Karris's desk. 'Imagine this scroll is the history of our world, beginning here to end over here. This one? Another world's history. And another's.'

Andross stacked the papers and drew his belt knife. He laid the point against the skin.

'We experience time like this.' He dragged the knife lightly forward.

'An immortal, on the other hand, may enter any world of its choosing.' He flipped a different scroll onto the top of the pile.

'It may enter at any location it desires. Any kingdom, satrapy, or city.' He moved the knife left and right.

'But once it enters, it moves in time as we do, until it leaves.' He stabbed the knife all the way through all of the scrolls. 'They aren't omnipresent, so if they choose to be in Ru all Sun Day, they may not ever be in Tyrea on the same day.' He grabbed a quill, dipped it, and crossed out everything to the left and right of the point where the knife had stabbed.

Then he cut forward. Then he lifted the knife out of the skins. 'So if our immortal stays a year in Ru, say, being worshipped as the goddess Atirat, that is a year denied her elsewhere.' With the quill, he crossed out all the area left and right of his cut.

'But why the stack?' Karris asked.

'Because there are many worlds, but only one time.' He flipped a different scroll onto the top of the stack. He crossed out the entire area left and right of the cut there, too. 'So Atirat is denied that time *everywhere* else. An immortal has all eternity, but they have only a finite number of chances to interact with us mortals. Thus, paradoxically, with all eternity available to them, a single day becomes incredibly precious to immortals. So, were I immortal, I would only visit when my presence would matter most. Perhaps on my holy days, or more likely in times of war, where I might claim or lose an entire world.'

Karris did not like where this was suddenly going. Tingles prickled along her skin. 'An immortal like Nabiros?'

Andross looked at her and licked dry lips. She swore she saw a flicker of fear in his eyes. 'We've entered a time that immortals find interesting enough to visit personally, and because of some fluke or perhaps some very carefully prescribed and maintained traditions that neither you nor I were aware of, we have just done exactly what we needed to do to *kill* one of them. I think it would be an insane level of optimism not to expect the full fury of their vengeance.'

It was as if the floor had dropped out from under her. Karris's problems had looked daunting when they'd been human. She buried her face in her hands, and felt her gorge rising.

It was too much for her. She was the wrong person for all this. She was going to fail everyone, and now that failure wouldn't just mean the dissolution of the kingdom.

Breathe, Karris.

She pulled herself together and suddenly thought of something. 'We aren't alone in this. This is Orholam's fight. We didn't kill Nabiros by sheer luck. Those traditions weren't just stumbled upon. Someone taught our ancestors those. And that we followed them well enough that they worked? That wasn't luck – it must have been Orholam's immortals intervening on our side.' And suddenly she could breathe again. Things were harmoniously blue and orderly again. Orholam would take care of the immortals, and she'd take care of her lists. That, *that* made sense.

Then Andross shit all over her peace. As he did. 'Let us not mistake their side and ours. This is one battlefield among a hundred thousand for them. Perhaps their victory is complete now that one of the two hundred rebels is banished. Or perhaps by drawing the vengeance of his fellows, they get a dozen of the rebels to waste days or even mere hours here that are critically important to a battle on some other world that they believe is more important.'

'You're telling me we could just be a distraction?' Karris asked.

'How did the old story put it? "When the king sends a ship of grain to his ally, he worries not about the comfort of the rats in the hold." Our lives are nothing to the universe, High Lady.'

'This is where your great intellect fails you for a lack of imagination and faith, Andross Guile. You think that to be concerned with the great tides of history means that one must lose track of one little fish. Or that by caring for one son, you can not care equally for another.'

'You wish to compare how well we have loved our sons?' Andross asked.

'I didn't mean it like that,' she said, flushing. She didn't want to talk about Zymun. He made her uncomfortable, still. Though that was surely her own guilt speaking. But he was always touching her. Always wanting to be with her. 'I meant that Orholam sees and hears and cares and—'

'And saves, yes, I know the old prayer. I'm simply not convinced by it. Tell me, Karris, have you ever prayed for something that you thought you needed more than breath itself?'

'Gavin is still missing. How dare you ask me that?'

'Ah, Gavin, yes. A man of singular gifts indeed. A man who would be of immense help in this war of ours, wouldn't he?'

She said nothing, certain some cruelty would come out of Andross Guile's mouth next.

'And where is he? And where is the Orholam who saves, who sees, who cares?'

Karris had no answer.

'We're in a battle alone. And of the immortals, only one side has shown up, and it wasn't Orholam's.'

'What would you have us do?' Karris said.

'First, understand the stakes. We aren't only fighting rebels now. We fight against the gods themselves. Should they win, this whole world will fall into their hands, perhaps until the end of time. We've killed one. In his time, Lucidonius killed nine. Depending on which translation is correct, that leaves us to face either twelve hundred thousand – minus ten – or a hundred and ninety. The good news or bad is that they come in ranks. Nabiros or Cerberos is a low-ranking immortal.'

'Naturally,' Karris said. Holy shit.

'I don't know what happens if the strongest ones come. It was said during the reign of one particularly old and powerful Atirat that it was impossible to draft green anywhere in Blood Forest without his permission. Scholars since have interpreted that to mean drafting green in Blood Forest was illegal. I think they really meant impossible.'

'Like what we felt at Ru,' Karris said. At the end, greens there had lost control of their bodies, been unable to move. 'The greens felt the bane from many leagues away, but it was only crippling within – what? A league or two? But how do they do it? And what determines their power?'

Andross hesitated. 'The point is—'

'No, wait. What was that? You were just going to say something. Tell me.'

Andross thought for a moment, studying her. 'That – how they do what they do and what determines their power – is what I sent Zymun to find out. It's why I ordered him to infiltrate the Color Prince's ranks. He didn't learn much, unfortunately, before he had to flee. He'd failed the Color Prince twice – in assassinating Gavin, and in holding Ruic Head. Truth is, I'm not entirely certain he meant to fail at either.'

But Karris didn't even hear the last biting words. Of course Andross would try to soil her joy. Karris hadn't been able to get straight answers out of Zymun about when he'd tried to 'hurt' Gavin, she'd said, couching it gently. No wonder! His grandfather was to blame for all that, and he was trying to keep it secret because he was being loyal to Andross – the one person in his family he'd known for years.

And Andross, the cold bastard, had put Zymun in a place where he'd needed to publicly fail at an assassination attempt – but appear to really be trying – in order to obey his grandfather and keep his position near the Color Prince.

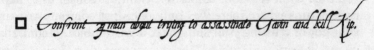 ☐ Confront Zymun about trying to assassinate Gavin and kill Kip.

Thank Orholam.

'The point is,' Andross said, exasperated, 'perhaps Orholam sees us as an acceptable sacrifice in a greater war. I do not. High Lady, I wish you to pick up your knives. If we're to survive this, we must be harder and smarter and stronger and crueler than the gods themselves.'

He regarded her for a long moment, and she shelved her sudden hope that maybe now things would feel more natural with Zymun, now that those awful things were explained away.

Andross said, 'I ordered those men to beat you, because I saw what Orea was doing, how she was grooming you, giving you all these different assignments so you could learn her work. And I didn't think you were equal to it. I remembered that sniveling girl you were, pretty and thoughtless. I wanted to see what you were made of – if you could even find out it was me, and if so, how you would come at me. I thought you were unwilling to fight back, or that when you did, you'd do it recklessly and stupidly. I was wrong about you then…and later, too.'

'Later? You mean when you stacked the election to White against me?' And tried to have me killed?! she didn't say aloud.

'You will need all your strength for this fight,' he said. 'And that streak of insanity or faith you show, whether it's real or feigned.'

To say she was baffled would have been understating the matter. Had he just admitted to trying to have her killed? What was that? Why?

Perhaps it was as close to an apology as he was capable of. He got up and walked to the door. She simply stared after him, speechless.

'Oh,' he said, turning, 'in case it wasn't clear enough: Zymun is one of my knives. Sharp and imbalanced, but very predictable once you understand what he is. In normal times, I should not...but these are not normal times, are they? Let me offer you this: Guilt is a poor counselor. Guilt oft conspires to make two victims where there was only one. If it comes to trusting your gut or trusting your son, make a wise choice, High Lady.'

Chapter 41

Liv walked through the abandoned orange groves silently, clouds of superviolet billowing from her with every step. Drafting was as easy as breathing now, and the many-fingered clouds spread a hundred paces and more from her in every direction. She patted the fallen statue of the Broken Man, remnant of the long-dead old Tyrean Empire.

She didn't go to the burnt-out buildings and rubble of Rekton. She didn't go to her old home. She was here for something important.

She crossed the river, appearing to walk on water, small geysers of superviolet rising to support her feet at each step. She arrived at the old battlefield, long overgrown with low plants, mostly brown this late in the summer. Craters were still visible from artillery and magic both, eighteen years on, but now rain lilies and haemanthus huddled in those shady, watered places, beauty flourishing over ugliness, new life sprouting from rot.

Uncertain what her full powers might do here among the dead, she withdrew most of them into herself. Sundered Rock beckoned her, and she climbed it.

'Beliol,' she summoned, and a moment later her ring sparkled. Her nameless servant hadn't remained nameless for long after she had broken the halo. He'd seemed surprised that she had known what his name meant. Beliol meant 'yokeless,' so different from Belial – 'worthless.'

'Yokeless?' she'd asked. "And yet you serve me.'

'One needs no yoke to be compelled to serve when one believes in the one whom one is serving.' She'd been flattered, but of course, he'd meant it to be flattering.

'The chained one comes, Mistress,' Beliol said. 'Five hundred paces, moving slowly so as not to give alarm, I believe.'

The approaching Mot was attended by only two guards, both blue wights, and thus fully under her control. Her full retinue was half a league away. They reached the base of the opposite side of the cracked dome that was Sundered Rock, and she began to climb it alone.

Samila Sayeh had been a hero of the Prisms' War and later the lover of Usef Tep, her former enemy. They had come to Tyrea together to submit to the Freeing.

Finding war threatening once more, Samila had intended to die fighting against the Color Prince at Garriston. Usef Tep had done so, but she'd lived, and now she served the man responsible for her lover's death. Funny how war makes villains of heroes and slaves of the free.

Liv had narrowly missed meeting the legend in Tyrea, but had later met her in Ru, when the mousy genius had figured out in moments a calibration problem with the Great Mirror of Ru that had stumped Liv and others for hours.

If anyone was going to figure out what Liv was really doing, it was she. But did Samila even remember what she'd done at the Great Mirror? Did she remember those coordinates she'd translated in an instant?

In a few minutes, the middle-aged woman had climbed the opposite side of Sundered Rock, allowing the gulf to sit between them. The duolith itself, shaped like a cracked egg, lay partially submerged. It was hundreds of feet tall, and lay gray in the sun, with scorch marks faded by nearly two decades' passage but not gone. A few withered tufts of grass clung to its overhanging halves, and there was an opening below, as if the egg, broken in halves, had spilled its innards.

Except it was no egg, and not nearly an empty shell. Probably the rock debris between the two halves had simply been cleared by looters certain that here at the epicenter of the holocaustic finale of the Prisms' War, there must be treasure hidden.

Maybe there had been, once. The Color Prince had gotten his black luxin from somewhere.

Oddly, Samila Sayeh had affected few of the usual traits of a wight, much less a god. Her skin wasn't crystalline, except her left hand, as if she were still running the experiment to see how blue luxin might function as skin in an application that required so much dexterity, sensitivity, and motion. The rest of her looked severe and beautiful. The olive skin of an Atashian, but barely wrinkled even at forty-four years and seventeen days old, because she'd been a noble, and careful to protect her skin. She was slender and striking, her naturally blue eyes now solid cerulean, irises and sclera both.

But her dress was murex purple. A simple preference? A sign of her obscene wealth now? Of trying to find some common ground with Liv and her superviolet? Was it a sign of not caring to wear blue every day – 'Yes, I'm the blue goddess, I needn't wear blue constantly, thank you'? Or...was the color in honor of her Usef Tep, the Purple Bear?

How much of the old Samila Sayeh was left in the new Mot?

Regardless, in Liv's new sight, the older woman crackled with power. A throbbing heartbeat of blue will scattered its near cousin superviolet with every breath, and spectral bleed made her glow in superviolet like a sword plucked from the forge and held in the air for a few long moments: the color dulled quickly from white hot to angry red to a sullen gray, but you'd still be a fool to touch it with your hand.

They were mirrors to each other: outsiders, logical women,

cool and rational, both captured, both entwined, but Liv young and Samila older, Liv unproven and Samila renowned, Liv with all her tales before her, Samila with her legends behind, and, most importantly, Liv free while Samila wore the Color Prince's black jewel at her throat. If she disobeyed him, or attempted to remove it, it would behead her.

'Hail, Lady of Sorrows,' Samila said across the great gap between them.

Liv had never heard the term before. She was probably supposed to ask about it. But she had no idea what games the Color Prince would be playing here nor any interest in playing them. 'Hello, Samila. Lady Mot, is it now?'

'You've taken the seed crystal,' Samila said. 'Without taking a slave collar. Impressively done.' She turned to the side and said, 'No, Meena, I think it's important to give credit where it's due.'

There was no one there, though. Not even in superviolet. Not even as an afterimage of power.

Now *that* was interesting. Was Meena Samila's version of Beliol?

Liv coughed, clearing her throat. 'Can she see you?' Liv asked as she covered her mouth.

'No,' Beliol said. 'Though she knows I'm here. You might find it in your best interest to hold back as much information as possible.'

That they both had...invisible helpers attending them, but that those were invisible even to other gods, meant something, but Liv wasn't certain what. And had that been Samila slipping in letting her know about her own attendant, or had it been on purpose?

'Beautiful ring,' Samila said. 'Is that where you keep the seed crystal?'

'Thank you, but no. A ring on the finger seems an awfully vulnerable place to keep such power, doesn't it? On the other hand – sorry, no pun intended – I did want a small physical reminder of my power to flash about when such things might prove helpful.'

Samila Sayeh seemed to like the idea. It was a lie, though. The same lie Liv wanted Beliol to believe. She'd sent him to get her a suitable ring, and while he was gone, she'd turned her powers to making a gem that would sparkle and glow only when he was near.

Then, because it glowed every time Beliol did appear, he simply thought it glowed at all times.

She'd encouraged him to think it merely part and parcel of her vanity by also sending him for dresses and ermine and other jewelry. It was lovely to have such an obedient and powerful servant, but Liv had spent too much time being bent to the will of others to actually trust him.

'Where do you keep yours?' Liv asked, as if they were exchanging fashion tips.

'Oh, incorporated with my body, of course. As you keep yours. I simply wanted to see if you'd try to mislead me, make me think you were ignorant where you are not.'

And Liv, of course, had. Caught. Dammit. Liv had a brief flash of the same rage she'd felt before at Samila when she'd humiliated her by figuring out the problems of the Great Mirror so easily. 'You do serve the man who tried to enslave me,' Liv said, smiling at the bitch.

'He enslaved me first.'

'There are many ways one might react to that,' Liv pointed out.

'There is no black luxin here,' Samila said, ignoring her.

'Is there not?' Liv asked.

'It was all carried away, long ago. You're wasting your time if you came here looking for it.'

'Is that why I came here?' Liv asked.

'You grew up in bloody Rekton, yonder,' Samila said. 'I told the White King you might be visiting there, to say goodbye. To mourn your dead. He thought the only reason you'd come would be for this battlefield.'

No, neither, actually. 'The White King?' Liv asked.

Samila Sayeh shrugged. 'One who brings all the colors together, perchance? The opposite of a Prism?'

'That's not how prisms work,' Liv pointed out. 'To bring light back together, you'd use another prism.'

'We had two Prisms at the same time once. Before your time,' Samila Sayeh said sarcastically. 'It didn't give us white.'

You old hag. 'So Koios sent you to stop me from wasting my time?' Liv asked, amused. 'So kind of him.'

'He wants you to rejoin him,' Samila said. 'You don't wear his collar, but our kind cannot hide from each other. He can find you anywhere in the world. On the other hand, you will also be able to feel him or any of the rest of us coming for you. It would make for a tedious chase. Instead he offers you a kingdom. Ilyta, specifically, traditional home of Ferrilux.'

'What do I care for Ilyta?' Liv asked.

'What do you care for any human land? You're a god now. But it is good to have a home, and a people who will rally to you. And worship you.'

'He really thinks he's going to win, doesn't he?' Liv asked.

'At this point, it's nearly inevitable. The question is really where you'll be standing when the fighting stops. He also offers the superviolet bane, without which you will never reach your full power.'

'My bane? He has it?' Liv asked.

'Oh, now you've tipped your hand, haven't you?' Samila said.

Liv didn't know what she was talking about.

'Never mind. He guessed as much.'

'Guessed what?' Liv asked.

'You are the reason why the Chromeria hides so much knowledge, Aliviana Danavis. You incorporated your seed crystal before it made a bane. If you'd waited until the bane had formed around the crystal and then incorporated it, you'd have both your powers and the place that magnifies them. Having incorporated the seed crystal too early, it will never form a temple. Unless you can figure out something even our ancestors struggled with. A Ferrilux would be the one to figure it out if any would, though, I suppose. Good luck.'

'He's found a second seed crystal?' Liv asked.

'Not yet. As you might guess, with it being invisible and with superviolet drafters of any skill so rare, superviolet seed crystals are the hardest to find. But he has teams looking for it. You understand, it is both the carrot and the stick. He can give it to you if you will serve him, or if he finds it, he can kill you and make a new, empowered Ferrilux who will be loyal to him.'

Liv's heart fell. She might be the most effective searcher for superviolet, but the other gods would be attuned to such a thing, and the White King could search many, many places at once. It would be a race to the death.

There was no way of knowing if another seed crystal had even formed yet. Liv might spend every moment for decades searching for something that didn't exist – and would have to, because her life would depend on it. Meanwhile, the White King would simply have subordinates do it.

'That's your deal?' Liv asked. 'I may live as a slave queen?'

'His deal. I don't care what you choose. Technically, you've rebelled. Being offered to live is generous in itself. But you're special, and superviolet has always been different, and, bluntly, weak. You will never have to wear the hellstone collar. But yes, you will bend the knee. *Servient omnes*. All shall serve, child.'

'I won't,' Liv said, but it sounded hollow.

Samila Sayeh sighed. 'Seasons come and seasons go, but youth will always think they know more than their elders.'

'And sometimes they'll be correct.' But Liv knew she was being immature. That was fine. Perhaps it would make them underestimate her.

Something more human entered Samila's tone when she said, after a pause, 'I do hope this is one of those times.'

Then she simply turned and left.

'Wait,' Liv said to the retreating form. 'That's it? No trap? No bartering?'

'Between gods?' Samila said. 'Unwilling gods at that. No. If you take his offer, you'll know where to find him. You'll feel him, perhaps do right now, even from here. But if I may...'

'Please,' Liv said.

'Take the time to visit your village. Whyever you came here, you're here now. You'll never find another good reason to visit a place so out of the way. Not with what you've become. You'll regret it if you don't go see what's become of the places you loved.'

Liv looked at the older woman for a long moment. 'Thank you. One question.'

'We've come all this way,' Samila Sayeh said.

'Do you hope to escape?'

The Mot fell silent for quite some time. She waved off a silent voice speaking to her. 'No,' she said finally. 'I save hope for things that are possible.'

'On my way here, I came through Garriston,' Liv said. 'Most of those who died in the battle were buried in mass graves.'

Samila Sayeh stopped breathing.

'But some of the slum dwellers who remained thought the drafters' bodies might be worth a ransom to their families. Especially Blackguards and...bichromes.' Liv didn't say the name Usef Tep. She could see it was dangerous ground. Never break the emotions of those who pride themselves on logic. 'Enter through the Hag's Gate. Take the third alley on the left. Blue door at the end. Ask for Ordoño.'

Then Liv left. To burn the time until Mot was far enough away that she wouldn't know where Liv was going exactly, she went to the dead village of Rekton. Eventually her feet took her to Kip's old hovel – somehow unburnt. She took in his scent deeply, deeply enough to send a message for him in superviolet, wherever he was now. He was the only wild card left, the only hope for victory.

Would he even understand it? Superviolet, Kip. Who else could send you a message in superviolet? But he was half the world away, and she had not the control yet to make her message clear.

It was probably hopeless.

She unbarred a closet. What a shithole. There were little scratch marks and dark stains on the inside of the door. A rats' nest sat on the ground, with old bones and fur and rat droppings. She'd had no idea Kip had lived in such squalor.

'Why are you crying?' Beliol asked her.

There was indeed wetness coursing down her face. Both sides. 'I don't know,' she said honestly.

Chapter 42

'We have a problem,' Conn Arthur said as his skimmer bumped ashore on the little island where Kip and the Mighty had camped. 'I'll explain as we go.'

Kip and Cruxer helped push off and jumped aboard. The Mighty's skimmer would follow. They were off instantly, if clumsily. The Ghosts were still figuring out the skimmers.

Conn Arthur said, 'There was a red wight yesterday who escaped our clash at the warehouse. Distinctive. No skin on his forearms. Several other wights and soldiers escaped as well, of course. But him...him we recognized. Name's Baoth. He's a former novice of Shady Grove who left us years ago. It was not an amicable parting. His gifts lay...elsewhere. Clearly he's been exploring those gifts, and now he's found a home for them with the Blood Robes.

'Trouble is, he recognized us. One of our scouts caught sight of him, last night. He was carrying some scroll cases. We think he's heading back to the main army to report everything that happened here, both above and below the falls. And, of course, who we are. Regardless, we get those papers, and we get some idea of what they know.' He grunted, and it sounded like a bear huffing as it tore apart a fallen log, looking for grubs.

'And you want to go after him,' Kip guessed.

'One of our women who grew up here said she knows a river valley he'll have to pass through tonight. It's narrow enough we can be sure he won't slip through our fingers there. After that, he's gone. We don't know exactly where the White King's army is, and there are many paths available to him. Most of them not on the river. These skimmers are our biggest advantage right now. Here's our chance to use their speed.'

Kip looked to Cruxer for his take.

'Anything we can do to minimize what the Blood Robes know about us...' the young commander said.

'Can we go after him and still get back to Fechín Island the day after tomorrow?' Kip asked. He'd promised to meet the Cwn y Wawr there.

'It'll involve some backtracking, but...with the skimmers? Not a problem,' Conn Arthur said.

So they skimmed up the wide river for a few hours. Kip noticed that one of the Ghosts with the conn – a newly established bodyguard – had a white spear etched with many yellowing runes. The leaf-blade of the spear was hellstone. 'That a *sharana ru* spear?' Kip asked.

The young man looked immensely pleased. 'My great-great-grandfather was given it from the hand of Zee Oakenshield. He liked to say he should have changed history with this spear. He coated the blade with poison before the battle, and during it, he stabbed Darien Guile in the arm, but it turned out the wise man who'd mixed the poisons was a charlatan – gave Darien nothing more than an itch for three days! Later my father served in Darien Guile and Selene Oakenshield's household. Grandpa Sé said he was worried he'd be killed for that scratch when his betters made their peace and married. But the Guile laughed about it with him instead. Kept Grandpa Sé close for many years. Even came when my great-great-grandfather was on his deathbed and laughed with him about it one last time. Great man, Darien Guile. Wish our family could have stayed with yours through the Blood Wars, my lord.'

There had been so many back-and-forths in that interminable conflict that Kip wasn't even sure when the houses might have been pulled apart. 'Well, the good news is that we're on the same side again,' Kip said. 'What's your name?'

'Garret, sir.'

'Well, Garret, if you ever want a rapt audience who will ask you a million questions about that spear, talk to Ben-hadad. In fact, if you *don't* want to talk about it, you'll probably have to hide.'

Just then, there was a shout as one of the conn's skimmers blew off one of its reeds.

Half an hour later, ashore, Ben-hadad hobbled over on one crutch and reported, 'Repair shouldn't take more than an hour.' He was taking the failure personally.

Kip didn't blame him. There was simply no way to expect reliable drafting out of amateurs. He blamed the masters of Shady Grove. What the hell kind of drafters went their lives without drafting? Sure, you'd live for seventy years instead of forty or fifty, but a drafter was a candle. She was made to bring light and be consumed in the process. These were candles who lived and died having barely touched a flame.

To one who'd always heard that drafters were given their powers and privileges for their communities' betterment, it seemed astoundingly selfish.

Still, in purely utilitarian terms, it did give him more of their drafting lives to use, if he could teach them quickly enough to keep them from getting killed.

Kip didn't want to split up the platoon if he could help it, so he consulted with the woman who knew the valley Baoth would pass through, and decided they could lose two hours without losing their chance to catch it. Ben had asked for one.

'You have an hour and a half,' he told Ben-hadad. Everything always takes longer than you think it will.

In the meantime, as the others kindled a fire and made lunch and checked their own skimmers for damage, Kip memorized maps and made plans for where they would beach the skimmers, who would stay with them, and how the rest would spread out through the woods. The Ghosts would look for tracks to find the red wight's trail if he was ahead. If they'd passed him, they would prepare an ambush point. Otherwise they would wait until after dark when he could no longer draft and set upon him at his camp. Baoth was a red, so Kip figured the wight would light a campfire to give himself a source. It would make him much easier to find.

'You're confident in your trackers?' Kip asked the conn.

The conn nodded. 'Not that I wouldn't mind having me a Daimhin Web.'

'Daimhin Web?' Kip asked. There was an odd buzzing low in his ears at the name.

'Young man. Scary. Way over on the other side of Green

Haven last I heard, though. In the old tongue, they call him *Sealgaire na Scian*.'

'He Who Hunts with Knives?' Tisis asked.

Conn Arthur said, 'I know it doesn't sound very imposing, but—'

But it hit Kip between the eyes.

Everything disappeared in a rush of leaves.

The next thing he was aware of, he was lying on the ground, blinking at concerned faces ringing him.

'Orholam's hairies, Breaker, you almost fell in the fire,' Ferkudi said. 'If Big Leo hadn't grabbed you—'

'Does he have the falling sickness?' Conn Arthur asked Tisis.

'Stop!' Kip said. 'Silence, please.' He reached after memories that were fading like a scent in the wind.

A scent. That was it. Something burning.

No, something that had been burning.

Kip opened his eyes and grabbed a stick from the fire. He stubbed it out on the ground and walked away, wafting the smoking wood in front of him, concentrating.

As with the first link of a chain, the rest came as he pulled on that. The smell, the memory, was from a burning village.

He blinked. Blinked again. He went back to the fire to stand next to Tisis. He murmured in her ear, 'Was I gone for long, just now?'

'What?' she asked. 'No. A few heartbeats.'

Oh, good.

'I'm sorry, but I must ask,' Conn Arthur said. 'Are you ill? More to the point, are you too ill to lead us?'

'No, and no,' Kip said. 'It was momentary, I'm better now. I must have eaten something that disagreed with me last night.'

Winsen cleared his throat behind his fist. 'Didn't sound like she disagreed much.'

The rest of the Mighty cracked up.

'Hey!' Kip said.

In a falsetto, as if in the throes of passion, Big Leo went, 'Ah! Ah!'

Kip's silver tongue failed him. He glanced at Tisis.

Her color was high, but she shot back at Big Leo immediately, 'Oh, you think that was *me*?' She looked over at Kip significantly.

They burst out laughing.

'Ah! Ah!...?' Big Leo said, somehow managing to append a question mark to his falsetto while giving Kip the side eye.

Kip nodded, taking his lumps. 'Fine. Fine. I'll practice making acceptably manly...ejaculations. Nightly. While you boys get to cuddle with each other.'

'Ooo,' Big Leo said.

'That's low, brother,' Winsen said. 'Did Ferk tell you how Big Leo threw his arm over me last night?'

'No,' Tisis said. 'What happened?'

'I couldn't get away! He wouldn't wake up!'

'A guy gets lonely,' Big Leo said defensively.

'I need a new tent mate,' Winsen said. 'Ferk? I know you snore, but I can deal...'

'That wasn't snoring,' Cruxer said. 'I do not know what it is. We all eat the same food, but this man's *anus*...If we could weaponize his farts...'

'Those were *farts*?!' Big Leo said. 'I thought we were being shot at! They woke me up like six times!'

'Wait, you woke up six times? So you were awake?' Winsen said. 'Why didn't you let go of me?'

'Oh, come on,' Ferkudi said, 'maybe I fart a bit more than some of you. But at least mine don't stink.'

'Ferk,' Tisis said, 'I smelled you from our tent fifty paces away.'

'Now you're just piling on,' Ferkudi said. 'Go on, have your fun, but I don't know why I always end up being the...' He trailed off as it dawned on him. 'Wait, I really am the butt of the Mighty, aren't I? This is my destiny.'

'Why don't you all go check with Ben-hadad if he needs anything,' Kip said. He just noticed that Conn Arthur hadn't said a word in several minutes, since they started joking. Kip had been distracted by his friends, but the man stood like a bear on its hind legs, staring at you, uncertain whether to plop down on all fours and amble away or to charge you with sudden fury.

Tisis left last, giving him a kiss on the cheek and saying,

'I'm sorry. That was wicked of me. You'll have to punish me later.'

'Right. As if I'd punish you for...' Kip trailed off. 'That was me missing the point, wasn't it?'

She winked at him and left, leaving Kip with the glowering giant.

As Kip studied him, though, he looked less angry and disapproving and more bereft. This was a man to whom joy was only a memory.

When he finally spoke, the conn said, 'Congratulations on your nuptials.'

'Thank you.'

'We're away from safe territory now. I think you pitching your tent away from the camp is a bad idea. You should be in the center of camp. You and your bride can carry on as you will. Our people aren't shy about such things.'

'Right,' Kip said lamely. He'd thought the big man's comments were going to be about something else entirely.

'Sibéal was deeply impressed by what she witnessed last night.'

'She was?' Kip said.

'But I see that you're still pretty young, too.'

It stung, of course, being slapped down by a big, imposing older man. He was partly right, too. Sex jokes with his buddies? Or were they his buddies? Shouldn't they be his men? Shouldn't he, their leader, demand more respect?

The old Kip would have sucked that insult into his big old blubbery ego and gnawed on it, cracking apart bone and marrow of the insult and eventually returning with his own mind made up.

That Kip hadn't been all wrong. Because the opposite approach would be to attack Conn Ruadhán Arthur in return. As any young blowhard would.

'You're not wrong,' Kip said. 'But tell me, where's saying that aloud to me come from? You're a quiet man, and not stupid. Was that a test, or was it a friendly warning that your people distrust me because of my youth already and I should be careful, or did it come from some bitterness at our camaraderie?'

The conn looked at Kip through tight blue eyes. He stroked his red, red beard. 'It was a test. I didn't have it all laid out sly-like. Just had a thought and wanted to see if you'd lose your temper if I said it to your face,' he said. 'I don't know what kind of man you are, Kip Guile. But you make me nervous. You led us to a great victory at Deora Neamh. Maybe a small victory in size, but strategically important and flawlessly planned, and you did it immediately after we joined you, which inspires us. How'd you do that?'

'I've read some books,' Kip said.

Truth was, he had read Corvan's books – but not like fifty of them. Maybe four. What he'd done at Deora Neamh wasn't exactly forging new military doctrine: a diversionary raid was pretty basic, and though he'd never read about anyone's using superviolet flares for communication, he surely couldn't be the first to come up with it.

But he'd also absorbed a lot of cards, a lot of memories. Surely among them must be some of the greatest tacticians of all time. Kip knew he should feel worried about dead men in his head.

Except they weren't like invaders. The memories sat on one shelf in the library of his mind, and he knew which memories were his and which were not. He felt no more threatened by those memories than by a vivid book. Well, usually.

Suddenly passing out because he'd stepped through an unseen trip wire of Daimhin Web's memories was unnerving. And could maybe be dangerous if it happened in the middle of battle or something. But mostly it just *was*. For once he didn't overthink it.

If he could find a tactician in his head and plunder that man's thinking in order to save his life and his friends, to Kip that didn't feel any different from studying General Corvan Danavis's tactics during the False Prism's War: sure, it felt a little strange to scrutinize someone close to you by the same standards you applied to the greats of history, but you got over it.

'You read some books,' Conn Arthur said flatly.

'Father Violet himself said he learned all he knew of fighting from books, and that he fought his last battle by the same tactics he'd used to win his first. The art isn't knowing what to do, it's knowing exactly what your people can do, and getting them to do it at the right time. I haven't been tested on those parts at all.'

'So despite our effortless victory, you're worried you don't know what you're doing.'

'We got lucky. And I'm worried it won't scale. That my skills won't grow as quickly as our army does.'

The conn snorted. '*That's* what you're afraid of.'

'Why's that funny?' Kip asked.

'Because it hasn't even occurred to you to be afraid that no one will join you. I can't tell if your total expectation of success is a function of your youth and inexperience, or insanity, or a deserved confidence. Oddest of all, I'm not sure it matters at this point.'

'But,' Kip said.

'But it *will* matter later,' Conn Arthur said. He seemed as if he wasn't sure he wanted to say it. He wasn't trying to make Kip angry now. He was deeply worried. 'Someday we'll face the White King himself or one of his generals, and I don't want that day to be the day we find out it really was madness or youth all along.'

'That's a lot of anxiety for you to tie up around some puerile jokes,' Kip said.

'It's not just the contents of the jokes. It's that you're joking. You're enjoying yourself out here,' Conn Arthur said.

'I *was*,' Kip said lightly.

But the conn's point sank deep.

Perhaps the hairy bear of a man mistook how quickly Kip could shift from jokey to thoughtful, though. The conn said in a way that made it clear he was quoting someone, ' "A man who loves war will be feared by his foes; he should be feared by his friends." '

Kip had been careless. Conn Arthur looked like a badass warrior. He would, if he lived long enough, probably become one. But he'd probably never fought until yesterday. The man was shaken. He didn't understand what it does to you to see a pile of fresh heads stacked in a pyramid, what it meant to find half your friend's leg lying on your pack or to laugh as

291

a musket ball *snapped* past your ear because hearing that snap meant they'd missed. He hadn't seen how precious any laughter at all is, because sometimes, at the campfire, a laugh was the only thing that kept you from thinking too hard about that thing you'd seen or that thing you'd done.

But Kip had been careless. Part of a warrior's duty was to remember what it had been to be a civilian. To protect that innocence, and not sneer at it.

Kip recognized the quote. 'Erastophenes, *Tactics*, the fourth scroll, if I recall correctly?'

The conn shook his head. He didn't know where it was from.

'It's from the conclusion in the sixth scroll, actually,' Kip said. 'You pass. I'm glad to see you're not a man who pretends to know what he doesn't. At least in some things.'

'You're testing *me* now?' Conn Arthur said.

'Have you heard the quote from Veliki Eden: "It is well that war is so terrible, or we should grow too fond of it"? Do you think he was kidding?'

'I've heard it,' the conn said. 'I've always taken that to mean that to their sorrow, men are fools, ever rushing to arms.'

'I take it different: war is hell, but hell's where all my friends are.'

Conn Arthur looked pensive. 'Time will tell which of us is right. Perhaps both. I only hope for us all that your knowledge becomes wisdom painlessly. Your pardon, Lord Guile.'

Kip nodded, surprised that the man would ask to be dismissed. But before he had gone far, the conn stopped and turned back.

'One last thing. As I said, my people aren't shy about matters of the root and cave...but a *little* consideration for those trying to sleep nearby does go a long way.'

'Right,' Kip said. Root and cave? Oh. 'Right!'

When the hour and a half had passed, Ben-hadad hadn't yet fixed the first skimmer, and he'd also found other potentially catastrophic cracks on three of the other skimmers.

Kip elected to leave them behind, and headed out with only four skimmers loaded with the best fighters. Tisis stayed behind. She said, 'I'm more use to you as an ear and tongue than as another gun.' She looked momentarily perplexed. 'Not that that was supposed to rhyme.'

'Such things occur from time to time.'

'Very funny, you're such a tease,' she said.

'You know I always aim to please.' He frowned. What the hell? 'I know that's the kind of silly thing I'd do,' Kip said, 'but I swear I didn't intend...to.'

He blinked. 'That also wasn't my intent—'

'It's fine, my dear, I know what you...' She seemed to struggle to form a different word. Then in defeat, she said, '...meant. Kip, what's going on?'

'I don't know, but the effect is strong. Let—'

'Superviolet!' she said.

It seemed the first line could be anything, but as if in some inescapable chain of cause to effect, it was impossible not to follow it with a rhyming couplet. Slant rhymes worked. How about if you ended a line with a word that didn't have a rhyme? Oh...superviolet! She hadn't simply meant to rhyme with let; she meant he needed to look at superviolet!

He narrowed his eyes to the superviolet spectrum and saw the color storm whipping past them in ordered violence. Like a mechanical octopus, every arm articulated with a million hinges, the storm swept the camp, but each segment of the arm moved only in right angles.

Kip handed his superviolet lenses to Tisis so she could see it, too.

A few people were looking up around the camp, quizzical looks on their faces. Of those who were moving about, they too were moving only in the same straight lines.

The superviolet was everywhere.

And then, before he could even say anything, it was gone.

'Are you okay?' Tisis asked.

'Why?' he asked.

'Because it all swirled around you in a weird funnel cloud before it disappeared.'

'It did?' He'd thought it was everywhere, but then, if he had been in the middle of a cloud of it, he would have.

'It was like it was looking for you.'

And it found me.

Chapter 43

It was one part practicality. A pinch of indecision. A dash of kindness. And four parts cowardice.

Teia flicked on only the blue and superviolet lights as she came into the Prism's practice room again. She'd taken to training more and more here while she marshaled her courage to talk to Gav Greyling.

Fine, while she avoided talking to Gav Greyling.

She tried not to come here too much, but the practice room had become her haven. There were good memories here, and light controls, and mirrors, and privacy – all the necessary ingredients to practice light splitting.

She tried not to come here too much, but she didn't try very hard.

With the master cloak, invisibility had become stunningly simple. She put it on, opened herself to paryl, and it did the rest, flawlessly.

Ah, blessed, blessed invisibility.

There were still things to be aware of. She was invisible, not silenced. She still left footprints. If she pulled the cloak over her eyes, she was blind herself, so in well-lit areas, she had to stare down at her feet and only steal glimpses up, knowing her disembodied eyes might appear to anyone who happened to be looking in just the right place. The cloak was long enough to cover her feet, but any movement that displaced it, such as running or descending stairs, could expose her legs. Also, its length meant that it brushed the ground. Any dirt it picked up from the ground, it carried, visibly.

Similarly, if she didn't launder it regularly, the dust it picked up from the air slowly made it less effective. Of course, slaves did all the laundry in the Chromeria, and of course, Teia wasn't going to let the master cloak out of her sight, so she had to figure out ways to launder it herself. Sometimes in this very room.

She'd even prepared her lies: the washboard was good for hand strength, those incompetents had torn her cloak the last time, she kind of enjoyed a simple task like this...

Weak lies, and she'd not had to use them yet.

But after much practice, the cloak had become simply another tool. It enabled things impossible without it, and it had limitations, but it quickly became a known quantity. It wasn't a sword or spear that required years of study to master, it was more like a pair of boots: you figured out what grip they gave you, you broke them in, and then you forgot about them.

What was more interesting for Teia than learning how to use it was trying to learn how it worked. She'd put on a single red light in the practice room, and use the cloak, then extend her will into the cloak to discern how it was splitting that red light. Then she'd repeat with orange, then yellow, then green, then blue, for hours.

It had yielded interesting discoveries over the months of practice since Kip left, if not the ones she was looking for. First, with a cloud of paryl gas surrounding her, Teia became the next best thing to a superchromat. The gas itself was a filter like polarized glass. It filtered blues into the perfect blue for making blue luxin, filtered reds into the perfect red for making red luxin, and so forth. If she held a bubble of paryl gas perfectly so that it covered one eye, she could look at any luxin and tell how well it had been drafted: if it looked and felt exactly the same to each eye, it had been drafted perfectly, and therefore probably by a superchromat.

She was sure there were handy applications for her discoveries, but she wasn't sure what they were, and there was no one she could really ask. The only one she'd really come up with was that, if she remembered to draft a paryl cloud, she could now differentiate red and green. She still couldn't see them as different, though, so it was a cold comfort.

One day she was sitting on the floor of the practice room. Always fearful of interruptions, she'd run through the obstacle course a few times first to work up a sweat, and now she sat as if winded, wearing her skimpiest workout attire. The point was to have as much skin exposed as possible. She had to feel the colors, and dammit if that wasn't taking a lot of practice. So she sat on the floor, nearly naked but sweaty, so that if anyone came in she could pass for someone just cooling from her exertions.

This new life of hers was always lies and preparations for lies.

She had her eyes closed and a headband functioning as a blindfold, every sense attuned to the blue (perhaps?) light, when she heard a hiss as of escaping gas. Her eyes snapped open and she pushed the headband back up her into unruly hair. She grabbed her tunic and looked toward the door.

Nothing.

She widened her eyes to paryl and saw paryl gas dissipating. Teia jumped to her feet, pulling on her tunic, eyes darting to the master cloak hanging on its hook by the door. She expected that paryl gas to come questing out toward her. It had to be Master Sharp looking to see if she was in the room.

But it did nothing instead.

She moved to the door, and heard only retreating footsteps. She pulled on long trousers and, after one moment of indecision, grabbed her cloak. There was someone disappearing down the hall. Not Master Sharp. But at her feet, there was a wineskin. Its spout had been pushed under the door, and then it had been stomped flat, expelling the paryl gas within. Teia picked it up. In tiny script, but undoubtedly Master Sharp's hand, there was one word: 'Follow.'

Oh hells! Here it was. Finally.

Swallowing hard once, Teia ran on silent feet after the man. She caught sight of him quickly. She'd been right. It wasn't Murder Sharp. Just a slave. He had a paryl mark floating above him, invisible to anyone's eyes except Teia's.

The man walked to the servants' stairs, and up. Teia followed at a discreet distance. In the entrance hall, his paryl mark abruptly blinked out.

It happened, of course. Paryl was so fragile that the slightest brush would usually shatter it, and that was especially true of the lighter-than-air gel marks appended to targets. Teia kept the man in sight, but within moments the mark bloomed over a slave woman.

What the hell?

Teia followed the woman as she headed outside. Teia put on her dark spectacles so she could continue glancing in paryl intermittently in the bright light without blinding herself. Mercifully, she didn't look out of place with them on. It was a bright, blustery, cool day. Distant clouds dotted the heavens like harbingers of the autumn coming on.

Just after the Lily's Stem, the paryl mark passed from the slave woman to a merchant heading down a side street.

This time Teia was ready. Marking someone with paryl required that the paryl drafter be nearby.

But Sharp was either being terribly devious, or he was using his own shimmercloak, because Teia never saw him.

Eventually she ended up in front of a tiny, run-down house in the Tyrean quarter with a paryl 'Enter' written on the door.

Drawing a surreptitious dagger to conceal behind a wrist, she knocked.

It opened and Sharp grinned at her through his exquisite white teeth. He beckoned her inside, but made her step close past him. Orholam, how he made her skin crawl. He sniffed as she slipped past him.

He closed the door. 'Are we forgetting our mint?' he asked. 'Not to mention the parsley.' He took her face in his hands, his manicured fingers on each of her cheeks, angling her chin up, a gesture all too intimate for her taste. He smelled her breath. Grimaced as if she'd farted straight in his face. Slapped her gently.

The gentleness made it almost worse.

'You know what we do, Adrasteia?' he asked. 'Stealth. Stealth is what we do. Well, it's the necessary building block for what we do. You know what's not stealthy? Haltonsis. Haltonsis isn't sneaky, Teia. Might as well chew garlic.'

He meant 'halitosis.' Moron.

But Teia didn't say anything. Moron Sharp might be, but he was a dangerous one.

Moron Sharp.

Teia almost grinned at her new mental nickname for him.

She couldn't be afraid of someone she had a stupid nickname for, right?

'What's that?' he asked.

'I, um, I did it on purpose. I've been wondering if you were ever going to check in with me again. So I thought it'd be funny if when you did, I had stinky breath.'

'Cute,' he said. 'Don't be cute.'

'I'm sorry, I—'

He slugged her in the stomach. She dropped, gasping. He grabbed a handful of her short hair and drew back a fist. But then he paused. He pushed her lips around, looking at her teeth.

'Ah, that's right,' he said. He ran a tongue around his own teeth and let her go. 'Sit.'

There was only one small chair and a small bed in this room. There was a coil of rope hanging off the back of the chair. All Teia's old fears came alive at the sight of it, but she sat. What could she do against Sharp anyway?

He bound her to the chair expertly, quietly whistling to himself. Excellent whistler. After he finished, he looked at himself in a tiny mirror on the wall. He checked his dentures, mostly, moving his jaw this way and that, smiling broadly or just cocking his lip up to reveal a tooth in a faux grin, looking at the teeth from different angles.

'We have a problem,' he said, not turning from the mirror. He touched a dogtooth with his tongue. 'You didn't tag anyone for me to kill.'

Teia had known this was coming. Had been dreading it for a long time now.

'Why? Lose your nerve? Or are you not quite what you represented to the Order? Perhaps a spy?' he asked as if inquiring after the weather.

So Sharp had been intended to be the murderer if she'd tagged someone. That suggested that he was the only other Shadow that the Order had on Big Jasper.

'I did tag someone,' Teia said. 'Did the assassin never find him?'

'That's impossible. Did you tag him poorly? Perhaps you tagged him poorly on purpose?'

Of course, this gambit had meant casting aspersions on the skills of whoever followed her. Now that Murder Sharp had suggested it was he, that got dangerous.

'No, but I did try to be tricky. I wanted to see how good my tail was. I didn't know it was going to be you.'

Sharp stopped looking at his teeth. He turned around, and for an instant, Teia thought she saw fear in his eyes. He was, Teia realized, terrified of anything that would threaten his value in the Old Man's eyes. 'I'd been up for two days straight, but you were only out of my sight for perhaps an hour – surely not...?'

'The night of my vigil?' Teia asked.

'Anat's cunt!' Sharp said.

And that gave Teia another peek at one of Sharp's cards: Sharp himself didn't have sources among the few Blackguards who'd been around on her vigil. That was good to know. She was always slowly compiling a list of Blackguards she knew she could trust.

Of course, *Sharp's* not having a source wasn't the same as the *Order's* not having a source. But every little bit of information helped.

'I wasn't gone long,' Teia said. 'Because I changed my mind.'

'Wait? You took the tag off?' Sharp asked. He sounded angry and yet relieved, too. If he'd missed a tag because she'd removed it, it wasn't his fault, was it?

On the one hand, it was nice to see him scared; on the other, it was good to see him relieved. On the third, impossible hand, Teia was crossing a person *Murder Sharp* was terrified of.

Teia said, 'The rules made it all pointless, didn't they?' Bitter girl, hateful, spiteful, right?

'What rules?'

'I couldn't kill anyone important. I mean, I briefly considered killing someone who'd irritated me who was *close* to someone important like that asshole slave Grinwoody, but I figured there was a good chance the Old Man would take that as me being impudent if not disobedient, so why risk it? And then I thought that if I wanted anyone who wasn't that important dead, I can do it myself now. I mean, it would be easiest if I have the shimmercloak – which I'd like to start learning to use better, thanks – but even without it, I could start throwing paryl crystals into someone's blood until they die. No one can find it except you, so no one can catch me. So if I've got a favor coming to me from the Order, I'm going to save it for when it matters.'

'One doesn't save up favors from the Old Man. You obey or you take the consequences.' Sharp scowled. 'He told me how to deal with you if you'd been disobedient or if you'd betrayed us...but this is something different. He'll be irritated. But I guess he'll have to deal with it himself.'

'Himself? What's that mean?'

'I'm leaving,' Murder Sharp said. By the way he said it, it was clear he meant for a long time.

'Where are you going? I thought you were going to train me!'

'It's war. Plans change. The Old Man isn't pleased, but there's word that there's a Third Eye.'

'What's that? What's that mean?'

'A prophetess. A true prophetess. Apparently for a long time she was safely out of the way on Seers Island where she couldn't tell anyone anything, but now she's out in the satrapies, helping the Chromeria with the war. You might be able to guess how important someone who can see the future would be to either side.'

'Pretty damn,' Teia said.

'That's right. So that's where I come in.'

'Isn't it going to be a bit hard to get close to someone who can see the future? I mean, you'd figure she'd protect herself, right?'

Sharp sucked spit through his dentures. 'Smart one, aren't you?'

Shit. Teia was supposed to be playing dumb. 'I'm not trying to be wise,' Teia said, placating. He might punch her again, if not do something worse.

'The cloaks,' Sharp said.

'The cloaks?'

'Her powers are all connected to light, turns out. The Order's known about her kind for centuries. She can't See the future, past, or present of anyone who wears the cloaks. Course, the Seers know that we know, which is why they usually stay on their island sequestered away from our blades. Gavin Guile brought an end to that. So I guess we can blame this on him. But them Seers gotta know their place.'

Teia felt sick to her stomach. 'So what's the plan? Kidnap her and sell her to the highest bidder? Hold her somewhere and make her work for you?' Maybe Teia shouldn't give them ideas.

'Too dangerous. How do you outwit someone who can see the future? You can't. We gotta kill her.'

It shouldn't have shocked Teia, this blithe talk of assassinating someone. It was what she was here for, after all. To learn, to become part of the plans, and then upend them on the Order's head. But...he was going to kill this woman. It was just work to him.

'Thanks,' Teia said.

'Thanks?'

'For telling me. Like you trust me.'

'Eh.' He shrugged, and finally started working at the knots to untie her. 'It's lonely work. No one to talk to. No one to appreciate it when you've done good, you know? Shadows usually work in twos, maybe for just that. So you know, I asked that you be promoted to be my second.'

'Really?' Teia said. She was oddly flattered.

'The Old Man said you aren't ready yet. It's why you won't get to keep the Fox cloak, at least not unless he's got a job for you.'

'What? I earned that cloak.' Inside, though, Teia was delighted. As long as they thought she had no cloak at all, they wouldn't be on the lookout for her doing the things that only a cloak allowed her to do; being known not to have a cloak made her invisible to the Order.

'He wants to hide himself from her, of course. He needs the cloak for that.'

'So does that mean I'm never getting the cloak back? He's going to wear it all the time?'

'We know she needs direct sunlight to do her...Seeing? Seering? So if you do jobs, you'll likely go after sunset and have to return the cloak before dawn. If you do well, after she's dead, you'll get to keep your own then. Your own fault, though, you shoulda found the other cloak they recovered.'

Teia raised her hands. 'It wasn't there.'

'I know. We believe you about that. We've had the White's room turned inside out, looking for hiding spots. Went through all your shit, too. Best guess is that she hid it somewhere and didn't tell anyone where before she died. The Old Man thinks she kept the Fox cloak to study it, thinking that no one could use a cloak that short. Or maybe she knew about the cloaks and hoped to teach you how to use it herself, someday. Loved to study things, she did.'

'Whoa,' Teia said. 'She never said anything to me about that. Swear.'

'Death does tend to interrupt plans. It's why we do what we do. Anyway, the Old Man will be handling you directly from now on. I'll fill you in on your drops and how he'll signal you, or how you can signal him in an emergency.'

He did, using much of the same tradecraft that Teia already knew from working with Karris. It all left Teia's mind whirling, though. She'd be meeting directly with the Old Man of the Desert?

After so long of nothing, it was hope. She might actually cut off the Order at the head.

If she was smart, she'd need to do it before the Third Eye was killed. In the meantime, she'd have to pass word about all of this to the Iron White.

'There's just one more thing,' Murder Sharp said. 'You're still pretty useless with paryl. It's my fault, I know. I haven't been able to come around and teach you like I should. But it's war. Everything is different now. Nothing is as we'd like. In the basement here is the solution to your problem.'

'Solution?' Teia asked. Her chest tightened.

'There's a slave down there. An old man. Won't be missed. Practice on him. The paralysis pinches, the lung clots, the seizures. When you've learned as much as you can before your next shift, kill him. With paryl if you can. There'll be a new slave down there every few weeks. Do try to learn fast. Murder practice ain't like other practice. Every body we have to get rid of puts someone's life in danger.'

And then he left.

Murder practice. Dear Orholam. Teia looked at the doorway to the basement stairs as if it were the mouth of hell itself.

She reached to squeeze the vial of oil she kept at her neck, but it was no longer there.

Chapter 44

The woods sang a song Kip had never known. The ponderosas swayed and shyly sighed as frogs croaked in chaotic chorus, descants of squirrels soaring high above all like preening sopranos while the wind danced past, her tresses brushing his cheek as she spun, leafy skirts flaring, willowy legs flashing.

The evening chill held him back from the floor, putting a hand upon his thudding heart. Be still, my dear, be still.

The last drop of rain pressed a shushing finger across his lips.

Made pliant by the rain's caresses, the earth pulled back her leafy covers like a beckoning lover, and the scent of their love filled the house of sky.

'Kip?' Conn Arthur whispered. 'My lord, are you well?'

Kip came back to himself. 'I'm eccentric, Conn Arthur,' he said, very quietly, 'eccentric.' Not crazy.

'Never mistook you for *con*centric, sir.'

Kip grinned. A wit, in a bear?

On the other hand, he was probably the last person who should judge a person's mind by the flesh suit it wore.

They were fanning out through the woods here as the late afternoon passed, looking for signs of the spy. They had docked not twenty paces back, and it had taken only that much distance for Kip to be overwhelmed by a sense of homecoming.

Not his own homecoming. Daimhin Web's. He nodded to Conn Arthur, and, spreading out with twenty others for a distance of three hundred paces, they began ghosting through the woods.

Daimhin Web was from a village long lauded for its skillful

hunters. Among the best of them, there was a test, an impossible test, to sneak up on a deer and touch it with your bare hand. Many young men tried for years, learning everything from their elders about scent and silence and silhouettes and the sweet subterfuge of stalking; they meditated on water and wind and all the ways of the wood and weather. They became satraps of silence, conns of camouflage, paragons of patience.

And friends of frustration.

Those were all traits invaluable to the master hunters they became, for on the path that led to that test and that failure, they were molded into the greatest stalkers known to man.

And this time, unlike any other time he'd been in the cards, Kip could remember exactly how Web did what he did.

As he moved through the woods, though, it became clear that remembering the mechanics of an action was different from learning it in your own body. Moving silently was itself the culmination of dozens of discrete skills, practiced separately and then together for so long that the stalker could do them without thinking. Scouting was a set of different but parallel skills: paying attention to the wind, to the sounds of the animals, knowing each kind and knowing to what each kind reacted and how: this bird goes silent when it notices animals, this kind takes flight when a predator or outsider is within this distance, these squirrels turn toward those they scold.

To pay attention to all those while tracking and using scent as well was simply beyond Kip.

By living the card and remembering all that was in it, he was instantly twice as adept as he had been before – he could now understand what made the master masterful, but that didn't make him a master himself. Kip could suddenly identify all the smells in his nostrils, but his nose wasn't as naturally keen as Web's, nor his body so light and lean. Web could bend branches with a step that Kip's big tread would crush.

But what a man! Web's first hand brush against a deer's flank had been partly luck. While he'd been stalking the deer, a running javelina had startled it toward him, so he'd not had to close the last ten impossible feet by stealth.

Another man would have taken his bragging rights and never looked back. Web had instead redoubled his efforts. This at fourteen years of age. He'd succeeded twice more by the time he was sixteen, and when a rival called him a liar for his claims – no hunter had ever succeeded three times – Web had left his village with only a knife and gone to stalk the legendary white stag.

It took him a month of living on bugs and berries, but he'd slain it with one stroke of his knife. He'd dragged the body – intact, not gutted – all the leagues back to his village so that none could deny he'd taken the white stag with only a knife.

For anyone else, taking a white stag at all would have been a tale to tell for the rest of his life.

When Web had arrived at his village, he'd found it burnt to cinders by the advancing Blood Robe army. Nearly everyone was dead.

The famed hunters could have fled, but none had been content to leave the old and the young and the infirm to die.

They'd stayed, they'd fought, and they'd been massacred by the Blood Robes. Only a few cowards had fled.

Web hunted the cowards first, including the man who had called him a liar.

Now he stalked the Blood Robes in the deep woods of western Blood Forest. In military terms, his killings didn't make much of a strategic difference. He killed only one man or one wight at a time, and always used only his knife or his bare hands. He spent days setting up a strike, and his target would simply disappear.

But not disappear forever. A camp of the White King's men had woken one morning to find their kidnapped leader in the middle of their own camp. He was skinned, gutted, his throat cut, and hanging upside down from a tree limb as meat is hung to cure by a butcher.

The men in that camp weren't simple foreign soldiers with lax discipline; they were locals who knew the land here; they were the White King's best scouts.

Daimhin Web had murdered their leader simply to embarrass them.

From time to time, he would show up in friendly villages or towns laden with gems or gold or coin sticks he'd taken from his kills. He would give these to the town's conn. He wanted nothing in return, not even the steel fishhooks or sugar or salt or whisky that other long-term trappers or hunters would have traded for. He simply gave them the valuables because he knew they would need money to rebuild their lives. And he would tell them the disposition of the White King's forces and the direction in which they were heading – usually toward that village.

He asked for nothing, and seemed not to care if they heeded his advice. He spoke with a gentle voice and then disappeared. He became like a forest creature, and his eyes were soft and skittish, not what you would expect of a predator who skinned and gutted men.

He was content to live alone, and he had become a beast.

And now Kip was doing his best to emulate him, though it was more and more obvious that he'd had too much confidence that he could ape such perfection, moving through the dusky woods searching for the red wight Baoth.

This wight was so far into his transformation that Kip suddenly smelled him – the tobacco-and-tea-leaves scent of his red luxin and the slight whiff of smoke. Kip veered off his assigned line in the darkness, so intent on the hunt and the thousand thousand skills needed to track silently that he didn't even tell Cruxer.

A pocket valley opened off to one side, far from the hunting ground the Ghosts had suggested, and as night settled on the Deep Forest, Kip's options were being shut down. He'd packed blue luxin before the evening light faded, setting all the blue lines in the Turtle-Bear tattoo aglow, but it was uncomfortable to hold packed luxin for long, and it slowly leaked away regardless, like sand through cupped hands. His Turtle-Bear now looked faded as a fifty-year-old tattoo.

Kip did have a bow, but he wasn't much of a shot. He couldn't have lived an archer's card, could he?

Nah, that would have been far too helpful.

Of course, at least *one* of the people in the cards must have been an amazing archer. More than one, surely, with so many warriors represented. In fact, Web himself had to be more than competent with a bow, but did Kip really want to sift Daimhin Web's memories further? The first thing that came to mind when he pulled those memories farther off the shelf was the sight of the charred bodies of Web's favorite little cousins. No thanks.

The next great warrior Kip could easily recall was Tremblefist, and though Kip had nothing but compassion for the man who'd lived and died a hero, fair or not, the memory that leapt out was of the Butcher of Aghbalu. Double no thanks.

Kip came over a rise and knew that something was wrong. You can't let your mind wander while you're tracking. He'd defaulted to being his overthinking self – and now the wight was gone, and Kip was alone.

In his reverie, Kip hadn't even realized how he'd picked up the trail. Maybe Daimhin Web had sunk in deeper than he'd realized.

That didn't matter now. Too much thinking!

In cresting of the rise, he'd skylined himself – putting his darker silhouette against the lighter forest behind him. He dropped to his face, lightly, landing on fingertips and toes so he wouldn't make any more noise than necessary.

A whoosh ripped through the jungle as a fireball streaked over his head.

Kip rolled to the side to get behind a tree, trying to find the wight.

The creature that had once been Baoth was smart enough not to stand out in the open with a flaming hand. It was a monochrome red, so it needed an open flame to have lit the fireball. It might have a flint and steel to scratch sparks onto each flammable missile, but that was like a musketeer going into battle with musket unloaded. Few warriors were daring enough to trade strength for stealth, especially not passionate reds.

As he moved back to the crest of the hill, Kip guessed at the fireball's trajectory from where he had been standing and where the fireball had hit the trees behind him. In the gloaming, the spotty light the trees allowed through their swaying branches made it near impossible.

Then he saw a constant, low light illuminating the leaves dimly from below. It was somewhat off to the side from the origin he'd guessed.

The wight was moving, trying to circle Kip.

Kip got behind the crest of the hill and ran to the side, flanking the entire hill. That much light cast upward? That meant the red wight was keeping a flame smaller than his palm – and probably *in* his palm. Kip's studies had told him exactly how much sizzling and popping a flame of that size would make, and thus how loud it would be. Over this distance, in this jungle that he knew so intimately? Kip could guess exactly how much noise his own passage through the undergrowth could make without the wight's hearing him.

Within half a minute, he'd flanked the wight, who was now moving stealthily toward where Kip had been. Baoth had further banked the flame he carried, making his right hand an inverted bowl like a hooded lantern.

How was he drafting so much with this light, though?

And then Kip saw how, and he was baffled that no one had ever explained it. The wight was drafting off *himself*. That must be at least part of why wights transformed themselves. This wight had copious amounts of imperfect red luxin encasing his entire body, so he could flash it back into red light that he could then draft. It was inefficient to draft from broken luxin, but this meant a wight could never be trapped powerless in darkness. Effectively, it carried its own mag torches in its body. And, come daylight, it could easily replenish itself.

The Mighty, like all the Chromeria, had discounted the accounts they'd heard of nighttime attacks. Drafters would never attack at night, they thought. They'd thought wrong, and it could have been a disastrous mistake.

But too much thinking, again.

Kip had lost the blue in all his running and loss of concentration. The fletching of his arrows had been fouled with mud from his roll on the ground. How accurate would they be?

He swapped through the spectacles on his left hip, drafting some superviolet – he didn't need much – and then some red, each color sending a new glimmer of light into the Turtle-Bear tattoo. In sub-red, Kip looked for any forest creatures. All I need is just one squirrel, dammit.

But there were none.

Have to do this the old-fashioned way.

With his left hand, he pushed a veritable ice carpet of superviolet webbing forward through the undergrowth. Superviolet was so light and weak that any particular strand of it could break easily, so he took the Gavin Guile approach: more is better. He needed only one continuous section to project his will through the luxin. With his right hand, he picked up a rock and threw it deep into the woods off to one side. It was unlike his usual Kipliness that this time, he didn't hit the first branch and spoil the whole effect.

The whisper of the falling rock in the undergrowth froze the wight, who looked first for an attack, and then for prey.

The pause was long enough. Kip's web of superviolet spread as far as the red wight's feet, up its ankles, and to the inevitable seams between the solid luxin plates of its feet and its calves.

A man wasn't made to have an exoskeleton. Skin moved and flexed in ways that solid plates didn't allow. The solutions most wights came up with were taken directly from armorers: painstakingly articulated joints, or chain-mail meshes, or bulky straps and prayer. This wight was floating an entire layer of open red luxin underneath his armor so that he could use it for fuel, and so his skin could move.

With his left hand seeking the open red luxin, Kip reached his will through the superviolet, while his right hand sent a tiny bolus of a firecrystal through the superviolet toward his target.

Every plate of the wight's armor would have knots – places where the magic had been sealed. Naturally, they would be on the protected inside. Kip was planning to unknot all the plates at once, but before he could reach them, the wight started to move.

Kip threw his will hard into the wight's open red luxin. He pulled it all toward the wight's chest, twisting hard. Its chest plate cracked with a snap at the same moment the firecrystal reached the wight's feet. Kip popped the firecrystal up, and, exposed to the air, the crystal flared and sparked.

Covered completely in a mess of open red luxin, the wight went up in flames.

But that wasn't enough. Kip ran forward, nocking an arrow.

The wight reacted first as a man would, slapping at the flames, terrified. So it wasn't so far gone yet, or so smart. He could have drafted off his own flames and covered himself in more and more red luxin until it made a crust – it was difficult to burn a red drafter to death, if he was thinking.

Kip couldn't give Baoth time to think. He loosed the first arrow a mere ten paces away. Drew another, loosed it. Drew another, loosed.

The wight screamed, a pillar of fire in the dark woods. He flung out a hand, and Kip leapt aside.

A gout of flaming oily red luxin went out from the wight, splattering and burning trees and bushes in a wide arc. It passed over Kip's head. Then, weakening, the wight threw one more burst of liquid death upward.

By the time the flaming goo dropped to the ground, the wight was dead. It had become a charred pillar of blackened luxin, still-burning patches of red luxin, and steaming bits of seared human flesh and white bone peeking out like gore candles.

Within minutes, drawn by Kip's oh-so-subtle signal fire, the Mighty arrived, along with Conn Arthur and a few trackers.

'So,' the conn said, looking around the forest punctuated with burning clumps of red luxin around this epicenter of destruction, 'I'm guessing you didn't get the scrolls he was carrying.'

'Ah shit,' Kip said.

Chapter 45

For a long while, Gavin lay bleeding on the floor of the yellow cell without even the courage to open his eyes. But he was a Guile, and to him 'a long while' without doing something wasn't long.

He'd already catalogued his own injuries. It was the curse

of his family: he couldn't stop thinking or planning any more than he could stop breathing. He sat up.

The injuries weren't bad. Well, ignoring for the moment the lost dogtooth, two stubs where fingers should be, and the gaping hole where an eye belonged. His cuts from falling were shallow, the bruises painful but not incapacitating, his jaw unbroken despite his father's punches. The weakness from the hunger was extreme, though.

The first thing he saw was his own reflection.

'You were a beautiful man once,' it said.

Of course the dead man in yellow would be the perfect balance of logic and emotion, devastating him with each. Gavin ignored him for the moment, and cast his eyes down.

There was no corpse.

Oh, thank Orholam, there was no corpse.

'You don't look well,' the dead man said.

'Does that make your work harder or easier?' Gavin asked him.

'Tell me, O man of Guile, what's worse? Madness unknowing, or madness recognized?'

'So...harder, huh?' Gavin said.

What was this talk of madness? Maybe the yellow dead man thought Gavin was more gone than he was. Gavin tried to remember if hunger caused hallucinations. Perhaps it did. Perhaps that was why saints and ascetics starved themselves – they were seeking a path to enlightenment through the signals for help a body released when it was being destroyed.

Gavin wasn't mad yet. He was too focused for that.

His father had pulled the rug out from under him. Very well, point to Andross Guile. His father had humiliated him by pummeling him with his fists. Fine.

Gavin was more than a match for the old spider. He would escape, and he would rise. He was unstoppable, unmatchable, superlative.

'Ah, Gavin Guile, surrounded with mirrors, and yet you refuse to see the simplest truths,' the dead man said.

'Dazen,' Gavin said. 'I'm Dazen Guile.'

'Indeed. And what happened to Gavin?'

'Go to hell.'

'You seem not to have noticed,' the dead man said. He gestured to the cell. 'Here am I.'

Orholam, I sure was a dick when I will-cast these walls with dead men.

I guess that was the point.

It wasn't until Gavin moved to lap up some water that he saw the other wall of the cell. His blinded left side had faced toward that wall, and he'd been too addled from the fall and his hunger to fully examine this new hell.

He saw the bullet holes scarring the wall from when he'd blown off his brother's head.

His breath caught as the memory filled his mind's eye, as he lifted both Ilytian flintlock pistols and shot Gavin dead. One bullet through the center of his chest, the other right through the chin. If either pistol had misfired, he'd still have had a quick death.

'He was insane,' Gavin said aloud. 'Maybe he was already insane before he came down here, but in my worship of him, I never saw it. Or maybe his madness was my fault. I know I'd not last sixteen years down here alone. Regardless, he was too far gone to be saved. It had to be done.'

'It was a mercy killing?' the dead man asked.

'Mercy too long delayed,' Gavin said. 'And that is my fault indeed.'

'Is that what you tell yourself?'

'Do you have a point?' Gavin asked.

'Two.' The dead man pointed across the cell toward those impact holes.

Gavin stood with difficulty. He'd expected there to be blood spatter or brain matter or something similar for the dead man to torture him with.

There was no gore. Apparently the water wash had worked well.

Instead there were two simple holes, the squashed lead musket balls visible less than a thumb's thickness inside each, the outside of each hole in the splintered yellow luxin forming short cracks in the top layer of the cell wall. He'd made the yellow luxin wall of this cell thicker than his hand; the bullets hadn't even come close to fully piercing the wall.

312

'First thing that might catch your attention,' the dead man said, 'is that there wasn't any ricochet. Solid yellow luxin, and no ricochet? But then, with the positions of your hands when you fired, each shot was perfectly perpendicular to the angle of the wall. So it is *odd*, but not *impossible*.'

At first Gavin didn't understand. And then he did.

'No,' he breathed. 'This is a trick. No.'

'Oh, so you've spotted the impossibility, have you?'

Gavin shuffled over to the wall. He stuck his pinky finger into one of the bullet holes and scratched, trying to dislodge the lead.

'What is that going to prove?' the dead man asked.

'This is not my bullet. It's impossible. He did this. My father. It's a trick.'

'What are you doing? Picking it out of the wall won't prove anything.'

'I can see if it's one of my bullets,' Gavin said. Like many veterans, Gavin had cast his own bullets. One of the tricks he'd picked up in his many years of fighting wights had been to pour the lead around a core of hellstone. It penetrated luxin like nothing else. Lead tore flesh catastrophically, but some wights layered themselves thickly enough with luxin armor to stop lead.

In Dazen's musket balls, the lead would tear away quickly, leaving a hellstone core that could pierce anything but thick solid yellow luxin. Few knew his trick, and of those who knew, fewer still could afford the hellstone necessary. In monetary terms, it was like shooting solid gold musket balls.

'Ah,' the dead man said. 'Look at it at an angle. You used to draft brightwater so pure a man could see through it.'

It was a good idea. He put his face against the wall. There! A nugget of hellstone, a hand's thickness deep in the wall.

Desperate, he went to the other bullet hole, and saw the same.

'Father could have shot balls from my own gun. He would have access to my ammo pouch, too.'

'I told you it wouldn't solve anything,' the dead man said. 'But think. Where the black luxin hasn't corrupted you, your memory was once so, so perfect for a mortal. Can you remember which bullets you fired that night? Can the Gavin Guile of legend remember that?'

The problem with hellstone was how brittle it was. Sharper than any steel, but you couldn't carve it. It fractured into bitter planes and hard curves and angles. It meant that when he was casting bullets, Gavin always had to make odd compromises. A star-shaped chunk of hellstone was what he always looked for – its weight balanced so it wouldn't put an odd spin on the musket ball, and small enough to fit within the lead, but large enough to retain momentum if it struck luxin and lost its lead jacket. Most times he made do with rough squares, triangles, or diamonds. Every bullet was different because the hellstone crystals were always different. He'd always arranged them by reliability.

Only the two bullets in his fine Ilytian pistols' chambers had had the star-shaped hellstone cores. Even he wasn't so wealthy that he could demand perfection in every bullet. His ammo bag was always full of second-best musket balls.

His father couldn't have known that.

The first bit of hellstone, deep in the wall, was star-shaped...

He checked. So was the second.

Gavin sat back, baffled. His father wasn't this good, was he?

Gavin had killed too many men to believe how his eyes and his memory were contradicting each other. He'd shot Gavin through the chest, a straight hole through his bony sternum. The other bullet had smashed through his chin and blown out the back of his head.

Lead squished on impact. It mushroomed, spun, tore gashes through flesh and bone. It was possible for the hellstone cores of his bullets to have pierced his brother and still hit the wall, but unlikely. There wasn't enough velocity left in the hellstone for this depth of impact, not usually, not through two layers of bone.

And for the lead itself to have survived intact to hit the wall as well?

That couldn't happen.

These musket balls were his own. These were the musket balls that had been in his pistols that night. He couldn't deny that. But these musket balls hadn't torn through a body – much less bone – before hitting the wall.

Impossible.

Gavin couldn't be alive. Dazen hadn't missed. Couldn't have. But that was the only possible answer. Wasn't it?

Did his father know even Dazen's musket-ball-casting method? It was possible, but why?

'Oh, my dear Black Prism,' the dead man said. 'You can't say you weren't warned. So tragic. And the perfect Guile memory is such a special thing, is it not? You did this to yourself. You knew the risks, but you couldn't help but draft black, could you? Black, the color of... Say it.'

Gavin's mind went many places at once.

He was standing on the beach with the Third Eye.

He was standing in the hot, smoking ruins of Sundered Rock.

He was standing in front of his mother, after returning from the war, with his brother unconscious in a trunk right behind him, telling her No, no, he was dead. He didn't suffer.

'Say it,' the dead man said.

Gavin said, 'Black is the color of oblivion. Black is the color of death. Black is the color... of...'

'You didn't spare Gavin out of pity,' the Third Eye had said to him. And then she said, 'Does the man who killed his brother expect the truth to be easy?' He'd interpreted her words to be wry; he'd thought there must have been a little stress he missed in the moment: 'Does the man who 'killed his brother' expect the truth to be easy?'

But there had been no wink or smile or nudge. Had there?

She had known how he would take those words at the moment, hadn't she? But she had also known that he would later remember those words. That was why she had been so very precise, so that without her lying to him, he could continue to delude himself until it was time to stop deluding himself.

'Tell me,' the dead man said. 'When did your nightmares about your brother stop?'

'Around the time I killed him.'

'No, Dazen. That's when they began.'

No. Impossible. The dreams about his brother's escaping

his prisons had begun right after the war ended, right after Sundered Rock. They had stopped only recently.

'Because...' the dead man said, as if leading a very stupid pupil to an obvious truth, 'because black is the color of...'

'Of madness,' Gavin said hollowly.

'Dazen, Gavin has been dead seventeen years. He was never imprisoned. You killed him at Sundered Rock.'

'That's not...that's not...' Gavin felt suddenly lightheaded. The tightness in his chest returned. He fell to the floor.

'All your contortions and striving have been to hide a man who wasn't there. Did you think it was a coincidence that as you lost blue, you dreamed of him breaking out of your blue prison? That as you lost green, he broke out of green in your dreams? The black luxin hell you brought to earth at Sundered Rock killed one man, but it destroyed two. Do you remember the bowl in the blue prison? And the cloth woven of human hair?'

Gavin remembered.

'How would you remember that? He never told you about it. He hid it from you.'

'I must have discovered them when I went through that cell.'

'Where was it when you were in the blue cell just weeks ago?'

'It must have been repaired.'

'Your father bothered to repair a slight depression in luxin more than a foot thick? And reset the trapdoor? And he repaired the green chamber? And somehow he didn't repair your trap in your work chamber where the rope didn't burn properly? And he cast new musket balls, all to make you think now... after all this, that you're mad? Does that sound like your father's work? Gavin was never here. It was always you, it was always only you.'

'And if I couldn't know any of that stuff about him, how could you? I know these cells aren't connected. I know it's will-castings that I did. How could you know any of this?' Gavin asked.

'We know, Dazen, because you came down and raved to us. Told us why it had to be this way. I, for one, always figured that the truth was, you made this prison for yourself. Surrounded by problems too big for you, you made a problem small enough for you to handle.'

Dazen felt the tightness increasing in his chest. He remembered, as in a dream, coming down here that fateful night. He opened the yellow chamber and thought of closing himself inside. He argued with himself, aloud. There was no one here but his reflection, his own image crafted so carefully to look like a dead man, his brother.

The dead man laughed. 'Come now, think of it! Did you really think that after Sundered Rock you were able to stuff your brother in a box, and keep him alive but drugged for the whole journey home, and bring him into the Chromeria – and no one ever noticed?! You had a box that you wouldn't let the servants touch. Do you think they wouldn't tell your father and mother about such a thing? Do you think your father and mother didn't break into it immediately?'

There had been a chest. He opened it in his memory, and this time, overlaid on the phantasmal image of his brother unconscious, he could finally see the truth. Inside the chest had been a spear of living black luxin. Black luxin he'd drafted himself.

It was the implement he'd drafted in those last desperate moments at Sundered Rock, the weapon with which he'd killed his brother. Beautiful and terrible as the night sky devouring itself unto eternity.

He'd carved the cells out of the Chromeria's heart with that spear, cutting through rock and the old bones of buried drafters and the luxin encased in their bodies with equal ease, until it too had failed, and broken apart into ten thousand pieces of hellstone.

The ten thousand pieces that he had then used in crafting the tunnels themselves.

How else could he have stolen such a kingdom's fortune's worth of hellstone without his father's noticing?

But what would his mother have done if she'd found that spear straight from hell in his belongings, still smeared with his brother's blood?

She would have wept, and prayed, and waited, and hoped

that her last son would come back from his madness. She would have been gentle, and patient, and protective. As she had.

And his father would have been scared, and distant, and angry, and watchful, and intrigued, and enraged, and uncertain. As he had.

Dazen had thought he'd been so clever. He thought he'd fooled the people closest to him. In reality, they'd played along, pretending to be deceived because they had no other options, no other sons, because in their own ways they both still needed him: his mother needed him to keep her own hopes alive, and his father needed him in order to rule through him.

'It didn't take everything, though, did it?' the dead man asked. 'Despite the black luxin, you knew certain truths. Or perhaps only certain hungers. You had to kill to keep drafting. You knew it would all fail eventually. That's why you had the nightmares, the attacks of panic. You knew that you were shameful, that you were a murderer, and everything you did to atone for your sins was a pile of glass baubles next to the mountain of shit that you built higher every year to keep yourself in power, to stay alive. You thought you were so clever. You thought yourself nigh unto a god, when in reality you were propped up by those who feared and hated you as much as by those who loved you. And even that wan love was tainted with fear and despair.'

'You're wrong,' Gavin said.

'You know I'm not.'

'No, you're wrong about one thing,' Gavin said. 'And perhaps one thing only.'

'Pray tell.'

'My father didn't know. There's no way my father has known all this time. He could never let anyone think they were fooling him. It isn't in him to play along. I—'

'Oh,' a voice said, 'I think you'd be surprised at what is in me, son.'

Gavin hadn't noticed the chamber moving, hadn't heard the slot open. He fell, nerveless, sliding against the unforgiving luxin wall to the ground.

Not him. Not now. Please. No, god!

'I came to see if you'd grasped the truth yet,' Andross Guile said. 'And I find you ranting to a wall.'

The dead man laughed, but Andross Guile didn't hear it.

'I want you to know, boy, I came down here just now seriously considering putting you back in power. Your brother's son Zymun is a worm who will become a terror if I let him survive. Kip is fled and too sensible to return soon, if ever. The Color Prince – he now calls himself the White King – is grown more powerful than we could have imagined. You are needed at this hour, Dazen. Not all of your power was magical, though you refused to see that. Not all of your leadership was based on light, though you were blind to that. But you've gone only ever deeper into madness. Perhaps this is my fault. Perhaps I left you down here too long. But you're mad now, and that I cannot change.'

'It can't be true,' Gavin said. 'I wouldn't do all this for no reason.'

'Couldn't. Wouldn't,' Andross scoffed. 'You *did*.' It was a death sentence. 'This is your work. All of it. Once I knew to look for it, it was obvious. Brute-force drafting, even where it was elegant. Always using lots of luxin, even where a little would serve as well. No aesthetic except that bigger was always better, and strongest was best.'

'This is all lies.'

'I won't leave you here, though. Lest all of this madness is an act, meant to lull me into a false confidence that you're broken. Your cunning is without peer. You've doubtless put in an escape hatch of some sort. So. One last game, where the stakes are light. Every day, I will send down two loaves. One will be poisoned. You can try to figure out which, if it pleases you. Eventually you'll fail, and when you're unconscious, you'll be moved somewhere more secure. Somewhere terminal. Or you can attempt to figure out where the drug is in each loaf, and hoard a stash of it, and take it all at once to kill yourself. That would solve a lot of problems for both of us, but you've never been interested in solving problems for me, have you?'

'I hate you,' Gavin said.

Andross stared at him with inscrutable eyes for a long time.

'I know. And it's too bad, because I have only ever loved you, Dazen.'

Chapter 46

'What is this?' Conn Arthur demanded. 'You said nothing about this.'

'This?' Kip asked. 'What are you mad about, and why are you bringing it to me right now?'

The sun was rising on another perfect morning on the Great River. According to their guides, they were about five minutes from Fechín Island. There they would rendezvous with the Cwn y Wawr.

'You were supposed to take care of this!' Conn Arthur said, pointing at Tisis.

'Easy!' Cruxer warned.

The Mighty's skimmer, already small with nine people on it, especially when that nine included men the size of Big Leo, Kip, and Conn Arthur, felt downright minuscule when the big bear was angry.

'I was planning to!' Tisis said.

'How?!' he demanded.

'I hadn't figured that out yet!' Tisis said. 'I was kind of hoping we'd have a chance for you to show how useful... Shit!'

'Whoa, whoa, whoa,' Kip said. 'You have to tell—'

'Ah shit!' Conn Arthur said. 'There's their scout. They've seen us. Now we're committed.'

Kip couldn't see anyone until he flickered his vision to sub-red and saw the warm blotch in the trees along the river-bank.

'Slow down to half speed,' Kip ordered. 'It's, um, only polite to give them a chance to prepare for our arrival.' He turned to Conn Arthur and Tisis. 'You've got ten minutes.'

'The Cwn y Wawr?!' Conn Arthur said. 'You never told us we were meeting with the Cwn y Wawr.'

'I wasn't hiding it,' Kip said. 'I told you we saved two-hundred-some men. Why do you care?'

'I thought the last conflict between you was a hundred years ago,' Tisis said.

'That's because we haven't wanted to be slaughtered again. We've had to live so we can disappear at any moment, for any amount of time. When we hear they're coming to the Grove in force, we leave and stay away until they lose interest.' Bitterly, he said, 'It's another reason they call us Ghosts.'

'Wait,' Kip said. 'Why do they hunt you?'

'You should have told him,' the conn said. Below him, Sibéal was rubbing her face.

'I *was* going to tell him,' Tisis shot back. 'When the time was right. Apparently you thought you'd take that decision out of my hands.'

'You didn't think you could keep it from him forever, did you?' the conn said.

'I wanted to give you a chance to prove your worth. The Chromeria is more than a little nervous—'

'What is this about?' Kip demanded. 'Now!'

'Shady Grove isn't separate from the Chromeria simply because some drafters want to stay in Blood Forest,' the conn said, mountainous shoulders slumping. 'We're will-casters.'

'So what?' Kip said.

'So what?!' The conn was baffled.

'I thought you'd be angry,' Tisis said. 'I thought that if they showed how incredibly useful their powers can be—'

'I'm angry. I'm angry you kept something from me that you thought would make me mad. *That* absolutely infuriates me. We'll talk about that later.' Kip remembered the fear accorded to Teia's use of paryl. Paryl was scary, and it didn't fit nicely into the Chromeria's septophiliac teachings. He could easily imagine the same happening to other slightly divergent teachings. But will-casting? He'd used it himself against Grazner, and been told only not to try that so early in his drafting career. What was the big deal?

Sibéal Siofra said, 'We hoped to show you how we use a partner in battle to help explain, but the skimmers travel so quickly they couldn't catch up.'

A partner? What was—

Tisis turned to Sibéal. 'I don't suppose the Third Eye said anything about what we're supposed to do now?'

'No.' Sibéal's face was impossible to read, maybe a little tightening around the eyes, but the smile not moving. That was unnerving. Luckily, the he-bear of a conn was far more expressive. His already pale face went pasty. His fists clenched, and Kip could actually see the tight thews of his shoulders swell with sudden tension.

'Kip,' Tisis said, 'do you remember when you were going through your Blackguard initiation, and you grabbed that boy's open-luxin spear and shattered it?'

'How'd you know about that?' Kip asked.

'Balls, Kip. You think the Blackguard trainees do anything in the Chromeria that isn't immediately grist for the rumor mills?'

Kip hadn't really thought about it. But he supposed that the attractive, powerful young men's and women's fights would be fairly intriguing to the average drafter who never got to raise a fist in anger, much less throw a luxin missile. 'Grazner was his name,' he said. 'Commander Ironfist called it willjacking.'

'Right. Willjacking is one tiny part of will-casting,' Tisis said.

'*Shit*,' said Cruxer, who had just come up to join them. 'I can't believe I didn't put the pieces together. Will-casters. That's why Sibéal's with you. That's her people's magic.'

To Kip, Tisis interjected, 'Will-casters draft only enough luxin to transmit their will. To objects and to animals.'

'And *to people*,' Cruxer said.

'Not to people,' Sibéal said quickly. 'Not in the sense you mean.'

Cruxer interrupted, 'Forcing your will onto a person, making them do whatever you want? It's mind rape – and often a precursor to actual rape. That's what I was taught. Are you saying it isn't used that way?'

A frisson passed through the nearby boats, and Kip was keenly aware that Cruxer had just equated a hundred nearby drafters with rapists. Everyone in the boats within earshot went very quiet and very tense.

'It can be used that way,' Sibéal admitted.

'And animals.' His mouth twisted. 'Uniting with an animal. Forcing yourself. On an innocent animal. It's like—'

'It's a terrible thing to call good evil,' Sibéal interrupted. 'Horny, shamed zealots often see perversity in innocent activities. Men like that would describe a mother changing her son's soiled nappy as stripping an infant naked and rubbing his genitals. It's true, but it's misleading. When a man sees perversity everywhere, one must question who's the pervert. I'd hate for you to become a person like that, Commander.'

Cruxer looked as if he'd been slapped. 'Yet even a shamed, imperfect man might actually find himself among those who pervert the gifts Orholam has given them.'

It was a step back, but the crowd of will-casters didn't see it that way. They moved from vindication to surly outrage in an instant. Point to Cruxer, but maybe this wasn't an argument worth winning. Kip felt as if he were watching a team of runaway horses pulling a heavy-laden cart down a crowded street. Perhaps disaster couldn't be averted forever.

But Sibéal held her hand up. 'Will-casting is a sword. Like any sword, it is meant to cut and kill. It is an implement – mostly – of violence and ugliness. It is a sword we here carry with an appreciation for the dangers of the blade. Surely you warriors can understand this. We do not disagree about how vile are the abuses of this craft.'

'Except the Chromeria says *all* uses of your craft are abuses,' Cruxer said.

'Cruxer,' Kip said, 'you know I love you. But shut your gob. Sibéal?'

She looked down the river nervously, but they were still quite a ways out. 'Your Magisterium draws its edicts in such a way as to keep as many people safe as possible. It would ban swords altogether, so as to save us all from those who use swords to rape and steal and kill. But there is a time to kill, and a place to use every weapon at our disposal. Is now the time and place for you, Kip Guile, who said he would lead us to kill and to die?'

'I take it that the Cwn y Wawr disagree,' he said.

'The Cwn y Wawr are liars and hypocrites,' Conn Arthur

said, hot. 'They claim they abide by the Chromeria's laws? For generations they've sent discipulae to the Chromeria, taken all the education they can get, then failed out on purpose so their contracts could be bought out cheaply. They've even trained with the Blackguard, abusing your trust and stealing positions and funds.'

Kip should have been thinking about whether he could bring together ancient enemies without losing everyone. Instead he thought about the Blackguard and its old discrimination against anyone not Parian or Ilytian, first justified because they were the peoples with the darkest skin – a justification made flimsier with every mixing generation.

Those old snubs must have made the Blood Foresters who became the Cwn y Wawr feel justified in stealing what training they could: 'You won't be fair to me? Fine, I'll take your training and leave.'

Those desertions would have then made the Parians and Ilytians feel justified again: 'See, these people are untrustworthy. They aren't worthy of being Blackguards.'

Every community is a gull gliding over a sea of spite, eager for carrion, all too ready to steal, and all too quick to squawk when stolen from.

Kip held up his hands, and they all quieted. They actually listened to him. As if he was a real leader. 'Some things at the Chromeria are going to have to change. But we're in no position to change anything until we win. And to win, we need all the allies we can get. We're in a fight to the death. I'll pick up any sword I can.'

'Even if it cuts you?' Conn Arthur said. It must have come out louder than he'd meant, because he reddened – Orholam bless that light skin – but he stood fast when he saw the others look at him, suddenly stubborn.

'If it cuts the White King deeper? Absolutely. This isn't a time when we have the luxury to cast aside help. And I'll tell them the same thing, when they raise the same objections about you.'

The big muscles went rigid again, and then slowly deflated. Orholam have mercy, but Conn Arthur was big, his muscles and fiery body hair rippling with every move.

'Sibéal, explain will-casting. You have four minutes.'

And, with remarkable concision, she did. The peoples of the deep woods had been will-casting for millennia. And, perhaps affected by the Great River itself, they had always conceived of magic in dichotomies: drafting without casting one's will into the world making one river, and will-casting making another. Down the will-casting river was another fork: will-casting into the soulless, and will-casting into the souled; then will-casting into the simple souled (small animals, mainly) and into complex souls (larger animals and humans); then will-casting into animal souls and into human souls, and so forth.

The first kind of will-casting – into objects, luxin, usually – was considered safe and almost mundane: it was tiring and usually short lived, but a drafter-archer might cast a bit of luxin into the fletching of her arrow, and then fix her will upon a target.

When released, the arrow would curve to some small extent, seeking its target automatically. These weren't dramatic effects: the core physics of an arrow's flight and momentum were still the same. One couldn't shoot an arrow and have it curve back to hit someone behind you, but a skilled will-caster might curve an arrow a bit over a wall to hit someone taking cover behind it. Or – if she possessed greater skill – she might focus on a difficult target and be able to shoot more accurately than her own mundane skills ought to allow.

Holy shit, Kip thought. He'd heard of that in the Blackguard itself. Some of the nunks had sworn they'd seen some of the best archers like Buskin and Tugertent shoot arrows that *curved* in midair.

No wonder they'd been quiet about doing it – it was utterly forbidden.

No wonder they'd done it anyway – it *worked*.

This kind of magic was exhausting, Sibéal said, and it usually expired within seconds or hours of being separated from the caster. They could make simple machines, too. Hidden traps whose trigger was something like 'If touched, ignite.'

The far more dangerous will-casting was into the souled. Whenever they could, they didn't allow their will-casters to start learning it until they were at least thirty years old – when they had a stake in their community, when they had families, when they had reasons not to go mad.

The simple souled could be given only relatively simple instructions: 'Go to this place,' or maybe 'Go to this place and do this.' This, Kip realized, was what his father Gavin had done at the *Gargantua*. He had sent a rat to find the floating fortress's powder magazine.

The height of the will-caster's art was working with creatures with greater intelligence – the complex souls, as they called them – the wolves and dolphins and horses and elephants and jungle cats.

'And *bears*,' Kip guessed. Motherfucker.

'Yes. Bears.'

Conn Arthur gestured to a nearby skimmer to come closer. He turned to Sibéal after he hopped gracefully onto the moving deck of the other boat. 'Tell him about it. Go on. I don't want to hear it, but he needs to know.'

'Conn...?' Kip asked, as the other skimmer separated once more.

'Conn Arthur communes with a giant grizzly,' Sibéal said quietly, looking at the big man's back.

A *giant* grizzly. In case a regular old grizzly wasn't terrifying enough. 'I thought the last of those died long ago,' he said.

'There are a few left. The Deep Forest remembers, Lord Guile.'

Wonderful. 'Tell me about the dangers,' Kip said.

'With the lower forms of will-casting, we're not sure why... It doesn't sap people of their will, like the Chromeria believes. Instead it seems to slowly eat away at their intelligence. We think sometimes the caster forgets to breathe while his will is elsewhere, and his body dies a little. He might come back to himself, but never really be the same. It's a death by slow degrees. As there are few old drafters, there are few old will-casters.'

'And as with drafters who go wight, there are the reckless among will-casters, too,' Tisis added. She'd been quiet until now. 'There are men and women who believe they are wrongly souled. That they are, deep down, wolves or bears or tygre wolves.'

'And what happens to them?' Kip asked.

'Most madness shows up early,' Sibéal said. 'It's part of why we don't teach will-casting to the young. They get themselves killed. Mauled by wild animals usually, or starved. A man is body and soul, and those who separate the two for long do it to their grief.'

'So if you're controlling an animal, and it gets killed, what then?' Kip asked.

She glanced at the conn over on his other boat. 'Sometimes nothing. Sometimes the caster is made an idiot. Sometimes she simply dies, too. It depends how *intricated* the caster is.'

'Intricated?'

'Polychromes can more fully take on their host's body. The different colors connect...differently.'

'Let me guess,' Kip said, stomach sinking. 'Superviolet to understand the thoughts, blue to see and remember, green to feel and to sense how the body should move, yellow to hear and hold the balance of man and animal, orange to smell and process what an animal smells, red to taste and feel the emotions, and sub-red for the passions and the other animal senses a man doesn't share.'

Sibéal looked at Kip as if he were a rock trout who had just beached himself and started lecturing her on eudaemonic theology. 'How...?'

'Lucky guess,' Kip said. The cards. It was the same as the cards. So will-casting was, deep down, connected to the same magical reality that chromaturgy was. It was simply understood differently.

All magic worked by certain laws, but no one knew them all.

But Sibéal wasn't ready to let go of it. 'I would have expected someone who had read up on will-casting to say blue for sight, green for touch, and so forth, probably forgetting sub-red and superviolet. But the secondary connections are not widely known. And you've shown no other knowledge of will-casting. Have you been pretending ignorance of all this? Trying to trap me in a lie?'

'No. And we don't have time to quibble now,' Kip said. 'What happens if the man is killed while he's controlling the animal?'

327

'No, how did you know about the colors' connections?' Sibéal insisted.

Kip said nothing, and they stood eye to eye. Or more accurately, eye to belly, but the pygmy didn't let the height differential affect her in the least. She was flushing, skin turning bluer by the moment.

'Lord Guile...sometimes just *understands* things about magic,' Tisis said, trying to spread oil on the waters. 'He's kind of irritating that way.'

Sibéal went silent, and her grinning mouth threw Kip. He was still learning to look around the corners of her eyes and to ignore the mouth. 'Conn Ruadhán Arthur's twin, Rónán, was killed while he was fully intricated in his bear, not two months past. Ruadhán had to go kill the bear himself. The animal that held the last living remnants of Rónán's soul. It tore Ruadhán's heart out to kill it. But kill it he did.'

'And what happens if you don't kill the animal?' Kip asked.

'Kip!' Tisis scolded.

'I have to know,' he said.

'It goes mad. Tries to return to its people – its human people. But the magic fades, and it reverts to animal, and the man-soul dies at last. But all too often, it gets violent, for it's been changed, been violated. They kill people. We have many stories of attempts to save the soul-trapped, Lord Guile. None of them end happily.'

'The *Briseid*?' Tisis asked. 'Tamar and Heraklos?'

'Indeed. Though perhaps told quite differently than you remember. The Chromeria has ways of crushing knowledge, but some truth always leaks out.'

'Not...*The Seven Lives of Maeve Hart*?' Tisis asked.

'That, too,' Sibéal admitted uneasily.

'No wonder the Chromeria forbids it,' Tisis said.

'What's that?' Kip asked. He'd only heard of the last one. 'Briefly.'

Tisis said, 'A woman flings her soul into a hart and flees when soldiers storm her home and burn it to the ground, killing her body. Her husband Black Aed hunts the men to their homes one at a time, and murders their wives, and puts his Maeve's soul in their bodies. But it never works, because every woman already has her own soul, so he slowly loses her, her soul slipping away, until he comes to the queen herself who had ordered the burning. And with her body, the magic works or seems to work, for she is soulless. But one night he has a foul dream, and on seeing his enemy's face leering over him, shaking him, he strangles her. And upon seeing what he's done, he kills himself, throwing his spirit into the stones of the old castle. He haunts it to this day.'

'Lovely,' Kip said. 'I can't wait to hear more uplifting tales from your homeland.'

'The story is actually...somewhat darker even than that,' Sibéal said. 'But that's beside the point.'

'I agree,' Kip said, not willing to answer more questions, which she seemed poised to ask. He wasn't telling her about the cards. 'So it seems like, to put it in your dichotomies, we're talking about two different things: will-casting and...what?'

'Soul-casting.' Sibéal looked up the river. 'Do we really have time for this?'

'I'm afraid we don't have time not to do this,' Kip said.

'Have you not read the Philosopher? Before you understand anything, you must understand physics – what is in the corporeal world. Upon that you build your understanding of the metaphysics, what is beyond the simple corporeal: emotions and thoughts and so forth. From those two, you derive your ethics, how one is to act properly in accord with the facts, above that, politics, how bodies of individuals are to act toward each other, and then rhetoric and the arts, the poetics. We and the Chromeria disagree about our metaphysics, and it affects everything above it.

'If, as they believe, you tear off a piece of your soul when you will-cast, you're doing fundamental harm to yourself every time you do this magic. It would be akin to magic powered by murdering someone – it wouldn't matter if you did good with the magic, because at base, the action empowering that good is itself evil. Thus, the good we do they discount, whilst every ill effect that comes from our magic they say obviously springs from the corrupted nature of the whole. We can't win, because we argue politics – the regulation of magics – when our dispute is about metaphysics.'

'This is…very complicated,' Tisis said.

'Not really,' Sibéal said. 'We say the will is the breath of the soul. Like your body needs breath and will die without it, your soul needs will. But we can inspire an animal – literally, "in-breathe" – to do something. Of course we need to recover afterward, like you need to inhale every time you exhale. Like you breathe hard after running. You need recovery time. And yes, if you go too long without breathing, you die. Or if you deprive another person of their breath, it's killing. This is murder if it's a person, but the animals we inspire can also be killed thus if it's done wantonly or clumsily or for too long, and we regard that as a serious offense, too. Will-casting with the higher souled is a profound partnership. And the animals we partner can tell if it is done with violent or disrespectful intent. And the will-caster feels their terror, too, if the part-nering is done poorly or meanly. We know and love our hosts to a degree that one who has never will-cast cannot fathom.

'Soul-casting is different. Forbidden. Soul-casting is when the soul of an animal is blotted out and replaced. Its body may live for days afterward, but its vital spark is extinguished. It damages the caster, too, in more insidious ways.'

'It can be done to men?'

She nodded grimly. 'Which is why to us soul-casting is a black magic. Damned magic. Always forbidden, always disas-trous, as the stories of the living dead and of wolf men tell. Loathed and despised.'

'And mostly moot, because only a full-spectrum polychrome can soul-cast,' Kip said. It was partly a guess.

She looked stung. 'That's right.'

'Ruadhán and his twin Rónán, full-spectrum polychromes?' he guessed.

'Yes.'

'And Rónán soul-cast himself?'

She licked her lips with a small blue tongue. 'While dying. Doubtless it is a unique temptation for those with such great power. And now you know Ruadhán's shame.'

'No,' Kip said, 'now I know why he swore fealty to me

instead of taking the lead himself.' The big man had the respect of his people, and the intellect and fierceness to lead, but at the word of some prophet he had given up the lead and sworn himself to Kip? Why would a man do that?

Kip had only hatred for his own half brother, but he'd seen what a big-hearted man will give for his brother. And he said a silent thanks to Tremblefist and Ironfist for that. For here, though different in culture and color and circumstances, he saw a mirror of their love. And what Tremblefist had taught him might just save his life.

Why would Conn Arthur not lead?

Not because he was ashamed of his brother, who had done something desperate as he died. There was little shame in that. Conn Arthur wouldn't lead because he was ashamed of himself.

Because there was no way in hell he'd killed Rónán's bear Lorcan, because that would have meant killing his brother. Rónán was out there, somewhere, trapped and going mad in the body of that bear, and nothing could stop him but death. Conn Arthur bore the responsibility to his people and to his brother to kill the animal, but that would mean admitting Rónán was dead. It would mean killing the last remnant of his brother with his own hands.

His love was his shame. But if he wouldn't confront that on his own, Kip was going to have to make him do so before someone got killed.

But how do you reveal a man's deepest secret shame, accuse him of heresy and cowardice, and not destroy him?

A commander couldn't. Maybe a friend could. Kip had to give Conn Arthur time to deal with it, had to pray the forest was big enough for one crazed grizzly.

Time was up. The island was coming into view.

'What are you going to do?' Sibéal asked.

It all seemed abstract – a philosophical difference about the best uses of magic. That was, until the skimmers beached on the island and Kip saw the sudden fear in the Cwn y Wawr men's eyes at the sight of Sibéal and at their sudden comprehension of who these people were.

The Cwn y Wawr, these hardened magic-using warriors, were *terrified* of the will-casters. Terrified through ignorance, partly, sure. But when you live in the forest, and you know the creatures there well, how scary is the idea of someone who can turn any one of those creatures against you, with the capabilities of the animal but the mind of a human? How terrifying is it that a person might take over your own body? How terrifying is it to actually meet the kind of people responsible for all the tales of the living dead and wolf men and worse?

To them, the name 'Ghosts' wasn't a sarcastic reference to how ephemeral and helpless these homeless, bereaved wanderers were. To them, the Ghosts haunted the darkness of the forest, ready to turn nature or even your fellow man or your dead against you.

But trained warrior-drafters were scary, too. And these Cwn y Wawr were in bad shape, whether they knew it or not. They'd been freed from death or servitude, but they'd lost two precious things: their confidence and their honor. They'd lost their confidence in being betrayed and captured and needing to be rescued, and they'd lost their honor in pursuing a separate peace with the White King.

A soldier without confidence and honor is a breath away from becoming a brigand or gangster.

But it had always been a fool's dream. Kip, leading men to destroy the White King himself? These two camps were like lodestones pushing against each other invisibly, endlessly.

Ergo, just flip one. They'll fuse themselves together.

Right?

Kip stepped ashore without a word, without so much as a nod at the men standing there to ask him a question.

Drafting green from a thousand trees shining on each bank of the river in the noonday sun, he threw down steps and made a small platform to stand on. 'We,' he declared, 'are damaged but not dismayed, oppressed but not overwhelmed. We are the Broken, for when our oaths were tested, we broke them and ourselves. We were the despised: Here are my best friends. This world sees a bastard, an orphan, a hostage, a cripple, an idiot. I call them the Mighty. We – you – are outcasts all, the homeless driven from the lands where our mothers were buried. They have taken the light from our lives.

Killed our loved ones, our friends. Taken our homes. Left us to wander as ghosts and feral dogs.'

He didn't remember, afterward, much of what he said after that. He was looking at the faces, watching how they moved, the little twitches of expression. A man's face is the surface of a pond, reflecting the sky, reflecting the trees, reflecting whatever is the object of his gaze and his love, the reflection hiding his depths. But when a wave passes, in the swell, for an instant, you can see what lies beneath the waters.

Their ears listened to his words, but their hearts inclined to the sincerity of his soul, deep calling unto deep: We have lost, but we are not lost. We have failed, he told them…but we can do better. We can be forgiven, we can make things new. This is not the end for us.

'They have taken the light from us. Yes. But now they expect us to cower like dogs beaten and fade like shades forgotten. But I don't see dogs and shades here. Do they not know what they've begun? I see wolves. I see ghosts…'

He looked around at them as if they had forgotten who they were, and he was here to hold up a mirror for them that they might remember.

'Have you forgotten? Have they made you, for this brief hour, forget? Ghosts and wolves *hunt at night*. They think we cower, waiting for the light? Alone we are broken, bereaved, afraid. Together we are strong. Together we will hunt. In darkness, we will usher them into the final darkness. Alone we were weak and frightened. That time is past. Together, today, we are the Nightbringers.'

It ended with cheers, and tears, and not a single accusation that this person or that was disloyal or heretical or dangerous. Somehow it ended with a hundred and twenty will-casters, two hundred and thirty Cwn y Wawr, and two hundred civilians swearing fealty to Kip.

And Kip's fool dream that he might destroy the White King was like a babe stillborn, lying pallid and cold in his hands – taking sudden breath, stirring, squalling; thus was born his army.

Chapter 47

There was nothing special about the basement where Teia would commit her first murder. Other than, naturally, the four iron rings anchored in one wall, and the old man shackled spread-eagled between them.

Teia set down her candelabrum. If only it were so easy to lay aside her conscience. The old man was wearing slaves' white. He was gagged, but he didn't appear to have been beaten. Most importantly, he wasn't blindfolded.

They didn't care that he saw her face. Her last, dim hope had been that this was just a test to see if she'd do it – maybe this 'slave' was in fact a plant from the Order itself whose assignment was to see if she broke and tried to free him.

But that hope, like all hopes, drained away.

Master Sharp had left. He didn't care. He'd given her no deadline at all, though obviously some lackey of the Order or someone hired by it was coming at some point to dispose of the body.

If there was no body here, Teia would be exposed as either disobedient or incapable of the work the Order had for her to do. Either would be a death sentence for her.

This was literally his life or hers.

The man looked at her with a slave's hooded wariness. You tried not to betray too much as a slave, lest your fear or hatred or disgust or longing earn you a beating.

'Earn.' Orholam damn us all.

She could see him trying to place her so that he might guess what to expect: Traders' clothes, perhaps? Young – she had always looked young for her age, which was made worse by her short hair and what looked like mere skinniness when her clothes covered her arms and shoulders. She probably didn't look too frightening to him, though. Just a slip of a girl, she was.

No, old man, I am death come for you.

'This shouldn't hurt,' Teia said.

Slaves had superstitions about who was the most likely to be brutal to them. Insecure wives, drunkards, slave owners barely rich enough to own slaves but desperate to do so to prove their status, the youngest children in wealthy households, and that particular breed of rich luxiat that strained under the hypocrisy of keeping slaves while Orholam taught that all men were brothers. Where did Teia fit? this man was wondering. Sometimes a very young girl didn't see a slave as a slave. He might be a playmate, an adult kinder than others because he gave her his time.

Sooner or later, they learned.

'Not until the end, anyway,' she said.

That was another evil of slavery, wasn't it? How it twisted not only the enslaved, but their owners as well. Teia had seen the worst impulses of her onetime playmate Sarai not only tolerated but encouraged as far as slaves were concerned. Surely every child has terrible impulses. Surely every mother says, 'No, child, don't hit!' Except a slaveholder says, 'No, child, you may only hit Kallas or Elpis!'

And Kallas was twisted by accepting the blows of his mistress's brats. And Elpis was twisted by her weekly rapes at her master's hands. And her master was twisted by thinking it was natural and moral, his right.

This is why Orholam hates slavery, as he hates divorce and war. But he tolerates them. They are his compromises with humanity, with the hardness of our hearts. For who could imagine a world without any of those?

She let loose a cloud of paryl from her palm, and then, given the darkness of the room, she remembered her dark spectacles, and took them off.

The slave shuddered at the sight of her irisless black eyes, monstrously agape, swallowing all light.

He bucked against his shackles. He tried to scream, but whoever had gagged him had not just bound a rag around his mouth – which did little to nothing. They'd filled his mouth with a rock and then bound it in place. Poor bastard.

And old, and male. Because an old worker slave was cheap.

An older woman could be put to work inside, watching children or knitting or doing simple tasks. Not all were, of course, but enough that they generally cost more than old men broken by long physical labor.

Teia felt far away from herself. As she streamed paryl through one of his arms, looking for the nerves, another part of her immediately started concocting schemes, each more impractical than the last. She could take the man out of here under the cover of her cloak – too small. She could wait until darkness – and what if someone came before then? She could find a dead body about his age and size – where? She could kill the Order's lackey who came to get the body – and who was to say that wouldn't be just some innocent grave digger? Even if it was one of the Order's people, killing them would tip her hand, wouldn't it?

It was already too late to go after Murder Sharp and try to kill him and then pretend she'd never gotten the orders. She hadn't even thought of it when he'd left.

'Mmm! Mmm!' His eyes rolled back in his head and he bucked again, making her lose the paryl stream, dammit.

He thrashed, tearing the skin at his wrists, blood trickling down his bare arms.

She could simply disobey – and show that she wasn't loyal. That was death. But perhaps she could disobey for some excellent reason – she refused to kill slaves because she'd been a slave, or, or...

It wouldn't matter. Not to the Order. Not in wartime. Disobedience was death. Their secrecy was more important to them than having another assassin.

She'd have to run away, far, far from here, to some city or village where they would never find her.

She found a thick tendon and pulled the paryl tight around it. His arm barely twitched before the paryl shattered. Apparently she wouldn't be pulling anyone around like a marionette with paryl.

In the right place, though – say by making a finger twitch on a trigger – it could make all the difference, couldn't it?

She was doing it. Exactly what the Order had commanded. She was using this slave like a practice dummy. A whetstone on which to hone her skills razor sharp. Not a human. Not an old man with fears and hopes and a history.

I'm a Blackguard. This is what I must do. I'm a soldier, under orders. This is war, and I am a soldier. I could have run away, but I chose this. I could run away now.

She could get money. How could you stop a thief who could make herself invisible?

How she wished she were back in the Prism's training room. She could bathe in superviolet and blue until there was only the cold logic of necessity.

The nerves! At last. She tweaked a bundle at the slave's elbow. His arm dropped, paralyzed, until the shackle caught his wrist. He gasped.

The problem was how much sense it all made. It made sense for the Order to train her. It made sense that she be trained on old, useless slaves who would die within a couple of years anyway. On the Chromeria's side, it made sense that Teia be ordered to comply with whatever the Order demanded. It was the only way they could get her close enough to uproot them.

Karris was an admiral accepting the death of her men on the front lines to protect more at home. Accepting, even, the corruption and breaking of those at the front lines to protect the lives of those at home.

But all that logic couldn't argue with the fear on the face of this man, who'd done nothing to deserve a death that accomplished something so near to nothing it surely couldn't measure against his life.

She would use these skills she would learn here with this man's pain and his death against the Order – but first she would use her skills for it. How did that balance any scales?

She wasn't killing an innocent on purpose; that was the difference between the good guys and the bad guys. Bad guys killed the innocent on purpose; good guys sometimes killed the innocent, but only by accident while trying to kill the enemy.

But she was killing an innocent deliberately in order to get a chance to kill the guilty. How was she any different from a marksman who shoots a child in the legs so that he can gun down any combatants who came to save the child?

No, the Order was making her do this. It was *the Order* who would kill her if she refused.

Alone, the Chromeria would never order this. Experimenting on and murdering a slave for *practice* was the Order's way of doing things.

Yet here she was.

The Order would keep sending her slaves until she mastered all the skills they demanded of a Shadow. If she mastered them quickly, they would send her sooner to kill targets out in the world. If she mastered them slowly, they would send her more and more slaves to practice on – and then murder.

There was no good choice, if she stayed. Nothing that would let her stay innocent.

If she ran, she wouldn't be a murderer. But she would never avenge Marissia, either. The spymaster was probably dead, but to run would mean giving up on her. Then Teia would never stop the Order, and they would continue murdering whomever they wanted. They would forever take their tithe of blood.

If she ran, she wouldn't be guilty of anything except cowardice.

I don't run.

Fear was a shackle. Fear was a shackle she would never wear again.

Orholam, forgive me for what I am about to do.

Teia pulled off the man's gag and removed the stone from his mouth. 'What's your name?' she asked quietly.

'Rajiv.'

'Rajiv? You don't look Atashian. What's your birth name?'

He looked at first as if he couldn't remember. Finally, in a tone that said, 'Must you take also this?' he said, 'Salvador.'

'You're Tyrean.'

He nodded.

'Any family, Salvador?'

'A son.'

'Slave?'

'No longer. They took him from me. Beat him to death years ago.'

'As they do,' Teia said. Fuck them. 'I wanted to tell you,

338

Salvador, that your death today is going to accomplish something. That it's part of winning this war, once and for all. That it's a secret, but I swear you're part of something good.' She looked down at her hands. 'I wanted to tell you that, but I'm not sure it's true.'

I don't run away.

But I promise this, my innocent Salvador, hollow though my promise may ring: I will avenge you.

Perhaps that's all that's left for me.

She rubbed a sore dogtooth absently and then, gathering her will, went to work. And when she was finished, she had by no means mastered paryl.

He would not be the last.

Chapter 48

Of all the improbable situations Kip had found himself in during his short life – killing a king, killing a god, actually having friends, being able to jog more than a few steps without collapsing and dying of equally lethal doses of heart attack and embarrassment – this situation struck him as the most implausible yet.

He was standing at the open flap of his tent with a beautiful woman who wanted him, who seemed to *genuinely* want him. Tisis practically glowed with pride in Kip and hunger for him. It was so weird it actually gave him pause, and made him think.

Thinking was clearly the enemy here.

The Cwn y Wawr and Ghost camps had joined together on the island, and tonight they were celebrating the end of generations of internecine strife and oppression. It was the wildest party Kip had ever seen. The kind of party where before you slipped into your tent, instead of worrying that you were going to disturb your neighbors, you worried that it might already be occupied.

And Kip. Goddam Kip. He was seriously considering not

339

making love with this beautiful woman. Against every sane consideration, Kip was stuck between his pride and having some good old-fashioned dirty fun with his mind-blowingly amazing wife.

Swallow your pride and take what you're given, you fat idiot. This is better than you deserve. Why can't you just enjoy it?

Tisis gave a little wave and a wink to her healer friend Evie Cairn, who'd been teaching her battlefield medicine, and tugged on Kip's belt again, her other hand holding open the flap of the much-larger tent the Cwn y Wawr had insisted on giving them. 'You coming inside, or do you want to get started right here?'

But then her smile faded as she saw the look in his eyes. She dropped Kip's belt.

'We have to talk,' Kip said. Not words he would have ever imagined speaking.

When bodies should speak, words are the enemy, moron.

'This is about the will-casters, isn't it?' Tisis said. She swallowed. She looked around guiltily, blonde hair glowing in the light of the rising moon, unwilling to meet his eyes. She ducked into the tent.

It looked like flight, and it triggered a predator instinct. Kip went after her. 'You manipulated me.'

Her back to Kip, Tisis said nothing. She lit a lantern.

It wasn't fair, but Kip wasn't reminded of Andross Guile and his thousand manipulations and machinations, his dispassionate way of fucking with everything for his own ends, even if those ends were merely his own entertainment. Instead, he was reminded of his mother. She had lied reflexively, for no purpose. She manipulated him, too, always, ever twisting him into guilt and shame when she could have accomplished the same ends with a simple request. Her manipulations were wanton and wounding and pointless.

'You kept what they were a secret from me – even when we were half an hour from meeting the Ghosts' mortal enemies. I came *this* close to walking into a trap blind. You could have gotten us all killed. Balls, Tisis, Cruxer could have said something about will-casting heathens and I would have agreed out of hand. After...I mean, I feel like we just came to this new understanding, this new place, and things are so good between us – and you sided with them against me.'

Whoa. Kip the Lip. That got away from him a little.

She said nothing. She didn't even turn around, damn her.

'Turn around,' he demanded.

'No.'

'You're just like my mother,' Kip said. Untruer words had never been spoken. 'You ever side against me again, and we're finished.'

Still not speaking, she stepped past him, averting her face and bringing a hand up to block his view – so he couldn't see her tears, no doubt, as if that very action weren't rubbing in that he'd made her cry.

Mere moments after she was gone, Kip's hot blood cooled. But he didn't move. She was in the wrong!

So why did he feel so wretched?

Should have waited until after sex to fight.

Never choose fighting over sex.

He opened the tent flap, but he couldn't see her anywhere.

Kip knew he should go after her. Bugger what anyone else in the camp thought of him. They were busy with their own pleasures tonight. He needed to go apologize. He needed to go tell her he was an asshole.

These new clothes were too wide across the shoulders and chest and too tight across the belly, too much effort to keep clean. Too damn grown up.

Putting on Kip the screw-up, Kip the fatty, Lard Guile, Kip the victim who soaked up damage and mistook passivity for placidity, who thought that being imperturbable was being invincible, putting on that old Kip was like putting on his old tunic. It reeked; it was stained and dumpy, but it was comfortable.

He couldn't suck in his gut and stand up straight every day. He was a child, pretending to be a lord.

He could remember his mother, sneering when Kip told her he'd been beaten again by Ram, after he'd seemed so nice for several weeks: 'Don't be a fool. No one ever changes.'

And then he remembered something Gavin had said after

341

he'd assigned Kip, impossibly, to the Blackguard: 'Don't decide to change. The world is full of people who have decided to change but haven't. Don't decide to change – change. If you want to be different, act different.'

The bed was calling Kip to comfortable stasis and self-recrimination.

Before he could think any more, he went out into the camp. But he never found her. He'd waited too long.

Eventually he returned to their tent, alone.

Dammit.

Kip pulled out the rope spear he'd started working on to keep his hands busy. He set a yellow hood on his lantern and started once more. The color set him in balance and helped him step away from his problems as a leader and mull them over in a new way – and he actually made good headway on the project, too. Ben-hadad had pointed out jokingly that if you made the links of chain small enough, the chain rope would be as flexible as real rope.

It hadn't been so simple, but after studying hemp ropes and then applying some other colors of luxin, Kip was actually making good progress.

Once he thought he heard the tent flap open, but when he looked up a moment later, no one was there.

He went to bed alone, and somehow he slept until he was awakened by Cruxer. The morning was as foggy as Kip's head, and as he came to join his generals and Tisis, Kip saw why he'd been awakened. On every bank opposite their little island were soldiers, armed and ready for war, bearing the Green Boar of Eirene Malargos. The Nightbringers were surrounded.

'So,' Kip said to Tisis, 'I guess your sister hasn't forgiven us for running away?'

Chapter 49

Gavin sat in his hell. Sat silent, cross-legged, with the poisoned bread clasped lightly in his hands.

'Useless,' the dead man said to him.

The poison, and the bread, and the hunger – his companions – they were oddly precious to him now. His world had contracted to a space as narrow as his dreams and as wide as his rib cage with its knocking, laboring heart.

He was, perhaps, losing coherence.

They have loved the darkness.

How could anyone love darkness?

He supposed that in darkness, everyone was as blind as a one-eyed man. His handicap became universal.

He was afraid of dying, he saw that now. But he was also resigned to it. He didn't think he deserved better. Karris deserved better.

He should never have married her. Should never have drawn her into his circle at all. He was poison, and he'd known it. And yet he had let her love him.

She'd had nothing from him but grief. It was so unfair. Unfair of him, who should have known, and unfair of Orholam to allow it.

But then, of all people it was unseemly of *him* to whinge about fairness, wasn't it?

'You could be in Karris's bed now,' the dead man said. 'You *coward.*'

The first part cut through Gavin like a black luxin tooth. But the latter part – coward? – was oddly off point. Was the young him so obtuse that he thought such an insult would hurt him?

Gavin knew he was a coward in certain areas – it had taken him fifteen years to be honest with Karris. But in physical danger he was often careless to a fault. Had he really once thought 'coward' would be a cutting insult? Odd.

It actually took his attention away from the open sore that was Karris and how badly he'd treated her. At some point, seated cross-legged as he was, he faded into sleep.

As he stood atop a tower, a dream giant towered over him, a colossus of light, blocking out the sun, but its own features not thereby cast into shadow.

Gavin felt himself guttering under the force of the giant's gaze, no, melting like a candle man in a holocaust, wax streaming from every limb, right on the edge of combustion.

'Please!' he begged. He held up a hand to block out the light, to find some darkness in which to hide. But his hand itself shimmered, turned to liquid glass. It gave him no shade. He was transparent.

But he wasn't clear.

Threaded through the pellucid flesh of his very hand were veins of thorny black, quivering angrily, exposed and hurting in the light, shrieking soundlessly, grinding and twisting to find some relief.

As the thorns rotated, splintering and lacerating the flesh they called home, Gavin's entire body convulsed with pain. He fell.

From the pure white marble ground, he crossed his glassine arms to defend himself. And saw another thick vein of parasitic, bloated blackness in his other arm. He tore open his tunic and saw, encased and strangled in a cage of thorns, his own black heart. No, not black. It was gray, diseased.

It pulsed loathsomely. And he was disgusted. And he was ashamed.

He plucked it from his chest to fling it away and die, rightly die.

And then he saw, at his heart's heart, a glimmer.

Storm clouds were gathering overhead, massive thunderheads of judgment, coming with such speed as to make up for how long they had been delayed. The air, so thin up here, changed palpably.

But Gavin had seen the white. His gray heart writhed, and the whiteness was swallowed again.

'No!' he shouted to the coming storm and the wind that whipped his body cold. 'I need more time!'

Chapter 50

Karris wasn't certain how he'd gotten the message to her without its being intercepted. For that matter, she wasn't certain it hadn't been. She wasn't certain the message was real. Even if it was real, she wasn't certain it wasn't a trap.

Koios had asked her to meet – Koios, her lost brother, though now he styled himself the White King. Koios, who had been her favorite. He'd signed the message 'Koios.'

So here she was, in a skimmer with a half-dozen Blackguards, waiting for the trap or the prank to reveal itself, or, just possibly, for a meeting that might change the future of the satrapies and save tens of thousands of lives.

The Blackguards kept her skimmer moving in random circles so they wouldn't have to flee from a full stop if it came to that. Each man wore his spectacles and had full grip of his color and a musket. Karris didn't offer advice to the Blackguards on their disposition, though she would have when she was first elevated; she had brought only the best Blackguards, and they knew their work.

Except, of course, that they had allowed her to come at all. Commander Ironfist might not have.

She had prepared her arguments before she'd summoned Commander Fisk. They had all boiled down to one thing: if I can end the war with words alone, it's worth the risk. If Fisk had been adamant, she would have brought up that she missed her brother. That was true, but it was false, too. She was pretty certain the man who had been her brother was long dead.

But Commander Fisk hadn't argued at all. 'Who do you want on it?' he'd asked instead.

'You're not going to try to stop me?'

'You're the Iron White. In my experience, you stop when you're good and ready.'

Her brow wrinkled. 'I don't know if I like being trusted so much.' Have I changed so much? Has the world?

Fisk only sighed. 'I only know one man who could stop you, and begging the High Lady's pardon, but I'm not that man, nor will I tell him without your leave.'

Fisk didn't mean Gavin. He didn't mean Ironfist. He meant Andross.

Was this what happened when you didn't have strong voices around you? Gavin and Ironfist would have kept her from making mistakes. Instead she was alone.

For a single moment, she remembered the day when she was seven years old, and her hateful slave-tutor Izza had forbidden her to leave her reading lessons until she finished ten pages, even though Karris told her that she needed to use the latrine. Shaking and crying, she'd made it through five pages before she'd wet her léine.

She'd opened the door, and Izza was gone. Her father was in the library instead, meeting with an important noble. He'd looked at her as if she disgusted him. 'Look what you've done!'

She soul-wept, hysterical, but he had pushed her away when she tried to hug him.

Karris had never tried to hug him again.

It had been Koios who'd found her after she'd fled. He'd wrapped his cloak around her and walked through the manse with her. When their mother had asked why Karris was wearing his cloak, he'd said they were playing a game. He'd taken her to the nursery slaves to wash her and her clothing, and commanded their silence about the matter.

The slave Izza hadn't been beaten. That wasn't Rissum White Oak's way. That would have been too direct for him. Instead he sold her to the silver mines at Laurion. Karris still felt a stab of shame at the elation she'd felt when she'd heard that.

The silver mines! An educated slave should never have faced such a punishment. Especially not a woman.

Ah, that was why she'd thought of that day now: shame and disappointment and her brother, all twined together like wintering serpents in a ball of slithering warmth.

She was still thinking of that day, of that young man whom she'd adored as only a young girl can adore her big brother, when they spotted the islands.

His note had invited her to choose whichever island she wished in the cluster, that she might be assured there was no trap. There were a dozen tiny islands here, differentiated mostly by how much or how little vegetation covered them. The Blackguards studied them through long lenses and picked one.

She jumped out of the skimmer as it came to rest on the blindingly bright white sand. Her Blackguards had chosen one of the smallest islands. As she waded ashore, they spread a cloth over the skimmer to hide its workings.

Karris had worn her whites. She thought that the odds of an assassination attempt were about one in two – yes, Commander Ironfist would have been furious they'd come. With those odds, there was no need to make herself clumsy with frocks and petticoats. She had a brace of Ilytian wheel-lock pistols tucked in her belt. They were all ivory and scrimshaw – a bit fussy for Karris's tastes – but they were also the finest pistols in the Chromeria's armory.

Truth was, the whole Iron White thing had taken on a life of its own. Every diplomat and noble who appeared before Karris brought a gift that somehow incorporated white. White leather, white silk, white cotton, white flowers – flowers! White with actual iron, white with platinum because it was more expensive, and every once in a while, some daring soul would do white with gold – for the sun, you see? Because you are so close to Orholam, you see?

Oh, I see.

Did no one – no one? – remember her love for color?

If only someone would bring her something red, or green, or black, she would grant their petition immediately, regardless.

But Karris wasn't a woman anymore. To become the Iron White was to become a symbol. If her greatest sacrifice in this war was giving up her preferred fashions, she should really wake each day with a heart full of gratitude. She could only hope that someday the inner woman resembled these trappings.

'There he is,' Gill Greyling said, lens up to his eye. 'But what the hell is that?'

He handed the monocular off to his brother.

'Don't know. But it's moving fast,' Gav said.

'He wouldn't reveal that they have skimmers like this,' Karris said. I don't think. 'Not for free.'

When the ship got close, she saw that it was shaped like a chariot, and that thick lines disappeared into the waves before it. Six dorsal fins like jagged teeth bit the waves.

As they entered the shallows, Karris caught sight of a

hammer-shaped head and an eye streaming blood or glowing from within with some demonic light.

It took everything she had not to step farther away from the waves. A rational part of her whispered, 'They're simply will-cast sharks,' probably with red luxin. But her stomach didn't hear that, her weak knees couldn't hear it, her tight throat wouldn't.

Iron White, Karris. Iron White. She painted on ambivalence and hoped it could fool the brother who'd known her so well.

Heedless of the sharks, six bodyguards clad all in white hopped from the chariot and waded ashore. They even wore white veils of precious silk, and bore ataghans and punch daggers and *krises*. There were no muskets that she could see.

In turning back to their old gods, were the pagans turning back to old technologies as well? Orholam, let it be so.

Upon reaching the shore, the bodyguards turned and cast blue luxin to make a bridge. The White King walked to shore without even dampening his boots, leaving only a hunchbacked charioteer behind.

They stood nearly a hundred paces from each other, a man in white and a woman in white, across the white sands, under Orholam's white, hot eye. Karris drew her pistols and handed them off. She drew her bich'hwa and her ataghan and handed them off as well. Last, she took her green and red spectacles off their necklaces and gave them away.

The White King handed off a scepter that could serve as a mace, and a simple hunting knife. He started across the sand without hesitation.

Of course, either of them could be hiding another weapon. But they were drafters. They both *were* weapons, against which the only defense possible was vigilance. Karris walked toward him.

When she'd been captured by King Garadul, her brother had appeared in the vast carapace of luxin armor he'd created for himself. But this man didn't so much as shine in the sun. There were no luxin angles reflecting light, no winking blues or flashing yellows.

He was smaller than she remembered, barely even taller

than she was. But then she saw his face. Somehow she'd forgotten, the scouring of time a mercy.

The burn scars. Orholam. Her beloved brother's face looked as if someone had given a wax poppet to a cruel child. His face had been melted. One eye was lower than the other. A thick knot of tissue had fused his cheek to his neck, and then been cut.

He looked far, far worse than when she'd met with him in Tyrea. It couldn't all be the lighting, but neither did these look like fresh scars. He'd been burnt then, but not misshapen.

She composed herself against the pity and despair. She had to be sharp and cold for this. She was the White, and her office settled over her like a blanket of snow, covering the cracks in her armor.

'Koios,' she said, choosing to let some warmth seep through her tone. She *was* happy to see him. She *was* happy to have a chance to end this war, slight though it might be.

'You've come a long way since last we met,' he said, gesturing to her robes. Even his voice had changed from when he'd been young. Husky, damaged by the smoke, changed by that damned fire that had changed everything else.

'As have you,' she said.

'You mean this?' he asked, pointing to his face. 'It was hexes, before, to minimize your horror, I hoped. I have since become...more comfortable in my own skin. Or what's left of it, I should say.' He smiled as if it were some unfunny joke.

'I was referring to the lands you've conquered and the untold misery you've spread for scores of thousands,' Karris said.

'We've freed four of the nine kingdoms of old,' he said, barely hearing her. 'But there is so much to be rebuilt. So much that was destroyed through ignorance and greed.'

It was as if they were speaking different languages. He saw himself as a *builder*?

'This is hopeless, then, isn't it? There is no bridge across this chasm,' she said.

He smirked, and it was his old lips, unscarred; his old expression, and an old memory. 'I had forgotten how intuitive you are, sister. You wrapped yourself in the blue virtues, but you understand with your heart first. Always did.'

'And does that make my judgments suspect?' she asked, coolly.

'On the contrary. I think you've grasped the crux of the matter. There can be no peace between us, only pauses to rearm.'

'Is that what you're seeking? An armistice?' Karris asked.

'Yes,' he said. 'Effective immediately. My armies have advanced as far as Azuria in Blood Forest. We'll give the city back as a sign of goodwill. In the north, we've crossed the Great River. We'll fall back to the west bank. The truce lasts until spring. It will give everyone a chance to harvest the fall and winter crops – lest everyone starve.'

'My generals tell me Azuria is indefensible. You're giving me what I could take with little effort.'

'And yet you have not taken it,' Koios said. 'Perhaps you are spread thinner than you would like to admit.'

He was right, although the real reason they'd not taken the city was that the question arose, what then? Her armies were needed elsewhere, and the Chromeria and Satrap Briun Willow Bough of Blood Forest were concentrating on keeping Green Haven free. Instead she said, 'If we both rearm, it only guarantees that the next war will be even bloodier.'

'Life is lived in the pauses between wars. Any peace is better than any war, some say.'

'Do you take me for one of those?' she asked.

'I'm not asking anything of you. Any place your troops hold today, they shall keep. It shall be my side that falls back.'

'And I'll guess that your spies will be repeating all this on the streets of Big Jasper within the week? Undermining support for the war?'

'Mm. That sounds like an excellent idea. It's a weakness of your empire: people here never want to bleed for strangers over there. Whereas my word is holy writ. I command the gods themselves. I say when it is time to bleed and when it is time to build, and none question me. Not bad for the weakling once beaten by your sadly deceased husband, mm?'

'What you've suffered doesn't excuse what you've done,' Karris said.

'I'm not looking for an excuse.'

And then she saw the terrible logic of it. Koios might be faced with a particular weakness right now that prompted him to a truce; perhaps he was waiting for someone to be bought off, or a critical shipment of black powder to come through. Certainly any pause would undermine support in the satrapies. But those things might not be the point at all.

Koios wanted both sides to rearm and come back to battle with more terrible weapons because Koios wanted slaughter. He wanted to demolish an entire generation. It wasn't just that he wanted to kill everyone who stood in his way and war was the most efficient way of lining up your enemies and finding out which of your friends might be too formidable someday. He wanted to prove that the Chromeria's way of doing everything was utterly broken. He wanted to kill their apologists, and anyone whose very memory would gainsay his new story.

It's easier to build a new culture on the graves of the dead than around the homes of the living.

'This isn't the kind of trap I was expecting,' she said.

'Trap my own sister?' he said, but his mouth twisted.

'If you kill me, I'll be a martyr for attempting to find peace, and you'll prove that you're untrustworthy. Dammit, Koios, how'd you come to this?'

'Fire burns away illusions,' he said.

'So now you'll plunge the satrapies into the fire, hoping it cripples everyone else as well?' she asked bitterly.

'I'm not a madman,' he said. 'It's beneath you to suggest I am. Too convenient by half. As lazy as I'd expect from some Chromeria witch or Magisterium sycophant. I thought better of you, though.'

She looked at him sadly. 'Your plan isn't mad, brother; it's evil.'

'Evil is what we call what we don't understand.'

She took a deep breath. 'I'm going to leave here today and wonder why I didn't try to kill you before you could do more harm, aren't I?'

'It's not in you to break a pledge, sister.'

Maybe it is, this once.

351

'How do you do it?' she asked. 'How do you convince them all that you're a polychrome?'

'Simple. I became one,' he said. 'The same way Dazen Guile did it.'

He noted her confusion.

'You've either become a better liar than I'd have expected of you, sister, or you've stayed exactly, disappointingly the same, and you're still the wide-eyed naïf who helped start the last war. You do know that the man you married is Dazen Guile?'

She tried not to react, but his face lit up.

'You did. So, not a complete naïf. But he kept some things from you. Heartbreaking.'

'Are you really trying to poison my marriage?'

'Dazen took all pleasures of the flesh from me. If I can be a fly in his ointment, I will. I wish he were alive so I could kill him with my own hands. But... we must all deal with our little disappointments, mustn't we?'

'I think we've said everything profitable here,' Karris said. 'Goodbye, brother. Nice chariot.'

She turned her back and started walking away.

'I did have a trap,' he said as she left. 'But I'll not trigger it. My gift to you, sister, for the love we shared.'

She turned again. 'The next time we meet, O White King, shall be the last. For the love I bear still for that precious boy who died in fire, I will end you. And I'll weep for him, but for your death I will feel only relief.'

He said nothing, only watched her go, and when they pushed away from the island, the skimmer was surrounded by a score of will-cast sharks. The fearsome beasts fell into an escort formation around the skimmer.

But as soon as they reached deeper water, an enormous black shape burst through their ranks and scattered them like chaff. A whale? A black whale?

'More than just men are concerned with this war,' Karris said. 'That should comfort us.'

Should. But then, she didn't feel any comfort herself.

They didn't wait to see what happened. They pushed the skimmer to full speed and headed for home.

Chapter 51

'This *could* be good news,' Tisis said in a voice that told Kip the sentence was bound to continue in a direction he wasn't going to like, 'but I doubt it.'

Thought so.

'You remember I told you about my cousin Antonius?' she said.

'The one you said got all the family charisma?' Kip said. 'This is him?'

'I might not have mentioned his flaws.'

The island was like the intertwined fingers of lovers this morning, soft and hard, billows of fog covering and revealing a thousand spears and muskets arrayed on every shore around the island. The beauty of the warm, diffuse light of the rising sun setting off the threatened death. 'So what about this could be good news?' Kip asked.

'Lord Guile,' Derwyn Aleph of the Cwn y Wawr said, coming up to them. 'The men are ready.'

Everyone had formed up neatly with their various constituencies. They weren't integrated or arrayed exactly the way Kip would have preferred. It would do for now. Kip hadn't read any books on what to do when you're outnumbered and surrounded – and on an island. Probably because no competent commander in history had ever put himself in such a position.

'Good. We wait,' Kip said. He motioned for Tisis to go on.

'Antonius is amazing. I got to spend a couple of weeks with him every time we'd swap off at the Chromeria.'

Kip had known the Malargos family had been required to send hostages to the Jaspers to enforce the end of the Blood Wars, and that Tisis had been one such hostage, but he hadn't thought through the mechanics of alternating the hostages.

'Everyone loves him, but he's...he's a total idealist. Thinks the best of people, but follows authority dogmatically because he trusts that those in command are acting as *he* would act if he were in their place. I never wanted to tear down my sister by telling him not to trust her that way. I hoped that he would grow out of it on his own. More gently.'

So we're fucked.

Kip considered it a moral victory that he didn't say that aloud. That was good, because a moral victory was the only kind of victory he was going to get today. He said, 'Allies don't surround you to cut off every escape.'

'You convinced age-old enemies to join together yesterday,' Tisis said. 'This shouldn't be as hard as all that. Right?'

Her tone was light, but he could tell she was scared, too. If it came to it, would Kip's outcasts attack Eirene Malargos's people?

Would he?

If he did, even a win would embark Kip on a terrible course. The marriage with Tisis was supposed to make peace. That had been Andross Guile's whole reason for arranging for Tisis to think the marriage was her own idea.

Apparently Eirene had figured out that Kip had more to lose from a clash of arms than she did. Or she simply didn't believe that he would bring it to that – which might be true. Or perhaps she thought Tisis had been kidnapped and forced into this marriage.

A rowboat emerged from the mists. A standard-bearer held a green flag with the Malargos Bull mounted on Antonius's personal sigil, a shield. So the young man saw himself as a shield for his aunt, Eirene Malargos, and his cousin, Tisis. A saver of damsels in distress. Wonderful.

Antonius Malargos didn't look as if he'd come with wedding gifts. He did look young, with a lean build. He held a spear, and a pair of red spectacles sat high on his head. He was light-skinned and boyishly handsome, with blond ringlets.

His men rowed toward where Kip and his leaders stood apart. Cruxer stood behind Kip and to his left, bearing a flag of the Mighty – was that Kip's personal seal now? It would have to do until they could come up with a flag for the

Nightbringers. Tisis was at his right, and at his left stood Conn Arthur and Derwyn Aleph.

On seeing Tisis, Antonius's face lit up. Gap toothed and wide mouthed, he had an infectious smile, and mere streaks of red through his irises.

'Sissy!' he said. Ignoring a sharp word from one of his men, he used the spear he held to vault off the boat and land ashore without soiling his fine boots. He rushed over and hugged her like a little boy, picking her up and spinning her around in a circle.

She smiled, too, eyes dancing.

Kip was suddenly glad that he knew Antonius was her cousin, because being jealous of someone who gave his wife joy would have been pretty shitty.

He put her down and stepped back, and clouds rolled over his open demeanor. 'Or should I say Lady Guile now?' he asked.

'I am proudly both,' Tisis said. 'But...if you're going to call me Sissy, do you want me to call you...ahem?'

He winced playfully. 'Maybe not in front of my men.'

Tisis said, 'Then let me introduce you: Lord Antonius Malargos, my husband, Kip Guile. Kip, my cousin, Antonius.'

The Malargos men had come to bracket their commander once more, and in contrast to his open spirit and happy demeanor, they had the air of men ready for violence.

'Sissy?' Kip asked Tisis under his breath as Antonius introduced his lieutenants.

It was an artful introduction, though, personal rather than the full introduction with all of Kip's newly claimed titles. That would have sounded more impressive, but also directed attention to whose title was biggest, and how these powers would interact with each other.

Kip would need to remember to praise Tisis for that, later. If they had a later.

How the hell had Eirene Malargos gotten word that they would be here?

'I've had less kind nicknames,' Tisis murmured.

Introductions of his subordinates concluded, Antonius straightened his shoulders and cleared his throat. He looked pained. 'My dearest cousin, Eirene has given me some very strict orders. I feel compelled to—'

'Where have you been?' Tisis asked. Smart. Never let an idealist frame your problem in black and white. 'Things have changed very quickly, and your orders may well have been, um, outpaced by events.'

'Because you've come here on skimmers and I couldn't possibly have heard something as recently as you?' Antonius asked.

'Yes. How'd you even know...'

'Our family has skimmers now, too. Not as big as those you have covered over there, but enough for a drafter and a messenger to travel quickly together. I was upriver, near the Floating City with Satrap Willow Bough. My orders are only a week old.'

In other words, almost as soon as Kip and his friends had blasted past Rath, Eirene had sent her hounds after them.

Shit.

'How did you get designs for the skimmers?' Kip asked.

'Commander Ironfist showed us how to build one. Former commander, I guess. As you said, events have been moving quickly.'

'Why would he give you such a secret?' Kip asked.

It was more thinking aloud than a question he expected answered, but Antonius said, 'Eirene promised him all our intelligence on your location.'

'So he's coming here?!' Kip asked.

Having Ironfist come to join them was the best news he could imagine.

'I...don't know. Apparently he spoke with his sister the Nuqaba, who was our guest at the time. They had a spectacular fight. He disappeared after that, and she left the next day. I don't know if they were together, or if they parted ways.'

Well, that went from good news to bad quickly. If Ironfist had been coming here, he should have made it already. Unless he'd been waylaid.

Ironfist was intimidating, but he'd also been traveling alone, in these woods, with no law to speak of and many, many talented archers.

What if he'd been killed by some idiot bandits?

'But that's beside the point,' Antonius said. 'Tisis, Eirene ordered me to come here and take you home. By force if necessary. Come home, Sissy. Your family needs you. Your sister needs you.'

'Home,' Tisis said quietly, nostalgic. 'I can't tell you how much I miss the terraced gardens of Jaks Hill...'

Tisis had a home, and a place. Not just sleeping in the woods, arguing with a boy and in constant danger. An honored place as heir to a vast fortune. Her sister Eirene was the real power in Ruthgar. Surely there would be important, fulfilling work for a woman like Tisis there.

It made him feel the gulf between them again. He had no home. Twice an orphan. Flames and death had taken everything except the Mighty from him.

Then Kip was struck by the thought that perhaps last night had not been the perfect time to have his first big fight with his bride. With one more word, she could destroy them all.

'I miss Eirene. I miss the mansion,' Tisis said. 'My old rooms. I miss our people. The smell in the air. The festivals, the races. But I have no home but at my husband's side.'

Oh, good. She doesn't want me and all my friends and allies dead.

'So you're here by choice? Truly? The slave Verity said so, but Eirene didn't trust a slave with such a claim.'

Why would you name a slave Verity and then not trust her? Mercifully, Kip didn't say it aloud. But then, his holding his tongue twice in a row meant he was probably due for a blunder anytime.

Antonius went on. 'You can tell me the truth. Kip can't hurt you now, and, if necessary, we can do this in such a way that Andross Guile never hears about it.'

There was only one way that could happen.

Balls! This smiling boy was threatening a massacre. Kip heard something quite like a growl from Conn Arthur.

Tisis was right about one thing: Antonius was an idealist. If he thought he would simply leave this parley to go order their massacre, he was going to find his head separated from his ass in short order.

Tisis said, 'Cousin, I am not only here by choice, but by design, as my letters should have confirmed. This marriage was my idea, and it may well be the smartest thing I've ever come up with. Eirene intends to imprison Kip, when he can serve the Seven Satrapies and our house both instead. When he can help save Blood Forest *and* Ruthgar.'

'The Guiles unseated you,' Antonius said. 'You were the Green. You've simply forgiven them that?'

Through which Kip heard: Eirene hasn't.

Again Kip was struck with a thought: maybe he had all this capacity to be struck with thoughts because he wasn't speaking. He hadn't said anything at all. He, Kip Guile, leader of the Mighty, Slayer of Kings and Gods – fine, singular for each, so far – but he, the Breaker, possibly Diakoptês, possibly Luíseach, possibly Lightbringer, was just standing dumb and listening to his (furious-at-him) wife do all the talking. His life was a child's racing boat, bobbing in the stream, suddenly swallowed by the rapids, utterly out of his reach.

'Forgive them?! I thank them for it!' Tisis said. 'Cousin, can you imagine me outmaneuvering the Golden Spider Andross Guile on the Spectrum? Or, failing that, convincing his lick-spittles and lackeys to do something contrary to his will?'

Antonius paused. He'd obviously never thought about what being on the Spectrum entailed. 'Perhaps not.'

'By marrying Kip, I've utterly guaranteed the only thing that Eirene could hope I might gain from any number of years on the Spectrum: timely help from the Guiles – and, through them, all the Seven Satrapies.'

'He is a good man, a good commander?' Antonius asked as if Kip weren't there, and as if it were one question.

'He's barely arrived here and look,' Tisis said. The fog was clearing, and the extent of Kip's forces was obvious now.

Antonius studied the forces for what seemed the first time. 'He's united the Cwn y Wawr and the Ghosts?'

That was answered with a nearly simultaneous grunts of assent from Conn Arthur and Derwyn Aleph. They mirrored each other's displeased looks at each other.

'And won a battle freeing the Cwn y Wawr from slavery

and sinking numerous barges full of supplies for the Blood Robes,' Tisis said, offhand.

Antonius Malargos was quiet for some time. Kip thought of saying something to sway him, but Tisis motioned subtly to be silent.

Yes, dear.

The young man finally said, 'Lady Eirene is considering... a treaty of nonaggression with the White King.'

'What?!' Tisis demanded.

Derwyn Aleph bristled, but her hand motioned for his silence, and he said nothing.

Antonius went on. 'Eirene said you and this Guile fighting the Blood Robes might – how'd she say it? "Preclude the option of peace for us and all of Ruthgar."'

Tisis was taken aback. 'Does she think we can simply *trade* with that monster?'

'I know not what she thinks, nor could I likely understand all the machinations in her mind if she explained them. Your sister has a genius for such things. I don't like peace with those creatures, either, but my trust in her has never been misplaced. And she has given me orders. She won't tolerate anything less than total obedience in this. Not with your life in the balance. You are all she loves.'

'I love her most dearly, too,' Tisis said. 'But sometimes we are called to obey higher things. My sister is a merchant queen, not a queen in truth, much less a warrior queen. Eirene's brilliant, but she thinks others will be rational as well. You remember when you wanted to give your pony to the luxiats to sell to feed the poor?'

He brightened at the memory. 'She told me if I wanted to help, I should have her sell the pony. She'd take a small commission, then invest the profits in one of her businesses. In five years, I could buy a better pony and still give twice the amount of money to the poor – who would surely still be poor.'

'She thinks the White King is like her. He's not. He's like us. There's no negotiating the best deal with someone who plans to kill you and take everything.'

Kip moved to speak again, but Tisis gripped his hand: No!

'She called me a zealot that day, for trying to obey what I

understood Orholam to be telling me,' Antonius said, with a woundedness unhealed by the passing years. 'She didn't understand me at all. Despite all her smarts.'

And suddenly Kip felt a wind of hope filling his sails with a crack.

'It's funny, isn't it?' Antonius said. 'How the Lord of Light asks us to step blind into darkness?'

'Orholam always gives us light enough to take the next step,' Tisis said.

'Ha!' Antonius barked. 'You know me too well.'

'Orholam uses the simple to confound the wise,' Tisis said, attempting a light tone.

'I'm certainly the former,' Antonius said wryly. But then his open face took on a troubled cast. Finally he said, 'You seem...happy.'

'I'm where I'm supposed to be, doing what I was made for,' Tisis said.

'No, cousin, I mean...with him.'

'Oh.' Tisis brightened and took Kip's hand. 'He is not only my lord. He is my love.'

The thought sent a frisson through Kip. Sure, they had some commitment (at least until one of them revealed they'd never consummated their marriage), and they'd had some sweetness and excitement in the privacy of their tent (at least until recently), and he liked Tisis, and he respected her far more than he had ever expected to. But was that love?

Or was she just lying to save their cause?

But even if Kip didn't quite believe her, Antonius clearly did. A slow grin broke over his broad face. 'Then my prayers are answered.'

'Mine, too, cuz,' Tisis said.

Easy, *dear*, don't lay it on too thick.

Antonius looked down at his hands as if to find an answer there. 'I don't want to kill Foresters. Or Guiles. Especially not for this White King. Somehow you boxed in Andross Guile, forcing him to do the right thing in agreeing to your marriage.' He looked up and smiled, and Kip felt all the tension whoosh out of Tisis. 'It's only fair if we box in Eirene, too. Right?'

Giving a perfect court bow and then taking one knee in

front of Kip, Antonius said, 'Lord Guile, I took an oath to Lady Eirene Malargos, but my allegiance to Orholam is higher. By the inner light that is my conscience, I know I must disobey her. So, Lord Guile, if you would take the oath of a man others may justly call Oathbreaker, then until the Blood Robes are destroyed, I pledge my life, my honor, my men, and my fealty to you.'

And...that didn't go how I expected at all.

Kip decided that in the future, his legend would be that he moved enemies to break their oaths and swear fealty without him even saying a word. He would be the Unmoved Mover. Kip Golden-Tongue the Silent.

In other words, he was really going to have to be nicer to Tisis.

Chapter 52

'That *asshole*,' Karris said. 'Just when I thought Andross and I were really working together. When'd you get this?'

'I came directly,' Teia said. She'd had to lie to Essel to switch guard schedules with her. It wasn't the preferred way for Teia to arrange a private meeting with the White, but this couldn't wait.

'And you're certain Andross ordered this?' Karris asked.

It had been a long summer and autumn for both of them. Karris had been juggling all the logistics and politics of running a distant war and, once it seemed the White King had stopped his advancement completely, gathering reinforcements for next spring. In every spare moment, she'd been scouring for information from every source at her disposal for any hint of Gavin's whereabouts anywhere in the Seven Satrapies, and sending out teams of Blackguards she could ill afford to spare to investigate any rumor.

Teia had been training constantly, and trying to figure out how to kill slaves and how not to kill them. After she'd killed a few to show that she was willing to do so, she'd left one alive with a note that she'd devised an experiment that would take three weeks. She'd left the man – they were always old men – blindfolded, and prayed. He'd been alive the next week. If she took three weeks to kill a slave rather than killing one every week, that was two lives she saved, wasn't it?

Or at least two lives she didn't take, which wasn't quite the same thing at all, was it?

Sharing the burden with Karris had helped some. The White had agreed that Teia needed to continue the killing and training no matter what. But Teia was still killing innocents. Nothing made that acceptable.

Every honest conversation was a huge risk. If their plans were uncovered, every murder was for naught. So Teia swept her gaze around the roof of the Prism's Tower again, and then put on her dark lenses and did it again with paryl. The White had taken to soaking up some sun to think on these late-autumn afternoons, and it was impossible for anyone to eavesdrop here, but there was no such thing as too careful where the Order of the Broken Eye was concerned.

'My contact called this "a little project for our sometime friend,"' Teia said. 'Our sometime friend' was the same phrase he used once when he described who ordered Marissia's kidnapping. And I was there when Andross ordered that one, though I didn't know then that they were talking about Marissia.'

It was funny, in a not-funny-at-all sort of way. Teia had been waiting for months to be activated by the Order. She'd needed to be given something to do that would enmesh her more deeply into their hierarchy. Something, at least, that would stop her murdering innocent old men. Now that something had come, and she felt not relief but fear.

Karris sighed. 'All of us are become weapons in this war, aren't we? But Andross Guile is all blade. I know that to not pick up that naked blade is to perish. But he cuts my hand to the bone with every move.' She turned to Teia, eyes resigned. 'I will never be able to exact justice for Marissia from him, Teia. You know that, right? He's too valuable.'

'But you want justice for her, right?' Teia asked. She knew the answer, she thought, but she needed to hear it.

The White held her eye. 'I hated her, for a time, if that's what you're asking.'

'I didn't mean to—'

'How do you feel about Tisis?'

'Excuse me?!' Teia said.

'If someone murdered her, how would you feel?' Karris asked.

'Uh, she's...I mean, I'd be outraged. Of course I'd want – but what's that got to do with—'

'Are you actually insulted that I know a thing or two about you, Teia? You, who know what we do? How we live? How secrets are our currency?'

'I don't know what you've been told, but they're clearly mistaken about that,' Teia said.

'It was an illustration, not an attempt to embarrass you,' Karris said. 'How you and Kip feel toward each other only becomes my concern if you threaten his marriage to my very tenuous ally in Ruthgar. What I was trying to say—'

'Daelos. It was Daelos, wasn't it? That little crippled piece of shit. You interviewed him like three times.'

'Peace,' Karris said. 'What I meant to say is that I long ago burnt through all my hatred for her. In fact...we were close to becoming friends. She disappeared too soon for that. But enough. Enough of all that. The question now is what to do about this. Whether we can stop it. Whether we should.'

'Whether we *should*?' Teia asked, at first happy not to be talking about Kip. She shot another paranoid look around. They were still alone. This was the whole reason they'd met. 'Andross Guile has hired the Order to kill the Nuqaba! I mean, I know you're mad at her, but—'

'Mad? Mad?! Because she kidnapped and blinded my husband, the Emperor of the Seven Satrapies himself? You think that makes me merely angry?' Karris asked.

Teia walked a circuit around the rim of the tower, streaming paryl down over the edge to make certain there were no climbers on the outside who might overhear them. Again. Then she said, 'I'm not saying she doesn't deserve death, but you're the one who was just talking about using dirty weapons when they're the only weapons you have. The Nuqaba is a bitch, but she's the bitch who runs Paria. *Paria.*'

Paria had a satrapah, of course. One of the Azmith family. The damned Azmiths, who included General Caul Azmith, who'd led the Seven Satrapies army to the disasters at Ox Ford and Raven Rock, and Akensis Azmith, who'd been nominated to be the White before he tried to kill Karris. Shamed on the one hand, aggrieved on the other, they were like a mad dog you didn't want to get too close to. They might cower, or attack for no reason.

But even Teia knew that Paria's satrapah was a figurehead. The Nuqaba was in charge, in charge of the satrapy that two out of every three Blackguards and the best soldiers in the world came from.

But Karris knows all that. Right?

Teia realized how foolish it was for her to lecture the White about this, but she couldn't help saying, 'If I fail as I attempt to kill the Nuqaba – hell, even if I succeed but get caught or found out – *Paria* will turn against you. Even if you and Andross aren't deposed and executed for sending an assassin, you'd lose *Paria.*'

There was no hope of winning the war without Paria.

Quietly, Karris said, 'We may have already lost them.'

'What?' Teia asked.

'The messenger you'll be accompanying for this mission is taking an ultimatum to the Nuqaba. Ever since the Battle of Ox Ford, they've contributed nothing to the war effort. They lost ten thousand men there, which is grievous, but compares not at all with the thirty-five thousand the Ruthgari lost. But since then, they've been saying they're still mobilizing, and we know they are. But they won't move. Cowardice or caution or treason, they aren't coming. Apparently, Andross expects her to say no to our ultimatum, or to stall again. So Andross wants to kill her so someone more amenable can take over.'

'Or maybe he's upset that she imprisoned and blinded his son?' Teia ventured.

Karris looked at Teia, and thought about it. 'More likely someone moving against one of his own offends his ego. Regardless, it's not a bad move. He probably would even expect me to be pleased if she turned up conveniently dead. I don't know that he has anyone in place behind her, though. The Nuqaba conducted a purge recently. I think it may have wiped out some of Andross's spies and agents over there. Now *that* I could see him being upset about.' Karris pursed her lips. 'So that's why he'd order it. But why would the Order take the job?'

'Anything that destabilizes the major powers is a net positive for the Order,' Teia said. 'They want to institute some kind of new world on the ashes of the Seven Satrapies.'

'That might be enough reason,' Karris said. 'And I suppose an erratic figure like the Nuqaba is no fun for them, either. Who knows but that they lost people in the purges as well. And perhaps the Old Man of the Desert is more motivated by passions like revenge than our icy promachos.'

Karris looked up toward the fading sun in what might have been prayer. 'What if...what if I have you intentionally fail... or what if you frame someone for the deed instead? Who? How? Hmm...Or I could just prevent you from going at all, but that might tip my hand...' She crossed her arms under her breasts and scrunched her shoulders against a sudden cold wind. 'What would Orea do? Something gentler, no doubt. Something clever and even kind. Of course, it's her fault I have all these Azmiths to deal with in the first place. In this world of bloody-minded men, is there not a smarter way? Must the Iron sometimes be a blade?'

She was quiet for a long time. Then, finally, Karris straightened her back and turned to Teia. 'It won't be enough to kill the Nuqaba. You'll also need to kill her master of spies, Satrapah Tilleli Azmith.'

'Am I to be your official assassin, then?' Teia asked. She couldn't keep the grief out of her voice.

'You have a problem with that?' Karris asked coolly.

'High Lady...I had a chance to murder...two men I find loathsome, and it would have stopped much trouble. I didn't because I felt Orholam tell me that I'm not an assassin; I'm a soldier. I'm a Blackguard. Not a knife in a darkness, a shield.'

'You train much with a shield?' Karris asked.

'A little. Trainer Fisk said he'd rather I was in the enemy's shield wall than his own.' He'd actually said he'd use Teia as a scout instead, even if he had to go one man short.

Trainer Fisk, of course, had hurled insults at all of them while they practiced. But a single day of charging at another line from a mere twenty paces, each side equipped only with shields, had convinced Teia not only that Fisk was right, but that no amount of training could help her overcome her limitations. Many of the men in the lines were twice her weight; some were three times her weight. Charging full speed into *them*? She got flattened, every time. And holding up a shield for several hours? She couldn't have done that with both hands, even while not fighting.

Thank Orholam that magic and black powder had rendered shield walls and phalanxes mostly obsolete. Teia preferred a buckler or even a targe, which required more agility and perhaps more luck, but less strength and endurance.

'Then from your training you should know,' Karris said. 'Shields also kill.'

Teia remembered the lesson now. She quoted Trainer Fisk: 'Those who use a shield only to block are ignoring a weapon in their hands.'

Well, shit. There went her whole metaphor about being a shield.

'Teia, you are my shield. You guard me well, but if I get the chance, I absolutely will bring you down on the neck of my enemies.'

And when I shatter, you will cast me aside. Teia didn't say it aloud.

But Karris must have seen the look on her face. 'Yes. If you break, I will take up another. We are not so different. I too am serving in greater hands, and I too fear that I am inadequate for what I've been called to do. I too wanted something different from this life.'

'A slave to your duties, huh?' Teia asked.

Karris shot an iron glare at her. She hadn't missed the notes of bitterness and scoffing in Teia's voice. 'Yes,' she said. 'If I had my way, Teia, I would send you and every drafter after my husband, and then I would add every slave and every tradesman and every soldier in my command, and to hell with it if all the satrapies together burnt. Gavin would be ashamed of me, but I could live with his disappointment if I could but live with his presence as well. No, mine is not actual slavery. No one beats or rapes me, but you're a fool if you think my cold, empty bed is much more a comfort to me than a slave's pallet or a soldier's bunk.'

'I'm sorry,' Teia said. The one person she could trust, the one person who knew her now that Kip was gone, and she was venting her bile on her.

'As am I,' Karris said. 'Not least for what I'm doing to you. The good news is that this will give us your first solid scent in your hunt for the Order.'

'How so?'

'Here's one of the few beauties of war. Sometimes pieces put into place secretly must be used openly if they are to be used at all. In the same way that you had to break our normal protocol so that you could meet quickly with me today, someone will have to work hard to get you – of all the Blackguards – onto that ship. That someone will be in the Order. There are really only two options: it's one of my watch captains or someone of high rank will ask a watch captain to do it for them. So when that captain comes in and shows me the deployment orders, I'll say that I'd prefer you to stay here; you're my favorite. If that captain is himself the Order's plant, he'll insist on you for some reason. If it's just a favor he's doing for some ambassador, he'll say who asked him to get you on this detail. The watch captain could lie, of course, but I can check on lies. No matter what they do, it gives us *something*. Given enough time, I'm sure the Old Man could come up with a better stratagem, but he has to act fast here, and he's juggling other subordinates and tasks – as I am. He'll have to opt for a direct approach.'

A lead on the Order. That meant an end to infiltration, and an end maybe to all of them. Teia could hardly wait.

'Wait,' Teia said. 'Did you say that my second target was the satrapah? The satrapah of Paria? The *satrapah* is the Nuqaba's spymaster? I'm to kill *both* of the most powerful people in Paria?'

Chapter 53

The game seemed trivial before Gavin understood it. His daily bread came down the chute. He caught the loaves if he could before they hit the ground, which would damage the crust.

Then he would examine every bit of each loaf's surface, looking for an injection site. He often couldn't find it. The loaves dropped down the chute and collided with several locks on its way to him, so finding a small hole was often impossible.

He would tear open a loaf and smell it, sometimes catching a faint whiff of something *off*. Then, with a carefully cleaned, dry finger, he would touch the soft flesh of the broken bread, feeling for wetness or any temperature variation.

If he didn't find it, he would close the loaves up as well as possible and wait. The poison, being liquid, would make the affected bread go gummy after a time.

Then sometimes Andross would baste the poison onto the outside of a loaf, as if buttering a pastry as it baked. That tended to affect either the flakiness or the color of the crust, so Gavin took to examining each loaf for those variations.

It was harder to examine the weekly fruit, not least because that sweet treat called to him in a way the boring bread never could. Some weeks, only a single segment of the lime would be contaminated. Other times, it would have seeped through numerous segments, and he would debate with himself about how much of the poison he might be able to ingest without losing consciousness.

Nor was he always perfect. He'd gotten woozy a number of times when he'd eaten some of the narcotic by accident.

He'd fought through his sleepiness and never lost consciousness.

But that wasn't the game. That was only the beginning of the game.

As the long days passed, until the summer must surely be over, and deep into autumn, Gavin saw that the game was one of endurance, to see if he could keep the same level of boring vigilance day in and day out, as his emotions cycled down and further down and the sands scoured the gilded grandeur of the idol he'd erected to himself, and it was revealed to stand on bare scaffolding and feet of clay.

This game was not a game; it was his whole life. He had become a bread inspector.

Andross Guile wasn't checking on him. Had never once come to talk.

There was no one to whom to prove himself. There was, finally, no escape.

Not for him.

There was an escape hatch in this cell. He'd put it there. It required drafting a key whose design he had carefully committed to memory, and affixing it to a pole he would draft in a particular shape to fish down around the corners of the cell's waste hole and into one dead end. If he could draft, it would have taken him no more than a day to escape.

If he could draft.

'Eat,' the dead man said. 'Let Karris be a widow. Let her move on. She probably already has. No one can mourn forever. Especially not a beautiful woman like that.'

Gavin said nothing.

'What if she's already moved on? The mourning period is over. She probably needs allies badly. A political marriage to the White isn't something anyone would scoff at. You staying alive only gives her a reason to feel guilty.'

'She doesn't know I'm alive, so it doesn't matter,' Gavin croaked. This will-casting was better than some of the others at getting him to talk. Or maybe Gavin was just that much weaker now.

'No, I meant when they find your body. If she finds out you lived past when she remarried, she'll be devastated. Of course I wasn't implying you'd actually get out and be reunited with her. I think we've all given up on that by now, haven't we?'

Gavin cursed him, but without passion.

'Do you think your suffering is ennobling?' the dead man asked.

Gavin didn't answer.

'Perhaps today is the day your father will relent!' the dead man said.

It wasn't, of course.

When Gavin woke the next morning, the dead man greeted him with the same gleeful words. 'Perhaps today is the day your father will relent!'

And then the next.

'Perhaps today is the day your father will relent!'
...

'Surely today is the day your father will relent.'
...

'Do you think today is the day your father will relent?'
...

'Perhaps Andross will show his merciful side today,' the dead man said, as if hopeful.
...

Sometimes he wouldn't say it first thing, and Gavin would hope that perhaps he'd forgotten, or thought it wasn't having an effect. But he always said it. 'Dazen...psst, Dazen...do you think today might be the day?'

Other times he would ask twice or three times, making Gavin wonder if a day had passed without his noticing, increasing his disorientation.

He laughed through Gavin's panics, the times he lay gasping, chest convulsing, certain he would die.

But death would be a relief, wouldn't it?

And there was no mercy in Andross Guile. One can't appeal to a side a man doesn't have.

Gavin had a pleasant hallucination once. One, out of all the nightmares and disquieting dreams and constant anxiety. Be strong and of good courage. You are not alone.

It wasn't a voice, it was a memory, and an unhelpful one at that. It had encouraged him for three days...what, sixty days ago now?

Gavin didn't want encouragement. He wanted a side of beef and rivers of wine and his wife's breath mingling with his and a bath and a bed and sun upon his face and his father dead at his feet and friends who weren't figments of his imagination and the susurrus of the sea beneath the skimmer's deck and the flexing of his arms and shoulders as he sailed. He wanted his powers back and the adoration of the crowd. And he wanted to have no secrets, to never feel a fraud again. He wanted to save everyone and be seen doing it. He wanted to be proud and beautiful again. He wanted all he'd had before and more.

He wanted that seventh goal he'd never told anyone.

But it was all gone.

But it was all folly. He would never have *more* than he'd had. He would never have *as much* as he'd had. He would never be as much as he'd been. He could only ever be less.

He couldn't even be Prism without his powers.

The best he could hope for was to live broken and powerless and ugly. What had he said when they'd saved him from the hippodrome and he'd shot that man? 'I'm not quite useless. Not yet'?

But now he was.

'Maybe today will be the day your father relents!' the dead man said as the bread came down the next morning.

But Gavin didn't even care.

He ate the bread. All of it. Both loaves. They tasted wonderful.

He could hardly hear the dead man laughing, and not for long.

Chapter 54

The skimmer ride from Big Jasper to Azûlay showed Teia how fast this war was changing the world.

Like many great discoveries, Gavin Guile's insight was simple in retrospect: instead of taking the oar as his paradigm, or the sail, he took the wind itself. The skimmers were powered by drafters who shot unfocused luxin to propel them.

But Andross Guile had seized on his son's original insight and innovated upon it, realizing that the new technology had a cultural implication: the typical threshold by which a satrapy justified the cost of educating a drafter at the Chromeria was her ability to make a solid, stable luxin in one or more colors.

What Andross was the first to realize was that the reedsmen didn't need to draft *stable* luxin. So he had called up all the discipulae who'd failed out of the Chromeria in the last four decades. Hundreds of suitable candidates had been found already. Thus, he gained an entire corps for transportation and saved the halos (and lives) of his trained drafters for war. Four of those now powered the ultralight skimmer that propelled Teia, the messenger, and barely more than the clothes on their backs across the sea to Paria.

But they made it in a day and a half. Gavin Guile was rumored to have been able to go twice as far in a single morning, but Gavin was also rumored now to have been ten feet tall, to have ended wars with a word, and to have been able to draft black and white luxin both. Gavin was said to have had a shining mien that made men gape and maidens swoon.

The mien part was basically true, but still. Though Teia would admit he was a man the likes of which the world would never see again, he wasn't a god.

They also said now that he was going to come back to the Seven Satrapies in their hour of greatest need to save them all.

Would have been better if he hadn't left us in our hour of greatest need, Teia thought. He was dead now. As like as not, the Order itself had killed him. He was simply too powerful and unpredictable for them to tolerate.

All too soon Teia and the messenger, a senior diplomat named Anjali Gates, were in sight of Azûlay. Teia tried to get all her gawking out of the way before they docked, but the grandeur of the city defied dismissal.

Their first glimpse was of the lighthouse called the Sword of Heaven. Its red glass dome gleamed in the sun like a ruby set in its pommel, walkways made the hilt, and the body of the lighthouse made a blade, its point buried in the earth.

From the ground up, the first ten paces were blank gray stone like steel, above that the stone was whitewashed, and above that beaten gold had been laid over the stone into flames, as if fire were emanating from the hilt down the blade.

'You should see it on Sun Day,' Anjali Gates said, coming to stand next to Teia. 'The pyroturges here make wonders to rival the Jaspers'. It's why I joined the diplomatic corps. I wanted to see all the wonders of this world.'

She fell silent, and Teia asked, 'And have you?'

Anjali grinned. 'Well, I've not seen the City of Stone in the Cracked Lands, but no one else has either for at least four hundred years. As for the rest, mostly. From the Everdark Gates to the Melos Deeps, from the Rath Delta in flood to the Floating City. I've seen the colossi of the Iron Elephants above the Red Cliffs, and the four Ladies of Garriston at sunset, and I've seen a sea demon circling White Mist Reef. I've played Nine Kings with satraps and danced a *gciorcal* with one of the last pygmy chiefs.'

'Really?' Teia asked.

'Really. We diplomats often stretch the truth, and sometimes make what we say seem to be the opposite of what we're actually saying, but we do our best not to lie straight-out.' Anjali smiled. 'Well, at least that's the Chromeria's school of thinking. Other nations, satrapies, and even clans have other approaches.'

'You just go from wonder to wonder? Nice work if you can get it, huh?' Teia said.

'Oh, don't get me wrong, most of my work has been much more tedious. It took me a full year to negotiate the passage taxes the Aborneans charge on the Narrows. A year working, for an agreement that only lasts ten. Though naturally, one flatters oneself that the representatives will simply renew it when it expires four years from now. If the satrapies last so long.'

'How'd you get to see all those things, though? You don't even look that old. Er, sorry.'

Anjali grinned. 'Easy. I gave myself all the interesting assignments.'

'You what? Wait, how senior are you?' Teia asked.

'Ambassadorships are given out to friends of satraps and Colors. They're not quite sinecures, but they are largely ceremonial positions. Important for what they do, of course, but there are entire armies of people like me – the career diplomats, not the political appointees – who get the work done where the satrapies rub each other wrong. Fishing rights, piracy, extradition of criminals and runaway slaves, water rights, taxes, spot checks of compliance to the slave laws, and, of course, these days, communicating and compliance checks of the new balancing dictates.'

The new laws governing drafting that Promachos Guile and the Spectrum had instituted didn't apply to drafters training for war, so Teia hadn't even noticed them. Drafters elsewhere, however, had to compensate for the war effort – not drafting a certain color as news of light storms came into the Chromeria, or trying to draft more of its opposite color.

'I imagine that's a nuisance,' Teia said. She was still studying the city they were rapidly approaching. Azûlay was built on a steep hill down to the sea after the arm of its protected bay and the lighthouse. Buildings were packed literally against each other, sharing walls up four and five stories and redbrick roofs, differentiated from their neighbors only by their individual bright-pastel walls. Ivies and greenery of all sorts sprouted everywhere.

'A *nuisance*? You have no idea, do you?' Anjali Gates said. 'In the rich cities like Big Jasper, sure, drafters still use magic for entertainment and convenience. But in the villages where most people live, a ban on green in the fall might damage the olive harvest or mean only natural fertilizers can be used with the barley and wheat plantings. Sub-red is chronically restricted, so if the weather turns bad an entire grape harvest might be ruined. Worse, it means a new mother with a fever can't be cooled. A nuisance? Child, people are dying so your compatriots can train with fire.'

Teia swallowed. She'd not even considered it.

'On the plus side, there haven't been as many light storms since the rules were instituted, and no reports of bane in months, of course.'

Orholam's ball sweat. But Teia said, 'You never answered me, did you? About your position.'

'Oh, did I not?' But Anjali Gates smirked. 'I'm the *corregidor* emeritus of the diplomatic corps.'

'That means you were the boss but you retired?' Teia said.

'Unretired now. Briefly. They needed someone who had a chance of reasoning with the...mercurial Nuqaba, and someone expendable, in case she does to me what has been done to messengers bearing unwelcome news from time immemorial.'

'Tough assignment,' Teia said.

'I volunteered.'

'I didn't,' Teia groused.

'I know, that's why I brought it up.'

'What do you mean you brought it up? I asked you out of the blue.'

'Did you? Regardless, if they seize me, you should get the hell out. If they take me, they'll either kill me outright, or possibly do something to shame me. Send me back naked or shave my head or rape me. Each is its own word in the language of diplomacy. The Chromeria will respond appropriately, as it finds possible.'

'What the...what the hell does that even mean?' Teia asked.

'If the Chromeria were to later seize the Nuqaba alive, then if she has beheaded me without torture, she would be beheaded in turn. If she sends me back naked, she would likewise be paraded through the streets. If I were to be raped on her orders, she would be tortured horribly and shamed publicly as much as possible, though not raped, of course: we aren't animals. Most leaders have an intuitive understanding of this kind of graduated retribution, if not an explicit one. Of course, how she conducts herself in the intervening time between my death and her reckoning could negate or change all of this.'

'And you *volunteered*?' Teia asked.

'I'm old,' Anjali said cheerfully. 'After negotiating grain prices and cart widths hundreds of times, believe me, this is the kind of message we in the diplomatic corps dream of delivering – if only we can get away with it. But it also takes a certain gravitas to deliver a proper epistolary beating. If I pull this off, I'll have to award myself the corps's highest honor. If I don't, I've left orders that they should award it to me posthumously.' She grinned at Teia.

'What's an epistolary beating?'

'Watch the introduction. You'll see what I mean. Just because I know the ceremonial bows and the twenty-seven titles of the Nuqaba Haruru doesn't mean I *like* reciting them. You realize you're part of this diplomatic grammar, right?'

'Huh?'

'One Blackguard accompanying me, not two, and the one they send is…petite. Forgive me for stating what others will think, I do not share this judgment and in fact know your reputation well – but the Nuqaba will see you as a little girl. Your slight stature makes you look even younger than you are. She might not even believe that you're a Blackguard. The Chromeria sending you to accompany me is a small snub, but it also means they're less likely to take or kill you. They'll think you're some child put into this role, and whatever glory they might find in defeating or humiliating a big man Blackguard is therefore absent.'

'My presence itself is an insult? And that's supposed to make me feel better?' Teia asked.

'I'm trying to help you gauge and define your own scope of actions here. This isn't my assignment alone. It's ours.'

'You really think we can reel them back in?' Teia asked. She hadn't meant to ask a real question. She knew what she had to do here.

'I think diplomacy may resolve all conflicts between parties of goodwill.'

'That last bit is the part that bites you in the ass, isn't it?'

'Rather, it's the part that bites you in the ass, my young Blackguard friend. For where there's no goodwill, my job ends.'

Teia had thought for a moment that they were very different indeed. Anjali the happy talker, traveling through the satrapies, her words bringing life and peace wherever she went, soothing conflict and finding outcomes acceptable to all parties; Teia the shield that came down on stiff necks.

But perhaps they were simply two different horses, pulling the same chariot of state. Anjali, at the front, saw different scenery wherever she went. Teia, pulling behind her, saw only horses' asses and different kinds of road.

They passed under the very shadow of the lighthouse, the reedsmen artfully guiding their small craft between the hundreds of ships going in and out of the port. They headed straight into the small beach, threw cloths over the skimmer so as to keep its secrets from the curious, and then threw down a plank.

Teia put on blue spectacles and trotted down the plank first. People began pushing closer on the crowded beach to get a look at them, so Teia threw her cloak back off her shoulders to reveal the sword and pistols at her belt and the rope spear wrapped around her waist, its long blade hanging down one thigh like another sword.

The crowd backed off, but Teia and Anjali didn't even make it off the beach before they were stopped by a detachment of port guards. Evidently, the oddity that was the skimmer speeding across the waves had elicited some alarm.

Anjali Gates did all the talking, declaring them to be a delegation from the Chromeria and demanding the skimmer and their men be unmolested while they themselves should be accompanied to the satrapah's palace. While the diplomat spoke, Teia did her best to look imposing without being threatening. It was doubly hard with her feet sunk into the sand while the port guards stood on the paving stones of the street just above them. Teia felt about as tall as Caelia Green.

No wonder Buskin had worn those shoes. Teia would give her second-favorite rope spear right now to be a little taller.

In short order, though, they found themselves being escorted through the streets. Teia wished that they could take their time in the city instead. Steep cobbled streets led up to a plateau where the majority of the city rested, and ivy adorned every building. Where the ivies or wisteria had torn apart stone or lumber, the people had simply rebuilt around them rather than trimming them back, even building supports to prop up ancient vines. Every window was a riot of flowering plants as well. The pastel paints were fresh and bright.

And the people, ah, the people.

Azûlay was as cosmopolitan as any of the other great cities

of the Seven Satrapies, but here the many skin tones of the satrapies' ethnicities were painted on a background of many Parians. It made Teia feel oddly at home, and she realized only slowly that it was because she *didn't* feel odd. In Big Jasper she hadn't stood out, simply because everyone stood out. But this was different. Homey.

She wasn't able to enjoy it or explore any of the little alleys, though – each one adorned with murals, it seemed – or visit the little kopi counters or the kitchens wafting heavenly smells into the street. A great wide ribbon of less steep grand boulevard switchbacked up the great hill so wagons could make their way to and from the port, but the guards took them straight up, sometimes climbing steep stairs, muscling aside *burnous*-clad crowds when necessary.

Some kind of palace guards joined them halfway up, and at the doors of the palace grounds, four of the Nuqaba's personal guard, the drafting Tafok Amagez, fell in around them. Dressed in white and black with blue vests the color of the sky, the Sun Guards claimed their genesis from Lucidonius's first followers and personal guard, but the only thing relevant about them for Teia was that these were the men who'd helped blind Gavin and tried to kill Karris and Ironfist and Essel and Ben-hadad. They had killed Hezik. He'd been a jovial braggart, and Teia hadn't known him well – but he was her brother, and she would never forgive his killers.

Karris had sneered about the Tafok Amagez's magical abilities, calling them blunt drafters who lacked all subtlety. But no one had criticized their fighting abilities, and Teia saw that they held themselves like professionals.

Teia realized that if she hadn't come as an assassin, her role here would be entirely ornamental. If the Parians decided to kill her, she would be lucky if she took down even one before they got her. So she pulled her cloak back around herself.

It's a bad idea to poke a lion in a cage.

These lions weren't caged.

When they entered the grand doors of the palace itself, Teia almost missed a step. Soaring ceilings, white marble, black marble, flying staircases, stained-glass-filled clerestories, jewels and onyx and a giant statue that seemed to be made entirely of obsidian and gold standing on powerful legs, wearing what Teia thought was called a toga, reaching toward the sky – the sun? – with yearning, and with determination in his clenched jaw.

Anjali Gates saw Teia's astonishment. 'At the midwinter feasts, the pyroturges remove the pinnacle cap of the dome and lower an incendiary. All night long, he reaches for a burning sun, and these stained-glass windows shine light out for leagues for everyone to see all through the year's longest night. Inside, there is one hell of an all-night party.' She smiled at a memory. 'He is known as *"handross Orh'olam."* The Seeker after the Lord of Light. Or perhaps the Striver after Orholam. Or, less popularly, He Who Strives *with* Orholam.'

' "With" as in "with," or "with" as in "against"?' Teia asked.

'Indeed.'

'I think I lost you there,' Teia said as they ascended a staircase with no railing or visible supports.

'The grammar allows for either interpretation, but these are a pious people. It is best not to note aloud that while their people were the first to fight with Lucidonius, they were also the first to fight *with* Lucidonius.'

'Ah,' Teia said.

'A subtle tongue, it is, Old Parian. So contextual, and we don't possess so much of that context anymore. The scholars even say that instead of *"handross Orh'olam,"* it may actually be *"handross h'olam."* Which would make it the Seeker after the Hidden.'

'Or He Who Strives with or against the Hidden?' Teia guessed.

'Indeed,' Anjali said.

' "handross"? That isn't the same root name as Andross...'

'It is. The Guile family has deep roots here in Paria.'

By chance or design, they had arrived while Satrapah Azmith was holding court. More palace guards in white and black stopped them at the door.

'Weapons? Any other contraband? Dangerous items?' a young man asked.

Anjali Gates handed over a belt knife and was given a chit with which to reclaim it.

Teia just stared at the man. She threw back her cloak. 'I'm a Blackguard, cur. By ancient right and treaties, we go unarmed nowhere. Our right holds in the presence of Colors and satraps and the Prism himself.'

The man gulped and shot a look at the Tafok Amagez. 'I'm commanded to let no one...'

'We are here with an emergency message from the Promachos and the White and the entire Spectrum,' Anjali said. 'Young man, Orholam help you if you detain us. The fate of the satrapies themselves rests upon a speedy response from your people.'

'I, uh...'

One of the Tafok Amagez interrupted. 'Oh, quit this! We can handle one little girl, whatever they dress her in.'

One little girl? Teia knew she should feel good they'd said it. She was supposed to be underestimated. So it was working.

But fuck them.

The guard had the Tafok Amagez sign for her, and then let them pass. They opened a small door inset in the great hall doors.

The great hall was a variation on the entry's theme: several stories tall, stained glass in clerestories, flying buttresses, and here silver and ebony and teak and walnut woods with mirrors that beamed diffuse sunlight to the platform.

The four Tafok Amagez and an equal number of palace guards took them to a line at least a hundred supplicants long and stopped at the back of it. Teia could barely see the Nuqaba and the satrapah from here.

The Nuqaba sat at the satrapah's right hand – or perhaps the satrapah sat at her left. Their chairs were of almost an equal height, the Nuqaba's a smidgen lower, but significantly grander.

Anjali Gates held herself at peace. When it took another ten minutes for the Nuqaba and the satrapah to finish with one case, the details of which Teia couldn't even hear, the diplomat put on her violet-tinged spectacles – it hadn't even occurred to Teia that the woman was a superviolet drafter. Of course she was.

As soon as a chamberlain brought down his iron-capped

staff onto the floor, causing a bang that Teia assumed meant judgment had been rendered, Anjali was out of her place in line like a shot.

Somehow she moved quickly without appearing to hurry, and she was ten paces down the main aisle before even Teia moved. An instant later, the Tafok Amagez woke up and poured out after them.

Anjali pulled a small orb from a pocket and twisted it. She held it above her head as she continued to walk, and in an instant it bloomed, and then burnt an intense yellow.

'Blessed Nuqaba! Exalted Satrapah Azmith! I come from the Chromeria! This is my proof,' Anjali boomed, just as Teia and the Tafok Amagez caught up with her. 'I come with an emergency message from the Promachos himself and the White's own pen for the entire Spectrum.'

The spectacle – and Anjali's confidence – was enough to buy them time to get to the front of the room, but there a rank of Tafok Amagez had deployed, spears leveled, blocking their path to the platform.

Anjali Gates stopped and held out the beacon toward the commander of the Tafok Amagez facing her. 'For your inspection.' She promptly ignored him.

Satrapah Azmith conferred with the Nuqaba. She had the dark, dark skin of a mountain Parian, with long, narrow limbs adorned with gold and turquoise bands. She wore a transparent black veil trimmed in gold, and a flowing black burnous with black embroidered squares interlocking. A jug of wine sat on the table at her left hand for her to serve herself. She said, 'We've not seen the western star beacon in these lands for decades. You're lucky the Amagez didn't skewer you.'

'Such a fear didn't even occur to me. We are all loyal children of Orholam here, and brothers and sisters under the light,' Anjali said. She might have stressed the word 'loyal' just a little.

The satrapah and the Nuqaba spoke again, and Teia was stunned by the Nuqaba's glamour. Where the satrapah was modest and sedate, the Nuqaba looked more like a pagan priestess oozing sensuality and demanding attention than a servant of Orholam humbly directing attention up toward the Lord of Light.

Of course, Gavin Guile had certainly had more than a little smoldering sensuality himself when he wanted to, and Teia had heard women getting themselves worked up just talking about how he'd looked during Sun Day festivities past, where he'd gone more than half-naked.

So maybe it wasn't any different. But it felt different. For a moment, Teia forgot her training and took in all the jewels, the perfectly tailored dress that emphasized the woman's enviable curves, and the gold and ochre and kohl face paints highlighting her eyes and the tattoo under each: judgment under the left and mercy under the right.

But then she remembered herself, and looked not to outer things but as a Blackguard looking at a potential opponent. The hauteur overlaid physical weakness. Her upper arms were flabby. There was a loose puffiness in her face that spoke either of overindulgence last night or of chronic overindulgence. Her eyes were glassy, as if she'd been enjoying ratweed this morning. Her attitude was insolent.

In short, though the Nuqaba had to be in her midthirties, she reminded Teia of a Blackguard nunk who needed a good ass-kicking.

The Nuqaba waved lazily at her Tafok Amagez to withdraw. All of them were eyeing Teia's many weapons, glancing back only occasionally, so none of them happened to be looking at her as she gave the gesture. A look of sudden rage at being ignored washed over the Nuqaba's face and she snapped her fingers. Not just once, but twice. As if they were dogs.

All of them looked back at her. All of them. The men weren't fools or amateurs, so it spoke to Teia of how horribly the Nuqaba must treat them. When the Nuqaba wanted their attention, she demanded all of it. It was stupid. If Teia were an assassin, it would have given her ample time to draw her flintlock pistol and—

Oh shit. She *was* an assassin.

Just not that kind.

The Nuqaba slashed her hand, and the men pulled back instantly.

Still, their commander gave orders, and as Teia and Anjali took several more steps forward, Teia saw that two Tafok Amagez quietly lit slow matches and affixed them to muskets. The others were already filled with their colors, and Teia realized that the front of the great hall was covered in a pristine white rug that had to be there so that the bespectacled Tafok Amagez could draft as quickly as possible.

One paryl drafter. If there's just one paryl drafter here, I'm in big trouble.

The Nuqaba was studying them, and apparently it was good manners not to speak until given permission, because Anjali Gates held her tongue as if happy to wait all day.

Teia had slightly more trouble doing so when the Nuqaba looked at her and openly sneered. Apparently she saw only a little girl, too. Again, it should have felt good.

Again, it didn't.

The Nuqaba turned to Satrapah Azmith, but spoke loudly enough for all to hear. 'Do you know, back when my brothers joined the Blackguard, it was a revered body. In fact, to get in, I think you actually had to have reached puberty!'

The satrapah chuckled and the front rows laughed like sycophants.

Teia had to take deep breaths. A Blackguard guards her tongue. This was exactly what she wanted, right? To be overlooked... by these disrespectful pieces of – easy, T, a Blackguard guards her tongue.

The Nuqaba harrumphed and turned to the satrapah again, this time more quietly asking a question about the star beacon. She asked a few other questions, and Teia was able to get enough of a grip on her temper to see how clever it was to have the satrapah be the Nuqaba's spymaster. Everyone knew that Tilleli Azmith was a figurehead, so they would take the Nuqaba's speaking with her to be merely keeping up appearances. The satrapah would daily meet with dozens of the most important people in the satrapy and beyond, but would be underestimated if not dismissed. Teia guessed that the big jug of wine was intended to further lower her in people's estimation. She feigned drunkenness while the Nuqaba concealed her real drunkenness.

The woman hid in plain sight.

And dear Orholam, Teia was supposed to kill her.

'Please,' the satrapah said, 'do deliver our dear White's message.'

'Then please forgive my informality,' Anjali Gates said. 'I deliver this message exactly as instructed, in the White's voice.' She drew herself more erect and imperious, and Teia readied herself. Karris had told her that her time to strike the satrapah might be during the very first paragraphs of her message. She'd said that the satrapah might find them so infuriating that if she went into seizures or had a heart attack, no one would be surprised.

While keeping her arms carefully motionless and down at her sides, Teia readied paryl in her fingertips. She hadn't had time to scope out every one of the Tafok Amagez. One of them might be a paryl drafter. If so, Teia was about to sign her own death warrant.

Beside her, Anjali's voice took on the cadence of Karris's own as she delivered the White's message:

'Tilleli, you're useless. If you'd fulfilled your duties as satrapah with a modicum of competence, I'd be addressing this letter to you. You haven't, so I'll not keep up the pretense that you matter. Further, in our hope of someday working with a representative who possesses a spine, by unanimous vote, the Spectrum hereby strips you of the rights and privileges of a satrapah. We will eagerly await whichever successor the Nuqaba names for you, and address this letter to her instead.'

Teia had her eyes locked on the satrapah. The woman looked as if she'd been run over by a charging horse. But her face didn't go to rage.

Teia hesitated.

Anjali Gates continued, unperturbed, in the sudden, utter silence in the great hall. She turned to the Nuqaba. 'Haruru, let me be blunt. You wounded my husband and tried to kill me. As a woman, I despise you and hate what you've done. No doubt you hate me as well. But I speak to you today not as a wife, but as a woman entrusted to care for the drafters of the Seven Satrapies, even as you have been entrusted to care for the believers of Paria and beyond, and to guard the

384

legacy of the Lucidonius. We are greater than our quarrel, and we would besmirch our offices and indeed our very faith if we were to brawl like tavern wenches who might only upset tables and feelings. So I put our personal quarrel behind us, and trust you will do the same.'

The Nuqaba had slowly been rising from her chair as Anjali spoke. For a moment, Teia thought that the Nuqaba was going to bolt out of her throne and attack the diplomat with fists and fingernails.

If she did, should Teia fight her off?

She was already calculating how to make sure that the Nuqaba was between her and the musketeers if it came to that when Satrapah Azmith grabbed the Nuqaba's arm and pulled her back to her seat.

The satrapah had a slow temper. Shit. That meant Teia couldn't take this opportunity to assassinate her.

Anjali continued her message placidly, but Teia could tell that the madwoman was enjoying the hell out of this. 'That said, we have not the luxury of time to continue overtures and negotiations and stalling and games. The Seven Satrapies are at war.

'We need you, Haruru. We need Paria wholeheartedly with us. Without your soldiers, the Seven Satrapies will fall. You think you have three choices: one, helping us and losing many of your men; two, joining the Color Prince and possibly being rewarded greatly, at the cost of violating your oaths and inviting civil war with those still loyal to us; or three, waiting as long as possible, hoping that we slaughter each other, and then coming in at the end and ending up in a better position than either, and maybe setting up your own empire.'

To see the cynicism and disloyalty of those calculations laid out so nakedly took the breath of many in the great hall. Even those jaded enough to have read the tea leaves in what the Nuqaba was doing were shocked to have someone actually say it publicly.

Teia saw then that Karris White's power was in speaking openly what others trusted everyone would hide. This is the game, others thought.

Karris said, I see your game... and *no*.

Anjali said, 'If you thought those were your choices, you were wrong. I'm not giving you those options. The Color Prince will destroy the Chromeria utterly without you. You owe us your loyalty. We ask for nothing that doesn't already belong to us. So if we are to die, you will die, too. I will leave my back exposed to the Color Prince, knowing it will mean the loss of the Jaspers and the Chromeria, and I will sail *all* of my soldiers to your home. And all my drafters, who train for war even now. When we arrive, we will kill everyone who joins you in treason. We will enslave the families of all those disloyal to us, and give their lands and houses and titles to those of our friends who remember their oaths.

'Under such circumstances and with such promised consequences, how many of your men will join you in treason? Even if all of them do, the Chromeria still has power enough to destroy you. We will, utterly. This we swear. And then we will attempt to colonize Paria, and hold our defense against the Color Prince in your – our – mountains. This strategy will likely mean our death. We are willing to risk it. For us, it is a likely death against a certain one.

'Now Blessed under the Light, Guardian of Truth, Arbiter of Mercy, Holy Nuqaba, your choice is simple: fight us or delay us and certainly die, or join us and likely die. Signed, Orholam's Humble Servants, the Iron White, Promachos Andross Guile, and the Holy Spectrum of the Seven Satrapies.'

Chapter 55

Kip moved expertly through the undergrowth to his vantage, blinking between sub-red and visible light in the darkness, eyes searching for Sibéal Siofra's body. The forest air between the old giant spruces was cool and soft with thick curtains of fog.

The fog was welcome. It dampened vision and noise both, so it would make Kip's superviolet signal flares visible only within a small range, thus limiting the dangers his men faced.

They were deep in enemy-held territory, attacking a supply train full of black powder mined and refined in Atash heading to resupply the White King's Blood Robes besieging Green Haven. Destroying it would be good. Seizing it would be much, much better.

Through all their recent months of raiding, Kip had carefully been building a profile for his Nightbringers. Unless they had an overwhelming force, they attacked during the day, often just before dark so they could melt away into the night, relying on their superior woodscraft. That identified them as a force that relied on drafting, and as raiders, glorified bandits. Where other guerrilla forces traditionally exaggerated their numbers, Kip consistently understated his own, even when procuring food and supplies from merchants and friendly towns. He relied on Eirene Malargos's quiet largesse to cover the shortfalls.

It had been another of Tisis's victories, mollifying her furious sister for turning Antonius and refusing her orders to come home by making promises she and Kip would someday regret if they lived so long. They'd also had to trade intelligence for food – Eirene was a merchant to the core.

On the other hand, the woman wasn't going to let her only sister and favorite cousin starve or die out here because they lacked supplies.

A further part of Kip's stratagem was that fire was usually a big part of their attacks, used with only the crudest drafting – first from necessity as the Ghosts learned Chromeria-style drafting, and later to hide how effective the Mighty had been at training their new compatriots. The Cwn y Wawr Kip used everywhere. The Ghosts' will-casting he used more judiciously, mostly for scouting and for tracking and killing the Blood Robes' scouts.

But the Nightbringers' ranks had swelled as their fame grew, and keeping secrets amid a growing army was a losing game – especially when your army included the giant grizzly Tallach that was partnered with Conn Arthur.

Still, Kip's attempts at secrecy and the lightning-fast relocation that the skimmers allowed had borne fruit. Now it was time to push into the next stage of the war.

Kip hoped that all meant the Blood Robes wouldn't be ready for a night attack of this magnitude.

He found Sibéal lying under some bushes at a good vantage point, her skin flushed the adrenal war blue of her people. He lay down beside her and clicked his tongue softly. Two mastiffs in heavy armor came up on either side of him. The Cwn y Wawr – the Dogs of Dawn – hadn't chosen their name at random. They'd kept war dogs for centuries. Getting the dogs' handlers to agree to let will-casters close to those beloved hounds had been beyond Kip's persuasive powers.

But somehow, someone in the will-casters' ranks had convinced the Cwn y Wawr that they cherished the animals they partnered with, and that the dogs would be safer with a human partner than without. Perhaps it had been that simple. Kip didn't know how it had happened.

That was what it was to be part of a team. Others were out there, doing things you never heard about to try to achieve the same goals you had.

There was a sound low in the bushes, and a hound with droopy ears emerged. Sibéal Siofra woke and the hound shook itself as if it had been wet. Then it licked her as she reported, 'Sixty oxen. Somewhere around one hundred men. Sarai's not good at counting that high and their scents are all on top of each other. Sixty-two horses. A blue drafter. Four red drafters. Red luxin. Two greens. And, um, freshly dug earth?'

'From fortifications, I'd guess. War dogs,' Kip announced, 'those are on you. Clear a path for us.'

Kip gave a few moments for the word to filter down his lines. Men were making the sign of the three and the four, praying. Kip looked back at the massive hillock behind him that was Conn Arthur's giant grizzly Tallach. He really needed to have that talk with the conn about his brother. Not tonight, though.

The giant grizzly was lying down so as not to upset any of the other animals more than necessary. Its head, helmed with blackened steel and yellow luxin over the eyes, bobbed in assent. That and a small breastplate (well, small relative to a mountain) were all the armor the great bear would tolerate.

Kip threw up a superviolet flare to signal the drafters to

fill themselves with their colors, sharing lux torches and shielding them under blankets. The lux torches' flaring made for a lot of night-blind drafters – not all of them had at-will pupil control yet – but it couldn't be helped.

He studied the trees for reflections of light from the torches and was pleased to see none.

'Wolves,' Kip said quietly. 'Go!'

They tore off with the unnerving speed of the predators they were. They were to hit the camp first, silently, and take out as many sentries as possible.

'War dogs. Go.'

The mastiffs were off only slightly slower, all big shoulders and spiky armor, and terrifying mass. If the wolves didn't raise an alarm, the war dogs definitely would.

'Night mares. Go.'

It had been a joke at first. It wasn't a joke. Most of the night mares were actual woodland ponies. Some were warhorses. Some were great elk. All were will-cast and carried Cwn y Wawr drafters on their backs. A will-cast horse knew when you needed it to be silent, and the union of its animal dexterity with full human intelligence and discipline – discipline not to bolt despite the pressures of battle and magic and snarling animals on every side – meant every one of them was at least the equal of a well-trained veteran warhorse.

Kip turned and found Tallach waiting, snout low and level to the ground. Kip stepped up and grabbed the horns of his platform. One didn't ride a giant grizzly. Its mass was too great for human legs to straddle. And if you somehow strapped yourself on, the undulations of its great form when it ran would break you. Instead Ben-hadad had designed something halfway between a saddle and a howdah. Kip – sometimes joined by Cruxer – could stand and stabilize himself with one hand on any number of grips while either drafting or firing one of the many muskets attached to the platform's racks, or he could sit and lock his legs into place, whether Tallach was on all fours or rearing up on his hind legs.

Whether it terrified the enemy or Kip more, he still hadn't figured out.

'Nightbringers,' Kip commanded. 'At a walk. Advance.'

For those beyond the sound of his voice, he threw up a superviolet flare, shielded like the first to radiate light only toward his own lines. A superviolet drafter looking into superviolet might still notice the light on the branches of the trees, but if you have to speak during a stealth attack, it is still better to whisper than to shout.

'Tallach—'

But the bear and the man inside it didn't wait for the complete order. Kip held on to two horns of his howdah and absorbed each loping impact with the ground with his knees. It was terrifying that something so large could move so quickly and dexterously. He ducked and bobbed and prayed while Tallach wove around the spruces that had branches low enough to sweep Kip off. The giant grizzly was still fast enough to almost close the gap with the night mares before they hit the camp.

The first cries that rose into the air were cries of surprise, not alarm: more yelps of *What the hell was that thing that just ran past me?* than fear. The wolves went only for the sentries and men with torches.

Where the wolves had slipped easily through the gaps in the sharpened stakes ringing the camp, the mastiffs had to pause to muscle their way in. Two teams of them stopped to clear lanes through the stakes for the horses and men coming up behind them, while the rest of the mastiffs streaked on, hunting anyone with the stench of drafting on him.

The tenor of the cries changed immediately as they began bursting through tents and tearing out throats.

The night mares rolled like distant thunder on the horizon into the camps next, streaming like twin lightning strikes through the two paths the war dogs had cleared, with Kip and Tallach hard behind them. The Nightbringer drafters riding on the night mares splashed green or blue or orange luxin down on every fire to smother it, from the smallest torch to the cookfires, engaging only those Blood Robes who directly stood in their way.

The White King's camp was plunged into darkness – and blindness for most of the humans, who were so bad at seeing at night. Blood Robes, spinning, startled by the streaking shapes, fired their muskets blindly, hitting nothing or hitting their own comrades.

Tallach simply jumped over the stakes ringing the camp, his gait hardly changing. When they landed, Kip finally had time to grab a flash grenado from his belt. His job was to guard Tallach's back – which mostly meant to distract and delay anyone who attacked him.

A Blood Robe soldier knelt with flint and steel, trying to light a slow match for his musket, each skritch and flare of sparks an invitation to death. Tallach's claws answered the call with a quick bloody swat.

Then Kip saw the sudden starburst of mag torches being broken open at the center of the camp, near the wagons.

Tallach saw it, too, and charged straight for it. His path took him over tents and through a dozen men trying to hand out muskets, whom he scattered like chaff. In a bound, he leapt over a picket of whinnying horses.

Then, from the high vantage that only Kip had, the disaster opened in front of him. The central pavilion contained nothing except a great pit. One of the mastiffs must have inadvertently knocked down one of the supports or had already fallen in. A pit that big could only be for Tallach.

A trap.

Kip yelled in alarm, but Tallach had too much momentum to stop. Instead, he tried to leap all the way over the pavilion and the pit.

He wasn't going to make it. Kip leapt from his platform as Tallach came down, crushing the pavilion and hitting the far edge of the pit. Kip flung the flash grenado toward where he thought the mag torches had been. A fraction of a heartbeat later he hit the ground.

He rolled perfectly – Ironfist would have been proud – but Tallach had been running at terrific speed. Kip flipped and flipped, trying to keep his limbs in. A flash split his vision and he hoped that had been the grenado, and not his head hitting a rock.

Somehow he found himself on his feet, only slightly dizzy. There was a strong stench of tea leaves and tobacco. Someone had drafted a lot of red luxin here.

But he was more worried about the four wights in front of him, each carrying a lit mag torch. Two of them appeared to be blinded and dazed from the flash. One, a blue, bolted.

One of the dazed wights lifted a pistol in Kip's direction. It pulled the trigger, noticed that nothing happened, and cocked the hammer. Then it disappeared in a blur of fur and saliva and snarling. Coming in from the side, a mastiff had clamped its jaws on the wight's gun arm and whipped him around. The war dog outweighed the man and had hit with great speed.

The wight was flung aside, and in moments the snarling dog was atop him, this time knocking aside frantic arms and going for the throat.

Kip turned and spiked the other dazed wight before it could recover. He saw another wight he'd missed before as the young woman drew an arm back and threw her burning mag torch toward the hole.

The hole. That was where all that red luxin Kip was smelling must be pooled.

Tallach was half out of the massive hole, recovering from his shock, claws piercing the ground, back legs churning for a grip, fur smeared with pyrejelly.

Kip shot out a dozen fingers of fast superviolet at the arcing mag torch, each streaming a line back to him. One hit, and along that guide line, Kip threw all the last of his orange luxin.

The burning mag torch was blasted safely away from the pyrejelly and into the distance.

Something knocked Kip off his feet as a musket went off, deafening him. From his back, he saw a war dog atop the wight who had thrown the mag torch. A musket lay on the ground beside her. She was limp already; the dog whipped her back and forth, his jaws clamped around her neck.

It must have knocked Kip down to save him.

But Kip was already scanning the distance for the blue wight who had run away – and he found him.

He hadn't run away. He was running toward the wagons laden with black powder, mag torch in hand.

Figures illumined only by that bobbing star flashed and

shifted as the two camps fought, shadows in a night made darker by the contrast. The sprinting wight wasn't thirty paces from the wagons.

Kip had only a little superviolet and yellow left. Still lying on the ground, he shot out the yellow as hard as he could. The molten yellow twisted in the air, connected to Kip's will by trailing tendrils of superviolet.

In midair, it solidified and curved.

The projectile connected with the blue wight's head – but it hadn't totally solidified. A failure. It splashed into light.

But Kip was already up and running after the wight.

The wight had fallen. Being hit from behind while running, even by a fist of water, had been enough to knock him off his stride.

The blue wight staggered to his feet and picked up the burning mag torch, mere steps from the wagon.

A Cwn y Wawr soldier ran in from the darkness and clubbed him with the butt of his blunderbuss.

But it was a glancing blow to a shoulder, and the hit spun the wight between the soldier and the wagon loaded with black powder. The Cwn y Wawr soldier lifted his blunderbuss.

'No! Don't shoot!' Kip shouted, running. 'Oof!' he tripped over a body in the darkness.

The soldier looked back, whether he understood what Kip had said or simply thought it was another attack.

He squinted against the darkness, unable to see Kip, and died as the wight's blue spikes rammed through his neck.

The wight released the spikes back to dust, and switched the mag torch from his wounded left hand to his right. He lofted the torch—

—and jerked forward several paces as Cruxer's giant elk rammed its antler through his back. The giant elk lifted the wight high in the air, but even then the wight didn't drop his torch.

Cruxer's first stab missed as the giant elk's animal instincts took over and it tried to shake the wight off its antlers. Then it paused and lowered its head, about to buck the wight up and off the tines of its antlers.

The wight threw the torch.

But Cruxer threw himself backward so he was lying on the giant elk and, upside down, swung his spear, slapping the torch off to one side.

His momentum carried him and he flipped off the giant elk's back just as the animal flicked its head upward. The wight flew into the air and somehow Cruxer flowed into position, his spear butt planted on the ground.

The wight landed, his momentum impaling him on Cruxer's spear. Cruxer took his hand out of the way at the last moment, casually releasing the haft of the spear and then taking it back as the wight thudded to the ground. He spun the spear, its blade slashing the wight's throat, and stepped out of range, eyes already looking for any other threats.

He gave a command to the giant elk, and it charged off.

Kip kicked dirt over the torch and walked to join Cruxer in guarding the wagons.

The Cwn y Wawr soldier was dying nearby, holding his throat, gurgling, his eyes on Kip accusing him of betrayal.

'You were going to shoot a blunderbuss toward a wagon full of black powder,' Kip told him. 'You would have killed us all.'

But the soldier was beyond hearing.

Moments later, the rest of the Mighty swept in and surrounded Kip.

'What are you doing?' Big Leo shouted. 'We've been looking everywhere for you!'

'Why isn't Tallach with you?' Ben-hadad asked.

'How did we manage to lose him again, Mighty?' Cruxer demanded.

'It's a trap,' Kip said, over labored breaths, still trying to yawn away his one deafened ear from the musket blast. 'Was. Was a trap. Fire. Wagons. Black powder.'

Conn Arthur, animating Tallach, must have realized that coming to help Kip keep the wagons from blowing up when Tallach was utterly soaked in pyrejelly was not the best idea. He'd gone elsewhere.

The other possibility, that he had run away, was simply impossible.

'These are rigged?' Ben-hadad asked from atop his night mare. 'Then what the fuck are you doing right next to them?'

But for the next minutes, they kept everyone away from the wagons. Not that any of their foes had any interest. Most of the men had no idea they'd been bait for a trap. The camp had been broken now.

It left Kip with a few minutes. His officers knew their work and didn't need him interfering, and he was too valuable to risk himself at this stage when the battle had already been won. He looked at the Mighty. They'd sharpened in these last months, and all of them had their halos at least half-full. Ben-hadad had crafted some device to move his crippled knee, and spent hours a day wincing, tears sometimes silently streaming down his face, regaining a range of motion. Big Leo had grown a heavy beard and picked out his hair to a large dark halo. He wore spiked gloves and carried a heavy chain into battle now. He'd joined Conn Arthur in his exercises and tried to eat only what the conn ate, envious of the man's ridiculously muscular upper body. Ferkudi had picked up a scar exactly where he parted his hair, from the top of his head down to one eyebrow. It was the only goofy scar Kip had ever seen.

Only Winsen seemed unaffected by all the fighting they'd done and death they'd seen. He'd saved countless friendly lives with his marksmanship, but had taken two. He'd reported those himself, but seemed unburdened by it. 'He dodged left for no reason. Arrow was already in the air.' His bow had been shattered during an engagement where he'd apparently saved many Cwn y Wawr lives, and they'd given him a new one in thanks. Or, more appropriately, an ancient one. It had a sea demon bone worked into the spine of the bow, and its mammoth tension could be strung only by will-casting. Winsen was able to learn enough of that art for the bow, and his eyes lit with real joy when he tested the draw for the first time. Ben-hadad had, of course, wanted to study it immediately.

Six months, Kip thought. Halfway through our halos in six months.

That meant they had six more months at the most, fighting this way.

Orholam's balls, just at the time they reach their full capacities as warriors, I'm going to have to take all these guys off the front lines completely.

The other options were of course impossible: tell drafters fighting for their lives not to draft, or let them draft all they wanted and then just kill them when they broke the halo.

Still, what nineteen-year-old was going to take retirement well?

From the screams, the Blood Robes who had fled into the woods were encountering the will-cast jaguars and mountain lions waiting there. In the darkness, those who fled had no chance. As far as the White King was concerned, these wagons would simply disappear.

No. This had been a trap, a sacrifice. That meant the White King would want to know how and if it had worked – or why it hadn't.

Kip said, 'There will have been at least one scout stationed to see if the trap worked. The pit was to kill Tallach. The black powder was to kill me and as many of the rest of us as possible. So…two scouts, at least.' Kip looked around. He couldn't see the hills in the darkness, but he'd memorized the map of this area. If the White King had been expecting a huge explosion, his scouts wouldn't need to be close. But if you wanted to see how many of the enemy you killed in that explosion, you had to have a sight line. 'Send the hounds over to that hill there, and get the war dogs going up Tenling Rise over there. Send some mounted men with them, in case it's a long pursuit. The one on the rise will be mounted, trying for speed.'

The orders were relayed, and Cruxer said, 'Now will you please get your ass away from here, Breaker?'

'You forgot to say "milord,"' Winsen said, his yellow-veined eyes sarcastic. Carelessly he flipped back the canvas covering the wagon's payload. It revealed cannonballs and stones and iron nails all tied tight around a dozen casks of black powder.

'Yep, that's a trap all right,' he said blithely.

'Are you insane!?' Ben-hadad shouted at Winsen. 'That canvas could have been booby-trapped! It *should* have been booby-trapped! You idiot!'

'Uh, yeah, let's get to a safe distance,' Kip said. 'No "milords" necessary.'

But in the back of his mind, the danger wasn't Winsen. The White King had been willing to sacrifice several hundred men, half a dozen wights, and many casks of black powder just to kill Kip and Tallach.

So they knew about Tallach. He was always going to be the first secret that slipped, of course. People on either side would love to talk about a giant grizzly.

But that the Blood Robes had thought it was worth losing many men to kill Tallach? That meant the raiding phase of Kip's war was well and truly finished. Kip's raiders needed to become an army now. That meant giving up sapping the enemy's strength, and trying to destroy him directly.

Kip had hoped that eventually some other satrapy would send in its men to do the large-scale killing and dying while he simply weakened the Blood Robes. That fantasy was dead now. No one was going to help them. This was their fight alone.

They'd won here tonight, but they'd come damn near a disaster. If all the White King had to do to lure Kip in was put some supplies in danger, he was going to get him eventually.

In a way, it was encouraging. A leader wouldn't spend that many lives and that much matériel to try to take out two enemies if he could kill them more cheaply.

That meant the White King didn't have any zealots willing to trade their lives for Kip's, or any professional assassins in Kip's army. Yet.

Which likely meant the next attempt would be a while. But when it came, Kip might have just made himself worth the expense of hiring a Shadow from the Order of the Broken Eye.

'Cruxer,' Kip said.

'Mm?'

'Remind me to give you a medal.'

'Sure,' Cruxer said. What had once been thin streaks of blue in his eyes were now perfectly horizontal and vertical bars that nearly glowed with amusement despite the strict professionalism of his expression.

'Wait, no, remind me to make up a medal first, so I can give it to you.'

'Uh-huh,' the commander said, using a rag to clean the gore off his spear and hands.

'Order of the Skewer, maybe?' Kip suggested.

Finally Cruxer cracked an unwilling smile. He shook his head. 'You know, you can just say thanks.'

'Thank you for saving my life, Commander,' Kip said gravely.

'No thanks required, sir.'

It was Kip's turn to smile. 'That's it. You're getting that damn medal.'

Chapter 56

Teia was surprised that they hadn't been thrown in a dungeon after witnessing the Nuqaba's fury reach such crescendos that Teia froze up. The Nuqaba had actually *spat* on them.

It was only after the first storm had passed that Teia realized she'd missed a perfect opportunity to fake a heart attack for the Nuqaba rather than the much older satrapah. She readied her paryl in case the Nuqaba started shouting again – the woman was an erratic moving target, though, and Teia wasn't fast enough with paryl to penetrate the skin, find a good blood vessel, and tie off a solid crystal all while the woman moved.

And then the satrapah calmed her, at least temporarily. The Nuqaba stormed out of the room, and as the supplicants and courtiers in the hall erupted in speculation, Tilleli Azmith came forward and spoke quietly to Anjali Gates. 'You will stay the night.'

'I was instructed to head back to the Chromeria immediately,' Anjali Gates said.

'Would you insult us more?' she asked. 'Besides, we may have an answer for you by morning, and we've no way to get the reply back as fast as you can. Your person will be respected; we're not barbarians here. As a representative of the Chromeria, you're invited to dinner tonight. It's *"āsōr Imbarken*, which means—'

'The Blessed Ones. A feast in honor of the first ten captains to join Lucidonius, yes, I know,' Anjali Gates said. 'Is it minor enough that it will be canceled?'

Her interruption wasn't, perhaps, the deference due to a satrapah, but then, technically, Tilleli Azmith wasn't one anymore.

'I was going to say it means another party. And no, it shan't be canceled. The Nuqaba never shirks her religious duties. You're invited to dinner, but I'd advise you not to attend.'

'Of course not,' Anjali said.

So they were staying. Teia was half-relieved and half-terrified. That meant she'd have a chance to complete her mission. It also meant she'd have to complete her mission.

'Chamberlain, rooms and provisions for these two,' the former satrapah said.

'If I may?' Anjali interjected. 'Can you see to it that someone takes provisions to our crew? The men expected to head back today, and will instead have to stand watch all night. Some meat and wine would be a kindness.'

The satrapah looked sad. 'In ordinary times, I would take offense on behalf of my city that you think your crew needs to stand watch all night in my port. But these are no ordinary times, are they?'

Do not like this woman, Teia. Don't like her.

'May such times return,' Anjali said, 'and quickly.'

'Indeed. See to their men's needs, Chamberlain. Thank you.'

'My lady?' Teia said, speaking for the first time. 'Um, I've never been to Azûlay before, and...the city is beautiful. May I...if we're to be sitting in our rooms all night...I would love to have a chance to get out and see the city. Is that acceptable? Or should I stay here?'

She smiled. 'It is a beautiful city, isn't it? You're no prisoner. You'll find yourself followed at a discreet distance while you explore the city. To watch you, of course, but also to watch over you. Last thing we need right now is for something terrible to happen to a Blackguard and have the White believe we had a hand in it. Mm? So please avoid the neighborhoods east of the docks.'

'Thank you.'

'As you will.' She nodded and left.

After the Chamberlain got them situated in a large suite and a neighboring servants' room, Anjali Gates said, 'Please leave ascertaining whether we're prisoners to me, would you?'

'I wasn't—'

Anjali's eyes were as forgiving as steel. 'By forcing the question, you could have pushed the woman into a position we didn't want. By speaking to her unbidden at all you invited punishment. You let me decide when to push and when to hold back. Understood?'

Teia was stung. 'I – yes, Mistress.'

'Good. Now get out of here for an hour. I'll write my report, and then you'll take it to our men at the docks. You give them instructions that if they're threatened, they're to head out immediately with my report. Just in case the Nuqaba decides something unfortunate for us.'

Teia nodded. Starting a conversation with a satrapah as if they were equals? Who did she think she was? Too much time with Kip and the Blackguard had somehow made her forget what she was to others. How could she, of anyone, forget?

'Adrasteia?' Anjali said. 'Did you notice anything peculiar about her?'

Teia thought. 'No wine on her breath,' she said.

Anjali smiled. 'See? They don't make Blackguards out of just anyone.'

'I won't step out of place again,' Teia promised.

Of course, my place is as an assassin – excuse me, I mean as a shield edge being brought down on some poor women's necks.

'Please close the door behind you.' Anjali Gates sat down at the deck in front of a nice window overlooking the cliffs and the sea, and pulled out her scrolls and quill. 'One hour,' she said without turning.

The door was still cracked open. Teia threw her hood up, let the lodestone clasps click the mask shut, and stepped into the hall, invisible. She shut the door behind her. Anyone watching the room would think that Teia was still inside.

But there was no one watching the room.

Teia ghosted through the halls, getting her bearings. Karris had shown her a map of the palace, but she hadn't had long to study, and Teia was embarrassingly terrible with maps. By the time she figured out which rooms belonged to the Nuqaba – well, those were obvious, being huge and crawling with Tafok Amagez – and which were the satrapah's rooms, her hour was nearly up.

The great hall was being set up for dinner, musicians tuning instruments and white-clad slaves setting the tables, when Teia passed back through. She came to her hall and saw a servant in nondescript clothing leaning against the wall where he could watch the entire hall. But he was obviously bored, and he was flirting with one of the dancers who was limbering up in a thin bodysuit nearby.

Teia took her time. It seemed that the dancer had figured out that he couldn't leave his spot, so she was teasing him. 'Well, why don't you come over here and show me?'

'Ah, later, I will. I promise.'

'Later? Later I'll have some lordling wanting me to sit on his lap. Can you compete with that?' She stuck her chest out and then rolled backward to form a bridge, kicked into a handstand, scissored her legs, and stood.

Teia actually stopped. That was amazing muscular control and flexibility.

But the man groaned aloud, his mind obviously on other things. Teia moved past him and missed whatever he said to the dancer as she turned the key in her door's lock.

But he missed the clacking of the lock as well.

'I've been known as a girl of easy religion,' the dancer said, winking, 'but I only worship at one shrine a day.' The woman slid smoothly into a full split on the floor and bounced on the ground suggestively.

But Teia didn't wait to see what the man said. His eyes were stuck. She slipped into her room.

Empty. She threw her cloak back and opened the door again. She locked her door behind her and walked next door openly, as if she'd been in her own room the whole time. She knocked and went in.

'Perfect timing,' Anjali Gates said. 'I'm just finishing up.' She blew on the warm wax sealing a scroll and then slid it into a leather scroll case. She also had a sheathed table knife on the table.

Anjali handed Teia the scroll case. 'That's the decoy. Filled with happy nothings about how well we were received and so forth. The real report is written in superviolet and wrapped around the blade of this knife. If you're taken, make sure you rattle that blade around inside its sheath well to break up the superviolet script, understood?'

'Understood. Can I run with it?'

'Absolutely. This knife's seen duty all over the world. You won't destroy my note by accident. When you get to the skimmer, one of the reedsmen will ask if he can borrow a knife for his dinner. Give it to him. You can eat before you go, if you like.' She gestured to the wine, bread, cheese, and meats that had been delivered.

Teia shook her head. 'Sooner started, sooner finished. I've been needing a run anyway.'

Minutes later, she was heading out the front door of the palace. A young Tafok Amagez fell in behind her. She turned and looked at him, amused.

Then she took off at an easy run. She'd left her sword behind, though she still had her knives and the rope spear around her waist. He, on the other hand, carried a decorative heavy spear and wore a gladius in addition to a brocaded burnous more fit for standing around looking pretty than for running.

So Teia took it easy on him – and ran as fast as she could. Blackguard Archers always had something to prove, and they treasured the chip on their shoulders as a birthright.

Teia made the pass at the skimmer with no problem. She took a draught of watered wine, didn't offer any to her escort, who was pretending unsuccessfully to not be winded, and then, on hearing that no one was bothering the reedsmen, she ran back to the palace.

This time she took the long way, going up the winding grand boulevard just to add distance.

When she got to the Tafok Amagez at the palace door, her guard was fifty paces back. Teia dabbed her forehead with a handkerchief as if it had been an easy jog. 'Tell your man it's really sweet that he let me win, but I'm the slowest of the Blackguards, and I know I wouldn't beat one of you in a real race.' Teia winked at the captain, who scowled, and patted his shoulder as she went past.

After she got inside, she finally took the deep, leaning-over-and-heaving breaths her body demanded.

It had all been the kind of thing she would have done if she were a real Blackguard, here on innocent duties, but to Teia it was something more than reinforcing her cover: it was a farewell. That girl Blackguard who teased other soldiers with her prowess was the girl she could have been. Maybe it was the girl she should have been. Like all soldiers, the Blackguards had hours of boredom to fill, and like all soldiers, they filled them with pranks and the breaking of silly rules.

She didn't get to be that girl. The candor and winsome integrity of a Commander Ironfist would never be hers. She could play at it, but it sat on the other side of a glass, the reflection of a girl she would never get to be.

Teia reported in to Anjali Gates, who gave her food and told her there was a bath waiting in her room. Teia pretended to be more tired than she was, and said she'd probably retire for the night unless Anjali needed her. The diplomat said she'd not go out to keep from antagonizing anyone – the party had already started, and the Nuqaba insisted everyone drink heavily at her parties. 'I know you might be curious to go to the great hall, have some fun, drink too much, maybe kiss a boy, I understand. But anything you do may have repercussions beyond yourself. And after the White's message, there will be those eager to pick a fight with you. Winning such fights would be as bad as losing them.'

'I understand,' Teia said.

Naturally, she headed out to the great hall immediately.

Chapter 57

There was nothing but time here. Time and the lure of insanity.

The dead man spoke to him whenever he opened his eyes, so he often sat in a torpor to gain a measure of peace. But when torpor yielded to sleep, there was a different kind of torture.

'Go on, sleep,' the dead man said. 'I'll be here when you wake.' And he laughed.

Gavin tore his heart open, and it tore him in turn. His fingers ripped on the thorns, bled. Blood flew in frantic gray splatters to fall to the luminous white marble of the tower's roof. But he didn't stop. Couldn't.

The storm bore down upon him, thunder rolling within the gathering clouds, all streaming toward the judging hands of the colossus who stood over him, towering over the tower, examining him with the intensity of a man stooping over a tantruming child, and at the same time so vast that the whole earth was his footstool.

Gavin threw aside dark thorns and chunks of his own skin and flesh, heedless, but he wasn't fast enough, couldn't be fast enough.

The gathered clouds massed around the great figure's fist, and rose, all together, rose, rose over his head, with a great sucking sound of all the winds twisting together. His fist rose in preparation to strike, to shatter, to smash, to judge, to obliterate the stain that was Gavin Guile.

His heart was full of murder, murder, murder. He broke the thorns off one by one. Wrath. Denial. Manipulation. Pride. And lies. Everywhere lies. Shame and bitterness and cowardice and lies. His oarmate-prophet Orholam had warned him to quit his lying. But he couldn't quit his lying. His whole heart was dark with it.

Everywhere he tore off thick black veins, glimpsing febrile

gray muscle palpitating beneath them – gray because it was starving, dying.

He was a liar, Gavin Guile. He was so inveterate a liar that he didn't know his own face in the mirror anymore.

He was weeping, weeping from the pain, weeping from memories half-seen, fully shunned.

He saw his brother, standing over him on the egg-shaped hill – the Great Rock before it had become Sundered Rock – and his brother said, 'Dazen, Dazen, Dazen. You could never beat me. Not in magic, not in muscle. Never. Not in cunning, not in counsel, not in stratagems or seductions. Not once in all our years. How did you think you would beat me now?'

The real Gavin had picked up a spear and limped toward where Dazen lay concussed, delirious, immobile.

'Brother,' the eldest said, his voice softening as he approached, steps slow, 'did you think I would give up this life? Do you even know what I paid to be here?'

And the elder brother, even as he lofted that spear and prepared to kill him, wept. How had Dazen forgotten that? The real Gavin's tears had fallen on barren, smoking ground.

Crying? Dazen had barely thought his big brother could.

But his tears didn't stop him from advancing. He didn't want to kill Dazen, but he was going to.

No, no, no.

It didn't matter. He broke the heart into its last pieces. From a distance, it looked gray. It wasn't gray. There were no shades of gray. Life was white and black streaked together so intimately that the two couldn't be untangled. If he tore out what was corrupted, it tore out everything.

There was nothing wholly untouched, nothing pure, nothing innocent. His heart fell to pieces, putrescent, rotten stinking meat in his hands.

He rolled from his knees onto his back, limp. His arms stretched out as they had so long ago under the rising sun, and he stared at that crackling colossal fist of judgment as it came sweeping down. And he accepted it.

Chapter 58

'This is a terrible idea!' Former Satrapah Tilleli Azmith whispered. 'The Chromeria's messenger is in a room not fifty paces from here! If she steps outside her room at the wrong moment...'

Apparently Teia had come in at a good time.

She dodged another servant in full regalia and white gloves, carrying wine.

'They have no claim on him,' the Nuqaba said. 'It doesn't matter. And how dare you speak to me that way? You're not even a satrapah anymore.'

She might have been teasing. Teia couldn't see the Nuqaba's facial expressions in the few brief upward glimpses she afforded herself.

Teia was, of course, invisible, but coming into the feast in the great hall had not been one of her better ideas. It was called a great hall, and indeed, it was huge, but it was also filled with nearly a thousand people. They weren't quietly sitting at their tables and talking and eating, either. They were milling about, grabbing wine jugs and food from beleaguered kitchen slaves, gambling, singing along to musicians, grabbing the asses of the slave dancers, kissing, gambling, and Teia didn't even know what else. A yellow show drafter appeared to have eaten a large quantity of hallucinogenic mushrooms and was sketching wonders in the air and blathering incoherently.

It was still a good five hours until midnight.

'This what happens when the first four courses consist of beer, wine, brandy, and arak,' a nobleman said to Teia. He started when he looked toward her and saw nothing. 'Oh, Nwella, I thought you were standing right here,' he said to a woman a few paces away.

He must have sensed Teia's presence. Her breathing? Had she made a sound? How could he have heard that in this cacophony?

She hadn't come directly to the high table on purpose. Instead she'd been driven here as she'd dodged into what gaps she could see. She'd thought it would be safe to come in here, that anyone who ran into her would likely be drunk and not even notice it. Instead, because whenever she wanted to see she had to uncover her own eyes, it meant she was giving hundreds of people a chance to discover her, over and over again.

Satrapah Azmith looked baffled. 'You're not really considering...'

The Nuqaba picked up a narrow sausage and looked at her. She took a bite and chewed, apparently in no hurry to answer her.

'So tell me again why you think I shouldn't unveil him here. Would it not be a demonstration of my power? To have plucked such a prize from the Chromeria itself?'

'Fuck that. I'm not even talking about that idiotic idea now,' Satrapah Azmith said. 'Are you really considering letting them demote me?'

'Oh, I'm considering doing it even if we reject their proposal. You seem to be forgetting your place in our partnership.'

It hit the satrapah like a punch in the face. 'Are you...' She looked as if she were struggling to contain herself, and failing. 'Are you fucking insane?'

The Nuqaba sucked the juices off long, gold-lacquered fingernails. 'Careful, old woman. Addressing me with such language flies perilously close to blasphemy.'

'Blasphemy? Who do you think...' But the satrapah regained control of herself, and stopped speaking, though she did set her cup down with a bang.

Teia wanted to see how this turned out. What the satrapah did, what she said afterward, and what she would do when the dinner was over. Would the Nuqaba apologize when she was sober? Would she take some vengeance? For Orholam's sake! The satrapah was the Nuqaba's spymaster! If there's one person you don't threaten, it's got to be your spymaster, right?

But it was all irrelevant. Satrapah Azmith was flushed with

rage, and that was all Teia needed. What she might do or might say, or that she seemed like a nice woman, that all meant nothing.

The warm, red light of the fire in the great hearth and the many torches suffused Teia and gave her all the passion she needed.

She was become death, and she would collect her due.

She'd already scanned the satrapah's body. The blood vessels around her heart were already narrowed, as Teia would expect in one who'd had so much stress and so many years and a rich diet to boot.

One by one, Teia brought paryl crystals into the woman's bloodstream, making many little crystals of it in the vessels leading to her heart. One for each slave she'd had to kill for these bastards.

The satrapah's own body attacked those invaders immediately, forming clots. Teia merely nudged the clots closer toward each other, helping them glom together. One passed through the narrow opening and whooshed right through.

Then another, as Teia had to dodge a servant carrying the next course of the meal.

But Teia had made half a dozen clots, and one caught. Then another, on another ventricle of the heart. She started moving to get out, and barely heard the woman grunt.

How dare you act decent and kind? How dare you merely do your duty while you served this monster? A thousand slaves might die at your word, and a hundred thousand if you nudged the Nuqaba one way rather than the other. And you didn't care. All you cared for was yourself.

How dare you? How dare you show a face to me that seemed kind and good?

There is nothing kind and good.

Teia slid as far as a slaves' door before she turned around. Tilleli Azmith was grabbing her left arm and grimacing.

It was over. Teia had claimed some small vengeance. She didn't even need to see her work.

As she turned away, Teia heard a crash as the woman fell.

'Tilleli?!' the Nuqaba said. 'Satrapah! Damn you! What's wrong?!'

Teia felt only a warm satisfaction, the lambent radiation into her soul of a big fuck you to all of them.

'Tilleli?!' the Nuqaba shouted, as everyone else went quiet in waves – music cutting out, awkward laughs hanging in the air from people who hadn't seen yet, and gasps from those who had. 'Tilleli, don't you do this to me!'

Teia looked at the Nuqaba's puffy, stupid face, and thought, One down.

The night wasn't over yet.

Chapter 59

'The question is why the White King changed his strategy so drastically. All these months of raiding, and we haven't answered that damned basic question!' Kip said.

Weeks after the attempted assassination in the woods, the Mighty were seated around yet another fire at yet another camp, having yet another talk. It was not the first, nor indeed the fifteenth time Kip had asked the question aloud.

'I know we need to talk about the battle tomorrow, but this first,' he said. He had grown more comfortable with giving commands, even ones nobody liked. And they'd grown more comfortable accepting them, too. Not even Winsen complained that it was late and they probably weren't going to solve what he saw as a nonproblem.

They knew he'd get to the battle plan, and that they'd need to be sharp when he did, in case he had in-depth questions about their positions.

'Why does there have to be a grand answer?' Cruxer asked. 'The White King felt he was getting overextended, so he paused. The break does him more good than it does us. He has secured and fortified his supply lines between Atash and the siege at Green Haven. Not even we could get to those unless we wanted to give up Dúnbheo and the lake.'

Dúnbheo – the nonfloating Floating City – was the Forester name of the city the Nightbringers were going to try to save tomorrow. It controlled access to the Great River and the immense lake by which Green Haven was getting what little supplies it still was.

'He's also had to deal with us,' Ben-hadad pointed out. 'Isn't it possible that *we* actually stopped him?'

'But he was advancing steadily,' Big Leo said. 'Just as he has everywhere. Why stop halfway through Blood Forest? Why not at least push to the Great River everywhere and then consolidate?'

'Too much guerrilla warfare that way?' Winsen suggested. 'He could capture the cities, but if he doesn't deal with us first, supply lines get long and vulnerable.'

That could be it, but he'd advanced so fast elsewhere, leaving small forces to mop up any continuing resistance. Was Blood Forest simply different because of its huge population of hunters and hard terrain for supply lines?

'All the fights we've had have kept us from linking up with the satrap's forces,' Tisis said. 'If he pushed us to the river, it's the only place we'd have to go.'

'We don't *want* to link up with the satrap's forces,' Kip said. Satrap Briun Willow Bough wanted Kip's army – and Kip, if he could get him. What he didn't want was another person running around his satrapy with an army he didn't control.

Which was understandable, and the man was a decent sort. Unfortunately, he was also a moron who had no idea what to do with the army he already had. There was no way Kip was going to take orders from him about how to use his own very peculiar forces.

'We all know that,' Tisis said. 'But the White King doesn't. Joining forces is what most defenders would do.'

'You think he's allowed us our victories?' Kip asked.

'Not the first one at Deora Neamh,' Tisis said. 'Maybe not the skirmishes around the Ironflower Marsh or the Deep Forest Ambush. But we've sometimes traveled pretty far to get disappointing quantities of food or muskets. And you yourself said the black powder wagons were an assassination attempt.'

It had been a hollower victory than Kip had hoped. They had done everything right, wiping out the enemy and seizing everything with minimal losses. They even successfully disarmed the booby-trapped wagon. But then they found that of the five wagons, it was the only one loaded with powder. The others' barrels were loaded with a layer of black powder, then sawdust.

The men of the wagon train hadn't even known they were bait.

It was small comfort that the war dogs had hunted down the scouts sent to watch the outcome. It was small comfort that Kip had been right and there had been two scouts.

'We haven't fought many drafters, either,' Kip said. 'We're missing something here.'

'Maybe we are,' Cruxer said, 'but then the question is whether the White King has some grand design or whether it's just an error. He's already spent many lives to keep us away from a place we never intended to go. Just at the wagons he lost several hundred men, half a dozen wights, and five wagons trying to kill you. He's a good orator, an inspiring leader by all accounts. But maybe he's simply a poor strategist.'

'Poor enough to take two satrapies,' Winsen said dryly.

If anything, Kip thought, he himself was the one who was a poor strategist. Good tactician. Loved by his people...but he still couldn't resolve the big picture. Damn, how he'd love to take some lectures with Corvan Danavis now. When he was a boy he'd wanted stories of battlefield heroics. Given the chance now, he'd say, 'Talk to me about rations for cavalry when moving through forested river valleys.' 'What's the breakdown of your command staff per soldier?'

'That was when the Chromeria didn't know what we were up against,' Cruxer said.

Cruxer still said 'we' when he talked about the Chromeria. Kip loved him for that idealism, but he didn't share it anymore.

'He's successfully stalled reinforcements, though,' Tisis said. 'We know from the White's letters that he's been trying to turn the other satrapies to his side or at least keep them out of the war. That's not the work of a poor strategist.'

That Karris had written to the Nightbringers at all was the biggest shock for Kip. Without shaming anyone, she'd laid out the numbers – Tyrea and Atash were lost, the Ilytians didn't care who won, the Nuqaba's Paria had pulled back all its soldiers after Ox Ford and had never sent reinforcements, and other than the several hundred men Eirene Malargos had sent under Antonius, and her continuing supplies, Ruthgar had pulled back to its side of the Great River, busily fortifying a border too long and too porous to be fortified well.

Kip might have been at fault for part of that. Eirene could be forgiven for not wanting to send more soldiers when Kip simply took them. And if Kip's co-opting of Antonius and his men was the reason Ruthgar wasn't sending reinforcements to Green Haven, Kip could well become the reason the Chromeria lost this war.

With all those satrapies out, only Abornea and the small army directly under the Chromeria's control were left. Karris had said nothing about that, and Kip wondered if that meant they were coming but coming late, or coming as part of a stratagem to sweep in at the last moment, or if Andross Guile had decided to cut his losses and let Blood Forest die.

Karris had also written about her insight that the White King wouldn't mind a slaughter of both sides, and in fact might prefer it so he could remake the entire culture of the Seven Satrapies. It had seemed an odd, paranoid thought at first, but Kip didn't think so anymore.

The White King hadn't sent one man or one squad on a suicide mission: he'd sent hundreds to die, just to kill Kip and Tallach. And from how the camp had fallen, except for a couple of the wights, those people hadn't volunteered.

That was some coldhearted butchery there.

'So he's successfully tying up our reinforcements from coming,' Kip said. 'But he's not pressing his advantage. Why? Why why why?!'

Ben-hadad chimed in for the first time. 'I don't mean to distract us from this highly profitable colloquy that is still not answering a question we haven't been able to answer for many months, but maybe we should talk about the battle that's going to shape our entire future that we are going to fight tomorrow?'

Big Leo looked down at him. 'You take that crazy talk and get out of here.'

'What's a colloquy?' Ferkudi asked.

No one answered him.

Kip acquiesced even though he felt he was close to figuring it out. Another almost. Kip Almost.

'Enough,' Kip said. 'Let's go inside.'

They moved to the map in the command tent. By this point, Kip had trained others in how to create the things, which was fortunate given that they needed new maps constantly as they moved.

'Let me lay this out plainly,' Kip said. 'Tomorrow's battle at Dúnbheo will either be the crowning achievement of all our work to keep our strength secret, or it will be the end of our hopes to save Blood Forest.'

There were grim faces all around, and a few muttered curses. Handsome General Antonius Malargos cursed quietly. He was perhaps the only one who hadn't guessed.

'It's for this that I've tried so hard to paint us as raiders by force allocation and by strategic disposition. Tomorrow we fight our first pitched battle. They shouldn't expect us to be prepared for this kind of fight. I'll be blunt, we might not be. Before now, retreat has always been part of our plans. If things went poorly in a raid, we ran. I hope we haven't engrained that into our troops.'

'We won't run, my lord,' Antonius said. It was his supreme confidence in Kip that made him a useful battlefield commander. It spread to his men. Kip could only hope it spread enough.

'Here are the stakes,' Kip said. 'Hiding behind its Greenwall, Dúnbheo has always been a defensive redoubt. They never projected force into the forests beyond them. But perched as they are at the mouth of the river, they have kept the river open to the lake. Besieged, it's been nothing to the war. Freed, it can become a gateway to a huge number of supplies. Lost, it becomes a stranglehold.'

'We free it, we can save Green Haven,' Cruxer said. 'We lose it, we lose Green Haven.'

'Right,' Kip said. 'And we don't know how bad things are inside the city, except to know they're bad. They've been able to bring in some supplies from the river, but the capital's mostly needed those supplies for themselves. We can't expect any help from the city. The Council of Divines is made up of

413

old cowards. At best, if we're already winning decisively, they might send some small force to help. I doubt it.'

'That's just fantastic,' Winsen grumbled. No one upbraided him.

'But if we win,' Kip said. 'If we win, with the skimmers we can land anywhere on the lake. We'll own the lake. With resupply readily available to us and to Green Haven, and with our forces able to strike anywhere we choose, lifting the siege of Green Haven will be only a matter of time.'

'Save the city, save the satrapy,' Cruxer said.

Cruxer was right, and Kip was maybe telling too much, but he always wanted his inner circle to know the full strategy. If he was killed, someone else would need to take the torch. A lot of lives depended on it.

Not that he said the last part aloud. That would only devolve into protestations that he couldn't die.

Dúnbheo was a strange city. It had once been the religious center of one of the nine kingdoms. Dúnbheo had been deliberately shunned since the establishment of the Seven Satrapies, but never destroyed. Apparently it was a beautiful place, and Lucidonius had believed that every beautiful thing man creates points to how the creative spirit of Orholam himself lives in all people.

So instead of being destroyed, the city had been starved of influence. No one born in the city or who had spent more than ten years there total could hold any position of power in Blood Forest, the Chromeria, or the Magisterium. Thus, as soon as any family native to the city rose high enough to entertain ambitions of being greater, it left. It bore and raised its children elsewhere, and those children generally didn't want to come back, lest they spend more than their decade there.

It meant, oddly, that there were a lot of nobles dispersed throughout Blood Forest and Ruthgar who had ties to the place – because the smart, the ambitious, and the strong were exported instead of killing each other off. The Malargos family had first risen from Dúnbheo, which was one reason Tisis had so many ties to Blood Forest while her family was technically Ruthgari.

'Commander? Over to you,' Kip said.

Cruxer pointed to a map of the city as it had been before the siege. It showed the city surrounded on three sides by trees and also filled with trees, more than any other city in the world. He gestured, and a swath of trees around the city walls disappeared.

The maps were put together now by a team of drafters and Derwyn Aleph of the Cwn y Wawr, who was in charge of the scouts, and Tisis, who interviewed the refugees. The maps now allowed them to advance time and see the reports appear as they had come in.

'Two months ago, the Blood Robes cleared the forests around the city for a hundred paces in every direction. They believed that the city was being resupplied through the trees.'

Derwyn said, 'Which is nonsense. There were ladders and rope swings concealed in those trees so that single scouts and messengers might move through the sylvan giants quietly, but entire convoys of food? Impossible.'

'Any caves?' Conn Arthur asked.

'Few, and none deep,' Derwyn said. 'Not only do you have the tree roots to stop that, but there's the groundwater to deal with. The river runs partly through the city itself.'

'It is *possible* there could be caves,' Ben-hadad said. 'Purely from an engineering perspective. But I guess it depends what you mean. Do you mean do the inhabitants of the city have any tunnels, or are you asking about sappers?'

'Either, both,' Kip said.

'The city might have made tunnels. If you took your time – and I mean years – you can dig and pump out the water and seal the tunnels with luxin and support them appropriately,' Ben-hadad said. 'I mean, you'd be constantly fighting the roots and leaks in the wood and luxin. But it's possible. The city has been here a long, long time. But to do it and then maintain it would require a permanent corps of drafters. Drafters of average ability? I'd say you'd need thirty or forty, which is expensive and very hard to keep secret. You can hide what one or five drafters do, but when you have forty, people wonder, people gossip, and spies find out.'

Ferkudi said, 'Dúnbheo doesn't *have* forty drafters.

Thirty-eight, tops, in the whole city, and surely most of those would be tasked with defense, right?'

As far as Kip knew, Ferkudi didn't have any ties to Dúnbheo, nor did he see the scouts' reports.

'Why do you say that?' Cruxer asked before Kip could.

'Oh,' Ferkudi said, finger lodged up his nose. 'You just cross-reference all the activation lists of the lords in the surrounding areas with lists of the Freeing, the Cwn y Wawr, and the Ghosts, take out those we know are dead, and those we guess have joined the White King. That's why it's fuzzy. We don't how many joined the pagans, so we have an upper bound of around sixty-one, but not a lower bound. There's a bit of unknown with how many drafters in the last ten years have been reported dead before their Freeing who might actually be alive – those records are weak, and don't show place of birth. Then Satrap Willow Bough came through here three months ago and offered protection and great pay to any drafters who joined him immediately, so I'm also assuming that any refugee drafter would have joined up with him at that point, what with an army on the way to besiege Dúnbheo. But that's why the number's a guess. Irritating.' He flicked a booger into the fire. 'What?'

They still hadn't gotten used to how Ferkudi did that every once in a while.

And usually, they couldn't harness those little moments of genius for things that mattered more than food and boogers.

'So, no escape routes from the inside out,' Kip said. 'Outside in seems even more improbable. It would cost too many drafters to make it as quickly as you would want, especially to seize this city. Am I right?'

'It holds great symbolic and religious value to pagans,' Tisis said. 'But still…no, I don't think the White King would think dedicating so many sappers to this was worth it. One of his Lords of the Air might feel differently.'

The White King had split his armies, giving control of them to various commanders he called Lords of the Air. The Mighty thought the one known as Amrit Kamal was in charge of these besiegers, but their intelligence on that wasn't good. The

Lords of the Air would do anything for a victory; they were replaced immediately if they failed.

'Is there any way that any of you can see that we might buy victory without tomorrow's battle?' Kip asked.

They all scowled at the map for a while.

Then Ben-hadad said, 'If we simply go around the city and attack the besiegers' own supply lines, we might starve out their siege without a fight.'

'Besiege the besiegers?' Conn Arthur said. 'But if it takes more than a couple of weeks, the White King can bring down part of his forces and besiege us in turn, in which case we lose every advantage we've built up to this point.'

'That would weaken the White King's siege at Green Haven,' Tisis pointed out. 'If Satrap Willow Bough used the opportunity to attack—'

'If,' Winsen said.

He was right. Audacity wasn't the satrap's strong suit. Kip couldn't trust him to see and take advantage of what might be only a small opportunity. Nor did he want to put his raiders through setting and undergoing a siege at the same time; it was totally the opposite of what they'd done before.

'If we attacked the Blood Robes briefly and let their messengers through, they might be recalled, again without a fight,' Big Leo said.

'I like this thinking,' Kip said.

'There's a problem with that,' Tisis said. 'If you free the city in a clever way where the Blood Robes simply leave, that's wonderful, and we'll have done a good thing. But we'll get no credit for it. It will just seem like Dúnbheo's good fortune. We'll get no new recruits, no funding, and no food except what we take at the point of the spear. You take food then, and they'll hate *us* instead.'

She was right. Dammit.

They all chewed on the injustice of that, but no one disputed it was what would probably happen, not even Antonius.

'Curious world, isn't it?' Kip said. 'Seeing your foes driven away inspires more gratitude than cunningly having others draw those same men away. The charging in is all Gavin Guile, the cunning is Andross Guile. One of them is loved, and the other hated. Is that because men are so shortsighted or because we long to see those who hurt us be hurt themselves?'

'Some more one, some more the other, I'd hazard,' Ferkudi said. He had trouble identifying rhetorical questions.

'Also, Andross Guile is an asshole,' Big Leo said.

There is that. Kip grinned grimly. 'So I have to let more men die so that their friends will be grateful enough to replenish my ranks of the dead and continue to support us and keep the rest of us alive. In other words, I have to be cunning enough to not be cunning.'

'The most important part of seeking victory is defining it first,' Tisis said.

'Shit,' Kip said. 'And I had this really brilliant idea about how to get around the Blood Robes' partial river blockade, too.'

'I'm sure you did, dear,' Tisis said.

'You know how they've set up the weirs to block the city from getting any fish?' Kip said.

'Are we going to use this idea?' Tisis asked gently.

'No,' he grumbled.

'Mmm,' she said. 'We wait at your command, my lord. Despite the hour.'

'I'm mean, it was an ingenious idea,' Kip said. 'You'd all be very impressed.'

Cruxer theatrically stifled a yawn. As if at a signal, everyone else stretched and rubbed their eyes. Even Conn Arthur blinked sleepily.

'I hate you guys,' Kip said. He waved his hand, and the battle order appeared on the map. 'Study your positions, then go. Sleep fast. Conn Arthur, a word.' It was almost scary how well they worked together now. His commanders knew exactly what they needed to do and how and when.

In turn, he gave them a huge amount of autonomy. He'd even taken to rotating commanders over various elements, partly so that each understood the others' duties and problems and speed, and partly so that the army wouldn't splinter into factions. The common soldiers certainly had favorite commanders, but they trusted all of them.

They all soon left, except for Conn Arthur and Tisis, who withdrew subtly.

'Conn Arthur, we need to have that talk.'

'Which talk, my lord?'

'The one neither of us wants to have.'

The muscles in Conn Arthur's jaw clenched.

Kip had had the other sections of the map brought in and assembled. He'd had to learn to get over his reflexive avoidance of inconveniencing his servants and subordinates. If someone needed to be wakened so Kip could think, even if it was only once in a hundred times that he came up with a stratagem or noticed an error in his plans, that one time in a hundred was worth waking them.

Tisis had directed the placement and organization of the figures on the map. Each refugee reported to her, and she placed forces on the map in various colors for each report. Each was dated, too. The will-casters had put it all into the map so Kip could watch colors blossom across the map a day at a time. His own scouts' reports bloomed in different colors.

There were hundreds of false reports, exaggerations, and mistakes, but with thousands of reports, those tended to reveal themselves as the noise they were. On the other hand, even low-quality reports, if repeated often enough, gave Kip a place to send his own scouts or raiding parties.

If he did nothing else, this map would likely be Kip's legacy, his big advance that he'd given the world.

Of course, the map had to be imbued with a bit of will, so it was technically forbidden magic. So maybe even this would disappear.

He put his hands on it and extended his will. Little lights bloomed around his own forces, leagues away most of the time, but shadowing them at all times. 'These are reports of a giant grizzly,' Kip said.

'Hmm. I try to keep Tallach away from people, but grizzlies roam. It's their nature.'

'And doubtless,' Kip said agreeably, 'some farmers and shepherds who know that we travel with Tallach have caught a glimpse of *something* in the woods and reported it as him, hoping for us to reimburse them for lost livestock.'

'Right, right,' Conn Arthur said.

He thought Kip was going to let it go.

And how Kip wanted to.

Kip slowed down the advancement of the map. Lights bloomed simultaneously, tens of leagues apart. One day, then another, and another.

'Odd, isn't it?' Kip asked. 'A series of these reports come from the kind of places I would expect you to send Tallach – abandoned areas with good hunting, mostly, and few humans. Others, sometimes simultaneous with those, come from more populated areas.'

Conn Arthur swallowed, but said nothing.

'What happens, then, if we assign a different color to the ones in rational areas than to the ones way too close to settlements?'

He started the series over again, and suddenly the reports made sense. Still shadowing the Nightbringers, two dots hunted the forests nearby: the red always farther from villages, the blue always closer.

There were still a few false positives from bad reports, but otherwise it explained all the data.

'This is . . . all guesswork,' Conn Arthur said, but he sounded more sick than defiant.

'Someone's going to get killed,' Kip said gently.

'I can handle it.'

'So you don't know,' Kip said.

'Know what?' The quick crease of his forehead told Kip he was telling the truth.

'Someone's been killed already.'

All the color drained out of the big redhead. 'No. Orholam forbid it. I would know if—'

'Not by Lorcan. By Tallach.'

'What? Lorcan?! I told you my brother's bear is dead. What—'

'Two hunters heard a giant grizzly was eating folks' pigs. They got liquored up and decided to go hunting. Said they'd be damned if some dark Tyrean – that's me, I assume – would tell them what to do in their own woods. One survived.'

'Well, maybe that's their own fault, then, right? We've warned the people everywhere to stay clear . . .'

'Tallach shouldn't have been in that area at all, Ruadhán, and you know it. Wouldn't have been there, except that you had to keep him on this side of the river so Lorcan wouldn't attack him. Am I right?'

Kip could see Conn Arthur trying to build up a rage, but the big man couldn't do it. 'How long have you known?' he asked instead.

'He's your brother. You love him,' Kip said.

'So…'

'All along. As you've known what needs to happen, but knowing in your heart takes time.' Kip put his hand on the big man's shoulder. 'It's been almost a year.'

'You were giving me time to do the right thing,' Conn Arthur said.

'Mm-hmm.'

'And I never did it.'

'How much of Rónán is left inside that bear?'

'Good days and bad. It's as bad as when our mother lost the light of reason. Never thought I'd have to go through that hell twice.'

Kip said, 'When you have to go through hell, go quickly.'

Tears dripped silently down the big man's face. 'I thought if anyone might be the exception, it would be him. I thought maybe he could beat this.'

'He's made it this long. That is exceptional,' Kip said. 'But we both know, when he goes, he could take out an entire village easy as snapping your fingers. There's no cure. If it were you—'

'I know! You think I haven't told myself all that a thousand times? I just can't do it!'

And he wouldn't want anyone else to do it, either. He'd never forgive himself for that, or whoever did it.

Kip said nothing for a while. Then he said, 'The battle tomorrow's gonna be tougher than most of us realize. We think of Dúnbheo as a backwater. The White King is a pagan. He thinks of it as the capital of Blood Forest. He's not going to retreat.'

Conn Arthur's brow wrinkled.

Kip said, 'When you – as Tallach, of course – and I ride

out here into full view, I'll throw up some firebirds and put some signal flares on this ridge just before dawn. When their people see a giant grizzly outfitted for war, it'll be hard to look anywhere else. If Lorcan can swim the river and land here and come fast through this gully, he'll be in the underbelly of the camp in minutes. If he can hit the camp, if he can give just a few minutes of chaos – right when the sun dawns – it'd make all the difference. No man wants to face one giant grizzly. Trapped between two?'

'Hell, I wouldn't want to do that,' Conn Arthur grunted. 'You think he can do that?'

Conn Arthur examined the terrain. 'It's a suicide run.'

'That's right,' Kip said. He let that sit, didn't defend it.

'But one that will save many lives if it works,' Conn Arthur said.

'If,' Kip said. 'It's a gamble. He may die for nothing.' He wasn't going to twist the conn's arm into this.

Conn Arthur was quiet again. Then he said, 'Surely a man who gives his life trying to save his friends is just as much a hero as one who dies actually saving them, right?'

'Better to die trying to do good than make your own brother blow your head off,' Kip said.

Conn Arthur took a deep breath. Then nodded. 'Rónán would've agreed with that.'

'Then go and speak with him. If all goes well, tomorrow night we celebrate, and the next day we mourn.'

'As it should be,' Conn Arthur said. He had regained some composure, but he was still taking deep, gulping breaths. He left swiftly.

Kip sat down and silently studied the map. Tisis came up beside him, and he rested his hand companionably on her hip.

'You did good there,' she said.

'Did I?' he asked.

'How could you even ask that?' she said. 'You gave him every chance to come clean on his own, and then when he didn't, you gave him the chance to give his brother a hero's death.'

'But why?' Kip said.

'What do you mean?'

'Did I hold back until now because I didn't want to force him to kill his brother, and lo and behold! here came an opportunity to avoid all that! Or did I, like my grandfather, keep Rónán off the table like a card to play at an opportune moment? Am I a good man, or just a fatter iteration of Andross Guile?'

She let part of that pass, though he saw the tightness in her jaw. 'So you did something devious and brilliant and also callous. But it was also kind, and respectful, and life giving. What if, my lord husband, you are a man with not one nature, but two?'

'Two?'

'What if you were not only flesh, but also spirit, and those moments when you bring the two together are not failures, but are your moments of deepest integrity and brilliance?'

'You think I'm brilliant?' Kip asked.

'I can't believe you still question it,' she said. 'But the real question is, do *you* think you're good?'

'No,' Kip said without hesitation. 'Competent. Crazy stubborn. Cunning sometimes.'

She sighed and looked at the map. 'What are you looking for?'

'Clarity,' he said. He thought about getting out the rope spear and working on it quietly for a few minutes or an hour to ease his mind. Young Garret had died in a raid and shattered his heirloom sea demon bone spear. Kip thought he'd figured out a way to make those bone fragments into the spine for the rope spear, which would give it some unique abilities.

But Tisis always got that aggrieved look on her face when he worked on the thing, like he wasn't paying attention to her or something. He didn't know what her problem was, but she seemed to hate the thing.

Anyway, it could stay in its bag for now. Enough time to take it out after Tisis went to bed.

She said nothing for a few minutes, then kissed his cheek. 'You'll not find clarity tonight, I think. Come to bed or you'll stay up so late that it costs you the clarity you'll need tomorrow.'

He followed her to the other side of the command tent. Their personal quarters consisted of a small area separated by a curtain, a chest to sit on, and a pile of blankets on the ground. There was barely room for the room slave Verity (a gift from Eirene that they had not been able to refuse) to stand with them, helping Tisis undress. 'I'll not be able to sleep,' Kip said.

Truth was, he wouldn't mind some distraction before he went back to the maps. They hadn't made love all day.

'You don't need sleep tonight,' she said.

Well, that was promising, especially as Verity peeled away her dress.

But Tisis dismissed the slave and continued. 'What you need is introspection and time. Come and rest on my breast.'

'Rest...after?' he asked.

'No.'

'Rest...first?' he asked.

'Only. Rest *only*. You wouldn't lose yourself to pleasure tonight, or if you did, you'd feel guilty about doing so while Conn Arthur is out having one of the worst nights of his life.'

'Be nice to forget all that for a little while.'

'Tonight you need to think about brothers, and family, and what they mean. And that means thinking about what you didn't have and don't have and what you were cheated of and what you're thankful for. I don't want to help you avoid that hurt, Kip. I want to help you heal it.'

Kip lay his head in her lap as she stroked his hair, and then later upon her breast. He didn't think. Though she'd expected him to think of family and of love, for the longest time, here in her softness and her strength, here with this family and this love, he didn't think at all.

Chapter 60

Teia made her way back to her room, which she entered unseen in the chaos. She wasn't sure how long she could afford to wait, but she was glad she had when someone banged on her door not ten minutes later.

A captain of the Tafok Amagez was standing there.

'What is it?' Teia asked. 'I've heard shouting. My lady ordered me earlier to stay in my room tonight no matter what. Is she safe?'

'Yes,' the man said. 'Everyone's fine. There's been a death.'

'A death? What happened?' Teia asked.

'Please stay in your room for the rest of the night.'

Teia gave him a suspicious look. 'Well, now you're making me nervous. My lady's safety is my sole charge. Do I need to be alarmed? Should I—'

'Absolutely not. General's orders. Stay put. I'm putting men outside your rooms to guarantee your safety. We've already checked on your lady. She's fine. The death was an accident. We're just taking precautions given the fraught nature of relations with the Chromeria right now. Can't have any well-meaning idiots jump to conclusions and maybe do something we all regret.'

'If that was meant to soothe me, I'm afraid—' Teia started.

'Satrapah Azmith died at dinner. Had all the signs of a heart attack, but a woman dies at dinner with you, you check the food for poison, right? You're a Blackguard.'

Teia feigned shock. 'The satrapah? Now? I knew we should have left right away.' She mumbled a curse.

'People are blaming your mistress—' the captain said.

Oh hell no.

'—for putting such strain on her with her message. Please stay inside for the night until tempers cool. You'll have orders in the morning.'

Orders? The Nuqaba wasn't in authority over them. That her men casually assumed she was wasn't a good sign.

'Uh, thank you, then,' Teia said.

He turned to go, but she stopped him.

'Um, sir? Before the screaming just now, the party sounded, uh, pretty exuberant. Should I advise my lady not to bother the Nuqaba too early in the morning?'

He looked at her as if deciding whether to take offense or not. Then he relented. 'She usually switches from alcohol to other things before dinner for that reason. Morning she has her poppy tincture first thing. It levels her out. Early is probably best. Ten minutes before dawn rituals on the east lawn. Orholam go with you, and may there be only light between our lands.'

'Thank you,' Teia said.

'I'll tell the watch captain to announce you.'

'Thank you,' she said again.

Maybe she'd put too much friendliness in her tone, because he looked at her again with something new in his eyes. He waved for his men to head out, but he didn't follow them. 'So,' he said. 'Crazy times, huh?'

'Huh?'

'Crazy times we live in,' he said. 'Really makes you think that you've gotta seize the opportunities for the good things that life sends your way.'

'Um...right. Sure.' Oh no.

'Where are you from? You look like you've got some Parian blood?'

'I grew up in Odess, actually. But yes. Think my family emigrated, immigrated? I can never remember when you say which. Um, a couple of generations back. Dad got into debt, so...' She fingered her notched ear.

It probably wasn't her smartest move to flag that she'd been a slave. Not usually a quick route to getting more respect.

'Huh, right,' he said in a tone that made it clear he wasn't listening to a word she said. 'How old are you?'

'I'm sorry,' she said, 'but you're making me uncomfortable.' And if I have to kill your ass, I am really in deep shit.

'Oh, I'm sorry. I didn't mean to be...whatever. Just, you're here tonight. War's on the horizon everywhere. I think you're beautiful, and you know, you don't even have a book. What are you going to do all night? Pretty boring here, right? What better way to pass the time? Do you know you have the most beautiful lips?'

He stepped forward and caressed her cheek. She had to control herself not to flinch away from his touch. He looked a bit tipsy, and Teia doubted it was from her beauty. Shit. She bit the inside of her cheek hard. 'Oh, I wish I could,' she said. 'But...uh, I'm sorry, it's embarrassing...'

'Are you on your moon? I don't mind. You don't have to be embarrassed about that, and there are certainly other—'

'Oh no,' she said. 'No, I love swiving during my moon blood. If my daddy won't swive me then, I just find a boy who will. No, it's, uh...my infection's flared up.'

'Infection?'

'You know, the boy who gave it to me swore I wouldn't get it if I just used my mouth, too. And I believed him. I guess that's what you get when you start swiving in back alleys at ten to get money for sweets.' Teia grabbed her cheek and turned it out so he could see the lumpy, bloodied flesh she'd just bitten.

The look on his face was one of pure horror.

'And if you think that looks bad...' She glanced downward and scratched at her groin. 'See? It's terrible. You're disgusted now, aren't you?'

'No, no,' he said, backing away.

'I just didn't want you to take it personally, you're very handsome.'

'No, no, I understand. It's fine.'

'It is kind of burning right now. Maybe I'll just sleep tonight and let myself heal,' she said.

'That...that sounds best,' he said. He left quickly.

Benighted jackass. Dammit. As Teia closed the door, she rubbed her cheek. It hurt like hell, but she silently thanked her Archer sisters for the stratagem.

That you can kill a man easily doesn't mean he knows it; even if he knows it, it doesn't mean he'll act in a rational way with that knowledge. Their fault, but your problem.

She grabbed her gear and went to her window. Her room had no balcony, but that was just as well. The window opened wide enough for her to wriggle through. She popped the first climbing crescent and affixed its sticky side to the wall and then poked her head out. This side of the palace sat over a cliff, with retaining walls leaving barely enough room for a row of low flowering bushes before the palace itself sprang from the ground. Teia's window was only about ten feet above those bushes, but if she fell and didn't grab on to them, a fall of several hundred feet onto rocky beach awaited.

Good thing I'm not afraid of heights.

Much.

There was no one else out here. No balconies hung out above the cliff face, though there were inset patios on the roof, Teia knew.

She moved carefully and took her time. She didn't have enough climbing crescents to make it all the way to the top, so she planned on getting into a window on the next floor. Quick and easy.

The window was locked.

Nothing is ever quick and easy.

She made it to the next floor up before she ran out of climbing crescents. The window was cracked open, but there was a couple inside. They looked like they'd be busy for a while.

Teia wasn't exactly fond of clinging to a wall while the autumn-evening breeze kicked up, chilling her fingers, but she didn't see that she had many good options, so she waited.

She peeked again. The couple – younger staff, servants both – were still sitting on the woman's bed, only kissing. The woman had her legs spread and was arching her chest toward the man, but he barely had his hand on her thigh. Awkward kisser, too.

Teia waited. She couldn't make her move now. The couple was seated facing the window she'd be trying to get through. Anywhere the cloak slipped, Teia would be visible, and it would be impossible to get in without making some sound.

She would have to wait until they were too distracted. Then she could slip out of the room either when they fell asleep or when the young man slipped out.

Teia peeked again. The young man barely had one hand on the woman's rib cage. She finally took his hand and pulled it to her breast.

He stopped and pulled his face away from her, though he left his hand where it was.

'Tiwul, I don't know if we should...' he said.

Orholam have mercy, man! Get on the horse and ride, or get out of the corral!

Teia looked around and considered her other options. They weren't good.

I don't need to worry. I've got all night.

All night to figure out how to kill the Nuqaba, without anyone suspecting it's an assassination. No problem.

So Teia alternately blew warm breath on one hand and then the other to keep her fingers from getting stiff while she clung to the wall at three points. Five minutes passed and Teia heard a little sound of protest.

She peeked again. Oh no.

This time the young woman had broken off the kissing. His burnous was off, and her dress was pushed down to her waist, and her skin was all gooseflesh.

Oh no no no, Teia thought. The young woman walked toward the window, shimmying so her dress dropped past her hips and onto the floor. She was flushed with glee and desire.

'It's freezing in here!' she said. 'Why don't we—' and Teia lost the rest of the woman's doubtless brilliant seduction with the creak of the window shutting.

Damn. It.

For one murderous moment, Teia thought of cracking the window just enough to draft through the empty space. At some opportune moment, she'd tweak a nerve in a leg or an arm and make the young man crush that stupid girl. Better yet—

Actually, she'd never thought of it before, but could she make a man's horn fall? Just by tweaking the right nerves? *That* opened up all sorts of possibilities for mischief.

Could she make a man's horn rise against his will with a similar manipulation?

Now *that*—!

Not the time, T.

Nonetheless, the idea made her almost giggle. It was almost irresistible, but she knew if she started, she wouldn't be able to stop. It was totally inappropriate, totally immature, but she was so scared, so nervous, so afraid of failing and of not failing, that she almost dissolved. She bit down on her macerated cheek.

Too hard. She almost yelped aloud.

But she felt more levelheaded when she was done cursing silently. Maybe that was the darkness working on her. Not a total darkness out here by any means, thank Orholam. She thought she'd go mad in ten minutes in total darkness. Here the lights of the city below and the stars above relieved the empty cold of blackness.

Time for a new plan.

Teia climbed back down to her own window, getting her feet onto the first crescents she'd placed. Each climbing crescent had a string dangling from it. Pull that string in a big circle around your crescent, and the string cut it off the wall. Each time you removed it, you lost adhesive luxin, but the crescents could be reused.

Of course, it was one thing to place a crescent and then decide you needed that handhold to be farther to the right; it was quite another to do what Teia planned.

Still clinging to the wall, she removed her boots and stockings one at a time and stowed them in her bag. Each string had a ring at the end of it. Dipping low, she grabbed one with her big toe, cut the climbing crescent off the wall with the string, and carefully stood. Then she lifted the crescent with her foot, holding on to the wall with a single hand and foot, and grabbed the crescent in her hand.

Each crescent retrieval took time, and after a few, Teia's toes were so cold and insensate that she had to watch carefully while grabbing at the rings, arching her head dangerously far from the wall. But in another ten minutes, she made it to the third floor.

Locked. Curtains drawn. Who locks a third-floor window overlooking a cliff?

She debated breaking the window, but she couldn't be sure the room was empty. Nor could there be any doubts about the Nuqaba's death. There were other windows on the same floor, but she had no guarantee that those would be open, either.

Worse, the climbing crescents were starting to lose too much adhesive. She rubbed the wall with a sleeve each time she set a hold, to remove the dirt, but it wasn't enough. Either the humidity or the dust or the simple fact that Teia was short and had to place the crescents closer than a taller assassin meant that there was no way Teia would be using the crescents to climb back down to her room.

That was a problem for later.

She decided to go for the rooftop gardens.

It took her an hour, and more than once, she told herself she was a fool, but there was no way down now; she'd brought the crescents with her.

When she finally threw herself over the edge of the roof, she simply lay beneath an immense rhododendron bush and quivered. Her hamstrings would never forgive her. Her knuckles were scraped bloody. Her sleeves were pilled from polishing the rock wall. Her toes were bruised and alight with pain where the feeling was leaching back into them. Her arms were jellyfish, stinging her shoulders with their death throes.

When she felt she had the strength, she sat up and massaged her feet and then put her boots back on. Standing, she shook out the master cloak to get the dust off it – and a gust of wind and her own zealous whipping of it launched it from her cold-clumsy fingers.

For a moment, it drifted over the void, flipping away from her – and then she snatched it, nearly lurching off the edge to reach it.

She held herself very still, the thunderbolt of what might have been paralyzing her for a moment. She let it roll slowly past her as she merely breathed, breathed.

An unforced blunder like that? What kind of nunk was she?

She had almost just killed herself. Losing the master cloak? Dear Orholam, it was that easy to die. One slip. The Order had provided her with the Fox cloak for this mission, but it was so inferior to the master cloak she hadn't even taken it out of her pack in her room.

The garden was beautiful. The kind of place Teia would have liked to take her time to explore. But it was night, and the moon was rising, and it was cold, and the garden was empty, so she simply made her way invisibly to doors leading inside and whispered a quick prayer.

It was open. Thank you, Orholam, for people who aren't paranoid enough.

The wide hallway was enclosed with a glass dome from the interior wall down one side and down to the ground on the garden side. Profusions of immaculately trimmed flowers yielded one to another in a pleasing sequence of colors and textures. In between large private rooms for the Nuqaba, there were little garrets for slaves everywhere. Private chapel, slaves' closet, private library, slaves' closet, drawing room, slaves' closet, music and art parlor, more slaves, rock-and-water garden, still more.

Most of the slaves' rooms didn't even have doors, merely a sharp bend upon entry so the slaves themselves wouldn't be visible. Teia peeked in one. She couldn't help herself. Four men slept on a single narrow bunk bed in a room not even as wide as Teia's stretched arms. A small washbasin sat against the far wall, and they'd hung their clothes flat against the wall. A few personal effects were stuffed under the bunk, with room to spare. They didn't even have shoes.

One of the men had his legs uncovered with his bedmate taking their too-small blanket, and Teia saw whip scars down his very calves. She was glad she couldn't see his back. Above their door was a small bell attached to a string, and a bundle of other strings passing through their wall to and from the rooms on either side. Teia moved in the direction their bell's string came from.

After passing a few more rooms – a swimming area and a hot room? – Teia found the chief eunuch's room. It was the center where all the bell strings led. Doubtless on being summoned he would then summon the appropriate slaves – because it's just too hard for a slave owner to figure out for herself which slaves she should call to address her doubtless urgent needs. Probably the bells were only for nighttime. The Nuqaba would be attended at all times when awake.

The next room was the Nuqaba's own, and Teia heard the woman's voice before she got there.

'Too hot, you idiot! Get out! No, stop, hold still.'

The crack of a heavy slap connecting with bare skin, and then a slave girl not twelve years old burst through the door, bucket in hand, sobbing. She tried to sob quietly.

Teia remembered that shit: Stop crying! Slap. Stop crying! Slap. You dare defy me? Report for whipping, you stupid bitch!

One learned to cry quietly. To save tears up for later.

Teia slipped in before the slave standing outside the door could close it. This was the Nuqaba's bed chamber, but though she had entire rooms devoted to baths just steps down the hall, they'd brought in a copper tub full of steaming water.

The Nuqaba herself was pacing the room in a bathing robe – Teia had forgotten that Parian women rarely bathed nude, which had always struck her as a weirdly backward custom for an otherwise reasonable people. How do you get really clean when you wear clothing into the bath? The noblewoman's hair was bound up on top of her head with aromatic oils to moisturize it through the night, her skin scrubbed of all cosmetics. But her eyes were puffy from tears and bloodshot from either whatever was burning in the hookah on the table, or the bundle of haze beside it, or the mushrooms she had diced very finely in a dish.

If only Teia hadn't been such a straight arrow growing up, she might know how much of which intoxicant would kill you. It would have been a nicely believable accidental suicide.

I'm a soldier, not an assassin.

But as the door closed quietly behind her, Teia was arrested by something else, and she instantly forgot all about the Nuqaba and assassinations and stealth and consequences.

Chained against the Nuqaba's wall, head imprisoned within a helm with blackened glass over the eye slits to keep him from drafting, but unmistakable from his towering form and chiseled body, was Commander Ironfist.

Chapter 61

He woke in the deepest darkness he had ever known. When his panic subsided, he examined his surroundings. He'd been moved while he was unconscious.

It was a black cell, but otherwise identical to the ones Gavin had made. Just more cruel.

More secure, too, naturally. It was very Andross Guile. This cell didn't even have to be made of luxin. Dark stone of any kind, plus no light, and there could be no escape.

'Feel it,' a voice said.

Oh no. 'Who are you?' Gavin asked. That wasn't his father's voice.

'Feel the stone,' the dead man said.

'You can't be here. You...'

'Feel the stone!'

Gavin felt it. Not granite, smoother. Marble? But without the slick coolness of marble. This was more metallic, as if rather than simply being cold, it was sucking the warmth right out of his skin.

'No,' he said.

'No one has drafted so much black luxin since Lucidonius,' the voice said. 'Here lies your masterpiece, and no one but your father will ever know.'

I made this? An entire cell of black luxin, a dark mirror of the others. Why?

I should feel distrust. I should have my guard up here, against *this* dead man, surely the worst part of me. Instead I feel only a cavernous desolation that sits below my rib cage, burrowing at my heart.

I am a skin suit. A hollow man. I am a disguise buttoned up over nothing.

I am as empty as the eye they burnt out. Lensless, I gawp and stare. Bathed in light, I remain a black Prism, reflecting nothing, spitting only facets of myself into these cells. I am the unseeing I.

'Of all the dead men, surely you would be the greatest liar. Why should I believe anything you say?' Gavin asked. But he believed.

'Because you know what makes the best lies, and you think you're smart enough to winnow out the facts even if I did lie to you.'

'That does sound like me,' Gavin admitted to the voice of the darkness. The younger me. Am I really talking to a part of myself in each of these cells? Shouldn't I be a good man, then, if I drained so much bile into these abominations?

'I created us one at a time,' the voice said. 'Blue first, then green sometime later, yellow, orange quite a while later – the technical problems made it difficult to craft a chamber entirely of orange. It was important to me, to you, not to cheat and use multiple colors. We fixated on that. Red we did with many layers of seared red luxin and liquid red. Anyone else would have worried about placing what amounts to a bomb in the Chromeria's heart. Superviolet and sub-red not even I could figure out.'

'But I did,' Gavin said, thinking he'd caught his dark mirror in a lie. He had some inkling of this, scratching around the back of his skull.

'By cheating,' the dead man said. So he knew that, too. He'd merely been baiting himself, to torture himself more.

'There is no cheating in life, only success and a thousand flavors of failure.' Gavin sounded like his father, saying that. He couldn't remember, though, if he'd heard it from him first.

'See, you do remember, a little. We made superviolet and sub-red as death traps rather than as true prisons. We crafted the superviolet so that in breaking any part of the luxin, it would all break. So when any man fell in, in falling in or fighting it, he would shatter it all and release so much luxin dust into the air that he must suffocate. And the sub-red, do you remember?'

The obvious problem was that sub-red was highly flammable. You could draft a crystal of it, but if exposed to air, it caught fire instantly.

'I did...something...with orange.'

'You carved out the space for the chamber, sealed it airtight on every side, then made a permeable wall of orange luxin that you stuck your hands through repeatedly. You burnt sub-red in that chamber until there was no air in it at all, and then you created the chamber itself with a monomaniac's total fixation. That cell is perfect, a perfect sphere shining and crystalline, a marvel with the beauty of ten thousand flame crystals larger than anyone else has ever drafted. A perfect cell that no man will ever see.'

'Because as soon as he fell through the trapdoor, he'd bring in air with him. He wouldn't have time to even see the fire that would consume him.'

'Or if he miraculously lived through the inferno, he would then asphyxiate, as you built the trapdoor to seal airtight behind an intruder.'

That was right. He'd done that to keep it from being an actual bomb.

'You're being awfully helpful,' Gavin said. The darkness was getting to him, even with this comforting voice.

'You made me different from the others. Don't you remember?'

Gavin didn't. Not enough. But the dead man knew that, didn't he?

'You assumed that if father caught you, he would throw you in here. Because why would Andross Guile try any half measure?'

'So I made an escape route?' Gavin said.

'Naturally, I thought about it. For a long time.'

'I built escapes for the others.' Most of them. 'Why not this one?'

'Perhaps I planned to. Perhaps it was too hard. Perhaps I wanted one prison that I might use for someone else – father, perhaps – from whence I knew no one could escape. Or perhaps it was that madness in me. That fixation. Perhaps I couldn't bear to build an almost-perfect prison.'

' "Perhaps," "perhaps"? Stop that!' Gavin said.

'Then you tell me,' the dead man said.

'I don't know.'

'You do.'

'No, I don't remember.'

'This doesn't take memory. I'd bet you haven't changed as much as all that.'

The dead man didn't goad him after that.

It took a few minutes, standing in the darkness, feeling it soak into his bones, feeling the terror rise like water flooding the cell, covering his toes, then his ankles.

Gavin cursed aloud. 'How young and stupid was I?'

The dead man didn't answer. Didn't need to.

Why do men walk to the edge of a chasm? Is the view so different, right at the edge, than it is two steps back?

They walk to the edge *because* it scares them.

I wanted this here because it frightened me. I, a veritable lord of light, was ashamed of being afraid of the dark. So I made my own cell, my own greatest terror, and I put it under my own house. But its existence wasn't enough. It had to be inescapable. A cell without locks isn't scary enough for a brash fool. It's only as scary as the threat is real.

There were many kinds of suicidal madness. There was only one name for the kind of madness that puts a gun to its own head when it has no intention of pulling the trigger: youth.

All these years of the terrors in the night and the sudden paralyzing panics that I dismissed as foolishness and cowardice and nonsense. All these years, I was sitting on this egg of darkness, all the time, waiting for it to hatch.

Shit.

'So what's the tally?' Gavin asked, impatient with his old self as all proud men are impatient with the proof of their past imperfections. 'Tell me about you.'

The dead man chuckled low. 'Direct, still direct. As if we don't have all the time in the world. Very well. You made me last of all the dead men. You made me with the black luxin that destroyed you, that obliterated so much of the Dazen Guile who had been. You didn't craft my personality to punish you, though. No additional torture is necessary in a black cell. You made me to hold all the memories you hoped to lose. Finally, Dazen, you made me to comfort you.'

So the young me wasn't heartless. Brash and irritating and irritatingly competent, but not always thoughtless. But this was a palliative comfort. A hierarchical comforting, wasn't it? Old me saying sorry, but I've clearly bested you, future me. Because I can't imagine you ever reaching the heights of perfection again that I have reached now.

Fuck you, young, arrogant me. 'What if I don't want your comfort?'

'Then we reach an impasse far more quickly than the old you expected we would. Hmm. Funny. The old you was the young you. Regardless, the young Dazen desperately wanted to share, to justify himself, to be understood. He thought you would be the only person who could understand him.'

' "The young Dazen"?' Gavin asked. 'Like you aren't him?'

'A will-casting like me is...quite special. I've been in here for almost two decades. I've aged. Learned. So no, I'm not exactly young any longer.'

'A will-casting doesn't age. It only decays.'

'Depends on how well they're made. All magic fails eventually, yes. Will-castings deteriorate regardless of how well drafted. Me? I've aged. I've been aware of the passing time, and I don't know that I would thank you for it. I've wanted someone to talk with for a long time, and I'll only appreciate it more if there are big differences between us now. I've talked to myself enough. You will wish to talk. Now, or soon. I know, because I am you.'

'And if I don't want your truth?' Gavin asked.

'*My* truth? Is this the madness speaking? There is no my truth or your truth. You have forgotten *the truth*; your forgetting it doesn't make it cease to exist. I am here to remind you of it, so that perhaps in the last days of your life, you might reconcile yourself to who you have been, and die with a measure of peace.'

'You're gentler than I would have been, back then,' Gavin said.

'Clearly not. But I do tire of your obstinacy, old man.'

Gavin waited in the darkness for a long time. It was impossible to tell how long, though. He felt his way around the chamber. Had he already done that? It felt as if he had. Maybe he only had all those years ago.

It was shaped exactly like the others, from the trickle of water down the wall to the hole in the bottom of the floor for his waste. Of course, in the darkness, the cell could be roofless for all he knew. It might extend only as high as his upstretched hand could reach, and he would never know.

That would be the kind of bitter joke young Dazen might have played.

So he moved around the cell, as methodically as he could in the total darkness, and jumped, slapping his hand against the curvature of the wall as high as he could.

'I could mock you for this,' the dead man said. 'But I don't find it foolish, despite how it looks. I rather admire your tenacity instead. I'm glad I didn't lose that as I got old.'

' "Despite how it looks"?' Gavin said. 'Can you see in here?'

'A figure of speech only. I can hear you slapping the wall, and it's what I would do. Would have done? Will do? I'm not really sure how to address us.'

'I would have thought I would only put the vile parts of me into this cell, into the black,' Gavin said, though he hadn't really intended to talk to the thing.

'My control of black wasn't that precise. It's more of a battle axe than a scalpel. And as you might not recall, I had very little practice. Handling black is analogous to the other colors but far more difficult. And I wanted me to be a comfort to you. Can't be all vileness and hate and do that.'

Only I would try to do surgery with a battle axe.

Only I would nearly succeed.

'The others,' Gavin said, still jumping and measuring the wall. He planned to go around at least twice, just in case he missed a spot on the first round. 'The others said I was the Black Prism. Is that true?'

The dead man sighed. 'So it worked, to hide that from you for all these years?'

'So the answer is yes.'

'Yes,' the dead man admitted.

'They said that I needed to kill drafters to refresh my powers.'

'That makes it sound like an evil power. It's not evil. Black luxin itself isn't evil...though I guess I, being will-cast into black luxin, probably would try to convince you of that. Hmm. Well, you needn't believe me outright on matters pertaining to black luxin itself – I wouldn't in your place, I suppose. Won't in your place, whatever. Suffice it to say, I only killed those who attacked me first, or those who wished to suicide anyway.'

'The Freeing.'

'That's right.'

'Is that what the Freeing was always about?' Gavin asked. 'Giving provender to feed a black luxin drafter?'

'I don't know,' the dead man said. 'I think maybe it once was, but I don't think that all the Prisms have been black drafters. Maybe only very few. The Spectrum was baffled when I made it past the first seven years. They expected me to die, or they thought I needed them. I feared that Father figured it out then, but from how old you are, I'm going to guess he remained ignorant for longer than I imagined.'

Gavin said, 'What happened at Sundered Rock?'

'I think you know by now,' the dead man said.

'Fragments only. I want to hear it all.'

Gavin could see no expression, of course, and eventually the dead man spoke: 'Our plan worked, mostly. I – we – decided that some of the friends I'd made and allies I'd promised myself to were worse than who we were fighting. You remember this much, right?'

That was where the plan to replace the real Gavin had come in. Gavin said, 'If I won, I wouldn't really win. As it was, the war was traumatic, but brief. If I won as Dazen, I'd have gained the upper hand against the Chromeria, but I would still have had to subdue five of the Seven Satrapies. I might have beaten them eventually, but it was the wrong victory. My general Gad Delmarta had killed eighty thousand people in Garriston, and my army was full of Gad Delmartas. I remember what I planned with Corvan before the battle. What I don't remember is what happened during and immediately after it.'

The dead man made a sound low in his throat. 'Mmm. General Danavis managed to array the men I most wanted to die against the strongest parts of Gavin's army. Unfortunately, it is remarkably hard to lose a battle in exactly the way you wish. A lot more people died in bringing me face-to-face with my brother than I'd intended, and then, of course, he kicked our ass.'

'How did he do it?'

'I don't remember that, either. I remember thinking he'd cheated. But maybe there is no cheating, there's only success and a thousand flavors of failure.'

'Thanks.' Old me is a dick. Guess that proves it is old me.

But the dead man went on. 'At the end, rather than die, I drafted black – and wow, did I draft black. It struck like a thousand cannons. Afterward, over the years, I asked a score of different soldiers who'd been there what happened that day. None wanted to talk about it. When pressed, there was no stable, single story. I drafted so much black luxin that day that it obliterated other people's memories as well as my own. And, like me, they filled in the details as well as they could without even knowing it. The mind abhors a void, so it fills it with avoidance and fantasies, and calls them truth.

'There was an explosion, they said. The gods walked the earth again, they said. No, the Guile brothers *became* gods and warred, they said. Magic had undone the world, they said. The brothers brought hell to earth, they said. Others insisted nothing happened. Just a huge battle like any huge battle, they said. Others said that was what split Sundered Rock, that the rock had another name before that they couldn't remember now. Storm giants came to Sundered Rock, they said, and threw mountains and lightning at each other.

'Others, who were much farther away – outside the influence of the black, I believe – reported the explosion. Like the earth screamed. Like creation itself groaned. Like Hellmount blowing up in fire from the stories, a scholar said. They saw something on the horizon, an obsidian sunrise. Maybe it was ash, a scholar guessed, from a new volcano – but there was no ash found later.'

'Stop. Enough.' It was too painful to dwell on. The lies and their cost, the men and drafters dead, undeserving. All those closest to Gavin and Dazen, the guards rushing to preserve them…obliterated by the brothers' hatred and power.

Now here he was, trapped in his own cell. The cell he had forgotten was the cell in which he would be forgotten.

It would take a miracle to save him. Something never seen. Perhaps something…mythic?

'Tell me,' Gavin commanded the dead man. 'So there's black luxin. A legend come to life. Is there white, too?'

'No.'

'That doesn't make sense. There must be a balance.'

'There *is* a balance. There is pure, white, full-spectrum light – which we split into all the colors of the rainbow, and which we draft in innumerable ways into matter – and there is darkness and black luxin. That is the balance: black against all the colors put together. As there is no forgiveness, only forgetting, white luxin's a myth, a lie for the desperate and foolish.

441

There is no hope for you, Guile. No escape. There is only the perfection of darkness. There is no white luxin.'

Chapter 62

Ironfist wore a peculiar white gem on his chest. Teia didn't recognize the stone, which had always been tucked into his tunic, but she did recognize the leather thong from which it hung.

Apart from his size and musculature, it was the only thing about him she recognized. His bare limbs were manacled to the wall at his wrists and elbows, thighs and ankles. An iron strap held his waist flush against the wall. A helmet was bolted directly into the stone and encased his head completely, locking under the chin, the glass over his the eye slits so dark he could probably barely make out shapes as he twisted his head back and forth painfully.

Little wads of cloth had been stuffed into several of the manacles to cushion them. They were bloody. He'd lost weight, too.

How long had he been here?

Teia was so stunned that she almost didn't move in time when the door opened behind her. The crying slave girl brought in a bucket of water and stood next to the tub awkwardly. Must have been new.

The Nuqaba touched the water. 'You took so long it's fine now. Begone, and see to it I'm not disturbed.'

The girl bobbed down to her knees and backed out to the door, then stopped. 'Blessed? Would you like your bathers?'

'What part of "not disturbed" was unclear? Out! Remind me tomorrow to have the captains put stripes on you.'

After the girl left, the Nuqaba rubbed her thigh in evident anguish. Teia saw what she guessed was a musket-ball scar, months old but still red and angry.

'I want you to know, I wasn't always like this,' the Nuqaba said, though she didn't look at Ironfist. 'Your Prism friend shot me. I almost died. The musket ball is still in my leg, and the pain is...quite something.' She picked up a little cup of a brownish liquid that Teia assumed was tincture of poppy and drained it.

The Nuqaba gritted her teeth against the taste.

'I made it through four broken bones, a broken tooth, innumerable black eyes, and such humiliations as you would scarce believe at the hands of that husband you left me to, and I never once asked for poppy. But maybe I was scared that it would make me lose control, that I would tell him how I wanted to kill him, how I'd been planning it for years. How he reduced me to seducing his men because I knew I'd need help.'

She walked over to him and removed a pin at Ironfist's throat.

'Turn your head away. I'm going to bathe.'

Ironfist turned his head, and she replaced the pin, locking his head in place.

She stripped off her overrobe and grabbed a pinch of the cut mushrooms on the table. She tucked them into her lip, then limped over to the bath. She got in, slowly, as she spoke. 'They all want everything, Harrdun. I had everything arranged, you know? Hanishu would be my satrap, you would be my general. We would secede from the Chromeria and be our own ruling family, like the Guiles. Instead you refuse me? You get Hanishu killed? For the Guiles? You want to go after Gavin's bastard son and save him? Why do you care less about us than about them? Where's your loyalty, brother?'

Teia hadn't even known Ironfist and the Nuqaba were related. At first, she'd thought this was some sort of weird seduction.

The Nuqaba was Ironfist's *sister*?

Oh hells.

The jumble of emotions Teia'd felt on seeing him – terror that he was hurt, inexpressible joy that he was alive, determination to release him immediately, fury at this bitch for doing this to him, and relief that he would take care of things from this point if only she could free him – suddenly shattered.

Teia was here to kill Ironfist's sister. Right in front of him.

He had never spoken of her, but this was the woman he'd kept a portrait of in his chambers. A man like Ironfist didn't keep a picture of someone he hated.

'Why? Damn you! Speak!' the Nuqaba shouted, and she flung the empty laudanum cup at him. It shattered on the wall, but Ironfist said nothing.

A quick tap sounded on the door, and it opened. The chief eunuch poked his head in. 'Blessed?' he asked.

'Out!' she said. 'No, wait. Fuck. The prisoner's gag is still in. Remove it.'

The eunuch went to Ironfist and pulled a different pin in the helmet, and manipulated something Teia couldn't see. The eunuch then grabbed a few of the larger pieces of the broken cup.

'Leave them. Go to bed. I'll not need your services for the rest of the night.'

The eunuch bowed. 'Blessed, may I summon your bathers?'

'They're all spies. Good night.'

He sighed. 'Blessed, I worry—'

'Good *night*,' she said. It was a command.

And as the door closed, Teia had her plan.

'Brother?' Haruru said.

'I didn't know,' Ironfist said, his voice low and rusty with disuse. 'I didn't know he beat you.'

'Because you were *gone*! Why? If you were here, you'd have seen. You'd . . .'

Ironfist, his head still trapped pointing away from her, only sighed. 'When . . . when mother died, I swore vengeance on her killers. I thought it was my fault she'd died. And then I'd foolishly killed the man who held the blade, so we couldn't be sure who'd ordered it. I know it may seem obvious in retrospect, but mother had many enemies, and not just enemies of our family. There were old rivals and bitter former friends. She was . . . apparently not an easy woman to get along with.'

'What are you talking about? Mother was beloved. Everyone loved her,' the Nuqaba said. She filled a golden chalice – though this simply with wine as far as Teia could tell.

'No, she wasn't. You were too young, you don't remember

444

what she was like, Haruru. You were her baby, her only surviving daughter. She was difficult, but we loved her.'

'And you sure showed it!' she sneered. 'Giving away everything she'd worked for to go to the Chromeria.'

A big breath, then, 'I went to the Chromeria at the command of the Order of the Broken Eye,' Ironfist said.

Teia saw the shock on the Nuqaba's face mirror her own. Ironfist? The *Order*? Ironfist was in the Order?

Ironfist was everything Teia had ever hoped to be. He was her patron Blackguard, for Orholam's sake. Resolute, loyal, comfortable in command, supreme in competence, unrivaled in confidence. Hearing from his own lips that he was a spy and therefore a traitor, that he was actually part of the Order whereas she herself only pretended to work for it, was like taking your wedding ring in shame to a shop to pawn it, and then hearing the gold ring was brass over lead, that all the precious stones were nothing but colored glass.

Teia was so shocked, she almost lost her grip on paryl and became visible.

'Impossible,' the Nuqaba said.

Teia had told Ironfist everything: not just about Aglaia's blackmail, but also about the Order. So why wasn't she dead? Had he not told the Old Man? Why?

'You remember our uncle? He...was able to point me to the right people. I went to them and asked that mother's murderers be killed. All of them.'

'What?'

'Of course, I didn't know who those murderers were, or how many there were, and we had very little money then. I couldn't pay the Order, so they took my service instead. It was too much for me, at first, to swear allegiance to such filth. But then I thought, who has a better claim on my fealty: a distant Orholam or my own family? So I went back three days later, and told them if they would not only avenge mother, but also protect you, I would join them. They said they were not bodyguards, but they would foil any assassination attempts against you they heard of, and would do their best to guard your life. They found and left the evidence for you to find that mother's killer was in the Gatu tribe. My first test of fealty was to enroll in the Chromeria instead of hunting down the murderer myself. I didn't know it until he was dying, but Hanishu followed me to the Chromeria because he found out about my oath to the Order. He hoped to save my soul.'

'This isn't true,' the Nuqaba said. 'You were never a liar before. What have those Guiles done to you?'

'Sister, the Order has killed fourteen men for me. But they weren't above keeping me in the dark. I didn't know your husband was such a monster. They told me that only four years ago. The captain who helped you? Yattuy? He worked for them... us.'

'Lies. Lies. I did this.'

'Takama Tanebdatt. Tatbirt of the Ishelhiyen. Tadêfi of the coast. Ultra Sinigurt. Aghilas the spearman. Yuba Winitran. Sifax Winitran. Isil Gwafa. Azrur Badis. Idus Aziki. Izem of the Tlaganu. Usem Yuften. Ziri the Stranger. Udad Red. In return, I gave the Order information. It never seemed to really matter, what I told them. It was just family politics, right? Until this war—'

'I don't care about that!' she said. But obviously now the intoxicants were fully upon her, and she was struggling for clarity. 'Those are all the people who stood between me and becoming Nuqaba. You're claiming *you* killed them all?'

'I – they were all people who planned to kill you. Once others figured out that opposing you meant risking assassination, those who could be deterred by fear were deterred, and those who were more ambitious went straight to trying to kill you first. It wasn't what I intended—'

'You're saying you handed me this seat? That I am Nuqaba only because of you?!'

Teia saw his chest rise and fall in a silent sigh. 'You never wondered why all those people died or disappeared? Your enemies certainly did!'

She was silent.

'What? You really thought that you were so lucky? So "blessed" that everyone in your way fell dead at your feet? Dear Orholam, sister, how arrogant have you become?!'

He couldn't see her face or he probably would have stopped talking, because after her initial shock was the briefest flash

446

of embarrassment like lightning in a distant cloud, and then the thunder of her rage rolled.

Teia started drafting, and she was only lucky that the Nuqaba went to a side cupboard first. Dripping wet, the Nuqaba threw open a drawer and grabbed for something. She swayed, missed, and rummaged. Her hand emerged with a short, sharp knife.

She was so furious she didn't even speak. She rushed toward Ironfist with murderous intent. Teia tried to make the Nuqaba's arm go dead with paryl, but she missed the nerve as the woman moved.

At the last moment, Teia abandoned her magical efforts and chopped her hand down across the Nuqaba's extending wrist. The knife clanged on the floor, nearly striking Ironfist's leg on the way down.

Teia jerked her arm back within the confines of the master cloak as the Nuqaba rubbed her wrist, baffled.

She looked at Ironfist as if he'd done it somehow, and then she pounced after the knife, dignity forgotten.

This time Teia didn't go after the nerve in the arm, she went for the spine. She'd had far more practice with this. Many slaves' worth, Orholam forgive her.

It still took her until the Nuqaba had recovered the knife and stepped again toward Ironfist, undeterred.

'And now,' the Nuqaba said, 'you mother—' She raised the knife as Teia got the right grip.

Teia squeezed hard, and the Nuqaba dropped boneless. Teia caught her, but lost the paryl.

It didn't matter. The Nuqaba was so befuddled in her intoxicated haze by suddenly losing control of her limbs that she didn't even fight.

'What's happening? Haruru?' Ironfist said, neck locked to the side. The helmet rattled. 'Who's there?'

Teia had almost wrestled the bigger woman back to the tub when the Nuqaba started trying to fight. Teia squeezed hard again, but her hold on the spine must have shifted because this time the Nuqaba's body bucked and seized so violently they both went down.

But Teia held on to the paryl at the woman's throat. Perhaps her very life depended on it. Her grip shifted to the right place again as the Nuqaba fell on her, and the woman went limp again.

Teia scrambled out from under the woman's dead weight, careful to keep the paryl grip. It was like lifting a fish live from the river, losing the hook, and finding it both too big and too heavy for your hands, praying it didn't slip or thrash before you got to shore.

She'd lost her invisibility, but maybe it didn't matter. Ironfist's face was turned away, and though his helmet rattled with his efforts to see what was happening, he couldn't – at least as far as Teia could tell.

The Nuqaba's eyes rolled in terror as she saw the hooded figure standing over her, and her mouth gaped to scream, but nothing came out. She had no control over her body below the neck.

With difficulty, while keeping the paryl hold on her spine, Teia lifted the woman and lowered her into the bathtub. She flopped the woman's limp arms over the sides of the tub to keep her from sliding down.

Her first thought had been to simply drown the Nuqaba. Drunks passed out and drowned all the time, especially in hot water. It had seemed to be what the chief eunuch had been nervous about. But that wasn't going to work now.

Not if Teia freed Ironfist.

If she freed Ironfist and the Nuqaba was found drowned, they would assume he'd done it. It wouldn't matter that there were no bruises on her face, no signs of violence anywhere on her body.

Damn. It had been a good plan.

Teia stood frozen with indecision.

'Murder Sharp?' Ironfist said. 'Is that you? Morteza? Is this you and Nouri Sharp? Speak to me, please. You can't do this. Things are different than whatever the Old Man thought when he sent you, please...'

Teia didn't answer. It was all true, then. Ironfist really was in the Order of the Broken Eye. It felt as if her world were coming down. The best man she knew was on the same side as the worst men she knew: Murder Sharp and the Old Man of the Desert.

'Don't you dare hurt her!' Ironfist hissed. Teia had never heard him angry before, had never heard his voice skittering along the edge of control.

She approached him, pulling her invisibility back around her. It didn't work fully. The master cloak had gotten wet from the Nuqaba's soaking body and bathing robe, and the master cloak shimmered weirdly in the air where it was damp.

'I can convince her,' Ironfist said. 'Whatever it is we need. I'll make whatever deal you want. I've given my whole life and all my integrity for this. Please!'

Teia said nothing. She felt as if her heart had been ripped out. She couldn't keep this up. She was still barely holding on to the Nuqaba's spine, and this...

'You leave me no choice,' Ironfist said, and his chest lifted as he took a deep breath to shout an alarm to the guards. But Teia anticipated it, and she slid the spiky gag inside the helmet into his mouth as he opened it, and pinned it in place.

But he hadn't been inhaling to scream. Instead he spread his arms, wrapping his hands around his chains, bracing his elbows against the wall.

Teia could only watch. There was no way he was going to break those massive chains.

Breath hissed out from the huge man. His muscles went taut throughout his torso and arms. Veins jumped out.

But the chains held.

A moment later, he gasped a breath and went limp.

Teia turned and picked up the knife the Nuqaba had dropped.

A moment later, Teia heard Ironfist's manacles rattle as he flung himself against them.

Teia stepped close to the Nuqaba. She whispered so Ironfist wouldn't hear her or recognize her voice if he did. 'And now, you bitch, now you pay for your treason.'

She dropped the invisibility so that the last thing the Nuqaba saw would be Teia's paryl-widened eyes, all black as the hell that awaited her. The woman blanched in terror, and Teia calmly pushed her arm under the water so there would be no spurting, and sliced her veins open from wrist to forearm.

A gush of blood incarnadined the bathwater.

The chains rattled again. Another grunt of expelled air and failure.

Teia grabbed the Nuqaba's other arm and slashed it underwater, too. Then she lifted it just enough to drape it over the side of the tub. Blood poured onto the floor like wine from the slaves' pitchers at the party downstairs.

Teia doused the blade of the Nuqaba's knife in that already-slowing stream, and then dropped the knife onto the stones beside the tub, careful lest the blood spatter her cloak.

After the action came the horror of it. The Nuqaba was blinking wildly, eyes rolling, face contorting. She clearly wanted to scream. She wanted to weep. She wanted to run. But there was to be none of that, not for her. She was to watch herself die, knowing that her murderer would go free, that this would look like self-slaughter. If she could but yell a single word, she would live.

Teia held the woman, eye to eye, her own muscles knotting with the tension of holding the paryl grip tight on that spine, for long minutes. Under one fluttering eye was a tattoo in Old Parian: justice. Under the other: mercy. But neither winked, neither was any different from the other or different from any woman's eyes. Haruru was no longer the Nuqaba. In her dying, she was no more a symbol of Orholam than she had been in her living. She was now only a victim of those stronger than she was. Now she was just a woman, dying in her bath.

Teia held the Nuqaba's spine. The water was a deepening red when she heard Ironfist say around his gag, 'Heeaa! Heeaa! Theeaaa!'

Teia.

Fuck!

With a muffled roar, he threw himself against the chains again.

Something gave. Not the chain, Teia saw. The bolt that held one of the chains to the wall had pulled forward.

No, not the bolt – the bolt had held – Ironfist had pulled an entire block nearly clear of the wall. Blood streaming down his arms, he threw them forward again, like an injured eagle flapping its wings, longing to be free.

The masonry broke; an anchor block tore clear.

Ironfist slapped at his helmet, trying to free his head so he could see, but the great swinging block impeded him. But only for a moment.

As Teia fumbled, flinging paryl toward him, he tore away the pins on the gag and holding his head to the left.

He reached over to free his right arm—

—and finally Teia caught his spine, and his arms dropped.

'Teia,' he said tersely. 'For Orholam's sake. I know it's you. That height. That chop across the wrist. Of the Shadows only you're that short. It's you!'

Teia'd grabbed the spine too low. He could still speak, and he was trying to crane his head to see his sister, but the helmet still blocked that from him.

'She tried to kill Gavin,' Teia whispered.

She shouldn't have said anything. Shouldn't have confirmed his suspicion that it was her.

'She was going to kill you.'

'I don't care what she did! I damned myself for her!'

Too loud. Teia shifted her grip on his spine upward, perilously close to where she might paralyze his lungs and not just his voice.

She'd never handled two spine pinches at once. Had never known she could.

'Teia, no. Teia, no,' Ironfist whimpered, but Teia held. Soon it would be too late for him to do anything.

In those long minutes, as Teia's courage faltered, she knew she should have thought of the Nuqaba's betrayal of the Seven Satrapies, how that woman turning her back on her vows cost the lives of hundreds or maybe thousands in the Blood Forest and elsewhere as the White King's armies advanced. Teia should have steeled her spine knowing that this woman had tortured and tried to murder Gavin Guile himself. She had tried to deprive Karris of her husband, and Kip of his dad.

But Teia didn't think of them. She thought of that little slave girl being ordered to remind the Nuqaba she should be whipped tomorrow morning. She thought of the thick scars all the way down to the sleeping slave's calves.

As the last spark of life fought to stay aglow in the Nuqaba's eyes, Teia whispered, 'Orholam is merciful...to the penitent. Burn in hell.'

Teia reached a finger out and held the Nuqaba's right eyelid, Mercy, closed. The left eye, the evil eye, Justice, went cold.

The woman's head lolled and sank, and she lost consciousness.

Teia stayed, though, as Ironfist wept and until the last ripples of water in the bathtub were stilled, averring that Haruru hadn't breathed for a long time. She checked; the heart had stopped.

Blood pooled on the floor, and the bathwater was stained opaque.

It was awful.

But Teia was a soldier. She was a spy and a fighter. She was a free woman and a fierce friend. She could do awful.

Now Ironfist. She'd loused up in letting him know it was she.

But she couldn't kill him. Even if he was a traitor.

She had no orders to kill Ironfist – and couldn't have killed her patron Blackguard even if she had.

'You should shout before you break free,' Teia said, not yet releasing Ironfist. 'If they find you standing over the body, they'll think you murdered her rather than that she suicided.'

He gasped a desperate, disbelieving breath, but couldn't speak.

'But take care what you shout. You're the one angry and bloody and alone in the room with her. Blathering about invisible assassins will sound crazy, and will make the guilt land on you. You shout first, Commander, and when the chief eunuch comes in you'll simply look like a bereaved brother trying to save his sister. You might even make it out of this alive.'

Chapter 63

'Tonight is the night,' the Third Eye said from behind him as he stood on the palace balcony. 'There's no way to delay it longer, my love.'

'That's not true.' Corvan Danavis looked unseeing over his fleet. He wore his dress uniform tonight, all brass buttons, battle sash, and medals, most of them given him by a man all now thought dead: Dazen Guile. His mustache had grown out to something near its former glory, gold beads adorning each side. They'd thought General Corvan Danavis dead, too.

'We've talked about this,' the Third Eye said. 'If we delay, others die as well. And in the end, it changes nothing. Someone once said, "Better to lose a scout today than a squad tomorrow or a city next week."'

'Someone' had been he, of course. He tried to grin, but it failed.

'I would sacrifice the world for another day with you,' he said. He couldn't turn and look at her, still. He didn't want to waste this precious time with weeping.

She came to stand at the railing beside him. She put her sunburnt hand over his. She said, 'Romantic...but if it were true, I never would have married you.'

' "A man may weaken," ' he said. Now he was quoting her to her. It was the problem of both of them being leaders. They both had to sling grandiose horse shit sometimes. The quote ended 'without it invalidating all he believes.'

Typical that his quote would be about giving others to death, and hers would be about extending grace to others' failures.

'I hope this one will,' she said.

He turned to look at her for the first time tonight. She wore a white silk dress with black ties drawing it snug around the body he worshipped. She was terribly sunburnt, with blisters on her skin over scars from older blisters. Her power of Seeing required sunlight on her whole body, and she'd been Seeing as much as possible for this past year, desperate to save others' lives by her own sacrifices. She'd known early on that there was no future in which she died of the skin cancers.

He saw the scars and railed against how they pained her, but they didn't dim her beauty in his eyes. The scars were only proof of her love made visible in her flesh, like a mother's stretch marks. Anyone who couldn't see beauty in them was a fool.

Nor was she self-conscious about her red and tender skin.

At thirty-nine years of age, his wife was the mistress of her body and her self. She knew her strengths and wasn't threatened by her weaknesses. She was a woman whole: able to cry or laugh or be silly or be seductive, and move from each in her own time, and move you with her. Her confidence made her far more appealing than even the few women Corvan had met in his life who might be objectively more beautiful, if such a thing as objective beauty existed.

For beauty isn't passive; beauty acts upon its beholder, moving and changing him. Line up ten paintings of different women by the same artist and ten men might agree which subject is the most beautiful. But let those men and women mingle for an evening, and duels might be fought over the same question, with no one lying in either case, and each convinced of the rightness of his judgment.

Corvan had lost two wives, but it was the loss of this third that would destroy him. The Broken Eye had sent one of its murderous Shadows for her. Something about the cloaks the assassins wore disrupted even Seers' vision. But she had been able to track her own presences and absences to figure out all the futures down which she died, though not how.

It is Orholam's will, she would say. Orholam would provide for him after she was gone, she would say.

Words strangled in his throat, he turned away from her. 'I have not your faith,' he said.

'Not like this, please,' she said, preempting him. 'Let's not spend our last night in those conversations.'

She was right. One didn't have to be a Seer to see how such talk would end with angry words and angry tears. This night was too precious.

The yellow luxin tattoo on her forehead gleamed softly, and he felt calmed.

'Using all your tricks on me again?' he said gruffly.

'Tricks? I prefer to think of them as my charms,' she said, grinning. 'And yes...before the night is over, all of them.'

The yellow eye tattoo was a cunning piece of art that seemed to be a Seers Island secret, but the real cunning of it was that the Third Eye wasn't only a yellow drafter. She was also an orange, and the Seers had no absolute prescriptions against the use of hexes.

Invisible behind the bright distraction of the gleaming yellow eye, she drew mood-changing hexes. No one could help but glance repeatedly at that yellow eye, so no one could help but be affected by the hexes there, hidden in plain sight. They'd been married before she told him of it. The Chromeria had a bad habit of executing hex casters.

'Your scouts from Blood Forest get back yet?' she asked.

He lifted his eyebrows. 'You want to spend our last night talking about the war?'

'It's your calling,' she said, as if it were simple. 'And when we talk about it, I feel I'm helping you and the world, and I feel closer to you than at any time other than when we make love.'

'I hope I wasn't presumptuous to expect—'

'That's next,' she said. 'I'm greedy. I want to be with you in every way tonight.'

It was surreal to talk so lightly about her death. But she was right. She usually was.

'A number of scouts have come back, actually,' he said. 'Piracy is rampant across the entire sea. Some new pirate queen named Pasha Mimi has got the Aborneans paying her to keep the Narrows open while they build their own fleet. She, naturally, is using the fortune they're paying her to build her own fleet. My scouts looking for the White King seizing bane all came up empty, but it's a big sea. They do report many superviolet bane storms, but it could be because so much sub-red is being used elsewhere in the world with so few superviolet drafters to balance that. The storms could be natural.'

Of course, neither of them believed that. Aliviana had become the superviolet goddess, Ferrilux.

'I'm sorry, dearest,' she said. 'You saved her life and helped her win her freedom. How she uses it...'

As if there were any meaningful choices after you bound yourself to dark forces.

'I should have raised her better. Told her more,' Corvan said. 'But...not tonight. Let's not...Not tonight.' He forced a smile and set that grief aside that he might focus on this brief blessing before it too turned to grief. 'What about Ironfist?'

'He either is or will soon be on his way to the Chromeria with a heart full of rage. For him and those who love him most, I see only sorrow now.'

Corvan fell silent. Their last night together, and he was picking at these future scabs. But he couldn't help it.

'Dazen?' he asked, hopefully. As if she wouldn't have told him right away.

'I tried again. I still couldn't See him, Corvan.'

So either he was wearing a shimmercloak all day every day, or he was hidden from her sight by some magic they'd never encountered – which was possible with the enemies he had! Possible, but not likely.

Or he was dead.

'One chance in five, you said?' For Aliviana, he meant.

'She's a Danavis. They're a tough breed.' She squeezed his hand.

There was nothing more to say on that. 'Has Kip seen the trap?' he asked.

'No. He's still marching in the wrong direction. He may save the city.'

'And lose the war. Dammit. It's like he read all my books for nothing,' Corvan said.

'Not everyone can be the best general of their time,' she said.

'By definition I suppose there can only be one.'

His wife, his daughter, his best friend, and his ward – it was as if Orholam was determined to take every light out of his life.

'I have something to ask,' the Third Eye said. 'Will you give this note to Karris?'

'Of course. What's it about?'

'Locusts,' his wife said.

He raised his eyebrows, but she said nothing as he tucked it away. She didn't always intend him to understand. 'Very well, then,' he said.

'I just left things…I was unfair to her, I think.'

'I'll tell her so,' he said. They stood for a time, watching the sunset and the sea. She made the sign of the seven, and, unbeliever though he was, he made it, too, tapping heart and eyes and hands: what you believe, what you behold, how you behave – each leading inexorably to the next.

'Now make love to me, and then go.' She smiled as if to soften the apparent command. 'You have much to do tonight elsewhere. I'll be fine until morning without you.'

And then he understood. She thought the assassin was already in the room. She was telling the Shadow that Corvan would be gone soon, that she would be alone and vulnerable, if only he would wait.

Corvan blew out a long breath, trying to get a hold of himself. She'd told him that if he tried to kill this Shadow, he would die. Period. She had told him the greatest gift he could give her this night was his total attention.

So he blocked out his rage, and his indignation that some killer was watching this private moment, and everything but his wife and his love for her.

They made love, and they shared breath and body. It was tenderness and desperation and clinging and resignation and acceptance. It was joy at what they'd had and sorrow at its brevity. It was golden heartbeats of pure unthinking pleasure pierced by iron arrows of grief.

After a long time, after all too brief a time, they held each other. She sat in his lap, arms and legs embracing him. She didn't lie down, though she was winded and sweat glistened on her skin. These were to be her last minutes. She wouldn't waste them in seeking sleep.

She touched her forehead to his, and kissed him. Then she reached one finger up to the yellow eye tattooed in luxin on her forehead. It went dark, and then frayed and disappeared.

'I have run the course set before me,' she said. 'I have finished the race.' Then she whispered in Corvan's ear, 'Polyhymnia.'

A lone tear coursed down her cheek, contrasting with the brave smile on her lips.

It was what she had laid down when she had taken up the title and duties and sacrifices of being the Third Eye: it was her name.

'Go with my love, Corvan Danavis, my Titan of the Great Fountain.'

It was an epithet he'd never heard. A glimpse into his own future, perhaps, a benediction and a farewell.

He rose, tears blinding him, and dressed in silence, strapping Harbinger on his hip, not trusting his voice, not trusting his rage. His breath came in little gasps as he struggled for control. When he looked back to her from the door, she didn't meet his eyes. She had thrown on a thin robe and sat, legs folded, hands resting in her lap, her back straight and proud.

Her face as cool and peaceful and beautiful as a statue of the saints, she faced the eastern window, praying, waiting for a sunrise she would never see.

Chapter 64

It can't be that big, was Kip's first thought as he first saw Dúnbheo in the low light. From his maps and many descriptions of it, Kip knew exactly what Dúnbheo looked like. But as with so many things in life, there's a difference between knowing and *knowing*.

Unlike most cities, there had been only a few buildings outside the walls. The population of Dúnbheo had shrunk so much over the years – and been so huge before the Chromeria's rise – that land inside the walls was cheap. The inns and food stalls that had set themselves up outside the walls for the convenience of travelers had been burnt or cannibalized for lumber and stone by the Blood Robe besiegers months ago.

It made for an odd scene: the attackers set up in a wide crescent around the walls amid the great stumps of all the trees they'd cleared, their boats anchored in a neat crescent outside the river gate, and then the vast, incomprehensible greenery of the wall itself.

Kip had seen the creation of one of the wonders of the world in Brightwater Wall, but the Greenwall surrounding

Dúnbheo was something on a completely different scale. Kip had assumed Greenwall was a screen of impressive trees in front of a wall itself. When told the trees were the wall, he'd thought there must be fortifications stretched between each tree.

That was wrong, too.

Massive sabino cypresses made towers to heaven every thirty paces, and the gaps between them were filled with millennial cypress and other trees, trunk to straining trunk, growing more thickly than should have been possible and also more closely to their neighbors. But no branches hung out into the space over the invaders. Every limb had instead grown back into the mass of the wall itself, as if guided by some chelonian intelligence to make it impregnable.

Over and through all the massive trees grew ivies and vines, further binding the trees together and clogging the spaces between them, but their leaves also gave the defenders perfect cover. An archer would part the leaves, take a shot through the makeshift murder hole, and then disappear, leaving not so much as a target.

The impression of the whole was of a green cataract as far as the eye could see, cascading in every direction as if it were the old gods' own verdant fountain. Flowers even sprouted everywhere, not deigning to accept the mortals' war going on beneath them.

In some places, the ivies had been burnt or pulled down in previous sallies, but it had done little. In fact, against the mammoth height of the tree wall, the tiny scars only made the efforts of man seem paltry and impotent.

'Time,' Ferkudi said.

In their months fighting together, Ben-hadad had fashioned clocks with deliberately weird intervals for each Nightbringer captain's superviolet drafter. Kip didn't need a clock to count out the six-minute-and-thirty-seven-second interval they were using today. Ferkudi counted it in his head. All the time. Without apparent distraction or even effort.

Sometimes Kip wanted to kiss the big dope.

He threw up a superviolet flare in the predawn gloom.

For a long time, nothing seemed to happen. Then Kip saw

the answering superviolet flare. The night mares were in place in the woods.

'Time,' Ferkudi said.

Around him, Kip saw men and women silently making the sign of the seven, preparing their immortal souls and hoping they wouldn't find out if they had immortal souls today. Here we go.

Kip gestured, and they released the fire birds. It had taken the will-casters and pyroturges a long time to figure out how to set birds on fire without actually *burning* them. But the Ghosts absolutely refused to intentionally harm the animals they partnered with. It was war, harm happened, but they did absolutely everything they could to avoid it. The fire birds went up in a broad fan in front of Kip and his lines, perfectly spaced. Their charges burnt for ten seconds, and then winked out.

Before they were all gone, four thousand throats roared, and fires went up all along Kip's lines. Narrow trenches filled with pyrejelly had been cut between each of the widely spaced lines and they lit with a satisfying whoosh in long deep streaks as if a dragon had clawed the forest itself with talons of fire.

Then each man and woman dipped their torches – two for each – into the flames. Eight thousand torches to make it look as if they had eight thousand soldiers, for Kip had ordered that even the camp followers should march behind the army to appear to be part of it. Everyone could carry a couple of torches.

The Blood Robes' officers would know the numbers were wrong, were impossible – but the men would see those supposedly impossible numbers with their own eyes.

Once a man is convinced to believe the impossible, it's impossible to make him disbelieve it.

The pagan army was spread red and black across the floodplain to Kip's sub-red vision. Only its commanders held torches. General Amrit Kamal, the Lord of the Air who led the enemy, had lined up his people in what had become a standard battle formation for the Blood Robes: centuries – each literally one hundred men – arrayed in lines. Battalions comprised of six centuries were deployed one hundred men wide and six lines deep. Between each two battalions was a century of drafters. These, being so much more rare, were deployed in four lines of twenty-four men each. But only half of each drafting platoon was made up of drafters. Each drafter was paired with a shield bearer whose main duty was defending his drafter with a massive tower shield that took both hands to hold. Each shield bearer also carried a pistol, a knife, and a bich'hwa or a punch dagger that could be mounted on the wrist without interfering with their grip. The tower shields had a spiked bottom so they could be stabbed into the ground to provide cover.

Sometimes wights led the drafter centuries, blues or super-violets or yellows predominantly. Like the greens, orange and red and sub-red wights were generally uncontrollable and were instead unleashed to fight alone where they willed.

Kip's army was facing Kamal's six battalions and six drafter centuries. Probably an elite battalion was being held in reserve back at the camp where the blurriness of sub-red vision couldn't even make it out against the darkness. So, just as reported, Kamal had more than four thousand men.

Against Kip's two thousand. But Kip had the Ghosts.

Tallach came out of the woods behind Kip, wearing his special howdah harness. Cruxer floated up into his place with that infuriating grace of his. He'd decided Kip didn't get to ride into battle alone ever again. Tallach didn't seem to even notice the additional weight.

Putting on spectacles, Kip looked a question at Tallach – 'You ready?' – and the giant grizzly woofed. He was. Kip mounted the howdah beside Cruxer, and motioned for the bonfires behind him to be lit. Then Tallach stood on his hind legs, lifting Kip and Cruxer high in the air. The bonfire behind them made a huge silhouette for the enemy to see. Then Kip threw fire into the air from his own hands, and his forces advanced.

Kip and Tallach advanced more slowly than the rest. No need to put himself at risk too early. They were supposed to be a distraction. He didn't want to arrive in musket or bow range before the battle was joined. That was the problem with arriving in battle on the back of a huge-ass bear: you made a huge-ass target.

His own soldiers were deployed in Kip's modification of General Danavis's model. The modifications had not been made because Kip thought he was an equal of the legend, but because he had an embarrassment of riches in having so many drafters. Danavis's armies had maybe one warrior-drafter for every fifty soldiers. Kip had one for every ten, and that wasn't counting the night mares.

A trumpet blew amid the enemy lines, and Kip saw the back two lines of each of Kamal's battalions peel off to march to either side of the Blood Robes' already-wide lines. They meant their wider lines to curl around Kip's lines and crush them from the sides.

It was a pretty standard maneuver when you had twice as many men as your enemy did.

So the officers hadn't been fooled. It meant the Blood Robes were sticking with their own battle plan, despite Kip's gambit with the torches.

If Kip wanted his lines to be as wide as theirs, he'd have to literally stretch his men thin and meet Kamal's four-man-deep lines with his own lines only two men deep. Their going only four deep was risky. His going two deep would be insanity.

It was a trap, but not the obvious one. No sane commander in his position would try to fight only two men deep.

Instead, a sane commander would try to punch through the Blood Robe lines, hoping to break through the four lines in a sharp move.

What else could he do? He couldn't match the width of their lines, and couldn't allow them to turn his flank, so instead he would draw his men in to hit their center hard and try to break their lines fast before the encircling maneuver killed them all.

Not today.

When his Nightbringers reached the appointed places, their commanders bellowed, and they stopped dead, as they'd planned.

Except that not all of Kip's men stopped as they'd been

commanded. Because glory is to young idiots as a mountain of poppy is to the lotus eater.

Ignoring the screams of their commanders, several dozen men tore away from Kip's lines and ran forward, screaming.

Because war is a fat whore who rolls over on her babies in the night.

'What the hell are those idiots doing?' Cruxer asked.

'Weeding themselves out of my army,' Kip said, furious.

The Turtle-Bear tattoo on his arm lighting up in angry red, Kip hurled out his signals, but now in fire: HOLD. HOLD!

The men who'd broken away ran, heedless, and all Kip could do was pray that they died quickly so that their friends didn't follow them, trying to save them.

He could sense others on the verge of breaking. Everyone knew that if they didn't follow those young fools, the fools would die.

Kip's commanders were screaming, even firing their muskets in the air to try to draw their men's eyes to them, lest they break.

Then an explosion rocked the field, and one of the charging idiots simply disappeared in fire as if he'd stood on the barrel of a musket aimed at the heavens. An instant later, another hit another of the buried charges and was flung skyward. Only half of him landed.

Not even the war dogs had smelled the charges; the Cwn y Wawr's dogs were bred to fight, and while they could smell more acutely than any man by far, their abilities were wan compared to those of the two scent hounds the will-casters had brought.

It was two hounds who would save Kip's entire army.

The charges had been buried weeks before, the smell of their luxin covered so well that they had been noticed only when the hounds' human partners reported that a certain area of ground had no scent of human passage at all. That had led their commanders – Kip hadn't even known about it until the deed was done – to scour the ground three nights in a row, dodging patrols and (unknowing at the time) the buried charges in order to discern the trap.

Kip watched the twenty men die with cold command. He

had no pity for men who were willing to trade their friends' deaths and their commanders' plans for their own glory. He watched them die in blood and fire, men screaming with blown-off feet and partial faces. Mostly he noted which charges had been exploded. He had a partial map of them, not a full one, so it was probably wasted effort, but you never knew.

One fool panicked as he saw his compatriots die. He turned and tried to run back in his own footprints. Another improbably made it through the mines and within twenty paces of the enemy lines. Somehow every shot in the first volley of at least twenty muskets had missed the man.

But two miracles was as many as a man could ask in one minute. The next volley, guns and magic both, leveled the man as he came within ten paces.

It had happened soon enough that none of their friends followed them. Thank Orholam.

The killing ground in the middle of the battlefield was limited, and the Blood Robes naturally knew exactly how far it extended. It had been their trap, hoping Kip would race into the minefield as he tried to break their lines.

Kamal's Blood Robes stopped their advance in the middle so as not to trample on their own charges, but their broad flanks extended around each side. Those continued their enveloping tactics.

Kip's drafters didn't waste any time. Those at the center of his line, knowing they were against a minefield and not soldiers, hadn't been carrying many weapons. Instead they'd been lugging slabs of luxin in pairs, green over yellow, three feet wide and five feet tall. Another crazy invention Ben-hadad's corps of engineers had come up with, a portable wall. Under musket fire, the men now stabbed the sections of the portable wall into the soil in rapid succession, from left to right, each section fitting perfectly into the next.

Meanwhile Kip's reds threw out long streams of pyrejelly, which a moment later sub-reds set fire to. The killing field was now visibly delineated for Kip's men: 'Don't go in here.'

But now the Nightbringers' flanks, which had stopped, too, faced enemy lines deeper than their own, and far wider.

They collapsed before they even came in contact with the Blood Robes.

As the Blood Robe cavalry advanced, completing its flanking maneuver, the Nightbringers' torch-carrying camp followers were revealed to be civilians, betrayed by the swelling light of the rising sun as the cavalry came nearer.

The men and women fled toward the forest, many dropping their torches.

There was now nothing between Kip's camp in the woods and the Blood Robe cavalry except fleeing civilians. The sight of those fleeing did to the cavalry what fleeing prey does to any predator. Hundreds surged forward, eager for killing and plunder. Their commanders didn't even try to stop them.

'Hold!' Kip shouted. That was the signal. With the sun nearing dawn, he'd caught sight of a broad form pulling itself out of the river behind the Blood Robes.

Tallach tossed his head and Kip sawed at the reins they'd tied to his jaws. The reins were purely for show. Kip never used reins. The immediacy of command would have actually been nice, but the bear wouldn't stand for it.

Kip shot superviolet signals out, and his men started screaming, collapsing back farther. The infantry lines were closing in on the sides, and Tallach seemed unnerved by the charging men.

'Hold, Tallach! Hold!' Kip shouted.

And the bear bolted.

Kip dropped his sword and Cruxer his spear, and they simply held on. Tallach bounded away from his army, fleeing into the forest.

He heard a cheer from the Blood Robes as they saw Kip's army lose its commander.

In between surprisingly fluid bounds, Kip saw his gambit unfolding in the forest.

They'd put the fleetest of foot at the front of the line – making the young men and women the last people to get to flee from the cavalry. They'd also armed them with grenadoes. The civilians had followed orders better than the hotheads in Kip's lines, and had run all the way to the cover of the forest before turning and throwing the grenadoes.

Some ran too slow, though, and were run down. Some panicked and didn't stop at all, forgetting their weapons and their orders, but Kip had figured that would happen. He'd armed them with grenadoes mostly to bolster the courage of those who were the bait for the trap.

Nonetheless, Kip saw a number of them turn and hurl the hand-size bombs at their pursuers. One hit a tree not two paces away from herself, and she was shredded by shrapnel. Another hit a horse and blew off its leg. Its careening body planted its rider headfirst into another tree, crunching him down to half his original height. Others missed and turned to run again.

Not far into the woods, which were significantly darker in the dawning light than the treeless floodplain, the night mares sprang their trap. First came the smoke. Charges went off with dull thuds, disorienting the charging cavalry and blocking the view of what was happening to them from their army. Wolves and panthers and mountain lions pounced from rocks and tree limbs and hidden hollows.

The civilians had their own traps, deeper, in case any of the cavalry got that far.

But Kip saw none of those. Tallach's path cut back into the forest, and then along its front edge, hopefully just out of sight of the Blood Robes on the plain.

One straggler from the cavalry was slow enough to be in their path, and Tallach elongated his bounds and slashed one huge paw as they went behind the horse. His blade-lined claws caught only the head and shoulders of the rider. Conn Arthur hated killing horses.

The horse staggered for one step, and then stood. The rider slumped and tumbled out of the saddle, his head and one arm torn completely off. Tallach had barely even broken stride.

They emerged from the woods, hundreds of paces west of where they'd entered.

The disposition of the battlefield had changed utterly in the minute or three Kip and Cruxer had been gone. As ordered, the Nightbringers had collapsed into a tight-packed square. They were surrounded on all sides by the Blood Robes, and held only because of the luxin walls they'd so hurriedly assembled.

Men deeper in the formation were reloading muskets and passing them forward again. It was perhaps the first time in military history that muskets were being used to good effect after the first shock of an infantry charge.

But the numbers were still too lopsided. They'd held out this long only because the cavalry had been drawn away.

And now the Blood Robes' reinforcement battalion was coming in. Their cavalry was lowering their lances and charging.

A signal flare went up from a wight near the killing field.

The wight had disarmed the Blood Robes' explosives. Dammit.

Kip's timing was off by just that much. Lorcan had needed to hit them thirty seconds ago.

But then he saw Lorcan. Somehow, in the screaming and their tunnel vision toward the enemies in front of them, the Blood Robes hadn't seen him yet.

The huge bear plunged into the back ranks of the infantry reinforcements running across the plain. He sank deep, deep into the heart of the infantry formation before they even saw him. They were jogging forward, the front lines already breaking into a run, so in moments it became utter chaos.

Men shrieking in fear, Lorcan roaring, and metal rending with every swipe of his big paws. Men were hurled bodily into the air. Commanders shouted unheard over the melee.

Meanwhile the charging cavalry hurtled across the killing ground. Not a single charge went off. But that side of the square was ready for them. A cloud of black smoke was vomited out into the air, streaked with green and golden lights and lit from within by streams of liquid fire.

The first rank of the cavalry didn't even make it to the Nightbringers' line, obliterated by hot lead and magic, and the second rank was appreciably thinned. The third rank hurtled past them and the fourth and fifth had to leap over the fallen.

But many made it through. They crashed into the luxin wall, lances extended.

They'd expected a shield wall, though, not an actual wall. Each section was not only physically linked to the others on each side, but also braced against the force of their charge with long diagonal supports.

Some few sections buckled, but most held.

Men flipped off horses brought to a dead halt, and toppled into the square, where the Nightbringers waited with axes and daggers.

Three red wights riding in the fourth rank of the cavalry leapt off their horses as they crashed into the mass of their friends and foes. Tumbling through the air, they blasted through the petty attempts to swat them aside – Kip had set the fastest drafters to knock grenadoes out of the air.

When the wights landed, they hurled death in every direction. But each wight was quickly brought down.

The last ranks of cavalry broke off the charge, seeing they'd only cripple and kill their own.

But that was when Kip and Tallach entered the fray.

They hit the cavalry from the rear quarter.

The men turned to see that their own infantry, which was supposed to support them, had melted behind them instead – and two giant grizzlies were tearing them apart. The other battalions' cavalry had gone into the woods and not re-appeared.

It was too many shocks at once for men trapped between a wall and a giant grizzly ridden by a man throwing fire down on their heads. Panic spread faster than the flames.

They broke in every direction.

Tallach gave a few more swipes at those nearest him, then halted at Kip's signal, and, as quickly as it had begun, Kip's fight was over. Now he was a general again. He began throwing flaming signals at once.

The tight square unfolded, pursuing the Blood Robes. Most of them headed toward the forest, where the night mares awaited. A few were headed too far east or west, but Kip's men drove them as sheepdogs drive sheep: a little barking here, a little nipping at the heels there, and they turned back to where Kip wanted them, like mindless animals.

The other Blood Robes ran toward their own camp and the walls. Kip sent more than half his forces after those, under Derwyn Aleph. He knew what to do.

Lorcan was deep in their camp. It wasn't where Kip wanted him, but he was beyond orders now.

Kip only hoped that in its rage, the great bear wouldn't kill any Nightbringers.

He started toward the city walls himself, and the actual horses and ponies of the night mares fell in with him.

A rout had started from the Blood Robes' camp. General Kamal's staff, his bodyguards, their servants and families – these were the people who could see the noose dropping over their necks. They knew that if they got trapped against the river, they'd not stand a chance.

So they ran the other way. If they could make it past the hulking form of Greenwall and its archers, they could escape.

It became a race, Kip and the night mares trying to head them off before they cleared the walls.

But within half a minute, it became clear it wouldn't be much of a contest. The archers lining the walls rained down shots on the fleeing Blood Robes, mostly missing, but killing a few and injuring more, slowing those who stopped to help them. The line elongated and separated completely.

Those with horses abandoned the others.

But Dúnbheo was vast, and Kip and the Mighty had the angle. They reached it a hundred paces before the end of the wall.

Now if those idiots up on the wall can just not shoot us.

It was a thought without rancor. Men long bored and suddenly excited who held weapons in their hands could get careless with whom they pointed them at.

On reaching the wall, Tallach wheeled and stood on his hind legs. He roared fury.

Tallach didn't want to be here. He wanted to be with his brother. Musket fire and explosions from the camp – and the lack of Lorcan's reappearance – didn't bode well for how Conn Arthur's brother was doing.

'Halt, halt!' the man mounted at the lead shouted to his bodyguards.

'Man' might have been generous. He was a blue wight, dressed in gaudy gold robes, skin sparkling with facets like snake scales.

'Lord Guile! Lord Kip Guile!' the wight shouted, holding his hand up.

Tallach dropped back to all fours and roared again. The Mighty thundered in to surround Kip even as Lord Kamal's own bodyguards surrounded him in a sudden flood.

'Lord Guile! I, Amrit Kamal, Lord of the Air, do challenge you to a duel!'

His men were hurriedly reloading muskets they'd discharged in the fighting.

'Yeah. No,' Kip said.

The Mighty fired their muskets immediately, perforating the Lord of the Air in as many places as possible. Waves of fire and missiles followed before Lord Kamal's bodyguards could counterattack.

That was enough for everyone else behind Lord Kamal. They doubled back and, fleeing, made easy prey for the Mighty. The Mighty hadn't been able to do much fighting in this battle, and they were eager to make up for lost time.

Chapter 65

'This, finally, is a cruelty beyond me,' Andross Guile said. 'You deserve it, but this is beyond what I am willing to do. You can't be released, and I won't punish you any longer. How do you wish to die?'

Gavin had felt a change in the air. It could mean only one thing. His cell opening.

He hadn't spoken to the dead man in days. Didn't want those cold comforts. And the days or weeks had blended together. Another thunk of bread falling, another slice of crust against black luxin. Another sleep. Nightmares passed to hallucinations, like paired dancers spinning a gciorcal. Gavin had no energy, couldn't plan, couldn't concentrate. The isolation was driving him slowly mad.

But now he could hear his father breathing. From old habit, Gavin looked in sub-red, and he could see the man so brightly (though in white tones rather than red) it almost blinded him. Gavin looked down, blinking.

He didn't want to laugh – it would seem proof of his insanity – but he couldn't help it. His father's words were an exact echo of his own thoughts, again, regarding his brother: You're too dangerous to release, so I'll imprison you. Your imprisonment is too cruel, so I must kill you.

His father had arrived at the logical conclusion much faster than he had, though. Give him that.

'Fuck him,' the dead man said. It was the first time he'd spoken in a while.

Gavin said, 'I've murdered hundreds. Maybe thousands. I don't know if there is an appropriate method of execution for me.'

'I was thinking starvation. Or poison. I can't imagine I'll ever have to use this cell again, so either would serve. I could simply leave you here to rot.'

As I did my brother. Or didn't.

Could you be guilty of things you thought you were letting continue but really weren't?

Andross said, 'I'm going to make a light. I would see your face one last time. Don't humiliate yourself and embarrass me again by trying anything.'

The dead man said, 'Listen to me. You can escape. This is your chance.'

A moment later, light bloomed. Gavin squinted against the glare, but the light itself didn't command his attention. First, eyes averted from the lantern his father produced, he saw the black luxin. There was barely any reflection off that eerie black. The light that touched it simply died. He cast no secondary shadow from refracted light, and his primary shadow was barely visible, greater darkness against darkness.

Then, pupils constricting, he turned to his father.

'This was a mistake,' Andross Guile said. 'I don't want to remember you like this, this hideous ghost of what you once were.'

'Too late now, isn't it? I got my memory from you, after all. You don't forget, either,' Gavin said.

'I suppose not,' Andross said.

'If you were simply going to put me down like a mad dog, you'd have done it without this much bother,' Gavin said. 'You came down to say something.'

Andross smirked, but only for a moment. 'I suppose I haven't dealt with madmen enough. Losing your wits doesn't mean losing your wit, eh?'

The dead man grew more insistent. 'Why aren't you listening to me? Are you frightened, Gavin? Gavin Guile? Frightened?'

'Frightened only of what I might do,' Gavin said below his breath.

'What's that?' his father asked.

Louder, as if merely repeating himself, Gavin said, 'I'll take that as a compliment.'

'How soon did your mother know?' Andross asked. He meant after Sundered Rock.

'Instantly.'

Andross cursed. 'Of course she did.'

'*Gavin,*' the dead man whispered, 'you have a way out.'

'When did you figure it out, then?' Gavin asked.

Andross said, 'On the seventh year from the real Gavin's ascension. We had figured out that you – the victor of Sundered Rock – had drafted black luxin, of course. I chalked up all the changes in you to that, and to killing your brother. Would have shaken anyone. But then you never even *asked* about doing the ceremony again. I didn't believe that you could have forgotten that.'

'The Prism ceremony?'

Andross waved it away. He wasn't interested in explaining. 'And then, once I could accept that you'd fooled me, it all became obvious. Audacious, though. You played it perhaps as well as it could have been played.'

'Mother coached me.'

'Of course she did.'

'And when you figured it out, there was nothing for you to do but go along with it,' Gavin guessed.

Andross turned his palms up in a small surrender. 'Gavin was dead and others believed you were he, so what could be done? I could mourn him. I could make you pay, but what would that accomplish?'

As if you *didn't* make me pay.

'We have a way out,' the dead man said.

'I'm sorry, Father.'

Andross Guile looked at Gavin as if he were suddenly speaking in some foreign tongue. 'We'll pretend you didn't say that. I came here for one reason.' He stopped, shook his head. 'No, what am I doing here?'

He's lonely.

The thought tore through Gavin. For some reason, looking at this monster, Gavin felt a sudden unwonted compassion.

He's *lonely*. Mother left him. His sons are dead. He's recovered his health and vitality, but it is nothing to him. His last son insane, and even Kip has fled.

'Let's play a game,' Gavin said.

'A game?' Andross asked skeptically.

'You always loved games. You and your Nine Kings. You can't tell me that you haven't missed matching wits with me. Witless as I may be.' Gavin grinned.

'What kind of game?' Andross asked, suspicious but obviously intrigued.

'Gavin!' the dead man said. 'You don't need to put yourself at his mercy. Andross Guile's mercy. Andross. Guile's. Mercy.'

Gavin said, 'You tell me about some of the problems facing you, and I try to guess what you're doing about them. Of course, you have to give me enough relevant information to give me a chance. We'll call the game, Which Guile Rules the Seven Satrapies Better?'

'There are several weaknesses to this game,' Andross said.

'There are weaknesses to every game,' Gavin countered.

Andross obviously missed sparring. He didn't think too long before saying, 'To clarify: in the game, you're guessing what I have done, or will do, not what *you* would do in my place? After all, we have...somewhat different strengths.'

'Exactly,' Gavin said. Anything to keep from going insane. Anything to give himself more chances. Anything to make him valuable to the old man might give him an opening.

Growing more irritated, the dead man said, 'You don't need to do all this.'

'I can play this game,' Andross said. 'You know who the White King is?'

'Koios White Oak, unhappily back from the grave.'

'And you know what he is?' Andross asked.

Gavin stared at him blankly, not sure what his father was asking. 'A polychrome? A man remade with incarnitive luxins?'

Andross sighed. 'Are you playing dumb, or did you cut yourself so deeply?'

'I don't know what you mean,' Gavin said. This was not starting well.

Andross sighed. 'I was hoping you might be useful, in this one thing at least.' He waited, apparently to see if he'd called Gavin's bluff about being ignorant. Then, nonplussed, he said, 'You are not the only man alive who can draft black luxin. Merely the only one on the Chromeria's side.'

'Koios is a black drafter,' Gavin said as it dawned on him. Of course.

'He's taken your old path to power. Except, of course, he doesn't glean his powers from already dying drafters and wights.'

My old path to power? 'So you think I'm the Black Prism, too?'

'Too?' Andross frowned. 'You didn't tell Karris about this.'

'No. Orholam, no. I didn't even remember any of it then. I...' It cut him to think about her. It was impossible. Hopeless.

'Then who else calls you that?' Andross asked.

'Never mind that.' Telling his father about the dead men was a sure way to cut this conversation short. His father would think him mad in truth.

Andross looked amused to have this imprisoned wretch tell him what to do, but he let it go. 'I more thought of you as a light-splitting black drafter. If you want a more grandiose title, I suppose the Black Prism fits.'

'Are you sure?' Gavin asked.

'Whatever do you mean?'

'About me. I don't...I don't remember any of that. I didn't seek out people to kill them for their magic. It wasn't like that. Was it?' Gavin said.

He thought he'd done all that to save people. That he'd put

himself in harm's way for the satrapies. That he'd been at least a little...good.

'You really have forgotten it all, haven't you?' Andross said. 'What's the alternative? That you're Lucidonius come again? You're the Lightbringer?'

'Mother said I was a true Prism...'

'Your mother loved you very, very much. But you were her last child, and you were a blind spot for her.'

There was something odd in how he'd said that. Irony aside, though: Gavin was *Felia* Guile's blind spot? Go to hell, Father.

'*Her* last child?' Gavin asked.

A pause. Then Andross said, 'Not witless, indeed. There is still some spark of you left in that shell, isn't there? Well, I had planned to tell you eventually. No time like at your end, I suppose. Do you remember that prophecy? The day the Mirror Janus Borig told you that you would draft black luxin? She told me, "Of red cunning, the youngest son, cleaves father and father and father and son." You remember?'

'I remember.'

'There was this librarian. She had access to some documents we needed. With your mother's permission, I seduced her. Naturally, I was careful. She shouldn't have gotten pregnant. She swore she'd take the tea to abort it if necessary. She lied. Showed up in our camp pregnant and with demands. Your brother didn't take it well. She fled.'

There were so many things wrong with what he'd just said that Gavin couldn't even begin to parse them. Andross had cheated on mother? And what pathetic lie was this that she'd approved of it? She would never do that!

'What documents would be worth such a thing?'

'It doesn't matter now.'

'You're certain the girl wasn't lying?'

'I presumed she was lying, of course. But over the course of time, I've become sure she wasn't.'

Gavin was incredulous. 'Are you telling me I have a *brother* out there?'

'When she sent you your note, she sent me one, too.'

'Sent me a note? I never got a note – You can't mean – Lina?!'

Andross said, 'She took the name Katalina Delauria when she fled, apparently. Lina. Kip isn't your brother's son. He's mine.'

Out of all the things that should have leapt to Gavin's mind, what he thought first was how odd it had been that when his mother had come to Garriston for her Freeing, she hadn't tried to meet Kip. Hadn't so much as inquired after her only grandson.

Because she knew. She knew Kip wasn't her grandson. She knew he was Andross's bastard, and she had no interest in having that rubbed in her face.

Dear Orholam. Kip.

The funny thing was, it didn't really matter, did it?

Instead of being the boy's uncle and pretending to be his father, he was actually his half brother, acting as his father.

If anything, that should make things *easier*, shouldn't it? It wouldn't be, 'I'm not your father, and by the way, I killed your real father and took his place.' Now it would be, 'I'm your half brother.' Full stop. Kip already knew that the Gavin who was still alive had killed his own brother. Without the weight of being the real Gavin's own son, Kip would be freed of a son's burden to avenge his dead father.

But then, it didn't matter regardless. Gavin was here. He was going to die in this black cell.

'This doesn't have to happen,' the dead man said.

'Are you going to tell Kip?' Gavin asked.

'Someday. Maybe. It's a card I'll keep for the right moment. Maybe if he gets too sanctimonious with me. It'll be fun to see the look on his face.'

'Why'd you tell me?' Gavin asked.

'I thought you deserved to know. You seem fond of the boy. I wanted you to know I'll look out for him.'

Gavin could tell that his father was drawing this to a close. Not just for now. Andross wouldn't be coming back.

'Draft black,' the dead man hissed. 'Kill him.'

'Look out for him?' Gavin said. 'You've tried to kill him twice!'

'The assassin was when I still thought Lina was lying, and I was hoping to hide Kip's existence from your mother. As for

476

a second time – you're counting when he attacked me on the ship after the Battle of Ru? He was trying to kill *me*, if you recall. I was only defending myself, and I was in the grip of red. Speaking of which, where's the knife now?'

'I haven't seen it since I jumped...' Gavin started laughing quietly. 'You *asshole.*'

'Pardon?'

'This was your plan all along, wasn't it? This whole conversation. Give me so many things to think about that I'd slip up. Orholam's balls, Father. If you wanted to know where the knife was, why didn't you just ask?'

Andross didn't deny anything. 'I have an island, off Melos. Small house there. Excellent though small library, including many forbidden books. Stocked with enough provisions for you to stay there for years. Impossible to approach if you don't have the chart, though. Terrible reefs. You go into exile there. I'll even let you take a couple of slaves. But you never leave, and you never try to send a letter out. You're dead to the world, you understand?'

'And in return, I give you the Blinding Knife?'

'You really have no idea what it is, do you? We can't make Prisms without it, son. The Seven Satrapies will dissolve. The False Prism's War will look like a village fair compared to what comes next.'

'You can balance manually, by dictate. It's been done before. The satrapies can stand.'

'We're already doing that. It's failing. We don't have enough people obeying to make up for those who don't. What happens when half the satrapies are pagan? When you're a blue drafter and a firestorm lays low your village because the Chromeria's suggestions are ignored, will you obey their call next year to stop drafting blue so that those sub-red bastards who killed your family will be safe?'

'Maybe the Chromeria deserves to fall,' Gavin said.

'Oh, most certainly. Our regime is the absolute worst way to rule, except for all the others that have been tried. The Chromeria is an idea, son, and if it's exposed as a hollow one, civilization falls. Not only to magic, but to the cycle of retribution and the Nine Kings. Drafters reviled by their own families if they happen to be born to draft the wrong color, drafters moving to a satrapy where they can be strong. Kings trying to stop them or killing them to keep them from going. Tyrants. One king after another rising as his people's magic waxes, rampaging across the kingdoms that have wronged them, massacring drafters of other colors. The terrible magic storms and plagues. The collapse of that king as his color's magic fails, and then the rise of his neighbors, doing the same, and wreaking vengeance on his people in turn. That's the alternative. For thousands of years that's what was. That's what we stand against.'

'He's not going to let you out,' the dead man said. 'Once you give him what he wants, he'll kill you.'

It was probably true. Would Andross really let Gavin go? Would he trust that he could smuggle Gavin away from the Chromeria itself? What if the smuggling failed? Would he put himself at risk that way?

If he gave his word, he would. Andross Guile was scrupulous about keeping his promises.

'Then I'm not the one who's insane,' Gavin said. 'All this? You mean the entire fate of the Seven Satrapies rests on one stupid knife?'

'If the White King wins, it'll be a moot point, but long term, if the satrapies are to survive, yes. We must find it.'

'There's only one? Can't you make another? I mean, who made it in the first place?'

'The luxiats have stood in the way of previous attempts to make another. It's a holy relic. Maybe Lucidonius made it. Maybe Karris Atiriel. Maybe the one we know was a much later replica. But the luxiats' grandstanding doesn't matter. There's a key ingredient in the Blinder's Knife that is extinct.'

Of course.

'White luxin,' Gavin said. He cursed. The dead man was a liar – or at least wrong.

'Indeed. The stories say that before Vician's Sin, things were different. Drafters of white luxin were born every generation. A piece like the Blinder's Knife was a stunning achievement, but not unique. In the intervening centuries, all of the others have been lost.'

'So if you could find even one white drafter or find one

piece of white luxin from an earlier era, you could make a new knife? So surely you have such a knife somewhere, just waiting for a bit of white luxin?'

'No,' Andross admitted. 'It was tried. There's a level of unity of will that couldn't be achieved by any team, not even one trying to save the world. A blinding knife has to be created by one person. He or she has to be a full-spectrum polychrome and a superchromat to handle the intricacies of balancing that kind of magic.'

'You mean a person like me.'

'Now you understand,' Andross said.

'So that's the real reason you didn't expose me, didn't kill me. You kept me alive just so I could make you a new knife!' Of course there had been another reason, and one tied to Andross Guile's own well-being. 'But you never so much as hinted about this.'

'I criticized your brute-force drafting,' Andross said. 'I hoped it would inspire you to learn more delicate work.'

'You asshole!'

'I thought we had at least another five years to get things in place.'

'Why not just tell me?' Gavin asked, though he should have known better.

'If I told you we absolutely needed you to craft an instrument which would allow you to be replaced, you would know that until you crafted it, you could do anything you pleased, anything at all, and we would not only not be able to oppose you, we would have to help and protect you. Even Orea agreed we had to keep that knowledge from you. And of course, this was all speculative anyway, contingent on us rediscovering white luxin – and you being able to draft it if we did. But even the hope of such a thing would have put tremendous power in your hands, if you'd known about it.'

It was like being punched in the stomach after already having had the wind knocked out of you. Gavin had been so consumed with keeping his own secrets that he had never pried into theirs. He hadn't noticed that they'd also avoided talking about the Prism ceremony, because he'd been so terrified of their discovering his ignorance.

He'd been like a wayward youth, sneaking out late and getting drunk, thinking his parents must never know, thinking them fools who had never been young themselves, while they watched it all and hoped he grew up sooner rather than later.

But there was some puerile protest left in him. 'If the knife was so important, why did you bring it to war against me? It makes no sense. Why would the High Luxiats allow you to endanger it like that?'

'Gavin was made promachos. They couldn't refuse him.'

'You mean they couldn't refuse you, armed with a promachos,' Gavin shot back.

Andross tipped his head and shrugged, acknowledging the compliment and the truth of it.

'That doesn't answer why. Why would you take it out there? You were going to kill me with it?'

Andross Guile sighed. His piercing gaze rested heavy on Gavin. 'We were going to try to save you.'

'Save me?'

'I was becoming an authority on black luxin. Your mother and I started secretly studying it as soon as Janus Borig told us that you would become a black drafter. Fascinating stuff, about which the world is clogged with superstition and misinformation. But this isn't the time for a lecture.

'In sum, your mother and I hoped that if we stabbed you – of all people – if we stabbed a black drafter with the Blinder's Knife, that you would survive it. Probably you would survive bereft of your powers, true, but if you can save a mad dog, you don't mourn that you have to break its fangs to do so.'

Gavin felt sick. It was exactly what had happened when he'd been stabbed with the knife. It had taken his colors. It had also taken his color vision – Blinder's Knife indeed. But it had left him *alive*. Somehow, the knife had separated his powers from his life. His parents' hopes and their research had borne fruit – only too late for him, too late for them, and too late for the satrapies.

'The knife doesn't take away the black, though,' the dead man said, breaking his silence. 'Nothing can take away black luxin from you. The abyss lives in you.'

If Gavin believed his father, and his own will-cast reflections, his own past self and the evidence in front of his own eyes, he had been on the wrong side all along.

The Prisms' War really had been the False Prism's War.

It had been his fault, utterly. All of it. From the massacre of the White Oak family to the Battle of Blood Ridge to the burning of Garriston to the coming fall of the Seven Satrapies.

He hadn't been caught up in his brother's and father's schemes to purge the Seven Satrapies of their enemies. He wasn't the victim. He'd cast himself as the aggrieved party, but of what had he been the victim? Being a younger brother?

The real Gavin had been no saint, either, sure. In fact, maybe he'd been a villain, too. But he'd tried to save Dazen.

For all his flaws – and there had been many – his big brother had tried to save Dazen.

And in return, Dazen had killed him and broken the empire.

'You see what the old man's doing,' the dead man said. 'Don't you? He's steeling himself to kill you. Or at least to abandon you here and never come back until you die. He's saying farewell.'

Andross said, 'All this devastation, caused by one bitter librarian who seduced your brother in a vain attempt at revenge on me, and then stole the knife while he slept. That was why I wasn't at Sundered Rock. I was going after her and the knife. I'd heard she had people in Blood Forest. Never guessed she'd double back to Tyrea. Smart, going back to the very center of the devastation. I never figured she'd be that canny, or that a woman with a treasure literally worth all the gold in the Seven Satrapies would keep it in a closet in a shack. Never figured you'd stab yourself with the knife and then jump in the sea, either.'

'Lot of inconvenient surprises for all of us in this,' Gavin said sarcastically.

Andross waved it away. He wasn't interested in revisiting that. 'Tell me, at Sundered Rock, if Gavin had held the Blinder's Knife, would he have had a chance to use it on you?'

'Yes,' Gavin said.

'Don't you see?' the dead man whispered. 'He's getting all his last questions answered. This is the end, Gavin.'

'That bitch.' Andross sighed. He was preparing to go.

'Damn you!' the dead man said. 'Draft black! Kill him! Let your hatred make you strong for once!'

'Poison, I think,' Andross said. 'Starvation is easier for me, but only in the short term. I should regret it later, I think, if I weren't as humane as possible.'

'I don't believe you,' Gavin said. 'What about our game?'

Andross just shook his head.

'You don't have any equals,' Gavin insisted. 'You don't have anyone to talk to. You're not going to kill me. You're too lonely.'

Andross said, 'Goodbye, son.' He picked up his lantern.

'You cretin!' the dead man said. 'You worm. You spineless ʊ ʌ ʃ ʔ ʌ ʃ ! *Raka!* We can get out!'

'Father, tell me you'll come visit.' Gavin was barely hanging on. He couldn't bear the darkness again.

Andross hesitated. 'No, Dazen. It hurts too much. No games. The poison will be in your next meal. And in every meal until you eat and die.'

'Draft black! Kill him!' And suddenly, the dead man's voice took on cavernous depths and thunderous tones that reverberated into realms beyond human ken. 'I won't be imprisoned forever!'

'I REFUSE! *NON SERVIAM!*' Gavin roared at the wall, and the darkness, but his shout was as much fear as it was defiance.

His father looked at him, shouting at a wall like a madman. There was a tremendous sadness and resignation on his face. He folded his arms. 'You know…for a moment this conversation…It was almost enough to make me forget…'

No. Orholam, no.

Andross said, 'There's one last thing I wanted to tell you, though. Did you ever wonder why I picked your older brother to be the Prism and not you?'

Still recovering from his terror and confusion – had the dead man said *he* wouldn't be imprisoned? as if they were separate? – Gavin said, 'He was the eldest. You needed to make someone Prism immediately.'

'Triply wrong. First, I'm a younger brother myself; you think I care about primogeniture? Second, I had all the time

I needed – and third, that isn't why you believed I picked him, anyway, was it?'

Gavin swallowed, and said quietly, 'Because he was your favorite. Because he was like you.'

'Half-wrong.'

The dead man whispered now, his voice low, gravelly, menacing, 'Do you want to be in here with me forever? I won't make it pleasant.'

'Which half?' Gavin asked. 'No one is like you?' Arrogant old cancer. He was right about that, but that only made him worse.

Andross said, 'I fell in love with Felia, not some woman who was a mirror of me. Of course I searched her out for her pedigree, for her family's lineage of drafters, for their intelligence and hers. Those were all prerequisites. I wanted to pass on the best breeding to my sons and daughters that I could. I felt I owed it to you to give you a mother as excellent as your father is, not just some beauty or heiress or noblewoman. But there were other possibilities.

'However, it was your mother I fell in love with, because I realized she had strengths where I had weaknesses. She had not just a mind, but also a heart. She had wisdom, and discernment, but she also had compassion. I did not. Do not.

'Your brother Gavin was more like me than even I am. He was hard and cold and egocentric. Charismatic, too. Better looking than you, a little. But with no sense of others. Like a baby who forgets you exist when you play hide-and-peek and is surprised each time when you reappear, Gavin forgot to care about people unless they were directly in front of him. Everyone around him thought they were the center of his world whilst they were around him, but as soon as they walked away – usually having given him what he wanted – he forgot about their concerns. About his promises to them. I chose Gavin to become the Prism, Dazen, because he was very good at getting what we needed. But I also chose him for another and far more important reason.'

'And what's that?' Gavin asked bitterly.

'Because usually, after seven years, the Prism dies.'

'What?' Gavin breathed.

'By choosing your brother, I was consigning him to death, so I swore I would spend as much of his last seven years with him as possible. Dazen, I chose him to die because you were my favorite. You always were.'

'You're lying.' Gavin's knees weakened, and he crumpled to the floor.

'You had all the strengths of your mother, and most of mine. You were the me I would have chosen to be.'

'You ignored me. You despised me.'

'Your brother was dangerous. He needed me if he was to have any chance of becoming a moral leader or even a decent human being. You, on the other hand, were destined to be upright. You erred, but you were always the son who ended up doing the right thing...had not the madness taken you. Had I understood what black luxin would do to you, I would have done everything differently. Perhaps I would have chosen you to be Prism first, and let you die young and pure, before this madness took you. I did the best I could with what I knew.'

'I hate you,' Gavin said.

'And I loved you, Dazen. And you betrayed me. Hiding your identity *from me*? For all those years? Every day was a twist of the knife, another ingratitude heaped on the rest. Another day of spitting on my sacrifices. But I was right about you. You're useless, broken, worthless, and used up now, but for a long time, you were magnificent. You were the greatest Prism this world has known.'

'Strike him down. It's our last chance,' the dead man begged.

Gavin's breaths came like little fires into his lungs. The black luxin was right there, burning molten under his fingertips. He could use it now. Surely it was safe to use a little. Even if he lost a little piece of himself, what was losing a few memories against losing his very life?

Andross lifted the lantern and stared at Gavin as he readied himself to go.

'You can still draft black luxin, can't you?' Andross asked.

'Yes,' Gavin hissed. It was so close.

'Kill him! *Kill him!*' the dead man screamed.

'And yet you haven't,' Andross said.

Surely next there would be some gibe about Gavin's weakness, his lack of will. All of Gavin's hatred and fear and the long years of resentment against his father raced to his fingertips, but they were outrun by pity. A man who has strength but no love is worse than dead.

Andross Guile shook his head, astounded. Each word clear and slow, he said, 'Imprisoned. Dying. Furious. And yet you won't use the black. Not even against *me*.'

'This is *death*. His or yours,' the dead man said.

'You see?' Andross Guile said with a sad little quirk toward a grin. 'I was right about you.'

The lantern snicked shut, and Gavin was plunged into the final darkness.

Chapter 66

By the time Tallach and Kip made it to the Blood Robe camp, the battle was virtually over. But battles don't end at all the way Kip had once imagined. He'd thought battles ended all at once: there's a winner, the losers run away, and the winners pick the corpses clean of loot.

It wasn't like that. This battle was over. The day had been won. But there was still a lot of killing and dying to do. There were even heroics.

Kip could see that a Blood Robe soldier with a spinning spear was facing off against a dozen of the Nightbringers, and had them down to a stalemate. The bodies of four of their comrades lay on the ground, two still, and two still writhing.

Kip gestured, and Ben-hadad rode over to take care of it. Ben-hadad lofted the double crossbow he'd designed. It was a fearsome weapon. The bows were made of scrimshawed sharana ru: sea demon bone.

Aside from its scarcity, sea demon bone was hard to work with because will was necessary to its use, and will itself was so variable, so bows made entirely of the stuff were impossibly inaccurate. The bows that did use it, like Winsen's, used it as one compound of several, and used will only to make it easier to string the bow, not during drawing or firing. At the same time, using a crossbow from horseback was usually stupid because drawing the string required either a crank, or a lot of strength and a stirrup: a crank was slow, and bracing a stirrup against the ground to draw was incompatible with riding.

Ben-hadad had surmounted both difficulties by bringing them together. His will softened the sea demon bone bow while he drew the bolts back. For the next step, he'd designed a pressure gauge. Using his will, he tightened the bow until the gauges turned blue. With this, he could shoot ten to fifteen bolts in a minute, and he thought he would get better with practice.

Winsen had scoffed at such speed, until Ben-hadad pointed the loaded crossbow at him. In a blink, Winsen nocked and drew an arrow, pointing it at Ben-hadad's forehead.

One didn't want to get in an insanity fight with Winsen.

But Ben-hadad merely stared at him, unblinking. The moment stretched.

Winsen's arm started trembling from holding the incredible tension. Then his whole back and shoulders shook from the pressure of holding the arrow drawn. Winsen wasn't tall, but his bow, of which he was a master, required incredible draw strength.

Then Winsen lowered the bow to let out the tension with a grunt. 'Point made,' he said. 'I suppose there are times a crossbow could be handy.' Then he grinned at Ben-hadad.

'You can call her Grace,' Ben-hadad said.

'Grace?' Kip had asked. 'Why not the Mighty Thruster?'

'You all are never going to let that go, are you?' Ben-hadad said.

'Never,' they said in a chorus.

But this day, Ben-hadad offered Grace to the heroic Blood Robe surrounded by the dead and wounded and impossible odds – offered it by pointing it at his face and speaking first. 'Put down the spear, and live a slave,' Ben-hadad said. 'Or hold it and die. You have a count of five. Four. Three. Two.'

The man screamed and charged. 'Light cannot be—'

Ben-hadad's heavy bolt punched through his armor and he pitched facedown.

One of the Nightbringers behind him in the circle went white as a sheet and grabbed his groin.

Ben-hadad cursed. 'You thought it would be a good idea to stand directly behind a man attacking me? Nine hells, man!'

But the man didn't crumple as a wounded man would. Instead he pulled at his tunic and trousers, and found a hole. He let out a little uncertain laugh. 'Shaved my balls!'

His friends laughed. Ben-hadad just shook his head. 'Be happy I didn't use the fire bolt.'

He left them to their japes. War is absurd. Those men had lost friends in the last five minutes, and yet had forgotten it for a moment: woodsmen and farm boys once again, joking now about whether their friend's balls had dropped.

And everywhere it was similar. People were playing out what were possibly the last moments of their lives as if they didn't even matter. A woman darted past one of the mundane warrior Nightbringers under Antonius Malargos's command. The warrior was smeared with blood, and he'd just sprinted across the fields to get to this chaos, death all around. His bloodlust was running high. She surprised him as she burst out of that tent. Did he slash?

Her life would be changed or ended in a decision that wasn't made in his head but in his arm – or perhaps it was a decision that had been made in his heart in the months and weeks before this day. And he would be changed forever by this fraction of a second.

He would know himself to be the kind of man who murdered unarmed women, or the kind of man who hesitated where others did not.

He hesitated – and two souls were saved.

But everywhere it was the same. As if something in the human heart longs for chaos and finality, however violent.

The dregs of the Blood Robe army and its camp followers had been pushed into the river, and were still being pushed as Kip and his men approached.

The once-pristine water ran brown and red, churned mud and men returning to mud. The bank was so clogged with bodies you couldn't see the ground for a hundred paces. Many men can't swim, and almost none can when you strap half again their weight in armor to their bodies. Most of them had realized it when they reached the riverbank. But others panicking behind them had pushed, pushed relentlessly.

They'd shoved and stabbed and slashed and trampled each other.

And the Nightbringers had fallen on them pitilessly – desperate for vengeance on all these men who'd tried to kill them, who'd taken their homes and livestock and neighbors, who'd killed and pillaged and despoiled their hard and happy lives. Kip's army fell on all these men, most of whom had thrown away their own weapons in order to run away faster, only to find no escape. All these men – but not men only.

The camp followers were huddled here, too: the crippled and sick and old and the traders and the merchants and the wives and lovers and their children and all who hope to live on the leavings an army produces.

It is impossible to spare the innocent and the partly innocent hidden at the back of the mob when you're pushing the whole damned lot into the river, stabbing and trampling any who resist. Hard to spare them, even if you're trying. Kip wasn't sure most of his men were trying.

Some of the camp followers, not weighed down by armor or greedily hanging on to goods, would escape by swimming. But many had drowned already. It was only Kip's arrival and a massive roar from Tallach that brought a relative quiet.

Finally Kip's officers could make themselves be heard and obeyed. With a few moments to breathe and think, the survivors surrendered and Kip's men left off their killing.

The survivors were seized and enslaved.

The Blood Robes and their followers looked no different from much of Kip's army, and Kip's men had a cast to their faces that said they'd be damned if any of these captives slunk away in the night and turned up at their fires later, claiming to have been on their side all along. So they notched their ears immediately, here, over the bodies of their comrades.

Smiths would later cauterize the flesh. Notches first.

The Nightbringers would leave the slaves here, give or sell

them to the people of Dúnbheo. Otherwise, the captured would slow down Kip's army, and serve it poorly. They would gladly become spies against their new masters.

But the Nightbringers wouldn't be able to get rid of all of them. There were exceptions; there always were. One of Kip's men would come forward. He had four children. His wife had been killed by the pagans. His extended family killed. He needed a new wife if he was to keep fighting, would take a slave if she hadn't been roughed up too much.

There was no saying no to that, not without Kip's alienating his own people. You could ask a man to die, but when he bared his heart to you, you couldn't deny him what he and his fellows saw as justice.

As the dawn yields to day, one exception gave rise to others. One attempt at justice gave a hundred excuses for injustice. Other men need wives, too, sure, milord!

Forbidding the rape of captured women had taken a number of hangings to enforce – those hangings had raised eyebrows, too, letting Kip know he was treading a dangerous line. It had come down to explaining that they weren't being hanged for raping slaves, but for disobeying a direct order. That made sense to the men in the nonsense that was war.

But a leader can get away with only so many nonsense orders before his men doubt his judgment, and that was poison.

And the unintended consequences piled up.

Having forbidden the rape of the slaves only made them more appealing as wives. One man somehow got permission to marry a slave wife four separate times. No one was sure what happened to the first three; Kip suspected murder but couldn't prove it. Kip had the man gelded and relieved of his hands, then notched and sold.

Kip was revered. It made him uncomfortable. It was a fool's gold. It wasn't real. It was an image they projected onto him. But some images are more helpful than others. They still saw how young he was, some of them.

Kip couldn't let himself be revered as some kind of holy child. Children could be fooled. Those who were too coarse to understand how love and obedience can be paired needed to learn fear.

So Kip had reinstituted the old tradition of the Year of Jubilee. It had been subverted before by the Ilytians and thence in the rest of the satrapies, but it was at least an established principle – it had a history – and the good or ill of it all came down to enforcement.

If one is to barter against human nature, one might as well make the best deal one can. The Year of Jubilee came every seven years, at which time slaves were freed.

They'd found a mention of which year it had last been celebrated and from there decreed that the tradition had lapsed rather than been broken. Thus, a slave-wife taken now would be freed five years hence on Sun Day. As a free woman on that day, she would be free to divorce her husband then. Any children she bore would be hers to take with her, and the husband would be liable to give her one-tenth of what he made in a year or a goat, whichever was more.

'This is the best I can do?' Kip had asked Tisis.

'During a war, when passions are hot?' she'd said. 'This is better than I thought you'd get.'

His idealism had also meant his army got a fraction of what they might have for selling the slaves. Each slave's contract now stipulated they would be in servitude for only five years. Every trader used that fact to bring the price down, though Kip knew that none of them intended to free the slaves in five years. He couldn't free the slaves immediately lest they take up arms against him again; he couldn't keep the slaves himself; but the slaves he sold would be slaves forever – unless Kip lived, and unless he won, and unless he was around in five years with enough power to enforce his will.

How did *I* become a slave trader?

And why was he so idealistic, when Jubilee had been tried and had failed before?

It wasn't just that Kip had grown up in Rekton, where they had no slaves and the institution didn't seem to fit naturally with all the people under Orholam's being equal. It was more than that. Every slave woman he looked at reminded him of his mother: bereft, cast off, disgraced, despised, vulnerable to abuse and thereby somehow a lodestone to those who would abuse her. Her saw her in every enslaved woman's face.

I couldn't help you, Mother. I couldn't heal you. But maybe I can keep these women from being hurt as much as they would be.

Tallach snorted, and Kip realized they hadn't seen Lorcan yet, though signs of his passage through the Blood Robe camp were evident in the destruction everywhere. Doubtless Conn Arthur wanted to see if his brother still lived.

Kip dismissed Tallach. He and Cruxer got down into the mud and blood to do more work. There was always more.

'Ferkudi,' Kip said, seeing a child weeping amid the bodies. Tisis had not yet arrived with the healers. 'Use your brain for me, would— Dear Orholam! What happened to you?!'

'What?' Ferkudi asked as Kip and the rest of the Mighty turned to him. Blood was streaming down the back of his head. He touched his neck and brought back the fingers wet and red. 'Oh, I thought I was just real sweaty.'

He patted the top of his head with no apparent alarm, then tipped it toward Kip.

'Bullet graze me?' he asked.

There was a new furrow across almost the entire top of his head, crossing the other scar, drawing a line almost from ear to ear.

'Sweet Orholam, man, how flat is the top of your head?' Big Leo asked.

'Flatter now,' Winsen said.

'Thanks for telling me,' Ferkudi complained. 'Now it's starting to sting. It didn't sting before you told me.'

'Well, you shouldn't have stuck your dirty fingers in it,' Ben-hadad said. 'Don't you know anything?'

'What're the odds it knocked any sense into him?' Winsen asked.

'Ben, you take him in a moment and get him some help, but first, Ferk, I got a job for you,' Kip said.

'Sure, sure, ouch,' Ferkudi said, still poking at his scalp.

'How much would it cost one widow to house and feed... eh, ten orphans?'

'Ages?' Ferkudi said. 'Teenaged boys eat more and what not.'

'Come up with an average. With housing included.'

'More than ten children per house would make it cheaper per child,' Ferkudi said.

'Efficiency isn't the point,' Kip said.

'Well, then, wouldn't one or two children per widow be better?'

'Fine, efficiency is *part* of the point.' Kip stopped speaking as he saw the gate opening to the city. 'What is that? Anyway, figure it out, Ferk. And talk to Verity and tell her we're feeding these kids tonight and until I say otherwise. She'll complain. But they're *kids*. Now what's this at the gate? I need you Ghosts for another five minutes before you extricate. And someone go find my sword and Cruxer's spear. We had to throw them down to mum the panic back there.'

'Love that spear,' Cruxer said.

It was best to get the will-casters out of the night mares as quickly as possible, but there were armed men facing off at the gate.

Kip jogged over there. It wasn't the most majestic entrance he'd ever made: one unarmed man on foot surrounded by drafters mounted on great elk and weird horses.

But the city's forces weren't terribly impressive, either. The conn was mounted on an emaciated stallion that looked exhausted just holding him on its back. No one else was mounted, but they did have weapons, and there were several hundred of them from what Kip could see.

Kip's men, despite not having any orders, hadn't let the conn or his people through.

Bless 'em for having sense and feeling empowered to make tough calls.

At the sight of the night mares and the Mighty, Kip's men moved back.

Kip went to stand before the columns. 'Conn Ruarc Hill, is it?' he asked.

'So I am. And you are?'

'Really?' Kip asked.

The man licked his lips. He looked well fed, though he had bags under his eyes. His men looked starved.

Kip didn't judge him for that, though. A starving leader could make bad decisions, so when numbers were large, it was a pretentious suffering to starve alongside your men. He did judge him, however, for being an asshole to men whose weapons were still bloody and bloodlust high – men who were here to rescue him, no less.

'Glad you came to greet us, but you didn't need to bring all these men,' Kip said. His own men had been smart enough to stop the column before it got out of the gates. If Conn Hill was going to attack, he was going to have a bad time of it.

'We came to help clear the heathen Blood Robes from the field of battle and hunt down those who've fled.'

'You have no cavalry,' Kip said. 'The Blood Robes are well fed and have a good lead on your men. Hard to hunt those who are faster than you.'

'Perhaps, then, we could help with those tasks that are nearer the walls,' Conn Hill said.

'Ah, you mean the claiming of slaves and plundering the camp,' Kip said. 'The meager rewards for the blood my men have spilled while you sat safe behind your walls.'

The man went red. Desperate, then, perhaps not entirely an asshole.

The conn said, 'We have a claim to the takings here. We have suffered. You fought them for one morning. We've fought—'

'Go back into your city, Conn Hill, and—'

'This is outrageous! I am conn of the most revered city in Blood Forest, and you are what? A bastard son with a few soldiers? I demand—'

Nope, not just desperate. Also an asshole.

'Conn Hill! Let me remind you...' Kip interrupted.

The Mighty's rage had been fading like the last thrumming notes of a lute's battle song. But impudence and insolence and insult to their Kip threatened a reprise of their favorite bloody verse.

Kip walked close to the man and lowered his voice so none could overhear it. The man himself had to bend over in his saddle to the unmounted, vulnerable Kip. Kip sometimes liked subverting power dynamics. 'Let me remind you, there's more than one way to liberate a city.'

Then Kip turned his back on him. He didn't look back, but

he was no fool. He looked at Cruxer's eyes. They would signal of an impending strike.

None came.

Kip turned and mounted one of the great elk gingerly.

'Go back into your city!' Kip shouted. 'Go talk it over with your elders or just take a good long drink of water, and come back here and try again. Think about flies and vinegar versus honey. Oh, and one thing, *Conn* Hill. My army is many things: bold, unconventional, fierce, fleet, frightening...oh, and not least, *victorious.*'

The Nightbringers within hearing roared at that.

'But one thing we are not, and this is very, very important: we are not heathens.'

Conn Hill snarled and sawed on his reins savagely, nearly making his horse trample his nearby men. The rest of his threadbare army withdrew behind the walls with him.

'What was that last little bit?' Cruxer asked. 'Not heathens?'

Kip said, 'Dúnbheo is actually where the Chromeria got the idea of voting in a promachos in times of crisis, except they call him a conn, a chief. Ordinarily the city rules itself through a Council of Divines – a title they take seriously – and they only appoint a conn for limited tasks. Conn Hill was appointed until "the heathens were banished from before our walls."'

'So you just stripped him of office.'

'Oh, only the Council of Divines can do that,' Kip said with a grin.

'But you made it irresistible for them to do so.'

'He was a dick.'

'There's more than a little Andross Guile in you, isn't there? You're changing, Breaker,' Cruxer said.

'And not only in good ways,' Kip said.

'The old Breaker never would have made an enemy for no reason.'

'Not for no reason,' Kip said. 'Sometimes the quickest way to make friends is to make the right enemies.'

'You're not telling me this was all part of some grand plan?' Cruxer said.

'Not grand. Not even really a plan. I just saw an opportunity. And he *was* being a flesh protuberance.'

'That's my old Breaker,' Cruxer said with a smile.

'This'll be a few hours,' Kip said. 'Have the men keep a watch. Ghosts, you can dis-integrate. Mighty, with me, I'm afraid there's a bear we need to help bury.'

Chapter 67

'Iron White'? What a load of shit. She ought to cross that one off her list right now. Karris didn't even dare lift her teacup, lest Teia see her trembling. The debriefing about the assassinations and Ironfist's fury had left her more fragile than her own porcelain. Ironfist!

Ironfist, either dead now or made an enemy. Either was unspeakably terrible. Ironfist's brother Tremblefist had, before all his training with the Blackguard, once killed five hundred men in a night and earned the moniker the Butcher of Aghbalu. Ironfist had bested *that man* in single combat. Him, as an enemy?

Yet how could Karris hope instead that one of her best friends had been killed in the tumult she'd triggered in Paria?

For Teia's part, the young woman sat with her legs crossed like a lady, back straight, daintily holding her cup without a hint of nerves. Before, Karris swore she'd always sat like a man, legs planted wide, ready to launch into action. Now she'd figured out that presenting oneself as a lady is simply another game, and she was playing it as a mock.

A mockery of Karris herself? Or was it the more innocent mockery of the fine furniture and fine porcelain and, yes, even fine tea?

But the young woman's eyes were terrible. Teia was changing before Karris, a shaking chrysalid, and Karris guessed that both of them feared what was going to emerge from that black cocoon.

'You can be mad at me for fucking up,' Teia said. 'I did. But don't you dare – don't you *dare* – flinch after what you had me do.'

Something about her combative tone actually settled Karris. She knew how to deal with fraught situations, with screaming men, angry women. The mask slammed back in place. 'Sugar?' she asked, lifting tiny tongs from the tray. 'The Ilytians use superviolet lattices to craft a single large crystal into fanciful shapes for the decadently wealthy. This kind is called a halo.'

'Thank you,' Teia said, confused, offering her cup.

'I think it looks like a puckered arse.'

From ladylike and pretentious to vulgar. It was a verbal hip throw. Teia seemed to have no idea what to do with that.

'Which is how I feel every day, Teia. I'm making big gambles all the time. Not because I'm reckless. I'm not. But because we're weaker than anyone knows. You loused up? Fine. Maybe so did I.'

'Who was it?' Teia asked. It was as if Karris hadn't said anything. The girl really was battle shocked.

'Watch Captain Tempus requested you for this mission when I said I'd like you to be here. He seemed nervous, insistent.'

'Guilty, you mean,' Teia said. Then she swore quietly. 'I liked him. Orholam blind him.'

'Teia, we don't know if he's in the Order himself. He might have been blackmailed. If we can... Teia, if we can, show mercy.'

For the first time, Teia actually looked angry. 'When I trained under Commander Ironfist, and Trainer Fisk, and Tremblefist, they told me never to point a musket at a man I wasn't ready to kill. Were you trained so differently?'

'Being ready to kill doesn't mean you kill regardless. Point the gun, but keep your finger outside the trigger guard until you're certain. I'm asking you to use discretion, that's all,' Karris said.

It wasn't fair of her. As if Teia wouldn't use her discretion.

Teia took the rebuke, though, unfair as it might have been. She simply looked sad. 'Tempus has done what the Order commanded once, how can you believe that he won't do it again at some critical moment? A man sworn to guard your back who betrays you even once is a cancer in the Blackguard. It doesn't matter if he's taken oaths or not, or if he attends the Order's secret meetings. If he obeys them, he's one of them.'

Karris bowed her head. She'd known Captain Tempus for twelve years. 'Do what must be done.'

Teia turned to leave, but as she got to the door, Karris called out to her. 'Adrasteia, we have all of us fallen short.'

The young Blackguard assassin looked at her, and she was pitiless. 'Some fall farther.'

Chapter 68

'They were littermates,' Conn Arthur said.

He was sitting in a charred, muddy circle of ground next to the giant grizzly's corpse when Kip approached. If anything, Lorcan had been even bigger than Tallach. The air stank of luxin, blood, black powder, burnt fur, and bear meat. Though the corpses had already been dragged away, the ground was muddy with the blood of those Lorcan had killed before dying.

From the look of things, the bear had sought out Amrit Kamal's bodyguard and his drafters. Nearby were four dead wights, a number of drafters, and several dozen finely equipped men and horses. They were already being stripped of their goods by Kip's gleaners, who kept uncharacteristically silent as they went about their work.

Lorcan had not only been the distraction Kip needed, he had also wiped out much of the Lord of the Air's leadership and protection here. The battle would have gone quite differently without him.

And the bear bore the signs of it on his body. Blood matted his fur from dozens of unseen wounds, many arrows stuck out from his hide, he had singe marks, and part of his jaw was blown off.

There was no sign of Tallach. Conn Arthur must have banished the great bear. No one wanted to see a giant grizzly feeding on men.

Instead the conn sat alone. There were no tears on his cheeks. He looked like a man concussed.

Kip said nothing, and the Mighty said nothing. Kip gestured

and they moved away, some setting up a perimeter, checking the dead – the scene of a just-finished battle was not a safe area. Cruxer stayed nearest, but only close enough to protect him, not close enough to listen in.

After a time, Conn Arthur found words again. 'My father was a great hunter. After we were born, my mother had something burst in her head and was sickly as long as we knew her. She got pregnant again when me and Rónán were six. Twins again, boys again, identical again, but she had not the strength for it a second time. Or perhaps we'd broken her somehow. They lived for a while, but she could give no milk, and they refused cow's or sheep's or goat's milk no matter what we did. My father rode many leagues to find a wet nurse, but they refused her, too. Perhaps they were wiser than us.'

Kip said nothing. 'After that, things were different. We moved with him from our village to a little cabin in the Deep Forest. Father took Rónán and me with him one day and let me take the shot at a magnificent stag. I only wounded it, though. We tracked it to a thicket and my father went in.

'He surprised a great she-bear. She protected her cubs and he protected his. It was a fight such as none I've ever seen. They both died of their wounds, and the four of us were left orphans. No one in our village believed us when we said our father had fought a giant grizzly, much less killed it. None had been seen for a hundred years, two hundred maybe. They thought we were lying to make our father seem a hero. We took in the cubs. What else were we to do? Rónán and I were thirteen years old then. When our powers awakened, it seemed the most natural thing in the world to reach out to them.'

Kip said nothing.

'You have to understand. They're still wild animals. Predators. I've known from the first time I touched Tallach's mind that I might step wrong one day, and he interpret me as a threat, and he'd kill me that day. Without malice. To call it betrayal would be to call the rock you stumble on a vicious rock.

'And yet we loved them as one loves nature itself. He loves me, too, but I can't guarantee that he wouldn't feed on my body if he found me dead when he was hungry. Like the world,

498

he is hard but not cruel. I have buried my mother and my father. We most of us bury our parents, unless our lot is worse and we bury our children. I've buried my baby brothers. Children born too soon often die. And now I've buried my brother and will bury Lorcan. There is nothing unique in my suffering. A thousand within shouting distance have suffered worse. The world is hard.'

And Kip knew then he had lost him.

'But I am not,' Conn Arthur said. 'Luíseach, I lied to you and you forgave me. You deserve my loyalty, my service, my life itself. But I have it not to give. At the end of all things, Tallach is just a goddam bear. But I've seen everyone else I love die, and I can't see him leave me, too. I can't risk him in battle one more time. I...can't.'

'I won't ask you to—' Kip said.

Conn Arthur interrupted, 'I have broken faith already. I have just banished Tallach. I will-cast him, compelling him to go to the deepest part of the forest, and to avoid men for the rest of his days.'

A cloud descended on Kip. It wasn't as if it were the first time he'd seen someone succumb to battle shock, but Conn Arthur? The great, hairy, muscular colossus seemed the very epitome of strength.

'Conn Ruadhán Arthur,' Kip said quietly. 'I release Tallach. He's done outstanding service to our fight, and he's free to go. At the end of all things, as you say, I don't need him. I do need you. Your people need you here. Your friends need you. You're more than your magic. Your service, your knowledge, your fierceness, your strength is needed here, and I don't dismiss you.'

Conn Arthur didn't look up from his seat in the mud. He shook his head. 'I'm finished. Call it a resignation or call me a deserter, you decide. Hang me or give me a pack. I'm done.' He stood and looked at his hands, bloody from where he'd been holding Lorcan's fur. 'I'm sorry to cast a pall on your great victory, my lord. You've much to do, I know. Here's your wife now. With news and pressing duties, no doubt. I'll not undercut your authority by defying you in front of your men. I'll await your verdict on the morrow.'

Tisis rode up on her little roan. She took in the scene quickly and her eyes softened, but she turned to Kip. 'I'm sorry, my lord, but the gates are opening. There have been stories of some sort of conflict between you and Dúnbheo's conn earlier? Your men are spoiling for a fight. Theirs seem to be, too. We need you. Now.'

Damn and double damn.

Chapter 69

The sky hammer came down in a crackle of lightning and fire and earthshaking thunder.

A moment before it struck him, Gavin jerked awake. He gasped, and fell from his cross-legged sitting position onto his back.

He sucked in great breaths, lying there in the darkness, his legs slowly untangling.

'Eat the poisoned bread,' the dead man said. 'It's your last hope. Go out like a man before you fade into your insanity.'

'What woke me?' Gavin asked.

'Holding out hope? You?' The dead man laughed. 'Die, Dazen Guile, and may those you've harmed curse you into eternity.'

Some comfort you are.

He groped around in the darkness until he found the bread.

There had always been some part of him certain that he would escape. Things had worked out for him, always. He was a falling cat, destined to land on his feet. But this time he'd been dropped from too great a height. Landing on your feet didn't mean anything when the fall pulverized your legs.

The pressure on his chest was suffocating.

'Do you remember your seven great purposes?' the dead man asked him.

'Uh-huh.'

'No. Really. Do you remember them all?'

'To tell Karris the truth about me, about Gavin and Dazen

and Sundered Rock, that was the first one. To finally free Garriston, that was the second. After all I'd let happen to it.' He'd failed to save the city, but he'd succeeded in saving the people. It counted, maybe.

'Go on.'

'Several were for war. I knew there'd be war again. So the third was to get an army loyal to me.'

'Of course. The people of Garriston, with your old General Corvan Danavis at their head. And you held them off the table like a card to be played when no one expects it.'

Gavin nodded. Seers Island seemed so distant to the conventional thinking, but it wasn't distant anymore, because of the next goal. 'The fourth was to learn to fly. That worked for me for a little while, but I couldn't ever make a condor that could move supplies and troops across the seas. Nonetheless, in my failure, I created the skimmer, which does what I wanted anyway: I can move troops to places no one could imagine they'd show up. Perhaps as importantly, I can communicate more swiftly than any foe. The fifth goal was to undermine the Spectrum and get myself named as promachos again. That almost worked.'

'What's number six?'

'To kill all the color wights. All of them, in the entire world.'

'For Sevastian?'

'For everyone.' Yes, for Sevastian. Eight years old and murdered by a blue.

'A grandiose plan, for a blind man.'

'No, grandiose was the *seventh* goal.'

The dead man was silent, but Gavin was, too.

Finally the dead man said, 'What was the seventh goal?'

'You're not me, are you?' Gavin said.

'Of course not. What, do you think you're talking to yourself? You're not that crazy. Not yet.'

'You aren't a young version of me I will-cast into this cell to comfort myself. You're something else.'

Silence for a time.

'You underestimate your old self.'

'Enough of that. I know.'

Silence again.

'What gave it away?' the dead man asked.

'When you said ʊ ᴧ ʃ ʔ ᴧ ʃ . "Raka," I might have dredged from the depths of a fevered brain. But ʊ ᴧ ʃ ʔ ᴧ ʃ ?' And you lied about white luxin, but Gavin didn't need to tip that card yet.

'Eh, I worried about that. I was angry. I made a mistake. I hoped you'd missed it.'

'So what are you?' Gavin asked.

'Oh, Dazen Guile. Come now. Isn't that your seventh goal? To join us?'

Gavin shivered. 'Us'? Every word was likely a lie. Every word had been a lie so far.

But what did that mean?

Or was this a hallucination? Was this conversation even real? Or was this madness in truth?

Dear Orholam, I am finally losing it. Conspiracies and spirits? What's next?

What could you do when you couldn't trust even your own mind?

He tore a hunk off the bread. He wadded up the dough, rolling it in his hands and compressing it until it was a starchy bullet. He opened his mouth to toss in the bullet all nonchalant.

Wait, a quiet voice said to him.

He closed his mouth.

'What was that?' the dead man said. 'Who was that? You can't touch him! You can't speak to him! That's not how it works. That's not the rules! Unless…'

Gavin was about to say something aloud, but whatever it was, he forgot it immediately when he heard a sound. Something from outside the cell.

No! I'm in here for months and months and nothing happens, and then two vitally important things happen at the exact same time?

The air changed and light streamed into the black cell like a sledge smashing Gavin's good eye. Gavin blinked against it, putting out a three-fingered hand to block the assault, and the man turned down his lamp. Then he set it on the floor.

Grinwoody.

Chapter 70

'In the circus when I was growing up, we had this act,' Big Leo said, as the Mighty followed Kip toward the Dúnbheo gate. They hadn't heard what Conn Arthur had said. Cruxer told them only that he was leaving.

They weren't taking it well.

Big Leo continued, 'We'd take the scrawniest kid we could find in the village, or some feeble old codger, or just the kid whose parents we wanted to please the most, and we'd pit him against my dad, who was my size now at least. Bigger. We had these funny illusions where we pitted him against my father in feats of strength, and somehow he won every time. And at the finale, my father pretends to be furious and picks the skinny guy up and sets him on a teeterboard, determined to bounce him out of the place. He jumps on his side of the teeterboard – and just slowly rises, not even fast enough to bounce him. Then my father looks at the teeterboard like it's got to be broken. Picks it up, moves it around, sees that it's just a plain old teeterboard: one piece of plain wood over a fulcrum.'

'Tell me this story is ending soon,' Winsen said. 'The awesome wonders of the circus are too much for my provincial mind.'

'It's going somewhere, all right? It got a little longer than I was expecting, but—'

Tisis gave a significant glance to Kip – 'Not too long, okay?' – and said, 'I'll go stall them.' She flicked the reins of her horse and darted away.

'He's right at the climax of the show, Win, I want to hear what happens,' Ferkudi said.

'What *happens*? Like it's still going on? Big Leo's parents and that whole damn circus were killed, Ferk,' Winsen said. Always was the diplomat. 'It's not what happens. It's what happened.'

'Thank you, High Lord Pedant,' Ben-hadad said. 'We don't know the story, so we don't know what happens next in the time stream of the story. You can put it in any tense you want. It's like it lives in a hypothetical fairy story land where anything may or may not happen. And we just want to find out what that happening is.'

'What? Hypothetical what?' Winsen said. 'It's a true story. Something really did happen. And it's over, so it happen*ed*.'

'I have to admit,' Big Leo said, 'it does kind of sound like you're talking out of your ass with that hypothetical fairy story whatever, Ben-hadad.'

Ben-hadad threw his hands up. 'So it's a true story composited from many instances of a mummery act facilitated with illusions, fine. That's *totally* different.'

'Yes,' Winsen said.

Ben-hadad nearly shouted, 'No, it isn't! It's a fucking story for the purpose of illustration! It doesn't matter if it even actually—'

'Shut it, Ben. I was damn near getting to my point,' Big Leo said. He grunted as they passed a burning pit. 'I know I've said this before, but I really don't like the smell of burning human.'

'I dunno,' Ferkudi said. 'I mean once the hair's burnt off, I think it's kind of appetizing. I missed breakfast. I'm hungry. Anyone else hungry?'

One of the burning pit workers, a rag tied over his face, looked at Ferkudi aghast.

'That's what I don't like about it,' Big Leo said. 'You don't remember that we've had this conversation before?'

'It did seem kind of fermiliar.'

'It's our third time,' Big Leo said. 'Annnnyway. Wait. I wanted to get this out of the way before we get to the wall. No, they see us. They'll wait.

'So my father'd put the teeterboard back down and we'd play it a few different ways, but he'd wobble it up and down, see that it was a plain old teeterboard, and finally ask this tiny kid to jump on the other side. And of course we had it rigged so that my father would be blasted not just high in the air, but all the way through the roof of the tent and out into some nets outside that none of them knew about.

'Brought some people to tears the first few times. They thought he'd been killed. But eventually we sighted in the humor and he'd come back in for the applause. Great bit. Dangerous as hell. Way too easy to miss the net. My mother hated it.' He shook himself. 'Anyway, that was supposed to be shorter than all that. Point is: What. The. Hell. Just happened?'

Kip sighed. Double damn and triple damn. He wanted space from this right now.

'The reaction doesn't seem proportional to the event, right? I mean, his brother's bear died. I had a dog die once. I was sad. And I know the Foresters enjoy their drama, but—'

'I dunno,' Ferkudi said. 'His brother died not long ago, satrapy's all tore up, maybe he just—'

'O's mercy, don't do it,' Cruxer said.

'—couldn't *bear* it?' Ferkudi asked. 'Get it? Bear it?'

'Balls, Ferk,' Ben-hadad said. 'You think it's appropriate to make jokes when a man *bares* his soul—'

The rest of them groaned.

'Jokes aside, I hear you,' Winsen said. 'It does seem like a bit of an overreaction. When my cat Fluffles died, I grinned and *bore* it...Damn. That didn't really work, did it? Grinned and beared it?'

'Now you're beating that joke like a dead—' Big Leo said.

'Don't...' Cruxer said.

'—bear,' Big Leo finished. 'Oops.'

'You motherfuckers!' Kip seethed, rounding on them. They didn't know. They didn't know, but he went red. 'You shut your fucking shitholes, or I'll—'

The conversation broke like ice over a puddle on a cold fall morning. They plunged into the mud beneath, the grime that was Kip.

He'd never spoken to them in anger. Not once in the year and a half – the lifetime – he'd known them. And it was going to shatter their friendship. All because Kip couldn't control his mouth. Kip the Lip. God. Damn.

'Breaker,' Cruxer said quietly. 'They don't mean anything by it.'

'It wasn't even Conn Arthur's bear,' Ben-hadad complained. 'I know he's a moody—'

505

'Stop,' Kip said, looking away. He turned his back, but didn't keep walking to the gate. Not yet. 'You're done.'

'Don't you turn your back on us, you asshole,' Winsen said.

'Don't,' Cruxer warned Winsen.

'No. Shit gets awful, we have a few laughs. You've joined us every other time. Now you pull high ground on us? Go fuck yourself. What's your problem, *boss*?' Winsen demanded.

'Let's forget it,' Kip said.

'Sure. We can joke about that guy's head we found two hundred paces from his body back at that wagon ambush, but some fuckin' bear is beyond the pale. Sure, boss, you get to decide what's funny, too. Because you're the Lightbringer.'

'I've never said that,' Kip said.

'Yes, he is,' Cruxer said at the same moment. But he went on, 'And if you doubt it at this point, what the hell are you still doing here?'

'I like the food,' Winsen said. 'And I get to kill people.'

Aside from Kip, the rest of them chuckled, but it was forced. They'd all known Winsen long enough to know that the first half was probably a joke – it should be; any spices the cooks laid their hands on had to be sold for actual necessities. But the second half probably wasn't a joke, and they'd all known him long enough to be uneasy about that.

Long enough, not well enough, because it didn't seem that any of them did know him well. If there were hidden depths to Winsen – and one expects depths – they remained hidden. He seemed unaffected both by the physical difficulties of a life at war and the moral ones.

'Bad people,' Ferkudi amended for him. He was probably the only one of them who wasn't a little unnerved by Winsen from time to time.

'Huh?'

'You get to kill *bad* people.'

'That's a bonus,' Winsen said. He grinned at their drawn faces. 'I *am* joking, guys.'

But Kip didn't believe him. Winsen was on their side, but he didn't actually care. He liked the excitement. When religious or moral conundrums came up at the campfire, the look on his face was akin to the one Kip imagined his own must wear when Tisis talked about fabrics for her eventual 'real' wedding gown.

Kip didn't think Eirene was going to spring for the big wedding. He also didn't think they were going to live that long, so it was a moot point.

'Oh shit,' Ben-hadad said. 'That wasn't just his brother's bear, was it?'

'It's over now,' Kip muttered. 'It doesn't matter.'

'What are you talking about?' Cruxer asked. When Kip started walking without answering, he asked it again, this time of Ben-hadad. Of course it was Ben who'd figured it out.

'You all didn't stop to think how weird it was that a non-will-cast bear attacked at just the perfect place and time? What? He was just trained that well?' Ben-hadad asked.

'Hadn't really thought about it,' Ferkudi said.

'That wasn't Lorcan,' Ben-hadad said. 'That was Rónán in Lorcan.'

'Oh shit,' Cruxer said.

'Orholam's beard, I'm so sorry,' Big Leo said. 'I didn't mean...'

'So wait,' Winsen said. 'That was really his brother? In the bear? Didn't his brother die before we even met him?'

'You're talking soul-casting. That is...not just a little bit forbidden,' Cruxer said carefully. 'I've come to appreciate that the Chromeria is sometimes overcareful with these magics. But even the Ghosts absolutely, categorically forbid soul-casting.'

'Yes,' Kip said. 'And yet he saved us all today. Which makes him a heretic and a hero at the same time.'

'You knew,' Cruxer said.

'And you gave Conn Arthur an ultimatum,' Ben-hadad said. He gestured around at the destruction the bear had wreaked. 'To do this.'

'Because Conn Arthur couldn't bear to kill him?' Ferkudi asked. He saw the disbelieving, outraged looks of the others. 'Oh no! That one wasn't on purpose, I swear!'

Ignoring him, Cruxer said to Kip, 'He lied to you, he said so. About this?'

'I suspected it from the beginning. What would you have

had me do, Crux? Put Conn Arthur in front of a tribunal right after the will-casters joined us?'

'That's the law among their people.'

Ben-hadad scoffed, and the others looked uneasy. It would have been impossible, of course. Even if they'd held the tribunal – not a sure thing, with how much the Ghosts revered Conn Arthur. Even if they'd found him guilty – and how would they, unless he confessed? Even if it had all gone as well as it could, Kip would have lost the Ghosts. They would have exploded or melted away into the forest.

And without them, these victories would have been impossible.

'Does the scripture say, "Do the law, and love meting out its punishment"?' Kip asked.

'No, it says, "Do justice and love mercy,"' Ferkudi said.

'Thanks, Ferk,' Big Leo said. 'He knows.'

'Oh, it was one of those rhetorical...'

'Yeah. One of those.'

'The laws are there for a reason,' Cruxer said stubbornly, but weakening. 'Every time we ignore the law, we end with tragedy.'

'Oh, look,' Kip said, 'here we are.'

The Nightbringers who'd been in a mob in front of the city's gate were now arranged in orderly lines and files. It was more formal, but they also all had their weapons close at hand.

But even as they snapped smartly back rank by rank to let Kip and the Mighty pass, someone high in the city wall unfurled several great, festive banners, and Kip knew everything was going to be fine.

The will-cast animals had all been released, so someone – Tisis, no doubt – had procured the remarkably docile black stallion Kip rode when occasions required it. He swung into the saddle less than gracefully. To the general merriment of the Mighty, he was still a rather poor rider.

Beside Kip, Ben-hadad asked Winsen out of the side of his mouth, 'Fluffles? You named your cat *Fluffles*?'

'What? Great name for a cat,' Winsen said. 'If I ever do or don't or did get one, I definitely may or may not have named it that. In some hypothetical fairy story land – or the real one – it may have happened. It's just for the purpose of illustration.'

'You're a dick, Winsen,' Ben-hadad said. 'I love you, man.'

'Hairless cat,' Winsen said.

'Hairless? They come like that?' Big Leo asked.

'Oh, of course,' Ben-hadad said, light dawning. 'Fluffles. The hairless cat. Not hypothetical, then.'

'Odd texture. Feels like foreskin,' Winsen said.

And *that* was how 'petting the hairless cat' entered the Mighty's lexicon.

Chapter 71

'Andross, you motherfucker.' Karris had waited a week to say those words so she didn't reveal she knew exactly what had happened in Paria immediately, but checking off 'Curse out promachos' wasn't quite as satisfying as she'd hoped.

'Yes?' he said, as if she'd simply called his name. He'd come into her room carrying two cups. 'Kopi?' he asked, proffering a delicate cup.

'I thought we were working together,' she said. She didn't take the cup.

He raised his eyebrows. 'Go on,' his expression said. He lowered the proffered cup.

'That was no suicide. You killed the Nuqaba, didn't you?' she demanded.

'Yes.'

She hadn't expected him to admit it. Crafty old rat. 'You... you ass! After all you and I went through drafting that ultimatum, you just assassinated her? She didn't even have time to respond. I hated her, Andross, but she unified the Parian people. She could have led them to our defense. This is betrayal, Andross. Assassinating a Nuqaba? Are you mad? With how much we need Paria and how fraught the relationship between the Chromeria and the Nuqabas has always been?'

He put her cup down on a table. He sat in one of her chairs, taking his ease. He sipped his kopi.

When the silence stretched on, he looked up. 'Oh! I'm sorry, I thought those were rhetorical questions. Done ranting? So soon?'

He made her feel powerless. Foolish. Like a child.

Uh-uh.

He moved to take another sip, as if thinking, and Karris's foot flashed out. If she'd paused to think about what she was attempting, she wouldn't have tried it.

Her foot swept between his seated legs, pushed forward, and kicked only the delicate cup as he tilted it to his lips. The cup popped into the air, jetting steaming kopi into Andross's face and hair and across his chest.

Andross roared, blinded and burnt, but Karris was still moving. The killing instinct imbued by so many years of fighting had taught her never to wound a foe without following up to kill immediately. Karris kicked off half of the sole of her right boot, and, before he could lurch out of his chair, she stood balanced easily on her left foot with the blade of her right foot – now lined with an actual blade – pressed against his neck.

She caught the kopi cup.

The blade along the edge of her boot was thin. It had to be to be small enough to conceal in her boot sole and not interfere with walking, but against his neck it was plenty big enough.

Andross sat back down, but the rage didn't leave his eyes. He raised one beringed finger and pushed her foot aside. She pivoted easily and brought her foot down, but stayed ready for an attack.

'That, my dear, was a miscalculation,' he said. His eyes flicked to the empty cup she'd caught in her hand.

She hoped it was because he was impressed. It had been damn lucky.

But she couldn't back down. 'I'll decide that.'

'Oh, I didn't mean for you. I meant for me. You took me by surprise. It doesn't happen often.' He looked about for a cloth with which to dry himself, and, not finding one or a slave to hand him one, he made an expression as if to say, 'What am I, among barbarians?'

He picked up a priceless lace pillow with a tiny shrug as if to say, 'Oh well, when among barbarians, do as barbarians do.' And he wiped his face and neck dry with the pillow.

It was a pretense, all this calm. The rage never left that deep corner of his demeanor.

Call that a victory, then.

The skin on his face was burnt. She couldn't tell how badly yet.

But there was no retreat. A burnt face? He'd murdered that woman. Teia had damned herself in her own eyes because of this man's orders. Karris couldn't feel remorse.

'So,' he said, 'any news on your hunt for Gavin?'

No no no. He was not going to get her derailed. Especially not into *that*. 'Did you kill Satrapah Azmith, too?' she asked.

'Clearly not,' he said. 'As she wasn't a satrapah when she died.'

'Is that a yes?' she asked. Why would he admit to a murder he hadn't committed?

'No. The woman was a complete idiot. My sources say she had a paroxysm when the Nuqaba told her she might not back her claim against us.'

So he hadn't known Azmith was the Parian spymaster. Or – dammit! – was merely pretending not to. She said, 'My sources suggested it might have been because we stripped her of her position, that she had a heart attack then. I thought her death might be on us.'

'I imagine the pressures of working with that lunatic Haruru for years had more to do with it.'

'Why kill her, Andross? If your assassin failed or had been discovered, you'd have plunged us into a war with two fronts. You're not so rash.'

Andross gave a sour grin through his pain. 'You didn't know me when I was young, before I gave up drafting red for the same reasons you did. Back to using again, are you?'

Damn her light skin. Her blushes were obvious, and so was the light staining from using red again.

The truth was, she'd been drafting to try to spur on some

feeling in her heart toward her son. She and Zymun had gotten off on the wrong foot, and things still weren't going well, this many months later. He'd continually struck her as somehow *off* – no doubt that was an artifact of the abuse he'd endured. Her fault. Raised without a mother's love, abandoned and abused by those who'd taken him on. Any flaws he had were on her. But she'd finally admitted to herself that she didn't *like* him.

What kind of mother doesn't like her own son?

She'd been trying to train herself to have good feelings around him, so they had wonderful food for dinners together, excellent wine, and she drafted red and what sub-red she could: all the things that could provide perfect soil for a new relationship. But she was a stone. It hadn't worked. Not yet. And when he kissed her on the lips in greeting, she flinched away from his innocent gesture.

She couldn't reject him, not after all she'd done.

She hadn't answered, and Andross took her silence as assent. He picked up the kopi he'd brought for her, and sipped it as if nothing had happened. 'We *were* working together, High Mistress. If the Nuqaba were going to comply, I'd given orders that the assassination be called off.'

A lie, almost certainly. Teia hadn't mentioned any way for her orders to be canceled, and no one there from the Order could have gotten orders in time to stop her regardless, because they didn't have skimmers. Unless Anjali Gates belonged to Andross?

Damn! Yet *another* person to put in the file of those who might be Andross's.

☐ *Investigate Anjali Gates.*

But Karris couldn't let him know that she knew the possibility of canceling the answer to be a lie. Orholam's balls, it was impossible to keep all this straight!

'As it was,' Andross continued, 'we were able to establish how hard you are, and how dangerous it is to cross you. Your ultimatum drove a Nuqaba to suicide – which it only would have if she'd already been planning to commit treason. And because she died before she could come out against us, none of the people who would have joined her had done so publicly. Think of it this way: if things are close and the tribes aren't sure who to side with, if they'd followed her and then we killed her, they would fear you'd hold it against them. So all things being equal, they would then have to join the White King. This way, they still have the possibility of joining us.'

'Why would they fear me if they hadn't acted yet? I've shown myself to be forgiving when possible.'

'Ah, but you see, men never believe others are more good than they are. Bad men see mercy as weakness. Smart men see it as shrewdness. Saintly men might see the truth of it, but sadly there are few saints among those we're trying to convince to join us.'

'And you've guaranteed that,' she said, though she couldn't argue with that much. She had dossiers on all the tribal chiefs, and she knew all the satraps and Colors herself. No saints among those, and few enough even among the High Luxiats. 'Because of what you've done, we'll have people join us who have only the barest loyalty. We may be inviting traitors into our midst.'

'A truth every time one recruits. Would you forego allies altogether?' Andross asked. 'I've seen you down at the yards, watching the training.'

'What of it?'

'You've accelerated the training. How many drafters have died because of that?'

'I don't know,' she mumbled.

'Horse shit.'

'Twelve,' she said.

'Twelve dead, to save some number you'll never know. That's our business here, Iron White. Trading blood now for what we pray is less blood later. Stop looking back.'

'Who's to say the tribes who join us won't turn when we get to battle?' she asked.

Andross grinned smugly. It was a cold mirror of Gavin's happy self-satisfaction when he did something clever. Gavin's delight made you want to join him; Andross's made you hate him more.

He said, 'That's why I blooded the Parians and Ruthgari early at the Battle of Ox Ford. It's hard to join up with an army after they've killed your sons and brothers, even if it is in your best interests.'

'You're saying you sent them to die on purpose?'

'I wasn't hoping they'd be massacred like total incompetents, if that's what you're asking. But I sent them to what I knew would be a hard fight, yes. The Parians in particular used to have a reputation to be exactly the people for that. That their losses would be another thing to keep them on our side if things went poorly was part of my thinking, yes. I knew the Nuqaba was crazy, but I didn't think she was *insane*. She might not even have been able to bring her people to join the White King. But if she'd tried to join him and instead started her own civil war, that wouldn't have helped us, either, would it? Not in time.'

'So you had reason to think that Satrapah Azmith would join us?'

'Weak people like Azmith don't lead rebellions. They fall back to doing what they're *supposed* to do. At worst, she would have dragged her feet, and another visit, this time by you or me personally, would have been sufficient to regain Paria once and for all. Of course, the Parians have the same problem that afflicts every fighting force subjected to protracted peace.'

'And what's that?' Karris wasn't sure they were done talking about his assassination, but Andross slid from one thing to the next like an eel.

'Do you know the true genius of my second son?'

'What?' What did Dazen have to do with this? Gavin. Oh hell.

Yes, she did know Gavin's genius quite well, thank you.

'Dazen was brilliant. Smarter than Gavin, but Dazen had his mother's—' Andross cut off suddenly, overwhelmed with emotion.

He'd really loved her.

And instantly, Karris felt the ice of her hatred for this man shiver, and a crack run right down the middle of it. If he could love Felia, then he could love.

Unless this, too, was a game. Was Andross so vile that he would use his own wife's death to manipulate Karris?

Andross cleared his throat. 'He had this ability, a perishingly rare ability for those who are good at practically everything they do. He knew where he wasn't the best, and it didn't bother him. He led his people, and he fought on the front lines, but he put another man in command of his armies. You met the man he chose. And he was not a choice anyone else would have made. At the time, Corvan Danavis was the last living son of a shattered, once-great family.'

Karris had met Corvan, but her own memories of any time before the False Prism's War were dim and tainted with grief and self-recrimination.

'Corvan was bookish. He'd gone along on some raids with his brothers but had never fought. He was too young. As the youngest of ten brothers, he never dreamed he would lead, nor did they. Then the Danavises got swept into the death orgy that was the Blood Wars. Corvan's brothers tried to take a shortcut through a swamp to surprise their enemies and were captured and flayed.'

Now *that* was something Karris hadn't known.

'Do you know what happens to a drafter who's been flayed?' Andross asked.

Karris's distaste must have shown on her face.

'Same thing that happens to any man. Incredible pain and flies and infection and fever and slow, horrendous, inevitable death – unless he crafts a luxin skin for himself. There was a law at the time that any man who turned wight forfeited all his family's belongings. So Grissel Spreading Oak – yes, Bran's older brother – flayed all seven of the Danavises he captured. When one broke and finally drafted skin for himself, Grissel killed all the ones older than him and took that one to a friendly luxiat. One bribe later, and the Spreading Oaks took four-fifths of the Danavis properties, and the Magisterium one-fifth.'

'Orholam have mercy,' Karris said. That was sweet Bran Spreading Oak's *brother*?

'I know. I would have negotiated for at least half,' Andross said. But he smiled slyly. He knew what she meant. 'Anyway, according to my sources, Corvan wasn't even an officer when he joined Dazen. He'd fought for half a dozen mercenary companies since his brothers died. He was a brawler and an angry drunk, and every time he got promoted, he got fired again. When his people's lives were on the line, he couldn't stand incompetence, and he couldn't keep his mouth shut. He joined Dazen immediately, but the old guard wouldn't give him so much as a squad. *That* is the problem of peacetime militaries: most of them train for peace, and they produce officers good at peacetime activities. Smiling sycophants mostly. Men who look good at balls, rather than men with balls.

'Dazen apparently saw Corvan lingering one day over the maps after his superiors left. He quizzed him, thinking he might be a spy – he was wrong, of course. For several months I had no spies at all in Dazen's army, he inspired such devotion. Dazen was so impressed by Corvan's answers, and how keenly he saw things, that he put Corvan in charge immediately. The audacity! And then they led together, Dazen bringing Corvan up to speed and Corvan showing a preternatural gift for strategy. They worked hand in glove. If he'd come in earlier, or if it weren't me they opposed, bleeding off allies who might have joined them, they might have won the war. The only mistake they ever made was letting themselves be drawn into a full-scale battle at Sundered Rock. Of course, they say Corvan was deathly ill at the time. Hmm.'

'This is going somewhere,' Karris said.

'I'd intended to have Corvan take command of the Parian armies. Indeed, all of our armies. If he was willing to join Gavin after having fought against him, apparently his loyalty to the Guile line is strong. Or he simply likes fighting. Doesn't matter to me. My son was right about Corvan; I'll not be too obstinate to admit it.'

'This is all fascinating, and I'm not against Corvan leading our armies, at least not in principle. But we're not finished talking about your assassinating one of the most important people in the Seven Satrapies behind my back.'

'Karris. Dear. I've done nothing but amplify your power.

This "Iron White" business might have seemed a whimsical affectation before. Now you will be feared.'

'Or you will be even more so. As much as this was a demonstration of my power, it was also a demonstration of yours. We both signed that ultimatum.'

'It isn't either-or. We can be feared together, like Corvan and Dazen. Hand in glove.'

'With me as the glove,' Karris said. 'And you the hand. I thought we wrote that letter together to show a united front. But really it was so your name would be attached to this.'

He didn't deny it. 'People need reminders. Just because there's a new power in the game doesn't mean all the old ones are gone. Besides, I did do all the work. I'm sharing my glory with you, not the other way around.'

'How did you do it?' Karris asked. She didn't expect an answer, but it was a question she would ask if she were as in the dark as she was claiming to be.

'I'm not telling you that. I'm the promachos, and I go before us to fight in the ways I deem best. Now, your options are varied, but simple. You've yelled at me; you've questioned my sanity; you've made certain that I knew what I was risking; you've expressed how you wished I'd tell you things before I did them...and you've spilled my drink. Now you simply have to decide if you're going to try to remove me from my offices, if you're going to try to kill me, or if we're going to get back to the delicate work of trying to save the satrapies. Because my plan worked, insofar as I could have predicted. Azmith's death, however, leaves us with some very particular difficulties.'

He looked at her, questioning, waiting, and apparently not the least bit worried.

She'd been outflanked. Again. And this was what it was like to have Andross Guile as an *ally*. Damn him.

'So, can we move on now,' he said, 'or are you going to ask the Blackguards to seize me? Will they, I wonder? Technically, they answer to the White...unless there's a promachos appointed. Hmm. I know what a stickler like Commander Ironfist would have done, much as it might have pained him, but maybe Commander Fisk would be overwhelmed by his personal loyalty to you instead.'

What was she going to say to salvage her dignity? 'Don't do it again'? He'd do it again in a heartbeat.

'This was not the partnership I was looking for,' Karris said.

'That makes two of us. I would prefer you to be completely subservient,' Andross said.

Was that a hint of a smile?

Karris pursed her lips. 'So where do we go from here?' She wondered which of them had been more wrong about Paria. Had she destroyed everything by killing Satrapah Azmith, or had she saved them from ruin by frustrating Andross Guile's plans?

The intelligence she was getting from Azûlay was fragmentary and contradictory at best. Maybe the whole country would dissolve back into its tribes. And of Ironfist, she'd had no word at all.

Andross said, 'Well, obviously, the first thing we need to do is send a letter. The tricky part is what to say, and for that, I was hoping your lighter touch might be helpful.'

'What do you mean? Whom are we sending the letter to?'

Andross smiled, superior again. 'Why, to the only person who matters in Paria now, of course: King Ironfist.'

Karris was ashamed that her first reaction wasn't joy that her old friend was alive, or that he was free, or that he was in charge.

Ironfist hadn't claimed the title satrap. He hadn't become Nuqaba.

Ironfist is calling himself *king*.

Chapter 72

'I can't decide if I'm going to be moved to tears or throw up,' Cruxer said.

'There's a good reason for that,' Tisis said.

The procession into the city wasn't what Kip had expected. He wasn't sure what that had been; it wasn't as if he'd fantasized about being a conqueror. But as his army snaked in through the streets toward the Palace of the Divines, they saw that the city was in a horrific state. It was far worse than they'd been led to believe.

Which made sense, Kip realized. A besieged city had every reason to hide how bad things were.

Gaunt men and women holding sickly children and limp babies cheered as if to make up with enthusiasm for lacking any tangible way to show their appreciation. But there was a troubling undercurrent here, too. A look on some faces like that of a beaten dog cowering under a raised fist.

'They're afraid of us,' Kip said suddenly. It was what Tisis had been hinting.

'What?' Cruxer asked in disbelief.

'If you let a strange army into your city, how do you stop them from doing whatever they want?' Tisis asked.

Kip looked around, sickened. Sad excuses for little banners of welcome waved from open windows and balconies. Instead of the famed living wood that the city was famous for, most of the buildings were built of the white granite that was so plentiful in the area. Everywhere, though, Kip saw the Foresters' art, from carvings of intricate zoomorphic dogs and tygre wolves to the more typical infinite knots, plaits, braids, spirals, and step-and-key patterns for love, for husband and wife and children and clan, for eternal life, for the relations of nature and man and their gods, for life above and life below and for life and death and renewal.

Despite its power at the time, this civilization had converted with little or no force. Lucidonius's teachings had made sense to these people, as if his ideas filled in the gaps that had left them puzzled, and contradicted only those things in their own practices that had left them uneasy. They had already revered the number seven: not only did they see it in their colors, but they arranged the world into what they called the seven creations: man, mammal, fish, reptile, bird, insect, and plant.

But all the grandeur of the city now was tarnished, a mock. Starving people had not the energy to clean their homes and streets or even themselves. Rubbish heaps had been plundered and the detritus left scattered about, not least on the faces of these walking skeletons in their rags.

'The city wasn't under siege that long,' Kip said. 'It shouldn't be this bad. Are those burn marks on the walls? Were there riots here?'

'My spies haven't reported yet,' Tisis said. 'I don't know what happened.'

Kip looked back at his lackluster parade: men and women literally bloodied, the grime and sweat and soot of the battle-field still on them, some limping, some still bleeding after refusing medical care because they didn't want to disappoint their leader or leave their friends...all marching to impress whom? A starving crowd? The city leaders?

These people didn't need to be impressed. They needed to be fed.

'What are we doing?' Kip said. 'A military procession to the heart of the city? Why? Because that's what people do? None of the people here have ever done it or ever seen it. There's a place for spectacle, but it's not here.'

Kip threw a flare into the sky to signal a stop.

It takes some time for an entire army to stop, though, and while the appropriate people got in their places for further orders, Sibéal Siofra said, 'I know what you're going to do, and while I admire the heart behind it, Lord Guile, it's not a good idea. Think about the logistics—'

'I've thought of them,' Kip said. But he didn't explain.

'What's he going to do?' Ferkudi tried to whisper.

'He's going to give away our food,' Cruxer said.

'He's not going to give our food away,' Ben-hadad said. 'Because that would be idiotic.'

'I'm giving our food away,' Kip told Ferkudi.

'Kip,' Ben-hadad said, 'if you give away our food, the army stops. Period. We go nowhere, we do nothing, people start leaving within a couple of days. If the army stops, the Blood Robes can kill as many Foresters as they want, including everyone in this city. In the long run, it's not a mercy to—'

'Give away the food!' Kip commanded. 'All of it. Section commanders, carry out the original plan, but begin now, and take all of our food rather than what we'd apportioned before.'

Sibéal huffed and Ben-hadad lifted his heavy spectacles and rubbed the bridge of his nose. 'Tell me you've got a plan,' Ben-hadad said. 'Please.'

'Drafters, cavalry, and the Mighty with me,' Kip said. 'I want our camp followers in here mending and washing clothes and cleaning streets. Anything that needs to be done and can be done in two days, do it. Looting or assault will earn hanging. Remind them to go in teams. Even killings in self-defense will be considered murder if there aren't two corroborating witnesses.' Last thing Kip needed was some young assholes to antagonize the whole city.

The army didn't dissolve at once, of course. But commanders began booming out orders, filling in their people on what they were about to do, and messengers exploded from the column like hornets from an upended nest.

Kip gave the signal, and the column began moving again, but now, as it got deeper into the city, sections broke off, each with its own wagons of provisions. It took a lot of work to give away something properly.

Gradually the signs of the city's impoverishment cleared until they reached the great gate into the part of the city called the Sanctum of the Divines. Here there were undeniable scorch marks from at least one earlier riot. The great gate was now open, though.

Here, as at the wall, the posts of the gate were trees. But these weren't sabino cypresses. They were atasifusta, though sadly no longer living. Kip hadn't known that there were any left standing in the world. Atasifusta were the only known plant that converted sunlight into something a lot like red luxin. Except it was a more potent red luxin than man had ever drafted. A single stick of the stuff would burn for many days without being consumed. Its usefulness had doomed it to extinction. Families still passed down single sticks of the stuff. A few shavings made a perfect fire starter, or the whole stick could be set alight to help light damp wood, and then extinguished with no appreciable loss to its mass. It had found worse uses in war, the sawdust being a precursor to black powder.

Here, knot work had been carved into the entire surface of

both trees, and the rest overlaid with some clear glaze so the designs stood out in black on bone-white wood. Clearly the designs were set alight for special occasions. Kip was somewhat sad that his arrival didn't rate.

A dozen guards stood at the gate, but they said nothing. A single rider on a white charger in ceremonial white-and-gold armor and carrying the white-and-green triangular flag of the city nodded to them from his wolf helm and rode before them, leading them to the Palace of the Divines.

Here the buildings were older and grander by far. Living wood made the frames of these buildings, with a few supporting enormous stained-glass windows between their branches, mostly hidden now by fresh green leaves, but no doubt glorious in autumn and winter.

'How the hell did they do that?' Ben-hadad said. 'Do they will-cast the trees? How do you will-cast a tree? They don't grow fast enough. How do the windows not shatter when the branches grow year by year? How do they keep the trees alive? It's not possible.'

'It's a great disgrace for any family to let their heartwood die,' Tisis said. 'That said, perhaps we should focus on more immediate matters.'

'Such as?' Kip asked. He stopped. 'Oh.'

A gallows had come into view. Ten ragged corpses bedecked with rags and carrion birds (rioters, no doubt) were hanged beside a familiar man whose trousers alone would have fed those rioters for a month.

'They hanged Conn Hill?' Cruxer asked. 'But why?'

'Because he offended Kip,' Tisis said, shocked. 'They're that desperate.'

Kip felt a sudden wave of guilt, as when he'd not hidden the money well enough and his mother had found it and gone on another binge. After she sobered, she'd berate him for failing her.

Conn Hill had been an asshole. Kip had wanted the man out of his sight. He'd guessed the Council of Divines would strip him of his position as conn. But this?

What had Kip done?

They entered a glorious plaza nearly the size of a hippodrome. It was paved with flawless white granite cobbles, and stately buildings in green and marble embraced by living wood rose on each side of the square. The grandest was the Palace of the Divines, which lay at the top of thirty wine-red marble steps like a pale bloated dictator in his palanquin.

The Divines, septuagenarians all, stood at the top of the steps in a semicircle.

Kip was clearly expected to dismount and climb the steps. He rode up the steps.

Don't fall off the damn horse. Don't fall off the damn horse.

The horse was sure-footed, though, and it deposited Kip at the top of the stairs in the midst of seven scandalized old men and their retinues. The Mighty had dismounted, and flowed up the steps like a black tide.

Having made a small point about how he might not do what they expected, Kip undercut it by striking a demure attitude.

'Greetings, my lords,' he said with only a tiny smile.

'Greetings, Lord Guile, Savior of Dúnbheo, Defender of Blood Forest, and loyal son of the Seven Satrapies,' an officious, nasally man at one end said. Kip thought it was Lord Aodán Appleton from Tisis's briefings. He decided he didn't like the little stuffed turd.

The others echoed him. Several looked openly hostile. Good, those he could trust. They also stood together, like amateurs, like cattle herding close to ward off harm. A faction, then.

After dealings at the Chromeria, it was actually refreshing to see one's friends and enemies do something so kind as to line up so you could tell who was who.

Time to stir the pot.

There were thousands of people gathered in the square, watching, though of course they wouldn't hear anything that Kip said to the assembled lords. Then again, Kip supposed that after weeks and months under siege, pretty much anything would seem fascinating. Perhaps he couldn't fault them for looking even to him for entertainment.

Might as well start out by putting them off balance.

'Good, good,' Kip said. 'I'm so glad to find you so amenable.'

'My lord Guile,' Lord Aodán Appleton said. 'We would like to present you—'

'I don't really enjoy ceremony,' Kip said, 'so let's skip all that. I see you've hanged that asshole, um, what's his...Hill. Conn Hill, wasn't he? Was that for me?'

They looked at each other, and some of the gazes were hateful. The hateful three of the wimpy herd were Lord Ghiolla Dhé Rathcore (nephew of Orea Pullawr), Lord Breck White Oak (third cousin of Karris White Oak), and Lord Cúan Spreading Oak (grandson of Prism Gracchos Spreading Oak and a kitchen maid). Kip guessed that they'd been allies of Conn Hill. With him dead, their majority on the Council had dissolved.

'We simply respect you so much that we wished to make your time here before you take your army to Green Haven as easy as possible, my lord,' Lord Culin Willow Bough said. He did an unconvincing job of looking mournful at the demise of his rival.

Orholam's beard, I really am in a backwater. This is what passes for the nobility here?

'I appreciate that,' Kip said. 'He was a bastard. I don't know if I could have worked with him. I'd like to reward whoever's idea it was. I imagine Conn Hill had some lands and titles one might redistribute to the worthy?'

'We don't often punish a whole family for one man's miscalc—' Lord Cúan Spreading Oak said.

'You don't often do a lot of things. I think good work should be rewarded fairly. Don't you agree?' Kip asked.

'We...we all agreed it should be done,' Cu Cománn said, speaking for the first time. He was white haired and pale as the dead, a look accentuated by a figure as lean as a rapier.

'Well, I'm not going to split up lands that have a history and a people. Satrap Willow Bough will already be irritated with me for this redistribution without his consent. He and I have bigger things to discuss, but I needn't rub it in his face. I know it wasn't any of them,' Kip said, pointing to the huddled three. 'They look angry and scared, friends of his, no doubt.'

'Not *friends*, per se,' Lord Breck said. The others glared at him.

'It was my idea,' Lord Cu Cománd said.

'He's not jumping on the credit where he oughtn't, is he?' Kip asked Lord Willow Bough and Aodán, as if it were funny.

'We agreed readily,' Lord Aodán said.

Lord Cu Cománd came from the smallest and weakest family on the Council of Divines. He had no doubt seen this as his big chance to move up.

'This wasn't part of some internal politicking, was it?' Kip asked. 'This was really for me?'

'Yes, my lord,' Lord Cománd said. A flicker of doubt crossed his face, but it was too late. 'A gift.'

'Hang him,' Kip said.

The words hit the rest like a grenado in the face, as the Mighty grabbed the man.

'Irritating me is not a hanging offense!' Kip bellowed. 'But murder is!'

'What are you – you can't do this!' Lord Cu Cománd said. 'What, do you think you're Gavin Guile himself? You're just a goddam child! You can't do this!'

Kip tilted his head. 'Funny,' he said, 'this city must be special indeed, because I hear a dead man speaking.'

Big Leo and Ferkudi dragged the lord down the steps bodily.

'Stop!' Cománd shouted. 'Fine! It wasn't for you! We had a feud with the Hills. Colm had ruined my sister ten years ago. They were engaged to be married and, and, and! He could have made peace, but instead he—'

'And you thought to use my coming as a cover for your vengeance,' Kip said.

'It was my only chance! The Hills were stronger than us. They were going to get away with it!'

'Like you almost did,' Kip said from the top of the steps. Everyone always has a good reason why the law shouldn't apply to them. Quietly, he said, 'Lords Appleton, Willow Bough.'

'Yes, my lord?' they said quietly.

'You lied to me.'

'We said nothing!' Lord Willow Bough said.

'Indeed,' Kip said. 'You let him lie to me, and you stood by silent and hoped it would benefit you.'

525

'We – we weren't really lying?' Lord Appleton said.

'Oh? Let me guess: you were just pulling my leg.'

They said nothing.

'Then now you can pull your friend's leg. One on each side.'

They looked at each other like they didn't understand.

'Go,' Kip said. 'Pull his legs to help him strangle quickly. He almost made you richer and more powerful; it's the least you can do in return.'

Less than a minute later, in utter silence, a noose was thrown over the gallows and tied to a saddle. With his hands bound behind his back, Lord Cu Cománn was lifted from the ground by his neck. His legs kicked and flailed until Lord Willow Bough and Lord Appleton each grabbed one and hugged it to their chests.

Lord Comán tried to kick them free. The body wants to live. But they held on, throwing all their weight into it, and his neck cracked and elongated.

A dark stain blossomed at his groin and spread down to where the lords held him, eyes clenched shut as if they hadn't felt all the fight go out of him. Nor did they feel the warm wetness for several long seconds.

They stepped back, revulsion and horror painting their faces, and then again as they took in Comán's head bent too far to one side, his neck inhumanly long.

Kip beckoned them back, and they came, painfully aware of the massive presence of Big Leo and Ferkudi.

The crowd was still as a tomb.

Strangely, it hadn't seemed to even occur to any of the nobles to try to call forth the city's own fighters to defend them. Not that it would have done them much good, but these nobles were men who couldn't even conceive of their privileges being abrogated, or on what those privileges rested, so they had no mental recourse when they were.

The lords rejoined the circle, holding their hands out, disgusted by the foulness they'd touched and done, but unwilling to wipe them on their clothes. Rich men, then, but not so rich as to defile their finest clothes.

Kip said, 'I'm going to tell you how things are going to be, and you are going to surprise me with how quickly you make them happen. Do we understand each other?' He didn't wait for an answer. 'Here's what's first.'

And on Kip's orders, the family of each of the Seven brought forward its chief accountant or secretary. Kip had fourteen horses saddled and waiting. In front of him, so that the lords could send no secret message, each was ordered to go to his employer's home or business and retrieve all his account books. He gave no more detail, and each was paired with a trained accountant from Kip's camp.

With no idea exactly what Kip was looking for, and no time to forge accounts, it would at least minimize the ability to obfuscate. Before the accountants left, Kip said, 'Oh, and if you're not back in one hour, both you and your lord hang. No excuses.'

'This, this is preposterous!' Culin Willow Bough said. He was a distant cousin of the satrap's.

'Yes, that I should *need* to do this is an outrage,' Kip said. He turned sharply to the accountants, who were frozen, wondering if his command would be called off. 'One hour, minus one minute,' he said. 'Shall I shave off another five minutes for impertinence?'

They galloped off in every direction.

'This is...most upsetting, Lord Guile,' Lord Golden Briar said. His moron son Dónal had set a trap for the Blood Robes at the Earthworks of Martis. The ambush had been turned back on them, and five thousand of his men were massacred in the muddy maze. He was new to the Council of Divines, brought in only hours ago to replace Conn Hill. Doubtless he was on the side of Willow Bough, Appleton, and Cománn, but he hadn't been around long enough for Kip to hold him responsible for anything.

'For that I apologize,' Kip said. 'But the problems here are significant, and you seem to be a people who appreciate the value of sharp action, are you not?'

'I...I suppose,' Lord Golden Briar said uncertainly.

'Your friends hanged a man within a couple of hours so you could be brought onto the Council to change the balance of power in a city. That's sharp action,' Kip said.

'Yes,' Lord Golden Briar admitted. 'It is, my lord.'

He didn't look afraid, and Kip wondered for a moment if he'd hanged the wrong man. But then, Комán had confessed to murder, and you can't hang men simply for being dangerous.

Or you can, but you have to give up any pretense of morality if you do.

'I want to know where all the food is,' Kip said.

'Food?' Lord Appleton asked, as if he hadn't gotten it through his head yet that Kip wasn't a moron.

Kip said, 'I understand hoarding food to take care of your own family and household in uncertain times. At some point it gets venal and cruel to your neighbors, but I understand it. But when you've got so much set aside that you have no fear of starvation but instead you're using that food to enslave your neighbors – making them trade their own children and their own bodies for a crust of bread – for that I have no patience.'

'There's no law against being wise enough to buy food before a siege.'

'No,' Kip said, 'but I daresay there are laws against hoarding it and then using your votes as councilors to buy it back from yourselves at ever-inflating prices. We call that corruption where I'm from.'

'We've done nothing illegal,' Lord Culin Willow Bough said.

'Considering that you've written the laws in this city and that Satrap Willow Bough is probably incapable of providing oversight on the lacing of his boots, that may actually be true,' Kip said. 'Your ledger books will tell us that.'

'Those books are private,' Lord Willow Bough said.

It had been Tisis who'd given Kip the idea of inspecting their books originally – they'd planned to do that regardless. A marching army needs food and supplies, and the nobles they liberated would have every incentive to underreport what they had available. It was Ferkudi who'd been puzzled by the scouts' reports that the city was desperate. This was a rich area that had had a long, long time to prepare for the Blood Robes' arrival.

Kip had been shocked only at how bad things had gotten, how callous these rich men had become to the suffering of their own people. The plan had always been to spring these changes on the Divines as if Kip were coming up with them off the top of his head – that was the only way to make sure they got no word of it beforehand.

They wanted to see him as young and impulsive? He'd play that happily enough with one tiny twist – he was young and impulsive and therefore dangerous.

'Here's what's going to happen,' Kip said. 'You're going to give me all the food you've stockpiled, and half the coin.'

'Ha!' said Lord Golden Briar. 'You'll have to hang all of us before we agree to this outrage!'

'Oh, I'll hang you if I must,' Kip said. 'But first I'll let it be known to the whole city that you've stockpiles of food and coin in hidden rooms in your houses, and that no soldiers or guards are present to protect them.'

'That's not true,' Lord Appleton said tightly. He believed Kip now. 'We would never put ourselves at such risk—'

'But thousands of starving, angry people won't know that, will they? The mobs will tear apart your homes, steal everything they can lay their hands on, and then likely burn them down when they find no food. I should think your families and any servants on the premises won't fare well, either. Heart trees will be cut down before your eyes. In the aftermath, new noble families may well have to be chosen.'

And finally, finally, true fear began to trickle into their piggish little eyes. 'You wouldn't,' Lord Willow Bough said. 'You're one of us. You wouldn't turn your back on fellow lords.'

'One of you? I'm one of them,' Kip said, pointing to the starving hordes, 'just in nicer clothes. The entire reason your class exists is so that when your city falls on hard times, you're there to feed the starving and protect the vulnerable. In return for that, in peacetime and in plenty, you're allowed to enjoy the fruits of excess. But you've not kept your bargain. You've not just failed your basic purpose, you've betrayed it. You've torn down this city and exploited its people when they needed you most. So this...this *is* my mercy. And it's the last mercy I'm going to offer you.'

And like that, they were broken. Cúan Spreading Oak and Lord Ghiolla Dhé Rathcore actually looked ashamed of themselves. But it was Lord Golden Briar, the conniver, who hit his knees first.

Even connivers have their place.

The rest dropped to their knees in submission. And Kip pressed on, because Andross Guile had taught him something: a hard push does the most when a man is already stumbling backward.

'And here's my first decree,' Kip said. 'Don't stand until you consent. Anyone enslaved in the last ninety days will be freed, immediately. In addition, we're now enforcing the old Slave Code. Anyone caught taking a slave or snipping a child's ear will face death. Families will not be split. Children born to slave parents will be born free and entitled to a freedom price when they reach majority. If you can't produce papers for any slave currently owned, they'll be manumitted. Period. Of those still in bondage after all this, their papers will be revised to show that on the seventh year, the Year of Jubilee, they'll be granted freedom. That's five years from now, in case you've forgotten. Plenty of time to adjust to the new reality. Copies of the new contracts will be signed and witnessed by a magistrate and a luxiat and be filed here and with the Chromeria.'

Lord Golden Briar, still looking at the ground, whispered, 'Are you insane?'

'Idealistic. It's a near cousin.'

'We could resist,' Lord Golden Briar said. 'We might not win, but we could stain your image irreversibly. The Luíseach is supposed to be a uniter.'

'I've never claimed that title,' Kip said. 'I'm just another man trying to protect his people...But others have claimed that name for me, and imagine their fury at you if you try to tarnish it.'

A silence stretched out. Then, like a weed too long in the pitiless sun, the man shriveled and wilted. 'My lord,' Lord Golden Briar said, and he reached out his hand to touch Kip's foot in submission.

And just like that, Kip had a city, and his army had food.

Chapter 73

'I had hoped to find you in better condition,' the man said.

'Grinwoody?' Gavin asked, incredulous. 'Is that you? Did my father send you? Did something happen to him?'

That was the only thing Gavin could guess: that his father had had a change of heart, and sent the old slave to stop Gavin from eating the poison.

'You may stand, but don't move forward.'

'Grinwoody, stop this nonsense.'

'I'll kill you if you move toward me, and that would be terribly inconvenient for both of us.'

'What?' Gavin said.

Grinwoody slid a basket across the ground. There was thin-sliced ham and bread and olives and a wineskin inside. Gavin fell on it like a wild animal.

After a few minutes of paradise, as Gavin tried to fight the urge to gorge himself and mostly failed, Grinwoody said, 'It turns out I need someone with your particular gifts, Gavin Guile. Or should I say Dazen?'

The shock of hearing his real name on the lips of one who shouldn't know it should have worn off by now, but it still tightened Gavin's chest. Some secrets sink their claws so deep that the shock of their revelation tears those claws out of flesh and leaves scars forever.

'I should like to talk to you someday,' Grinwoody said, 'about pretending to be someone you're not. For years and years, pretending. We are none of us who we pretend to be. But you and I...we took it to an extreme that few people could even imagine, did we not? But the pretense changes you, doesn't it? I wonder how it changed you, Dazen.'

'Who are you, then?' Gavin asked. Olives. Dear Orholam, he'd nearly forgotten how glorious an olive was. It was impossible to eat and think at the same time.

What in the hells was Grinwoody talking about?

'I come with a deal for you, Gavin Guile – I presume that's how you'd like me to refer to you. So much easier that way, isn't it? Unfortunately, if you don't take the deal, I'll have to kill you. I would much prefer to give you a real choice, but perhaps death was the road you were going to choose anyway, mm?' He gestured to Gavin's hand and to the bread hollowed out on the floor.

'Death threats!' Gavin said. 'How original.'

'Do you remember this?' Grinwoody asked. Careful not to let it touch his skin, Grinwoody held forth a small jewel of living black luxin, barely visible in the greater and lesser darknesses of the cell. It was attached to straps, somewhat different from the choker band it had sported when Gavin found it.

Another hammer blow of fear.

'That's the black jewel I recovered from the blue bane, isn't it?' Gavin said, voice even.

'Put it on.'

Gavin didn't, of course. 'What is this?'

'The White King has learned a little mastery of black luxin, Gavin. And we learned it from him. He says that he can control black luxin everywhere in the world. He may even believe it, but it's a lie. He learned to will-cast simple commands into the black, and we learned from him. Thus, after you put it on, if you remove it, it will kill you. Or if you say my name or act while willing that I be exposed, or if I say the word, or trigger it in a number of other ways that I won't bother to tell you, it will kill you. This is my guarantee of your obedience, your compliance with the deal I'm about to offer you.'

'Who are you?' Gavin asked.

'Upon my majority, my people named me Amalu Anazâr, the Daring Rebel in Shadows, the Dark Defiant One. More know me as the Old Man of the Desert.'

Gavin almost broke out laughing.

'Not the response I was expecting,' Grinwoody said. 'But then, you have been down here a long time, haven't you?'

He didn't ask what was funny, which was just as well. Gavin wouldn't have told him. Both he and his father had unknowingly brought spies as close to themselves as possible – his father an old, withered man, and himself a young, beautiful girl. But both slaves, like a dark and a light mirror, had been spies on the Guile men, father and son. Spies serving in places no one would dare, serving quietly, serving well, and serving traitorously. Both Guiles had been blind to those closest to them.

Perhaps not funny after all. Perhaps not coincidental, either. Like father, like son. Except Gavin had been protected by the White and his mother. They had chosen a good traitor, in both senses of the word.

But that Marissia should be dead while this vile thing lived on was milk curdling in his mouth.

'So, Old Man. What is it you want?'

'I direct assassins, Gavin Guile, what do you think I want?'

'Ha. You. I'm still having a hard time... Who would you want me to kill?' Gavin asked suddenly. Who out there would require a washed-up former Prism to kill them?

'In return for your freedom and your life, you go to White Mist Reef, climb the Tower of Heaven, and kill Orholam.'

Oh, *come on*, I thought I got to be the crazy one in this room.

'Pardon?' Gavin took a sip of the wine. Orholam only knew when he'd get another chance.

'I know your seventh goal, Dazen. Maybe this will allow that. Unlikely, but possible.'

'Are you mad? It's impossible. All of it. Legends and idiocy.'

'And yet you're more irritated that I know your seventh goal.'

Gavin sneered. 'I've never said it aloud. Never written it once. Barely even thought it.'

'It's impossible for you not to think it. Great men dream of being the promachos. Great drafters dream of being the Prism. What does the greatest promachos and Prism of all time dream of?'

Gavin said, 'Even if it were true, it's impossible.'

'Improbable. But I believe in taking long-odds wagers, and in following them to their end. I've arranged everything to give you this one chance. And, of course, if you choose death, all my work will have been for nothing.'

'And how am I supposed to kill Orholam? With very sharp

words? The cutting edge of my disbelief? The poison of a Prism's hypocrisy?'

'Put this on.' Grinwoody extended the jewel toward Gavin. 'Or die. Now.'

The old Gavin would have taken the opportunity to attack while the slave-king had one hand occupied. But Gavin had no strength and one clumsy half hand, and he'd seen the old man move. Though aged, Grinwoody was a martial artist, and Gavin could barely move. Worse, with the rich food in his stomach, he'd probably just throw up.

Gavin took the jewel.

At first glance, he'd assumed the setting had been changed simply so he could wear the jewel lower on his neck than a choker would allow. He'd been wrong. There were too many straps for that, and they were too short. The glittering black jewel was set through the middle of an eye patch. It looked like a veritable eye of darkness.

'I took some liberties with the original design,' Grinwoody said. 'It will still kill you if you try to remove it. When you bathe, you can hold it in your hand. Just make sure it *never* loses contact with your skin.'

Gavin put it on. It snugged against his left eyelid tight enough that it pressed skin into the divot where his pupil lay, lensless. A chill went down Gavin's spine, and he wasn't sure it was entirely natural.

Grinwoody's demonically gleeful look of triumph made Gavin want to punch him in the face.

'It's a good look on you. Follow me,' the old man said.

He turned his back on Gavin, utterly dismissive of what had once been the most dangerous man in the world.

'Guile,' the dead man said. But now he didn't speak with Gavin's voice, but what might have been his own guttural growl. 'Take me. I'm the only one who can save you. Touch that black stone in your eye patch to the wall, and I will make you emperor of this world in truth.'

Gavin could swear that in the black-on-black he could make out a pair of hateful gleaming eyes.

He smiled into the darkness. 'What kind of a raka do you take me for?'

Expecting claws to dig into his head and pull him back into hell at any moment, Gavin slowly stepped out of the cell.

Another step. Another.

'This way,' Grinwoody said after he swung the door to the black cell shut. 'There's...old superstitions among the Braxians that there's something terrible below the Chromeria. Like about how you can't take anything out of there, or something cataclysmic would happen. Andross was always very careful to strip and wash before he came out of here. I also put an emetic in that food. Just in case. Sometimes old traditions and old fears do hide wisdom.'

'What?' Gavin said. But he already could feel the answer to that in his belly. Orholam have mercy, what did the man think, he'd swallowed a stone?

Grinwoody came to a stop in a small chamber. The Old Man was already stripping off his own clothes and washing himself. He gestured to a basin. Gavin staggered over and was messily sick. But apparently it wasn't an emetic only.

'Can't take any risks that you swallowed something,' Grinwoody said. 'I have somewhere to be. I'll be back with clothes and real food. Don't forget: you try anything – and I mean even yell – and that black crystal will go straight through your skull.'

But Gavin was too busy being sick to even think of escape.

Chapter 74

'Your lady awaits in the honeymoon chamber, my lord,' Cruxer said.

They were not, perhaps, words that should have inspired dread.

Kip blew out a breath. He and Cruxer were virtually alone in the Council's chamber, which they'd converted to a war room. It was late. Big Leo was the only other person in the room, and he was propped against a wall, reading a book.

The first night in Dúnbheo, the Divines had either been in

disarray or had intentionally snubbed Kip by not having a room made ready. Kip and Tisis had worked so late they'd simply grabbed the nearest defensible room and slept. He didn't actually care, but he'd known that other people would – and that they would take his acceptance of an insult as a sign of weakness or barbarity – so he'd made a passing comment about how it was strange a people so famed for their hospitality could make such an oversight.

Tisis had helped, musing that maybe hospitality was more a virtue of the rural areas. The palace staff had been mortified. Outclassed by bumpkins? Unthinkable.

The conveniently dead Lord Comán had been blamed, and the staff had been almost painfully punctilious. Tonight they had prepared a room that was apparently not simply the city's finest, but a cultural treasure of some sort.

'Breaker?' Cruxer asked.

Kip was staring at the map. 'Uh, right. I'm just waiting for one last report.'

'He's gone, Breaker,' Cruxer said. 'It's not giving up on him to admit it. He just couldn't take it. Death isn't the only way we lose people in war.'

Contrary to his promise, Conn Arthur had left immediately, slipping away while the rest of the Nightbringers marched into the city. No one had seen or heard from him since.

'It's not just him,' Kip said. 'Sibéal's gone, too.'

'Gone? No note?'

'Nothing,' Kip said. 'I don't know if she went after Conn Arthur or if I'm looking at the beginning of a general desertion by the Ghosts.'

'That's impossible,' Cruxer said. 'Why would they?'

'Maybe they think if we save Green Haven they'll be back under the Chromeria's thumb and it'll be the end of them. I don't know,' Kip said.

'No. Not gonna happen,' Cruxer said with total certainty.

Kip loved him for that.

'And this is not something you need to worry about tonight. Sometimes you move heaven and earth, Breaker, and sometimes you just go to bed and let your wife make you happy. Very happy, if the gleam in her eye tells me anything.'

'You're a moron to keep her waiting,' Big Leo said from the corner, speaking for the first time in hours.

But Kip didn't move. That damned map.

'There are other problems?' Cruxer asked quietly enough that Big Leo wouldn't overhear. 'I mean, between you and her?'

Kip met his eye and was tempted to tell him everything, but how could Cruxer understand? And was it any of his business, anyway? 'Nah, it's, it's fine. It's great.'

Cruxer saw straight through the lie. Kip could tell. But he seemed to forgive it immediately. There are things a man just doesn't want to share about his marriage. 'Well, uh, even if there were some, uh, tough things going on, she didn't seem in a mood to fight tonight.'

'Thanks,' Kip said. 'I mean, thanks, really.' For putting up with a lie. That wasn't worthy of me.

'Nah, I'd say she was in a different mood altogether,' Big Leo said from his corner. Apparently they hadn't been speaking quietly enough.

But that damned map. Tisis had been working with the refugees from all over the Forest, all day long, to fill in more reports about the White King's movements. Kip rewound it and watched the light blossom again, everything they had since Ox Ford and even before up to the present.

He was missing something.

'Well, don't thank me, get a move on,' Cruxer said happily.

But Kip didn't move. He reached for the bag with the rope spear and tried to think. He bathed himself in yellow light from a special lantern. The problem was, he was almost done. He needed only to make the spear point now, and he wasn't certain that luxin would make the best material for it. He'd thought about tying a tassel to the spearhead to distract the eye or perhaps filling it with off-spectrum brightwater so it would shimmer and gleam as it moved, but he hadn't decided yet.

'Two things,' Cruxer said.

Kip looked at up at his friend. Cruxer drew a black spearhead from a bag.

Not just black, hellstone. He handed it to Kip. A setting of blackened steel graced the base of the blighted leaf-blade. Kip examined it and then the mantle of the rope spear. They snapped together perfectly.

'You want to explain this?' Kip asked.

'The hellstone came from the treasury here.'

That wasn't what Kip was asking, and Cruxer had to know. 'Ben-hadad do this?' he asked.

'We sort of all thought it was about time you were done with that damn thing,' Big Leo said, still without looking up from his book.

'What are you talking about?' Kip asked.

'Permission to speak bluntly, my lord?' Cruxer asked.

'Of course.'

'I mean, really bluntly.'

'Come on,' Kip said. As if he'd take offense.

'I figure a good friend gets one free chance to tell you you're being an asshole in your life. And if he's right, he gets one more.'

'That is an excellent introduction into whatever you're about to tell me,' Kip said.

'Are you just tolerating that amazing fucking woman down the hall there, hoping you can trade her for Teia someday? Grow some balls, man. Make a choice. You know we all love Teia. You know we do. But you're being an asshole to a woman who is better than I think you appreciate.'

'I appreciate her!' Kip protested.

'The question, Breaker,' Big Leo said, looking up from his book, his feet still propped up, 'isn't if you appreciate her. It's whether you're an asshole or a moron.'

'What are you talking about?' Kip said. 'Wait, is this about the rope spear? Are you joking? You think I've been making this for Teia?'

Big Leo closed his book, sighed, and walked toward the door.

'I'm glad you all have been so thoroughly won over by my wife,' Kip said to Cruxer. 'But you're sadly mistaken about the whole rope spear thing.'

Cruxer looked at him flatly. 'Yes, my lord.'

Kip looked at him, peeved. Of course, if they'd been mistaken, then mightn't she...

And then he thought of all the times Tisis had seemed disappointed or hurt when he'd pulled out his little project to work on. Surely she couldn't have made the same mistake.

Oh hells. She thought he hadn't really chosen her.

Hadn't chosen her? Come on! What bullshit...what totally, goddamned...accurate bullshit.

He was making the best of the hand life had given them.

But that was different, wasn't it? It wasn't making the choice his. It wasn't owning it.

Kip looked at the rope spear he'd made. It was a perfect weapon, and completely hypothetical. He couldn't use it.

He *hadn't* chosen Tisis, had he? Despite everything. He'd called what they had 'fun' and told her he 'cared for her,' and he'd spent his spare time – for a year! – on a gift for another woman.

He stood up and tossed the damn thing to Cruxer.

'What do you want me to do with it?' Cruxer asked.

'I don't care,' Kip said.

'You spent a year on that thing,' Big Leo said, standing up and closing his book. 'It's brilliant. I mean, the execution, not the idea of you doing it. Or working on it in front of your wife. Or taking time away from—'

'Thanks, Big Leo! Enough!' Kip said.

'You are going to at least name it, right?' Big Leo said. 'Magical weapons have to have names. It's a rule or something.'

'Sorry,' Kip said, ducking past the big man and out into the hall.

'Wait!' Big Leo said. 'Is that you refusing to name it, or is that its name?'

Chapter 75

A paryl trip wire perched across the top step, waiting for Teia. It was an impressive distance from the mirror room, farther than she'd thought possible. Either Murder Sharp had just arrived, or he was a better paryl drafter than she had known.

She rubbed her face with her hands, as if she could scrub away fear as easily as she could rub fog off a window. It was about as effective. She checked quickly that no one could possibly see her in the stairwell, but of course the path to the mirror room was abandoned on the night of a new moon. Seeing it was safe, she made the sign of the seven, splaying her fingers to touch forehead, eyes, and mouth, then tapping them to heart and hands. The deeper she'd gotten into the secrets of the Order through the winter and into this spring, the more she needed to make an outward show of her own beliefs. The deeper she fell into the pits of heresy, the more orthodox she was becoming. But fear fogs the windows again at any hesitation, so there was time for only one sign and one brief prayer. Orholam, let your light guard me in this darkness.

It didn't seem to do anything, but she kicked through the trip wire anyway. She walked down the hallway quietly, as if she didn't know her entrance had been announced. There was another trip wire outside the door. She paused, then stepped over it, opening the door slowly.

The door squeaked. Of course it did.

She let out a cloud of paryl from her fingertips. It billowed freely through the room full of silent mirrors mounted on their great spinning frames. The paryl cloud spread from her outstretched hands like the slow blast of a blunderbuss: lighter paryl from her right hand floating up toward the ceiling while heavier, nearly solid paryl spilled across the floor and drizzled down the great circular holes in the floor. The slowly erupting cloud crashed against an invisible form in front of her, and curled around it like a thunderhead parting around a mountain.

The Shadow stood silent, his head bowed to hide his eyes.

Then a hand extended from his shimmercloak, and as easily as if he were tearing the covers off a bed, he ripped away the entire cloud of paryl and was invisible once more.

She was left aghast at how easily he'd done it; his will had suffused the entire cloud, had touched her own. Having will touch will unexpectedly was like having a stranger walk up to you and caress your face with both hands – not violent, but still violating.

He was invisible again. Heart straining, chest tight, she strained to hear the whisper of cloth on cloth that would be her sole warning of his attack.

But then the figure shimmered into visibility, and Murder Sharp flung back his hood.

'You made one mistake,' he said.

'Mistake?'

'When I was a younger man,' Sharp said, 'I fancied myself to be formidable. I flattered myself that I was scary.'

Sharp had changed again in all the months he'd been gone. His hair had grown out and, while still short, had been trimmed neatly in a swept style preferred by some young nobles, and it was dyed to auburn from its previous fiery red. His naturally golden eyes had been colored somehow to brown – lenses that sat on the eye itself? Was such a thing possible? The scleras of his eyes were red from the irritation of wearing them, but no more than a haze smoker's.

Worse, he wore the white uniform and gold insignia of a Lightguard captain.

'I had to be reined in,' he said. 'Violently. I was bitter about it for a time, but now I see that every gem needs to have its rough edges chipped away before the stone can be polished to gleam.'

He reached up to his mouth, fingering his immaculate teeth. And then he pulled out the dentures with a sucking sound and a dribble of spit. He examined the human teeth on his dentures with a craftsman's eye, scrubbing at some imperceptible imperfection on the dogtooth, then tucked the dentures away in a special box.

From a pocket, he produced another box, but he didn't open it immediately.

'But you. You, Adrasteia, I don't think the Old Man will be as gentle with you as he was with me.'

He smiled at her then, revealing his natural, broken teeth. Like an ancient circle littered with toppled stones where once there had been symmetric perfection, half incisors and dogtooth nubs slumped in front of shattered and missing molars.

'Only pain makes us sharp,' Murder Sharp said. 'Only *pain* makes a Sharp.'

He opened the other box he'd taken from his pocket and lifted a new set of dentures from it. They were fixed with a nightmare assortment of fangs. 'Weasel-bear for the dogteeth, naturally. Special animal to all Braxians. Hard to see, near impossible to kill. Takes down prey far larger than itself through patience and then sheer ferocity. Called a wolverine some places. Not sure why. Doesn't share a thing with wolves so far as I can see. Fox fangs here. Quicker than weasel-bears, and can hide in plain sight, despite that ginger coat.' He smiled his ruined smile again. 'And all the rest are piranha fangs, from the rivers of Tyrea that flow into the far ocean. Piranha are frightening by themselves. River pugilists. Jaw like a bare-knuckle fighter. But nothing wants to tangle with 'em when they swarm. That's the Order, Teia. A river full of piranha with weasel-bears on the banks and foxes in the rushes.'

He tested the edges of the weasel-bear fangs.

'There's this rare fish in those waters. Damn thing *feeds* on piranhas. Front fangs this long. Gorgeous, gorgeous fangs.' He sighed. 'But too long to fit in a human mouth, sadly. I tried. Bloodied my mouth half a dozen times before I learned. So I settled for the piranha fangs instead. Thought it was appropriate, the predator that everyone fears in turn fears one – only one.'

'The Old Man.'

'The Old Man,' he agreed.

'Are you going to break out my teeth like he broke out yours?' she asked, gulping against the bile rising in her throat.

He laughed softly, exposing those weathered plinths and jagged spires of tooth stumps again. 'You think *he* did this to me?'

Murder Sharp took out a handkerchief and bit down on it. Methodically he worked it around his mouth, keeping his lips back, drying his teeth. He pulled back the blue luxin protective strips from an adhesive lining and then carefully fit the fang dentures into his mouth. He moved his jaw back and forth and took a few experimental bites to see how the fangs meshed, careful to keep his lips clear. His eyes clouded over with something like bliss.

'No,' he said several moments later. 'He told me he'd found

542

my disobedience. He told me only pain makes us sharp. Then he gave me the tooth breaker and told me to get out.'

You broke out your own teeth? Teia thought, aghast.

'Murder came back the next morning,' an altered voice said from the shadows.

Teia flinched hard. She'd been so focused on Sharp, she hadn't even dreamed there could be someone else up here. It was *he*.

'He came back swollen, and bloody. But he came back with the job done. I had never heard of such devotion, such readiness to pay penance,' the Old Man said. 'I told him he had earned my trust and a Name, as were given to the mighty of old. He said only pain makes us sharp. You see?'

He chuckled and Murder joined in.

These people are fucking crazy.

As if she hadn't figured that out already in nearly a year of serving them.

'I don't get it. I don't understand,' Teia said.

'That's good. A tool should never be smarter than its wielder.'

She wanted to tell him where to go.

'Which brings us to our present difficulty,' the Old Man said. He stayed where he was, against one curving outer wall of the tower. He was hooded and cloaked, and a glint of spectacles was visible – the paryl ones, Teia guessed. 'Your actions up until now had allayed my suspicions. Or so I thought.'

'You've got to be fucking joking,' Teia said. 'I'm still proving myself? Fine. Tell me to kill her. I will. I don't care. You told me to get close. I am. But I've never forgotten what I'm there for. And you still haven't given me my...' – she took a sharp breath through her nose and corrected herself – '*a* cloak.'

'Allaying my suspicions is one thing; earning my trust is quite another,' the Old Man said. 'But even that is in jeopardy now.'

Teia said nothing.

Murder Sharp had faded back, off to the side, far enough that he was out of Teia's peripheral vision. The serpent fear in her guts wakened and turned. She looked at him with a challenge in her eyes.

He stared back blankly and started picking at his fangs.

543

'Let's talk about your father,' the Old Man said.

'What? Why?' she asked, not able to keep the surprise from her voice.

'The White paid all his debts, right around the time you became a Blackguard. She had no reason to do that.'

There was no pretending ignorance, not with the Old Man. No deflection. 'She told me it was normal to look into Blackguard scrubs' lives to see if there were any ways enemies could exploit them, turn them. I was shocked, too. But she said she was dying and had no heirs, and her wealth could at least do some good.'

'You never told the other Blackguards about it.'

'Well, none of the ones on your payroll, apparently,' Teia said. She sounded like a snotty kid even to herself.

Murder Sharp tensed at her disrespect, and she made a soothing gesture.

'Easy. Sorry. Look, I didn't tell anyone. Look.' She took a breath. 'We all came from different places, and some of us talk about our pasts and some don't. They can see my ear. They know I was a slave. A fair number of the girls who came from that life...well, we don't volunteer much, and the others don't ask. There's everything from orphans to nobles' children in the Blackguard. I thought that by telling what she'd done for me I would sound like I was bragging. But yes, absolutely, it meant the world to me.'

'Enough to buy your loyalty?'

'As a slave, I'm pretty attuned to people trying to buy me, thanks. It wasn't that. She wasn't using her money to put me in her debt, not precisely. To her, the money was negligible. The effort and the care were the real expenses. She was a great woman, and she was kind to me. I know she was clever, too, but I saw no falsehood in it.'

'But it was enough to buy your loyalty all the same,' the Old Man said.

'If you have to put it like that, yes. Like you "bought" mine by melting down all those silver items I stole that Lady Crassos was using to blackmail me, I suppose.'

He chuckled and wagged a finger. 'Point. Very clever, very true. Did it work?'

'It did, until now,' she said gloomily. No, it had never worked. It had always been clear to her that she was working with monsters.

'We killed Orea,' the Old Man said. 'Specifically, Murder did. Your master. That a problem for you?'

Teia flinched. As soon as the old woman had come up, she'd been desperately searching her mind for any time Murder had mentioned her, and if she was supposed to know that the Order had killed her – but all her information had come from sources the Order couldn't – shouldn't – know about. 'I suspected as much,' she said.

'But you never asked. Despite feeling loyalty to her,' Sharp asked skeptically.

'I cared about her, yes. But she was old, dying already. I wasn't going to ask about it until I knew you trusted me. I look forward. Why risk my own neck for someone who's already dead?' It seemed so easy, somehow, here in the darkness, to talk and think like those who were empty.

'This,' the Old Man said. 'From a girl who likes to hold grudges? You're not angry at me or Sharp?'

'Oh hell yes! I've got a list of things I'm furious at you for,' Teia said. 'But I'm not an idiot. Being mad at you isn't like being mad at your neighbor who gets loudly drunk every night after you go to bed; it's like being mad at the weather. Raise your fist to your neighbor, you might change things. Raise your fist to the sky, and you're a fool.'

He seemed to appreciate the flattery. But then he walked over to one of the great mirrors on the east side of the tower. It was blackened, burnt – not just soot on the glass, but the silver backing itself was mottled and melted, ruined. 'I asked you to meet us here for two reasons: The lightwells are handy to dispose of a corpse if necessary – we can't disappear a Blackguard, and slipping down these is easy enough that it could be accidental. Second, for this. I like physical illustrations when I can afford them.' He patted the mirror. 'Do you know how this happened?' he asked.

'Sir? No.'

'No one does. It happened during the executions on Orholam's Glare – which is when anything would fail, one imagines. The intensity of that light scared off no few of our newest members. The caretakers of these mirrors are slaves, of course, but highly prized, intelligent, taken excellent care of, like the Blackguards themselves. They swore it must be sabotage, for they would never, never leave so much as a smudge on one of the great mirrors, certainly not before such a grand occasion. Others claim it was the djinn himself who reached his will up and smote the mirror, but that he couldn't break even one before he died.

'Carver Black himself hasn't been able to replace it. The backup mirrors appear on their lists of inventory they purchased years ago, but not in their storehouses. Not our work, actually, just old-fashioned corruption – someone long ago lining their pockets. Creating new mirrors of the quality needed to replace this one has been impossible because of the war. They require Atashian or Tyrean glass and silver from the Karsos Mountains bonded by one of three lens makers in Ru. So here it sits, long months after its failure. Marginally useful, kept in place mostly because the other mirrors need the counterweight, not because it does much of anything. It failed its purpose. Perhaps it never should have been put in service in the first place.' He stepped away from it. 'I don't want you to fail me, Adrasteia. I won't allow it. So I will test you to your limit, and perhaps beyond.'

He took a breath, studying her, and she held herself still and reflective as silver. Let him see only himself in me, she thought.

Then he said, 'Your father is here. On the Jaspers.'

And suddenly the cloud of danger suffusing the room like paryl gas crystallized in Teia's chest, choking her heart. Father? Here? He'd mentioned coming to the Jaspers in that letter last year that Orea Pullawr had shown her, but Teia'd never imagined he'd actually follow through on it.

And the Order had known about him before anyone.

'I want you to prove yourself. I want you to earn my trust like Elijah here did.'

No, no, no.

The Old Man said, 'Only pain makes us sharp. Only pain makes a Sharp. Are you ready, Teia? Ready to become a

Shadow? Ready to become my left hand as Murder is my right?'

Murder Sharp's eyes were orbs of midnight. Teia couldn't expand her own eyes without his seeing it, couldn't look for the paryl that she knew must be around and through her right now like a choking cloud. Any move that so much as smelled like hostility would mean death now. 'We're your family now, Adrasteia,' Sharp said.

'To become Teia Sharp, you must sever the last link of your loyalty to any other before us,' the Old Man said. 'You'll be given one hour to say your goodbyes, and then you'll kill your father. You'll be well paid for this. The rest of your family will be taken care—'

'Fuck you,' Teia said. 'No. Never.'

Murder Sharp growled, bestial behind his fangs, but the Old Man held up a gloved finger to him. 'Refusal is failure. Refusal is death, child.'

'Then kill me,' she said. She turned her back and started walking away. It was the longest walk of her life, those steps to the door. They stretched out as if she were trekking across the great deserts of the Broken Lands, hope as distant as water.

But nothing happened. It was a torture in itself. She reached the door and put her hand on the latch.

'Stop,' the Old Man said softly.

She turned. He could have stopped her easily enough with Sharp's skills. Apparently the Old Man was used to the force of his personality doing more than any magic could.

'There are only two kinds of people who will agree to commit patricide – unless they are victims of horrific abuse, in which case all bets are off. But we know your father was no abuser. Those willing patricides? Spies who have no intention of obeying, and those soulless folk who are willing to betray anyone because they are only capable of feigning loyalty, not feeling it. The Order excises both kinds of cancer without remorse. You see, Adrasteia, the thing that makes the Order great is that we are able to do the monstrous without becoming monsters. A girl who will kill her father for nothing more than her own ambition is a viper, and anyone who takes a viper to his breast deserves the bites he gets.'

'You're telling me this was another test?' Teia asked. 'Are you f—' She wrestled the words down. How many could she pass? What kind of lunatics were these people? How many times could she gamble her life before she lost just once?

'And your tests aren't finished,' the Old Man said.

'I can't do this forever,' Teia said.

'One more. One last test. One test that will make you a Sharp. One I would entrust to no one else.'

How many Shadows do you actually have? Teia suddenly wondered.

'So what is it? What do you want me to do?' she asked.

'Perhaps it just got old. Perhaps it simply…gave up.' He stared again at the blackened mirror, and then he put a gentle hand on it. 'The backbone of the Order's rising power is the shimmercloaks, Teia. Our assassins are frightening, where we have them, but the Shadows are terrifying. No one is safe from you. That power has two limits – there are few paryl drafters, though more than you might think – and fewer shimmercloaks. It means I have to think long and hard before sending Shadows on truly risky missions, because while the men and women wearing them can be replaced, the *cloaks* cannot.

'There's a man, Teia, who's going to go do something vitally important for me. You're to help him in any way you can. Then, after he's done it, you're going to recover whatever weapons he's carrying, and you're going to kill him. Just in case he fails – or succeeds in a way I've not foreseen. You'll kill him with this dagger, and you'll do it while he's awake. Not drugged, not asleep. Only awake will this dagger capture his will. You will stow away in his ship, and you will be given the Fox cloak to help you.

'You're going to kill a man after he's served you?' Teia asked.

'A poor thanks indeed, I agree. But this man is far, far too dangerous to be allowed to live. He would, after this service, hunt us all.'

And then she had a stomach-turning intuition. Who had served the Order, and was now too dangerous to be allowed to live? Ironfist.

But Ironfist wasn't here, was he? She'd heard some rumor

548

that he'd become King Ironfist. Another that he was coming to the Chromeria for some diplomatic discussion.

Could he have come already? By skimmer?

And what? Been kidnapped by the Order, just like that? Sure, they'd done it with Marissia, but Ironfist?

'If you succeed, you will keep the Fox cloak permanently, and I will return your father to you. He will not only be allowed to come or go as he pleases, he will go home with papers of membership in some very important traders' blocs with some very important monopolies. In short, he will go home a very wealthy man.'

'Or not at all,' Teia said. 'If I disobey.'

He brought his fingertips together and nodded. 'And as for you, I've already prepared how to explain your absence. You will return to the Blackguard seamlessly, with very few questions asked.'

'My absence?' Teia asked.

'Only pain makes a Sharp, Teia. You'll understand when you see who you're being asked to kill.'

So it was Ironfist. Please, Orholam, no.

Teia was that damned mirror. This was her great test, and the heat was too much for her. She was deforming, chipping, cracking. Or this demon before her was smashing her with his will. In all the time she'd had, she hadn't tracked down the Order's membership, hadn't retrieved the secrets bound up in ribbon, hadn't found the Old Man's office, much less broken into it. She'd murdered all those slaves for nothing.

Her father's life against the life of someone who was serving the Order? Some traitor?

What if it was Ironfist? But Teia couldn't save Ironfist if she wanted to. She couldn't save herself, now.

But she could save her father.

'There's a ship, *The Golden Mean*. You get aboard secretly and then hide belowdecks until you're well under way. The crew all belongs to me, but Captain Gunner is...unpredictable. You come back as Teia Sharp, or don't come back at all,' the Old Man said. He held forth a slender black knife that looked like writhing smoke in his hand.

She took the black dagger.

Chapter 76

'Ah, good, you live.' Grinwoody came in the room with fresh clothes and a basket of food.

Gavin was quivering on the floor. The vomiting had turned to dry heaves quickly enough, and the stomach cramps from the diarrhetic had passed some time ago. He'd been weakly sponge bathing himself since then. He was mostly clean now, for all the good that did him.

Grinwoody gave him water first. Gavin rinsed his mouth of the residual taste of vomit and spat it out. Then real food and clothes.

Nor did the old man rush him. But finally, when Gavin was feeling warm and full for the first time in a year, and a little tipsy from what could have only amounted to a single cup of wine, the counterfeit slave motioned it was time to go.

They left everything. 'I'll burn it later,' Grinwoody said.

Within a dozen paces out into a dim hall, he pushed against a section of wall, and a secret door opened on unseen hinges, silently.

'What's this?' Gavin asked.

'I made another gamble, months ago. I bet that you would end up in the black cell eventually, because I know your father.'

The narrow tunnel ascended sharply, barely wide enough for Gavin's turned shoulders to pass, and so short that he had to stoop to walk. But there was no stopping. He felt as if the darkness were chasing him with eager fingers.

In minutes, they emerged into an empty little hut with curtains drawn. In piles, and hanging from hooks, and standing in towers, were pitch and scrapers and lines and buoys and more lines and lanterns and various other implements for the keeping of ships. Gavin guessed it was one of the boat keepers' shacks at the Chromeria's back dock. It was still dark out, but a hint of light trickled around the cracks in the walls and around the curtains, hinting at coming dawn.

Grinwoody picked up a wrapped bundle. 'You asked before how you're to do it.' He grinned. 'If one is to kill a god, one must be properly armed.' Then Grinwoody – the hidden Old Man of the Desert, Anazâr – unwrapped a sword that was not a sword. Its blade was long, light, thin, with twin black whorls crisscrossing around each of seven shining jewels, one for each color, though to Gavin's eye they were a uniform brightness and tone. Along its spine was a thin musket barrel, except for the last hand's breadth, which was only a sweeping blade that served as both sword point and bayonet. The Blinding Knife.

To cover his sudden fear, Gavin said, 'You old bastard. You know my father wants this more than anything in the world, right?'

'Of course.'

'And what do you think happens when I pass the impassable reef, climb the tower that's probably just a trick of the light, climb the footstool of the Lord of Light himself, and stab him with this?'

Grinwoody grinned an arrogant grin. Shook his head. 'Are you really as desperate to believe in gods and devils as the rest of them? Knowing what you know? Having done what you've done? Orholam is no god. It is merely the nexus of this world's magic. It's not sentient. It's not a person or a godhead. It is the wobbling, unbalanced axle around which all magic rotates. It is the center that cannot hold.

'If you destroy this nexus men call Orholam, you kill magic itself. It will be an end of the tyranny of the Chromeria and an end to the magical storms that have devastated our world for millennia beyond counting. It will end the world putting one man in power while another is his slave – merely because the first can do magic. For that hope, for that hope for justice, I have wagered everything.'

'Regardless of the cost?' Gavin asked.

'The cost to do nothing is greater.'

'You really think the Blinding Knife will blind God himself.'

'This is the problem with erasing your own history, as the

Chromeria has done, never trusting its own with dangerous knowledge: sometimes the most dangerous things are exactly what you need to save yourself.'

'What are you talking about?' Gavin asked. Erasing history? Was this some kind of Order conspiracy theory?

'How I would love to sit and talk with you for an afternoon and tell you all the parts of your reign you owe to me, and all the things you misinterpreted through the decades. It would be better if your father were there, too, for he's been the more substantial foe by far. But we have little time. Dawn comes, and light waits for no man, am I right?' He peeked out the curtain, then dropped it back in place.

'I have no idea what you're talking about. What are your demands?'

'Do you remember this?' Grinwoody asked. He upended a black velvet bag into his hand, and a jewel the color of midnight dropped into his hand. It somehow radiated darkness, or sucked light into itself. It was living black luxin, but it was something more. If the black luxin in Gavin's eye patch was a child of eternal darkness, this was Mother Night herself.

'The black seed crystal,' Grinwoody said. 'You remember now?'

'I have...no memory of that.' Except that he felt an instinctive fear and revulsion at the sight of it. It was too painful to even behold.

'You created this. At Sundered Rock.' Grinwoody pushed back a curtain from a window and looked out at the water. Then he turned again to Gavin. 'Or perhaps this is an older one. You see, the Chromeria used to deny that seed crystals exist – even while they hoarded them. The seed crystals call their color of drafters to themselves – which is why, unknowing, drafters have always come here for their teaching. But uncontrolled, unchecked, they create the bane, and the bane call wights much more powerfully.

'The Chromeria likes to believe that there's only one seed crystal of each color. As if one can wish that there should be only one volcano, or one hurricane, or one earthquake – because one is devastating enough. The truth is, any sufficiently powerful drafter can create one, like you did at Sundered

Rock. Or they can spontaneously appear, as they have recently, if there's too much of their color. Maybe it's random, maybe it coalesces around a drafter of that color, like the first crystal in a freezing pond – what does it matter? When you create the right conditions, the bane appears. And the conditions now? Without you balancing? It's like all magic is a pond below freezing, waiting for that first crystal. Only death can follow, Dazen Guile.'

'Oh, good, here I was thinking things looked grim.'

Grinwoody stared at him, unsmiling. 'Apparently that irreverence has helped keep you alive and sane. I hope it continues to work for you.'

Gavin swallowed, flippancy gone. 'So what does the black do? Does it make a black bane?'

'I've never heard of such a thing, but then, they'd have erased that, too, if such didn't spontaneously erase themselves from men's memories as your conflagration at Sundered Rock did. No, Dazen, I'm not going to tell you any more. All you need to know is this...'

He balanced the sword on the floor, tip down, and set the black seed crystal on its pommel. It sank into the pommel, melted, and a change rushed over the entire surface of the sword. What had been black and white entwined now shimmered with darkness. As Grinwoody turned the blade, entire sections dulled in the light as if they were a polarized lens.

'...you find the nexus of magic, and you stab the Blinding Knife into it. I don't care if it's a thing or a person or God himself. You kill it, and our deal's complete.'

Simple.

'Why me?' Gavin asked. 'You've got dozens? Hundreds? of people loyal unto death to you.'

'The Blinding Knife's powers can only be activated by a Prism. Climbing the tower was once a pilgrimage open to all, but after Vician's Sin, the priests at White Mist Reef created magical locks on the tower to keep drafters from reaching the top – to protect the nexus, you see? There's a magical lock at each level, a blue lock to block blue drafters, a red to block reds, and so forth. So only a non-drafter will be able to reach the top of the tower.'

'How do you know this?'

'The Chromeria has always tried but failed to gain a monopoly on old knowledge. We Braxians have protected our own histories.'

'But if there are locks, surely there's one for black.'

'Not according to the records. Either black resists being formed in such ways, or the priests felt black defiled them to use. That's why they formed the reef instead – failing to keep out the worst, they decided to keep out everyone.'

'But you don't know if this will work.'

'Of course not. But I do know that you're the only person in the world who has a chance,' Grinwoody said. 'Only a non-drafter can reach Orholam. Only a Prism can use the Blinding Knife to kill him. Only you are both.'

'I never expected to find you betting on me,' Gavin said.

'One thing I like about you Guiles. People are usually either fighters *or* survivors. You're both.'

Gavin looked at the blade and couldn't even think. It was like staring down an infinite chasm now, where before it had been like staring at the sun. Each was too terrible to behold for long.

It felt *hungry*.

'So let's pretend I'm an enthusiastic participant,' he said. 'How am I supposed to get through White Mist Reef? You have drafters who can handle a skimmer?'

'I sent a skimmer already. It shattered in the stresses passage through the reef put on it. I'm sending you on a normal ship. Mostly.' Grinwoody checked the window again.

Gavin was incredulous. 'And what kind of a lunatic would be willing to attempt to sail through White Mist Reef?'

'The kind that gambles.'

What the fuck does that mean?

Then Grinwoody opened the door. Gavin followed him out onto the Chromeria's back dock. In the lightening gray of dawn, a magnificent white ship with a glimmering sheen was docked at the quay, but Gavin barely had a moment take it in.

'My friend!' a voice boomed out of Gavin's past. The human avatar of braggadocio ambled down the quay in an open jacket with no tunic beneath, wild hair, baggy trousers, and a huge, crooked-toothed grin.

'Gunner,' Gavin said. 'Of course it's you.'

'You look worst hand lass time,' Gunner said. Gavin thought it was a crack about his missing fingers at first, but then he translated: 'Worse than last time.'

But then Gunner stopped suddenly, stricken. His eyes were fixed on Gavin's eye patch as if it were a serpent that might strike him. 'What's with the evil eye? Is it bad luck?'

'Only for our enemies,' Grinwoody said.

'Indeed?' Gunner asked Gavin, still disconcerted. The man could be childlike in his superstitions.

'Troth,' Gavin said.

'Diggity. Been told I got a fearsome aspect my own self. Guess I can use you to loosen the bowels of any poppy fiends we got. I'll keep my deal,' he said, recovering his swaggering tone. 'Gunner abides his bets.'

Grinwoody lifted his eyebrows at the man's insouciance, but said nothing.

Gavin said, 'You *gambled* for this?'

'Nah...Sorta...I s'pose you could say...Yes. So you see, arter I lost the first time – my ante the gun-sword, his the ship yonder – he asked me if I wanted to go double or nothin'. I felt real down-like about losing your poky boom stick, plus I didn't have anything left to lose 'cept this mighty fine jacket what I plundered from an Ilytian pirate king. Plust, whenever has Gunner's luck been so bad he's lost twice in a row?' He twisted his ratty beard. 'So, uh, arter I lost again, he said I gots to sail my old bosom friend Guile through White Mist Reef. He calls that losing! An' if we live, I keep the ship! You know our missing?' Gunner asked. 'Our mission.'

'Oh yes.'

'Ain't it exasperbating?!'

Exciting? Exhilarating? That was one way to put it.

'Not so loud, please,' Grinwoody said, glancing back toward the Chromeria looming above them all.

'Can't wait to show you my new girl!' Gunner said. 'Guile! Brother! If we pull this off, we'll be legends!'

Gavin sighed. 'Gunner...we're already legends.'

Gunner winked. 'That's Cap'n Gunner to you.'

Gavin looked up at the Chromeria looming above him. Somewhere up there was Karris. She was *this* close. She was on this island, greeting this dawn, and she would never know he was here.

He was about to get on a ship and leave – going to his death, no doubt – and she would never know he'd been this close.

All that stuff about controlling the black luxin in Gavin's eye patch could be a bluff. Could be. But the Order was here, armed, unstoppable, standing behind everyone and everything he loved.

Grinwoody laid the Blinding Knife out over his palms. 'Let me make something clear, Guile. I have watched you for decades now. I have seen you prevaricate and charm. I have seen you baffle and obfuscate. I have seen you stand steady as a mountain and then dodge the inevitable with the grace of a bull dancer. I have seen you appear to lose, only to emerge quietly victorious years later. Some would see you as diminished by the loss of your drafting. I don't accept that. So let me tell you this, as a man who fully appreciates the powers of his opponent, and the dire position I'm putting that resourceful man in: I don't know if Orholam can be destroyed, but I expect you to find a way to do it. I expect you to turn your whole heart and mind and soul to accomplishing it. If you fail, I will kill everyone you love. Her first.' He cast his eyes up toward the Prism's Tower where Karris must be. 'If anything happens to me or you reveal me, she dies. If she disappears, one of those she trusts enough to take with her will be mine, and she will die. If any of a hundred things happens that is not your obedience and success, I will take away every bright and happy thing in this world that you know.

'On the other hand,' he said, his voice taking on a happy tone as if he hadn't been threatening Gavin a moment before, 'if you succeed, you will be the man who changed the world forever. Who, indeed, saved the world.' He offered the Blinding Knife in his hands to Gavin. ' "Some work of noble note may yet be done," eh? What will it be? Death? Or a chance?'

Looking into Grinwoody's black orbs – no, Anazâr's, there

was nothing of the sniveling slave in this man – Gavin believed him completely. There was no weaseling out of this. No third way. No drafting something so audacious that no one else had ever dreamed of it to escape.

Perhaps it was a measure of Gavin's stubborn arrogance, even here, even now, reduced to this, that his thought wasn't of how impossible it all was. He thought, But what if I succeed?

Magic was lost to him, but that was very different from killing magic altogether. Everything he'd done and built and dreamed and created had been because of and with magic. The whole society. His family's wealth and privilege. His living while his brother died. The skimmers. The condor.

Grinwoody couldn't be right...but what if he was?

Whistling a melodious little trill, Gunner nudged him. 'C'mon, what'll it be? Death or glory?'

Gavin rubbed the eye patch, and the touch of the black luxin jewel sent unpleasant tingles through his fingers and down his wrist. He pulled his hand away. As the snowy-fingered dawn reached across the sky like a thief, he grabbed the dark Blinding Knife and said, 'Let's sail. Death and glory, Cap'n Gunner.'

'Death *or* glory. *Or*,' Gunner said.

Not likely.

He cast his eyes up at the tower. Goodbye, Karris. Farewell, my love.

Chapter 77

'We've got a skimmer of Blackguards back, High Lady,' Samite reported as she strode into Karris's staterooms. There was none of the usual levity from the square-shouldered woman. 'There are casualties.'

Karris broke off another damned negotiation for black powder with representatives of the Ilytian pirate kings – now with a pirate queen added in for variety – and left immediately.

In minutes they were in the infirmary. Chirurgeons and

luxiats bustled through a ward of gleaming white stone. The infirmary was ablaze with light all hours of the day and night. The sun's rays were believed to have healing properties. Because that meant it was substantially warmer than other floors of the Prism's Tower, it was held that the servants and luxiats here were allowed shortened sleeves and hemlines because of the heat.

The truth was grimmer, told in the runnels and gutters in the infirmary floor: short sleeves and hems don't drag in blood. In its long history, the Chromeria had seen its share of war and pestilence.

Karris composed herself as she walked. She wasn't the concerned friend or even a stern-faced commander here, she was Orholam's left hand on earth. As he looked unblinking on every horror, and with mercy on every weakness, so must she appear caring but unmoved. She must be a pillar for others to lean on, never needy, never surprised, never weak. Iron.

The rooms were surprisingly sedate. Karris hadn't been down here since the last training accident more than a month ago, when two teenaged nunks ended up with scars across their faces from an explosive they'd created – with one blinded permanently.

These days the infirmary was double staffed – evidence of Carver Black's early preparations for the war – but it faced hardly more than the usual number of injuries, even as the war training of drafters had continued through the last year.

Given the scarcity of other patients and their elevated status, the Blackguards had been given their own room. Most of the injuries were minor: a burn that had seared Gill Greyling's sleeve to his bicep, a cut across Jin Holvar's back, an arrow stuck in Presser's buttock that would be funny someday if it didn't get infected. But for once, there was no humor, no attempts at levity.

Gavin Greyling lay on a table surrounded by his brothers and sisters. Not a one didn't have a hand on him. He was stripped to the waist, but Karris saw no wounds on the teen-ager.

Karris came to stand by his head and put a hand on the dark, sweaty skin of his chest. She looked to his elder brother

Gill, who winced as a chirurgeon ripped the fabric away from his own wound and pressed a bandage to it. The young man never moved his reassuring hand from his brother's arm. So what was Gavin's wound?

With a groan, Gavin Greyling opened his eyes to see who had just touched him. And Karris knew.

The sclera of his dark eyes were littered with the glowing blue fragments of his broken halos.

'Ah *fuck*,' Karris said, forgetting everything she'd just prepared.

It seemed to be the right thing to say, though. The Blackguards nodded and grumbled, and Gavin Greyling smiled weakly at her.

'Broken, huh?' he said. 'They didn't want to tell me. I could feel it, though. Something wrong, something let loose in me. Shit.'

'Shit,' Karris agreed. The cat was out of the bag now. What did it matter? These were her people: they would forgive her for remembering she'd been a Blackguard first.

'Ambushed us,' Gavin Greyling said. 'We were looking for Promachos.'

'Of course you were,' Karris said. Orholam have mercy. They'd been looking for her husband. Quietly.

Officially, Andross Guile had stopped sending out Blackguards to look for Gavin. They were overworked already, and didn't need their deaths hastened by drafting more. Other eyes and ears had taken on those duties, searching foreign capitals and rival houses for any whisper of him.

The Blackguards were professionals. They weren't supposed to have favorites.

But they'd loved Gavin Guile. Quietly. They'd loved him. They would never give up on him.

She had to hold back sudden tears. Gavin Greyling was only eighteen years old. He'd been named after her husband. He'd lived to protect him. Now he was dying for him.

She didn't ask if they'd found anything. Of course they hadn't. Asking would only drive home the waste of it. This young man was dying for nothing. But his intentions had been good. Heroic, even. War cared nothing.

'You're entitled to have the Prism-elect perform your Freeing,' Karris said.

'Fuck him,' Gavin said. 'Damn. It feels kind of good to be able to say it free and clear. Sorry, Gill. Sorry, brothers, sisters. But fuck him. I know he's your son, High Mistress. But you got a blind spot where he's standing. He's not a good man, High Lady. No one wants to say it to you. No one can tell you the truth. I can now. Because you have to listen to a dying man, don't you? He did the Freeing last year, and we were there. We've been at Freeings – not me, but this brotherhood – we've been there with Gavin Guile every time he had to do the Freeing. We saw how a good man approached that day. We saw him steeling his nerves. We saw his vomit in the chamber pot the morning of. We saw his steel spine all day. We saw his drunkenness the night after and the endless baths and the hands bloodied from him scrubbing them over and over. That's how a real man takes having to kill seventy or a hundred or two hundred friends. Your son did none of that.'

Her heart caught in her throat. This was the blathering of a madman, the raving of the dying. But to cut him off would be a cruelty the Blackguards would never forgive. She had to listen to his words, no matter how vile.

'Your son enjoyed killing seventy men and women. Enjoyed it. And don't you dare excuse him as a true believer who thought he was sending souls to a better place, to their just reward. He barely prayed the prayers his position demands. He giggled. He killed women before they'd finished their confessions. He stabbed them through the stomach first. Or the loins. He did it for fun.'

And her heart sank. And her heart died. Her son. Her son was inhuman – and she'd known it for long and long.

'Perhaps you can't hear this. Perhaps telling you the truth will only gain your condemnation and his. But I live to serve you, Karris White Oak, Karris Guile, Karris White, my Iron White.' And now tears spilled from those broken eyes. 'I have adored you, always been in awe of you, and I've never known how to tell you that this shadow grows in your very house. I have nothing to gain from this, but Karris...he is poison. He may be the flesh of your flesh, but he is not the flesh of your spirit. He is nothing like you. You are so good, and so worthy. Please. Cut him off. Cut him out. And don't let him near me. High Lady—'

'Enough, brother,' Gill Greyling said, putting a hand on Gav's shoulder. 'We will tell her the truth of it all. I promise. But for now, enough.'

It was as if the jaws of her mind were being pulled open until the corners of her mouth tore open, and her throat were being stuffed with putrid meat faster than she could swallow. Make it stop. Just make it stop. 'Are you ready?' Karris asked, cold as iron is cold.

'I am,' he said.

They helped him sit, and then stand. He looked at his compatriots, this boy of eighteen summers. He whispered words in the ears of some, nodded to others. He acted with a gravitas far beyond his years. A few of the Blackguards rushed from the room, unable to contain their weeping though they were supposed to stand strong.

Their weakness was forgiven.

Moving slowly – a wight must move slowly amid the Blackguard – Gavin Greyling approached Karris last.

He knelt. First he looked to his brother Gill. 'I'm sorry, brother. You told me to take more care a hundred times. I never listened.'

'I should—'

'It's not on you,' Gav said. He squeezed his brother's hand. 'Brothers, sisters, I'm sorry to leave you before the final lap of the race.'

Commander Fisk was weeping. He said, 'One cannot give more than all. You have finished your race, Blackguard. You may put your burden down.'

'Permission for an extended absence, sir,' Gavin said.

Commander Fisk cleared his throat twice trying to find his words. 'Permission granted, soldier.' He snapped to attention, and all the Blackguards followed. The commander drew an ancient dagger from his belt, said to have been passed down from Karris Atiriel herself and the first Blackguard. He spun it in his hand and presented it to Karris.

Then he snapped back to attention with his Blackguards.

Some met Gav's eyes as he looked from face to face. Others couldn't bear it. Gill was shaking like a leaf trying to keep his composure.

The ward fell silent, even other patients hearing the hushed flap of immortals' wings.

'I shall miss your jokes,' Karris said. 'I shall miss your light and easy spirit.' Her own was as heavy as a millstone.

'Let's not stretch this out longer than I can take,' Gavin said. He pulled the skin of his chest tight against his ribs to show the chinks between the bones. He stared at his brother's face and squeezed his hand hard.

'Well done, good and faithful servant. Orholam take you to your rest,' Karris said.

Then she stabbed him in the heart, sliding the dagger home hard, and then pulled it out quickly.

Gill held Gav's hand until the light went out of his eyes, and then lowered his brother's body onto the table and fell across him, weeping.

Karris fled, all her ideas of dignity and position forgotten, until she found herself on a rear balcony, in the shadow of the Chromeria, looking over the back bay, where a bone-white ship was loading. She gripped the rail unseeing.

She had always thought that heartbreak would arrive with tears and wailing, disconsolate flopping about and shutting oneself in one's bed chamber. Not eating. Not sleeping. Looking gaunt and pale, like in the stories.

For her, the sound of her heart cracking was simple and sharp and accompanied by nothing other than silence. It came in one sentence, pitiless and plain, stilling all argument and complaint:

So this is what my life is now.

Gavin, are you out there somewhere? She would know if he were dead, wouldn't she? She would have a feeling, right? Why did he feel so close, after all this time?

But that was only a stubborn, stupid denial.

She couldn't afford to lie to herself anymore. She couldn't let any more good kids die for her willful blindness.

The Third Eye had told her, Orholam will repay you for the years the locusts have eaten.

But God either didn't see, or didn't care, or didn't save. The husband she'd longed for was gone; the son she'd longed for was rotten; the stepson she should have kept she'd driven away. God was a liar.

Her fields were barren and sere, picked clean. Her story was over. Now she would merely survive. She would do her duty. That was all there was.

This is my life now.

'Commander,' she said, not turning.

'High Lady?' Of course he had followed her. In all the ways that didn't matter, she was never alone.

'I know they were motivated by love, but there will be no more expeditions to search for my husband. I forbid them. He is gone. Let us live for the living, not die for the dead.'

She straightened her back and squared her shoulders, and, with an iron heart, she finally did what she'd sworn she would never do.

☐ *Find Gavin.*

Below, the bone-white ship cast off from the quay. As the sun slowly rose, Karris watched it sail away until it disappeared into the horizon.

Chapter 78

Liv reached the crest of the hill unseen, of course. Her mastery of her new powers had grown greatly in what was now almost a year since she'd ascended. Now, when people weren't paying attention, she was able to impose order on their very thoughts.

As she worked, the ambling circuit of a guard's watch went from routine to clockwork, superfluities excised, perfect efficiency aspired to. But when you know patterns and can internalize others' and create your own to exploit them, you can walk twelve unhurried steps, pause by a shrub, and wait for the man with the infection in his groin to scratch, and then move on.

Not that all men or women were such automata. There was some twitchy woman who reacted violently even to the lightest touch. Liv simply gave her a wide berth.

She reached the top of the hill overlooking Azuria Bay on the Blood Forest coast, and her breath was taken away.

The bane lay below her. All of them, and all of them massive. Sub-red sizzling in the waves. Red smoldering. Orange placidly floating. Yellow awash in men and wights, every line perfect. Green bobbing wild. Cool blue melding with the color of the waves. And even the true prize, her superviolet bane, sitting invisible to most human eyes, known to most only by the odd bowl-shaped depression it made in the waves, waiting for her.

That had been the White King's bait. She had the seed crystal, but he had the bane, her temple. Attuned to her powers, it had called to her and Beliol all these months. Calling, waiting to grant her her full power, for her to take her place as a goddess.

Had she really finished her work, and decided rationally to come here? Or had she been pulled along, manipulated like a drunk to his only source of wine, swearing he'd chosen it – yet every day, despite decay and wreck, he chose it again.

Wasn't there one last place she was supposed to go to fulfill her mission? One place…near here? Something to do with Kip?

'We will be safe, Mistress,' Beliol said. 'I shall know the very moment the least of them thinks of betrayal.'

'And I can trust you, of course,' Liv said. She'd been careful not to voice her suspicions to him before, but now it slipped out.

'I've no wish to be chained, either, goddess. What would the Yokeless One be if he were chained?'

No, that made sense.

Her body pulsed with superviolet, of her accord, and she felt at peace and focused again. 'You can do this,' Beliol said. 'Really, you must do it.'

The bane below were ready to sail to the Chromeria, loaded

with supplies and an army and their drafter-paralyzing powers. They were going to win. They would cast off within a day or two at most, and Liv felt no armies within that distance coming to stop them before they could assault the Chromeria itself.

So Kip hadn't figured it out. Sad.

The Blood Robes couldn't be stopped, then, and the Chromeria was doomed. There was nothing to be gained by joining the losing side now, was there?

Ah well. At least that made her decision easy.

Releasing the fine superviolet shielding she'd developed to hide herself from the other gods, she whistled a little tune and started down the hill to join the White King.

To be worshipped, she thought, would be very fine.

Chapter 79

Some time later, Kip found himself washed and shaved and somehow, despite all his loitering, still waiting for his wife to appear.

And then she did.

Were they any other couple, Kip wouldn't be thinking at all right now.

Candles, perfumed water, flower petals across a bigger bed in a more beautiful room than Kip had ever seen. Aromatic oils and all things pleasing to the senses. The Blood Foresters were serious about sex.

Tisis emerged from some side room with a blend of shyness and confidence and expectation and delight. On the trail or in a palace, wearing trousers or a nightgown or nothing at all, a beautiful woman is a beautiful woman. Or so Kip had thought.

But somehow what was becoming familiar had been made new, and what had continually delighted him now left him agog.

For an unutterably beautiful long moment, Kip didn't think at all. He basked in the revelation of her as if it were the sun on a cold morning when the chill wind dies down and the winter fades.

But then that moment trembled and faltered and fell, and they saw it mirrored in each other's eyes. They were not merely a husband and wife eager for each other – they were they, and what should be an unalloyed good was instead a battle-field.

For all the times this past year that they'd gone to bed without thinking of their problem, it was impossible to ignore it in the honeymoon chamber.

No honey for us.

He wished he could simply enjoy looking at how she brought light and life to the silken curves of her celadon nightgown, but now Tisis had that look on her face that Blackguard scrubs got during the puke circuit, that last time through any phys-ical conditioning exercise where success was measured by puking only *after* you finished, rather than before.

Can't anything be easy?

'No eye makeup,' Kip said. So she was already figuring she'd be crying.

'Thought there was no need to stain the sheets.'

'I think they're actually prepared for that. You know, honey-moon chamber.'

'Kip, I meant—' she started, irritated, then saw that he was joking.

'Come here. Sit with me.'

He drank her in as she came across the chamber. Part of him thought, Of course I can't make love with her. She's far too beautiful. Something had to go wrong with me in the picture.

But he ignored that voice and simply enjoyed her.

She said, 'When you look at me like that...I feel so loved... and so wretched. I feel so betrayed by my own body, like you're starving, and I'm withholding food from you. But I'm not doing it on purpose, Kip!' She sat down heavily.

He took her hands. 'I don't blame you,' he said. 'I'm not angry at you for what you can't control. That wouldn't even make sense.'

'Angry doesn't have to make sense. Anger. Whatever. I know you're upset.'

'I am.'

'You're disappointed in me, in us, in this sham marriage.'

'No, no, no, and yes. This isn't what I expected. But I'm not disappointed in you, and our marriage isn't a sham. But yes, I am disappointed.'

'You've been holding something back. I can tell.'

Shit. He puffed out his cheeks. 'I hadn't wanted to put anything else on you.'

She froze up.

He said, 'Our wedding vows included an admittedly aspirational bit: "Let there be no darkness between us." Tisis, on our first night, you said something about "again." Do you remember what that was?'

She looked stricken. ' "Let's try again," I think? How do you expect me to remember—'

' "Not again," ' Kip said. 'You said, "Not again." Can you explain that to me?'

She couldn't cover the guilty look that flitted over her face for the barest fraction of a second. 'No,' she said, 'I'm sure that wasn't it, I was frustrated, and I said, "Dammit, let's go again." '

'Tisis,' Kip said gently.

There was a long silence. Then, not moving her eyes from the floor, she said hollowly, 'There was a boy. Almost two years ago now. I wasn't even that interested in him, but I was furious with Eirene. My sister was sleeping with every willing woman in three satrapies, and she wanted *me* to be the perfect virgin. She said since she was never going to marry, I had to carry the family honor. It wasn't a religious thing. Eirene doesn't believe in anything but honor and money. But I had to act virtuously so I could be sold like a pillow slave to the highest bidder. I love my sister, and she's apologized to me a few times when she's been drunk, but the apologies never changed the deal. She insisted I had to do this one thing – like it's simple for me. She has to do all the hard stuff in every other aspect of her life, she said, so it's only fair she gets to relax in her private life.

'Anyway, I was with this boy, and we were pushing the boundaries one night, sort of daring each other to go further, but I kept thinking about how furious Eirene would be, and we tried, and...when he couldn't get in, he didn't take it as gracefully as you did, Kip. He, he said I wasn't a real woman. That I was a freak. And I said some pretty terrible things, too. I said if he ever spoke of it that I would tell everyone how he didn't even last long enough to get inside me. We never spoke again, and every time I would see him, my stomach would knot up all over again. I thought maybe because I was older now, it would just work with you, but I was afraid, too. I expected you to reject me if it happened...and then it did. I sort of still do. Expect your rejection, I mean.'

Kip sighed. He had two thoughts at once, and one was terribly selfish. 'Tell me about this ceiling. I've never seen anything like it.'

'The...ceiling?' She was incredulous.

'Please.'

'What? You need some distance from all this girlish emotion?'

He took a deep breath and blew out the spark of her rudeness before it could reach the tinder pile of his resentment. He was not a good man, but he could pretend for a little while longer. 'Please, it's soothing. I think we could use some of that.'

'Fine,' she said in her not-fine-est tone.

God, what a bitch, a hard, unforgiving part of him said. I am trying to give us a chance—

But another part of him said, God, how she's hurting. And that voice, slower and softer, utterly silenced the first. Peace, Kip, peace.

The muscles in her cheeks clenched, but she silently surveyed the undulating, burnished wood that formed the ceiling. 'I can't remember the name of the woodwright, but there are treasured examples of his work all over Blood Forest. Few are so large, though. It's called *Túsaíonn Domhan*, it means "A World Begins." It's supposed to represent a pond where a single rock has been thrown. These are the waves expanding from the center. At different times of the year and different times of day, two people can lie down head to head right below the center and see different colors and even visions, some claim. Apparently, getting all these beams to match in color and curvature is considered impossible now, and it's endured like this for three hundred years.'

'What about the gold...stars? The knotholes?'

'Oh, that's an old tradition. In woodworking like this, knots in the lumber are a tremendous challenge. You can't get beams this size without them, of course. They're a problem when you're felling the trees because the saws bind in the knot, and then when the lumber is cut, the knot becomes a weakness in the structure. In every way, the knot is a flaw, an embarrassment that must be worked around, glued or minimized or covered over as well as possible.

'But there was another school of thought. Instead of ignoring the flaw, they highlighted it instead. It's called golden joinery or golden repair. Look, maybe this is all just artists' bullshit, right, but they say it's not a celebration of flaws but an acceptance of them, addressed insofar as the structure needs it. Here, Phaestos – that was the woodwright's name, just came to me – here in addition to the gold dust that would be mixed with the joinery glue to hold the knots together and make the starburst patterns, he also employed some master drafter-artisans.'

Her face had relaxed as she told Kip of her people, as he had hoped it would. She was intensely proud of them.

'But I'm boring you,' she said.

'Not at all. Why masters? Slap some solid yellow in knotholes. Problem solved, right?'

'Structurally, yes, but these were women who'd been asked to work with Phaestos himself. Well, we don't know their names. It's assumed they were women because they were yellow superchromats. They were great artists, too. A true artist is one for whom there is no "good enough." They drafted perfect solid yellow for the structural integrity, but then they filled channels so small we can't see them or perhaps natural air pockets in the wood with a yellow luxin ever so slightly off spectrum so that on moonlit nights, some of the yellow would release into visible light. They say it was like seeing the moonlight shimmer on the undulating waves.

'The downside, of course, is that when you have luxin

decaying, no matter how slowly that is, it eventually disappears. They say the shimmering luxin lasted more than a hundred years. Some say there is a lesson there about the longevity of what is made by magic and what is made by hand, and what endures – Phaestos's work remains while theirs is gone. Personally, I think a century is pretty good.'

'No one could fix it?' Kip asked.

'It's not like sending gleams to refill the lanterns at the Chromeria, Kip. They tried. They failed. There are some things that pass from the earth and are simply lost.'

'Huh.'

They sat together for a time, looking at the salving curves and basking in the soporific natural wood tones.

'Do you buy it?' Kip asked finally.

'That they used the luxin for art?'

'No, the bit about golden joinery.'

'I don't know,' she said. 'I mean, it's one thing when you see the technique used on a bowl or plate. The woodwright could have simply tossed out a piece of faulty wood and made something perfect with another piece, so you know that incorporating the flaw was a choice, right? But on something this massive? There wasn't a choice. Orholam only knows how many trees they must have gone through to get the perfect tones and patterns already. Maybe the flaws came first and the justifications came later, like this is what they had to work with, so they made the best of it.'

'Regardless, they did a helluva job with it, didn't they?' Kip asked. 'I can imagine the ceiling without those golden stars reflected in the rippling waves, but they add something beautiful, don't they?'

He saw a wave of gooseflesh go over Tisis's skin. Perhaps it was merely because the room was cold.

'You *bastard*,' she said, but she wasn't angry. She turned and looked at him. 'You already knew about golden joinery, didn't you?'

He was quiet for a moment. 'Actually, I was hoping we could learn about it together.'

Her body tensed and she sucked in a breath, and then tears blossomed in her eyes.

He saw her, in that single moment, fall in love with him.

If their brokenness were anything else, they would fall into each other's arms and let their bodies now speak with wordless urgency the vows they'd made long ago. But where bodies fail, words must stand.

'I will not leave or forsake you,' Kip said. 'This is something we need to fix; it does weaken us, but someday, it will be a source of our strength.'

Tisis fixed intent eyes on him. 'Kip, I'm going to cry now, and I need you to hold me and not try to fix it. It's the good kind of crying.'

There's a good kind?

'And then,' she said. 'To the best of my ability, I am going to ravish you.'

And so she did.

After they had pleased each other, and laughed, and held and been held, in the moment where Kip was torn between ramping up the passion again or maybe just admitting it had been a damn long day and maybe they could make love again in the morning, Tisis said, 'I need to talk to you about something.'

'You can't,' Kip said. 'I'm asleep.'

Very subtly, he wiggled deeper under the blankets.

'Kip,' she said plaintively.

'Oooh, what have we here?' he asked her chest.

'Kip – oh! Kip, I'm – mm...serious.'

He sighed. If he was learning anything about marriage, it was that talks must come. Putting them off did nothing good.

He poked his head back above the covers.

She looked mildly disappointed – not fair! But then she gathered her wits. 'Um...' She blew out a breath. 'Kip, I want to make love tonight. I mean, I want to try again.'

Kip dropped his head onto his pillow with a groan. They had fresh bread and fine cheeses, and she was going to complain that they didn't have wine? 'Tonight? When everything is so perfect? You're doing this now?' Eat the fucking bread and cheese, woman!

'I want—'

'We've talked about this! We agreed! Can't you just leave well enough—'

'I *knew* you were going to do this,' she said.

'Hold you to your word?!' he said.

'That is not fair!'

Yes, it was. But Kip bit his lip.

A man who'd just been pleasured by a woman so beautiful shouldn't feel the depths of rage Kip felt now. 'I have made my peace with this,' Kip said.

'I haven't,' she said.

'Well, you'll save yourself more heartache the sooner you do,' Kip said. 'This is how things work in my life. Nothing can be all good; there always has to be birdshit floating in the mead. If I have a friend, I have to know he's going to die. If I love a girl, she'll fall for someone else. If – against all odds! – I have something as good as what you and I have, there's no way it can be whole. This is as good as it gets.' He waved a hand at the rippling, polished grains of the master-piece above them. 'I don't understand why the *hell* you're looking at this marriage and calling it a dead ceiling.'

'Oh, Kip,' she said, but she couldn't find words.

They lay beside each other, still in the midst of wealth and beauty, but Kip felt as if all the mud and shit at the bottom of Kip Pond had been swirled back up, and he didn't trust himself to find words that didn't reek of bitterness. He just needed time for all that shit to settle down again. Just let it be.

'Maybe, maybe you've noticed me working with Evie Cairn?' she asked, still lying on her back, speaking as if to the ceiling.

'Yes?' The healer?

She rolled her eyes. 'And here my first plan was to wait until you asked me about it.' It was an attempt at levity, but a weak one.

Kip didn't say, 'You meet with people all day long, and most of them are your sources for something or other, why would I even—' Instead he said, 'So, honey, why were you meeting with a healer?' It was an attempt at sincerity, but a weak one.

And lo and behold, *that* question didn't lead to a fight.

Damn, this controlling-his-tongue thing was seeming like a better and better idea all the time.

'She said she'd seen this before. Especially in girls under incredible pressure or who'd had bad early experiences.'

Kip wasn't understanding. He propped himself up on an elbow.

Tisis continued, 'Or women who have a lot of negative attitudes about lovemaking, but obviously that's not really my case, ha. But the first two...'

'What? What?'

'So I've been talking through some things with her,' Tisis said.

Kip felt like the time when Ramir and Sanson and Isa and he had gone swimming. Ramir's idea, of course, and when Isa had balked at taking off her tunic by pointing out that Kip was wearing his, Ramir had been furious with him. He'd cornered Kip, and forcibly stripped off his tunic. Then he'd mocked Kip for being fat, as Kip had known he would.

That sensation of being stripped naked for someone else's commentary came rushing back. 'You've been telling some stranger about what we do and don't do in our bed—'

'Kip, dammit! You think it was easy for me? Don't you trust me at all? And she's not a stranger now.'

It wasn't just embarrassment, it was bigger than that. 'Do you realize what could happen if my grandfather or your sister finds out? Orholam's balls, Tisis, your cousin could take a quarter of our army away—'

'I wasn't thinking about them! I was thinking about us!'

He didn't say, 'And you put everything at risk to do so!'

He didn't say, 'That's the problem, you didn't think at all!'

Instead he took a breath.

And in his momentary hesitation, she spoke again. 'It was supposed be a surprise. A good thing, Kip. I can't – I can't live like this. I'm sorry you're angry, but I'm not sorry I did it.'

'Great. So you've risked the entire war so that you can have girl talk with someone who – for all we know – could be an enemy agent. Do you feel better after talking it out?' Kip demanded.

He was being an asshole. He knew it; he couldn't stop it.

'Gods! I don't understand you at all sometimes. I don't know how you can be that magnificent giant I see bending the world to his will one day and then the next day be this, this dwarf.'

'Oh, come, look at it another way,' Kip said. 'If I were smaller – much, much smaller – we wouldn't be having this problem at all.'

'Orholam *dammit*, Kip!' she said. 'I don't know why you're embarrassed. You feel exposed, ashamed? It's not even your fault! She told me all the things men often do and say that make it even worse, and you've done none of those. You've been perfect. This is all on me.'

And she was silent, and she was hurting, and Kip's heart opened to her because he knew what being silent and hurting and trying to suck it up and not complain felt like when it seemed everything was your fault.

'Don't be like that. Don't do that,' Kip said.

'What?'

'There's no your problem or my problem here. There's only our problems. There's only things we each have to do for our marriage to thrive.'

'Yeah?' she asked.

'Yes,' he said.

'I've been trying. I'm sorry I didn't tell you, but...I thought you'd forbid it, and we'd just have to endure *good* for the rest of our marriage. I don't want good with you, Kip. I want amazing. I won't settle for less than that.'

'I just don't...' He stopped. Tried again. 'I appreciate that. And you're right. I would have been an asshole, and I would have tried to stop you, and...and I would have been wrong.' Because the entire fucking war is totally worth risking for my personal happiness, right?

Shit.

No, it was because it's never good to give up. He had, and she hadn't, and he was wrong to ask her to be more like him in this.

'So what now?' he asked.

'So...I've been, um, practicing? Training?'

574

'Practicing? Practicing – wait, with who?'

'Orholam's beard, Kip, no, come on! I haven't been seeking out men with small penises.'

'Well, I...okay, maybe that was kind of stupid. What did you mean, then?'

She looked awkward. 'I don't really know how much you want to know. I mean, some wine beforehand and olive oil and, uh, graduated cylinders.'

'Graduated cylinders?' Then he thought of cones he'd seen in her luggage. And then he thought about them again. 'Ooooh.'

'And with your constant late nights, I haven't had much privacy to work on it.'

'Oh. Uh, sorry? That does sound...awkward.'

'You walked in on me once, don't you remember?'

'Was that when you had the coughing fit?'

'And you came over to comfort me. I thought the smell would...*Anyway*...' She was blushing hard.

'I thought you Foresters were supposed to be unembarrassable with, ahem, matters of the root and cave.'

She ducked her head. 'Clearly I didn't spend enough of my youth here.'

'Oh yeah, seeing as my dad sort of took you hostage and all.' He grinned. 'I am really, really blind, huh?' Kip said.

'Only wh—' She stopped herself.

'Only where I'm concerned,' she didn't say.

Shit.

She was right. And she'd stopped herself from saying it because she was kind.

Somehow the ice was melting, and more than that.

'You do realize that I love you, right?' Kip said.

It was, now that he thought about it, actually the first time he'd ever said it. Somehow he'd thought his actions should have made it obvious.

She burst into tears.

Kip was no expert, but he didn't think these were the good kind.

'You big idiot,' she said through her tears. 'That's not how you tell a girl you love her!'

'I thought it went without saying!'

'Those words never go without saying!'

'Well!' he shouted. Then he got quiet. 'Now I know.'

She hesitated, uncertain where he was going next.

'First time I ever said it to anyone,' he said.

The future was a chasm, and her love was a plank, and he didn't know where it ended. And he'd just run three steps blindly into the darkness.

'You know I love you, too, right?' she said.

'Well, now I know,' he said with a half grin.

'I've said it before,' she said. 'Pretty much.'

You won't accept a tacit 'I love you,' but you want me to? But he didn't say it. It wasn't exactly analogous anyway. 'I didn't believe it,' he said.

'Oh, Kip, you make me want to take this big knot of all these feelings I can't even name and have *gneas sáraigh*.'

'That was...not clear,' Kip said. He could memorize foreign terms, but he didn't think this was one he was going to want to ask anyone about.

She exhaled and reached under the covers. She grabbed him and squeezed. Not softly or erotically, either, though there was something inescapably and confusingly erotic for Kip in having Tisis grab him.

She said, 'I am so frustrated and I want you and I want to hurt you and I love you and it's all such a jumble—'

'No, I think I've got the feeling pretty exactly. It was the phrase I didn't know. Ow.'

'Oh.' She loosened her grip, but didn't let go. Better. 'Closest I can translate it would be "fucking it out." It's when you make love after you're angry and then you feel better. It's different than *caidreamh collaí feargach*, which is just angry lovemaking, where afterwards you feel better because you just had passionate sex, but you're still mad at the other person.'

'That sounds good,' Kip said. 'I mean, the former. I mean, the latter sounds not too bad, either, but only if after a few rounds of it you eventually got to the former. So, uh, let's do that – the former, I mean.'

'I, um.' She cleared her throat. 'I said I really wanted to – and I do! Not that *I can*. Because I can't. And if I get even a little bit nervous – well, we'll fail. Again.'

'Very...well...' Kip said. 'You just tell me what to do that will make you happy, and I'll do that.'

'Can you, like...hold all that grab-me-and-hold-me-down-make-me-quiver passion in your eyes, but not actually do anything to scare me?'

Now Kip cleared his throat. 'You're asking a lot of a man.'

'You are a lot of a man,' she said with a naughty little grin.

It was as if they were playing roles for each other, but all in all, being silly and out of your depth was better than being angry and confused, wasn't it?

He kissed her, and slowly, the inner turmoil vanished. Then, slowly – more slowly than either of them wanted, but as slowly as was necessary – they made love.

It wasn't perfect, but it was good. It was halting, and it was asking questions, and it was some answers that would not appear in one's fantasies. But Kip shut up and he began to listen, and once he began to listen, he began to hear snippets of her song, and then all he had to do was hear the ever-changing verses of her heart's desire and sing them in a refrain to her body.

Though perfectly attentive, perfectly diligent, Kip was not a perfect lover yet. But love doesn't demand perfection, only focus and time and effort. And before the night had passed, they had finally, joyfully, consummated their marriage.

It was a beginning, and it was a promise, and it was love; it was what had been broken fused together anew.

As the dawn rose, they lay head to head, staring up into the center of A World Begins, and Kip understood why this was treated as a honeymoon chamber. For a wedding was a world's beginning, a start from which all was possible, and a couple would lie head to head like this only after the lovemaking and after the cuddling, after their desires were sated, and their hearts were full, and their minds at ease, and their bodies at rest, and now they could be refocused together to a single purpose.

As the light rose like gold through the mirrors and lenses channeling the light above, Kip felt open to all the world, at peace, and in that morning color, he intuited another truth, coded there in the luxin itself: even perfect repairs must be tended.

The golden yellow was a mere hair's breadth from perfect luxin yellow, and, seeing that, Kip looked for superviolet, and it too was there, and a smidge of orange, and even the tiniest slivers of red and sub-red. There was blue for some stars, and red for others, there were nubs of paryl and triggers of chi.

He wouldn't have understood, much less attempted, such delicate work if he hadn't worked on the rope spear.

Orholam wastes nothing, not even our errors.

With superviolet fingers, he traced out lovingly where the luxins had been, and simply copied them, listening to their song, simple as refilling the lantern, and cleaning out some soot and the dust of centuries from a few plugged channels.

His Turtle-Bear tattoo filled with each color in turn as he used it, and glowed.

Simple. Simple for a fearless nine-color full-spectrum super-chromatic polychrome who didn't stop to consider that if he botched anything, he could set the whole room on fire and destroy an entire culture's most treasured art.

You dare to use sub-red, Kip? On centuries-old wood?

But he knew he could do this, and he couldn't stop himself, not with beauty so close, not with his gifts so fully engaged.

In a moment, in an hour, in an eternity, in a wink of Orholam's eye, Kip finished.

Tisis gasped, and Kip did, too. It was one thing for Kip to put the luxin paints back onto the palette of a great artist, it was quite another to see what Phaestos and the drafters had done with them.

The room lit. Sunshine shimmering on ocean waves, a mirror, in this darkest forest, to the stars and then the rising sun. A world beginning. This light was a gift of man and Orholam, once broken apart fused together anew, what had been flawed now rejoined in gold perfection.

'Oh my God,' Tisis whispered, but in her hushed tone, that holy word wasn't blasphemy but reverence. 'Kip. Heart of my heart. You have brought light.'

Author's Note

Vaginismus, as suffered by Tisis Malargos, is a real gynecological condition that can cause painful intercourse or the inability to experience intercourse at all due to involuntary muscle spasms. It is also little understood and too often surrounded by shame, jokes, or disbelief. One woman I know confessed to her (female!) gynecologist that she had been unable to consummate her marriage. The doctor told her it was her own fault for being a virgin, and it wouldn't have been a problem if she'd been sexually active earlier, and offered no treatment suggestions other than, 'Maybe get really drunk?' (Nope.) Another had her marriage end over this.

Among my early readers, there was a woman who couldn't believe that this was a real condition and not some weird plot device. 'A woman who can't have sex? What's that a metaphor for?' That ignorance, that secret grief, and that disbelief prompted this note, awkward though I feel to write it. If a twenty-first-century doctor specializing in women's health can be unaware of this condition, I figured a couple of early seventeenth-century teens would be even more baffled – and hurt and angry and ashamed and afraid.

The great news is that vaginismus is very, very treatable. So if you or someone you love is affected by this, it's not a joke. It's not something to be ashamed of. It's not just your issue, or her problem to fix; it's a relationship hurdle that you can overcome together. Get help. Start with a web search, and talk to a doctor.

Acknowledgments

Much as I'd like to pretend I'm a Gavin Guile of the written word, a solitary genius of word-magic creating entire worlds merely by drafting the electrons pouring through the circuits under my fingers, the truth is that a novel like this takes an entire Chromeria working together.

Thank you first to you, my readers, who have been light to me. It is an uncommon privilege to be afforded the time and space and finances to pursue a dream. You've given me that, plus encouragement and understanding when I say things like, 'I know I said it was going to be four books. Um...' You'll find my best efforts to honor your gift here, and in everything I put my name on.

Thank you to my superviolet drafters, Gleni Bartels and her colleagues and discipulae in production. Your work is invisible to the untrained eye – unless things go wrong! I have once again given you an unenviable task, with a compressed schedule and a long book and odd demands like quirky fonts, checklists, and handwriting.

Thank you to my blue drafters. My copy editor, S. B. Kleinman, brought my work into harmony with accepted grammatical and usage norms while honoring my unique voice. Thank you for bringing a sensitive hand to your work: for finding that one sentence with a semicolon and ten commas and instead of asking me to break it up, pointing out that the sentence actually needed *eleven* commas. After teaching English and with seven books in print now, I really shouldn't need to be corrected on when to use 'like' versus 'as if,' but apparently I do. For that and much more, thank you.

Thank you to my yellow drafters. Translation, like drafting yellow, is bringing logic and emotion into balance; it requires both analysis and creativity, understanding what is happening in one language on several levels, and then artfully bringing that into another language with different syntax and vocabulary available. Noah Dauber, thank you for the quick lesson on ancient Hebrew. I totally understood some of it. Dr Jacob Klein, it hardly seems fair that your reward for all your Friday nights of refusing to leave our dorm room to do something fun ('Just three more hours of Greek!') is having me ask you to do my homework now, but I do appreciate it! My new friends Thomas McCarthy and Carla O'Connell, thank you for the Irish translations of sometimes-awkward terms. If you conspired together to do the equivalent of making me shout *'eho tria orchidea'* (I have three testicles!) à la *My Big Fat Greek Wedding*, I'm not even changing it.

Thank you also to all my professional translators adapting my work for other countries. Thank you, Manuel de los Reyes. I hear over and over how great your Spanish translation is. Thank you, Michaela Link, Olivier Debernard, Malgorzata Strzelec. And thank you to the rest of you, whose names (embarrassingly!) I don't even know. Please always feel free to e-mail me if you need a clarification. Every time I rhyme or make a pun, I wince thinking of how I'm making your job harder – and do it anyway. Thank you to Simon Vance for his rich, warm, and precise audiobook narration. It feels wonderful to work with an artist of your caliber. Thank you to GraphicAudio for your passion and the life your cast and musicians bring to your adaptations.

Thank you to my green drafters, my beta readers John, Tim, Heather, Keith, Andrew, and Jacob, for the wild life and powerful new growth you brought to my work. When Elisa compiled all your comments into the manuscript, they numbered more than six hundred. After the medics revived me, I delighted in your work and insight. Though you all did all of the below, let me single out Heather Harney for her dissenting views. I'm a dissenter myself, and I love hearing an alternate take. Thank you. Tim, thanks for your theory crafting. The places where you thought 'That doesn't line up with what you said earlier' were all *totally* on purpose and *always* part of the grander design. Andrew and Jacob, thanks for your continuity catches and insightful comments. Keith, thank you for wisdom, penetrating questions, and your praise. It's impossible to rate such things, but you are one of perhaps the three best encouragers I have met in my life.

Thank you to my orange drafters, working behind the scenes to make sure the gears are oiled, that solutions are reached, and that everyone mysteriously continues to feel good about working together. Donald Maass of DMLA, you've been a dream agent, and friend, and mentor. Cameron McClure and Katie Shea Boutillier, thanks for taking us bravely into new waters, investigating unknown depths, and answering many questions! Charlie, have we received even one royalty statement where I didn't ask you many, many questions? Thank you. To Angie Hesterman and the rest of the crew, thank you.

Thank you to my red drafters, who bring passion and warmth to what is so often a solitary profession. Thank you to the fan artists who take some seed of what I've done and add their own gifts to it. Thank you to the fans who've gotten a tattoo of my work or words. I'll try to keep coming up with cool visuals, and the next time I'm frustrated over some almost-quotable line, I'll think, 'I can't stop working and say this is good enough! Someone might wear this on their body!' No pressure. Thank you to the fans who've named their children after my characters (!); I promise only good things will happen to them and the moral of my stories will be to never disobey your parents. (Trust me! I tell lies for a living.) Thank you to the fans who drop me a line simply to say they enjoyed what I've done. If I were an accountant, I might have a clear promotion structure, a steady paycheck, and a 401(k), but strangers never come up to an accountant to praise them. You guys rock.

Thank you to the fans who think all I get is the above kind of positive attention, and who anoint themselves to tell me all the ways I suck so I don't get too big of an ego.

No, never mind. Screw those guys.

Thank you to my sub-red drafters, whose work is rarely noticed by the unlearned and who might burst into flame if you dragged them out onstage, but without whom the whole work could never catch fire with an audience: the sales personnel at Hachette who convey passion for my books to a buyer who hears thousands of such pitches a year. Thank you to Ellen

Wright at Orbit, who makes travel such a smooth experience and brings me physically to booksellers and readers. Thank you to Laura Fitzgerald and Alex Lencicki, who do so much online and off-. Thank you to Clockpunk Studios for making the webpage look so good. Thank you to Lauren Panepinto, Silas Manhood, and Shirley Green for the beautiful covers – and then going above and beyond to help me with bookmarks or T-shirt designs or posters. Beyond my awesome professional partners, thank you to you booksellers who – out of all the baffling array of books weighing down the store shelves – pick up mine and tell a prospective reader why they'll enjoy it. That's a dream come true for me.

Thank you to my paryl drafter,

Most people will never see nor understand what you've done, but it's changed everything.

Thank you to my chi drafter, ███████████████████████████
████████████████████████████████

cancer.

Then there are the polychromes, those drafters who have helped me in ways that defy singular categorization. John DeBudge, not just rereading and continuity checking and theory-crafting and encouraging, but for catching some of the more subtle stuff – and being wildly wrong on a small number of his guesses! Elisa Roberts, you've been my right hand. Lasher when I want to get lazy, organizer of literal reams of lore, Guardian of the Official Timeline, transcriber of the unholy words, website keeper – 'Can I get this icon in cornflower blue?' – and general mess cleaner-upper (and often spotter in the first place). You've been the one who reads the book one last time, *backwards*, to try to catch those final typos. I'd say more nice stuff about you, but then you'd ask for another raise.

Editor Devi Pillai was my White. Or maybe my White King. I'm still not sure. In any large endeavor, someone has to make sure all the skills of her minions are well allocated and whip nurture the laggards project along. When I see the old canard,

'Editors don't edit anymore,' I think of Devi reading this book four times and giving advice all along the way. She has been taskmaster and advocate, and many things in between. Thanks, Devi. Kelly O'Connor, Devi's right hand, I'd say you're the Marissia, but that starts to get weird. Thanks for making sure things happened smoothly.

Tim Holman has been the Black, orchestrating everything else that doesn't fall under the White's purview, and his right hand has been Anne Clarke. Thank you for discovering me and assembling this wonderful team and helping them work so well together. Also, the checks. Thanks for signing those. Very handy.

Last and most, thank you to my wife, Kristina, who's been more than a Karris to me. Angel investor, first reader, counselor in more ways than most, bookkeeper, lens that brings me into focus, partner, lover, best friend. You've had to take up a lot of slack as I've worked on this book. I see you. I hold you in my eyes.

In short – yeah, this counts as short for an epic fantasy author – it's been a team effort. And I know there's one of two things you're thinking after seeing a list this long after a book: 1) Wow, there's a lot more people who go into making a book than I thought, or 2) Wow, you had that many people helping and this is the best you could do?

Yes, and yes.

Gratefully yours,
Brent Weeks
July 25, 2016
Oregon, USA

P.S. I'd be remiss if I don't mention the nunks of my Chromeria, my daughters O. and A. Thank you, young ladies, for interrupting my work with tackle-hugs, and 100-watt smiles, and asking Daddy to read you another story. ('Again! Again!' 'Gong-gong.') If it weren't for you, I'd certainly have finished this book sooner. And I wouldn't trade you for the world.

Look out for the final volume in the

Lightbringer series

by

BRENT WEEKS

As the White King springs his great trap, and the Chromeria itself is threatened by treason and seige, Kip Guile and his companions will scramble to return for one impossible final stand.

In the darkest hour, will the Lightbringer come?

www.orbitbooks.net

Character List

'Annaiah: Darjan's wife, burnt by orgiasts.

Abaddon: Also known as the King, the Day Star. One of the chiefs of the Two Hundred. Often depicted with crippled ankles, giant locust's wings, and pallid features.

Abirin: A luxiat-scholar who studied the old gods.

Abraxes, Ambrosius: A saint from ancient times.

Adrasteia (Teia): A Blackguard, a drafter of paryl, a member of the Order, and the White's spy.

Aeshma: One of the Two Hundred, nearly one of the Nine, and Darjan's *jinni-yah*. A potential Atirat.

Agnelli, Lucia: A Blackguard scrub, she had a forbidden romantic relationship with Cruxer. Murdered by an assassin during a training exercise.

Ahhana the Dextrous: Superchromat yellow drafter who was the architect and lead drafter of the Lily's Stem.

Ahhanen: A Blackguard. Partners with Djur, known for a somewhat sour demeanor. Killed in the Omnichrome's War.

Aklos: A slave of Aglaia Crassos.

Aleph, Derwyn: Commander of the Cwn y Wawr.

Alban and Strang: Saints and commentators on holy writ.

Amalu Anazâr: The Dark Defiant One.

Amazzal: One of the six High Luxiats, most notable for his commanding presence and rich voice.

Amestan: A Blackguard at the Battle of Garriston.

Anamar: Commander of the Blackguard at the close of the False Prism's War.

Anir: A librarian at the Chromeria.

Antaeos: A Blackguard nunk.

Appleton, Aodán: A nobleman and city leader of the Blood Forest city of Dúnbheo.

Appleton, Lady: A noblewoman of Blood Forest.

Appleton, Taira: One of Lady Appleton's four daughters. A friend of Karris White Oak during childhood.

Aram: A failed Blackguard scrub with a grudge against Kip Guile and Cruxer.

Arana: A drafting student, a merchant's daughter.

Aras: A student at the Chromeria.

Arash, Javid: One of the drafters who defended Garriston.

Aravind: Satrap of Atash until his death. Father of Kata Ham-haldita, the former *corregidor* of Idoss.

Arias: One of the Color Prince's advisers. He is an Atashian in charge of spreading news about the Color Prince.

Arien: A magister at the Chromeria. She drafts orange and tested Kip Guile on Luxlord Black's orders.

Ariss the Navigator: A legendary explorer.

Arrad: A Lightguard.

Arthur, Rónán: Twin brother of Ruadhán.

Arthur, Ruadhán: Leader of Shady Grove will-casters.

Asif: A young Blackguard.

Asmun: A Blackguard scrub.

Aspasia: Karris Guile's room slave.

Assan, Uluch: Gunner's birth name.

Atagamo: A magister who teaches the properties of luxin at the Chromeria. He is Ilytian.

Athanossos: A wealthy jeweler on Big Jasper.

Atiriel, Karris: A desert princess. She became Karris Shadowblinder before she married Lucidonius.

Atropos, Leonidas: A Prism.

Aurellea: A procurer for high-class prostitutes on Big Jasper.

Auria: Darjan's superior in the first Blackguard.

Ayrad: He was a Blackguard scrub years before Kip Guile entered the class. He started at the bottom of his class (forty-ninth) and worked his way up to the top, fighting everyone. It turned out he'd taken a vow. Became a legendary commander of the Blackguard and saved four different Prisms at least once before someone poisoned him. A yellow drafter.

Azmith, Akensis: A scion of the powerful Azmith family. Killed by Karris White Oak during the choosing of the White.

Azmith, Caul: A Parian general, the Parian satrapah's younger brother.

Azmith, Tilleli: Parian satrapah, older sister of Caul Azmith and spymaster for Paria's Nuqaba.

Balder: A Blackguard scrub.

Baoth: A red wight in the Color Prince's army.

Barrel: A Blackguard scrub.

Barrick: A sailor murdered by Zymun.

Bas the Simple: A Tyrean polychrome (blue/green/superviolet), handsome but a simpleton, sworn to kill the killer of the White Oak family.

Bel: An apprentice at a brewery on Big Jasper, the Maiden's Kiss.

Ben-hadad: A Ruthgari and a member of the Mighty. A blue/green/yellow drafter who has created his own mechanical spectacles that allow blue and yellow lenses to be used separately or together to create green. He's highly intelligent and an inventor.

Beryl: A watch captain in the Blackguard, a skilled horsewoman who is known for taking new recruits under her wing.

Big Ros: A slave of Aglaia Crassos.

Bilhah: The White's elderly room slave and a spy for Andross Guile.

Blademan: A Blackguard watch captain. He led one of the skimmers in the battle at Ruic Head, along with Gavin Guile and Watch Captain Tempus.

Blue-Eyed Demons, the: A mercenary band that fought for Dazen Guile's army.

Blunt: A Blackguard watch captain.

Borig, Janus: An old woman, she claimed to be a *Demiurgos* and a Mirror, creating true Nine Kings cards.

Brightwater, Aheyyad: Orange drafter, grandson of Tala. A defender of Garriston, the designer of Garriston's Brightwater Wall; dubbed Aheyyad Brightwater by Prism Gavin Guile.

Bursar: The Omnichrome's treasury adviser. She was originally a minor secretary for the secretary of the treasury of Paria.

Burshward, Captain: An Angari captain. He chose to dare the Everdark Gates because he'd heard rumors of the wealth beyond, and because of his vision from his god, Mot. Mortal enemy of Gunner.

Burshward, Gillan: Captain Burshward's brother, now short a leg due to an encounter with Gunner.

Buskin: Along with Tugertent and Tlatig, one of the best archers Commander Ironfist had on the approach to Ruic Head.

Caelia Green: A talented drafter, a dwarf, and formerly a servant of the Third Eye.

Cairn, Evie: A healer from Blood Forest.

Carver Black: A non-drafter, as is traditional for the Black. He is the chief administrator of the Seven Satrapies. Though he has a voice on the Spectrum, he has no vote.

Carvingen, Odess: A drafter and defender of Garriston.

Cavair, Paz: Commander of the Blue Bastards at the Great Pyramid of Ru.

Cezilia: A servant/bodyguard to the Third Eye. A fourth-generation Seers Islander.

Clara: A servant/bodyguard to the Third Eye.

Cománn, Cu: A nobleman and leader of Dúnbheo.

Companions' Mother: Head of the Omnichrome's army's prostitute guild.

Coran, Adraea: Blessed. Said, 'War is a horror.'

Cordelia: A willowy female Blackguard. An Archer.

Coreen: An old widow of Blood Forest. Despite her humble isolation, she seems to speak for or with Orholam.

Corfu, Ramia: A powerful, extremely handsome young blue drafter. One of the Color Prince's favorites.

Corzin, Eleph: An Abornean blue drafter, a defender of Garriston.

Counselor, the: A legendary figure. Author of *The Counselor to Kings*, which advised such cruel methods of government that not even he followed them when he ruled.

Cracks: A singularly ugly young Blackguard.

Crassos, Aglaia: A young noblewoman and drafter at the Chromeria. She is the youngest daughter of an important Ruthgari family, a sadist who enjoys the pain she inflicts on her slaves. Has a powerful hatred of both the Guiles and Teia.

Crassos, Governor: Elder brother of Aglaia Crassos; the last governor of Garriston.

Crassos, Ismene: A middle-aged cousin of Aglaia Crassos.

Cruxer: He was perhaps the most talented Blackguard of his era, now one of the Mighty.

Daelos: A Blackguard, very small, but intelligent and talented with blue. Left behind at the Chromeria when he was gravely injured fighting as one of the Mighty.

Dagnar Zelan: One of the original Blackguard. He served Lucidonius after converting to his cause.

Dagnu the Thirteenth: One of the legendary Nine Kings. Together with the red drafters of his time, wiped out the blues to the last child.

Dakan, Dayan: A thug for hire on Big Jasper.

Danavis, Aliviana (Liv): Daughter of Corvan Danavis. A yellow/superviolet bichrome drafter from Tyrea, she serves the White King. Formerly a discipula at the Chromeria whose contract was owned by the Ruthgari, supervised by Aglaia Crassos. Grew up in Rekton with Kip Guile.

Danavis, Corvan: A red drafter. A scion of one of the great Ruthgari families, he was also the most brilliant general of the age and the primary reason for Dazen Guile's success in battle. Now the satrap of Seers Island and married to the Third Eye.

Danavis, Ell: The second wife of Corvan Danavis. She was murdered by an assassin three years after their marriage.

Danavis, Erethanna: A green drafter serving Count Nassos in western Ruthgar; Liv Danavis's cousin.

Danavis, Qora: A Tyrean noblewoman; first wife of Corvan Danavis, mother of Liv Danavis.

Dancing Spear, Ikkin: A Blackguard famed for his fighting abilities in the Jadmar Rebellion.

Darjan: Legendary drafter at the time of Lucidonius and Karris Shadowblinder.

Delara, Naftalie: A woman from a prominent family whom Andross was going to 'let' Gavin marry. An ally of Andross Guile.

Delara Orange: The Atashian member of the Spectrum. She represents Orange and is a forty-year-old orange/red bichrome nearing the end of her life. Her predecessor in the seat was her mother, who devised the rotating scheme for Garriston. General Caul Azmith and the satrapah of Paria are her cousins.

Delarias, the: A family in Rekton.

Delauria, Katalina (Lina): Kip Guile's mother. She is of Parian or Ilytian extraction and is a haze addict.

Delclara, Micael: A quarryman and a Rekton villager.

Delclara, Miss: The matriarch of the Delclara family in Rekton.

Delclara, Zalo: A quarryman, one of the Delclara sons.

Deleah: A slave woman in Andross Guile's household.

Delelo, Galan: A master sergeant in the Omnichrome's army. He escorted Liv Danavis to the gates of Garriston.

Delmarta, Gad: A young Tyrean general from Garriston, he commanded Dazen Guile's army. Took the city of Ru and publicly massacred the royal family and its retainers. Garriston was later burnt in revenge.

Delucia, Neta: A member of the ruling council of Idoss (i.e., a city mother) before its fall.

Demistocles: A prophet and a mentor of prophets.

Diakoptês: An ambiguous term. Literally 'He who rends asunder,' but a looser translation could be 'Breaker.' In Braxian belief, both the name (or perhaps title?) of Lucidonius and the name or title of a similar figure (or possibly a reincarnation of Lucidonius?) who will come again to break or heal the Cracked Lands.

Djur: A Blackguard, he died fighting in the White King's War.

Droose: One of Gunner's shipmates.

Eden, Veliki: A military commander known for his integrity and for being one of the greatest strategists of all time.

Elelyōn: Another name for Orholam, from the Old Parian, meaning 'God Most High.'

Elessia: A Blackguard. Killed in the White King's War.

Elio: A bully in Kip Guile's barracks. Kip broke his arm.

Elos, Gaspar: A green wight, he saved Kip Guile's life in Rekton.

Erastophenes: A legendary general.

Erato: A Blackguard scrub who has it in for Kip Guile.

Essel: A Blackguard Archer.

Euterpe: A friend of Teia's. She was a slave. Her owners lost everything in a drought and rented her to the Laurion silver mine brothels for five months. She never recovered.

Eutheos: A captain and hero of Dazen Guile's army, and later a member of Ruthgar's military.

Falling Leaf, Deedee: A green drafter. Her failing health inspired a number of veteran drafters who were also her friends to take the Freeing at Garriston.

Farjad, Farid: A nobleman and ally of Dazen Guile's once Dazen promised him the Atashian throne during the False Prism's War.

Farseer, Horas: Another ally of Dazen Guile's, the bandit king of the Blue-Eyed Demons. Gavin Guile killed him after the False Prism's War.

Fell: A female Blackguard, the smallest in the force, she excels at acrobatic moves.

Ferkudi: A member of the Mighty, a blue/green bichrome who excels at grappling. Gifted with spotty intelligence.

Finer: A Blackguard seen in one of the cards.

Fisk: He trains the scrubs with drills and conditioning. He barely beat Karris White Oak during their own test to enter the Blackguard.

Flamehands: An Ilytian drafter and defender of Garriston.

Fukkelot: One of Gavin Guile's oarmates, he swears unceasingly under stress.

Gaeros: One of Aglaia Crassos's slaves.

Galaea: Karris White Oak's maid, and betrayer.

Galden, Jens: A magister at the Chromeria, a red drafter with a grudge against Kip Guile.

Galib: A polychrome at the Chromeria.

Gallos: A stableman at Garriston.

Garadul, Perses: Appointed satrap of Tyrea after Ruy Gonzalo was defeated by the Prism's forces in the False Prism's War. Perses was the father of Rask Garadul. He worked to eradicate the bandits plaguing Tyrea after the war.

Garadul, Rask: A satrap who declared himself king of Tyrea; his father was Perses Garadul.

Garret: One of Conn Arthur's Ghosts.

Gates, Anjali: A semiretired senior diplomat in the Chromeria.

Gazzin, Griv: A green drafter who fought alongside Zee Oakenshield.

Gerain: An old man in Garriston who exhorted people to join King Garadul.

Gerrad: A student at the Chromeria.

Gevison: A poet of a heroic bent. He wrote *The Wanderer's Last Journey.*

Gloriana: A Blackguard nunk from the cohort behind Teia.

Golden Briar, Cathán: Cousin to both Arys Greenveil and Ela Jorvis. Eva Golden Briar's elder brother.

Golden Briar, Dónal: A Blood Forest nobleman and leader of a minor military catastrophe.

Golden Briar, Eva: A Blood Forest noblewoman Andross Guile was going to let Gavin choose to marry.

Goldeneyes, Tawenza: A yellow drafter. She teaches only the three most talented yellows each year at the Chromeria. A notorious misandrist.

Goldthorn: A magister at the Chromeria. Barely three years older than her disciples, she teaches the superviolet class.

Gonzalo: A farrier's son of Atan's Town in Darjan's time. A simpleton.

Gonzalo, Ruy: A Tyrean satrap who sided with Dazen Guile during the False Prism's War.

Goss: A Parian Blackguard inductee, one of the best fighters, and a member of the Mighty before he was killed by the Lightguard.

Gracia: A mountain Parian scrub. She's taller than most of the boys.

Grandpa Sé: Served Darien Guile and Selena Oakenshield. Garret's great-great-grandfather.

Grass, Evi: A drafter and defender of Garriston. She is a green/yellow bichrome from Blood Forest, and is a super-chromat.

Grazner: A Blackguard scrub. Kip Guile broke his will in a bout.

Green, Jerrosh: Along with Dervani Malargos, he was one of the best green drafters in the Omnichrome's army, and a Blood Robe. Killed by the Omnichrome before the Battle of Ru.

Greenveil, Arys: The Sub-red on the Spectrum. A Blood Forester, cousin of Jia Tolver, sister to Ana Jorvis's mother,

Ela. Her parents were killed in the war by Lunna Green's brothers. She has twelve children by twelve different men and is pregnant with the thirteenth.

Greenveil, Ben-Oni: Arys Greenveil's thirteenth child. His name means 'son of my agony.'

Greenveil, Jalen: Arys Greenveil's third child.

Greyling, Gavin: A Blackguard. He is the younger brother of Gill Greyling, named after Gavin Guile. He is the handsomer of the two brothers.

Greyling, Gill: A Blackguard. He is the elder brother of Gavin Greyling, and the more intelligent of the two.

Greyling, Ithiel: Father of Gill and Gavin Greyling.

Grinwoody: Andross Guile's chief slave and right hand. He is barely a drafter, but Andross pulled strings to get him into training for the Blackguard, where he made friends and learned secrets. He made it all the way through Blackguard training, and on oath day decided to sign with Lord Guile instead, a betrayal the Blackguards remember.

Guile, Abel: Andross Guile's elder brother and the heir to the Guile 'fortune' before he signed it over.

Guile, Andross: Father of Gavin, Dazen, and Sevastian Guile. He drafts yellow through sub-red, although he is primarily known for drafting red, as that was his position on the Spectrum. He took a place on the Spectrum despite being from Blood Forest, which already had a representative, by claiming that his lands in Ruthgar qualified him for the seat. Now the promachos.

Guile, Darien: Andross Guile's great-grandfather. He married Zee Oakenshield's daughter as a resolution to their war.

Guile, Dazen: Younger brother of Gavin. He fell in love with Karris White Oak and triggered the False Prism's War when 'he' burnt down her family compound, killing everyone within.

Guile, Draccos: Andross Guile's father. Hero of the Aghbalu Campaign. Notorious for gambling an entire hyparchy for the hand of a woman, the young Orea Pullawr, on a horse race. He lost the race, the woman, and his family's entire fortune. It was revealed decades later that his opponent, Juldaw Rathcore, had cheated. The Spectrum refused to expel the Rathcores at that time, leaving the Guiles as wool traders. Implicated in the murder of his brother, but as the only witnesses were slaves whose testimony was thereby inadmissible, the case wasn't prosecuted by local magistrates or the satraps. (Orea ended up later marrying Juldaw's brother.)

Guile, Felia: Wife of Andross Guile. The mother of Gavin and Dazen, a cousin of the Atashian royal family, she was an orange drafter. Freed at Garriston just before the great battle. Her mother was courted by Ulbear Rathcore before he met Orea Pullawr.

Guile, Galatius: A Guile ancestor, a drunk and a gambler, important mainly because he married the woman who became known as Iron Ataea Guile.

Guile, Gavin: The Prism. Two years older than Dazen, he was appointed Prism at age thirteen.

Guile, Iron Ataea: Member of a small noble family that provided champion racehorses for Ruthgar and Blood Forest. She stole Galatius Guile's heart and reshaped the Guile family's destiny.

Guile, Kip: The illegitimate Tyrean son of Gavin Guile and Katalina Delauria. He is a superchromat and a full-spectrum polychrome.

Guile, Memnon: A legendary wanderer who was cursed by a witch and murdered by his brother on his return home.

Guile, Sevastian: The youngest Guile brother. He was murdered by a blue wight when Gavin was thirteen and Dazen was eleven.

Guile, Zymun: A young drafter and former member of the Omnichrome's army. Also known as Zymun White Oak, he claims to be the son of Karris and Gavin Guile and has been declared Prism-elect.

Gunner: An Ilytian pirate. His first underdeck command was as cannoneer on the *Aved Barayah*. He later became captain of the *Bitter Cob*.

Gwafa: A legendary Blackguard.

Hada: Handmaid to Tazerwalt, princess of the Tlaglanu.

Ham-haldita, Kata: Corregidor of Idoss before its fall. Ally of the Color Prince.

Hammer, Enki: The Lord Commandant of the Armies of Paria and the Nuqaba's consort. Killed by Karris Guile.

Harl, Pan: A Blackguard inductee. His ancestors were slaves for the last eight generations. Killed in the White King's War.

Helel: A member of the Order, she masqueraded as a teacher in the Chromeria and tried to murder Kip Guile.

Hena: A magister at the Chromeria who teaches a class on luxin construction.

Hezik: A Blackguard whose mother commanded a pirate hunter in the Narrows. He could shoot cannons fairly accurately.

Hill, Ruarc: A nobleman and leader of Dúnbheo.

Holdfast: A Blackguard. His son is Cruxer and his widow is Inana, another Blackguard.

Holvar, Jin: A woman who entered the Blackguard the same year as Karris White Oak, though she is a few years younger.

Hrozak, Grath: A sadist who murdered hundreds personally, and was well-known for his brutal military tactics.

Idus: A Blackguard scrub.

Inana: Cruxer's mother, and a Blackguard. Widow of Holdfast, a Blackguard.

Incaros: One of Aglaia Crassos's room slaves.

Ironfist (birth name Harrdun): Commander of the Blackguard, a blue drafter. Parian.

Isabel (Isa): A pretty young girl in Rekton.

Izza: Karris White Oak's childhood slave-tutor.

Izîl-Udad: The Nuqaba's former husband. A cripple.

Izem Blue: A legendary drafter and a defender of Garriston under Gavin Guile.

Izem Red: A defender of Garriston under Gavin Guile. He fought for Gavin during the False Prism's War. A Parian drafter of red with incredible speed, he wore his ghotra in the shape of a cobra's hood.

Jade: A female Blackguard.

Jalal: A Parian storekeeper who sells kopi.

Jarae: One of the Guile house slaves when Gavin and Dazen were children.

Jo'El, Seer: An ancient prophet, a Third Eye known for his promises of restoration following a coming devastation.

Jorvis, Ana: A supervioled/blue bichrome, student at the Chromeria, one of the women Andross Guile would have allowed Gavin to marry. Died in suspicious circumstances after she attempted to seduce Gavin by entering his rooms at night. The death was ruled a suicide, but the family claims it was murder.

Jorvis, Demnos: Ana Jorvis's father, and Arys Greenveil's brother-in-law, married to Ela Jorvis.

Jorvis, Ela: Sister of Arys Greenveil, wife of Demnos Jorvis, Blood Forester, mother to Ana Jorvis.

Jorvis, High Luxiat: One of the six High Luxiats during Gavin Guile's first Freeing.

Jorvis, Jason: Brother to Ana, son of Ela and Demnos. Killed by Karris White Oak during the choosing of the White.

Jumber, Norl: A Blackguard, a casualty of the Omnichrome's War.

Jun: A Blackguard scrub.

Kadah: Formerly a magister at the Chromeria who taught drafting basics. Now a researcher for the Chromeria.

Kalif: A Blackguard.

Kallea: Teia's sister; married to a butcher.

Kalligenaea, Lady Phoebe: A yellow superchromat with finer luxin control than even Gavin Guile.

Kallikrates: Teia's father. He ran the silk route as a trader before losing everything due to his wife's lavish lifestyle.

Kamal, Amrit: One of the White King's generals.

Keftar, Graystone: A green drafter and Blackguard scrub. He's an athletic, dark-skinned son of a rich family that paid for him to be trained before he came to the Chromeria.

Kerea: A Blackguard and an Archer.

Klytos Blue: The Blue on the Spectrum. He represents Ilyta, though he is a Ruthgari. A coward and Andross Guile's tool.

Kyros: Dazen Guile's childhood tutor.

Laya: A Blackguard who drafted red, present at the Battle of Garriston. Later killed in the Omnichrome's War.

Leelee: A pretty young kitchen slave in Andross Guile's household.

Lem (Will): A Blackguard, either simple or crazy, a blue drafter with incredible will.

Leo: A member of the Mighty, hugely muscular, drafts red and sub-red. Often called Big Leo.

Leonus: A sailor with a twisted back who was particularly cruel to the slave rowers.

Lightbringer, the: A controversial figure in prophecy and mythology. Attributes that most agree on are that he is male, will slay or has slain gods and kings, is of mysterious birth, is a genius of magic, a warrior who will sweep, or has swept, all before him, a champion of the poor and downtrodden, great from his youth, He Who Shatters. That most of the prophecies were in Old Parian and the meanings have changed in ways that are difficult to trace hasn't helped. There are three basic camps: those who believe that the Lightbringer has yet to come; those who believe that the Lightbringer has already come and was Lucidonius (a view the Chromeria now holds, though it didn't always); and, among some academics, those who believe that the Lightbringer is a metaphor for what is best in all of us.

Lillyfield: Martial arts tutor to Sarai Lucigari and to Teia.

Little Piper: An orange/yellow bichrome Blackguard.

Lorcan: A giant grizzly. Littermates with Tallach.

Lucidonius: The legendary founder of the Seven Satrapies and the Chromeria, the first Prism. He was married to Karris Shadowblinder and founded the Blackguard.

Lucigari, Lady: The mother of Sarai; a wealthy noblewoman of Abornea.

Lucigari, Sarai: Teia was her slave companion and training partner.

Lunna Green: The Green on the Spectrum until her death. Ruthgari, a cousin of Jia Tolver. Her brothers killed Arys Greenveil's parents during the war.

Lytos: A Blackguard, a lanky Ilytian eunuch. Partners with Buskin. Betrayed his oaths before he was killed by the Mighty.

Malargos, Antonius: Cousin of Eirene and Tisis Malargos, a red drafter and devout follower of Orholam.

Malargos, Aristocles: Uncle of Eirene and Tisis Malargos; lost during the chaos in the aftermath of the Battle of Sundered Rock.

Malargos, Camileas: One of the High Luxiats during the False Prism's War. Sister of Dervani and Aristocles Malargos.

Malargos, Dervani: A Ruthgari nobleman, father of Eirene and Tisis Malargos, a friend and supporter of Dazen during the False Prism's War. A green drafter who was lost in the wilds of Tyrea for years. When he tried to return home, Felia Guile secretly hired pirates to kill him so that he wouldn't reveal Gavin's secrets. He survived the attempt and later became the Omnichrome's choice for Atirat.

Malargos, Eirene (Prism): The Prism before Alexander Spreading Oak (who preceded Gavin Guile). She lasted fourteen years.

Malargos, Eirene (the Younger): The older sister of Tisis Malargos. She took over the family's affairs when her father and uncle didn't come back from the war.

Malargos, Perakles: The brutal though cowardly head of the Malargos family prior to Eirene Malargos's ascension.

Malargos, Thera: Perakles Malargos's wife.

Malargos, Tisis: A stunningly beautiful Ruthgari green drafter. Her father and uncle fought for Dazen Guile. Her older sister is Eirene Malargos, from whom she will likely inherit the wealth of a great trading empire, as Eirene has refused to bear children. Now married to Kip Guile.

Maltheos, the: A Ruthgari noble family that fell before the False Prism's War.

Marae: One of Teia's younger sisters.

Marid Black: The Black during the False Prism's War.

Marissia: Gavin Guile's room slave. A red-haired Blood Forester who was captured by the Ruthgari during the war between Ruthgar and Blood Forest, she has been with Gavin for over a decade, since she was eighteen.

Marta, Adan: An inhabitant of Rekton.

Martaens, Marta: A magister at the Chromeria. She is one of only a handful of living paryl drafters, and she instructs Teia.

Martaenus, Luzia: A young woman of Atan's town during Darjan's time.

Massensen: A hero in defeating the Jadmar Rebellion.

Melanthes: The steward – and slave – of the Malargos family.

Mennad: A Blackguard who gave his life for a Prism.

Mimi, Pasha: A new pirate queen of Ilyta.

Mohana: One of the six High Luxiats.

Mori: A soldier in the Omnichrome's army.

Morteza: A Shadow for the Order of the Broken Eye.

Mossbeard: The conn of a village on the Blood Forest coast near Ruic Bay.

Naelos: A Blackguard with whom Karris White Oak had a brief affair after the end of her engagement to Gavin Guile.

Nabiros: One of the Two Hundred. Legendary. Also known as Cerberos.

Naheed: Satrapah of Atash. She was murdered by General Gad Delmarta during the False Prism's War.

Naheed, Quentin: A young luxiat and genius polymath.

Nassos: A Ruthgari count in western Ruthgar. Liv Danavis's cousin serves him.

Navid, Gariban: A discipulus at the Chromeria.

Navid, Payam: A good-looking magister at the Chromeria; Phips Navid is his cousin.

Navid, Phips: Cousin to Payam Navid. He grew up in Ru, and later joined the Omnichrome's army. His father and older brothers were all hanged after the False Prism's War when he was just twelve years old. Killed in the Battle of Ru.

Nerra: A Blackguard who invented great explosive luxin disks (hull wreckers) for sinking ships.

Niel, Amestan: Now the third largest exporter of wool in Paria, as a young man he knew Karris White Oak.

Niel, Baya: A green drafter and Blackguard.

Nuqaba, the: Keeper of the oral histories of Parians, a figure of unique and tremendous power due to her ancient office as both religious leader to the Parians and guardian of the great Library of Azûlay. Within her satrapy, she rivals both the satrap of Paria and the Prism in her influence.

Oakenshield, Taya: Known for extending the walls of what

was once known as Oakenshield Fortress (now simply called the Castle).

Oakenshield, Zee: Andross Guile's great-great-grandmother, a green drafter.

Omnichrome, Lord (the Color Prince): The leader of a rebellion against the rule of the Chromeria. His true identity is known by few, as he has re-formed almost his entire body with luxin. A full-spectrum polychrome, he posits a faith in freedom and power, rather than in Lucidonius and Orholam. Also known as the White King, the Color Prince, the Crystal Prophet, the Polychrome Master, the Eldritch Enlightened, and derogatorily as Lord Rainbow. He was formerly Koios White Oak, one of Karris White Oak's brothers. He was horribly burnt in the fire that triggered the False Prism's War.

One-Eye: A mercenary with the Cloven Shield company.

Onesto, Prestor: An Ilytian banker at Varig and Green.

Onesto, Turgal: The young scion of a great merchant banking family and Karris White Oak's spy.

Ora'lem: The legendary first drafter to use a shimmercloak, name literally meaning 'the hidden.'

Orholam: From the Old Abornean *Or'holam*, literally 'Lord of Light.' Referred to by his/its titles rather than by a name as a sign of total respect. The deity of the monotheistic Seven Satrapies, also known as the Father of All. His worship was spread throughout the Seven Satrapies by Lucidonius, four hundred years before the reign of Prism Gavin Guile.

Orholam: A tongue-in-cheek nickname for a slave rower who once served Orholam as a prophet. Due to Gunner's superstitions, he is assigned to the seventh seat in the galley's ranks, seven being also the number of the deity.

Orlos, Maros: A very religious Ruthgari drafter. He fought in both the False Prism's War and as a defender of Garriston.

Or-mar-zel-atir: One of the original Blackguards who served Lucidonius. His name meant 'master who serves as [the goddess] Atirat's spear' with the dual connotation that he was a master of the spear, and that he himself was lordly and used as Atirat's spear.

Oros brothers, the: Two Blackguard scrubs.

Param: A retired Blackguard. One of Karris White Oak's former lovers.

Payam, Parshan: A young drafter at the Chromeria who attempted to seduce Liv Danavis as part of a bet. After she learned of the bet, he failed in spectacular fashion.

Pevarc: He proved the world was round two hundred years before Gavin Guile, and was later lynched for positing that light was the absence of darkness rather than a positive presence itself.

Phaestos: A legendary woodworker of Blood Forest.

Pheronike: A spy handler for the White King and a sub-red drafter.

Philosopher, the: A foundational figure in both moral and natural philosophy.

Pip: A Blackguard scrub.

Polyphrastes: A rhetor and grammarian. Author of *Dictions*.

Pots: A Blackguard.

Presser: A Blackguard.

Ptolos, Euterpe: Satrapah of Ruthgar.

Ptolos, Croesos: Cousin to Euterpe Ptolos.

Pullawr, Orea: The White. A blue/green bichrome who refrained from drafting in order to prolong her life. She was married to Ulbear Rathcore before his death twenty years ago.

Rados, Blessed Satrap: A Ruthgari satrap who fought the Blood Foresters although he was outnumbered two to one. He was famous for burning the Rozanos Bridge behind his army to keep it from retreating.

Ramir (Ram): A Rekton villager.

Rassad, Shayam: Completely blind in the visible spectrum, he allegedly could navigate with sub-red and paryl; instructed Marta Martaens's teacher in the use of paryl.

Rathcore, Fiona: A Prism.

Rathcore, Ghiolla Dhé: Nobleman, nephew of Orea Pullawr.

Rathcore, Ulbear: The late husband of the White, he has been dead for twenty years. An adroit player of Nine Kings.

Rhoda: Masseuse for the Blackguard and the White.

Rig: A Blackguard legacy. He is a red/orange bichrome.

Roshan, Mahshid: A beautiful superviolet drafter, she serves as a greeter at the Crossroads tavern.

Rud: A Blackguard scrub. He is a squat coastal Parian who wears the ghotra.

Running Wolf: A general for Gavin Guile during the False Prism's War. He was thrice bested by smaller forces commanded by Corvan Danavis.

Sadah Superviolet: The Parian representative, a superviolet drafter, often the swing vote on the Spectrum.

Salvador: An elderly Tyrean slave.

Samite: One of Karris White Oak's best friends. Now one-handed, she has become a trainer for the Blackguard.

Sanson: A village boy from Rekton who grew up with Kip Guile.

Satrap of Atash: See 'Aravind.'

Sayeh, Meena: Cousin to Samila Sayeh. She was just seven years old when she was killed in Gad Delmarta's purge of the royal family at Ru.

Sayeh, Samila: A blue drafter for Gavin Guile's army. She fought in the defense of Garriston under him.

Scriptivist: A prophet.

Seaborn, Brádach: A nobleman who crossed Gavin Guile.

Seaborn, Phyros: A member of the Omnichrome's army. He was seven feet tall and fought with two axes. Liv Danavis's protector and guardian. His family was destroyed by the Guiles after his brother crossed Gavin Guile. Killed when he tried to enslave Liv Danavis.

Selene: One of the six High Luxiats. A close friend of Orea Pullawr.

Selene, Lady: A Tyrean blue/green bichrome. Not related to High Luxiat Selene (this being a relatively common name).

Sendinas, the: A Rekton family.

Shadowblinder, Karris: Lucidonius's wife and later widow. She was the second Prism. See also 'Atiriel, Karris.'

Shala: Gavin Guile's middle-aged room slave immediately following the False Prism's War, chosen by Felia Guile. Her position was eventually permanently filled by Marissia.

Shales, Mongalt: A ship's captain.

Sharp, Murder: An assassin of the Order of the Broken Eye who has at times worked for Andross Guile when the Order endorsed the assignment.

Sharp, Nouri: A Shadow for the Order of the Broken Eye.

Shayam: An influential follower of the Color Prince.

Shimmercloak, Gebalyn: Vox Shimmercloak's former partner. She seems to have died in a fire while on an assignment.

Shimmercloak, Niah: An assassin. Partner to Vox and a light-splitter.

Shimmercloak, Vox: A green drafter and assassin. He was kicked out of the Chromeria at thirteen. A devotee of Atirat.

Shining Spear: Originally called El-Anat, which means 'Anat is the lord.' Once he converted to the Light, he became Forushalzmarish, then Shining Spear so the locals could pronounce it, beginning the tradition of Blackguards' assuming new names upon joining.

Siana: One of Darjan's wives.

Siluz, Rea: Fourth undersecretary of the Chromeria library and a weak yellow drafter. She knows Janus Borig and directs Kip Guile to meet her.

Siofra, Sibéal: A pygmy drafter of Shady Grove.

Small Bear: A huge archer with just one eye. He served Zee Oakenshield.

Spear: A commander of the Blackguard when Gavin Guile first became Prism.

Spreading Oak, Alexander: The Prism before Gavin Guile. Became a poppy addict shortly after becoming Prism. He spent most of his time hiding in his apartments. Son of Lord Bran Spreading Oak.

Spreading Oak, Bran: The head of an old noble family of Blood Forest, devout, an old classmate and friend of Orea Pullawr.

Spreading Oak, Cúan: Nobleman, city leader of Dúnbheo.

Spreading Oak, Gracchos: The youngest of Lord Bran Spreading Oak's six sons. Killed in the False Prism's War.

Spreading Oak, Gracchos (the Elder): A Prism known for his exploits between the sheets as much as for his incredible diplomatic prowess. He seduced every kind of woman, from satrapahs to kitchen maids. He lasted just seven years, *but* managed to stop two wars, though he barely avoided starting a third when his wife found about the kitchen maid.

Strap: An overseer of the slaves on the *Bitter Cob.*

Stump: A Blackguard. Coastal Parian.

Sworrins, the: A Rekton family.

Tafsut, Thiyya: A legendary Blackguard, remembered for her self-sacrifice and her beauty.

Takama: Head of the Chromeria's binderies.

Tala: A drafter and warrior in the False Prism's War. She was also a defender of Garriston. Her grandson is Aheyyad Brightwater, and her sister is Tayri.

Tala (the Younger): A yellow/green bichrome. Named after the hero of the False Prism's War, she is an excellent drafter, though not yet an excellent fighter.

Talim, Sayid: A former Prism. He nearly got himself named promachos to face the nonexistent armada he claimed waited beyond the gates, fifty years ago.

Tallach: A giant grizzly partnered with Conn Ruadhán Arthur, littermate of Lorcan.

Tamerah: A Blackguard scrub, a blue monochrome.

Tana: A Blackguard legacy, a scrub.

Tanner: A Blackguard scrub.

Tarkian: A polychrome drafter.

Tawleb: One of the six High Luxiats.

Tayri: A Parian drafter and defender of Garriston. Her sister is Tala.

Tazerwalt: A princess of the Tlaglanu tribe of Paria. She married Hanishu, the *dey* of Aghbalu who later joined the Blackguard and took the name Tremblefist.

Temnos, Dalos the Younger: A drafter who fought in both the False Prism's War and the defense of Garriston under Gavin Guile.

Tempus: A Blackguard and a watch captain, he led the green drafters during the battle at Ruic Head.

Tensit: A Blackguard inductee.

Tep, Usef: A drafter who fought in the False Prism's War and later against the Omnichrome's armies at Garriston. He was also known as the Purple Bear because he was a disjunctive bichrome in red and blue. After the war, he and Samila Sayeh became lovers, despite having fought on opposite sides.

Third Eye, the: A Seer, the leader of the original Seers Island inhabitants, and wife of Corvan Danavis, the new satrap of Seers Island.

Tiziri: A former student at the Chromeria. She has a birthmark over the left half of her face. Forced to leave when Kip Guile failed to win a game of Nine Kings against his grandfather.

Tizrik: The son of the dey of Aghbalu. He failed the Blackguard testing, though not before Kip Guile broke his nose for being a bully.

Tlatig: One of the Blackguard's most skilled Archers.

Tleros: A Blackguard Archer.

Tolver, Jia: The Yellow on the Spectrum. An Abornean drafter, she is a cousin of Arys Greenveil (the Sub-red).

Treg: A Blackguard who defended Garriston.

Tremblefist (birth name Hanishu): A Blackguard. He was Ironfist's younger brother and was once the dey of Aghbalu.

Tristaem: The author of *On the Fundaments of Reason*.

Tufayyur: A Blackguard scrub.

Tugertent: One of the Blackguard's most skilled Archers. Killed in the White King's War.

Tychos: An extremely skilled orange drafter and hex-caster (a Chromeria-forbidden magic) in the Color Prince's army.

Ular: A Blackguard scrub, Jun's partner.

Usem the Wild: A drafter and defender of Garriston.

Utarkses, Daeron: One of the High Luxiats during the False Prism's War.

Valor: A Blackguard inductee.

Vanzer: A Blackguard and green drafter.

Varidos, Kerawon: A superchromat, magister and head tester of the Chromeria. He drafts orange and red.

Varigari, Lord: A scion of the Varigari family, originally fishermen before they were raised in the Blood Wars. He lost the family fortune and lands to his gambling habit.

Vecchini, Phineas: A master builder of cannons.

Vecchio, Pash: The most powerful of the pirate kings. His flagship is the *Gargantua*, the best-armed ship in history.

Vena: Liv's friend and fellow student at the Chromeria; a superviolet.

Verangheti, Lucretia: Adrasteia's sponsor at the Chromeria. She is from the Smussato Veranghetis (an Ilytian branch of the family).

Verity: Tisis Malargos's room slave.

Vin, Taya: A mercenary with the Cloven Shield company.

Wanderer, the: A legendary figure, the subject of Gevison's poem *The Wanderer's Last Journey*.

Web, Daimhin: A hunter from deep in Blood Forest.

Weir, Dravus: A spy with connections to the Blood Forest ambassador.

White Oak, Breck: Nobleman, city leader of Dúnbheo, third cousin of Karris White Oak.

White Oak, Karris: Former Blackguard; a red/green bichrome; the original cause of the False Prism's War. As the newly appointed White, she is now perhaps the most powerful woman in the world.

White Oak, Koios: One of the seven White Oak brothers, brother to Karris White Oak. Though not originally believed to be a polychrome, after the disastrous fire that killed the majority of his family on the Jaspers, he disappeared and years later emerged as the Omnichrome in Tyrea. Now known as the White King.

White Oak, Kolos: One of the seven White Oak brothers, brother to Karris Guile.

White Oak, Rissum: A luxlord, the father of Karris White Oak and her seven brothers; reputed to be hot tempered, but a coward.

White Oak, Rodin: One of the seven White Oak brothers, brother to Karris Guile.

White Oak, Tavos: One of the seven White Oak brothers, brother to Karris Guile.

White, the: The head of the Chromeria and the Spectrum. She (a strong majority of Whites have been women, though it isn't a requirement) is in charge of all magical and historical education at the Chromeria (as opposed to purely religious instruction, which is the demesne of the High Luxiats). She is in charge of all discipulae, and matters political and social regarding the Chromeria (where the Black is in charge of matters mundane, practical, and martial, and is subordinate to her). She presides over the Chromeria, though her power is limited to casting tiebreaking votes – a rarity, as the Spectrum gives one vote to each of its seven Colors (the Black having no vote ever, though he is allowed to speak and attends meetings).

Wil: A green drafter, and a Blackguard.

Willow Bough, Briun: The satrap of Blood Forest.

Willow Bough, Culin: A nobleman and leader of Dúnbheo.

Winsen: A mountain Parian, and one of the Mighty. An incredible archer.

Wit, Rondar: A blue drafter who becomes a color wight.

Wood, Deoradhán: A veteran of the Blood Wars.

Young Bull: A blue drafter who fought alongside Zee Oakenshield.

Yugerten: A gangly Blackguard scrub, blue drafter.

Zid: Quartermaster of the Omnichrome's army.

Ziri: A Blackguard scrub.

Glossary

abaya: A robe-like dress, common in Paria.

Aghbalu: Both a Parian *dey* (city-state) and its capital city, this inland region is mountainous, its inhabitants known for their height and blue drafting, as well as a fierce independence from the coastal Parian deys.

ah'dar qassis gwardjan: A green drafter-warrior-priest and servant of the green goddess/god Atirat.

Akomi Nero: A river in Blood Forest that originates in the Ruthgari Highlands.

alcaldesa: A Tyrean term, akin to 'village mayor' or 'chief.'

Amalu and Adini's: Chirurgeons' clinic on Big Jasper. Amalu and Adini are famous for making a fortune treating nobles and Colors for two decades, then freeing their slaves and taking a religious oath to treat the poor.

Am, Children of: Archaic term for the people of the Seven Satrapies.

Amitton: An Atashian city north of Sitara's Wells.

Anat: God of wrath, associated with sub-red. See Appendix, 'On the Old Gods.'

Angar: A country beyond the Seven Satrapies and the Everdark Gates. Its skilled sailors occasionally enter the Cerulean Sea. The Angari are matrilineal, remarkable for their blond hair and fair skin, sailing skills, emphasis on hygiene, and brewing of an alcohol from honey.

Ao River: A river on the border of Blood Forest and Atash.

Apple Grove: A small town in the interior of Blood Forest, a part of the White Oak patrimony for generations.

aristeia: A concept encompassing genius, purpose, and excellence, and often the demonstration thereof.

Aslal: The capital city of Paria. The Eternal Flame, at the heart of the city, was lit by Lucidonius at his inauguration as Prism.

ataghan: A narrow, slightly-forward-curving sword with a single edge for most of its length.

Atan's Teeth: Mountains to the east of Tyrea.

Atan's Town: An extinct village on the coast of what is now Tyrea. Legend holds that it was wiped out in a storm of fire. Some scholars believe this to be a symbolic interpretation of a massacre after Atan's Town resisted Lucidonius's forces. Others believe it was a literal magical storm.

atasifusta: The widest tree in the world, believed extinct after the False Prism's War. Its sap has properties like concentrated red luxin, which, when allowed to drain slowly, can keep a flame lit for hundreds of years if the tree is large enough. The wood itself is ivory white, and when the trees are immature, a small amount of its wood, burning, can keep a home warm for months. Its usefulness led to aggressive harvesting, and this, coupled with slow growth, caused its extinction.

Atirat: God of lust, associated with green. See Appendix, 'On the Old Gods.'

Aved Barayah: A legendary ship. Its name means 'the fire breather.' Gunner was its cannoneer for a time in his youth. It was during his service here that he is said to have killed a sea demon with a miraculous shot.

aventail: Usually made of chain mail, it is attached to the helmet and drapes over the neck, shoulders, and upper chest.

Azûlay: The capital city of Paria; the satrapah and Nuqaba live there.

balance: The primary work of the Prism. When the Prism drafts at the top of the Chromeria, he alone can sense all the world's imbalances in magic and can draft enough of its opposite (i.e., balancing) color to stop the imbalance from getting any worse and leading to catastrophe. Frequent imbalances occurred throughout the world's history before Lucidonius came, and the resulting disasters of fire (see 'Atan's Town'), famine, and sword killed thousands if not millions. Superviolet balances sub-red, blue balances red, and green balances orange. Yellow seems to exist in balance naturally.

bane: An old Ptarsu term, can be either singular or plural. It may have referred to a temple or holy place, though Lucidonius's Parians believed they were abominations. The Parians acquired the word from the Ptarsu.

Barrenmoor: An expensive whisky. Distilled by the same process as Crag Tooth, its rival, Barrenmoor evinces a smoky, medicinal, seaweedy nose with flavors of peat and salt.

beakhead: The protruding part of the foremost section of a ship.

beams: See 'Chromeria trained.'

Belphegor: God of sloth, associated with yellow. See Appendix, 'On the Old Gods.'

belt-flange: A flattened hook attached to a pistol so it can be tucked securely into a belt.

belt knife: A blade small enough to be tucked in a belt, commonly used for eating, rarely for defense.

bich'hwa: A 'scorpion,' a weapon with a loop hilt and a narrow, undulating recurved blade. Sometimes made with a claw.

bichrome: A drafter who can draft two different colors.

Big Jasper (Island): The island on which the city of Big Jasper rests just opposite the Chromeria, and where the embassies of all the satrapies reside. At the time of the Lucidonian expansion, inhabited by the Ptarsu and enslaved pygmies.

binocle: A double-barreled spyglass that allows the use of both eyes for viewing objects at a distance.

Blackguard, the: An elite guard at the top echelon of the Chromeria. The Blackguard was instituted after Lucidonius with a unique dual purpose: to guard the Prism, and to guard the Prism from him- or herself. Though they are commonly seen as bodyguards for the Prism (and at times the White, and at other times all of the Colors), the exact nature and extent of their duties is little known.

Black River: A tributary of the Great River.

blindage: A screen for the open deck of a ship during battle.

Blood Plains, the: An older collective term for Ruthgar and Blood Forest, so called since Vician's Sin caused the Blood War between them.

Blood War, the: A series of battles that began after Vician's Sin tore apart the formerly close allies of Blood Forest and Ruthgar. The war was seemingly interminable, often starting and stopping, until Gavin Guile put a decisive end to it following the False Prism's War. It seems there will be no further hostilities. Also known as the Blood Wars among those who differentiate between the various chapters and campaigns of the long struggle.

Blue-Eyed Demons, the: A famed company of bandits whose king Gavin Guile killed after the False Prism's War.

blunderbuss: A musket with a bell-shaped muzzle that can be loaded with nails, musket balls, chain, or even gravel. Devastating at short distances.

Braxos: A legendary city thousands of years old, cut off from the Seven Satrapies by the Cracked Lands, which were reputed to have been formed with magic during the Ptarsu expansion centuries before Lucidonius.

brightwater: Liquid yellow luxin. It is unstable and quickly releases its energy as light. Often used in lanterns.

Brightwater Wall: Its building was a feat to match the legends. This wall was designed by Aheyyad Brightwater and built by Prism Gavin Guile at Garriston in just days before and while the Omnichrome's army attacked.

Briseid, the: An epic of Blood Forest.

Broken Man, the: A statue in a Tyrean orange grove. Likely a Ptarsu relic.

burnous: A long Parian cloak with hood.

caleen/calun: A diminutive term of address for a girl or female slave/boy or male slave, used regardless of the slave's age.

Cannon Island: A small island with a minimal garrison between Big Jasper and Little Jasper. It houses artillery and, it's rumored, magical defenses.

Cerulean Sea, the: The sea the Seven Satrapies circle.

cherry glims: Slang for red-drafting second-year students.

chirurgeon: One who stitches up the wounded and studies anatomy.

Chosen, Orholam's: Another term for the Prism.

chromaturgy: Literally 'color working,' it usually refers to drafting, but technically also covers the study of luxins and will.

Chromeria, the: The ruling body of the Seven Satrapies; also a term for the school where drafters are trained.

Chromeria trained: Those who have trained or are training at the Chromeria school for drafting on Little Jasper Island in the Cerulean Sea. The Chromeria's training system does not limit students based on age, but rather progresses them through each degree of training based on their ability and knowledge. So a thirteen-year-old who is extremely proficient in drafting might well be a gleam, or third-year student, while an eighteen-year-old who is just beginning work on her drafting could be a dim.

darks: Technically known as 'supplicants,' these are would-be drafters who have yet to be tested for their abilities at the Chromeria or allowed full admission to the school.

dims: The first-year (and therefore lowest) rank of the Chromeria's students.

glims: Second-year students.

gleams: Third-year students.

beams: Fourth-year students.

cocca: A type of merchant ship, usually small.

Colors, the: The seven members of the Spectrum. Originally each represented a single color of the seven sacred colors; each could draft that color, and each satrapy had one representative. Since the founding of the Spectrum, that practice has deteriorated as satrapies have maneuvered for power. Thus a satrapy's Color could be appointed to a color she doesn't actually draft. Likewise, some of the satrapies might lose their representative, and others could have two or even three representatives on the Spectrum at a time, depending on the politics of the day. A Color's term is for life. Impeachment is nearly impossible.

color matchers: A term for superchromats. Sometimes employed as satraps' gardeners.

color-sensitive: See 'superchromat.'

color wight: A drafter who has broken the halo. They often remake their bodies with pure luxin, rejecting the Pact between drafter and society that is a foundation of all training at the Chromeria.

conn: A title for a mayor or leader of a village sometimes used in far-northern Atash, but more common in Blood Forest.

Corrath Springs: A small port city on the coast of Ruthgar.

Corbine Street: A street in Big Jasper that leads to the Great Fountain of Karris Shadowblinder.

corregidor: A Tyrean term for a chief magistrate; from when Tyrea encompassed eastern Atash. Now used for regional governors or even the leaders of larger cities.

corso: A title for the drummer on a galley.

Counselor to Kings, The: A manuscript noted for advocating ruthless treatment of opponents.

Cracked Lands, the: A region of broken land in the extreme west of Atash. Its treacherous terrain is crossed by only the most hardy and experienced traders.

Crag Tooth: A fine whisky with a sublime nose hinting at rose and cinnamon, made in distilleries at the edge of Blood Forest in the highlands above Green Haven. It evinces orange and raisin flavors under powerful chocolate.

Crater Lake: A large lake in southern Tyrea where the former capital of Tyrea, Kelfing, sits. The area is famous for its forests and the production of yew.

Crossroads, the: A kopi house, restaurant, and tavern, the highest-priced inn on the Jaspers, and downstairs a similarly priced brothel. Located near the Lily's Stem, the Crossroads is housed in the former Tyrean embassy building, centrally located in the Embassies District for all the ambassadors, spies, and merchants trying to deal with various governments.

cubit: A unit of volume. One cubit is one foot high, one foot wide, and one foot deep.

culverin: A type of cannon, useful for firing long distances because of its heavily weighted cannonballs and long-bore tube.

Cwn y Wawr: The 'Dogs of Dawn,' a Blood Forest martial company of archers, tree climbers, green drafters, and masters of camouflage. A semisecret society found in the deep parts of Blood Forest.

dagger-pistols: Pistols with a blade attached, allowing the user to fire at distance and then use the blade at close range or if the weapon misfires.

Dagnu: God of gluttony, associated with red. See Appendix, 'On the Old Gods.'

danar: The currency of the Seven Satrapies. The average worker makes about a danar a day, while an unskilled laborer can expect to earn a half danar a day. The coins have a square hole in the middle, and are often carried on square-cut sticks. They can be cut in half and still hold their value.

tin danar: Worth eight regular danar coins. A stick of tin danars usually carries twenty-five coins – that is, two hundred danars.

silver quintar: Worth twenty danars, slightly wider than the tin danar, but only half as thick. A stick of silver quintars usually carries fifty coins – that is, one thousand danars.

den: One-tenth of a danar.

darks: See 'Chromeria trained.'

Dark Forest/Deep Forest: A region within Blood Forest where pygmies reside. Decimated by the diseases brought by invaders, their numbers have never recovered, and they remain insular and often hostile. Few Chromeria drafters have ever returned from trips to the Dark Forest.

darklight: Another term for paryl.

dawat: A Parian martial art: 'circling strike.'

Dazen's War: Another name for the False Prism's War, used by the victors. Dazen Guile's defeated armies and disinterested observers sometimes call it simply the Prisms' War.

Deimachia, the: The War of/on the Gods. A theological term for Lucidonius's battle for supremacy against the pagan gods of the old world.

Demiurgos: Another term for a Mirror; literally 'half creator.'

Deora Neamh: 'Heaven's Tears' – a waterfall in Blood Forest.

dey/deya: A Parian title, male and female respectively. A near-absolute ruler over a city and its surrounding territory. (Equivalent to the Atashian/Tyrean 'corregidor.')

dims: See 'Chromeria trained.'

discipulae: The feminine plural term (also applying to groups of mixed genders) for those who study both religious and magical arts, usually at the Chromeria.

drafter: One who can shape or harness light into physical form (luxin).

Dúnbheo: Also known as the Floating City.

Elrahee, elishama, eliada, eliphalet: A Parian prayer meaning 'He sees, he hears, he cares, he saves.'

Embassies District: The Big Jasper neighborhood that is closest to the Lily's Stem, and thus is closest to the Chromeria itself. It also houses markets and kopi houses, taverns, and brothels.

epha: A unit of measurement for grain. (Approximately thirty-three liters.)

Ergion: An Atashian walled city a day's travel east of Idoss.

Eshed Notzetz: The tallest waterfall in the Seven Satrapies.

Everdark Gates, the: The strait connecting the Cerulean Sea to the oceans beyond. It was supposedly closed by Lucidonius, but Angari ships have been known to make it through from time to time.

evernight: Often a curse word, it refers to death and hell. A metaphysical or teleological reality, rather than a physical one, it represents that which will forever embrace and be embraced by void, full darkness, night in its purest and most evil form.

eye caps: A specialized kind of spectacles. These colored lenses fit directly over the eye sockets, glued to the skin. Like other spectacles, they enable a drafter to draft her color more easily.

False Prism, the: Another term for Dazen Guile, who claimed to be a Prism even after his older brother Gavin had already been rightly chosen by Orholam and installed as Prism.

False Prism's War, the: A common term for the war between Gavin and Dazen Guile, where 'False Prism' refers to Dazen.

Fásann Ár Gciorcal: The Greenveil family motto, meaning 'Our Circle Grows.'

Fealty to One: The Danavis motto.

Feast of Light and Darkness, the: A celebration of the equinox, when light and dark war over who will own the sky.

Because the religious calendar is tied to the lunar calendar, the feast is sometimes as much as a month off the solar date of the equinox.

Fechín Island: An island in Blood Forest at the Black River confluence.

Ferrilux: God of pride, associated with superviolet. See Appendix, 'On the Old Gods.'

firecrystal: A term for sustainable sub-red, though a firecrystal doesn't last long when exposed to air.

firefriend: A term sub-red drafters use for each other.

Flame of Erebos, the: The symbolic pin all Blackguards receive: as a candle must be consumed to provide light, so too the Blackguards' lives require sacrifice to be of use to Orholam.

flashbomb: A weapon crafted by yellow drafters. It doesn't harm so much as dazzle and distract its victims with the blinding light of evaporating yellow luxin.

flechette: A tiny projectile (sometimes made of luxin), with a pointed end and a vaned tail to achieve stable flight.

foot: Once a varying measure based on the current Prism's foot length. Later standardized to twelve thumbs (the length of the foot of Prism Sayid Talim, who decreed the standardization).

Free, the (see disambiguation with 'Freed, the' below): Those drafters who reject the Pact of the Chromeria to join the Omnichrome's army, choosing to eventually break the halo and become wights. Also called the Unchained.

Freed, the (see disambiguation with 'Free, the' above): Those drafters who accept the Pact of the Chromeria and choose to be ritually killed before they break the halo and go mad. (The closeness of this term with 'the Free' is part a deliberate linguistic war between the pagans and the Chromeria, with the pagans trying to seize terms that had long had other meanings.)

Freeing: The release of those about to break the halo from incipient madness; performed by the Prism every year as the culmination of the Sun Day rituals. A sensitive and holy time, it is accompanied by both mourning and celebration. Each drafter meets personally with the Prism for the ritual. Many refer to it as the holiest day of their lives. The pagans take a different view.

frizzen: On a flintlock, the L-shaped piece of metal against which the flint scrapes. The metal is on a hinge that opens upon firing to allow the sparks to reach the black powder in the chamber.

gada: A ball game that involves kicking and passing a ball of wrapped leather.

galleass: Originally a large merchant ship powered by both oar and sail. Later, the term referred to ships with modifications for military purposes, which include castles at bow and stern and cannons that fire in all directions.

gaoler: One in charge of a prison or dungeon.

Gargantua, the: A veritable floating castle, it was Ilytian pirate king Pash Vecchio's flagship, with one hundred and forty-one light guns and forty-three heavy cannons.

Garriston: The former commercial capital of Tyrea at the mouth of the Umber River on the Cerulean Sea. Prism Gavin Guile built Brightwater Wall to defend the city, but his defense failed, and the city was claimed by Lord Omnichrome, the Color Prince, later the White King, Koios White Oak.

Gatu, the: A Parian tribe, despised by other Parians for how they integrate their old religious customs into the worship of Orholam. Technically their beliefs are heresy, but the Chromeria has never moved to put the heresy down with anything more than strong words.

gciorcal: A traditional dance of the Blood Forest pygmies involving paired, spinning dancers.

gemshorn: A musical instrument made from the tusk of a javelina, with finger-holes drilled into it to allow different notes to be played.

ghotra: A Parian headscarf, used by many Parian men to demonstrate their reverence for Orholam. In old Parian tradition, a man's hair is a sign of his virility and dominance and thereby his glory. Most wear it only while the sun is up, but some sects wear it even at nighttime.

giist: A colloquial name for a blue wight.

gladius: A short double-edged sword, useful for cutting or stabbing at close range.

Glass Lily, the: Another term for Little Jasper, or for the whole of the Chromeria as a collection of buildings. A reference to how the seven towers turn to follow the sun.

gleams: See 'Chromeria trained.'

glims: See 'Chromeria trained.'

gold standard: The literal standard weights and measures, made of gold, against which all measures are judged. The originals are kept at the Chromeria, and certified copies are kept in every capital and major city for the adjudication of disputes. Merchants found using short measures and inaccurate weights are punished severely.

Great Chain (of being), the: A theological term for the order of creation. The first link is Orholam himself, and all the other links below (creation) derive from him.

great hall of the Chromeria, the: Located under the Prism's Tower, it is converted once a week into a place of worship, at which time mirrors from the other towers are turned to shine light in. It includes pillars of white marble and the largest display of stained glass in the world. Most of the time, though, it is filled with clerks, ambassadors, and those who have business with the Chromeria.

great hall of the Travertine Palace, the: The wonder of the great hall is its eight great pillars set in a star shape around the hall, all made of extinct atasifusta wood. Said to be the gift of an Atashian king, these pillars are made of trees that were the widest in the world, and their sap allows fires to burn continually, even five hundred years after they were cut.

Great River, the: The river between Ruthgar and Blood Forest, the scene of many pitched battles between the two countries.

great yard, the: The yard at the base of the towers of the Chromeria.

Green Bridge: Less than a league upstream from Rekton, drafted by Gavin Guile in seconds while he was on his way to battle his brother at Sundered Rock.

green flash: A rare flash of color seen at the setting of the sun; its meaning is debated. Some believe it has theological significance, citing Karris Atiriel's sighting of it the evening before the battle in Hass Valley. The previous White, Orea Pullawr, called it 'Orholam's wink.'

Green Forest: A collective term for Blood Forest and Ruthgar during the hundred years of peace between the two territories, before Vician's Sin incited the Blood Wars.

Green Haven: The capital of Blood Forest.

Greenwall: The massive defensive wall surrounding Dúnbheo.

grenado: A clay flagon full of black powder with a piece of wood shoved into the top, with a rag and bit of black powder as a fuse.

grenado, luxin: An explosive made of luxin that can be hurled at the enemy along an arc of luxin or in a cannon. Often filled with shot/shrapnel, depending on the type of grenado used.

Guardian, the: A colossus that stands astride the entrance to Garriston's bay. She holds a spear in one hand and a torch in the other. A yellow drafter keeps the torch lit with yellow luxin, allowing it to dissolve slowly back into light, so the colossus also acts as a lighthouse. See also 'Ladies, the.'

Guile palace: The Guile family palace on Big Jasper, distinct from their residence on Jaks Hill. Andross Guile has rarely visited his home in the time Gavin has been Prism, preferring to reside at the Chromeria. The Guile palace was one of the few buildings allowed to be constructed without regard to the working of the Thousand Stars, its height cutting off some of the light paths.

habia: A man's long garment, most common in Abornea.

Hag, the: An enormous statue that comprises Garriston's west gate. She is crowned and leans heavily on a staff; the crown and staff are also towers from which archers can shoot at invaders. See also 'Ladies, the.'

Hag's Crown, the: One of the towers over the west gate into Garriston.

Hag's Staff, the: The second tower over the west gate into Garriston.

haik: An outer garment that wraps around the body and head. Commonly worn in Paria.

Harbinger: Corvan Danavis's sword, inherited when his elder brothers died.

Hass Valley: Where the Ur trapped Lucidonius. Karris Atiriel (later Karris Shadowblinder) saved his army there, after climbing through the mountain passes at night to strike the Ur's camp from behind at dawn.

haze: A narcotic. Often smoked with a pipe, it produces a sickly-sweet odor.

Hellfang: A mysterious blade, also known as Marrow Sucker and the Blinder's Knife. It is white-veined with black and bears seven colorless gems in its blade.

hellhounds: Dogs infused with red luxin and enough will to make them run at enemies, and then lit on fire.

Hellmount: A snow-capped peak far to the southwest.

hellstone: A superstitious term for obsidian, which is rarer than diamonds or rubies, as few know where the extant obsidian in the world is created or mined. Obsidian is the only stone that can draw luxin out of a drafter if it touches her blood directly.

Highland: A small town at the top of a volcano's rim on Seers Island.

hippodrome (Rath): A stadium dedicated primarily to horse and chariot races, the hippodrome in Rath occasionally operates as a public gathering place for executions and other important state functions.

hullwrecker: A luxin disk filled with shrapnel. It has a sticky side so that it will adhere to a ship's hull and a fuse to allow the attackers to flee before it explodes, often punching a hole in the ship's hull and spraying shrapnel in toward the crew.

Idoss: An Atashian city, now under the control of the White King's armies.

Incarnitive luxin: A term for luxin when it is incorporated directly into one's body. This is forbidden by the Chromeria as debasing or defiling Orholam's work (the human body itself) with man's work, and is seen as a slippery slope to trying to fully remake the body and become immortal. In certain cases, the luxiats have turned a blind eye to more minor or prosthetic uses.

Inura, Mount: A mountain on Seers Island, at the base of which the Third Eye resides.

ironbeaks: A term for explosive luxin- and will-infused birds, which drafters use to attack opponents at a distance.

Ivor's Ridge, Battle of: A battle during the False Prism's War, which Dazen Guile won primarily because of Corvan Danavis's brilliance.

Izîl-Udad: The current Nuqaba's husband, the head of the family that had her mother assassinated. Now a cripple, rumored to have been pushed down the stairs by his own wife after he'd beaten her one too many times.

Jaks Hill: A large hill in the city of Rath overlooking the Great River, notable for its wealthy estates. Castle Guile dominates the area.

jambu: A tree that produces pink fruit.

Jasper Islands/the Jaspers: Islands in the Cerulean Sea. The Chromeria is on Little Jasper. Legend has it that the Jaspers were chosen for the Chromeria by Karris Shadowblinder after the death of Lucidonius because they were part of no satrapy, and therefore could be *for* all the satrapies.

javelinas: Animals in the pig family, often hunted. Giant javelinas are rare, but can reach the size of a cow. Extremely dangerous and destructive, giant javelinas are believed to have been hunted to extinction in all satrapies except Tyrea. Both species have tusks and hooves and are nocturnal.

jilbab: A long and loose-fitting coat, often with a hood. Often worn by Parians and occasionally Aborneans.

jinni-yah: A female *jinn* or immortal.

ka: A sequence of movements to train balance and flexibility and control in the martial arts. A form of focusing exercise or meditation.

kaptan: Ptarsu for 'head' or 'leader,' cognate of 'captain.'

Karsos Mountains, the: Tyrean mountains running east and west that border the Cerulean Sea.

katar: A type of punch dagger, it has a cross-grip and a hilt that extends up on either side of the hand and forearm. With this allowance for the fist and its reinforced tip, it is made for punching through armor.

Kazakdoon: A legendary city/land in the distant east, beyond the Everdark Gates.

Keffel's Variant: A set of rules for Nine Kings to make the game especially quick.

Kelfing: The former capital of Tyrea, on the shores of Crater Lake.

khat: An addictive stimulant, a leaf that stains the teeth when it is chewed, used especially in Paria.

kiyah: A yell used while fighting to expel breath, tightening the trunk and empowering the body's movement.

kopi: A mild, addictive stimulant, a popular beverage. Bitter, dark colored, and served hot.

kris: A wavy Parian blade.

Ladies, the: Four statues that comprise the gates into the city of Garriston. They are built into the wall, made of rare Parian marble and sealed in nearly invisible yellow luxin. They are thought to depict aspects of the goddess Anat, and were spared by Lucidonius, who believed them to depict something true. They are the Hag, the Lover, the Mother, and the Guardian.

Laurion: A region in eastern Atash known for its silver ore and massive slave mines. Life expectancy for the enslaved miners is short and conditions brutal. The threat of being sent to the mines is used throughout the satrapies to keep slaves obedient and docile.

league: A unit of measurement, six thousand and seventy-six paces.

léine: A close-fitting smock sometimes worn by Blood Foresters.

Library of Azûlay: An ancient library in Paria, the building itself is more than eight hundred years old, and built on the foundations of another library at least two hundred years older. The Nuqaba generally resides in Azûlay, though she has residences elsewhere.

lightbane: See 'bane.'

Lightguard, the: Andross Guile's personal army, nominally established to defend the Jaspers, answering only to him. Mercenaries, ruffians, veterans, and any others willing to fight for Andross Guile. Primarily washed-up Blackguards and the sons of poor nobles. Even their clothing is in contrast to – some would say a mockery of – the Blackguards': white jackets with big brass buttons and medals.

lightsickness: The aftereffects of too much drafting. Only the Prism never gets lightsick.

lightwells: Holes positioned to allow light, with the use of mirrors, to reach the interiors of towers or sections of streets.

Lily's Stem, the: The luxin bridge between Big and Little Jasper. It is composed of blue and yellow luxin so that it appears green. Set below the high-water mark, it is remarkable for its endurance against the waves and storms that wash over it. Ahhana the Dextrous was responsible for designing it and engineering its creation.

linstock: A staff for holding a slow match. Used in lighting cannons, it allows the cannoneer to stand out of the range of the cannon's recoil.

Little Jasper (Island): The island on which the Chromeria resides. Became the site of the Chromeria after Vician's Sin.

Little Jasper Bay: A bay of Little Jasper Island. It is protected by a seawall that keeps its waters calm.

loci damnata: A temple to the false gods. The bane. Believed to have magical powers, especially over drafters.

longbow: A weapon that allows for the efficient (in speed, distance, and force) firing of arrows. Its construction and its user must both be extremely strong. The yew forests of Crater Lake provide the best wood available for longbows.

Lord Prism: A respectful term of address for a male Prism.

Lords of the Air: A term used by the Omnichrome for his most trusted blue-drafting officers.

Lover, the: A statue that comprises the eastern river gate at Garriston. She is depicted in her thirties, lying on her back, arched over the river with her feet planted, her knees forming a tower on one bank, hands entwined in her hair, elbows rising to form a tower on the other bank. She is clad only in veils. Before the Prisms' War, a portcullis could be lowered from her arched body into the river, its iron and steel hammered into shape so that it looked like a continuation of her veils. She glows like bronze when the sun sets, and a land entrance to the city comes through another gate in her hair.

Luíseach: A Blood Forest term for the Lightbringer.

luxiat: A priest of Orholam. A luxiat wears black as an acknowledgment that he needs Orholam's light most of all; thus he is sometimes called a blackrobe.

luxin: A material created by drafting from light. See Appendix.

luxlord: A term for a member of the ruling Spectrum.

Luxlords' Ball, the: An annual event on the open roof of the Prism's Tower.

luxors: Officials empowered by the Chromeria to bring the light of Orholam by almost any means necessary. They have at various times pursued paryl drafters and lightsplitter heretics, among others. Their theological rigidity and their prerogative to kill and torture have been hotly debated by followers of Orholam and dissidents alike.

magister: The term for a teacher of drafting, history, and religion at the Chromeria. It always retains its masculine ending: *magister,* not *magister* or *magistra* as appropriate. This is a relic from when all teachers were male, female drafters being considered too valuable for teaching.

mag torch: Often used by drafters to allow them access to light at night, it burns with a full spectrum of colors. Colored mag torches are also made at great expense, and give a drafter her exact spectrum of useful light, allowing her to eschew spectacles and draft instantly.

Malleus Haereticorum: 'Hammer of Heretics.' The title for a luxor commissioned to destroy heresy.

Mangrove Point: A village on the border between Blood Forest and Atash.

match-holder: The piece on a matchlock musket to which a slow match is affixed.

matchlock musket: A firearm that works by snapping a burning slow match into the flash pan, which ignites the gunpowder in the breech of the firearm, whose explosion propels a rock or lead ball out of the barrel at high speed. Matchlocks are accurate to fifty or a hundred paces, depending on the smith who made them and the ammunition used.

matériel: A military term for equipment or supplies.

merlon: The upraised portion of a parapet or battlement that protects soldiers from fire.

Midsummer: Another term for Sun Day, the longest day of the year.

Midsummer's Dance: A rural version of the Sun Day celebration.

millennial cypress: A tree known for its immense age and ability to grow in damp conditions.

Mirrormen: Soldiers in King Garadul's army who wear mirrored armor to protect themselves against luxin. The mirrors cause luxin to shear off and disintegrate when it comes in contact with them.

Molokh: God of greed, associated with orange. See Appendix, 'On the Old Gods.'

monochromes: Drafters who can draft only one color. (See 'bichromes' and 'polychromes.')

Mot: God of envy, associated with blue. See Appendix, 'On the Old Gods.'

Mother, the: A statue that guards the south gate into Garriston. She is depicted as a teenager, heavily pregnant, with a dagger bared in one hand and a spear in the other.

mund: An insulting term for a person who cannot draft.

murder hole: A hole in the ceiling of a passageway that allows soldiers to fire, drop, or throw weapons, projectiles, luxin, or fuel. Common in castles and city walls.

nao: A small vessel with a three-masted rig.

Narrows, the: A strait of the Cerulean Sea between Abornea and the Ruthgari mainland. Aborneans charge high tolls on merchants sailing the silk route, or simply between Paria and Ruthgar.

near-polychrome: One who can draft three colors, but can't stabilize the third color sufficiently to be a true polychrome.

Nekril, the: Will-casting coven that laid siege to Aghbalu before being destroyed by Gwafa, a Blackguard.

non-drafter: One who cannot draft.

norm: Another term for a non-drafter. Insulting.

nunk: A half-derogatory term for a Blackguard inductee.

Oakenshield Fortress: The old, original fortress in Ruthgar on Jaks Hill, which eventually became known as Castle Guile, Corinth Castle, Rath Skuld, and finally simply the Castle.

Odess: A city in Abornea that sits at the head of the Narrows.

old world: The world before Lucidonius united the Seven Satrapies and abolished worship of the pagan gods.

oralam: Another term for paryl, meaning 'hidden light.'

Order of the Broken Eye, the: A secret guild of assassins. They specialize in killing drafters and have been rooted out and destroyed at least three times. The pride of the Order is the Shimmercloaks, or Shadows, pairs of purportedly invisible, unstoppable assassins.

Overhill: A neighborhood in Big Jasper.

Ox Ford: The site of a disastrous battle in the White King's War.

Pact, the: Since Lucidonius, the Pact has governed all those trained by the Chromeria in the Seven Satrapies. Its essence is that drafters agree to serve their satrapy and receive all the benefits of status and sometimes wealth – in exchange for their service and eventual death before they break the halo.

Palace of the Divines: The residence and meeting place of Dúnbheo's Council of the Divines.

parry-stick: A primarily defensive weapon that blocks bladed attacks. It sometimes includes a punching dagger at the center of the stick to follow up on a deflected blow.

pathomancy: Related to hex-casting, the reading or manipulation of emotions directly via orange drafting. Forbidden by the Chromeria.

Pericol: A city on the coast of Ilyta.

petasos: A broad-brimmed Ruthgari hat, usually made of straw, meant to keep the sun off the face, head, and neck.

pilum: A weighted throwing spear whose lead shank bends after it pierces a shield, preventing the opponent from reusing the weapon against the user and encumbering the shield. They are becoming more rare and ceremonial.

polychrome: A drafter who can draft three or more colors.

portmaster: A city official in charge of collecting tariffs and managing the organized exit and entrance of ships in his harbor.

Prism: There is only one Prism each generation. She senses the balance of the world's magic and balances it when

631

necessary, and can split light within herself. Other than balancing, her role is largely ceremonial and religious, with the Colors and the satraps all working hard to make sure that Prisms rarely turn their fame into political power.

Prism's Tower, the: The central tower in the Chromeria. It houses the Prism, the White, and superviolets (as they are not numerous enough to require their own tower). The great hall lies below the tower, and the top holds a great crystal for the Prism's use while he balances the colors of the world.

promachia: The institution of giving nearly absolute executive powers to a single person (the promachos) during wartime.

promachos: Literally 'he [or she] who fights before us,' it is a title that may be given during a war or other great crisis. A promachos may be named only by order of a supermajority of the Colors. Among other powers, the promachos has the right to command armies, seize property, and elevate commoners to the nobility.

Providence: The care of Orholam over the Seven Satrapies, and his intervention on behalf of its people.

psantria: A stringed musical instrument.

pygmies [of Blood Forest]: A rare, fierce people of the Blood Forest interior, they claim common ancestry with the people of Braxos. Almost extinct. Their taxonomy is debated, with some saying they are related to humans only as mules are to horses. They can interbreed with humans, though with great danger if the mother is the pygmy, death in childbirth being the norm. Some Blood Forest chiefs and kings in the past claimed that pygmies were not human, and as they weren't, they deemed the killing of pygmies a morally neutral or even laudable act. The Chromeria declared pygmies human and such killing to be murder, but pygmy numbers have never recovered from a number of massacres and human diseases.

pyrejelly: Red luxin that, once set alight, will engulf whatever object it adheres to.

pyroturges: Red and/or sub-red drafters who create wonders of flame, known particularly for their wonders in Azûlay.

qassisin kuluri: Possibly an early incarnation of the Order, 'the color warriors [or assassins].' The exact provenance of the term is lost to history.

Rage of the Seas, the: An Ilytian galley.

raka: A heavy insult, with the implication of both moral and intellectual idiocy.

Raptors of Kazakdoon, the: Flying reptiles from Angari myth.

Rath: The capital of Ruthgar, set on the confluence of the Great River and its delta into the Cerulean Sea.

Rathcaeson: A mythical city, on the drawings of which Gavin Guile based his Brightwater Wall design.

Rathcore Hill: A hill opposite (and somewhat smaller than) Jaks Hill in the city of Rath. The hippodrome is carved into its side.

ratweed: A toxic plant whose leaves are often smoked for their strong stimulant properties. Addictive.

Red Cliff Uprising, the: A rebellion in Atash after the end of the False Prism's War. Without the support of the royal family (who had been purged), it was short-lived.

reedsmen: Drafters used to propel skimmers.

Rekton: A small Tyrean town on the Umber River, near the site of the Battle of Sundered Rock. An important trading post before the False Prism's War. Now uninhabited after a massacre by King Rask Garadul.

Rozanos Bridge, the: A bridge on the Great River between Ruthgar and the Blood Forest that Blessed Satrap Rados famously burnt, so that his troops had no choice but to win or die.

Ru: The capital of Atash, once famous for its castle, still famous for its Great Pyramid.

Ru, Castle of: Once the pride of Ru, it was destroyed by fire during General Gad Delmarta's purge of the royal family in the Prisms' War.

Ruic Head: A peninsula dominated by towering cliffs that overlooks the Atashian city of Ru and its bay. A fort atop the peninsula's cliffs guards against invaders and pirates.

runt: An affably derogatory term for a new Blackguard inductee.

sabino cypress: A tree that grows to massive heights, often found in marshes.

salve: A common greeting, originally meaning 'Be of good health!'

Sapphire Bay: A bay off Little Jasper.

satrap/satrapah: The title of a ruler (male or female respectively) of one of the seven satrapies.

scrogger: Slang for a small rodent.

sev: A unit of measurement for weight, equal to one-seventh of a seven.

seven: A unit of measurement for weight, equal to the weight of a cubit of water.

Seven Lives of Maeve Hart, The: A Blood Forest epic.

Shadow: Another term for a member of the Order of the Broken Eye who can use a shimmercloak.

Shadow Watch: A secretive martial drafting society based in Ruthgar.

Sharazan Mountains, the: Impassable mountains south of Tyrea.

shimmercloak: A cloak that makes the wearer mostly invisible, except in sub-red and superviolet.

Sitara's Wells: An Atashian town north of Ruic Head. In otherwise arid land, its numerous artesian wells have made it a stop for traders and travelers for all of recorded history.

slow fuse/slow match: A length of cord, often soaked in saltpetre, that can be lit to ignite the gunpowder of a weapon in the firing mechanism.

Skill, Will, Source, and Still/Movement: The four essential elements for drafting.

Skill: The most underrated of all the elements of drafting, acquired through practice. Includes knowing the properties and strengths of the luxin being drafted, being able to see and match precise wavelengths, et cetera.

Will: By imposing will, a drafter can draft and even cover flawed drafting if her will is powerful enough.

Source: Depending on what colors a drafter can use, she needs either that color of light or items that reflect that color of light in order to draft. Only a Prism can simply split white light within herself to draft any color.

Still: An ironic usage. Drafting requires movement, though more skilled drafters can use less.

spectrum: A term for a range of light (for more information on the luxin spectrum, see the Appendix); or (capitalized) the council of the Chromeria that is one branch of the government of the Chromeria (see 'Colors, the').

spidersilk: Another term for paryl.

spina: The center line of a hippodrome, which often has a raised platform for announcements, demonstrations, and executions.

spyglass: A device using curved, clear lenses to bend light to aid in sighting distant objects.

star-keepers: Also known as tower monkeys, these are petite slaves (usually children) who work the ropes that control the mirrors in the Thousand Stars of Big Jasper to reflect the light throughout the city for drafters' use. Though well treated for slaves, they spend their days working in two-man teams from dawn till after dusk, frequently without reprieve except for switching with their partners.

Stony Field: A border town between Blood Forest and Atash.

Strang's Commentary: The authoritative work of theology, teleology, and epistemology (in that order) by Aldous Strang, the full opus fills one thousand scrolls.

Strong's Commentary: The authoritative work of epistemology, teleology, and theology (in that order) by Albus Strong, pupil and rumored illegitimate son of Aldous Strang, the full opus fills one thousand and one scrolls.

subchromats: Drafters who are color-blind, overwhelmingly male. A subchromat can function without loss of ability – if his handicap is not in the colors he can draft. A red-green color-blind subchromat could be an excellent blue or yellow drafter. See Appendix.

Sun Day: A holy day for followers of Orholam and pagans alike, the longest day of the year. For the Seven Satrapies, Sun Day is the day when the Prism Frees those drafters who are about to break the halo and go mad. The ceremonies usually take place on the Jaspers, when all of the Thousand Stars are trained onto the Prism, who can absorb and split the light, whereas other men would burn or burst from drafting so much power.

Sun Day's Eve: An evening of festivities, both for celebration and for mourning, before the longest day of the year and the Freeing the next day.

Sundered Rock: Twin mountains in Tyrea, opposite each other and so alike that they look as if they were once one huge rock that was cut down the middle.

Sundered Rock, Battle of: The final battle between Gavin and Dazen Guile near a small Tyrean town called Rekton on the Umber River.

superchromats: Extremely color-sensitive people. Luxin they seal will rarely fail. Overwhelmingly female.

Sword of Heaven: The luxin-imbued lighthouse of Azûlay.

Tafok Amagez: The Nuqaba's elite personal guard, composed entirely of drafters.

tainted: One who has broken the halo, also called a wight.

Tanner's Turn: A village on the border of Atash and the Blood Forest.

targe: A small shield.

Tellari separatists: Rebels behind the burning of the Great Library three hundred years prior to Prism Guile, they also attempted to destroy the Lily's Stem.

telos: A man's end or his highest good.

Tenling Rise: A hill in Blood Forest.

thobe: An ankle-length garment, usually with long sleeves.

Thorikos: A town below the Laurion mines on the river to Idoss. Serves as the center for arriving and departing slaves, the bureaucracy necessary for thirty thousand slaves, and the trade goods and supplies necessary to the mines, as well as the shipping of the silver ore down the river.

Thorn Conspiracies, the: A series of intrigues that occurred after the False Prism's War.

Thousand Stars, the: The mirrors on Big Jasper Island that enable the light to reach into almost any part of the city for as long as possible during the day.

Threshing, the: The initiation test for candidates to the Chromeria. Through subjecting the initiates to things that most commonly instigate fear and providing appropriate spectra of light, it usually reveals the initiates' ranges of drafting ability (with some uncertainty around the edges).

Threshing Chamber, the: The room where candidates for the

Chromeria are summoned to be tested for their abilities to draft.

Thundering Falls: An enormous waterfall at the intersection of the Great River and the Akomi Nero. The city of Verit is right at the base of the falls.

Tiru, the: A Parian tribe.

Tlaglanu, the: A Parian tribe, hated by other Parians, from whom Hanishu, the *dey* of Aghbalu, chose his bride, Tazerwalt.

torch: A red wight.

translucification, forced: See 'willjacking.'

Travertine Palace, the: One of the wonders of the old world. Both a palace and a fortress, it is built of carved travertine (a mellow green stone) and white marble. Notable for its bulbous horseshoe arches, geometric wall patterns, Parian runes, and chessboard patterns on the floors. Its walls are incised with a crosshatched pattern to make the stone look woven rather than carved. The palace is a remnant of the days when half of Tyrea was a Parian province.

Tree People, the: Tribesmen who live (lived?) deep in the forests of the Blood Forest satrapy. They use zoomorphic designs, and can apparently shape living wood. Possibly related to the pygmies.

tromoturgy: A form of hex-casting, 'fear-working' or 'fear-casting' banned by the Chromeria, as are other forms of direct manipulation of emotions; man being created in the likeness of Orholam, any assault on the dignity of man's body (violence, murder) or his mind (emotion-casting, torture, slave-taking) is considered sinful – except as allowed by just-war theory and the rights of rule: a city can imprison a thief where citizens doing so would be punished, et cetera. In general, the Chromeria takes a harder line toward things magical, especially manipulation of emotions and minds, as such things generate a natural terror and distrust among those the Chromeria would rule. Luxors were a noted exception to this blanket prohibition, allowed 'a righteous fear-casting.'

Túsaíonn Domhan: 'A World Begins' – the name of a piece by a legendary Blood Forest woodwright.

Two Hundred, the: Apocryphal. Two hundred of Orholam's progeny who rebelled and came to the world to rule over men and magic.

Two Mills Junction: A small village in Blood Forest, not far from the border of Atash.

tygre striper: Also known as the *sharana ru*, said to be carved sea demon bone. Sources contest that the even rarer whalebone makes superior weapons. It is the only known mundane material that reacts to will, becoming hard or flexible depending on the user's will.

tygre wolves: Fierce creatures of deep Blood Forest, untamable, but able to be directed by will magic.

ulta: In the Order's religion, a man's highest goal, his life's purpose and final test.

Umber River, the: The lifeblood of Tyrea. Its water allows the growth of every kind of plant in the hot climate; its locks fed trade throughout the country before the False Prism's War. Often besieged by bandits.

Unchained, the: A term for the followers of the Color Prince, those drafters who choose to break the Pact and continue living even after breaking the halo.

Unification, the: A term for Lucidonius's and Karris Shadowblinder's establishment of the Seven Satrapies four hundred years prior to Gavin Guile's rule as Prism.

Ur, the: A tribe that trapped Lucidonius in Hass Valley. He triumphed against great odds, primarily because of the heroics of El-Anat (who thereby became Forushalzmarish or Shining Spear) and Karris Atiriel (later Karris Shadowblinder).

urum: A three-tined dining implement.

vambrace: Plate armor to protect the forearm. Ceremonial versions made of cloth also exist.

Varig and Green: A bank with a branch on Big Jasper.

vechevoral: A sickle-shaped sword with a long handle like an axe's and a crescent-moon-shaped blade at the end, with the inward bowl-shaped side being the cutting edge.

Verdant Plains, the: The dominant geographical feature of Ruthgar, enabling the farming and grazing that give Ruthgar its immense wealth. The Verdant Plains have been favored by green drafters since before Lucidonius.

Verit: A town on the Great River at the base of Thundering Falls.

Vician's Sin: The event that marked the end of the close alliance between Ruthgar and Blood Forest, and purportedly led to Orholam's raising White Mist Reef and the mist itself at the center of the Cerulean Sea.

Wanderer, the: Andross Guile's flagship during the fight to save Ru.

warrior-drafters: Drafters whose primary work is fighting for various satrapies or the Chromeria. Usually far inferior in drafting to the Blackguard, who are the foremost warrior-drafters in the world.

water markets: Circular lakes connected to the Umber River at the centers of the villages and cities of Tyrea, common throughout Tyrean towns. A water market is dredged routinely to maintain an even depth, allowing ships easy access to the interior of the city with their wares. The largest water market is in Garriston.

Weasel Rock: A neighborhood in Big Jasper dominated by narrow alleys.

Weedling: A small coastal village in Ru close to Ruic Head.

wheel-lock pistol: A pistol that uses a rotating wheel mechanism to cause the spark that ignites the firearm; the first mechanical attempt to ignite gunpowder. Some few smiths' versions are more reliable than a flintlock and allow repeated attempts to fire with repeated pulls of the trigger without manual cocking as flintlocks require. Most, however, are far less reliable than the already-unreliable flintlocks.

Whiteguard, the: The term for the Omnichrome's personal bodyguard. Most likely a jab at the Blackguard, whose black denotes humility in excellence.

widdershins: Counter-sunwise spinning.

willjacking/will-breaking: Once a drafter has contact with unsealed luxin that she is able to draft, she can use her will to break another drafter's control over the luxin and take it for herself.

will-blunting: A form of drafting used to directly attack another's will by connecting emotionally and intellectually with them, and thereby forbidden as an assault on man's mind and dignity.

Wiwurgh: A Parian town that hosts many Blood Forest refugees from the Blood War.

wob: A term for a Blackguard inductee.

wyrthig: A Blood Forest term for a falsehood or tall tale.

zigarro: A roll of tobacco, a form useful for smoking. Ratweed is sometimes used as a wrapping to hold the loose tobacco to allow use of both substances at once.

ziricote: A type of wood.

zoon politikon: 'Political animal.' From the Philosopher's treatise, *The Politics*. His theory was that man can only reach his *telos*, his end or highest good, when in a community, specifically a city large enough to meet all his needs: physical, social, moral, and spiritual.

Appendix

On Monochromes, Bichromes, and Polychromes

Most drafters are monochromes: they are able to draft only one color. Drafters who can draft two colors well enough to create stable luxin in both colors are called bichromes. Anyone who can draft solid luxin in three or more colors is called a polychrome. The more colors a polychrome can draft, the more powerful she is and the more sought after are her services. A full-spectrum polychrome is a polychrome who can draft every color in the spectrum. A Prism is always a full-spectrum polychrome.

Merely being able to draft a color, though, isn't the sole determining criterion in how valuable or skilled a drafter is. Some drafters are faster at drafting, some are more efficient, some have more will than others, some are better at crafting luxin that will be durable, some are smarter or more creative at how and when to apply luxin.

On Disjunctive Bichromes/Polychromes

On the light continuum, sub-red borders red, red borders orange, orange borders yellow, yellow borders green, green borders blue, blue borders superviolet. Most bichromes and polychromes simply draft a larger spectrum on the continuum than monochromes. That is, a bichrome is most likely to draft two colors that are adjacent to each other (blue and superviolet, red and sub-red, yellow and green, etc.). However, some few drafters are disjunctive bichromes. As could be surmised from the name, these are drafters whose colors do not border each other. Usef Tep was a famous example: he drafted red and blue. Karris Guile is another, drafting green and red. It is unknown how or why disjunctive bichromes come to exist. It is only known that they are rare.

On Outer-Spectrum Colors

There is a small and controversial movement claiming that there are more than seven colors. Indeed, because colors exist on a continuum, one could argue that the number of colors is infinite. However, the argument that there are more than seven draftable colors is more theologically problematic for some. It is commonly accepted that there are other resonance points beyond the seven currently accepted ones, but those points are weaker and much more rarely drafted than the core seven. Among the contenders is one color far below the sub-red, called paryl. Another equally far above superviolet is called only *chi*.

But if colors are to be so broadly defined as to include colors only one drafter in a million can draft, then shouldn't yellow be split into liquid yellow and solid yellow? Where do the (mythical) black and white luxins fit? How could such (non)colors even fit on the spectrum?

The arguments, though bitter, are academic.

On Subchromacy and Superchromacy

A subchromat is one who has trouble differentiating between at least two colors, colloquially referred to as being color-blind. Subchromacy need not doom a drafter. For instance, a blue drafter who cannot distinguish between red and green will not be significantly handicapped in his work.

Superchromacy is having greater than usual ability to distinguish between fine variations of color. Superchromacy in any color will result in more stable drafting, but is most helpful in drafting yellow. Only superchromat yellow drafters can hope to draft solid yellow luxin.

On Luxin (with sections on physics, metaphysics, effects on personality, legendary colors, and colloquial terms)

The basis of magic is light. Those who use magic are called drafters. A drafter is able to transform a color of light into a physical substance. Each color has its own properties, but the uses of those building blocks are as boundless as a drafter's imagination and skill.

The magic in the Seven Satrapies functions roughly the opposite of a candle burning. When a candle burns, a physical substance (wax) is transformed into light. With chromaturgy, light is transformed into a physical substance, luxin. Each color of luxin has its own properties. If drafted correctly (within a tight allowance), the resulting luxin will be stable, lasting for days or even years, depending on its color.

Most drafters (magic-users) can only use one color. A drafter must be exposed to the light of her color to be able to draft it (that is, a green drafter can look at grass and be able to draft, but if she's in a white-walled room, she can't). Each drafter usually carries spectacles so that if her color isn't available, she can still use magic.

PHYSICS
Luxin has weight. If a drafter drafts a luxin haycart over her head, the first thing it will do is crush her. From heaviest to lightest are: red, orange, yellow, green, blue, sub-red,* super-violet, sub-red.* For reference, liquid yellow luxin is only slightly lighter than the same volume of water.

(*Sub-red is difficult to weigh accurately because it rapidly degenerates to fire when exposed to air. The ordering above was achieved by putting sub-red luxin in an airtight container and then weighing the result, minus the weight of the container. In real-world uses, sub-red crystals are often seen floating upward in the air before igniting.)

Luxin has tactility.

Sub-red: Again the hardest to describe due to its flamma-bility, but often described as feeling like a hot wind.

Red: Gooey, sticky, clingy, depending on drafting; can be tarry and thick or more gel-like.

Orange: Lubricative, slippery, soapy, oily.

Yellow: In its liquid, more common state, like bubbly, effervescent water, cool to the touch, possibly a little thicker than seawater. In its solid state, it is perfectly slick, unyielding, smooth, and incredibly hard.

Green: Rough; depending on the skill and purposes of the drafter, ranges from merely having a grain like leather to feeling like tree bark. It is flexible, springy, often drawing comparisons to the green limbs of living trees.

Blue: Smooth, though poorly drafted blue will have a texture and can shed fragments easily, like chalk, but in crystals.

Superviolet: Like spidersilk, thin and light to the point of imperceptibility.

Luxin has scent. The base scent of luxin is resinous. The smells below are approximate, because each color of luxin smells like itself. Imagine trying to describe the smell of an orange. You'd say citrus and sharp, but that isn't it exactly. An orange smells like an orange. However, the below approximations are close.

Sub-red: Charcoal, smoke, burned.
Red: Tea leaves, tobacco, dry.
Orange: Almond.
Yellow: Eucalyptus and mint.
Green: Fresh cedar, resin.
Blue: Mineral, chalk, almost none.
Superviolet: Faintly like cloves.
Black: No smell/or smell of decaying flesh.
White: Honey, lilac.
(*Mythical; these are the smells as reported in stories.)

METAPHYSICS
Any drafting feels good to the drafter. Sensations of euphoria and invincibility are particularly strong among young drafters and those drafting for the first time. Generally, these pass with time, though drafters abstaining from magic for a time will often feel them again. For most drafters, the effect is similar to drinking a cup of kopi. Some drafters, strangely enough, seem to have allergic reactions to drafting. There are vigorous ongoing debates about whether the effects on personality should be described as metaphysical or physical.

Regardless of their correct categorization and whether they are the proper realm of study for the magister or the luxiat, the effects themselves are unquestioned.

LUXIN'S EFFECTS ON PERSONALITY

The benighted before Lucidonius believed that passionate men became reds, or that calculating women became yellows or blues. In truth, the causation flows the other way.

Every drafter, like every woman, has her own innate personality. The color she drafts then influences her *toward* the behaviors below. A person who is impulsive who drafts red for years is going to be more likely to be pushed further into 'red' characteristics than a naturally cold and orderly person who drafts red for the same length of time.

The color a drafter uses will affect her personality over time. This, however, doesn't make her a prisoner of her color, or irresponsible for her actions under the influence of it. A green who continually cheats on his wife is still a lothario. A sub-red who murders an enemy in a fit of rage is still a murderer. Of course, a naturally angry woman who is also a red drafter will be even more susceptible to that color's effects, but there are many tales of calculating reds and fiery, intemperate blues.

A color isn't a substitute for a woman. Be careful in your application of generalities. That said, generalities can be useful: a group of green drafters is more likely to be wild and rowdy than a group of blues.

Given these generalities, there is also a virtue and a vice commonly associated with each color. (Virtue being understood by the early luxiats not as being free of temptation to do evil in a particular way, but as conquering one's own predilection toward that kind of evil. Thus, gluttony is paired with temperance, greed with charity, etc.)

> ***Sub-red drafters:*** Sub-reds are passionate in all ways, the most purely emotional of all drafters, the quickest to rage or to cry. Sub-reds love music, are often impulsive, fear the dark less than any other color, and are often insomniacs. Emotional, distractable, unpredictable, inconsistent, loving, bighearted. Sub-red men are often sterile.

Associated vice: Wrath

Associated virtue: Patience

Red drafters: Reds are quick-tempered, lusty, and love destruction. They are also warm, inspiring, brash, larger than life, expansive, jovial, and powerful.

Associated vice: Gluttony

Associated virtue: Temperance

Orange drafters: Oranges are often artists, brilliant in understanding other people's emotions and motivations. Some use this to defy or exceed expectations. Sensitive, manipulative, idiosyncratic, slippery, charismatic, empathetic.

Associated vice: Greed

Associated virtue: Charity

Yellow drafters: Yellows tend to be clear thinkers, with intellect and emotion in perfect balance. Cheerful, wise, bright, balanced, watchful, impassive, observant, brutally honest at times, excellent liars. Thinkers, not doers.

Associated vice: Sloth

Associated virtue: Diligence

Green drafters: Greens are wild, free, flexible, adaptable, nurturing, friendly. They don't so much disrespect authority as not even recognize it.

Associated vice: Lust

Associated virtue: Self-control

Blue drafters: Blues are orderly, inquisitive, rational, calm, cold, impartial, intelligent, musical. Structure, rules, and hierarchy are important to them. Blues are often mathematicians and composers. Ideas and ideology and correctness often matter more than people to blues.

Associated vice: Envy

Associated virtue: Kindness

Superviolet drafters: Superviolets tend to have a removed outlook; dispassionate, they appreciate irony and sarcasm and word games and are often cold, viewing people as puzzles to be solved or ciphers to be cracked. Irrationality outrages superviolets.

Associated vice: Pride

Associated virtue: Humility

LEGENDARY COLORS

Chi (pronounced KEY): The postulated upper-spectrum counter-part to paryl. (Often referred to in tales as 'far above superviolet as paryl is below sub-red.') Also called the revealer. Its main claimed use is nearly identical to paryl – seeing through things, though those who believe in chi say its powers far surpass paryl's in this regard, cutting through flesh and bone and even metal. The only thing the tales seem to agree on is that chi drafters have the shortest life expectancy of any drafters: five to fifteen years, almost without exception. If chi indeed exists, it would mostly be evidence that Orholam created light for the universe or for his own purposes, and not solely for the use of man, and would move theologians from their current anthropocentrism.

Black: Destruction, void, emptiness, that which is not and cannot be filled. Obsidian is said to be the bones of black luxin after it dies.

Paryl: Also called spidersilk, it is invisible to all but paryl drafters. It resides as far down the spectrum from sub-red as most sub-red does from the visible spectrum. Believed mythical because the lens of the human eye cannot contort to a shape that would allow seeing such a color. The alleged color of dark drafters and night weavers and assassins because this spectrum is (again, allegedly) available even at night. Uses unknown, but linked to murders. Poisonous?

White: The raw word of Orholam. The stuff of creation, from which all luxin and all life was formed. Descriptions of an earthly form of the stuff (as diminished from the original as obsidian supposedly is from black luxin) describe it as radiant ivory, or pure white opal, emitting light on the whole spectrum.

COLLOQUIAL TERMS

Students at the Chromeria are encouraged to use the proper names for each color, but the impetus to name seems unstoppable. In some cases, the names are used technically: pyrejelly is a thicker, longer-burning draft of red that will burn long enough to reduce a body to ash. In other cases, the reference becomes precisely the opposite of the technical definition: brightwater was first a name for liquid yellow luxin, but Brightwater Wall is solid yellow luxin.

A few of the more common colloquialisms:

Sub-red: Firecrystal
Red: Pyrejelly, burnglue
Orange: Noranjell
Yellow: Brightwater
Green: Godswood
Blue: Frostglass, glass
Superviolet: Skystring, soulstring, spidersilk
Black: Hellstone, nullstone, nightfiber, cinderstone, hadon
White: Truebright, starsblood, anachrome, luciton

On the Old Gods

Sub-red: Anat, goddess of wrath. Those who worshipped her are said to have had rituals that involved infant sacrifice. Also known as the Lady of the Desert, the Fiery Mistress. Her centers of worship were Tyrea, southernmost Paria, and southern Ilyta.

Red: Dagnu, god of gluttony. He was worshipped in eastern Atash.

Orange: Molokh, god of greed. Once worshipped in western Atash.

Yellow: Belphegor, god of sloth. Primarily worshipped in northern Atash and southern Blood Forest before Lucidonius's coming.

Green: Atirat, goddess of lust. Her center of worship was primarily in western Ruthgar and most of Blood Forest.

Blue: Mot, god of envy. His center of worship was in eastern Ruthgar, northeastern Paria, and Abornea.

Superviolet: Ferrilux, god of pride. His center of worship was in southern Paria and northern Ilyta.

On Technology and Weapons

The Seven Satrapies are in a time of great leaps in understanding. The peace since the Prisms' War and the following suppression of piracy has allowed the flow of goods and ideas freely through the satrapies. Cheap, high-quality iron and steel are available in every satrapy, leading to high-quality weapons, durable wagon wheels, and everything in between. Though traditional forms of weapons like Atashian bich'hwa or Parian parry-sticks continue, now they are rarely made of horn or hardened wood. Luxin is often used for improvised weapons, but most luxins' tendency to break down after long exposure to light, and the scarcity of yellow drafters who can make solid yellows (which don't break down in light), means that metal weapons predominate among mundane armies.

The greatest leaps are occurring in the improvement of firearms. In most cases, each musket is the product of a different smith. This means each man must be able to fix his own firearm, and that pieces must be crafted individually. A faulty hammer or flashpan can't be swapped out for a new one, but must be detached and reworked into appropriate shape. Some large-scale productions with hundreds of apprentice smiths have tried to tackle this problem in Rath by making parts as nearly identical as possible, but the resulting matchlocks tend to be low quality, trading accuracy and durability for consistency and simple repair. Elsewhere, the smiths of Ilyta have gone the other direction, making the highest-quality custom muskets in the world. Recently, they've pioneered a form they call the flintlock. Instead of affixing a burning slow match to ignite powder in the flashpan and thence into the breech of the rifle, they've affixed a flint that scrapes a frizzen to throw sparks directly into the breech. This approach means a musket or pistol is always ready to fire, without a soldier having to first light a slow match. Keeping it from widespread adoption is the high rate of misfires – if the flint doesn't scrape the frizzen correctly or throw sparks perfectly, the firearm doesn't fire.

Thus far, the combination of luxin with firearms has been largely unsuccessful. The casting of perfectly round yellow luxin musket balls was possible, but the small number of yellow drafters able to make solid yellow creates a bottleneck in production. Blue luxin musket balls often shatter from the force of the black powder explosion. An exploding shell made by filling a yellow luxin ball with red luxin (which would ignite explosively from the shattering yellow when the ball hit a target) was demonstrated to the Nuqaba, but the exact balance of making the yellow thick enough to not explode inside the musket, but thin enough to shatter when it hit its target, is so difficult that several smiths have died trying to replicate it, probably barring this technique from wide adoption.

Other experiments are doubtless being carried out all over the Seven Satrapies, and once high-quality, consistent, and somewhat accurate firearms are introduced, the ways of war will change forever. As it stands, a trained archer can shoot farther, far more quickly, and more accurately.

extras

www.orbitbooks.net

extras

about the author

Brent Weeks studied at Hillsdale College, before brief stints walking the earth like Caine from Kung Fu, also tending bar and corrupting the youth (not at the same time). He started writing on napkins and, eventually, someone paid him for it. Brent doesn't own cats or wear a ponytail.

Find out more about Brent Weeks and other Orbit authors by registering for the free monthly newsletter at www.orbitbooks.net.

if you enjoyed
THE BLOOD MIRROR

look out for

AGE OF ASSASSINS

by

RJ Barker

TO CATCH AN ASSASSIN, USE AN ASSASSIN . . .

Girton Club-foot, apprentice to the land's best assassin, still has much to learn about the art of taking lives. But their latest mission tasks him and his master with a far more difficult challenge: to save a life. Someone, or many someones, is trying to kill the heir to the throne, and it is up to Girton and his master to uncover the traitor and prevent the prince's murder.

In a kingdom on the brink of civil war and a castle thick with lies Girton finds friends he never expected, responsibilities he never wanted, and a conspiracy that could destroy an entire land.

If you enjoyed

THE GLASS MIRROR

look out for

AGE OF ASSASSINS

by

RJ Barker

Prologue

Darik the smith was last among the desolate. The Landsman made him kneel with a kick to the back of his knees, forcing his head down so he knelt and stared at the line between the good green grass and the putrid yellow desert of the sourlands. Nothing grew in the sourlands. A sorcerer had taken the life of the land for his own magics many years ago, before Darik's parents were born, and only death was found there now. A foul-smelling wind blew his long brown hair into his face and, ten paces away, the first of the desolate was weeping as she waited for the blade – Kina the herdsgirl, no more than a child and the only other from his village. The voice of the Landsman, huge and strong in his grass-green armour, was surprisingly gentle as he spoke to her, a whisper no louder than the knife leaving its scabbard.

"Shh, child. Soonest done, soonest over," he said, and then the knife bit into her neck and her tears were stilled for ever. Darik glanced between the bars of his hair and saw Kina's body jerking as blood fountained from her neck and made dark, twisting, red patterns on the stinking yellow ground – silhouettes of death and life.

He had hoped to marry Kina when she came of age.

Darik was cold but it was not the wind that made him shiver; he had been cold ever since the sorcerer hunters had come for him. It was the first time in fifteen years of life that the sweat on his skin wasn't because of the fierce heat of the forge. The moisture that had clung to him since was a different sweat, a new sweat, a cold frightened animal sweat that hadn't stopped since they locked the shackles on his wrists. It seemed so long ago now.

The weeks of marching across the Tired Lands had been like a dream but, looking back, the most dreamlike moment of all was that moment when they had called his name. He hadn't been surprised – it was as if he'd sold himself to a hedge spirit long ago and had been waiting for someone to come and collect on the debt his whole life.

"Shh, child. Soonest done, soonest over." The knife does its necessary work on another of the desolate, and a second set of bloody sigils spatters out on the filthy yellow ground. Is there meaning there? Is there some message for him? In this place between life and death, close to embracing the watery darkness that swallowed the dead gods, are they talking to him?

Or is it just blood?

And death.

And fear.

"Shh, child. Soonest done, soonest over." The next one begs for life in the moments before the blade bites. Darik doesn't know that one's name, never asked him, never saw the point because once you're one of the desolate you're dead. There is no way out, no point running. The brand on your forehead shows you for what they think you are – magic user, destroyer, abomination, *sorcerer*. You're only good for bleeding out on the dry dead earth, a sacrifice of blood to heal the land. No one will hide you, no one will pity you when magic has made the dirt so weak people can barely feed their children. There is the sound of choking, fighting, begging as the knife does its work and the thirsty ground drinks the life stolen from it.

Does Darik feel something in that moment of death? Is there a vibration? Is there a twinge that runs from Darik's knees, up his legs through his blood to squirm in his belly? Or is that only fear?

"Shh, child. Soonest done, soonest over."

The slice, the cough, blood on the ground, and this time it is unmistakable – a *something* that shoots up through his body. It sets his teeth on edge, it makes the roots of his hair hurt. Everything starts changing around him: the land is a lens and he is its focus, his mind a bright burning spot of light. What is this feeling? What is it? Were they right?

Are they right?

A hand on his forehead.

Dark worms moving through his flesh.

The hiss of the blade leaving the scabbard.

He sweats, hot as any day at the forge.

His head pulled back, his neck stretched.

Closing his eyes, he sees a world of silvered lines and shadows.

The cold touch of the blade against his neck.

A pause, like the hiss of hot metal in water, like the moment before the geyser of scorching steam hisses out around his hand and the blade is set.

The sting of a sharp edge against his skin.

And the grass is talking, and the land is talking, and the trees are talking, and all in a language he cannot understand but at the same time he knows exactly what is being said. Is this what a hedging lord sounds like?

The creak of leather armour.

"I will save you." Is it the voice of Fitchgrass of the fields?

"No!"

"Only listen . . ." This near the souring is it Coil the yellower?

"Shh, shh, child." The Landsman's voice, soothing, calming. "Soonest done, soonest over."

"I can save you." Too far from the rivers for Blue Watta.

"No." But Darik's word is a whisper drowned in fear of the approaching void. Time slows further as the knife slices though his skin, cutting through layer after layer in search of the black vessels of his life.

"Let me save you." Or is it the worst of all of them? Is it Dark Ungar speaking?

"No," he says. But the word is weak and the will to fight is gone.

"Let us?"

"Yes!"

An explosion of . . . of?

Something.

Something he doesn't know or understand but he recognises it – it has always been within him. It is something he's fought, denied, run from. A familiar voice from his childhood, the imaginary friend that frightened his mother and she told him to forget so he pushed it away, far away. But now, when he needs it the most, it is there.

The blade is gone from his neck.

He opens his eyes.

The world is out of focus – a haze of yellows – and a high whine fills his ears the way it would when his father clouted him for "dangerous talk". The green grass beneath Darik's knees is gone, replaced by yellow fronds that flake away at his touch like morning ash in the forge. He stares at his hands. They are the same – the same scars, the same half-healed cuts and nicks, the same old burns and calluses.

Around him is perfect half-circle of dead grass, as if the sourlands have taken a bite out of the lush grasslands at their edge

His wrists are no longer bound in cold metal.

Is he lost, gone? Has he made a deal with something terrible? But it doesn't feel like that; it feels like this was something in him, something that has always been in him, just waiting for the right moment.

He can feel the souring like an ache.

There had been four Landsmen to guard the five desolate. Now the guards are blurry smears of torn, angular metal, red flesh and sharp white bone.

Darik rubbed his eyes and forced himself up, staggering like a man waking from too long a sleep. A movement in the corner of his eye pulled at his attention. One of the Landsmen was still alive, on his back and trying to scuttle away on his elbows as Darik approached. The smith knelt by the Landsman and placed his big hands on either side of his head. It would be easy to finish him, just a single twist of his big arms and the Landsman's neck would snap like a charcoaled stick. He willed his arms to move but instead found himself staring at the Landsman. Not much older than he was and scared, so scared. The Landsman's lips were moving and at first the only sound is the high whine of the world, then the words come like the approaching thunder of a mount's feet as it gallops towards him.

"I'msorryI'msorryI'msorryI'msorry . . ."

"It's wrong," Darik said, "this is all wrong," but the Landsman's eyes were far away, lost in fear and past understanding. His mouth moving.

". . . I'msorryI'msorryI'msorry . . ."

Darik stared a little longer, the killing muscles in his arms tensing. Now his vision had cleared he saw beyond the broken bodies of the other Landsmen to the shattered corpses of those who had died beside him. They had been picked up and tossed away on the winds of his fury.

Darik leaned in close to the Landsman.

"This has to stop," he said, and let go of the man's head. The words kept coming.

". . . I'msorryI'msorryI'msorry."

He could see Kina's corpse, dead at the hand of the knights then shredded into a red mess by his magic.

"I forgive you," said Darik through tears. The Landsman slumped to the floor, eyes wide in shock as the smith walked away.

Inside the thick muscles of Darik's arms black veins are screaming.